D0454920

THE
DEAD

CHARLIE HIGSON

Hyperion
New York

Copyright © 2010 by Charlie Higson
First published in Great Britain in 2010 by the Penguin Group

All rights reserved. Published by Hyperion, an imprint of Disney Book Group. No part of this book may be reproduced or transmitted in any form or by any means, electronic or mechanical, including photocopying, recording, or by any information storage and retrieval system, without written permission from the publisher. For information address Hyperion, 114 Fifth Avenue, New York, New York 10011-5690.

Printed in the United States of America

First U.S. paperback edition, 2012

1 3 5 7 9 10 8 6 4 2

V475-2873-0-12074
ISBN 978-1-4231-3422-0

Library of Congress Control Number for Hardcover Edition: 2011379156

Map illustration by Kayley Le Favier

Visit www.hyperionteens.com

For Alex

I have a lot of help from some wonderful people in researching parts of this series, but I would especially like to thank:

> *James Taylor and Terry Charman at the Imperial War Museum.*
> *David Cooper at the Tower of London.*
> *Daniel Armstrong at Waitrose Holloway Road for helping me to understand how supermarkets work.*
> *And Jon Surtees at the Oval for a great guided tour that was slightly wasted on a non-cricket fan like myself.*

I would thoroughly recommend a visit to any of these fine institutions, whether you want to check out the locations from the books or whether you are interested in English history and culture.

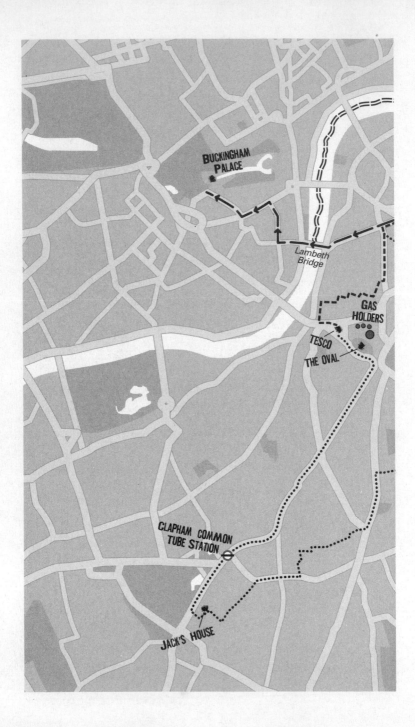

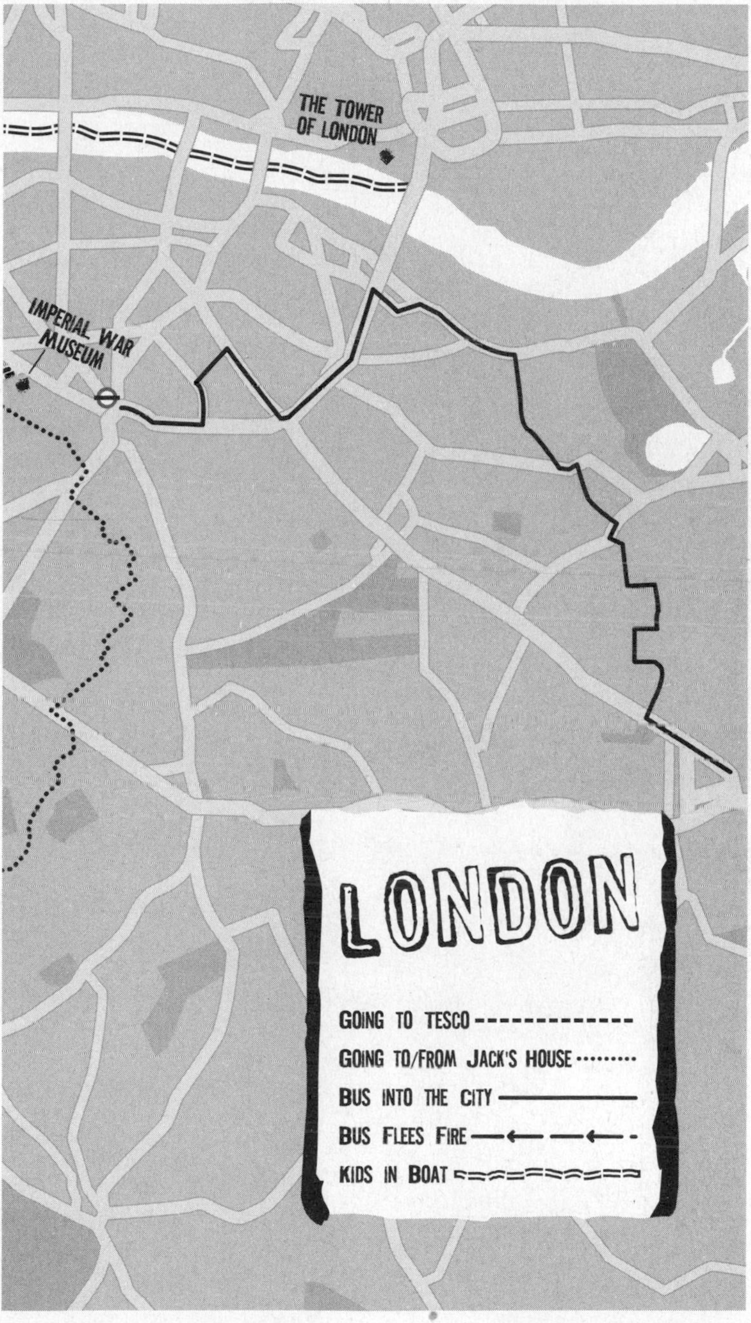
THE TOWER OF LONDON
IMPERIAL WAR MUSEUM
LONDON
GOING TO TESCO
GOING TO/FROM JACK'S HOUSE
BUS INTO THE CITY
BUS FLEES FIRE
KIDS IN BOAT

THE
DEAD

THE SCARED KID

When the video is posted on YouTube it's an instant hit. Within days everyone's talking about it.

"Have you seen the 'Scared Kid' video?"

"It's really freaky."

"At first I thought it was a joke, but it looks so real."

"It's definitely fake, but it's still scary."

"I can't watch it. It's too frightening."

"Who is he? Do you know who he is? Who's the Scared Kid?"

"Nobody knows. . . ."

Maybe it's a clever trailer for a new horror film? Maybe it's a viral ad for something. A new car or a chocolate bar? Or just maybe it's real. . . .

There's something about it. Something about the kid. No ten-year-old is that good an actor. And if someone's playing a trick on him, they are *really* sick and they've done way too good a job. Who would do that? Who would deliberately scare a young kid that much? And why has nobody come forward to explain it all?

Even after everything that happens, when the whole world changes forever, when everyone knows that the video wasn't a hoax but the start of something terrible, people will remember the Scared Kid. His poor frightened little face.

It's like the last thing everyone saw before the lights went out.

He sits there at his computer, talking into a webcam. It's clear he's been crying for ages, his eyes are red raw, his face streaked with tears. He's shaking uncontrollably and his teeth are actually chattering. You can hear them. It would be funny if it wasn't so weird. He can hardly get his words out. They tumble over each other.

"I don't know what to what to do I don't know they've killed Danny and Eve they killed Danny and Eve Danny and and Eve and Eve and and . . . they're outside now I can see them I can see them outside there are three mothers and a father. . . ."

That's the freakiest part, the part that sticks in people's minds, that he calls them mothers and fathers.

"They came to the house and they killed they killed Danny and Eve there's blood omigod—omigod there's blood three mothers and a father they've killed Danny and Eve make them go away please make them go away. . . ."

Then he picks up the webcam and turns it to point out of the window. It veers all over, lights smearing the screen. Now you can see the street. It's nighttime. The picture's awful, but you can just see these four people under the streetlights— *three mothers and a father*—three women and a man, and near them what looks like a dead body. The body of a child.

There's something not right about the people. They don't seem like actors. The way they're standing. And when one of them looks up at the camera it's the most awful thing . . . a dead-eyed stare, like an animal. Are they actors? The picture's so bad it's hard to tell.

Then the Scared Kid's voice again.

"Can you see them? They've gone crazy—three mothers and a father—they've been trying to get back in the house but Danny and Eve they're dead they're dead and I don't know where my mom and dad are there's nobody else here they've all gone it's only me. . . ."

The camera moves again. You can hear crashing and smashing in the background. Shouting. Now the kid's back at his desk, staring into the lens like he's staring into the grave. Even more terrified than before. Shaking. Shaking.

"I'm going to post the video—Danny showed me how—they killed him three mothers and a father I have to do it quickly I don't know what's happening I don't think anyone will help me I think I'm going to die like like—"

And that's the end of it.

Some other kids do impressions of him, and post them. There's a remix of the kid done to a death metal sound track. But the thing is—the video is scary because it seems so real. People watch it over and over, trying to understand it. And when adults start dying, when it becomes clear that some terrible new disease is striking everybody over the age of sixteen, the Scared Kid begins to look like some kind of prophet.

Within a very short time, "Scared Kid" becomes the most watched YouTube clip ever. After a month it's taken down. There's a message saying it's been removed. The day after that, the whole YouTube site is taken down without any explanation.

And the day after that, the Internet stops working.

It just disappears.

That's when people finally realize that something serious is happening.

THE ACTION IN THIS BOOK BEGINS JUST OVER A YEAR BEFORE THE INCIDENTS DESCRIBED IN *THE ENEMY*.

1

Mr. Hewitt was crawling through the broken window. Sliding over the ledge on his belly. Hands groping at the air, fingers clenching and unclenching, arms waving as if he were trying to swim the breaststroke. In the half-light Jack could just make out the look on his pale yellowing face. A stupid look. No longer human. Eyes wide and staring. Tears of blood dribbling from under his eyelids. Tongue lolling out from between cracked and swollen lips. Skin covered with boils and sores.

Jack stood there frozen, the cricket bat held tight in sweating hands. He knew he should step forward and whack Mr. Hewitt as hard as he could in the head, but his right arm ached all the way down. He'd been swinging the bat all night, and the last time he'd hit a teacher it had jarred his shoulder. Now it hurt just to hold the bat, which felt like a lead weight in his hands.

He knew that wasn't the real reason, though. When it came down to it, he couldn't bring himself to hit Mr. Hewitt. He'd always liked him. He'd been Jack's English teacher for the last year. He was one of the youngest and most popular teachers in the school, always talking to the boys about films and TV and video games, not in a creepy way, not to get in with the kids, simply because he was genuinely interested in the same things that they were. When the disease hit, when everything started to go wrong, Mr. Hewitt had done everything he could to help the boys. Trying to contact parents and make arrangements, keeping their spirits up, comforting them, reassuring them, always searching for food and water, making the buildings safe . . .

And when it had gotten really bad, when those adults who'd gotten sick but hadn't died had started to turn on the kids, attacking them like wild animals, Mr. Hewitt had helped fight them off.

He'd been tireless, and it had looked like he might escape the sickness.

He'd been a hero.

And now here he was, crawling slowly, slowly, slowly into the lower common room like some huge, clumsy lizard. He raised his head, stretching his neck, and wheezed at Jack, bloody saliva bubbling between his teeth. Jack could see two more teachers behind him, attempting in their own mindless way to get to the window.

Jack swallowed. It hurt his throat. He hadn't had anything to drink all day. They were running low on water and trying to ration it. His head throbbed. This was the second night the teachers had attacked in force. Jack's second night without sleep. The stress and the tiredness were turning him slightly crazy. His heart felt all fluttery and he was constantly on the edge of losing it, breaking down into uncontrollable sobbing, or laughter, or both. He was seeing things everywhere, out of the corner of his eye, shapes moving in the shadows. He would shout a warning and turn to look and there would be nothing there.

Mr. Hewitt was real, though, something out of a waking nightmare, slithering in, inch by inch.

The last hour had been a chaotic panicked scramble of running around in the dark from room to room, checking doors, windows, battering back any teachers that got past the defenses. And then they'd heard breaking glass in the lower common room, and he and Ed had come charging in to see what was happening.

And there was Mr. Hewitt.

Jack couldn't do this alone. He looked for Ed and saw him crouched down behind an overturned table, his gray face poking over the top, eyes white-rimmed and staring. Ed, his best mate. Ed, who everyone thought was cool. Clever without being cocky or a suck-up. Good-looking Ed, who all the girls went for. Ed, who beat him at tennis without really trying. Jack had always felt second in line to him, even though the two of them did everything together, hung out all the time, shared books and comics and music, played on the same football team, the same cricket team.

Last year the school had produced a glossy booklet advertising itself to new parents, and there on the front cover was Ed—the boy most likely to succeed. The happy, smiling, confident face of Rowhurst.

Well, this was the new face of the school, hiding behind

a table, scared halfway to death, while the teachers crawled in through a broken window.

Ed reminded Jack of someone.

The Scared Kid.

Ed was totally bricking it, and his fear was making him next to useless.

"Help me," Jack croaked.

"I'm keeping watch," said Ed, a slight catch in his voice.

Yeah, right, keeping watch. . . . Keeping safe is more like it.

Jack sighed. His own tiredness and fear were turning him bitter.

"If you won't help," he said, "at least go and get one of the others."

Ed shook his head. "I'm staying with you."

"Then do something," Jack shouted. "Hewitt's nearly through. I need help here."

"What . . . ? What do you want me to do?"

Jack rubbed his shoulder. He'd had enough of the school. He'd had enough of this mess, night after night, the same bloody ritual. Right now he'd rather be anywhere else than here.

Most of all he wanted to be at home, though. Back in his own house, in his own room, with his own things. Under his comforter, with the world shut out.

Home . . .

He tossed the bat to Ed. It bounced off the table and ended up on the carpet.

"Hit him, Ed," he said.

"I'm not sure I can," Ed replied.

"Pick up the bat and hit him." Jack felt tears come into

his eyes. He squeezed them tight and pinched the wetness away. "Please, Ed, just hit him."

"And then what?" Ed asked. "They just keep coming, Jack. We can't kill them all."

"Hit him, Ed! For God's sake, just hit him!"

2

Ed looked at the bat, lying in a strip of moonlight on the worn-out carpet. The electricity had gone off three weeks ago. Nights were blacker than he had ever known they could be.

He didn't know what to do. He knew he should help Jack, but he was paralyzed. If he did nothing, though, wouldn't it be worse? The teachers would get him, just as they'd gotten Jamey and Adam and Will. They'd come in with their horrible filthy nails and their hungry teeth. They'd grab him. . . .

Maybe that would be better. To get it over with. All he could see ahead of him was a never-ending string of dark nights spent fighting off adults, as, one by one, his friends were all killed.

Get it over with.

Shut your eyes, lie down, and that would be that. . . .

He saw a hand reaching out toward the bat. As if he were watching a film. As if it were happening to someone else. The fingers closed around the handle.

His fingers.

He picked up the bat and raised himself to a standing position. The blood was pounding in his head and he felt like he was going to throw up at any moment. If he came out from behind the table and ran forward now, he could get Mr. Hewitt before he was fully through the window and on his feet. He could help Jack. They'd be okay.

Yes.

He pushed the table out of the way and crept forward. What if Mr. Hewitt sped up, though? What if all the diseased adults weren't slow and confused? It was easy to make a mistake. Every boy who'd been taken had made some stupid mistake. Had been careless.

Ed raised the bat just as Hewitt flopped onto the floor. For a moment he lay there, unmoving. Ed wondered if he was dead. Then the teacher rolled his head from side to side and forced himself up so that he was squatting on the sticky carpet. He belched and vomited a stream of thin clear liquid down his front. It smelled awful.

"Hit him, Ed."

Ed glanced over at Jack. He was stooped over, breathing heavily, his eyes wild and shining. Exhausted. The strawberry birthmark that covered one side of his face and gave him a permanently angry look was like a splash of blood.

"Hit him now."

When Ed turned his attention back to Mr. Hewitt, the teacher had straightened up and was shuffling closer. There were three long jagged rips down the front of his white shirt. Ed's eyes flicked to the window frame, where a row of vicious glass shards stuck up along the lower rim. Mr. Hewitt must have raked his torso across them as he crawled in, too stupid to realize what was happening. Blood was oozing from behind the rips and soaking his shirt. His tie had been pulled into a tight, stringy knot.

There was a noise from outside. Already other shapes were at the window, jostling with each other to get through.

Hewitt suddenly jerked and lashed out with one hand. Ed staggered back.

"Hit him, Ed," Jack hissed angrily, on the verge of crying. "Smash his bloody skull in. Kill him. I hate him. I hate him."

The thing was, Ed hadn't hit a single one of them yet, and he didn't know if he could. He didn't know if he could swing that bat and feel it smash into bone and flesh. He'd never enjoyed fighting, had always managed to avoid anything serious. The fact that most people seemed to like him and wanted to be his friend had kept him out of trouble. He'd grown up thinking it was wrong to hit someone else, to deliberately hurt another person.

And not just any person. It was Mr. Hewitt, who until about two weeks ago had been friendly and normal. . . .

Normal. How Ed longed for things to be normal again.

Well, they weren't ever going to be normal again, were they? So swing that bloody bat. Feel the bone break under it. . . .

He swung. His heart wasn't in it, though, and there was no force to the blow. The bat bumped feebly into Mr. Hewitt's arm, knocking him to the side. Hewitt snarled and lunged at Ed, who cried out in alarm and jumped backward. One of the table legs poked him in the back, winding him and knocking him off balance. He fell awkwardly, his head bashing against the table. He lay there for a moment in stunned confusion until a shout from Jack brought him back to his senses.

Where was the bat? He'd dropped the bat. Where was it?

It had fallen toward Mr. Hewitt, who had stepped over it. Ed couldn't get to it now and neither could Jack. Not without shoving Hewitt out of the way.

And Hewitt was nearly upon him. There was just enough light to see the pus-filled boils that were spread across his face. He raised both his hands to chest height, ready to make a grab for Ed, and his shirt pulled out of his trousers.

"Help me, Jack!"

But before Jack could do anything, there was a bubbling, gurgling sound, like a clogged-up sink unblocking, and an appalling stink filled the room. Mr. Hewitt howled. The glass had evidently cut deeper into his belly than any of them had realized. He looked down dumbly as his skin unzipped and his guts spilled out.

Now it was Jack's turn to vomit.

Mr. Hewitt dropped to his knees and started scooping up long coils of entrails, as if trying to stuff them back into his body. Jack moved at last. He kicked Hewitt over, grabbed the fallen bat, then ran to Ed.

"Come on," he said, seizing Ed's wrist and pulling him to his feet. "We're getting out of here."

3

They bundled out into the corridor, and Jack pulled the door shut.

"I'm sorry," said Ed. "I can't do this."

"It's all right," said Jack, and he hugged Ed. "It's all right, mate, it's all right."

Jack felt weird; it had always been the other way around. Ed helping Jack, Ed cool and in control, gently mocking Jack, who worried about everything. Jack never sure of himself, self-conscious about his birthmark. Not that Ed would ever say anything about it, but it was always there, like a flag. What did it matter now, though? In a list of all the things that sucked in the world, his stupid birthmark wasn't even in the top one hundred.

"Should we try to block the door somehow?" said Ed, making an attempt to look like he was in control again.

"What with?" said Jack. "Let's just get back upstairs to the others, yeah?"

"What about the teachers?" said Ed, glancing fearfully at the door.

"There's nothing we can do, Ed. Maybe the rest of them will be distracted by Mr. Hewitt. I don't know. Maybe they'll stop to eat him. That's all they're looking for, isn't it, food? You've seen them."

Ed let out a crazy laugh. "Listen to you," he said. "Listen to what you're saying, Jack. This is nuts. Talking about people eating each other. It's unreal."

But Ed *had* seen them. A pack of teachers ripping a dead body to pieces and shoving the bloody parts into their mouths.

No. He had to try not to think about these things and concentrate on the moment. On staying alive from one second to the next.

"All right," he said, his voice more steady now. "Let's get back to the others. Make sure they're all okay. We've got to stick together."

"Yeah."

Ed took hold of Jack's arm. "Promise me, Jack, won't you?"

"What?"

"That whatever happens we'll stick together."

"Of course."

Ed smiled.

"Let's go," said Jack, dragging his flashlight from his pocket and shining it up and down the corridor. There were heavy fire doors at either end that the kids kept shut to slow down any intruders. This part of the corridor was empty. They had to keep moving, though. They had no idea how long the other teachers would be delayed in the common room.

Ed suddenly felt more tired than he'd ever felt in his life.

He wasn't sure he had the energy just to put one foot in front of the other. He knew Jack felt the same.

Then one of the fire doors banged open and Ed was running again.

A teacher had lurched through. Monsieur Morel, from the French department. He'd always been a big jolly man, with dark wavy hair and an untidy beard; now he looked like some sort of mad bear, made worse by the fact that he seemed to have found a woman's fur coat somewhere. It was way too small for him and matted with dried blood. He advanced stiff-legged down the corridor toward the boys, arms windmilling.

The boys didn't wait for him; they flung themselves into the fire door at the opposite end, but as they crashed through they collided with another teacher on the other side. He staggered back against the wall. Without thinking, Jack lashed out with the bat, getting him with a backhander to the side of the head that left him stunned.

Jack and Ed came to a dead stop. This part of the corridor was thick with teachers. God knows how many of them there were, or how they'd gotten in. Even though they were packed in here, there was an eerie silence, broken only by a cough and a noise like someone trying to clear their throat.

Ed flashed his light wildly around, almost as one the teachers turned toward him. The beam whipped across a range of twisted, diseased faces dripping with snot, teeth bared, eyes staring, with peeling skin, open wounds, and horrible gray-green blisters.

They were unarmed and weakened by the sickness, but they were still larger and on the whole more powerful than the boys, and in a big group like this they were deadly. The boys had fortified one of the dormitories on the top floor where they were living, but there was no way Jack and Ed could make it to the stairs past this crowd.

They couldn't go back and try another way, though, because Monsieur Morel was even now pushing through the fire door, and behind him was a small group of female teachers.

"Coming through!"

There was a loud shout, and Ed was dimly aware of bodies being knocked down, then Morel was shunted aside as a group of boys charged him from behind. At their head was Harry "Bam" Bamford, champion prop forward for the school, and bunched next to him in a pack were four of his friends from the rugby team, armed with hockey sticks. They yelled at Jack and Ed to follow them and cleared a path between the startled teachers, who dropped back to either side. The seven boys had the muscle now to power down the corridor and into the empty entrance hallway at the end. They kept moving, Ed running up the stairs three steps at a time, all tiredness forgotten.

They soon reached the top floor and hammered on the dormitory door.

"Open up! It's us!" Bam yelled. Below them the teachers were starting to make their way onto the stairs.

There were muffled voices from the dorm and sounds of activity.

"Come on," Jack shouted. "Hurry up."

Monsieur Morel was coming up more quickly than the other adults, his big feet crashing into each step as his long muscular legs worked like pistons, eating up the distance.

At last the boys could hear the barricade being removed from the other side of the door. They knew how long it took, though, to move the heavy cabinet to the side, shunting it across the bare wooden floorboards.

There had to be a better system than this.

Jack turned. Morel was nearly up.

"Get a move on." Ed pounded his fists on the door, which finally opened a crack. The boy on the other side put an eye to the gap, checking to see who was out there.

"Just open the bloody door," Bam roared.

Morel reached the top of the staircase, and Jack kicked him hard in the chest with the heel of his shoe. The big man fell backward with a small high-pitched cry, toppling down the stairs and taking out a group of teachers on the lower steps.

The door swung inward. The seven boys made it through to safety.

4

The adults were scraping the dormitory wall with their fingers and battering at the door. Now and then there would be a break, a few seconds' silence, and the boys would hear one of them sniffing at the doorjamb like a dog. Then the mindless frenzy of banging and scratching would begin all over again.

"Do you think they'll give up and go away?" Johnno, one of the rugby players, was standing by the heavy cabinet that the boys had used to barricade the door. He was staring at it as if trying to look through it at the adults on the other side.

"What do you reckon?" said Jack, with more than a hint of scorn in his voice.

"No."

"Exactly. So why ask such a stupid question?"

"Hey, hey, hey, no need to start getting at each other," said Bam, stepping over to put an arm around his friend's shoulder. "Johnno was just thinking out loud, weren't you, J? Just saying what we're all thinking."

"Yeah, I know, I'm sorry," said Jack, slumping onto a bed

and running his fingers through his hair. "I'm all weird inside. Can't get my head straight."

"It's the adrenaline," came a high-pitched, squeaky voice from the other side of the room. "The fight-or-flight chemical."

"What are you on about now, Wiki?" said Bam, with a look of amusement on his broad, flat face. Wiki's real name was Thomas. He was a skinny little twelve-year-old with glasses who seemed to know everything about everything and had been nicknamed Wiki, short for Wikipedia.

"Adrenaline, although you should properly call it epinephrine," he said in his strong Manchester accent. "It's a hormone that your body makes when you're in danger. It makes your heart beat faster and your blood vessels sort of open up so that you're ready to either fight off the danger or run away from it. You get a big burst of energy, but afterward you can feel quite run-down. It's made by your adrenal glands from tyrosine and phenylalanine, which are amino acids."

"Thanks, Wiki," said Bam, trying not to laugh. "What would we do without you?"

Wiki shrugged. Before he could say anything else, there was an almighty bang from outside, and all eyes in the room turned back to the door.

Ed looked around at the grubby faces of the boys, lit by the big candles they'd found in the school chapel. Some of these boys had been his friends before, some he'd barely known. They'd been living in this room together now for a week, and he was growing sick of the sight of them.

There was Jack, sitting alone chewing his lip, the fingers of one hand running back and forth over his birthmark. Bam with his four rugby mates, Johnno, Piers, and the Sullivan brothers, Damien and Anthony, who had a reputation for being a bit thick and had done nothing to prove that they weren't. Little Wiki and his friend Arthur, who almost never stopped talking. A group of six boys from Field House, across the road, who stuck together and didn't say much. Kwanele Nkosi, tall, elegant, and somehow, despite everything, always immaculately dressed. Chris Marker, sitting by the window, reading a paperback (that's all he did now, read books, one after another; he never spoke) and "the three nerds," who were all in Ed's physics class.

Nineteen faces, all wearing the same expression: dull, staring, slack, slightly sad. Ed imagined this was what it must have been like in a trench in the First World War. Trying not to think about tomorrow, or yesterday, or anything.

Apart from the nineteen boys in this room, Ed was alone in the world. He had no illusions that his mom and dad might still be alive. About the only thing the scientists had been able to say for sure about the disease, before they, too, had gotten sick, was that it only affected people sixteen or older. His brother, Dan, was older than he, eighteen, so he'd probably be dead, or diseased, which was worse.

The last contact Ed had had with his family was a phone call from his mom about four weeks ago. She'd told him to stay where he was. She hadn't sounded well.

There were probably other boys around the school, hiding in different places. He knew that Matt Palmer had taken a load over to the chapel, but basically Ed's world had shrunk down to this room.

These nineteen faces.

It scared him to think about it. How shaky his future looked. He felt like a tiny dot at the center of a vast, cold universe. He didn't want to think about what was outside. The chaos in the world. How nothing was as it should be. It had been a relief when the television had finally gone off the air. No more news. He had to concentrate on himself now. On trying to stay alive. One day at a time. Hour by hour, minute by minute, second by second.

"How many seconds in a lifetime, Wiki?" he asked.

Wiki's voice came back thin but sure. "Sixty seconds in a minute, sixty minutes in an hour, twenty-four hours in a day, three hundred and sixty-five days in a year, actually three hundred and sixty-five and a quarter because of leap years, so let's say the average life is about seventy-five years, that's sixty, times sixty, times twenty-four, which is, er, eighty-six thousand four hundred seconds in a day. Then three hundred and sixty-five days times seventy-five makes, let me see, twenty-seven thousand three hundred and seventy-five days in seventy-five years. So we multiply those two numbers together . . ."

Wiki fell silent.

"That's a big sum," said his friend Arthur.

"Never mind," said Ed. "It doesn't matter."

"It's a lot," Arthur added, trying to be helpful. "A lot of seconds."

And too many of them had been spent in this bloody room. They'd dragged beds in here from all around the House, so that they didn't get split up, but it meant it was crowded, stuffy, and smelly. None of them could remember the last time he'd washed, except perhaps Kwanele. He had

had his school suits specially made by a tailor in London and used to boast that his haircuts cost him fifty quid a shot. He was keeping himself clean somehow. He had standards to maintain.

The room was made even more cramped by a stack of cardboard boxes at the far end. They'd once contained all their food and bottled water, but there was virtually nothing left now. They had supplies for two more days, maybe three if they were careful. Jack was looking through the pile, chucking empty boxes aside.

There came an even bigger bang, and the cabinet appeared to shake slightly. They'd packed it with junk to make it heavier, and it would need a pretty hefty shove from outside to knock it out of the way, but it wasn't impossible.

"We've got to get out of here," Jack muttered.

"What?" Ed frowned at him.

"I said, we've got to get out of here." This time Jack's voice came through loud and clear, and everyone listened. "It's pointless staying. Completely pointless. Even if that bunch out there backs off in the morning, even if they crawl back to wherever it is they're sleeping—which we don't know for certain they will do—we're gonna have to spend all day tomorrow going around trying to block up the doors and windows again. And then what? They'll only come back tomorrow night and get back in. We can't sleep, we can't eat. Luckily, none of us got hurt tonight, but . . . I mean, if the teachers don't get us, we'll basically just starve to death if we stay here."

"Yeah, I agree," said Bam. "I reckon we should bog off in the morning." His voice sounded very loud in the cramped dormitory. He had always had a tendency to shout rather than speak, and before the disaster the other boys had found him quite irritating. He was large and loud and boisterous. Blundering around like a mini tornado, accidentally breaking things, making crap jokes, playing tricks on people, laughing too much. Now the others couldn't imagine how they'd cope without him. He never seemed to get tired or moody; he was never mean, never sarcastic, and totally without fear.

"We need to find somewhere that we can defend easier than this," Bam went on. "Somewhere near a source of food and water."

"The only source of food around here is us," said Jack.

"They might go away," said Wiki's friend Arthur. "They might all die in the night—lots of them are already dead. If we hold on long enough, they'll all die, they'll pop like popcorn. You see when Ms. Jessop, the science teacher, died? She was lying on the grass in the sun, lying down dead, and her skin started to pop like popcorn, the boils on her kept bursting like little flowers all over her. You know like when flowers come out in a speeded-up film? Pop, pop, pop, and after a while there wasn't anything left of her, she was just a black mess, and then a dog started to eat her and the dog died, too." Arthur stopped and blinked. "I think we should stay here until they all go away or pop like popcorn."

"They're not going to go away," said Jack, going over to the window where Chris was still reading his book, his eyes fixed on the pages. There was a bright moon tonight, and it threw a little light into the room, but Jack doubted if it was enough to see the words properly. Not that that stopped Chris. Nothing could stop him now.

Jack looked down into the street. There were two teachers down there and an older teenager, maybe seventeen or eighteen. They were hobbling along, walking as if every step hurt their feet.

"Some of them die from the disease and some don't," he said. "Who knows why?" He turned back from the window to point toward the door where one of their attackers was rattling the handle. "And who knows how long that group out there are going to take to die? Could be weeks, and in the meantime they know we're here, and they won't give up until they've got us. They're going to keep on attacking every night, soon as it's dark, every bloody night. Most of the other boys left ages ago. Us guys, we stayed in case anyone turned up to rescue us. Ha, good one. Nobody *has* turned up, and, let's face it, nobody will."

"Two billion three hundred and sixty-five million and two hundred thousand seconds . . ." said Wiki quietly. "Roughly. In a lifetime. If you are lucky. . . ."

5

It took four of them to shift the cabinet in the morning. Aware that they were moving it for the last time.

Once the door was clear, Bam put his ear to it. He looked at Jack. Jack licked his lips, tense. "Well?"

Bam shook his head. "Can't hear anything."

"Go on then."

Bam grasped the handle, turned. It clicked and the door popped open a fraction. He checked that everyone was ready. A row of boys stood waiting. They'd pulled the metal bed frames apart to make weapons out of the struts and heavy springs, and they'd packed up whatever supplies and belongings they had left into backpacks or bundles made out of sheets.

"Ready?"

The boys nodded. Bam took a deep breath and tugged the door open.

A pale, sickly light washing in from the small windows showed that the area outside was empty.

The teachers were gone.

One by one the boys filed out onto the landing, wary and alert. They were shivering. Their combined body heat had kept them reasonably warm in the dormitory, but it was early March, and the air out here was noticeably colder.

"Look at that." Johnno nodded toward the door. The outside of it looked like it had been savaged by a pack of wild animals. There were gouges and great dents, long gashes as if from claws. It was worst around the handle. The teachers had almost managed to scrape right through the wood. The walls were similarly scarred, with chunks missing and a pattern of bloody handprints.

"Looks like we only just made it out in time," said Bam. "One more night and they'd have been on us."

It stank on the landing. There was evidence that at least one of the teachers had used the carpet for a toilet. There was torn wallpaper down the stairs and a fresh splash of blood up one wall. Maybe they'd been fighting among themselves.

"Come on." Bam led the way down. Behind him came Johnno and his other mates from the rugby team, carrying vicious metal lengths of bed frame, with ripped-up sheets wrapped tightly around the ends to protect their fingers. Next came Jack and Ed, Jack with the cricket bat, Ed with a hockey stick. Behind them were Arthur and Wiki, chatting away to each other, wobbling bedsprings up and down in their hands. Then Chris Marker, still reading a book as he walked, a makeshift pack slung over his back crammed with yet more books. Then the three nerds, carrying wooden clubs made from chair legs. After them came Kwanele, immaculate as ever in his suit and tie, lugging an expensive suitcase and suit bag, filled with his favorite outfits. Finally the six boys from Field House, watching their rear and armed with an odd assortment of garden tools.

At the bottom of the stairs the carpet was black and sticky, as if a tub of molasses had been poured into it. The boys' sneakers stuck to the floor and squelched as they lifted their feet. It smelled worse down here, a foul brew of blood and dead flesh and unwashed bodies. Sweet and sour and putrid.

The main way in and out of the building was through two big double doors. The first thing Mr. Hewitt had organized when they'd decided to secure the House was nailing the doors shut with planks of wood. They'd been using an alternative exit through the back of the kitchen as a way in and out, because it was quicker to open and close and easier to lock. They had keys for the back door as well as the kitchen door, so had an extra line of defense. It had turned out to be a complete waste of time, though, as the sick teachers soon found other ways to get into the House.

Bam put a hand over his mouth to block the stink.

"This way," he said, leading the group down the corridor that led toward the kitchen.

It was dark in the corridor and they walked quickly. All the boys wanted to get outside as quickly as possible. They soon arrived at the kitchen door, which had a small reinforced-glass window set in the center, crisscrossed with a wire mesh.

Bam strode up to it, as eager as the others to be out of here. He took a big bunch of keys from his pocket, selected the right one, and slotted it into the lock. He was just about to turn it when Jack pulled him back.

"Wait a minute."

Bam stopped. A flash of irritation. Then a little laugh.

Jack sighed. "Come on, Bam, you could at least check it before you open it."

"Sorry, old mate, brain not in gear. Never did work at a hundred percent, to tell you the truth, turned to mush now. Still asleep, I think." He knocked the side of his head with his fist. "Wakey, wakey!"

Jack stuck his nose to the little window and peered into the kitchen. It was dark; the sun was rising on the other side of the building, and its light hadn't reached this far yet. He could see no movement in the gloom. Then he spotted that the back door was half open. Someone had definitely been in there during the night.

"What do you reckon?" Bam asked. "Is it safe?"

"Hang on a minute. Can't tell."

Jack's eyes were slowly growing used to the light. He was picking out more details in the kitchen. There was a scarlet smear of blood on the window over the sinks. And there, on the table, what looked like a slab of meat. He realized there was an arm still attached to it. He swallowed, trying not to retch.

"I'm not sure we should go this way," he said.

"Are there some in there?" Bam asked, trying to see over Jack's shoulder.

"It's hard to tell."

"Here, let me look." Bam shoved Jack aside and took his place at the window.

"Not a pretty sight, is it? Don't think there's anyone in there, though. . . . Whoa!" He leapt back as a female teacher hurled herself at the door, squashing her face against the glass and smearing it with pus. It looked like Ms. Warlock, from the English department, but it was hard to tell.

The shock made Bam burst out laughing, and soon most of the other boys had joined in. Jack just stared at the door, which shook on its hinges as Ms. Warlock repeatedly rammed herself against it with a whining and slobbering noise.

Ed crept forward and risked looking in.

"There's more than one of them in there," he said. "We'll have to go another way."

"You don't say," Jack murmured.

"And we need to be quick," said Ed, ignoring Jack. "They could break this door down if there's enough of them. Or they might just figure out that there's another way in—however they all got in last night."

They backtracked down the corridor, increasingly nervous and anxious to be out of the building that was feeling more and more like a trap. When they got back to the hallway, they headed for the doors.

Jack saw what looked like a football sitting in the middle of the floor. He had an urge to race forward and kick it, an automatic response. He took several paces, then came to a dead stop, almost overbalancing, like someone suddenly finding himself at the edge of a cliff in a cartoon film.

It wasn't a football. It was a human head. All that was left of Mr. Hewitt. His eyes were open, and he looked calm and at peace. He no longer resembled the deranged maniac he'd been when Jack last saw him.

Now Bam spotted the head. "Bloody hell," he said with a laugh. "Better get rid of that. Bit freaky."

He gingerly picked the head up by the hair, then lobbed it across the room toward a trash can that sat in a dark corner. Amazingly, it landed cleanly inside. Bam cheered and punched the air. "Shot!"

Jack didn't know whether to laugh or curl up in a ball and bang his forehead on the floor in despair. He stood there, drained of all energy, wishing he were a million miles away.

Bam, Johnno, and Piers, armed with bits of iron bed frame, set to work on the door, trying to lever the planks off. It was slow work, made slower by the fact that the boys had hardly slept again in the night and were strung out, awkward, and sluggish, their muscles not working as they should, as if the signals weren't getting through clearly from their brains. In the end Jack couldn't bear to watch them clumsily struggling to make any headway; he came back to life and went over to help.

As they worked, they could hear the teachers down the corridor, bashing and thumping against the kitchen door.

"Can't you hurry up?" said Kwanele, who was standing back, watching, his luggage sitting neatly at his feet, looking for all the world as if he were waiting for a train.

"We're going as fast as we can," said Bam.

"If you're in so much of a hurry," said Jack irritably, "why don't you help? Or don't you want to get your clothes messed up?"

"I'm not very good with my hands," said Kwanele, flattening a lapel on his suit jacket. "And, yes, I don't want to ruin my clothes. This shirt is Comme des Garçons."

Jack shook his head and tutted. If Kwanele weren't so ridiculous, the others would have lost patience with him long ago.

There was one last plank left to remove. Bigger and thicker than the others, with about ten fat nails fixing it to the door. The boys were getting in each other's way, and Johnno's weapon slipped, gouging Piers's hand. Piers sucked his fingers and swore at him.

There came an almighty crash from the kitchen.

Jack glanced back. *Had the door finally given out?*

"Come on, come on," he said, as much to the piece of wood as to the other boys. He was scrabbling at the plank with his fingers, trying to pry it loose, and he was so intent on removing it that he lost track of what was going on behind him. It was only when he heard a high-pitched scream that he turned around.

There were teachers in the hallway. Six of them, including Monsieur Morel, who had his hands at the throat of one of the Field House boys and was shaking him like a doll. The boy's friends were battering the teacher with their makeshift weapons. The rest of the teachers were being held back by the Sullivan brothers and the three nerds, who stayed in a tight pack, yelling and screaming abuse.

Ed was with the rest of the boys, who were milling in a frightened circle, not sure what to do.

Johnno gave his iron strut to Jack and snatched a fire extinguisher from a bracket on the wall.

"You get the door open," he shouted. "We'll deal with this bunch."

Ed ran over to help Jack, and between them they managed to get the bit of bed frame behind the plank. They pulled down on it with all their weight and, with a horrible squealing noise, the nails began to pull loose.

Johnno hit the plunger on the top of the fire extinguisher, and a stream of white foam erupted from the hose. He aimed it at the circling teachers, blinding them.

Monsieur Morel was still savaging the boy from Field House. The blows raining down on his back seemed to be having no effect.

With a final screech, the plank popped off the door. Jack grabbed one end and raced back to Morel.

"Out of the way!"

He swung the piece of wood at the man's head, and it stuck fast. One of the nails must have punched through his skull. Morel stood up, the plank hanging from the back of his head like a huge ponytail. He stretched out an arm toward Jack; then went stiff and shuddered before falling sideways, knocking over Ms. Warlock, who slipped and slithered about on the floor, unable to stand up in a pool of melting foam.

"Come on," Bam yelled from the doorway. "Let's go! Let's go!"

"We don't know what's out there." Ed looked worried.

"Can't be any worse than what's in here," Jack shouted as he ran over and pushed past Ed.

Ed closed his eyes and took a deep breath, trying to find some small scrap of courage hidden deep inside.

When he opened his eyes, he realized that he'd been left behind. The others had already gone outside. He hurried after them and found them in a tight pack, blinking in the early morning light. The boys from Field House looked shell-shocked. Ed realized their friend hadn't made it. He said nothing. Too sick to speak.

There didn't appear to be anyone else out here, but a low moan from behind him caused Ed to turn around. The teachers were emerging from the House, covered in foam. They were too sick to move fast, and the boils and sores covering their skin made them walk as if they were treading barefoot on broken glass, but the boys knew from experience that they wouldn't stop. Once they started to follow, they wouldn't give up.

"Leg it!" Bam shouted, and the boys raced across the open ground toward the main school entrance.

Ed stayed at the back, helping Wiki and Arthur. They were smaller than everyone else and slower. Ed didn't know what he'd do if one of them got left behind. He urged them on, shouting encouragement, aware all the time that the teachers were steadily lumbering along behind them.

They rounded the end of School House and headed toward the archway that led out into School Yard. Ed spotted Jack ahead. He was hanging back, staring at the administrative building by the main gates.

What now?

Ed was too scared to stop. He sprinted through the arch, but as he ran past, Jack grabbed hold of his jacket and pulled him back.

Wiki and Arthur ran on.

"What's the matter?" Ed's voice rasped in his throat.

"Can you see that?" said Jack, and he blinked, as if not wanting to trust his own eyes.

Ed turned in the direction Jack was looking. For a moment he could see nothing.

"What?" he said, scared and angry and desperate to get

away. "What am I looking for?"

"Over there. The office where the school secretaries work."

"What? What is it . . . ? Oh, my God."

There was a girl at the window, hammering on the glass, her mouth forming a silent scream.

Who the hell is it?"

"Dunno. Never seen her before in my life." Jack's voice sounded as dry and croaky as Ed's.

"We should keep up with the others," said Ed, nervously glancing over to the road where Wiki and Arthur were disappearing from view.

"We can't just leave her there," said Jack.

"No . . . I know . . . I didn't mean that."

"Then what did you mean?"

"I don't know." Ed massaged the back of his neck. Couldn't think of anything else to say.

"We're going to go and help her," said Jack. "Okay?"

Ed turned back toward the archway. There was no sign of the teachers yet, but it was only a matter of time before they came through.

"Okay," he said.

A look of relief flooded the face of the girl in the window as they hurried over to the building. She was thin, with long hair and a slightly large nose and mouth. Her cheeks were wet with tears, and her eyes were red.

The boys gestured for her to open the window. She shook her head and indicated that it was locked.

"Why doesn't she just use the door?" Ed asked as he and Jack went along to the front entrance. His question was immediately answered when they came upon a small pack of teachers on the porch at the entranceway, scrabbling to get inside.

The two boys backtracked quickly and, luckily, the teachers, intent on getting in, didn't see them. When they got back to the window, the girl was crying again and knocking uselessly against the glass with a shoe.

"That's no good," said Jack. "It's toughened glass."

Ed tried to control his fear, fighting the urge to suggest that they leave her, and then he spotted two big metal garbage cans on the other side of the yard.

"We could use one of them," he said, pointing. "Like a battering ram."

"We'll try it," said Jack, and they raced across the cobbled sidewalk to grab a can. All the other boys had gone down the road, and Ed realized he was alone with Jack in the yard.

No. Not totally alone. The first of the teachers who had attacked them inside was shuffling through the arch, still dripping with foam.

The boys trundled the garbage can across the cobblestones; it rattled and banged on its small wheels. The noise sounded like thunder, and Ed was scared it would attract the teachers on the porch.

"Stand back!" he yelled at the girl when they were close; then he and Jack hoisted the can up onto their shoulders and, still running, launched it at the window. There was a terrific bang as the window disintegrated. For a few seconds there was no sign of the girl, and then she slowly revealed herself in the empty window frame, looking pale and shocked.

"Can you climb out?" Jack asked.

"I think so," said the girl, her accent strange, foreign-sounding.

"Be careful of broken glass," said Ed, remembering what had happened to Mr. Hewitt last night. The girl disappeared again, and when she reappeared she was carrying some blankets, which she draped over the windowsill. Then once more she went off to get something.

"Get a move on," Ed murmured under his breath. The teachers were advancing across the yard, and as they drew closer, Ed got a good look at them. Their eyes were yellow and bulging, their skin lumpy with boils and growths, horrible pearly blisters nestling in the folds. They were streaked with foam, and one or two of them had bright red blood dribbling from their mouths. One had an ear hanging off. It flapped as he waddled along. Another had some sort of huge fleshy growth bulging out from his shirt, as if he'd swallowed a desk lamp. His whole body was twisted and misshapen.

There was a shout from the window. The girl was standing there with a large plastic carrying box. She passed it out to Ed, and he realized that there was a tabby cat inside, huddled, terrified and shivering, down at the end. Once the cat was safely out, the girl maneuvered herself over the window ledge, and Jack helped her to the ground. Her whole body was shaking, and her breathing was quick and shallow.

She flung her arms around Jack with a great sob and

buried her face in his shoulder, soaking his jacket. She kept saying the same thing over and over, her voice muffled. "Thank you, thank you, thank you . . ."

"We've got to keep moving," said Jack, pushing her away from him. "We've got to get away from here."

The girl nodded and took the cat from Ed. She peered inside the box, making little reassuring noises, and then spoke to the cat in what sounded like French.

Ed looked at the teachers. The girl hadn't seen them. They were getting closer by the second.

"We need to hurry," he said, and the girl tore herself away from the cat, her large eyes very wide. Even like this, her hair a mess, her face blotchy from crying, it struck Ed that she was pretty.

He tugged at her arm, but she resisted.

"My father," she said. "I don't know where is my father."

"Who's your father?" Ed asked, even though he knew it was a stupid thing to say.

"Monsieur Morel. He is a teacher here. He was looking after me. But yesterday he goes out. He is feeling sick, he goes for medicine, he does not come back. I wait for him. I wait all through the night. He does not come back."

The girl stopped. She had finally noticed the panic on Ed's face. She glanced over her shoulder and gasped as she saw the teachers, almost close enough to touch.

Jack snatched hold of her arm and dragged her along, forcing her to run at his side.

"You've got to forget about your father," he said. "All the adults, everyone sixteen or older, gets sick. They die, all right? Or they turn into . . . one of them."

"Is he . . . is he sick?" said the girl. Her voice was high-pitched with tension. "Is he changed?"

"No," said Ed as they ran out of the school gates. "No, he's not."

"Have you seen him?" asked the girl. "You must tell me."

"Yes." Jack exchanged a pained look with Ed. "We saw him. He's dead. Sorry."

"I knew it . . ." The girl choked out the words then wailed in despair. Jack shook his head at Ed. Best not to say any more. At least neither of them had lied.

Ed hadn't left the school grounds for a few weeks. It hadn't been safe. And it was strange seeing the main road with no traffic. Even on a Sunday there had always been cars going past at all times of the day and night. Now it was utterly still and calm. Birds were singing in the trees, oblivious to how the world had changed. Not caring about the humans and their problems.

How quickly everything had fallen apart.

In a strange clearheaded moment, Ed realized that for a while the world was going to be a better place for the birds, for all animals. No more cars, no more pollution, no more factories, airplanes, oil wells, coal mines . . .

There was a very strong chance that soon there would be no more humans. What chance did children have of surviving? What was the point of going on? What was the point of crossing the road? Running, fighting, hiding . . .

He didn't stop, though. Something inside made him keep on running, just as something had made him pick up the bat last night. He looked back. They'd left the teachers behind.

Nobody else had come through the school gates. Maybe they'd be safe for a while.

A little farther down the main street, on the other side of the road, was the school chapel. It was only about two hundred years old but had been built to resemble a small medieval church, complete with bell tower and stained-glass windows. It was easy to see why Matt Palmer had thought it might be a safe place to hang out. There were battlements around the top of the tower that made it look like part of a castle.

Matt had come over here about ten days ago with some other boys. If he could be persuaded to join them and look for somewhere better to hole up, they'd have safety in numbers.

As Jack, Ed, and the girl entered the gate and crossed the graveyard, they saw that the rest of the boys from the party were up ahead, huddled in the entranceway to the church. Why hadn't they gone in as they'd arranged?

"They won't open the door," Johnno explained when Jack and Ed ran up. "They won't even answer us." He stopped when he saw the girl, and frowned quizzically at Jack and Ed.

"This is Monsieur Morel's daughter." Jack gave a look to the boys that said *Keep your mouths shut*. "Don't know her name."

The girl seemed to have retreated into herself. Her hair hung down either side of her face like curtains, and she stared at the ground. Johnno went over to her. He was a good-looking lad and had always been confident and successful with girls. Not all the boys could say the same. Rowhurst was an all-boys school, and many of them had had little female contact.

Johnno squatted down so that he could look up into the girl's face.

"What's your name, love?" he asked. The girl remained silent.

"Come on, tell us your name. You're safe now."

"Frédérique," the girl muttered, barely audible.

Johnno put a hand on her arm. "I'm Johnno," he said. The girl didn't respond. Johnno looked around at his friends, eyebrows raised, not sure what to do next. They were pretty shocked by the morning's events, and if they hadn't been trying to tough it out and not seem weak in front of each other, they might all have turned in on themselves like Frédérique.

Ed had been taking a scout around. There was some evidence that teachers had been trying to get into the church, but the heavy oak doors looked almost indestructible, and the windows were too high to reach and laced with metal. He slammed his fists against the door.

"Matt!" he yelled. "Matthew! Open up! It's us! Open the bloody doors." He stopped and listened, head bowed. Nothing. Not a sound.

"Maybe they're not in there," he said. "Maybe they've all gone."

"We need to get inside," said Arthur. He was staring back at the road. Three of the teachers were crossing toward them. The man with the twisted body, Ms. Warlock, and Mr. Langston, an old history teacher. His gray hair was standing up like a crest on top of his head. He looked bewildered.

"There's a door at the side," said one of the Field House boys. "You can get in through the vestry. We use it for choir practice."

"Could we force it?" Jack asked.

The choirboy shrugged.

"Well, why mention it, then?" Jack snapped viciously. "What use is that to us?"

"There's a key," the choirboy muttered. "Mr. Lewis, the choirmaster, uses it sometimes. We're not supposed to know about it, but we all do."

"Why didn't you say that before? Show us."

The choirboy led them around to where there was a lower flat-roofed extension to the side of the chapel. A tiled over-hang protected the door. The choirboy put his hand up under the beams, felt around until he found what he was looking for, and brought down two keys on a ring. He quickly selected one, shoved it into the keyhole, twisted it, and pushed the door open.

A rush of air was sucked through the doorway as if the church were breathing in, and the boys started to cough as they crept cautiously inside, their eyes stinging. There was the smell of smoke. A thin haze hung in the vestry and they found it difficult to fill their lungs. The vestry was filled with stuff for the church like prayer books, choristers' robes, and the chaplain's bits and pieces.

"There's no oxygen," said Ed.

"You don't say, Einstein," Jack sneered.

Ed angrily turned on his friend and put a hand on his chest, holding him back as the others went on through to the church. "Quit it, Jack. For God's sake. Stop giving everyone a hard time. What's the matter with you? You never used to be like this."

"Yeah, I know. Sorry." Jack cleared his throat and spat on

the vestry floor, then he ran his fingers over the red birthmark on his face. "But *nothing* used to be like this, did it?"

Jack looked at Ed, defying him to argue.

"Well, it's the same for all of us," Ed croaked. "How does it help, you constantly sniping?"

"I said sorry, didn't I?"

"Did you? It didn't sound like much of an apology."

"What does it matter?" said Jack, shrugging off Ed's hand. "What does any of it matter? Hello, good-bye, please, thank you, sorry, I beg your pardon, can you pass the salt, please? What bloody difference does any of it make now? We're up to our necks in crap."

Ed couldn't think of anything to say, so he simply shook his head and followed the others to the chapel.

A metal wastebasket sat in the middle of the aisle with some smoldering wood in it, and a murky cloud of smoke clung to the roof beams. There were about fifteen boys in here. Some were lying in sleeping bags and under blankets on the floor; others were slumped on the pews.

"Are they dead?" asked Bam, scanning the lifeless bodies.

Ed didn't know if it was the foul air in the church, his fear, or simply exhaustion, but the blood felt tight in his head, which throbbed horribly. His lungs were burning. Without being conscious of it, he'd been holding his breath since his argument with Jack. He approached one of the boys on the floor and realized with a jolt that it was his friend Malik.

He reached out a hand. Malik looked like all the blood had been drained out of him. He was completely still. Ed touched his neck. It was damp and cool, but not cold. He knelt down by his side and put his ear to his chest. There was the faintest heartbeat, barely a flutter, a tiny rise and fall of his chest.

"No. They're not dead." Ed stood up—too quickly. He felt instantly dizzy and swayed on his feet.

"We need to get them out of here," said one of the nerds. "They need fresh air."

"There are no windows open," said Wiki, looking around. "If they've been burning wood, there'll be carbon monoxide. It's given off when there's not enough oxygen left for organic matter to burn properly. It's a deadly poison. It could poison us all."

7

The Sullivan brothers managed to unbolt the main doors of the church, and they threw them wide. Johnno and Piers, their friends from the rugby team, had picked up a comatose boy, but they hung back in the doorway.

They'd forgotten about the teachers.

The bigger of the two, Piers, looked back anxiously. "They're still out there," he said.

Jack strode over to where Piers had put down his weapon and snatched it up without stopping. He continued on outside. Bam followed, a grim look on his face. Mr. Langston, the history teacher, was trying to get the gate open, his swollen, mushy fingers unable to get a proper grip. Next to him, Ms. Warlock and the other teacher were shaking and moaning.

Jack kept on walking. Nothing was going to stop him. He went right up to Mr. Langston and swung the bit of iron hard at the side of his head. Langston went down.

Bam vaulted the wall, knocking Ms. Warlock over, and then took a swing at the third teacher. The blow jarred his head to a weird angle, but he stayed on his feet. Jack climbed over the wall and came up on the teacher from behind. There was a nasty wet crack as Jack hammered his club into the back of his skull.

None of the other boys could watch as Jack and Bam finished off the three teachers. But they could hear it. It sounded like men at work mending a road.

At last Jack came back over to the chapel.

"Get them out of there," he snapped, flinging the bloody iron bar aside.

Those who were strong enough began feverishly dragging boys out into the air, carrying them by their hands and feet. As soon as they dumped one on the grass they went back for another. As the limp figures drew clean air into their lungs they started to stir and wake up. Some just lay there groaning. Others sat against the gravestones of long-dead masters and churchmen, groggy, pale, and confused. One boy tried to stand, then collapsed to his knees and was sick on the ground.

Having made sure Malik was okay, Ed went back to find Matt, the boy who had led them all into the church. He discovered him curled up beneath the altar, one arm stretched out stiffly as if reaching for something. Clutched in his other hand was a sheaf of half-charred pages that had been torn from a book, a Bible by the look of it.

Ed slapped his face gently. Matt didn't respond, so he slipped his arms around his chest, ready to lift him. As he did, Matt suddenly came awake. He gripped hold of Ed with clawlike hands and looked up into his eyes.

"I've seen him," he said.

"It's all right, we've got you now," said Ed.

"I've seen him."

"Who have you seen, mate?"

"The Lamb. The Lamb is going to save us all."

"That's good to know," said Ed, humoring him while still trying to get him onto his feet.

"He came in a cloud of golden light, his shadow behind him. The Lamb. He's going to save us all. We have to prepare for his coming."

Bam came over to help, and they propped Matt up under each armpit and walked him outside, Matt babbling all the way, none of it making any sense.

They lowered him onto a bench in the graveyard and checked to make sure no more teachers had turned up.

It looked like the aftermath of a battle or gas attack. The boys from the church lay among the gravestones, puking and moaning, clutching their sides in agony. At least they seemed to be recovering, though.

The Sullivan brothers were the last out, carrying a skinny young lad between them. They gently put him down away from the others, and Anthony approached Ed and Bam.

"I think you should come look at this one," he said. "He won't wake up."

The little boy's face was chalk white, his lips slightly blue. Ed listened to his chest and peeled back his eyelids, then tried mouth-to-mouth, but there was no response. He was dead.

"His name was Jacob." Malik had revived enough to make his way over to the group of boys huddled around the dead kid. "He wasn't well before," Malik went on. "He had asthma, and his inhaler had run out."

"Poor little guy," said Bam. "What are we going to do with him?"

"We can't leave him out here. He'll be eaten," said Anthony matter-of-factly.

"But if we take him inside he'll start to . . . you know . . . smell. . . ." said Damien Sullivan, looking at his brother.

"We're in a graveyard, aren't we?" said Jack. "We'll bury him."

"The Lamb has taken him."

Everyone turned around. Matt was standing there, wrapped in a blanket, a strange drunken smile on his face.

"Taken him for his army," Matt went on. "Don't feel sad for him. The Lamb is going to save us all!"

It was cold in there at night. We couldn't get warm, so we broke up a couple of the pews and used the wood for a fire." Ed's friend Malik was sitting on a bench, drinking from a plastic bottle of water. His eyes were weepy and bloodshot and his hand was shaking. Ed was standing nearby, keeping watch for any teachers.

"I guess the smoke and fumes must have built up without us realizing," Malik went on, his voice hoarse.

"You're lucky you're not all dead." Ed relaxed and sat down next to Malik. "Carbon monoxide will kill you."

"I *feel* like death." Malik offered Ed a sickly grin. "I think my head's going to explode. And you want to watch out—I might spew at any second. Just don't ask me to stand up for at least three days. I'm dizzy enough just sitting here."

"You might have to stand, Malik." Ed was still scanning the road. "We're all right at the moment, but it's only a matter of time before more of the teachers figure out where we are and come sniffing around."

"I guess if it's a matter of life and death I'll make it

inside." Malik groaned and sank his head down between his knees, supported by his shaking hands. "Do you know if carbon monoxide can give you any permanent damage?"

"No idea," said Ed. "Wiki's the one to ask."

Malik made a face. "I don't want, like, brain damage or something."

Ed punched him lightly in the shoulder. "Wouldn't notice the difference," he said. "But, seriously, what's happened to Matt? Talk about brain damage. He's still coming out with totally random stuff."

Malik let out his breath slowly and noisily, then laughed through his nose.

"I think he's found God," he said.

"In a big way." Ed laughed as well now. "Was he a religious nut before?"

"Not that I know of," said Malik. "But stuck in there . . ." He nodded back over his shoulder to the chapel. "All we had to read were Bibles and prayer books. You know Archie Bishop?"

"Yeah."

"Well, one night he said we should all pray."

"He always was a bit like that," Ed interrupted. "His dad was a vicar or something, I think."

"Well, I'm a Muslim, as you know," said Malik. "So I pray every day anyway, at least I'm supposed to. So there we all were inside. I prayed to my God and they prayed to theirs. Even those kids who didn't believe in anything before got in on it. It sort of held us all together in a funny way. And Matt seemed to really get into it. Started reading parts of the Bible from the, you know, like, the pulpit thing. I didn't understand most of it, and I don't think he did either."

"What's all this stuff about the Lamb?" Ed asked. "Where did that come from?"

"Well, the thing was, as I say, it got really cold in there," said Malik, "and we'd started making these, like, fires, using anything we could find—pages from the prayer books and old Bibles and whatever to get it going. Then last night Matt, like, totally freaked out, said we shouldn't burn any more of the books, and he rescued a lot of pages from the burner we'd made, found us some charcoal instead. Bad idea. By the time we realized we were all being poisoned by the fumes it was too late—we were all passing out."

"Lucky we came over when we did."

"Too right," said Malik. "I was heading into the light, halfway to paradise. When you woke me up I thought you were God!"

Ed laughed, then Malik went on more seriously. "I reckon Matt's flipped," he said. "Can't blame him. It's been tough on all of us. Our food ran out three days ago, though we still had some water. I reckon we've all been seeing things, and Matt . . . well, Matt seems to think he's some kind of prophet or something now."

"Let's hope he doesn't freak any of the other kids out," said Ed.

"Too late for that," said Malik, rubbing his temples. "He's already got the younger kids following him around. We call them his acolytes. And Archie Bishop's become his, like, second in command."

Ed hauled himself up off the bench. "I'm going to go and see if he's all right."

• • •

Matt was sitting by himself away from the other kids. He was a tall boy of Ed's age with very little flesh on his bones. He was all angles and lumps, knobbly knees and elbows, sharp shoulders, pointy chin, and big nose. His usually very tidy hair was starting to grow wild. His skin looked gray. His eyes, sunk deep in purple sockets above high cheekbones, were bleary and unfocused.

Ed flopped down next to him.

"How you doing?"

"Better than ever." Matt smiled that weird spooky smile of his again. Maybe he thought he looked angelic; to Ed he just looked creepy.

"That's good. Listen, the reason we came over to the chapel to find you is we don't think we can stay here any longer. We need to find somewhere where there's food and water, and we, you know, we figured we should all stick together."

"Yes," said Matt, and his face broke into a huge radiant smile. "You've seen it too?"

"Seen what?"

"The vision."

Ed shook his head. "I haven't seen any visions, Matt."

Matt clutched Ed's arm, his fingers digging into the soft flesh. "I saw it. I saw it really clearly."

"Saw what?"

"A big church in London, bigger than any real church, as big as the whole city, with thousands and thousands of children inside it. Like an ants' nest. It was shining, the dome of the church was shining, and the Lamb was there. We have to be there to meet him."

"Meet the Lamb?"

"Yes. He'll look after us, and watch over us, as long as we follow him and follow what he's shown me, in the vision. . . ."

"You had a vision of a lamb telling you to go to London?"

"Yes. It was so clear, and it's all written here." Matt held up the torn and charred pages he'd been clutching when Ed had rescued him. Thrust them right into Ed's face. Ed tried to get up, but Matt still held on to him with his other hand.

"Listen," he said, and began to read: "*The throne of God and of the Lamb will be in the city, and his servants will serve him. They will see his face, and his name will be on their foreheads. There will be no more night. They will not need the light of a lamp or the light of the sun, for the Lord God will give them light. And they will reign forever and ever.* Don't you understand? He's left us a message, a new message. It was hidden in the pages of the old Bible, in the words, but this is a new message."

Ed tried not to laugh. "I don't get it," he said, frowning at the grubby sheaf of papers. "What sort of message?"

"I don't understand it all," said Matt, and he finally let go of Ed so that he could sort through the pages. "Not yet, but I'm working on it. I need to study the pages. Look, you see, the meaning has changed. . . . I need to get them in order. Some of the words have been burned away. . . ."

He waved a page at Ed.

"See this one here . . . *First begotten of the dead. Keeper of the keys of hell and death* . . . No, that's not the bit I meant, here, yes . . . *Then I heard a loud voice from the temple saying to the seven angels, 'Go, pour out the seven bowls of God's wrath on the earth.' The first angel went and poured out his bowl on the land, and ugly and painful sores broke out on the people who had the mark of the beast and worshipped his image.* Do you see? It's all in here. The disease, everything. It was all meant to be." Matt squinted at the lines of print and read out another passage. "*Men gnawed their tongues in agony and cursed the God of heaven because of their pains and their sores, but they refused to repent of what they had done.*"

"Yeah, look, Matt, I don't really get all this stuff. I'm not even sure I know what repenting is."

"The dead will rise again, Ed, but only the Lamb can save us."

"So you're saying Jesus will look after us?"

"No . . . Not Jesus, the Lamb."

"I thought the Lamb was Jesus."

"No . . . the Lamb is something new, a new kind of prophet, or a new God."

"You sound a bit confused about this, Matt."

"No. I saw him. I saw him clearly."

"Yeah? What did he look like, then, this Lamb?"

"He was one of us . . . a boy, a child, even younger. With golden hair. A child who isn't a child. In the vision I saw, he was walking out of the darkness, and all around him was light, and in his shadow walked a demon."

"A demon?"

"Yes, yes . . . I think so, but he was in darkness."

"What sort of demon?"

"He was in the form of a child as well, but dark-faced where the Lamb was alight. He was in shadow. They're like two sides of the same coin, heads and tails, yin and yang."

"Batman and Robin." Ed stood up and brushed his jeans clean.

"Don't make a joke of it, Ed; don't piss on it."

"Matt, I can't take any of this seriously. How can I? People don't have visions."

Now Matt stood, confronting Ed, standing too close. "We know hardly anything about the world, Ed. Isn't that clear? Isn't that really bloody clear now? Six months ago, if someone had said to you that everyone sixteen and older would either die or turn into a zombie, you'd have laughed at them. Wouldn't you?"

"Yeah, but . . ."

"These are strange new times," said Matt. "But it was all there, in the pages of the Bible. We just had to be shown it properly. We have to prepare. First there's the plague, then the fire, then the river of blood, and then—"

"All right. All right." Ed put up his hands in surrender. "I won't laugh at you, Matt. Just maybe keep this to yourself, though, yeah?"

"No, Ed, no!" In his excitement, Matt was spitting. "You have to listen to me. Everyone has to listen to me. We have to go to London! If you aren't there to welcome the Lamb, you'll be struck down like the other sinners."

"Maybe we don't all want to go to London!"

"I'm going to London."

While they'd been arguing, Jack had been listening in. Now he stepped between the two of them, keeping them apart.

"I'll go with you, Matt, at least as far as south London."

"Jack, we all need to stick together." Ed was trying to keep the emotion out of his voice. "It'd be crazy to go to London. There'll be more food and water in the countryside."

Jack shrugged. "I just want to go home."

"But there'll be nothing there, Jack."

"I don't care. I want to see my own home, my old bedroom. Get some of my old things, family photos; all my memories are there. I can't just let it all go."

"Jack, I thought we'd all decided last night," Ed pleaded. "We have to have a plan. And our plan was to go into the countryside. We have to stick together and we have to have a plan."

"I do have a plan," said Jack. "I'm going home."

Chris Marker opened his book to the page with the corner he'd folded down. He found that he could stop anywhere in a chapter and start up again at the exact same point without ever having to go back and reread anything. He never had to remind himself what was going on. It was as if there'd been no break between when he stopped reading and when he started again. In a funny way the story he was reading became the real world for him, more alive than the world he found himself in when he lifted his eyes from the page, blinking and lost. Real life was nothing more than a tiny interruption to his reading.

The kids were all assembled in the church, and they were talking, talking, talking. A repeat of last night in the dormitory . . . *We have to stick together, we need to find food and water, we should go to London, we should go into the countryside, we should go to the moon, blah blah blah. . . .*

So much talk. What difference did any of it make?

He heard a sniffle and a sob, and looked along the pew. The French girl, Frédérique, was sitting there with Johnno the rugby player, her cat-carrying box held tight in her lap. She hadn't spoken since they'd arrived at the chapel, but she seemed to like having Johnno with her.

There were raised voices, and Chris looked to the front. Jack and Ed were arguing again. Chris shook his head. Tried not to smile. He wondered if Jack was ever going to tell Frédérique that he'd nailed a plank of wood to her father's head.

They were very different, Jack and Ed. Ed, the poster boy for the school. He'd never had to worry about anything much before all this. Now he looked tired and scared all the time. Jack, whose strawberry birthmark had always made him look a bit angry, and who now really did seem to be in a permanent bad mood. Shorter than Ed, with darker hair, he had the feel about him of someone who wanted to start a fight.

Look at the two of them. Trying to take charge, to be in control. They were only fourteen years old. They were children. They were *all* only children. And out there . . . outside the chapel . . .

Chris didn't want to think about that.

Now Anthony Sullivan joined in.

"How far is it?" he asked. "To London? How long would it take to get there?"

"About twenty-five miles, I think," Jack answered. "Same distance as a marathon."

"It's twenty-one miles to Trafalgar Square," said Wiki. "So at an average human walking speed of three miles an hour, that would be roughly a seven-hour walk, if you did it in one go."

"What time is it now?" Anthony Sullivan asked.

"Quarter to eleven," said Matt. "We could be there by six o'clock."

"Provided there are no delays," Ed butted in. "You make it sound like it's a stroll in the park, 'Lah-di-dah-di-dah, let's all skip to London and take a sightseeing bus.' We don't know what's out there. If you go to London, you might have to fight every step of the way."

"You don't know it's going to be any easier going to the countryside," said Jack.

"I've never liked London," said Bam. "I grew up in the country."

"You're a yokel, Bam," said his friend Piers, and Bam grinned.

"Ooh arr!" he said, and the little kids laughed.

"I'm with Bam," Piers added. "I vote we go to the countryside."

Chris stayed with his head bent over his book.

He wasn't going to get involved in any stupid voting. He'd go along with whatever the others decided. As long as he had some books with him, he'd be all right. He had a sackload he'd looted from the school library. There'd be other libraries, bookshops, houses with bookshelves, a world of books. . . .

He'd always loved reading. Even before the disease, he'd retreated to the safety of stories. Books were a gateway into an alternative universe. They were magic. A book could hold anything inside it.

A book could hide Chris inside it.

He turned a page. He was reading a science-fiction adventure called *Fever Crumb*, set in London hundreds of years in the future. He found that reassuring. That there would still be something [in] the future, that the world wasn't about to end.

He smiled.

He was there, inside the walking the streets of London, living in the future city

And he was happy there.

The winter sky was a great slab of unbroken gray. The flat light made Rowhurst look like a picture laid out below him, not a real town at all. From up here in the church tower Jack had a clear view of the main street and the school buildings across the road. He was leaning on the battlements, wrapped in his coat to keep out the cold. A thin biting wind was carrying drizzle that settled on his hair and face and kept trying to run down the back of his neck.

The rain was staining the gray stonework of the school with dark, blotchy patches. The place had been founded four hundred years ago, but only a couple of buildings from that time remained. Most of the rest had been built in the nine-teenth century in a grand, heavy, and, quite frankly, ugly style. A row of black railings ran along the front, broken by the wrought-iron gates with the school's name in gothic letters across the top. Boys had been going in and out of those gates for nearly a hundred and fifty years. Too many boys to count. Jack wondered if any boys would ever come back here. Would this place ever be a school again? Or would the buildings slowly crumble and decay, split open by wind and rain and frost and the searching roots of trees and weeds? He'd never really enjoyed school that much. He'd struggled in class—his parents had hired a string of tutors to help him pass the entrance exam—and he'd always felt that he was never going to catch up with the other students.

Rowhurst had been his dad's old school. Dad had been very happy there and still kept in touch with his old school friends. . . .

No. Not anymore. Jack had to keep reminding himself that that world didn't exist anymore. The world of school reunions and dads going off on "boys' weekends," fishing and bike riding and whiskey tasting.

Welcome to hell.

A cold, gray hell.

In a funny way, Jack was going to miss school, though. It had been such a big part of his life, and if you didn't count the classes, he'd probably gotten a lot out of it. He'd made some good friends. He'd enjoyed the sports. He'd been a good all-rounder—football, running, tennis, cricket, swimming. Plus he'd liked acting in the school plays. He could cover over his birthmark with makeup, pull on a wig and a costume, and pretend to be someone else. He'd enjoyed playing villains most. He'd been Iago in a production of *Othello*. Kwanele had played the main part—he was the only black boy in the school. Kwanele was a bit hammy as an actor, and almost turned the play into a comedy, but audiences loved him and he had definite star quality. Everyone agreed that Jack's scenes with him were the best thing in the play, and it was the best theater the school had ever seen.

Ed had taken a small part, for a laugh, but he couldn't act to save his life. He just couldn't be anything other than himself. Good old Ed Carter. He was self-conscious and couldn't stop grinning in embarrassment.

Memories. That's all Jack had left now. That's all the school would become—a memory kept alive by however many boys survived. Would Jack one day tell stories of his schooldays to his own son as they huddled in the dark in some ruined building eating rats and drinking polluted water?

Ah, yes, son, the best years of my life . . .

Which they probably would be, of course. He couldn't see his life exactly improving from here on in.

Memories. You had to hang on to your memories somehow. That's why he wanted to get home—to try to grab a corner of the past and hang on to it.

He spat over the battlements, watching the spitball fall with the rain.

He certainly wouldn't ever forget the school. Not after all that had happened here in the last few weeks. How many teachers had he killed, he wondered.

He hadn't been counting.

Home, though, was a small precious memory that seemed to be slowly fading. A magical lost place. A place where the old Jack lived. The one who rode a bike and argued with his mom and dad and watched TV and spent hours on the Internet.

Very different from the new Jack, the one who cracked open the skulls of teachers and buried dead kids.

He was going to go back there, no matter what it took.

He'd come to the top of the tower to take a last look

around. See what might be waiting for him out there. The view was pretty good. He could see most of the school and a fair part of the town. The street was the main route in and out, and he had a clear view along it in both directions.

The town seemed quiet and peaceful from up here. If the sun had been shining, it might have been the picture on the box of a jigsaw puzzle. A typical small town in Kent with the sort of houses that children drew—red brick, pointy roofs, chimneys. If you didn't know, you would have no idea of the horrors that were going on all around you. If you looked closely, though, you could spot a couple of burned-out buildings, abandoned cars all over the roads. A dead body lying in the gutter. So far he hadn't seen another living soul since he'd climbed up here, though. The diseased grown-ups tended to stay inside when it was light. But they were there. Hundreds of them, thousands. . . .

It couldn't be any worse in London.

Jack looked north, in the rough direction he imagined his family home in Clapham to be. What lay between here and there? He wanted to get moving and find somewhere to sleep before it got dark.

"Is it all clear?"

Ed had come up the stairs and out of the little turret in the corner of the roof.

"Looks okay," said Jack. "You sure you don't want to change your mind? Come with me? Whatever happened to the idea that we were going to stick together no matter what?"

"There's nothing for me in London, Jack."

Jack felt like saying *There's me, your best friend, Jack,* but kept his mouth shut. Their friendship had become difficult lately; maybe it was time they went separate ways.

"I just think there's a better chance of survival in the countryside," Ed said. "It seems crazy to me to go into town."

Jack shrugged. "Maybe in London they're having twenty-four-hour parties with no adults telling them when to go to bed."

Ed smiled. "Maybe."

"You'll be all right," said Jack. "You've got Bam and all the rest. Bam knows how to take care of himself. If you stick with him you'll be fine." Jack didn't say it, but he knew that was what had decided it for Ed. He was going to stay close to Bam and the rugby players. Jack couldn't blame him. Survival was everything now. Stronger than old friendships, even.

He smiled and gave Ed a quick, awkward hug. "Take care."

"Yeah."

"How does that song go? 'I will survive'?"

"Yeah."

Ed looked pained, like he was struggling to say something. Whatever it was he didn't say it. They were both keeping their secrets to themselves.

That was how to survive.

What was the point of survival, though, if you became an animal? Scrounging for food, fighting, killing to stay alive? Jack's house, and all it contained, had become something special in his mind. Because what it contained was what made him human. He couldn't explain that to Ed. He wasn't sure he even understood it himself. He would never have had spacey thoughts like this before. Somehow, being close to death made you go deeper into your mind. Either that or you did what Bam did, shut your mind down, didn't think about anything, treated it all as a big joke.

Jack moved to the stairs.

"Please come with us," Ed pleaded. "Please, Jack."

"My mind's made up."

"You always were a stubborn bugger."

"Always will be. Now I've got to go."

11

Jack had put that song in his head and now he wasn't around to suffer the awful singing. Ed had started it; now they were all belting it out as they tramped along through the drizzle in a straggly line, for all the world like an unruly bunch of elementary-school kids on a trip.

Problem was, nobody really knew the words.

"I will survive . . . da-da-da-daa . . ."

Ed wondered if they would have been better off staying quiet and not attracting attention to themselves, but singing seemed to keep the shadows away, it gave them courage. As long as they were singing, they were invincible.

"I will survive . . . da-da-da-daa . . ."

They were marching south, out of the town, leaving the school and the church behind. None of them had been off the grounds in at least the last five weeks. For a while the town had been chaos, the streets overrun with crazies. Now the boys were goggle-eyed at how deserted everywhere was. The shops that had always been busy stood open-doored and empty, ransacked of all their stock. The houses were dark, lifeless, and neglected, with trash piled in the yards. Offices were silent. Cars abandoned. The only sign of life was when a dog ran out and barked at them. The shock had made them all jump, but after a moment's panic they'd burst out laughing and had mocked each other for being wimps. The dog was still tagging along behind, keeping a wary distance. It was skinny and scabby, with patches of fur missing.

But so far they'd seen no other people. Living or dead. They'd made it to the outskirts of the town. The shops had mostly given way to houses and small businesses. They passed a doctor's office; a dentist; the local pub, the Hop Sack, its windows blackened by fire. There was a big Tesco supermarket up ahead and, after that, beyond the common, was Futures Enterprise Zone, known by the locals as "The Fez," an ugly modern retail and industrial park, whose main occupants were a carpet warehouse and a tool-rental company.

Arthur and Wiki were walking along with a boy called Stanley, who had been part of the chapel group. They were having an intense conversation about whether you got wetter walking or running.

"Scientifically, the less time you spend in the rain, the less wet you'll get," Wiki was explaining. "So you're better off running. As long as you're running toward a shelter."

"We had floods last year," said Arthur, "at home. It rained really hard for two days and nights, and the river burst its banks; it was like the streets had become a river, you had to use boats to get anywhere; it was really fun, and I thought it would be probably the most exciting thing that was ever going to happen in my life, you know, like a disaster movie; you see them in the cinema and you think, that looks incredible, but it's never going to happen to me, because, mostly, living in England it used to be pretty boring; not anymore, though, this is more extreme than a flood, much more; it's maybe not as cool as a flood, and it's more, you know, terrifying, but it is like a real disaster movie, and I never thought that was going to happen."

When they got to Tesco, they stopped to take a look, but the place had been cleaned out and set on fire. All the food and drink had been looted from the gas station next to it as well, but there were a few useful items still on the shelves: flashlights, cigarette lighters, batteries, and a stack of road atlases.

Bam opened one out on the counter.

"Look," he said, pointing to the map with a stubby finger. "This is us, here, in Rowhurst. We're going this way, south-west, past The Fez. After that there are fewer and fewer buildings, and then we'll start to be in the countryside. Not proper countryside, though, still lots of town and villages and whatnot. We'll need to go more west to this open area here, toward Sevenoaks and Maidstone. That's proper farmland, that is. We'll get a pretty decent idea of what to expect once we're there. And it's near enough to some major towns if we decide the country life isn't for us after all."

"Looks like a plan," said Ed.

When they got outside, they found the group of boys from Field House throwing bricks at a glossy black Mercedes in the parking lot. They were trying to break the windshield, but so far the bricks were just bouncing off.

"Stand aside!" said Bam, and he picked up a huge block of masonry.

He ran at the car and hefted his missile at it with a grunt. This time the glass shattered, and the boys cheered.

The bang had seemed startlingly loud, as did the wailing alarm that followed it. It shrieked for about thirty seconds, then stopped.

The silence that followed was perhaps even more extreme. There were no angry shouts from adults, no sound of traffic, no airplanes overhead, no music. . . .

The boys, too, were quiet. Thoughtful. They were in a world of silence now, something that none of them had ever really known before. The comforting hum and buzz of civilization had ceased.

"Come on," Bam shouted. "Let's hear some noise! What's happened to the singing? We're on the road, a band of brothers, team effort and all that! How about a group hug before we go?"

"What?" Ed looked at him as if he'd lost his mind.

"Joke, okay?" said Bam, laughing "Don't lose your sense of humor, Ed me old mate. Now *ándale, ándale!* Let's get motoring."

As they marched off singing, the car alarm started up again as if cheering them on.

12

Jack was trudging along in the opposite direction out of town, wondering if he'd made the right decision. Aside from Matt and Archie Bishop and their six young acolytes, nobody else had come with him, and he was beginning to feel very alone.

Matt wouldn't shut up. He seemed to be able to talk tirelessly about his new religion. Spouting a nonstop stream of babble. To make it worse, if he ever paused, one of the acolytes would ask him a question and he'd be off again.

He was droning on now about what they could expect when they got to London.

". . . it will be changed by the Lamb to become a city of pure gold, as pure as glass, like transparent glass with twelve gates made of pearls, each gate made of a single pearl. You see? And there will be food, more food than we can eat, and clean water."

"But won't it be hard to get there?" asked Phil, the smallest acolyte.

"The Lamb will test us," said Matt, and he scrabbled through his scorched pages for a couple of minutes before he found the passage he was looking for. "*The first angel sounded his trumpet, and there came hail and fire mixed with blood, and it was hurled down upon the earth. A third of the earth was burned up, a third of the trees were burned up, and all the green grass was burned up. The second angel sounded his trumpet, and a third of the sea turned into blood, and a third of the ships were destroyed.* You see, we'll have to go through fire and rivers of blood."

"And a shipwreck?" asked another acolyte.

"Maybe."

"That sounds a bit scary," said Phil. "This is all a bit too real. It was all right in the chapel. I don't like it out here. It's like a ghost town."

"*Do not be afraid,*" said Matt, quoting again. "*I am the First and the Last. I am the Living One. I was dead, and behold I am alive forever and ever! And I hold the keys of death and Hades.* You see? The Lamb will look after us."

Jack sighed. He didn't have an iPod he could plug into his ears. The battery had long ago died on him. He wasn't sure he could put up with seven hours of this.

13

Ed was walking along with Malik and Bam. Bam as cheerful as ever. It seemed that not even the rain could spoil his good mood.

"Don't you ever get miserable, Bam?" Ed asked.

"Nope."

"Or scared?"

"Nope."

"Why not? What's your secret?"

"I have no imagination," Bam said in a very matter-of-fact way. "Never have done. Never will. Works just fine for me."

"Do you think we're doing the right thing?" Ed said quietly. "Going to the countryside and everything?"

"God knows," said Bam. "Just don't think about it, mate. Onward and upward and outward!" With that, Bam gave Ed a hefty slap on the back and strode off to catch up with his friend Piers.

"You worry about things, don't you, Ed?" said Malik. "You never used to."

"There's a lot to worry *about*."

"We're going to be all right, Ed. We'll find a barn to sleep in. A river to drink from. Maybe there'll be cows we can milk, sheep, and chickens."

"Pigs," Ed added.

"Technically I'm not supposed to eat pork," said Malik. "But I guess God might let me off if I'm just trying to stay alive."

"It'll be like going back to Victorian times," said Ed. "We can set up a sort of commune."

"We'll need to find some girls," said Malik.

"What, you mean to clean and cook?"

"No." Malik shook his head in exasperation. "That's not what I meant."

"All right, don't sound so misunderstood, Malik," Ed protested. "I know what your lot are like when it comes to women—keeping them in the home doing the housework and all that."

"We're not all like that, Ed. Just like you Christians aren't all the same."

"I'm not sure I am a Christian," Ed said.

"Whatever." Malik shrugged. "I meant we'll need to find some girls if we want to start repopulating the world."

"Fair point. We've got Frédérique for a start. We'll find others. Nice country wenches."

"Let's hope we can persuade them to join us," said Malik. "I don't know that much about girls."

"Do you ever wish you'd gone to a mixed-sex school?" Ed asked.

"My parents would never have allowed it," said Malik.

"They're not that strict Muslims, but there are some things they're quite old-fashioned about."

"They don't know about that girlfriend you had that time?"

"No way."

"Whatever happened to her, anyway?"

"She dumped me for an older boy," said Malik. "He had his own car and everything. Plus he didn't have any pesky Muslim hang-ups."

"How very shallow," said Ed, putting on a nasal nerdy voice.

"Indeed," said Malik, copying the voice. "How very shallow."

Johnno the rugby player was walking next to Frédérique, trying to get her to come out of her shell. She plodded along, head bent forward, hair hanging down like a veil. All Johnno could see of her face was the tip of her long nose, but he could tell that she was still miserable. Her shoulders were slumped and she barely lifted her feet as she walked, as if each step were a huge effort.

He tried asking her about her cat, about France, about her school, but he could get nothing out of her, not even a grunt. In the end he told her about himself. He thought at least it might distract her. He told her how he had grown up in Dover. How his dad worked for the customs department at the ferry port. How he had two sisters, his parents were divorced, and he'd got into the school on a sports scholarship. He explained how he lived for rugby. The French played rugby too, so he thought she might be interested in that, even though in his experience girls weren't really that much into rugby.

"I'm into music as well," he said. "Not just rugby. I don't much like indie music, though, and hate R&B. I like anything LOUD."

He couldn't remember when he'd last heard any music. You needed electricity to hear anything. Had all the music in the world just disappeared along with the power? What a weird idea, to think that there would be no more AC/DC, no more Led Zep and Nirvana and the Rolling Stones and the Stone Roses. . . .

Best not say anything about all that to Frédérique; he was meant to be cheering her up, wasn't he? He'd only bring her down even further if he started to point out all the things that no longer existed because there wasn't any electricity.

The Internet, music, TV, films . . .

Bloody hell.

They were coming up to the Futures Enterprise Zone—The Fez. A modern development of low brick buildings each with its own parking area in front.

Bam caught up with Johnno.

"I've been thinking," he said.

"Are you sure that's a good idea?" Johnno asked with a grin.

"Ha-ha, laughed the man," said Bam. "No, listen, there's that tool place in The Fez. We should check it out. We could really get tooled up, if you'll pardon the pun. Most of us have still only got bits of broken bed and sticks. There'll be axes in there, crowbars . . . *chain saws.*"

He said "chain saws" with such relish that Johnno smiled.

"Might be worth a look," he said.

"Come on, then."

Bam spread the news and they veered off the road into The Fez, which was as deserted as everywhere else in Rowhurst.

They passed the carpet warehouse, and there ahead of them was the tool-rental store. It looked untouched, though there was evidence of fire damage to the laminating factory to the right. The steel shutter over the loading bay was rolled up, and inside it was blackened and sooty.

Ed and Malik were in the middle of the party, still discussing girls. Not really paying much attention to where they were.

"We've got to think practically," Malik was saying. "We need to make sure the human race doesn't die out. It's hard to imagine—but us lot, we're the future."

Ed looked around at the others. "It's not much of a future, is it? A bunch of public school boys and a girl with a cat in a box."

"We'll find other kids," said Malik. "We can't be the only ones who've survived."

"Well, it's certainly looking that way so far," said Ed.

"No," said Malik. "You'll see. For the first time in weeks I'm starting to feel positive. Not too positive, mind, let's not get carried away here, but I really think that—"

Malik was gone.

One second Ed was talking to him, and the next . . .

It took Ed a moment to process the information, to make sense of what he'd seen—the brief flash of a face in the darkness of the factory doorway, a white face with black eyes and yellow teeth, two hands reaching toward Malik's neck.

He'd been pulled inside.

Before Ed had time to shout, to warn the others, bodies erupted from all around, from out of the doorway, from the gaps between buildings, from behind them, moving fast, hitting the boys hard.

There were screams coming from all around Ed now. And everywhere he turned there was a confused melee of writhing shapes.

What should I do? What should I do?

Malik was in the building. His friend Malik. Ed made a halfhearted move toward the doorway, and saw in the dim interior about ten of them, three or four crouched over Malik's body, the others coming straight for him, charging out of the gloom. Ed backed away, and the figures exploded into the daylight, arms flailing, teeth bared.

Teenagers. Boys and girls. They looked to be about seventeen or eighteen.

Ed turned and ran. Shouting to the other boys.

"Stay with me. Get away from here." But he had no idea if anyone could hear him, if anyone could do anything.

He saw Johnno go down, with three or four teenagers on his back, another two pulling his arms and legs. The Field House boys were in a huddle, panicked. The three nerds were backed up against a wall, sobbing.

The teenagers were faster and stronger and more brutal than the older teachers from the school. They were filthy, their clothes stained with blood and worse. Some wore hoodies, some were wearing only T-shirts, others were so ragged it was hard to tell what they were wearing—their clothes hung off them in tatters. A few were nearly naked, their bodies a mess of wounds and pus-filled boils. One or two of them were older boys from the school, wearing suits. Ed recognized a prefect. He'd lost most of his hair and one eye and looked more like an animal than a human now. He had a smaller kid, Stanley, one of the boys from the chapel that Ed remembered carrying out into the fresh air only an hour ago. The prefect was swinging him around by one arm, his face blank and emotionless.

And all the while the rain fell in a steady monotonous drizzle. It was a dull, damp, gray day. A typical English day. Boring and flat. A day for staying indoors and waiting for tomorrow. And here they were, dying on this dreary industrial estate.

Ed spotted Frédérique, still hanging on to her cat carrier. She was standing frozen, staring a hundred miles into the distance, while the fight raged around her. He grabbed her and pulled her away from where four teenagers had Johnno on the ground and were trying to bite his stomach. Then Ed saw Wiki and Arthur cowering behind a pile of boxes. Ed grabbed Wiki and hoped that Arthur would follow.

"We have to get away from here," he shouted, but there was nowhere to run. Wherever they turned there were more of the older kids.

Ed dragged his gang toward the Sullivan brothers, who had made it back to the road and were holding out, fighting back clumsily but effectively with their garden spades. There were just too many of the teenagers, though, and before Ed got to the brothers, he watched helplessly as a fat teenager got Anthony from behind and sank her teeth into his neck. Anthony yelled and clutched at the wound, dropping the spade. Instantly, two more were on him, girls with maniacal twisted faces covered in spots and blisters.

Damien tried to batter the girls off his brother, but he was overpowered by a mob of bigger boys, and he went down struggling and cursing.

Ed switched direction and bumped into someone running the other way. He went sprawling, pulling Frédérique and Wiki down with him. He let go of them and rolled to his feet. Both Sullivan brothers were on the ground now, and it didn't look like they'd be getting up again. And there was one of the Field House boys trying to run with two girls on his back and another with her arms around one leg. He fell over with a yell.

Ed made it out of the estate and into the road but was knocked over again and ended up with someone on top of him. He laid into them desperately with knees and elbows.

"Ow, stop it!" It was one of the nerds, his shirt torn half off his back. Ed apologized, and they helped each other up. The nerd—Justin—picked up a bit of bed frame that had been dropped by a rugby player and started lashing out around him in a blind, red-faced fury, keeping the circling teenagers at bay.

Ed looked around for Frédérique and the younger boys. Wiki and Arthur had disappeared, but Frédérique was standing frozen again. A slobbering, wet-faced teenager was crouched in front of her, sniffing her, his head moving up and down her body. For some reason he wasn't attacking her, maybe because she was standing so still he couldn't tell if she was alive.

Wasn't that what you were supposed to do if you were attacked by a bear? Play dead?

Whatever; the teenager was just dribbling and sniffing, and Frédérique wasn't moving.

Ed had just enough time to register this before he was flattened again. And no sooner was he up than he was down once more. There was such a confusion of sprawling bodies that he couldn't remain standing for more than a few seconds at a time. Sometimes he was knocked over by the older kids; sometimes it was one of his friends from school.

He was weeping in fear and rage and frustration.

He didn't want to die. Not here. Not like this . . .

14

As he walked, Jack constantly scanned his surroundings, keeping alert for any movement, any signs of danger. It felt very strange being out on the streets after all those long days cooped up in the school, and he had had no idea how dangerous the outside world was now. There were signs of violence. They'd seen wrecked shops and a few dead bodies, but so far no living ones. No kids, no adults. Nothing. Just a dreary parade of boring houses sitting gray and damp in the rain. Matt and Archie were so absorbed in their conversation about the Lamb that they seemed to have completely forgotten they might be in any danger at all. That wasn't clever of them. The sudden attack that came from nowhere was the most devastating. You had to be prepared.

Jack wanted to scream at the boys to shut up and pay attention, but feared they would only try to involve him in their discussion. There was no way of getting through to Matt— he was utterly obsessed. He really seemed to think that the Lamb, whatever the hell that was, would protect him from anything.

He was reciting something by heart as he walked, without needing to look at the pages, which he'd put away to keep them dry.

"I was dead, and behold I am alive forever and ever! He who overcomes will not be hurt at all by the second death."

"Will it be clear when we meet the Lamb what it is?" asked one of the younger boys. "What will it look like?"

"Not *it*," said Matt. "*He*. The Lamb is a boy like us. His hair is golden. His face is white and shining, and he walks with a shadow."

"You keep saying that, Matt, but what does it mean?" Archie Bishop asked. "Surely we all walk with a shadow."

"The Lamb's shadow is a living shadow, like a doppelganger."

"A what?"

"It's a fancy word for a double. It's like his dark half, his dark brother. He's a demon who speaks in tongues."

"My older brother, Robert, went on an Alpha Course," said Archie. "They speak in tongues. He did a bit for me. It sounded mad."

"Should *we* speak in tongues, do you think?" Matt asked, getting excited.

"We could try."

"How do you do it?"

"Well, you just sort of let the spirit guide you and you sort of go, blah laa laa, baba babala laaa la la al ba ba ba blaaa. . . ."

Matt joined in, going, "Blaa maa kaaa baa laaa . . ." but soon broke down into helpless giggles. "We need to practice that a bit."

The acolytes started up, and soon all of them were chirping away, laughing and spouting gibberish.

Great, thought Jack. I'm on marathon walk to London, likely to be ambushed by diseased nutters at any moment, and I'm stuck with a load of idiots who sound like they've escaped from the set of *In the Night Garden*.

15

When he was eight, Ed had gone on a family holiday to the west coast of France. There had been signs everywhere reading CÔTE SAUVAGE—wild coast—and the waves had been huge. One day his dad had taken him out to brave them. It had been amazing, rising up on the swell, diving through the breakers, bodysurfing, but then one had taken him by surprise and knocked him off his feet.

It had been terrifying, being rolled over and over, not knowing which way was up or down, a hideous churning confusion of water and sand. Whenever his feet had found the bottom, they'd been whipped away and he'd been spun again, like being inside a giant washing machine.

At last his dad had grabbed him and pulled him up.

That's how it felt being in this fight. And his dad wasn't here to rescue him today. His dad would never be able to help him again. Winded once more against the hard concrete, he didn't have the strength to get up. He drew in a painful rasping breath, rolled onto his back, and the next thing he knew one of the teenagers was on him. A sharp-faced boy who looked to be about eighteen. It was hard to tell, though, because his eyes were bulging out of his head, and his face resembled a Margherita pizza, livid red with crusty yellow patches, like the worst case of teenage acne Ed had ever seen.

With a mad, terrified burst of energy, Ed just managed to get his hands around the boy's neck and hold him off at arm's length.

The boy was snarling and snorting, which made green snot bubble from his nose. Pinkish-looking saliva foamed from between his rotten teeth, flecked with blood. It mingled with the snot and formed into a dribble that hung down like a rope, dangling over Ed's mouth. A drop fell from the end and spattered onto Ed's lips. He jerked his head to the side and spat. More warm dribble pooled in his ear.

Ed shook his head.

The teenager looked horribly diseased. Ed didn't understand how the sickness worked, nobody did, but the thought of catching it off this drooling, pizza-faced git was horrifying.

He lay there on his back, arms straight out, squeezing the boy's neck and trying to keep him away at the same time. He had a horrible image of one of those rubber toy heads that when you squashed them the eyes and tongue popped out. The teenager had shorter arms. He couldn't quite reach Ed, but he scrabbled wildly at him, scratching his skin with dirty black fingernails. Ed could do little to stop the crazed attack, and he felt his arms shaking with the strain. He wasn't sure how much longer he could hold out.

And then the boy would fall on him and press that gaping mouth into Ed's face.

There was a shout—"Look out, Ed!"

Out of the corner of his eye Ed saw Bam pounding over.

Bam shouted "PUNT!" and Ed let go of the boy just as Bam swung his leg in a mighty dropkick. His boot connected with the boy's head and sent him spinning over backward. Ed scrambled to his feet and glanced at his attacker, who lay still for a moment, then got to his knees and started to crawl about in circles, his head bent at a crazy angle. He appeared to be looking for something, and then Ed realized that the force of the kick had knocked one of his eyes out.

Ed felt faint and turned away to be sick. Bam caught him and held him up.

"No time for that, mate. Gotta keep moving."

"I can't," Ed sobbed. "I can't. I can't do this."

"Yes you can."

Before Ed could say anything else, a fresh group of teenagers jumped Bam, and he was at the center of a thrashing brawl, arms and legs working furiously to keep his attackers off him. He seemed to have lost his weapon and was fighting barehanded.

Ed had nothing left. He was alone. Exhausted. Terrified. He was sick of the sight of blood. His ears were filled with the sound of screaming. He fell to his knees, looked up at the sky and opened his mouth wide, but his throat had closed, his vocal cords had gone tight, and all that came out was a long, hopeless, silent shout of despair.

And then the screams of the other boys were drowned out by a rumble and a roar. Something huge was approaching down the road, looming out of the misty rain like a breaching whale. There was the blast of a horn.

Two of the teenagers let go of Bam and turned to stare,

dumbly. They were flattened with a bone-breaking crunch.

Ed's lungs had stopped working altogether. His chest was gripped by bars of iron. It felt like his heart had stopped as well. He couldn't move or make sense of what was happening as the hulking leviathan headed straight for him where he knelt in the middle of the road.

16

With a final mighty hiss and a screech of metal scraping against metal, the thing stopped inches from Ed.

It was a bus. A bloody monster of a thing, ten feet wide and twice as high. White, with smoked windows. Ed could feel the heat coming off it.

It seemed so out of place here. A thing from the past. Ed wouldn't have been more surprised if a dragon had just landed snorting fire and smoke. He scrambled around to the side, half crawling, half running, and the passenger door opened with a sigh.

Ed froze.

There was a man in the driver's seat. Stocky and round-faced with a big head and close-cropped fair hair. Thirty-five, maybe forty—Ed was never very good at judging. The thing was, though, he was a man. An adult. The enemy.

"Get in!" he barked at Ed.

Was this a rescue or a trap? The man didn't look diseased, but that didn't mean anything. You couldn't trust any adults at all. And yet he was driving a bus. None of the other adults, whose brains had been rotted by the disease, could drive a bus. Most of them could hardly even walk.

"Get in, or I'm going."

Before Ed could do or say anything, Wiki and Arthur pushed past him and scurried up the steps. Chris Marker and Kwanele, still lugging his designer suitcase, followed hard on their heels.

Ed turned back to where the last survivors were still fighting.

"Get on the bus!" he screamed. "Come on, quickly!"

He saw Frédérique and grabbed her again, almost throwing her up the steps. Then he got hold of Justin, the nerd who had fallen on him earlier, and dragged him away from three vicious-looking teenage girls. Four boys from the chapel pushed past, then Bam came barrelling over with his arm around one of his rugby players. It was Piers, his red hair soaked with blood. Ed helped them onto the bus, but as he climbed on board himself, he felt a hand close around his left ankle and tug him backward. He fell painfully on the steps.

"Stay down!" the bus driver shouted, and Ed did as he was told.

There was a flash and a bang. Ed felt something skim over his head, brushing his hair, and whoever had hold of him let go. He looked up to see the driver pointing a shotgun out the door, smoke rising from the end of its double barrels. Ed crawled up the rest of the way, the doors closing behind him, and the bus started to move.

He hauled himself to his feet and slumped into one of the front seats, too shattered to take another step. Every part of him felt bruised and battered.

"That's not everyone," he croaked. "There must be more?"

"I couldn't wait any longer, pal. Too risky by half," said the driver. "You'd better say good-bye to whoever you left behind."

"We have to check. We have to make sure."

"No we don't. We have to get away from here."

Ed felt the bus speed up. Heard the thump of bodies being hit.

"You're not safe yet, sunbeam," said the driver, grimacing as he wrenched the wheel around, and the whole bus jolted and juddered as its wheels ran over something—or someone. "Not till we've put this lot behind us."

Ed twisted around in his seat and looked along the length of the bus—how many of them were missing? Half? More?

"Look out!" the driver yelled, and Ed turned back just in time to see a teenage girl being squashed against the windshield like a giant bug. The driver turned a switch and the wipers sped up, smearing pus and blood over the smoked glass.

"That's the last of them, I reckon. Looks like a clear run ahead."

Ed was shivering. He pulled his knees up and huddled in a ball on the seat, trying to shut the world out. He looked at the man driving the bus. He had a thick slab of a body, with skinny legs and fat muscled arms. He seemed fit and healthy. Ed should have been curious. Who was he? Where had he come from? Why was he not sick like all the others? But he couldn't care less. The man might as well have been someone in a film. A boring film about a bus driver.

There was a boy sitting quietly behind him. He looked

like a smaller version of the driver—slightly fat, with a big round head and close-cropped hair. The only real difference, apart from the size, was that the boy wore a pair of wire-framed glasses.

The driver must be his dad.

Who cares? Who bloody cares?

The boy noticed Ed and gave him a shy smile.

Ed ignored him.

He closed his eyes. And the boy's smile was replaced by Malik's smiling face. Malik had one of those faces that always seemed to be smiling.

Terrible thoughts crowded in on him, and he couldn't keep them out. He'd left Malik behind. He'd abandoned his friend because he was scared. He was a coward. There was no other word for it. He was a stinking, useless coward. He slapped his hand against his forehead.

Coward.

He sniffed and brushed a tear from his damp cheek. He was in the grip of a dark shadow; it seemed to wrap around him like a physical thing. A black cloud of misery and despair. This was a new feeling for him. He'd always been a cheerful boy, untroubled by anything. His life had run very smoothly. He'd passed every exam, won every cricket match, gotten texts from every pretty girl, sailed along without a care, not really thinking about anyone other than himself. He'd been happy because there had been nothing to make him unhappy. There had been no upsets.

He had no way of dealing with being unhappy. He felt helpless and broken. With Jack and Malik gone, he didn't even have anyone to talk to, to share his problems with.

He slumped down in the seat, staring ahead as the wipers went left-right-left-right across the rain-flecked windshield, *clomp-squeak-clomp-squeak-clomp-squeak* . . . gradually removing all traces of blood.

Clomp-squeak-clomp-squeak . . .

The bus trundled on, back the way they'd just come. Past the common. Past Tesco. Past the dentist and the empty silent houses, the doctor's office, the Hop Sack, the little row of shops.

Clomp-squeak-clomp-squeak . . .

There was the school now, and a knot of teachers wandering in the road. Ed barely noticed as the bus plowed through them, knocking them aside.

Clomp-squeak-clomp-squeak . . .

"Where are we going?" he said, surprised by the low droning sound of his voice. He had only meant to think the question, not ask it out loud.

"London," said the driver. "The big smoke."

Ed gave a short bitter laugh. So much for his dreams of the country life. The sunny commune packed with wenches; milking cows, fattening pigs, collecting eggs, making babies, building a bright new future with Malik and his other friends. All gone now. All gone.

Clomp-squeak-clomp-squeak . . .

They drove along the highway. The driver had to slow down to maneuver the bus through a jumble of cars that had been left in the middle of the road. Once they were through the obstacle they sped up again and were soon passing the railway station and leaving town on the long straight road that led to the M25. There were buildings nearly all the way along here. The little villages that had once been distinct and separate had joined together into one continuous ugly strip of housing, garages, shops, and offices.

Clomp-squeak-clomp-squeak . . .

There were people up ahead. Walking down the road. Gray shapes in the rain. More crazies probably. Ed gripped the armrests of his seat, ready for the jolt as they were knocked aside.

As the bus drew nearer, the walkers must have heard it. They turned around, their faces white streaks.

"Wait!" Ed shouted, leaning forward, craning to get a better look.

"What's the matter?" the driver barked. "Sit down."

"Stop the bus. You have to stop. It's Jack!"

17

W hat's going on?"

The boys came warily up the steps. They looked wet and confused, but unharmed. Archie Bishop and Matt came first, with their younger followers. Then finally Jack. He turned to Ed, frowning.

"What is this?"

"We were attacked." Ed said it with a hint of shame in his voice, as if it had been his fault.

"Attacked? Who by?"

"Older kids. Teenagers, seventeen, eighteen, nineteen. There were too many of them for us. The bus came . . ."

Now Jack really looked at the driver for the first time, then back to Ed.

"Who is he?" he said with a hint of accusation.

"My name's Greg," said the driver. "Greg Thorne. And if you want to come to London, get off them steps and go sit down."

Jack still looked at Ed. "He's an adult."

"Hey!" Greg shouted. "You can talk to my face, sunshine, or you can get off my bus."

"I don't mean to be rude," said Jack.

"Then don't be," Greg snapped. "I've saved your sorry asses here. I think a thank you would be in order, don't you?"

"It's just . . ." Jack looked uncomfortable, hovering half-way up the steps. "Everything that's happened . . . you must admit it's hard for us to trust anyone older than we are."

"The door's still open," said Greg, nodding toward the outside world, where the rain was falling more heavily now. "You want to take your chances out there, that's fine by me. But make up your mind—you're letting all the heat out."

Jack came up one step and looked along the bus. Matt and his gang had already made their way to where the survivors from the chapel group were sitting, urgently catching up with what had happened.

"Do I look like I'm diseased?" Greg said, jutting out his jaw in a challenge. "Do I *act* like I'm diseased? Can any of those dozy sods out there drive one of these things? They can't even speak no more, let alone master a three-point turn. So I'm your best hope, pal. Your *only* bleeding hope. An adult with a clean bill of health and a bloody big bus."

Jack came up the last couple of steps. "Thanks, Mr. Thorne," he said stiffly.

"Don't bother with the Mr. Thorne crap. You can just call me Greg—everyone else does."

"Okay."

Jack sat down next to Ed.

"Did you see anyone else?" Ed asked. "Did you have any trouble?"

"No. The only trouble was being stuck with Matt and Archie and having to listen to their bull. So what happened to you?"

Jack said it as if Ed had had some minor upset. How could he have known what it had really been like? For Jack the last half hour had been nothing more than a boring walk through the rain.

"Did anyone get hurt?"

Ed stared out the window, unable to catch Jack's eye. "Yes," he said quietly.

"Badly?"

Ed couldn't hold it in any longer. All the bottled-up fear and frustration and rage came pouring out.

"Look around you, Jack, look who's here," he shouted. "Can't you see?"

"You lost people?"

Ed nodded.

"How many?"

"I don't know, I haven't checked. I can't face it, Jack."

"How many?" Jack jumped up and started to make his way down the length of the bus.

Ed followed him. "What difference does it make?"

"Who's missing?"

"They're not *missing*, Jack, they're dead." Ed grabbed Jack's shoulder and pulled him back. "There was nothing we could do, okay? If Greg hadn't come along, we'd *all* be dead."

"So it was all thanks to Greg?" said Jack.

"Yes."

"Not *you*? You didn't do anything?"

"What do you mean?"

"You didn't whack any of them?"

Jack stared at Ed. Ed tried to say something, but it just came out as mumbled nonsense.

"I've seen you, Ed, in a fight," said Jack. "Or should I say I've *not* seen you in a fight."

"Please, Jack."

"You can't hit them, can you? You won't get your hands dirty. You're bloody useless."

Before Ed could protest, Jack had turned away and was walking on down the aisle.

Ed felt like crying, but knew he had to hold it together. The thing was, Jack was right: he still couldn't bring himself to hit any of them. He'd hoped Jack hadn't noticed. But Jack didn't miss a thing.

"Malik?" Jack called out. "I don't see Malik."

Ed caught up with him.

"No," he said, the word catching in his throat. "He didn't make it. This is all that's left of us."

"Jesus."

Jack was trying to take it in. Who else was dead? He spotted Bam. At least Bam was all right. He was sitting with Piers, who had blood seeping from a head wound. Bam was trying to bandage him with a piece of ripped shirt.

"Where's Johnno and the others?" Jack asked him.

Bam just shook his head.

"All three of them?" Jack couldn't believe it.

"Yes."

"But they were hard guys. They were good fighters."

"You weren't there, Jack," said Bam, staring Jack down. "You don't know what it was like. They ambushed us. There was nothing we could do. It was a bloody massacre. You had no right to talk to Ed like that. Ed looked after the little kids and the girl. I saw him. He got us all on the bus. So you apologize to him. Right now."

Jack dropped his head, put a hand out, and squeezed Ed's arm. "I'm sorry, mate," he said quietly. "I shouldn't have said that. I was out of order. It's just . . . It's not real. It's totally freaked me out. I said good-bye to you all less than an hour ago. Who's left?"

He continued to check the seats. Ed walked behind him.

Justin the nerd was sitting by himself, his head in his hands. Both his friends were missing. Jack couldn't see *any* of the Field House boys.

"They can't all be dead."

"They are."

Matt was sitting with the remaining four boys from the church group who hadn't set off with him to London. "You should have come with me," he said as Ed went past. "The Lamb would have protected you."

"Shut up, Matt!" Ed yelled at him. "Your poxy made-up religion wouldn't have made any difference."

"But it *did* make a difference, didn't it?" said Matt, with a smug smile. "We weren't touched."

"That was just luck."

"Was it?"

"Leave it, Ed." Jack kept walking. "There's no point in arguing with him. I've tried it."

Frédérique was all right, as was Kwanele, and Chris Marker, who as usual had his head buried in a book, oblivious to the world. Arthur and Wiki were sitting together. They looked very pale and shocked, but at least they were unhurt.

Farther back were a little boy and a girl with long curly black hair, whom Jack didn't recognize. Greg must have picked them up earlier. They looked at Jack and Ed as if they were intruders, strangers who had gotten into their safe place, but then the girl smiled at them. A big open friendly smile showing tiny white teeth.

"Hello," she said. "My name's Zohra. I'm nine. This is my brother, Froggie. He's seven. I'm looking after him until Mom gets back. We're going to London. Everything's going to be all right there; Greg said so."

Froggie smiled too, now. The smile was so hopeful and trusting it broke Jack's heart. He was aptly named. He had big, slightly bulging eyes and a wide mouth. Jack wouldn't have been surprised to learn that he had webbed feet.

"Yeah," he said kindly. "Everything's going to be all right."

"I've never been to London," said Froggie. "I want to go on the London Eye."

Jack was about to say something to try to reassure the little boy, when he was stopped by a shout from the back of the bus that hit him like a slap.

"Hey, you. Ketchup face! What's your name?"

18

There were three girls half hidden behind a wall of cardboard boxes, as far back as they could get on the bus. There were more boxes stacked up around them, and crates of bottled water wrapped in plastic film.

Jack walked toward them. "Are you talking to me?" he asked as he got nearer.

"Don't see no one else with crap all over their face."

The girl sniggered, and a hot flush of anger passed through Jack, as if his blood had suddenly turned to acid. He glared at the girls. At first it was as if the three of them were one single creature, the way a gang of girls can be, stronger than their individual parts. They looked to be about his age, dressed in clothes that must once have been fashionable, but were now dirty and tattered. They were a riot of bright colors, big hair, too much makeup, broken accessories, and ripped tights, like a new girl band with an extreme image.

Apocalypse Divas . . .

There was an overpowering smell of cheap perfume coming from them. Presumably they'd drowned themselves in the stuff to hide the fact that none of them had taken a shower in ages.

Jack was suddenly aware of his own body odor in the cramped confines of the bus, made worse by the damp fumes rising from his soggy clothes.

It was the pretty blond one chewing gum in the aisle seat who'd shouted at him. She looked at him defiantly. Daring him to say something.

Jack just stood there, too angry to speak.

"You been in a fight?" she asked.

"Yeah, I've been in lots," Jack snapped. "But that's got nothing to do with this." He put a hand to his birthmark.

The girl kept staring at him. Like a fussy shopper wondering whether to buy something.

"So, what is that all over your face, then?"

"It's a birthmark."

"A birthmark? You mean you was born like that?"

"Yes."

"Does it hurt?"

"No."

"Why don't you do something about it, then? You know, get it removed? Like a tattoo? Can't you get it removed?"

Jack shrugged. His anger was fading away. At least this girl was direct and honest. Most people when they first met him were embarrassed and pretended not to notice anything different about him, and then they'd secretly stare at him when they thought he wasn't looking.

"So, what's your name?" she asked, her jaw working away at the gum.

"Jack."

"*Jack*," she repeated, trying it out. "Are you all, like, from the same school, or something?"

"Yes. Rowhurst."

"Never heard of it. Must be expensive. You look rich. Some of you is wearing suits. Only rich kids wear suits. Are you?"

Jack shrugged again.

The blond girl nodded to Ed, who was hanging back behind Jack. "Who's your friend?"

"I'm Ed."

"*I'm Ed*," she mimicked. "You're even fancier than he is. I bet you're a millionaire."

"Money doesn't really exist anymore, does it?"

"Yeah, but *were* you a millionaire?"

Ed laughed. "No."

"Was it horrible back there?" asked the girl nearest the window, whose black hair and dark skin were almost the opposite of her blond friend. "We couldn't look."

"It was pretty bad," said Ed. "We lost a lot of friends."

"I'm sorry." The girl offered him a sad smile.

"My name's Aleisha, by the way," she added, then nodded to her blond friend. "She's Brooke. She's got a well big mouth on her, but she's a'right."

"I ain't a'right," said Brooke. "I'm a right bitch, but I'm pretty so I can get away with it. Unlike Aleisha, who's an ugly little midget and has to be nice to everyone."

"Ha-ha," said Aleisha. "Everyone knows I'm prettier than you."

"On what planet? My *butt* is prettier than you, Mrs. Shrek."

The three girls laughed.

Jack felt self-conscious, awkward. He'd always been slightly nervous around girls, not helped by his birthmark. Ed was different. Ed was easy and relaxed with everyone. Didn't matter who. Already he was settling down comfortably on the edge of a seat, leaning forward, smiling at the girls' jokes. Jack stood there in the aisle feeling like an idiot, shuffling from one foot to the other. He wanted to go, but thought it might look like he was running away from them.

Ed wasn't hanging back.

"What are you called?" he asked, eyeballing the third girl.

"That's Courtney," said Aleisha.

"We're like a set," said Courtney, who was larger than her friends, not exactly fat, but not thin either. Her hair was scraped back and she had a nasty bruise under one eye that she'd tried to hide with makeup.

"Brooke's like white bread," Courtney went on. "Aleisha's black, I'm half and half."

"You're a sort of yellow," said Aleisha.

"I ain't yellow," said Courtney indignantly. "Do I look yellow to you?"

"Yeah, an' I'm not black neither," said Aleisha. "Black is like *black*, like black ink. My skin ain't black. It's brown. I'm African-Caribbean. Not like you. I don't know *what* you are."

"Who are you kidding, sister?" said Courtney. "You're black as they come."

"So how did you end up on the bus?" Ed interrupted before they got into another argument. "Were you all friends before?"

"This is our bus!" said Brooke.

"Your bus?"

"Our bus!" said Courtney and Aleisha together.

"We was on a school trip, near Bilbao, in Spain."

"Spain's a dump," said Courtney. "Don't go there."

"We was there when people started getting, like, sick," said Aleisha. "It was really scary, like a disaster movie or something. At first it looked like we was gonna be stuck there, but in the end our teachers said we had to try and get home. We drove all the way across Spain and France to get to the ferry, and all the time it was getting worser and worser. We heard it on the radio. Our cells wasn't working, so we couldn't speak to none of our families or no one."

"By the time we got to the ferry the port was closed," said Courtney. "The French ferry people was on, like, strike. They said they didn't want to spread the disease."

"We was in this, like, gross hotel for ages in Calais," said Aleisha. "With no food."

"Calais is a *dump*," said Courtney. "I am not *ever* going back to Calais, man."

Brooke picked up the story. "Some of the kids went off with a teacher to, like, try and get back on their own," she said. "But in the end the British government arranged for this, like, special ferry to bring everyone back who was stuck there. We was the last ferry out of France."

"It was horrible," said Aleisha. "People was going mad trying to get on, but because we was, like, children, they let us go, yeah?"

"Back in England it was worse, though," said Brooke. "The roads was all jammed, people getting sick and going nuts all over the place. We couldn't believe it. Half our teachers was losing it big-time. We had to get off the freeway in the end. Our driver was getting sick. We went to a place called Ashford."

"Ashford's a dump," said Courtney.

"Some more kids split when we got there," said Aleisha. "But we didn't know what to do. It was all happening so fast. That's what was really freaking us out. It was like the end of the world or something. Nothing was working and there was people everywhere, just sort of wandering about, and more and more of them was getting sick. It was horrible. Some of the kids got in a fight with some grown-ups. Then one of the teachers tried driving the bus. Took us to the, like, what do you call it, the countryside."

"The countryside's a dump," said Courtney.

"That was the last teacher," said Aleisha. "Mr. Betts. He was a'right. Looked after us, but then even he's got sick."

"We was stuck on the bus in the middle of the countryside," said Courtney. "With all these grown-ups around."

"It was like a what-d'you-ma-call-it, a siege or something," said Aleisha. "They was all, like, trying to get on the bus. Luckily Greg come along and sorted them out, but us three's the only ones who made it out of, like, a hundred."

"There was never a hundred of us," said Brooke.

"Well, there was a lot."

"Greg's rescued us last night," said Courtney. "We been a'right since then. It ain't so bad on here. We got food and water and a toilet. But it's bare slow because most of the roads is blocked. Is a nightmare. We got to keep going around other ways, stopping and starting, avoiding people, going back the way we come. I dunno how long it'd normally take, but Greg's already been driving for, like, hours."

"I reckon we'll be a'right now," said Aleisha. "There's more of us. Greg keeps picking people up. It's better with more people. And you boys look tough enough."

"You can stay," said Courtney with a snicker.

"So long as you do what we tell you," said Brooke. "Our bus, our rules."

"Where's Greg taking you all, though?" said Jack.

"He's gonna get us to London so's we can go home," said Courtney.

"Where was your school? Where are you all from?"

"Willesden."

"Where's Willesden?" Ed asked.

"You ain't never heard of Willesden?" Aleisha sounded amazed.

"Nope."

"It's in northwest London."

"It's a dump," said Courtney.

"I thought you might say that," said Ed.

For a while there was silence as the five of them thought over all that had happened recently. Finally Aleisha spoke.

"So we've all lost people," she said with a sad smile.

"Yeah."

"But we gonna be a'right. Here come the girls!"

Brooke, Courtney, and Aleisha laughed and bumped fists.

Ed felt weird. It was as if they were discussing losing a dog or a football match, not friends. It had been a terrifying few minutes of bloody carnage back at The Fez, and it sounded like the girls had been through hell themselves, but now here they were in this little bubble looking inward, trying to laugh it all off.

He'd noticed it before, the way people tried to pretend that things weren't as bad as they were. It was a way of keeping the horror away, he supposed. When it came down to it, they were none of them any better, any cleverer, any saner than poor little Froggie with his dream of going on the London Eye.

He was starting to feel a bit numb, pushing the memories to the side, where he couldn't feel them anymore. You couldn't keep on being sad and scared all the time, could you, or you'd go crazy.

Talking to these mouthy girls was helping take his mind off things. It was helping take him to a normal place. Boys and girls. Flirting. Text messaging. *My friend thinks you're hot. . . .*

They all knew it was a game.

Let's all pretend we're just a bunch of ordinary girls and boys meeting on a bus. There's nothing outside the bus. There's only the bus.

"You're quite buff, you know," said Brooke, giving Ed the eye. "Your friend would be all right if he didn't have that thing on his face. If I go with a boy, he has to be, like, *perfect*."

Now it was Jack's turn to laugh. "Ed's nowhere near perfect."

"He's better than you, darling."

"Well, maybe I don't want to be your boyfriend."

"That's good because you're not going to be," said Brooke.

"You can have Courtney. She'll take anyone, because she's fat. Although she's quickly becoming skinny now. Any more of this starvation diet and she'll turn into a supermodel!"

"You're so full of it, Brooke," said Courtney.

"Not as full of it as you. You look like you've eaten a *mattress* or something."

The bus swerved and Jack had to steady himself against a seat back.

"Sit down!" Greg barked from the front. "There's trouble up ahead!"

Ed swore. The bubble had burst.

19

Jack hurried to the front of the bus and leaned on the back of Greg's seat.

"Didn't you hear me?" said Greg. "Sit down. This could get bumpy."

"I wanted to see what's going on."

"I can cope all right by myself, thank you very much."

"Yeah, and so can I," said Jack. "I've gotten this far without you, and I've done that by not trusting anyone. Looking after number one."

"Yeah? Well, I'm number one now, pal," said Greg. "And don't you forget it. Now, d'you want to sit down, or do you want me to knock you down?"

"I'm sitting." Jack collapsed into a seat and fastened the belt, leaning forward to try to see what was happening ahead.

There were a truck and several cars in the middle of the road about four hundred yards away. One of the cars appeared to be on fire. Nasty-looking black smoke billowed and boiled across the road. Through the smoke, Jack could just make out some kind of fight taking place. It was hard to tell from this distance who was involved, whether it was kids or grown-ups or, most likely, both.

Greg swore. "We'll have to find another way around." He stamped on the brake and the bus snorted and shuddered to a halt.

"There might be kids up there," said Jack.

"Don't make no difference," said Greg, checking the rear-view mirrors. "It's too risky. We don't have any idea what's going on, or how dangerous it might be. Could be a full-scale war, for all we know. We can't risk the bus getting damaged. At the moment it's all that's keeping us safe. It's a fortress on wheels, and I aim to keep it that way. You want to go and see if there's any kids need rescuing, Batman, you can get out and walk."

The bus was too long to turn around here. Greg put it into reverse and started to laboriously maneuver it backward along the road. The warning system was giving out an insistent, irritating *beep-beep-beep-beep-beep-beep*.

Jack stayed silent, staring ahead. After a while he saw figures emerging from the smoke, limping, lurching, stumbling, swaying from side to side, but moving fast.

"You need to go faster," he said.

"No kidding," said Greg.

"They look sick, but they can run—"

"Shut it," Greg snapped. "I'm trying to concentrate here. I'm not a professional bleeding bus driver, am I? These things are a bugger to keep in a straight line."

The running figures were getting nearer and nearer.

They were close enough now for Jack to see that they

were definitely diseased. They were a mess, their skin blistered, their clothes hanging off them, smoke-blackened and blood-spattered.

Greg managed to reverse past a turnoff before the first of the attackers reached them. A lanky young man of about twenty. He hurled himself at the windshield and tried to get a grip. He tore off one of the wipers, and Greg cursed. Then the rest of them arrived, some scrabbling at the door, others jumping up and banging their fists on the windshield. A shrill high-pitched scream came from somewhere toward the back of the bus. Jack watched helplessly as the other wiper was ripped off.

"Right," said Greg, wrenching the gear stick into first. "You asked for it."

He floored the accelerator and the bus juddered forward, quickly picking up speed and shaking off the first wave of attackers, who slithered out of the way and ran alongside, spitting with fury. Two stragglers were batted to the ground as the bus smashed into them, and Greg spun the wheel, veering off onto a side road.

"It's been like this all the way," he said. "Every time I pick a route, I have to change it. And now we've lost them wipers, we're gonna be screwed if it rains much worse than this."

Ed came up to join Jack.

"Everything all right?"

"Can't you lot stay sat down?" Greg shouted.

"Is the road blocked?"

"We'll find another way."

"Looks like we can make a left about a mile ahead," said the boy who was sitting in the seat behind Greg. He was studying a road map, squinting through his wire-framed glasses.

"Thanks, son," said Greg, and he turned to grin at Jack and Ed. "That's what I need, practical help. Not you bunch of toffs flapping about."

"Tell us what you need us to do and we'll do it," said Ed.

"I need you to sit down and shut up." Greg glanced back over his shoulder at his son. "We're coping just fine, ain't we, Liam?"

"Yeah," said Liam quietly. He was a miniature of Greg in every way except that where his dad was loud and aggressive, he looked slightly shy, almost embarrassed by him.

"Good lad," said Greg. "He don't say much, but he's a bright one. Ain't you, Liam? All his teachers say so."

"Nice to meet you, Liam," said Ed. "I'm Ed and this is Jack."

Liam looked down at the floor and mumbled something.

"We could have used you earlier," Ed said kindly. "We needed a map reader and you look like a pretty good navigator."

"And he didn't learn none of that at school, neither," said Greg. "Everything he knows *I've* learned him."

"Where were you all going when we picked you up?" Liam asked softly.

"We were trying to get to the countryside," said Ed. "Thought it might be easier there."

"You're joking, aren't you?" scoffed Greg. "Where d'you think we just come from? You don't want to go to the country-side, pal, not unless you want to end up as dinner for some bunch of spotty Herberts."

"Can't be any worse than the towns," said Ed.

"You think? Everyone's had the same idea as you—get away as far as possible from other people, get out of town, go back to nature, live off the land. And what happens? They've all wound up in the great outdoors with everyone else. Don't know what they thought they was gonna do when they got there. The roads are absolutely chock-full of abandoned cars—that's why we've taken so long to get back up this way. City types. Useless. Didn't know one end of a cow from the other, most of them. Soon started fighting over what there was left, which wasn't much, I can tell you. It's all right when it's one bloke and his dog living off the land—not millions of blokes and their wives, and girlfriends and boyfriends and kids and bleeding hamsters. Millions of them, there was. That's why the towns are empty. You know what you would have found if you'd made it to the countryside proper?"

"What?" Jack asked.

"Fields and fields and fields piled high with dead bodies. Stinking, rotten, flyblown corpses. That's what you'd have found. Death and disease like you can't imagine. It's bloody chaos. I don't have the words to describe it. Maybe if I'd been to a fancy school like you I would. I could quote some poetry or some Shakespeare maybe. To be or not to be. I'm not a poet. I'm a butcher."

"A butcher?" Ed didn't know why, but he found this quite funny.

"Yeah." Greg nodded toward a black case in the luggage rack above the first row of seats. "You don't believe me you can check out me knives. Never go anywhere without them."

"I believe you," said Jack.

"Yeah, good, well, so I might not know much about words, but I do know about livestock. About animals. Dead animals, I'll give you that, but animals all the same. Meat. That's what I understand. Meat. You know what it says on my shop sign, my motto, like? 'Meat is life.' I run an organic butcher's in Islington. You probably heard of it—Greg's Organic Gaff. Well, your mom and dad might've. I been on the telly a few times, local news and that. My sausages have won more awards than you can count. Butcher of the Year two years running, I was. So don't tell me I don't know about meat. And to know about meat you got to know about animals. I got me suppliers, you see, organic farmers and that, and I have to visit them regular. See where the meat's coming from. Well, when this all kicked off, I was down there, on one of the farms near Maidstone, with Liam. He likes to visit the farms, don't you, son?"

Liam nodded.

"Good farm. Good meat. One of me top boys he was, the foreman, Big Paul McLaren. He said we could stay with him till things blew over. Reckoned we'd be better off there on the farm with him and his lads. Well, things never did blow over, did they? We fortified the place. Wasn't hard. Big Paul had guns and everything for shooting vermin. Came in well handy for shooting trespassers. Had like a smokery in a barn. We smoked enough meat to get by on, and we held out for a while, but it soon got silly. In the end, Big Paul and all his family start getting sick, don't they? Wasn't nice. Had to shoot *them* and all. All except his youngest boy, *Little* Paul. Then the animals started to get sick. I'm a butcher, not a vet, and without Big Paul we didn't know what to do. Couldn't risk eating them no more. I'll tell you it was nuts. Too many crazies turning up. Dead bodies rotting everywhere. We realized we had to get out of there. Thought we might as well try and get home, the boy and me."

"What happened to Little Paul?" Jack asked.

"Never made it," Greg said simply, and didn't explain any further.

"We found the bus after two days," said Liam.

"Only just in time," said Greg. "I drive me butcher's van all over, more of a truck than a van, really, so I know a bit about these things. I'm like Noah's ark on here, aren't I? Be perfect if it weren't for them three harpies at the back—Girls Aloud."

"What are you going to do when you get to London?" Ed asked, hoping Greg might have a plan.

"Dunno, but there must be food all over," Greg replied. "Lying around in shops and warehouses and people's kitchen cupboards. Everyone got into hoarding in a big way when it all started going belly-up, and then they all died before they could eat much of it. There's got to be more nosh stockpiled in London than in the countryside, I reckon. But the real reason we want to get back is . . . You tell 'em, Liam."

"We want to get back to see the Arsenal."

Ed laughed. "I don't think they're still playing."

"He knows that, smartass," said Greg. "He means the stadium. The Emirates, as was. That's like a church for me and Liam, a cathedral of dreams. We've spent our best days there, ain't we, son? We just want to get back home where we can see it."

Greg twisted around in his seat to study Jack and Ed.

"You probably think that's stupid, don't you?"

"No," said Jack. "Seems as good a reason as any to go to London."

"Yeah, well, I ain't stupid, pal."

"Didn't say you were."

"You gotta have something to believe in," Greg went on. "Keeps you going. Stops you from chewing on your own dark thoughts."

"Can I ask you something?" Jack asked.

"Fire away."

"You won't get angry?"

"Can't guarantee it. It depends if it's a stupid question."

"Why haven't you got sick like everyone else?"

"Don't know, don't care."

"But it's important," said Jack. "We thought everyone older was—"

"Listen," said Greg, interrupting Jack. "You must have seen it yourselves. Some of them, didn't make no difference what sex, what race, just so long as they was sixteen or more, they pretty much got ill straight away, and within a few hours they dropped down dead. Others took longer to die, a few days. Others didn't die at all. They're still wandering around out there dribbling and squeezing their spots. The disease takes everyone different. Me, I must have a special gene or some antibodies or whatever that's protecting me. Yeah? Or maybe I'm just stronger. I can fight it off. I mean, let's face it, nobody knows why you lot, you kids, ain't got sick. Look at you, all bright eyes and rosy cheeks. It's not bloody fair. Kids these days, spoiled, want everything on a plate. Well, now you got it, you've got the world to yourselves. How d'you like it, eh? Your dreams came true; you got your three wishes. No more pesky adults to mess up your spoiled little lives. Except for them out there. The nutters. The walking bags of pus. What was it the Scared Kid called them? The mothers and fathers. Ha-ha! Welcome to paradise. Have a nice stay. Turn out the lights before you leave. Now, I'm starving. I can't keep this up on an empty stomach. I gotta eat something."

He slammed on the brakes and reared up at Jack and Ed, a leery smile exposing two rows of neat little teeth. "How's about I start with you two, eh?" he snarled, then burst out laughing as Jack and Ed shrank away from him.

"Your faces!" he said. "What a picture." He chuckled and looked to Liam, who was smiling sheepishly. "Did you see them soft sods, Liam? What a picture. What a bloody picture."

He applied the handbrake and switched off the engine.

"Don't worry, lads," he said, standing up and stretching. "I never eat boys for lunch. . . I prefer a nice salad."

20

They'd stopped on a long straight stretch of open road with good views in all directions. If anyone approached them, they would be clearly visible.

Greg rationed out food from the cardboard boxes stacked at the back of the bus, moaning all the while that with the newcomers there was less to go around. Jack wondered why he'd picked them up in the first place if he didn't want them on board, but he reckoned Greg just wanted to make sure everyone knew who was in charge.

It wasn't as if their lunch was exactly five stars, either. It was bags of chips and Cheetos mostly, with some stale Nutri-Grain, although Jack noticed that Greg had his own separate food supply that he kept in a cooler stashed behind his seat. He and Liam sat up front, eating alone.

Jack was sitting halfway back with Chris Marker, who was eating chips while reading his book. Jack was happy with the arrangement. He didn't want to talk. He didn't want to think either, so he was reading the information on the back of his chips bag. He was surprised by how much there was to read.

He was just working out the calories when he became aware of someone standing next to him.

He heard a meow and looked up. Frédérique was holding her cat-carrying box at Jack's eye level, and he could see the tabby cowering suspiciously at the far end, its eyes wide and staring.

"You all right?"

Frédérique nodded, the curtain of hair around her face opening for a moment. Jack got a glimpse of eyes as wide and frightened as the cat's.

"Have you got some food for her?" he asked. "Him? Is it a male or a female?"

A voice came from behind the hair, so quietly that for a second or two Jack thought he'd imagined it.

"Female."

"Have you got some food for her?"

Frédérique nodded again.

"What's her name?"

"Dior." A whisper.

"Like the perfume?"

Frédérique shrugged.

Jack knew she wanted something, but couldn't work out what. At least she was speaking, though, coming out of her shell a little. It was a start. He gave her what he hoped was a reassuring smile. She'd tell him in her own time what it was she wanted.

At last she spoke again. "Dior must come out of her cage for a minute."

"Really?"

"She needs to go to the bathroom."

Jack's smile grew wider before he could stop himself. "She needs a crap?"

"Yes."

"Well, okay. Let's go outside. But won't she run off?"

"I don't think so. She is scared, though."

Jack got up. We're all scared, he thought, but said nothing. He led Frédérique up the aisle toward the front.

As he got nearer to Greg he saw that he and Liam had better food than the others. Proper cheese, crackers, a tin of cold beans, even some apples and slices of smoked meat. He watched as Greg offered some meat to Liam. Liam shook his head, concentrating on the handful of crackers he was munching his way through.

Jack paused and put a hand on Frédérique's arm. He didn't want to interrupt and wind Greg up any more. He waited for his moment, listening to their conversation.

"You gotta get some protein inside you," Greg was complaining to Liam.

"Cheese is protein."

"Meat is better."

"I'm all right. I don't want it. I don't like it."

"Go on—it's good for you. Look at me. I eat well and I'm healthy. You want to be like me, don'tcha?"

"I *am* healthy, Dad."

"You won't stay healthy if you don't eat proper balanced food."

Greg noticed Jack, and stopped talking. Jack stepped forward.

"We want to get off the bus."

Greg went back to his food. "You're walking from here?" he asked.

"No. We just need to go outside for a minute."

"Way too risky, pal. Don't even think about it."

"Oh, come on—we can see fine from here. If anyone comes, we'll get straight back on."

"What d'you want to get off for anyway? Fresh air?"

"The cat needs a dump."

Greg laughed like it was the most ridiculous thing he'd ever heard.

"I'll tell you what we can do with that cat," he said when he'd calmed down and taken control of himself. "We'll skin him, gut him, butcher him, and make him into some nice kebabs." He finally turned back around to look at the two of them. "How does that sound?"

Frédérique gasped and held the box more tightly to her chest. This made Greg laugh even harder.

"Only joking, love. Did you see her face, Liam? What a picture. But, seriously, that moggy's gonna be more trouble than it's worth. You can't get sentimental over pets, love, not since what's happened."

"The cat's all she's got," said Jack. "Bit like you and Arsenal."

Greg peered at Jack, trying to work out if he was making fun of him. In the end he gave him the benefit of the doubt. "Point taken," he said, and opened the door. "You want to go out there in the rain, that's fine with me. But the first sign of any trouble, I'm pulling up the drawbridge. The door closes and stays closed. Savvy?"

21

Jack and Frédérique stood by the bus in the drizzle. The rain had died down a little. There was just a general dampness in the air rather than actual drops falling. It had gotten colder, and Jack shivered. He watched as Frédérique squatted down and put her cat box on the ground. She carefully opened the front, then reached in to take hold of the cat. She eased her out and held her under her chin, stroking her and whispering soothing words into her twitching ear. Then she sneezed. Just her luck if she was allergic to cats.

Jack looked along the stretch of empty road ahead. They'd gone on a very roundabout route since leaving Rowhurst, and he wasn't sure whether they were any nearer to London than when they'd started.

Ed came down off the bus, zipping up his jacket.

"What are you doing?"

Jack nodded toward Frédérique. "Cat needs a crap."

Ed smiled. "Feels good to be out of there," he said, and glanced back to make sure Greg couldn't hear them. "It's a bit claustrophobic, if you know what I mean. Greg's kind of . . . well, he fills the space."

"I hate guys like that," said Jack. "Always trying to throw their weight around. He's a bully."

"Yeah, but remember, we'd all be dead without him. Those teenagers were—"

Jack shot Ed a look and nodded toward Frédérique, who was gently putting the cat down into the long grass by the side of the road. The girl was terrified; there was no point in making it worse by reminding her of how close she'd come to being killed.

Ed mouthed "Sorry," and Jack went over to Frédérique. The cat was looking around nervously, then she stretched her back and darted quickly under a bush, where she sat staring at Frédérique.

"You're sure she won't run off?"

"I have food. She will come back for food." Frédérique fished a small can of cat food out of her coat pocket and popped the lid. "I did not want to open it on the bus. I was worried that if anyone sees it they will take it. It is food, *n'est-ce pas?*"

"I'll make sure they leave you alone," said Jack. "That's your food—you can do what you like with it."

"Thank you. I will put it in her cage when she is finished." She said something to the cat in French. The cat checked out her surroundings once more, then walked daintily on stiff legs out from under the bush, tiptoeing a little deeper into the sodden greenery of the verge.

Greg was watching the three of them through the window.

"Look at those idiots," he said to Liam, and chuckled.

"They ain't even got the sense to be scared."

"Is it all right to be scared, Dad?" Liam asked quietly.

"A little, son, just a little. Keeps you on your toes."

"D'you get scared?"

"'Course I do. Wouldn't be human otherwise, would I? But you don't have to be scared, Liam, 'cause I'm always gonna be here to look after you."

"I try, Dad. I try not to be. But I ain't like you, really. You're a man."

Greg put an arm around Liam and gave him a bear hug. "Listen, Liam, everything I'm doing, I'm doing for you. I sound like that soppy song, don't I? But it's true. I don't really care about me, whether I live or die, quite frankly, and before you go getting all down in the mouth, I don't aim to be kicking the bucket anytime in the near future, okay? Not while I've got you to look out for. My job now is the same as it's always been, since the day you was born. To protect you. To stop you from being scared. To put my arms around you. It's a bad world out there, son, and without me you'd be dead in five minutes."

"I know, Dad."

"So you have to listen to me, do as I say. If anything was to happen to you, I'd go mad. Maybe that's what's keeping me healthy, eh? My love for you."

"Could be, Dad."

Greg rubbed the top of Liam's head with his fist. "You're a good boy. I'm so proud of you, son. So proud. You're all I live for."

• • •

Ed stood on the lowest step of the bus to get a better vantage point. He was nervous being out here, but he'd wanted to stay close to Jack, even though it was obvious that Jack didn't really want him around. He was trying to talk to Frédérique, and Ed felt like a spare part. Maybe if he kept watch he might appear to be useful.

Jack was watching the cat as she rooted around among the plants. "Listen, Frédérique," he said. "I know you've been through some bad stuff, we all have. But . . . if you want to talk about any of it, you know, it might help."

"I am scared," she said bluntly.

"We're all scared," said Jack.

"No. You do not understand. You cannot understand. I am so scared."

"I do understand. Since your dad died . . ."

"Yes." Frédérique gripped Jack's forearm. "Yes. You are right. Since my father died I am scared."

"But we're all together now, we're safe on the bus. I'll look after you. Greg will look after you. We'll all look after you. See, even Ed's keeping an eye out for us."

"Why is Greg not sick?"

"I honestly don't know." Jack shook his head. "He doesn't know either. Maybe the sickness doesn't affect everyone."

Frédérique smiled for the first time, and it was as if the clouds had lifted and the sun was beaming bright and warm. Her whole face changed, and Jack was with another person. She looked very beautiful when she smiled.

"Yes," she said, nodding her head. "Maybe not everyone will get sick. Maybe everything will be all right."

"You see," said Jack. "We don't need to give up hope."

"Yes." Frédérique was madly nodding, smiling and crying at the same time. Then there was a gust of cold wind, and she stifled a small cough, anxious not to alarm the cat.

"So, how did you end up at Rowhurst?" Jack asked. "I mean, I know your dad was there and everything, but . . ."

"My mother, she still was living in France. In Paris. But my father is walk out on her. They argue all the time. I was at school in Paris, but I miss my papa. My mother, she was one of the first to get sick. She send me to England to be with my papa. She thought I would be safer here. She thought maybe because England is an island it will be better. I came in the Eurostar. It was very difficult when I arrive. To get from London to Rowhurst take me a long time, and when I arrive is very bad. Papa, he try to keep me safe, we hide in the flat, keep the curtains closed all day, but . . . then . . . yesterday, he is go out and not come back. I know he is sick. I have seen the same *symptômes* . . . ? How you say *symptôme*?"

"Symptom," said Jack. "It's the same word."

"Yes. The same. I see that Papa is sick like Mama. That I think is why he leave me. He did not want to hurt me. But I don't see him again. Then you come. You save me, Jack."

Jack could see that Frédérique was going to lose it again, so he put his arms around her and held her. He felt pretty rotten that he'd been the one to kill her father, but he'd had to do it, and it wasn't like the man had even really been human anymore. He wondered if he would ever be able to tell her. Now was definitely not the time. Frédérique felt warm and damp, and very thin. She was trembling in the cold. He stroked her back, looking over her shoulder.

"She's not the only one. Here, puss-puss-puss . . . If you can see her, can't you just go over and grab her?"

"No—if I try it and she is scared she might then run away."

"Come on . . . we'll have to leave her."

"Hey!" Greg shouted from the bus. "All aboard who's coming aboard. There's some movement down the way."

"We're just coming," said Jack. "Hold on."

"Get out of the doorway so I can close it."

"No. It's all right." Ed sounded rattled. "I'm keeping watch. Those people are still a long way off."

"You saw them already, didn't you? Why didn't you say nothing?"

"They're miles away."

"Whatever—I ain't taking no risks. Now get out of my doorway so's I can close up."

"Here, puss-puss-puss . . ."

"Move it!"

"They just need to get the cat," said Ed.

Greg swore, calling the cat all manner of filthy names. Jack couldn't help but agree with him. He didn't want to get left behind for the sake of a pet, but he'd promised Frédérique that he'd stay with her.

"Here, puss-puss . . ."

He looked down the road.

Oh, Jesus.

The grown-ups weren't moving very fast, but they were tramping steadily toward the bus, breathing through their mouths, rotten flesh hanging off their faces. The mother who seemed to be leading them had bulging black-rimmed eyes like hard-boiled eggs. She was completely bald with a patch of bare skull on the top of her head surrounded by a ring of boils.

"Here, puss, come on, Dior, come on, cat . . ."

"I can see her."

"Where?"

The cat's face emerged from the long grass, and it sneaked toward Frédérique, sensing the tense atmosphere.

Frédérique was smiling at her and rubbing her fingertips together, making a dry rustling sound.

Thank God.

There was a hiss and a rumble as Greg fired up the bus, and the cat darted back into the bushes.

"You asshole!" Jack yelled.

Frédérique wailed. "She is too scared."

"You've just got to try and grab her," said Jack. "We can't wait. The bus is going to go."

They heard Greg yelling from the driver's seat. "Get out of the doorway or I'll kick you out."

"Hang on," Ed shouted back. "They've nearly got it."

"I can drive with the door open, you know!"

"Frédérique!" Jack snapped. "You've got to do something!"

22

Frédérique could just see Dior's tail sticking up out of the grass. The poor cat was spooked by the voices, by the noise. If Frédérique had only been left alone to do this by herself she could have gotten her by now.

How long did she have?

She looked down the road for the first time, and her breath caught in her ribs.

The silent mass of adults was almost there. They were bloated by disease, their skin tight, cheekbones massive, lips fat and pulled back from their teeth, as if they'd all had bad plastic surgery. Some of them were completely naked, their sagging flesh swaying from side to side as they staggered onward.

"Please, Frédérique." The boy, Jack, sounded like he was going to cry.

Frédérique felt awful. She didn't want to be responsible for anything bad happening.

All right, she told herself. It's just a cat.

Just a cat.

Papa would not have wanted her to die because of it.

She would try to pick Dior up. If she ran off, she would leave her behind. That was the only thing to do. Without thinking anymore, she slid forward quickly but smoothly, trying to make no sudden movements. Dior stared at her warily, ready to jump aside. At the last moment, Frédérique bent down and made a grab for her.

Dior jumped.

Too late.

Frédérique's hands closed around her. The cat struggled and kicked, gave a wild meow, but she was held fast.

Frédérique ran to Jack, who was holding the carrying case ready.

She stuffed Dior in, and Jack closed the gate.

"Get on the bus!" Ed shouted. "Hurry!"

The bus was moving. Ed leaned out and hauled Frédérique aboard. The bus picked up speed. Jack threw the cat box to Ed, who caught it neatly and dumped it inside.

"Come on, Jack!"

Frédérique stood up and watched out of the window.

Jack was sprinting, his feet slapping on the wet pavement, his clenched teeth bared in pain and desperation. He stretched out his hand. The bus was pulling away from him.

"Come on!" Ed shouted.

Someone pushed past Frédérique, the big boy, Bam. He took hold of Ed's arm. "Lean out!"

Ed swung out over the road, fingers plucking at the air. Jack roared and threw himself at Ed, who somehow managed to get his fingers around his wrist and pull him onto the step.

The three of them collapsed, Jack panting, Ed and Bam giggling hysterically.

"That was bloody close," Greg snarled. "If any of you lot mess with me like that again, I will throw you off this bus and not look back. You got it?"

"You could have waited." Jack's voice was tight with cold fury.

"You're not the only people on this bus," Greg spat back at him. "And don't you forget that. I don't mean me. There's other kids here. You put them all in danger back there. For a cat! A sodding cat!"

"Nobody was hurt," said Ed, trying to calm the situation down. "Nobody was in any real danger."

"Sit down and shut up," said Greg.

Jack insulted Greg under his breath. Greg realized he'd said something but couldn't tell what.

"You've been on my case ever since you got on this bus," he said, shifting up a gear. "And I am rapidly beginning not to like you, sonny boy. Not one little bit."

"The feeling's mutual," Jack muttered, and went to sit farther down the bus. Frédérique and Bam followed.

Ed watched them go. When it came down to it, Greg was right. Jack had put them all in danger. Ed was shaking uncontrollably. He'd been absolutely terrified and was still experiencing an adrenaline rush. It had taken every last scrap of courage he possessed to stay on that step as the grown-ups marched steadily nearer.

And when the bus had started to drive off . . .

He took a deep breath and swallowed the bile that had risen in his throat.

Greg swerved to avoid something in the road, and Ed nearly fell over. He looked for somewhere to sit. All the younger kids had moved to the front of the bus and were sitting with Liam, as close to Greg as they could get. Despite all that had happened, they still looked to grown-ups to protect them, and they found the big, powerful figure of Greg reassuring.

Arthur and Wiki sat across the aisle from Liam, Zohra and her little brother, Froggie, sat behind them, and next to Liam, a good head taller than the rest of them, was Justin the nerd.

The next three rows of seats were filled by crazy Matt and Archie Bishop and the other kids from the chapel. Ed settled down behind them, across from Kwanele and Chris Marker.

He smiled to himself.

The thing was, he hadn't left the step, had he? He hadn't let Greg close the doors. He'd pulled Jack onto the bus. This time he'd saved his friend.

This time he'd done the right thing.

At the front of the bus, Arthur was talking, as usual. He seemed to have an endless supply of words inside him, just waiting to come pouring out.

"I don't think they would have caught up," he was saying. "Those zombies were slow, not like the ones earlier, at The Fez—they were like superzombies, they were really quick; I wonder why some are faster than others, maybe the young ones aren't as badly affected by the disease. . . ."

"I didn't think zombies could run fast," said Froggie, a look of deep concern on his face.

"Yes, well, technically they're not zombies," said Justin.

"What d'you mean?" Froggie asked.

"I mean they're not zombies," Justin went on. "They're not the living dead."

"Yes," said Wiki, "but a real zombie isn't really dead either. Not a proper one. A proper zombie is someone who's been given a drug to make them appear dead, and then they're revived by the voodoo priest and they have to do his bidding."

"Well, they're not those type of zombies either, then, are they?" said Justin.

"No."

"So they're not any type of zombie."

"What should we call them, then?" Arthur asked. "We have to call them something. I mean, most of them are grown-ups, we could call them grown-ups because there aren't any normal grown-ups left, so we'd always know what we were talking about, or we could just call them mothers and fathers, like the Scared Kid did? That's what I think of them as, mothers and fathers, though not my real mother and father, they weren't zombies."

"These ones aren't zombies either," Justin insisted. "That's what I've just been trying to explain."

"We could call them ghouls," said Wiki. "Or demons."

"What about ogres?" Zohra suggested.

"Or savages," said Froggie.

"We could call them brutes," said Wiki.

"I like zombies best," said Arthur.

"Me too," agreed Froggie.

"But they're not zombies!" Justin was getting quite angry.

"I know they're not," said Arthur. "But they act like zombies, and they walk like zombies, except the ones who can run, the fast ones, and they're stupid like zombies, and they eat people like zombies."

"Are they a sort of vampire?" said Froggie.

"In a way," said Wiki. "They want human flesh, though, not just blood."

"Why do you think they do?" said Froggie, as casually as if he were discussing the eating habits of a pet guinea pig.

"That's a very good question," said Justin. "We should make a proper study of their behavior. If we can understand them more, we might be able to work out better ways of defending ourselves against them, maybe even defeating them. We're cleverer than them, so that should give us the edge."

"We may be cleverer," said Wiki, "but they're stronger."

"Clever beats strong every time," said Justin, pulling a small notebook and a pen out of his pocket. "So let's make a pact. We'll use our brains to work out the best way to survive. We'll be a brain trust."

"What's a brain trust?" asked Froggie.

"It's like a think tank."

"What's a think tank?"

"If we don't even know what it means," said Arthur, "I can't see us being the finest minds in the world."

"Well, we're cleverer than that lot out there," said Justin.

"You mean the zombies?"

"They are *not* zombies!"

"They're sickos," Greg growled from the driver's seat. "That's what I call them. Sickos."

"Yes," said Justin, smiling. He wrote the word down in his book and underlined it. "*Sickos*. That's a very good term for them. From now on they're officially not zombies, they're sickos."

23

Jack felt hot and sweaty. He'd landed badly when Ed and Bam had pulled him onto the bus. He'd scraped his shins on the steps, but he couldn't sense any pain yet. It would come, though. That much he knew. He sat down with Frédérique in the same row of seats as Bam and his injured friend, Piers. Piers had been slipping in and out of consciousness since they'd gotten on the bus. The piece of material that Bam had wrapped around his head was stained every shade of red from bright scarlet to almost black. It had stopped the bleeding, but Piers looked chalk white, and his face was streaked with dried blood.

Frédérique didn't look much better. She was shaking as if someone had stuck electrodes in her and was passing an electric current through her body. Jack realized he was shaking as well, and he had a hollow sick feeling inside. He put his head between his knees and took a few deep breaths. He closed his eyes and waited for the pounding in his head to subside.

Once he was feeling halfway human again, he straightened up. For a moment he saw dancing colored spots and blobs in front of his eyes, and his brain felt like it had come loose and turned light and fizzy. He had the sensation that he was floating up out of his body. He gripped his armrest, and slowly everything settled down and he was back on the bus.

"You all right?" Bam was giving Jack a concerned look.

"Hard to say." Jack rubbed his face. "How's Piers doing?"

Bam made a movement with his hands as if he were weighing something. "Could be worse. He's sleeping now. I got some water inside him and a bit of food. Chips, mainly, but it's better than nothing, I suppose. The cut's not too deep, as far as I can tell, but he's lost quite a lot of blood. It's going to be hard to get his strength back up."

"Have you put anything on the wound? Some antiseptic or anything?"

"Yeah. Greg has a box of stuff. I squirted some Savlon on; that's what my mom always used to do if I had a cut. Savlon and soup."

"Yuck."

"Not together. Savlon on the cut and then a hot bowl of soup. Cream of chicken. That's if I was badly mashed up in a match. Which was nearly every week. I'd kill for some chicken soup right now."

"Me too."

"Piers really needs some proper food, though. He can't live on chips. If we could get hold of some of that smoked meat Greg has stashed away in his cool box, that'd sort him out."

"You can try," said Jack. "He doesn't like me. I doubt it'll do much good, though. Despite what he says, he's only really looking after himself and Liam."

"That his Mini-Me?"

"Yeah."

Jack's seat jolted forward as someone bashed into the

back of it. There was a girlish laugh, and he was aware of bodies crowding behind him.

"Is she your girlfriend?"

It was Brooke and her two mates leaning over him, laughing and eyeing Frédérique up and down. Jack wondered why he had ever seen them as a set. They actually looked very different—Courtney big and awkward, Brooke thin and blond, Aleisha tiny and dark.

"Is she?" Brooke repeated.

"No."

"What's her name?"

"Frédérique. She's French."

"We had enough of the French when we was in Calais," said Courtney. "France is a dump."

Jack felt hot anger erupt from his guts. He twisted up out of his seat and confronted the girls, who dropped back in surprise.

"Why don't you all knock it off? Huh? Why don't you give it a rest? She's been through a lot. Her dad died this morning. She's a human being like you, okay?"

Brooke was the first to get her front back in place. She gave a long drawn-out *Oooooh*, eyebrows raised, mouth in a perfect little circle. "Definitely your girlfriend, then."

Aleisha put a hand on her friend's arm, making a concerned face. "He's right, Brooke," she said. "Leave it. You don't have to be a bitch all the time. We all need to be friends."

Brooke looked taken aback. She wasn't sure quite where she stood now. "I was only joking."

"Yeah, me too," said Courtney. "She looks all right. Are you okay, darling?"

Frédérique nodded without looking around.

Courtney passed her a half-eaten Mars bar. "D'you want this? I was saving it, but you can have it if you want."

Frédérique shook her head.

"She'll be okay," said Aleisha kindly, and she smiled at Frédérique.

"Look," said Brooke. "Touching moment and all that, but just so's we know where we all stand—is she your girlfriend or not?"

"Broo-ooke!" said Aleisha, jutting her head forward.

"What?" said Brooke. "We need to know."

"Why would you care?" said Jack. "Apparently I don't count in your world because of my birthmark. I'm just some kind of freak."

"So she *is* your girlfriend, then."

"Oh, forget it." Jack slumped back into his seat and the girls returned to their camp at the back of the bus, arguing loudly with each other.

Frédérique was shaking worse than ever, and Jack was about to put his arm around her to reassure her when he realized she was laughing. He couldn't help but join in. This whole situation was so ridiculous. The world was falling apart and people couldn't see outside the little boxes they'd lived in all their lives.

An image of Frédérique's father trying to stand up with a plank of wood nailed to his head came to him, and he laughed even harder.

The world didn't make much sense anymore.

He leaned across Frédérique and drew a smiley face on the window.

24

Chris Marker reached up to the luggage rack to get his bag of books down. He'd finished *Fever Crumb* and needed to start something new. He always felt a bit deflated finishing a book. He'd race to get to the end and then wonder why he hadn't taken it more slowly to make the enjoyment last longer. Of course he could always just turn back to page one and start all over again at the beginning, as he sometimes did. But right now he wanted something new. He searched through the books and chose one he'd grabbed at random in the library because it looked long. It was a heavy, fat paperback called *The Gormenghast Trilogy*. Three books in one: *Titus Groan*, *Gormenghast*, and *Titus Alone*. That should keep him busy for a while.

He sat back down, and Kwanele looked over to see what he'd chosen.

"I haven't read that," he said.

Chris grunted. As far as he could tell, Kwanele had never read *any* book, unless perhaps it was a history of fashion. Magazines were a different story. Kwanele must have read every fashion magazine ever published in the history of the world. And watched every program about fashion on TV. He'd already summed up everyone on board based on their clothing.

The three noisy girls at the back were "an unholy mix of Topshop, Juicy Couture, JD Sports, Accessorize, and Willesden market."

Zohra and Froggie were "classic Boden," whatever that was.

Greg and Liam were Next, plus "inevitably more JD Sports."

Frédérique, though, apparently "had style."

"That coat's an Agnès B," Kwanele had said approvingly.

He'd been quiet since lunch, drifting in and out of sleep, and Chris had taken the opportunity to tune in to the conversation that Matt and Archie Bishop were having about their new religion. His book was a prop a lot of the time so that he could spy on people without them realizing.

Matt and Archie seemed to be making it up as they went along, but they were still deadly serious about their religion, discussing each point at great length.

Matt was reading something out from one of his rescued scraps of Bible. *"And he carried me away . . . and showed me the Holy City. . . . It shone with the glory of God, and its brilliance was like that of a very precious jewel, like a jasper, clear as crystal.* What's a jasper?"

"A type of jewel, I suppose," said Archie.

"I think it's significant," said Matt. "Why choose a jasper, and not, say, a ruby or an emerald or one of the better-known jewels? It's a code of some sort, I reckon. Maybe we need to look out for a boy called Jasper."

"Maybe," said Archie, though he didn't sound convinced.

Matt continued reading aloud. *"It had a great, high wall with twelve gates, and with twelve angels at the gates. . . . There were three gates on the east, three on the north, three on the south, and three on the west. . . .* And look, here . . . *The foundations of the city walls were decorated with every kind of precious stone. The first foundation was jasper!* Jasper again. I told you it was significant."

"What else does it say?" Archie asked.

"Erm . . . *the second sapphire, the third chalcedony, the fourth emerald.*"

"There you are, then," said Archie. "He says emerald."

"Yeah, but listen to these others—I've never heard of them—*the fifth sardonyx, the sixth carnelian, the seventh chrysolite, the eighth beryl, the ninth topaz, the tenth chrysoprase, the eleventh jacinth, and the twelfth amethyst.*"

"I've heard of amethyst."

"What color is it?"

"Dunno. Red, maybe?"

"The twelve gates are important," said Matt. "Doesn't London have twelve gates? The old city of London."

"Don't know. Does it?"

"Yes. I used to know them all. There's Ludgate . . . erm, Old Gate, Newgate, Aldgate, Bishopsgate, Moorgate. . . . I don't remember the rest, but there's definitely twelve."

Chris shook his head. There were seven gates in London, not twelve. Matt was a fool.

"It's all in here, Archie," Matt was saying, his voice growing louder as he got more excited. "London, the Lamb, the plague, my vision."

"I wish I'd had a vision," said one of the acolytes. "I'd like to see what the Lamb looks like."

"He's beautiful and frightening at the same time," said Matt, and he stood up. "He's going to save us all!" he cried out.

"Sit down, Matt," said Ed, who was sitting across the way from Chris.

"I won't sit down. You all need to accept the Lamb if you want to be saved. The golden child, who is more than a child. I've seen him, walking out of the darkness, and all around him is light, and in his shadow walks a demon."

"Sit down, Matt."

Matt left his seat and went over to Ed. "You'll see," he said. "You'll see that I'm right. It's all in the pages, and if you can't see that, then you're blind. We're being tested. That's what all this is about, the disease, the dead, don't you see? God has sent a plague to wipe out the sinners, to kill the evildoers. We have to found a new Jerusalem in London, and welcome the Lamb, who will come to save us."

"And just how do we welcome him?" Ed asked.

"We have to make a sacrifice."

"A sacrifice?" Ed looked amazed.

"Yes," said Matt. "The Lamb is ready for sacrifice, but we don't sacrifice the Lamb, you see, we sacrifice the demon, the beast who walks at his side in the darkness, and then once he's been cast out, the Lamb will be free and we can all rise into God's kingdom here on Earth."

This was all too much for Ed, and he started to laugh. Matt stood there for a moment, his bony shoulders rising and falling heavily, then he turned away and stalked back to his friends.

Chris was secretly smiling. He didn't think Matt's new religion would catch on. After all, he was just a kid.

What did kids know about anything?

He focused his attention back on his book. He knew the others thought he was weird. Always reading. But the thing was, books were the future now. They held what was left of the world's knowledge. All the adults were either dead or sick. All those teachers with their knowledge, all those parents, scientists, historians, gone.

There were no more computers now, and wouldn't be again until the electricity came back on. And how long would that take? What did kids know about generating electricity? Well, if they wanted to find out, they were going to have to read books.

First read the books, then build the generators, then switch the computers back on. Probably wouldn't work after all that time. So they'd have to build new computers, which would mean reading more books. . . .

And in the meantime, all the gigabytes, zigabytes, mega-ziga-gigabytes of information that had once been stored in all the computers of the world would have vanished.

All that knowledge lost forever. They were back to square one. Well, perhaps not square one. More like the Middle Ages. Before electricity, before the Industrial Revolution, before cars and machines.

When there were just books.

If Chris knew one thing, it was that knowledge is power. And where was all the knowledge in the world right now? In books. So that meant that books were the most powerful objects in the world.

And he was going to use that power. He was going to keep on reading. He had to start collecting encyclopedias, science books, history, geography, books of facts and figures. He had to start planning for the future.

The scenery rolled past as the afternoon wore on, growing grayer and grayer. The drizzle never let up and their progress was painfully slow. Roads were blocked everywhere, and whenever the rain picked up, Greg had to slow down to a crawl because of the missing wipers.

Several times they had to stop altogether and the bigger boys would have to get out and physically move cars out of the way while Greg watched out for sickos with his shotgun. Some of the cars still had keys in the ignition, but most didn't. The boys smashed the side windows, and then it was Greg who showed them how to disable the steering lock by jamming a screwdriver in behind the steering column. They didn't bother trying to hotwire them, but simply put the cars in neutral and pushed them out of the way.

It was not quick work, though.

The sky steadily darkened as they crisscrossed the dreary streets on the fringes of south London, trying to find a way in. Despite the rain, there were fires smoldering everywhere, filling the air with smoke, which made their going even more difficult.

One by one, everyone on the bus fell silent, retreating

into their thoughts. Even the three girls at the back piped down. The only voice was Greg's as he muttered under his breath, cursing and swearing.

Liam sat staring at the great solid lump that was the back of his father's head. It was so familiar from countless drives. The pale bristles of his short haircut, the big crease in the skin that ran all the way across his scalp, the red rash where his collar rubbed against his wide neck. Greg always complained that most shirts didn't fit around his neck. The collars were always too tight.

The hours Liam had spent in the back of the car studying this great fleshy boulder. He took after his dad. He had the biggest head in his class. When he'd had his glasses fitted, the optician had been amazed. She said she'd have to give Liam adult frames.

He had a sudden flashback to a memory of when he'd been much smaller. Sitting in the car—not the new Jeep, the old one, the Shogun—and there being two heads in the front.

Mom and Dad.

It must have been a really long time ago.

Mom was gone now, back up to Coventry. She'd moved in with the man from the phone company. Daryl.

Liam visited her three times a year, once on her birthday, once at Christmas, and for two weeks in May when Dad went fishing with his mates.

It suited all of them. Mom had never much enjoyed being a mom, and Dad was more fun. He did cool things with Liam. They went to football, they went fishing, they watched DVDs together—old war films, mostly. They were Dad's favorites: *The Dam Busters*, *The Great Escape*, *The Longest Day*,

Sands of Iwo Jima, The Battle of Britain.

They walked Charlie on Hampstead Heath. Charlie was a boxer. They'd left him with Uncle Ray when they'd set off down to Kent all those weeks ago. They weren't allowed to take Charlie onto the farms.

Liam wondered if he was all right. Maybe Uncle Ray was like Dad. Maybe he wouldn't get sick. He *hoped* Charlie was all right. He loved him.

He loved his dad as well, even though he sometimes scared Liam. Dad could get really angry, and when he was "in one of his rages" as he called it, Liam had to try to keep out of his way. He was worst when he was driving. He would swear at other drivers and say the most horrible things. Once Liam had been with Dad when he'd got into a fight with another driver.

Dad had had a laugh about it afterward, but Liam had been really shaken up by it. Liam hated fighting and spent a lot of time at school trying to stay out of the way of bullies. He never told Dad when he was bullied, because he knew Dad would only make it worse. Go around to the bully's house and start a fight or something.

Liam watched as Greg coughed and ran a hand through his hair. A fine spray rose up as he did so, like a mist. Liam thought at first it was water, and then he realized it was a spray of Dad's hair, like when you go to the barber and they leave those powdery, itchy bits down the back of your neck and in your hair.

There was a bald patch where Greg had rubbed. And right in the middle of the patch was a spot. A single whitehead, glistening and fat with pus.

Liam held his breath.

He didn't want to look, but he had no choice; the spot drew his eyes like a target. And Greg kept scratching at it, scratching and scratching, rubbing off more hair and making the skin around the spot red raw.

Greg coughed again, like he had something caught in his throat. He reached for his plastic water bottle and drank half of it in one long swallow. Dad's party trick was to down a pint of beer in one go. He'd tried teaching Liam how to do it with a glass of water, but it always ended the same way, with Liam choking and Dad laughing.

"You're no son of mine!" he joked.

You only had to look at pictures of Greg as a boy to know that wasn't true, however. The two of them were identical. He supposed he'd be just like Greg when he grew up —strong and tough and not afraid of anything or anyone.

That would be nice.

He looked forward to getting home. It had been awful on the farm. With everyone dying and all that.

And then there was poor Little Paul, the farmer's youngest son. Liam had made friends with him.

He shivered at the memory. He couldn't help it.

Little Paul had gotten hysterical when his dad and all his older brothers got sick and Greg had to shoot them. Little Paul had been like a crazy person. Screaming, shouting, crying. And then he'd gone very quiet. Wouldn't move. Wouldn't talk. Stared at the wall.

Liam remembered how Greg had taken Little Paul out to the barn one night, and when he came back into the house, his hands were all wet. He'd washed them.

Little Paul never came back.

Greg coughed, a long fit of it, and spat into a paper coffee cup.

When he rubbed his head again, he exposed another bald patch.

There were three more spots on it, nestling in the crease of skin.

Liam felt a coldness creeping up his legs, as if his heart were sucking all the blood back into itself like a sponge. His vision was turning black-and-white, like an old film.

"Dad . . ." he said, just before he passed out.

25

"He's all right, he's all right, give him air. He's just fainted. Give him air. Liam . . . Liam . . . wake up, son."

Liam felt a damp hand slapping his face. His eyes fluttered open. What was he doing lying on the floor? Dad's big face looming over him. Boys and girls crowding around him.

"You fainted, son, is all. Nothing worse than that. You feeling all right? Get him some water, one of you, come on!"

"I'm fine, Dad. I'm fine."

"What set you off? What happened?"

Liam couldn't say anything. He looked up at his dad as if he were an alien. Someone already dead.

The spots.

The cough.

He couldn't say it. Couldn't say "You're getting sick, Dad." Couldn't say anything. Because saying it would make it real. And the reality of it was too terrifying to think about. If he didn't say anything, maybe it wouldn't happen.

Dad's face was covered with a thin film of sweat, and the whites of his eyes looked yellowish.

It had started like this on the farm. First Big Paul and his wife, and then the older boys.

It could be something else, though, couldn't it? Couldn't it? Maybe Dad just had a cold.

That was it. Just a cold.

Liam smiled at his dad, who smiled back. Greg coughed and sniffed and wiped his nose. Liam saw a thin smear of blood along his finger. Had anyone else seen it?

Please, no. Not Dad.

"Let's get you up from there, son."

Greg pulled Liam up off the floor, dusted him off, and took him to the front, where he sat him in the driver's seat and stood looking out through the rain-spattered windshield.

"I'm sorry, Dad," said Liam, feeling like he'd let his dad down and shown weakness in front of the other kids. "I didn't mean to. You've had to stop the bus and everything. I'm really sorry."

"We needed to stop anyway, soldier," said Greg. "It's getting late and it's getting dark. I wanted to try and push on over the river and get back to Islington tonight, but it ain't gonna happen. I'm knackered, London Bridge is blocked, and it's raining too hard. I can't see a bloody thing without the wipers."

"Can't we get home, Dad? If we go slowly?"

"It's too dangerous. Don't want to hit nothing and damage the bus. It's our lifeline. No, we'll kip down here and hope the rain clears by the morning." He pressed his face against the glass of the windshield. "Don't seem to be no one else about."

"No, Dad," Liam pleaded, "not another night on the bus.

We're so close. If you go carefully . . ."

Greg sighed. "I *said*, Liam, it's too dangerous. Look at it out there—it's coming down like stair rods. Plus I've got a banging headache. It's been a very stressful day."

"All right, Dad, you know best."

Greg turned and winked at him. "'Course I do," he said. "Besides, we need to work out what everyone else wants to do. Much as I love 'em all to pieces, I ain't taking them all back to our place. I don't want to be responsible for nobody but you."

Greg took a step up the aisle, looking at the rows of faces. "I don't know where you lot want to go," he shouted. "But this ain't a regular bus. I ain't dropping you off all over."

"I want to go to the London Eye," said Froggie, and Greg laughed.

"I want to go to the Tower of London," said Arthur. "I went there with the school; it was really cool, like a proper castle, I reckon you could be safe there, and there are, like, weapons and everything, and you'd be in a commanding location on the river, that's why William the Conqueror built it there, it's in a commanding position; you could fish for fish, I'm quite a good fisherman, my dad said so, we went this one time to Ireland and I caught a sea bass, it was quite big but the biggest one was—"

"Yeah, yeah, put a sock in it, will you, Jibber-jabber?" said Greg. "You've not shut up since you got on this bus."

"Yeah, Jibber-jabber," said Froggie, "you talk more than my mom."

"My dad said I could talk for England," said Arthur, "if there was only an Olympic event, like the talking marathon, you know, like talking instead of walking—"

"Jibber-jabber. Enough!"

"Sorry."

Ed had come to the front to see what was going on when Liam had collapsed into the aisle. He was now sitting with the Brain Trust. "I've always said we should stick together," he said. "There's safety in numbers. Maybe we should all go to Islington? I don't really know the area, but maybe there's somewhere that—"

"You don't really know the area?" Greg interrupted.

"No."

"You don't really know anything, do you, buster?"

"What?" Ed was taken aback. He gave a little unconvincing laugh. "I know a bit."

"No you don't," Greg sneered. "None of you do. I don't want you with me. You're a liability."

"That's not fair."

"*That's not fair.*" Greg mimicked. "Look at you with your floppy hair. Your silver spoon ain't gonna be no use to you now. And what use has all your fancy education been, eh? I'll tell you. No use at all. All Mommy and Daddy's money down the toilet. Is Latin gonna help you now, eh? Tell me that. You can't, can you? Because you're stupid. That school of yours ain't taught you nothing you can use in real life. I bet you can speak about ten languages, can't you? Maybe play the flute? Toot toot! Well, you're dealing with a new world now, a new enemy. That lot out there, the sickos, they can't speak French, or Spanish, or bleeding German, can they? They can't even speak English no more. All they can do is grunt. You're dealing with morons, and when you're dealing with morons, education don't mean nothing. Wake up and smell the blood, Hugh Grant, you can't just go waltzing into Daddy's firm in the city. You need real skills now."

Greg shouted down the length of the bus at the other kids. "You wanna come with me? That's fine. Just so long as you can get it into your pretty little heads that I'm in charge, savvy? Because I'm the only one here who can save you." He tapped his head and started to walk down the aisle.

"Me who left school at sixteen with no qualifications," he went on. "Because I know about real life. I know how to work with my hands. I know how to kill and gut an animal. Yeah? Could you do that? Any of you? If you had to? Which you might have to. Could any of you skin a cat?" He stopped and gave a meaningful look to Frédérique, followed by a mocking laugh. "There's no supermarkets now to serve you your nosh all nicely packaged up in cling film with the blood drained out of it. No more Marks and Spencer's ready meals. You wanna come with me, you're gonna have to learn and learn fast, learn about the real things that matter in life."

"We're not completely useless," said Archie Bishop.

"Yeah? You know how to pluck a chicken? Break a rabbit's neck?"

"I do, actually," said Bam. "I've been out shooting loads of times. My rabbit stew's the best in Kent. I might not have won any awards for my sausages, like you, but I make a mean stew. My barbecued rabbit kebabs aren't too sloppy, either."

"You having a laugh, Lord Snooty?"

"Not me," said Bam. "I'm a bloody good shot, if I say so myself. I grew up in the country, you see, always out yomping 'round the fields. Plus, last summer I went on an SAS survival course during the holidays. I can build a shelter, set animal traps, net fish. . . . I could live off the land if I had to."

"I'd like to see you try."

"No, seriously, I could."

Greg strode to the front and pulled the door open. "Go on, then," he shouted. "I believe you was on your way to the countryside when I picked you up. Why don't you walk all the way back there and start netting fish, Boris?"

"Change of plan since then," said Bam. "Looks like it's the city life for me in the foreseeable. Not sure if there are any rabbits in London, but I know there's foxes. I'm sure I could bag one of them. Can you eat a fox? I suppose in the end you can eat anything if you're hungry enough."

"You getting out or staying?" Greg asked.

"Staying, thanks," said Bam cheerfully. "All for one and one for all, and all that. You're stuck with me, I'm afraid, Greg."

"Yeah, well, as I said, just you remember who's in charge, and don't get cheeky or I'll give you a slap. This is *my* bus. *My* rules."

Nobody said anything.

"All right." Greg coughed. "Get some sleep. We'll push on in the morning. I'll take you all as far as Islington. After that you're on your own."

26

It was dark on the bus, very dark and very quiet. Except for when the silence was interrupted by distant shouts, or the sound of something smashing. And then there were the other noises, harder to identify, that could have been made by animals or by humans.

Hell, thought Ed, some of the sounds were so weird they could have been made by aliens. That wouldn't have surprised him one bit. Nothing could surprise him anymore. If strange green lights appeared in the sky and bug-eyed freaks with ray guns strolled down the street, he wouldn't think twice about it. For all he knew, the sickness had come from outer space. It was the first wave of an attack by an alien assault force. Soften everyone up, remove the military threat, and enslave the remaining young population.

It made about as much sense as Matt's ideas about the Holy Lamb.

Ed was walking slowly down the aisle, checking that everyone was all right. It was the least he could do. He still felt guilty that he had escaped from the attack at The Fez, and that good friends had been left behind.

Jack was sitting midway down the bus. "It's rubbish," he said when Ed drew level with him.

"What is?"

"What Greg was saying. About survival. Just total bullshit."

"How d'you mean? In what way?"

"Well, it's random, isn't it? Really? Who lives and who dies."

"Is it?" Ed checked to make sure there was no way that Greg could listen in on their conversation, and sat down next to Jack.

"Of course it is," said Jack. "It's luck, that's all. Makes no difference one way or the other what skills you've got, what training you've had, what school you went to. It's like in the First World War, when the soldiers were ordered to go over the top and march toward the German trenches—what difference did their training make? Would a professional soldier with ten years' experience be any less likely to be shot than someone whose first day it was at the front? No. It was pure chance whether you got killed or not. When a bomb goes off, it doesn't choose who it blows up. Do you think any of the survivors thought, Yeah, look at me, I'm great, I've survived because I was better than the man standing next to me? I don't know, some of them probably thought God had played a part in it, but from what I've read in history, most of the soldiers felt terrible; they felt they didn't deserve to live while so many of their friends had died."

"That's how I feel," said Ed. "Guilty."

Jack turned away. "I didn't mean anything by what I was saying, Ed."

"I know you think I've been a coward, and maybe I have, but . . ."

"I'm sorry for what I said earlier. I didn't mean it."

"Yes you did. And I understand why you said it. But . . . I can't fight, Jack. I can do everything else, but I can't fight. In a way Greg's right. Nothing in my life has made me ready for all this."

"But that's exactly what I'm saying." Jack was trying not to raise his voice. "Nothing you did *could* have prepared you for this. You could have left school at sixteen, like Greg did, and trained as an, I don't know, a plumber or an electrician, what difference would it have made? Look at the Sullivan brothers—they were big tough guys. They were both boxers. They both did a shedload of sports and now they're both dead. But two little wimps like Wiki and Jibber-jabber both made it through. What skills do they have that the Sullivans didn't? None. They were just luckier. That's all."

At the front of the bus, Greg was struggling into his coat. He zipped it up, pulled a flashlight from the pocket, and went over to Liam, who was sitting with the Brain Trust.

"I'm just going outside to have a smoke and give the bus a once-over. Check the tires and that."

"Dad . . ."

"It's all right, Liam." Greg smiled. "Nothing's gonna happen."

He winked at Liam and climbed down off the bus into the rain.

"He's wrong, you know," Justin the nerd said to Liam and the other younger kids when Greg was gone. He'd obviously come to the same conclusion as Jack. "It's not all about trapping rabbits and skinning cats. You don't just need fighters. You need people like us, people who know things, people who know about chemistry and biology and all that kind of stuff, people who can make machines work."

"But we *do* still need fighters," said Froggie.

"Yes, of course we do," Justin went on. "But you can't just have a society of warriors. What are they going to eat? Where are they going to live? What clothes are they going to wear? You need some fighters for protection, yes, but it'll be like any functioning society—you'll also need farmers to grow food, scientists and engineers and doctors to make things and to keep you healthy, you're going to need artists, musicians, and actors to entertain people."

"Jugglers," said Jibber-jabber.

"Jugglers? We won't need jugglers."

"But *they're* entertaining. I like jugglers."

"Well, learn to juggle, then," said Justin, "and you can entertain us all."

"Maybe I will."

"What about clowns?" said Froggie. "Will we need clowns?"

"We'll certainly need people to make us laugh," said Justin. "Now more than ever. But the thing is, we need lots of different people with lots of different skills. That's how we can survive, and why we'll defeat the sickos, because we're cleverer than they are, and we can build a society, but they can't. They will eventually die out. They must, because they can never be anything more than dumb animals. That's mankind's greatest weapon—our brains. There are cannibal tribes—there *were* cannibal tribes—that believed that if you ate the brains of your enemy you'd gain their wisdom and power."

"Lots of cannibals in Papua New Guinea were wiped out by eating human brains," said Wiki. "They all caught mad cow disease—well, the human form, CJD."

Liam was staring at Wiki with wide eyes. "Is it safe to eat other bits of humans?" he asked quietly.

"Well, it's not a very good idea," said Wiki. "We're full of diseases. Most farm animals are given injections and drugs, and they're specially bred to be healthy. Most humans are really unhealthy. We're walking bags of disease and germs. Compared to the average cow, anyway."

"But could you die if you ate someone?"

"Probably not. I don't really know. You'd have to avoid the brains to be sure."

"The sickos eat people," said Jibber-jabber. "And look at them. They're in a terrible state."

"But they were in a terrible state already," said Justin. "They were already sick, that's why they eat people, not the other way around."

"Why are you so interested, anyway?" Jibber-jabber asked Liam. "Are you thinking of eating someone?"

"No. I never would. That's why . . ."

"That's why what?"

"Nothing. But, Dad, you see . . . I don't know for sure . . . But the smoked meat . . ."

"Are you trying to say your dad's eaten someone?" said Jibber-jabber in a whisper. "That's gross."

"No. I don't know. I hope not. But . . . the adults and the older kids, on the farm, they all got sick . . . but Little Paul, he . . ."

Liam stopped as Greg got back on to the bus and took off his soggy coat. They could feel heat radiating off him, and he smelled ripe and meaty. None of them smelled great, but Greg was the worst. He put the coat on the back of his seat and joined the boys. He seemed to fill all the space around them, a featureless black shape.

"You lot need to settle down and go to sleep," he said. "Stop your yakking. You're disturbing everyone else."

"Sorry," said Wiki.

"And, Liam?"

"Yes, Dad?"

"You come and sit with me, son, back here. You need to get a proper night's rest. You was always the same when you had a sleepover. The other kids'd keep you up, and you'd be useless the next day."

Liam didn't like to point out that his dad had only ever let him have one sleepover.

"Okay," he said, and got up out of his seat.

The others all said good night, and he went with his dad to a quieter section of the bus, where they snuggled down next to each other. Greg tucked a blanket around Liam and slipped an arm across his shoulders, giving him a squeeze.

"That's better, isn't it?" he said, and started to cough, bent over, his whole body shaking, still holding Liam tight.

"Are you all right, Dad?"

"'Course I'm all right. It's the dry air on this bus. I wish we didn't have to have the heater on all the time. It dries me throat out, but if I turn it down the girls get cold. No, I'm fine."

"Good. I don't want you to get ill, Dad."

"Hey, hey, hey, that's enough of that. I'm the one supposed to be looking after *you*, remember. Not the other way around. Now, that's enough chat. You just need to get some sleep."

"I don't know if I can, Dad. I'm scared."

"Don't be scared. Nothing's gonna happen to you so long as I'm around." Greg coughed again, and Liam heard him swallow a mouthful of phlegm.

"But what's going to happen to us, Dad? When we get to Islington? I've always just been thinking 'Let's get home,' but what then? What are we going to do?"

Greg was about to say something when he was gripped by another attack of coughing. Afterward, he held Liam even tighter. His body felt hot and damp and he was sweating buckets.

Greg had always told him that there was no God, but Liam prayed now.

Please let him be all right. . . .

At the back of the bus, Courtney and Aleisha were asleep, but Brooke was wide awake. Staring out at a London that lay black and mysterious under the starless sky. She felt like she'd been on this bus forever, and she never wanted to leave it. She could live here quite happily till the end of her life, eating chips and candy. Safe. They had a loo. They had water. They could be like gypsies.

Except they'd grow fat and stinky, the water would run

out, the loo would overflow, they'd fight over the last packet of chips . . .

Stop it, Brooke. Don't think like that.

She wished she could sleep. She didn't like it when she was left alone like this. She needed the constant noise and distraction of her friends. She didn't want to think about anything.

She loved her friends. As long as they were all together, they were invincible. Too invincible sometimes. When she felt untouchable, she often went too far. She wished she didn't say such harsh things all over the place. But she didn't like anyone to get too close. She kept intruders out with sarcasm and insults and ragging. She wished she didn't do it, didn't try to own everyone she met. She did it without thinking, without really meaning to, even if she liked someone. Like the boys they'd picked up. Some of them seemed okay. All right, they were a bit stuck-up, but you couldn't be too picky these days. Ed was nice, fit-looking; Jack was okay—if he didn't have that ugly red thing on his face, she could have fancied him. For sure he was a bit moody, but she quite liked that in a boy. Sometimes the easy, happy ones could be boring. Maybe Ed was boring. She didn't know; she'd kept him away with her big mouth. She'd kept them both away.

As usual.

Well done, Brooke.

She told herself she'd make an effort tomorrow. Especially as it now looked like they were all going to be staying together. She'd never held out much hope for Willesden. She didn't really care if she never saw the dump again. There was nothing for her there, after all.

She looked across at the sleeping bodies of her friends, slumped against each other. Not a care in the world. What did they know about anything? Brooke had had to get used to sickness and death long before they ever did.

There it was. Every night she came back to this place. Thinking about her mom.

Missing her mom.

She'd been sixteen when she'd had Brooke. She had still been at school, though she left soon after. Brooke had never met her dad, and Mom never talked about him, just referred to him as "the tosser." Brooke and her mom had been very close, sharing everything, having a laugh, the two of them against the world. She was more of a sister than a mother. She'd been very pretty, always a new boyfriend on the go, with a flashier car than the last one, more money to throw around. They couldn't ever believe that Brooke was her daughter. One had even come on to her, but Brooke had told her mom, and she'd never seen him again.

Mom was like that. She looked after Brooke, always took her side, always believed her. Not like some of her friends' moms. They could be right cows. Mom had been tough and funny and kind and clever, all the things a mom should be, but what difference had any of that made when she'd got the cancer in one of her breasts?

People said she was very brave. But it didn't help. She had surgery and every kind of treatment the National Health could throw at her.

And eight months later she was dead.

Nothing had been right since then.

What use was all that love when the person wasn't there

no more? It just went bad. Brooke had turned hard and mean and nasty, not caring what she said to anyone. Not caring what anyone thought of her. Except her friends. They were a kind of family now, the three of them. Brooke was the dad. Aleisha the mom, always fussing over them, too nice for her own good. And Courtney was the grumpy teenager, moody and moaning about everything.

She didn't love them the way she'd loved her mom, though. She didn't think she'd ever love anyone ever again, not like that. She was never going to let anyone get that close to her, because people died, and there was nothing you could do to bring them back.

She missed her mom so bad. All that Brooke really wanted in the world was for someone to wrap her up inside their love. She'd cried when she saw Greg settle down with Liam.

Some people were just luckier than others, she supposed.

Greg was still holding Liam tight and murmuring into his ear, his voice low and soft, the voice he used to tell Liam bedtime stories. He always made them up himself, didn't really like storybooks. He was good at it; he made the stories really exciting, doing all the voices and sound effects. A lot of the stories were based on the war films they'd watched together, but he also told Liam about history: Nelson and Wellington, the British Empire, the Charge of the Light Brigade, battles won and lost, about brave soldiers, about Iraq and Afghanistan, and somewhere called Wootton Bassett. Liam didn't care what the stories were about; it was just nice being alone with his dad in the cozy darkness, and having him all to himself.

Greg wasn't telling a story tonight, though. He was trying to make Liam feel safe and unafraid. Dad would have made a good soldier, a brave captain or a general, looking after his men.

It felt good, hearing his voice, the same as all those nights for as long as he could remember. "I love you, Liam," he was saying. "I wouldn't never let anyone hurt you. You know that, don't you?"

"Yes, Dad."

"You're mine, see? *My* boy. And out there. Out in the world, there are people who want to hurt you. But they can't as long as you're with me. Nothing can ever hurt you. I'm your dad, Liam. That means a lot—a boy and his dad. Haven't I always done well for you, looked out for you? Haven't we always had a laugh together, eh? Going to the Arsenal, sitting side by side. Wish I could have taken you back when it was standing. What a crowd that was!"

"I'd like to have seen that, Dad."

"Yeah. I remember going with *my* dad. The two of us, squashed in, but I always knew I'd be okay, 'cause he was with me, watching over me. That's where a son should be, Liam, by his dad's side. That's why you had to stay with me when your mom walked out on us. She would never have known how to look after you, bring you up proper, bring you up to be a proper man like your dad."

"No."

"Only dads know how to bring up boys."

Greg coughed, and as he did so his arm tightened about Liam's neck.

"It's my job as a dad," he said when he'd recovered, "to

make sure that nobody can ever hurt you."

"Yeah . . . actually, Dad, you're hurting me a bit now." Liam gave a little laugh. But he was serious. Dad's arm was choking him.

"Nah. I ain't hurting you, Liam, you silly sod," Greg said, and he too chuckled. "I'm holding you. That's all."

"Yeah . . ."

"Everything's all right. See? I'm just holding you by my side. Where you belong. You'll always be by my side. A boy and his dad. You and me, eh, Liam?"

Greg groaned and dropped his head between his knees. He was shivering, although he felt almost too hot to touch. Liam was sweating where his dad's body was pressed against him.

"Are you sure you're all right, Dad?" he asked quietly, the words falling heavily.

"I've got a real bastard of a headache, son. Feels like my head's splitting open. Makes it hard to think what's the right thing to do, but I'm okay. I always do the right thing, don't I? Always do the right thing. Always look after you. My little whassname . . . whassname . . . God. Forgot your name for a moment there, son. Silly old fart. Losing my memory in my old age. Losing my marbles. Cuh, there's words in there, son, slippery as eels. I'm just trying to catch them. Eel Pie Island. Yeah . . ."

Greg fell silent and Liam didn't know what to say. Dad was acting strangely, not making sense. His arm felt as heavy as lead across his shoulders. For a long while Greg said nothing and didn't move, just sat there, breathing heavily. Liam wondered if he'd fallen asleep.

He tried to move his dad's arm away.

"Leave it," Dad mumbled. "I'm protecting you, Liam. . . . See! I know your name. Lee Am. I need to keep my arm around you, so's you're safe. Nobody is ever going to hurt you as long as I've got a breath in my body. The world was always a bad place and it ain't getting any better, but at least it's getting simpler. There's not so much to understand, just kill or be killed, survival of the fittest, eat or die. Meat Is Life. You know that, don't you? It's written on the front of my, whassname, ship."

"Your shop?"

"Yeah. We don't have to worry no more about taxes and laws and the congestion charge and *Newsnight* and *Question Time*, you won't never have to learn French at school or math—I've always been good at math; you have to be if you're a shopkeeper—and inflation, that don't exist no more, or the credit crunch, or sub-prime mortgages or nucular war. You don't have to worry about books and instructions and how to upgrade your phone and all that rubbish, none of it means nothing no more, just be strong and eat to live. I'll be strong for you, Liam. I know you find it hard to be tough, to be a little man, and maybe if we'd kept up with the footie training you'd have got good at it, but none of that matters no more now. All that matters is . . . What's the matter? What's the, er . . . Yeah, what matters is that you can't be hurt no more, you can't be scared no more. You can just lie there asleep in my arms, Liam, where you'll always be safe. . . ."

"Please, Dad, I can't breathe, you're hurting me, you're squashing my neck."

"Shh, shh, don't talk no more. Just go to sleep, Liam. As

long as you're asleep nothing can hurt you. . . ."

"Dad . . ."

Greg put his hand across Liam's mouth, silencing him. "There, that's better. Quiet now," he said, and whimpered softly, like an animal. "I can feel fingers inside my head, Liam, tearing it all away. And if I ain't here to look after you . . ."

Liam made a muffled noise, "D'd . . ."

"Go to sleep, my darling boy."

27

It was still raining when they woke up, stiff and cold, wrapped in an assortment of coats, blankets, sleeping bags, and whatever else they'd been able to find to keep warm under. Jack groaned and rocked his head on his neck, trying to ease out a knotted muscle. By habit he pulled his mobile phone from his pocket, then sighed. He showed it to Ed, who was coughing and sniffing at his side.

"Look at that," he said, holding up the blank, dead screen. "I'm so used to telling the time by my phone. Used to do everything on it. My whole life was on here. My photos, my music, all my contacts. Don't even know why I hang on to it. It's never going to come back to life, is it? I sometimes think about all those satellites up there, floating about uselessly, cut off from Earth. What do you suppose'll happen to them? Will they fall down? I never could get my head around satellites, how they stay in orbit."

"They'll stay up there." Ed coughed again, clearing phlegm from his sore throat. "Once you're in orbit you stay in orbit. They'll be dead, though, just like your phone. I chucked mine ages ago."

"Yeah, it's just a sort of comfort thing, I guess," said Jack, turning his battered old phone in his hands. "Like Floppy Dog."

"You've lost me. What are you talking about?"

"Floppy Dog."

"You say that like I'm supposed to know what it means."

"Come on!" Jack laughed. "I must have told you about Floppy Dog."

"Nope. Not that I can remember."

"It was this stupid stuffed toy dog I used to have when I was a kid. It had these long black fluffy ears that were kind of like silky. I used to stroke one of the ears, at night, in bed. It was very reassuring, the feel of it, the softness, the smoothness." Jack closed his eyes and smiled. "I can still feel it now. I rubbed its right ear smooth, rubbed it half away by the end. I couldn't live without him. It was a major alert if Floppy Dog ever went missing. National emergency."

"What happened to him?"

"In the end, it was weird, one day . . . I don't know how it happened . . . I went to bed without him, without even thinking. And that was that. Spell broken. I'm not gonna tell you how old I was, but after that—no more Floppy Dog."

"It's all right," said Ed. "Your secret's safe with me."

"It better be." Jack tossed his phone up and caught it neatly. "What time do you think it is, anyway?" he said.

Ed looked at his watch. "Nearly six o'clock," he said. They were all used to going to sleep and waking up at different hours these days, tuned to the rhythm of light and dark. Six o'clock didn't seem as barbaric as it once would have.

Jack looked out the windows. They were parked in the middle of the road on a faceless backstreet. What a miserable day. Rain was dripping off everything and splashing into the puddles that ran along the side of the pavement. There was no one to unblock the drains anymore. The water just lay there.

"What are you going to do, Ed?" he asked.

"How d'you mean?"

"You going to Islington with everyone else?"

"Suppose so. Best to stick together. Aren't you?"

Jack tapped on the window. "We're in south London, Ed. Haven't gotten across the river yet. Now's my chance. Clapham's just a few miles west of here. Wouldn't take me long to walk it."

"But you can't go there by yourself," said Ed. "I thought after what happened . . ."

"I haven't changed my mind." Jack sounded very sure of himself. "But I don't have to go it alone. You could come with me, you and Bam. Why's it going to be any different in north London? You've just got it into your head that it's safe on the bus and you don't want to get off it."

"I know. . . ." Ed ran his fingers through his hair, massaging his scalp. "I suppose I hadn't really thought beyond trying to stay as a gang. You really are a stubborn git, aren't you?"

"Quite frankly," said Jack, lowering his voice and leaning in toward Ed, "the sooner I get away from Lord Greg Almighty, the better."

"I know what you mean."

"So, come with me, eh?"

"I thought you didn't want me around, Jack. You reckon I can't fight. You think I'm a coward. Why would you want me along?"

"Look, I said some stupid things yesterday, Ed. I was tired. You know what it's like. The thing is, I *do* want you around. You're my friend."

"But I'm not any good in a fight," said Ed. "I'm just not."

Jack stood up. "You'll learn," he said.

"I'll need to talk to Bam," said Ed.

"We'll be okay, Ed." Jack squeezed past him. "The three of us. We won't have to worry about the smaller kids and the nerds."

"What about Piers? He won't get far with that head injury, and I don't think Bam would leave him behind."

Jack stopped, swore. "I forgot about him. Maybe the girls could look after him?"

Ed laughed. "I don't think so."

"Well, sort it out with Bam. Make a decision of some sort. I'm going to go and talk to his lordship up front."

Jack yawned and made his way to the front of the bus. He had to step over Liam, who was lying in the aisle wrapped in a blanket, Greg's jacket under his head for a pillow.

Greg was sitting in the driver's seat with his shotgun in his lap, staring straight ahead through the rain-streaked windshield. He was still as a statue, but as Jack got close, Greg suddenly burst into a wild coughing fit that ended with him spitting into the stairwell.

Jack stopped and took a deep breath. It wasn't good when

an adult coughed like that. It usually meant only one thing. He let his breath out slowly and stepped closer.

"Do you know exactly where we are?" he asked, hoping for the best.

Greg ignored him. Just sat there.

"Is this, like, Borough, or somewhere?" Jack pressed on. Nothing.

"Greg?"

Just the rain, tapping on the roof.

"Are you all right?"

There was a sound somewhere between a shriek and a sob. Jack turned round. Zohra was with Liam, trying to wake him.

"There's something the matter with him," she said. "He won't wake up."

"What?" Jack felt very cold suddenly.

"What's happened to him? Why won't he wake up?"

"Get some water, splash his face maybe."

"He won't move."

"Put him in the recovery position."

"LEAVE HIM ALONE!"

Greg's voice sounded uncomfortably loud in the cramped confines of the bus. Everyone fell silent.

Still Greg wouldn't turn around.

Jack went over to Liam and knelt down. He shook him. He felt frozen. Jack lifted his face. His lips were blue, his eyes wide open and staring, slightly bulging. There were red marks and bruising around his neck.

"He's dead," he said to nobody in particular.

"I said, leave him alone!" Greg snarled. "Don't touch him.

Don't go anywhere near him. I'm looking after him. You're none of you fit to be anywhere near him."

"He's dead," Jack repeated.

"He's all right."

"What happened?"

"Nothing happened."

"You were with him last night," said Jack accusingly. "What happened to him?"

"HE'S ALL RIGHT!"

At last Greg turned around and stood up. His face was greasy with sweat, his eyes and nostrils red-rimmed. There were white spots around his mouth. But the thing Jack found most disturbing was that he was wearing Liam's wire-rimmed glasses.

"Why are you wearing them?" he asked.

Greg put his hand to his face.

"The sun was too bright," he said, blinking. "I needed to put me dark glasses on."

Jack was gripped by a cold, hard fury. "You're sick," he said accusingly. "You've got the disease. You're just like all the rest."

"I ain't sick. I'm fine."

"Look at yourself, Greg. Look in the mirror. You've got the disease." Now Jack pointed to Liam's lifeless body. He was shaking with rage, his finger waving. He knew Greg was dangerous. He knew he should be careful, be clever like Ed, but he couldn't stop himself. "Did you do this?" he asked. "To Liam? Did you?"

"I was protecting him," Greg croaked. "So nobody can ever hurt him. If I ain't around to look after him, what was he gonna do? He was always gentle, my little Liam, never a tough nut like me. Couldn't take care of himself. He would have gotten hurt. He was the sweetest, kindest boy. And now he always will be."

"Greg . . ."

"Shut up! Sit down and shut up. I said I was going to get us all to Islington and I will. I'm taking Liam home."

He aimed his shotgun at Jack, who backed into a seat, shaking worse than ever.

"That's better," said Greg, showing both barrels to everyone on the bus. "Now, all of you, stay where you are, sitting down. Don't talk to the driver when the bus is in motion, or the driver will shoot you. Got that?"

Greg returned to his seat and started the engine. A spray of rain rattled down the side of the bus, which rocked as a blast of wind rolled over it. Jack realized with dismay that Greg would virtually be driving blind.

As the bus eased forward, Ed nipped up the aisle and tucked in next to Jack.

"He's lost it," he said quietly.

"Big-time."

"What are we going to do?" Ed asked.

"Just sit tight and wait for our moment. He's not gonna get far like this."

"He killed Liam?"

"Looks like it. And he'll probably kill the rest of us if we don't stop him somehow."

Greg shifted up through the gears so that they were soon thundering along through the cluttered streets of south London. Too fast. Greg was completely out of control.

There were a thump and a grinding crunch as they hit something on one side, but Greg just sped up. Someone screamed, and Zohra started wailing. They were all being thrown about in their seats. Jack pressed his face to the side window and tried to get his bearings.

"Where's he taking us?" Ed asked. "Can you tell?"

"Not sure. We're somewhere near London Bridge, I think. But I reckon we're heading south, away from the river. It's so hard to tell around here. None of the roads goes in a straight line."

There was another terrific bang, and the bus lurched sideways across the road. Greg wrestled with the wheel.

"This is crazy," Jack said, standing up and climbing over Ed.

"Jack, no . . ."

Jack fought his way to the front, rocking from side to side, stumbling into the seats.

"Stop the bus!" he yelled. By way of a reply, Greg flung an arm back and fired off a round from his gun. It went wild, peppering the ceiling with shot, but Jack threw himself to the ground and lay pressed against the carpeted floor.

"Sit down!" Greg yelled, still waving the gun around.

Jack stayed there, hoping that Greg might at least slow down. It was clear, though, that nothing short of a major accident was going to stop him.

Jack made a decision.

If the bus hit something head-on, he'd be thrown forward like a torpedo.

He started to crawl. Inch by inch along the floor. Hoping that Greg wouldn't notice him in the big convex mirror that gave the driver a view of the entire bus interior. He passed Liam's body, tried not to think about what Greg had done to him, kept going.

The bus went way too fast over an obstacle, a speed bump maybe, and Jack was flipped up into the air and landed with a thud. He heard something scraping the underside. Still he crept forward, his eyes fixed on the shotgun that Greg was waving blindly in the air.

Greg couldn't drive properly like this, and neither could he aim properly. Sooner rather than later, either they were going to crash or Greg was going to loose off a shot that would hit one of the kids.

Jack had to keep going.

At last he reached the front. Greg was close enough to touch. Jack picked his moment and then forced himself up from the floor. He shunted Greg's gun arm out of the way and grabbed his wrist. There was a bang as Greg squeezed the trigger. Shot raked the windshield and punched a hole in the door.

But that was it. The gun only held two shells at a time. If Greg wanted to shoot again, he would have to reload first, and Jack wasn't going to give him the chance. He wrenched the weapon out of Greg's grasp and butted the stock into the side of his head. Green snot exploded from Greg's nose, and he fell away from Jack as the bus slewed across the road, hurling Jack down the steps. For a few seconds the bus plowed on sideways, filling the street from curb to curb, its tires screaming. Then there came a final almighty smash as it hit some parked cars, and they at last stopped moving.

From his position sprawled in the stairwell, Jack could

see smoke and steam rising outside.

Ed unbuckled his belt, ran along the aisle, and pulled Jack up out of the stairwell and onto his feet.

"Well done!" He grinned at his friend, who looked shaken and a little disorientated.

But Greg wasn't finished. With a roar, he surged out of his seat and punched Ed out of the way with a meaty forearm, trying to get to Jack.

Jack aimed a wild kick at Greg; it got him in the knee. Greg yelled and swung back at him, a vicious right hook that, if it had connected, would have knocked Jack's head off. But Jack managed to duck and scurry backward up the aisle, dragging Ed with him.

Greg went into a low crouch, arms outstretched, his red eyes burning with hatred and rage. There was blood drooling from his mouth—whether from Jack's blow to his head or from internal bleeding, it was impossible to tell. He coughed, spraying blood and mucus over the kids at the front of the bus, who were up out of their seats and retreating from him in a pack like startled ducklings.

Greg belched, causing a big brown bubble to form between his lips. It burst, filling the bus with a foul stench. He wiped his mouth and then spat a gobbet of rubbery mucus against a window, where it slowly crawled down like a fat yellow slug.

"If Liam ain't gonna live," he slobbered, "none of you deserves to live. NONE OF YOU. I'm gonna rip you to pieces."

28

Brooke was lying in a confusion of spilled and scattered boxes at the back of the bus, half buried beneath bags of chips and cookies. A can of beans had hit her in the back of the head, and for a moment she wasn't sure where she was. Then Courtney pulled her out, and she quickly caught up with what was going on. Greg was advancing down the aisle, forcing the panicked kids ahead of him. Brooke swore and looked for some way to escape the chaos.

Fixed above the window was a little metal hammer thing in a glass case.

"Look," she said, twisting Courtney around. "Let's smash the glass and get out of here."

"Do it!" said Courtney.

Brooke jumped on the seat and used her elbow to break the thin glass covering the hammer. Then she fumbled to remove it from the clips that held it in place. "Let go, you stupid thing."

At last she got her fingers around it and tore it free.

"Hurry up!" Aleisha was watching Greg slowly make his way up the bus. Kids were spilling from their seats and falling over each other to keep ahead of him.

Brooke swung the hammer.

Too weak. It just bounced off.

Useless.

"Harder!" yelled Courtney. "Do it harder."

"I know!" Brooke snapped. "Give me a chance." She pulled her arm back, bared her teeth, and grunted like a tennis player as she swung again. This time there was a satisfying crack as the window turned into a thousand glittering diamonds. Another hit and the bits of shattered glass dropped out, clattering and tinkling.

Brooke bustled to the window, then jumped back with a cry.

There were sickos outside.

About ten of them crowding around the bus, mothers and fathers, a couple of teenagers, in a much worse state than Greg. One of them reached up toward the broken window and took hold of the sill. He was a mess. His cheeks had either been torn through or had rotted away so that his lower jaw dangled down, no longer attached to the upper jaw. His head tilted back and his long pink tongue poked out like he was a living Pez dispenser.

"We're trapped," Brooke yelled, swiping at the father's fingers with the hammer.

The other two girls crowded around her to look outside. The sickos were getting excited. They started whining and battering the sides of the bus with their fists. *BANG-BANG-BANG-BANG-BANG-BANG . . .*

Greg came on down the aisle, dribbling, coughing, belching, arms wide.

Matt was standing his ground in the aisle as the smaller kids surged past him. He was clutching a handful of the torn pages from his Bible. "Greg! Stop!" he said, raising an open palm. "It doesn't have to be like this. I can help you. The Lamb can cure you. He can make you better. The Lamb can—"

Greg lashed out at him with a scything backhander. The slap took Matt full in the face, and Greg's signet ring tore a bloody gash from his eyebrow up into his hairline. Matt went flying and fell down heavily between the seats.

Zohra, Froggie, and Jibber-jabber used the distraction to run to the toilet. They wrenched the door open and darted inside, frantically scrabbling to lock the door behind them.

Greg snarled and punched his fist through the top of the door. It stuck there, halting him for a moment. He tugged and bellowed and shook like a dog arguing over a bone. Splintered chipboard and plastic tore at his forearm as he tried to pull it free. The cries of the little kids sounded small and distant inside the toilet.

Greg let out a string of obscenities and looked like he might wrench the whole door off its hinges.

"Out of the way! Coming through!" It was Bam, charging down the aisle, head lowered, shoulder braced, as if he were on the rugby field going into a tackle.

Greg looked around just as Bam barged into him, and the two of them collapsed in a tangle.

"Get the gun!" Bam yelled, trying to keep Greg down. Bam was big and strong and heavy, but Greg was heavier and filled with a mad fury. He flailed and spat at Bam, who clung on to him.

BANG-BANG-BANG-BANG-BANG-BANG . . . The sickos outside continued their hammering on the side of the bus.

Jack vaulted over the writhing bodies in the aisle and sped to the front of the bus. He picked the gun up from where it was lying on the floor and looked around for some shells.

There was a messy driver's shelf full of tissues and old candy and CD cases and maps. Jack tore into it, tossing stuff aside, his hands feeling slow and clumsy. It was hard to think straight with the screams of the kids, the banging from outside, the rain lashing the roof. "Come on, come on . . ."

There. He'd picked it up and tossed it aside before he realized what it was. A box of shotgun shells. He'd never loaded a gun before, but he'd seen it done enough times in movies and on TV to have a pretty good idea what to do. You sort of bent the gun in half and shoved the cartridges in the back end of the barrels. He couldn't for the life of him work out how to open the gun, though.

He let loose a string of obscenities.

It must have a catch or a lock of some kind.

There was a shout, and he looked around to see Greg forcing himself to his feet, throwing off Bam. He moved awkwardly. It looked like the arm that had been stuck in the toilet door was dislocated. He turned his whole upper body to his right, as if his head could no longer swivel on his neck.

Chris Marker was sitting there, frozen in the act of reading his book.

Two pairs of eyes locked.

Chris slowly stood up and backed away until he was flattened against the window, his book open in his hands.

Greg was breathing heavily, blinking, angry, and bewildered. He glared at the book, focusing all of his hatred on it.

Chris calmly closed the covers and then, in one swift movement, smashed the book's spine into the bridge of Greg's nose like a brick, knocking the lenses out of Liam's glasses. Greg grunted and staggered back on stiff legs before collapsing on the seats on the other side of the aisle.

"Come on," Ed yelled, helping the little kids out of the toilet. "Everyone off the bus."

"No!" Brooke shouted. "There's more of them out there."

BANG-BANG-BANG-BANG-BANG-BANG . . .

Bam limped over to Jack and took the gun from him. He quickly found the release catch and thumbed it forward. He grinned at Jack and broke the gun over his knee before slotting two of the shells into the twin barrels.

He looked back at Ed, who was halfway down the bus.

"I'll clear the way outside. You bring Piers!" he shouted, shoving the rest of the shells into his pocket. He kicked the damaged door open.

"Stay with me!" he commanded, and stepped off.

There were two blasts.

"Quickly!" Jack jumped down after Bam, and the others followed, jostling each other to get off the bus before Greg recovered.

Ed put a hand on Kwanele's shoulder as he pushed past, wheeling his luggage. "Help me," he said.

"Me?"

"Yes, you! I can't carry Piers by myself."

"He's bleeding. It'll ruin my suit."

"Just shut up and help."

They each took one of Piers's arms and pulled him up out of his seat. He felt like a dead weight. Kwanele cursed as his suitcase got entangled in the legs of one of the seats. Piers gasped and winced in pain, his eyes flickering open.

"It's all right," said Ed. "We're getting you off the bus, mate."

They dragged him along the aisle, blocking Brooke and her friends, who were struggling forward over the scattered boxes.

"Hurry up," Courtney wailed.

Brooke was shaking uncontrollably. She'd seen what was outside. The boys hadn't. If they got split up, it would be a disaster, and she definitely didn't want to be left on the bus by herself.

As they passed Greg, he looked up at them. "Stay where you are," he said, his voice rattling with mucus. He lunged up toward Brooke, who shrieked and punched the hammer into his gut. The air went out of him with an *OOF*, and he doubled over in pain.

The girls pushed past Ed and ran the rest of the way to the doors, nearly falling down the steps in their hurry. Outside in the rain, Bam was reloading the shotgun. There were two sickos lying on the pavement, a mother and a teenager; the rest were cowering near the back of the bus. Pez was with them. His head rocked back and his horrible pink tongue stuck out.

"Move it," Bam shouted at the girls. "Get away while you can."

29

Ed and Kwanele had nearly made it to the doors, but it was hard going. Piers had passed out again, and Kwanele was having trouble holding him up with one arm and wheeling his suitcase with the other. He called for help, but everyone else was already running away from the bus.

"They've forgotten about us," Kwanele wailed.

"Shut up and keep going," Ed grunted. "We can't just leave him."

There was a noise behind them. Greg was up again. Trying to work out where everyone had gone.

He spotted the boys.

"Forget it," said Kwanele. "I'm out of here."

He dropped Piers. Ed screamed at him, but Kwanele bolted off the bus and ran after the others.

Ed was left holding Piers's arm. "Piers," he sobbed. "Come on, Piers, help me . . . help me . . ."

But Piers was dead to the world.

Greg was moving slowly toward them. He looked cross-eyed, more confused than ever, his face a mask of blood and pus. Liquid was gurgling in his throat. His breath was rasping and harsh.

With a superhuman effort, Ed got Piers as far as the doors, but then he wouldn't budge any farther. Ed tugged and tugged at him, but it made no difference. In his panic he couldn't figure out what had happened. He hadn't spotted that Piers's jacket had caught on a handle.

"Piers," he shouted. "Piers, come on. Wake up!"

Greg was getting nearer by the second, his lips curled back from his bloody teeth. He reached out with his good hand toward Ed and seemed to smile.

Ed looked out. Three big sickos were approaching the doorway. In another moment his way out would be blocked altogether. There was no sign of his friends.

"Piers," he yelled, uselessly jerking the boy's body. Ed was crying in desperation. Greg was so close now he could smell him.

Ed let go.

"Sorry," he said, relieved that Piers was unconscious and would have no idea what was going on.

He jumped off the bus, shoved past the sickos in the street, and ran for it. Behind him, he could hear Greg raging and roaring, fighting the other adults over Piers's body.

Ed kept moving, all the while glancing wildly around for a glimpse of the others. There was a bang, and he turned toward the sound. The kids were a little way along the road. Most of them were scrambling over a fence beside a tall white gatepost, while Bam and Jack fought off a second, smaller band of sickos. The noise had been Bam shooting at one of them.

"Hey!" Ed shouted. "Wait for me."

They either didn't hear him or they ignored him.

Ed sprinted to catch up, feeling sick that he'd abandoned Piers. Bam and Jack were frantically trying to keep the sickos back. There were about six of them, clawing at the boys, snapping their yellow teeth. They were too close for Bam to fire the gun again, and he was using it as a club.

With a yell, Ed piled into them, scattering them and knocking two of them over. Bam saw his chance and shot another one.

"Get over the fence," Jack shouted. "They can't follow us."

Ed vaulted the fence into the small park on the other side. Ahead of him were two massive gray naval guns that were a good twenty feet long. They stood in front of a building, making it look like some weird stranded battleship. The building was grand and classical in design, with six pillars across the front and a very tall, narrow, green dome jutting straight up at the top.

With a shock of recognition, Ed realized he'd been here before with his prep school. It was the Imperial War Museum.

Jack and Bam followed him over the fence. Bam reloaded and turned to fire a last shot at the sickos on the other side. Not that it mattered. They didn't have the sense to figure out how to get over.

The three boys charged down the path toward where their friends were waiting for them by the naval guns, lungs burning, rain stinging their faces, their feet slapping on the wet paving stones. Jack and Ed ran side by side, Bam slightly behind.

"What happened to Piers?" Jack panted.

"You didn't wait," Ed replied.

"You left him?"

"Kwanele ran off. I couldn't do it by myself. You should have stayed."

"I was helping the others."

"You should have stayed." Ed arrived at the steps to the museum and stopped, doubled over, resting his hands on his knees. The rest of the kids were hammering on the doors. Kwanele was with them, looking sheepish, his suitcase at his side.

Ed gave him a dirty look. "Thanks for your help, Kwanele."

"What difference would it have made?" Kwanele protested. "Even if we *had* got him off the bus? We couldn't have gotten away."

"That's not the point."

"The point is we are both still alive."

"Which is more than can be said for Piers."

By now Bam had registered that Piers was missing. "Where is he?" he asked accusingly.

"We had to leave him on the bus," Ed explained. "We couldn't move him."

Before Bam could say anything, there was a cheer. Someone inside the building had opened the doors. The kids bundled noisily inside.

Ed hung back for a while, regaining his breath, pulling himself together, not wanting to have to face Bam and Jack. Then he walked slowly into the museum, past two boys in old army uniforms who were holding the doors open.

Inside, he crossed a small entrance area, went up some

more steps, and came out into the main atrium. There were planes dangling from the ceiling. Jack recognized a Spitfire among them. The white-tiled floor was littered with tanks, vehicles, and artillery pieces of all shapes and sizes.

The rest of the kids from the bus were gazing around in openmouthed awe. A small group of boys were staring sullenly at them from one side. Like the two boys who had let them in, they were dressed in military uniforms that they'd obviously borrowed from an exhibit, and they were heavily armed.

"Who is it?" came a voice from behind one of the tanks.

"Dunno, some kids," said one of the boys in uniform.

Brooke walked around the tank, followed by the rest of the bus party.

Three boys, about thirteen years old, were sitting cross-legged on the floor, wrapped in blankets. They looked like village elders around a campfire. All three of them were equipped with rulers, dice, and notebooks, and spread out around them on the gleaming tiles were hundreds of miniature metal soldiers and an odd assortment of bits and pieces that were being used to represent a landscape—trees and buildings and roads. They were evidently in the middle of an elaborate war game.

One was a chubby kid wearing a World War I German helmet with a spike on the top. Next to him sat a black kid wearing plastic-framed glasses held together at the nose with putty. He stared, unblinking, at the intruders. The glasses made his eyes look massive, as if they could see right through you. He had a serious expression, verging on blank, and there was a stillness about him. The third boy couldn't have been more different. He was pale, wiry, fidgety, animated, like a pot of boiling water. He scratched his armpit, picked his nose, and grinned like a monkey at the new arrivals.

"Fresh meat," he said. "Yum yum! Groovalicious."

"Ha-ha," said Brooke, with all her usual sarcasm. "Very funny."

"I like to think so," said the skinny boy. "I like to think I ain't lost it."

"I doubt you ever had it," said Brooke.

The skinny boy jumped up and offered his palm to Brooke. She refused to slap it.

"I'm DogNut," he said. "But you can call me Babe."

Brooke shook her head and moved away from him.

"Watch where you're walking," said the black kid in the glasses.

"Ooh, we don't want to mess up your toys, do we?" said Brooke.

"No," said the boy matter-of-factly, but combined with his cold hard stare, it came across as strangely menacing. Brooke faltered, unsure whether to push it any further. There was something about the boy that told her to be careful, an air of authority and quiet power.

"Listen to what the bad man says," said DogNut. "Believe me, you don't never want to get on the bad side of Jordan Hordern."

"That your name?" said Brooke. "Jordan Hordern."

"Yes," said the black kid. "What of it?"

"Nothing. Is a good name. Rhymes."

"Yes," said Jordan Hordern. "I know."

"Will you be staying for tea?" asked DogNut in a mock fancy voice.

"They're not staying," said Jordan Hordern, turning away from them and concentrating on his game.

"Who says?" Brooke asked.

"If the man says you ain't staying," said DogNut, "you ain't staying. Like, sorry and all, but no one argues with Jordan Hordern, get me?"

"Hang on a minute," said Jack, pushing past Ed. "You don't own this place. You can't just kick us out."

"Can't I?"

"No way," said Brooke. "We just escaped from a whole mess of sickos out there, man. First we was trapped on a bus with a father who went psycho on us and tried to batter us all, and then there was these, like, freaks in the street and—"

"What were you doing with a father on a bus?" Jordan Hordern interrupted.

"Well, duh, he was, like, *driving*, wasn't he?"

"Don't you know they're all mental?"

"We know that now, but he looked okay; he saved me and my girlfriends, and he swore he wasn't gonna go sick on us."

"And you trusted him? You're more stupid than you look."

"Yeah? And you're a prick," said Brooke.

Jordan Hordern looked at her curiously and then shrugged. "You still ain't staying."

"Why'd you let us in in the first place, then?" Ed asked.

"Good question." Jordan Hordern turned his gaze onto the two guards who had opened the doors. "Why *did* you let them in?" he asked. "You know the rules."

The boys looked at their feet, not sure what to say.

"They let us in because they wanted to help us!" said Jack angrily. "Because we're kids like you. Human beings.

Assuming you *are* human and not some kind of macho robot asshole."

Jordan Hordern's expression didn't change.

"Come on," said Brooke. "You can't kick us out. We wouldn't last five minutes out there. We'll be massacred."

"Not our problem."

"Well, what *is* your problem?" said Jack.

"It's very simple. And it's nothing personal," said Jordan Hordern. "We've got enough food and water here for ten people to live an okay life. We've got security and heat, and we're well defended. Any more than ten of us, though, becomes a problem. That clear enough for you?"

"And how long is your food gonna last?" Jack asked.

"It'll get us through the winter if we're careful. With any luck, when it warms up, all the adults will have died off and we can go out and get more."

"We only being reasonable," said DogNut. "We looking after number one. That's how it works now, blood."

"Have you turned other people away?" Bam asked. He was bruised from his fight on the bus, and had a gash in one cheek, as well as a nasty wound in his left hand where Greg had bitten him.

"A few," said Jordan Hordern.

"Well, you're not throwing us out." Bam sat down in the middle of their game, crushing a battalion of German soldiers.

"Oh, don't do that," DogNut moaned. "I was winning for once."

"We're not leaving," said Bam. "You can try and make us, but we're staying put."

Jordan Hordern stared dispassionately at Bam for a few seconds, then clapped his hands together. Five more of his boys came over. They were carrying swords and truncheons.

"Come off it," Jack scoffed. "It's one thing hiding in here and not opening the doors to a few stray kids, it's another thing to actually kill them. Is that what you think you're gonna do? Kill all of us? Or maybe you were thinking you might just beat us up and throw our bleeding, semiconscious bodies out of a window."

"Wait up," Brooke interrupted, jutting her jaw out at Jordan Hordern. "You said there's ten of you, yeah?"

"Yes."

"Are you all boys, then?"

"What of it?"

Brooke laughed. "Then we got something you need," she said, eyeing Jordan defiantly.

"What?"

Brooke made a display of herself, arms out to her sides, and said, "Ta-daa!"

"Broo-ooke!" Aleisha rolled her eyes, scandalized.

"I don't mean like that," said Brooke. "You've got a dirty mind, Aleisha. I just mean we got skills that might come in useful."

"Yeah, I can think of a few," DogNut sniggered.

"In your dreams," Brooke sneered.

"You already are," said DogNut.

"We don't need girls," said Jordan Hordern.

"Whoa-whoa-whoa, wait a minute," said DogNut, dancing on the spot and dropping his blanket. Underneath it he was wearing a brown leather American flying jacket, a screaming eagle painted on its back. "Let's not be too hasty here. She does have a point, Jordan."

"No, she doesn't. We're not taking in any more. Now get them out of here so we can finish our game."

Jack exploded with rage. He barged his way over to Jordan and leaned over him, jabbing a finger in his face. "You're worse than the bloody grown-ups. You know that? At least they don't know what they're doing. You're just cold. We've got little kids with us—eight, nine years old—you gonna smash their brains out, are you? You gonna cut us all up? Well, you can bloody try. We've climbed a mountain of crap in the last two days and we're not gonna go down without a fight. We're not asking to come and live with you forever in your precious bloody museum. We just need shelter until we can get ourselves sorted."

"Don't point at me," said Jordan. "I don't like people pointing at me."

"Oh, don't you? So why don't you get one of your little soldier boys to hack my finger off? Cos I don't think you've got the balls to do it yourself, have you?"

At that, Jordan threw off his blankets and stood up. He was wearing a smart black officer's uniform, complete with gold braid and medals. He was taller than Jack and moved like an athlete. Before Jack could react, Jordan had grabbed his wrist and was twisting it to the side.

Jack winced, evidently in a lot of pain. Jordan kept on turning his wrist, forcing Jack to the ground. Jack tried to pull away, but Jordan held him with an iron grip. Once Jack was on his knees, Jordan spoke, his voice low and quiet.

"I don't care what you say to me, I don't care what you

think about me, but don't ever point at me again. All right?"

"All right, all right, you can stop now. I've got the general idea."

Jordan squeezed harder. Jack yelped.

Now Ed spoke up. "I think this has gotten a bit out of hand," he said. "We should all calm down and talk about it."

Jordan looked around at Ed without letting go of Jack.

Ed went on. "Jack's right. All we need is somewhere to stay until we've worked out what we're going to do. Maybe only for one night. Maybe not even that. Okay? You don't need to give us any food if you don't want. We're not trying to take over or anything. We all just ran in here after a fight to get away. There's still sickos out there."

Jack gasped. He was kneeling on the tiles, his lips pulled back in a grimace of pain.

"Can we at least just talk about this sensibly?" Ed pleaded.

Jordan let go of Jack, who rolled away and sat down against a tank, rubbing his arm.

"I'll think about it," said Jordan. "We'll finish our game, then we'll talk. You can have some water, but no food. Sort yourselves out and I'll listen to what you've got to say. I'm only going to talk to one of you, though. Who's in charge?"

"Nobody," said Ed.

"Then I'm appointing you." Jordan turned back to his game and started straightening the troops that had got knocked over.

30

"Let's get this out in the open." Ed banged his hands on a tabletop. "And then I don't want to hear any more about it. Not from you, Bam, not from Jack, not from anyone." Ed looked around, daring the other kids to catch his eye.

They were all in the museum café, off to the side of the atrium, spread out among the tables. The place had been ransacked and no one at the museum had bothered to tidy up; there was litter everywhere.

The Brain Trust was sitting shivering at one table—Justin the nerd, Jibber-jabber, Wiki, Zohra, and Froggie. Mad Matt was with Archie Bishop and the other kids from the chapel. There was an ugly black-and-red scab across Matt's forehead where Greg's ring had raked his skin. Brooke, Courtney, and Aleisha sat in one corner, in a cloud of perfume and attitude. Chris Marker was by himself. He had inevitably gone back to reading his book, but the others viewed him differently after what he'd done to Greg on the bus. He wasn't totally useless. Jack, Ed, and Frédérique were at another table with Bam. Bam was the only one of the rugby players still alive, and he'd obviously been hit hard by Piers's death. This was the first time anyone had seen him down and lacking his cheery optimism. Kwanele sat by himself, straight-backed and defiant.

While they'd been waiting in here, Bam had been on Ed and Kwanele nonstop about leaving Piers behind, and Ed had had enough.

"Have any of you ever tried to carry someone who was unconscious?" he asked. "People are heavy. Piers was heavy. Greg came after us and Piers's body got caught on something. If I'd stayed any longer, Greg would have gotten me, and then the other sickos outside would have made it onto the bus and that would have been that. And why? Because you all had disappered and left me to it. Thanks."

Kwanele obviously thought Ed was referring to him. "Piers was badly wounded," he protested. "He probably would not have lived anyway, not without medicine, and doctors, and things like that."

"So that's it, is it?" said Bam. "Like DogNut or whatever his name is out there said, look out for number one. If you're hurt, forget it."

"It wasn't just Kwanele!" Ed shouted. "You all left me behind."

"We were fighting off sickos," said Bam. "I was trying to get everyone to safety."

"Exactly," said Ed. "We've all got excuses."

There was a long silence before Bam spoke.

"All right," he said. "Maybe we were all to blame. It happened too fast."

"It's basic survival now," said Ed. "Getting from one day to another. This place is well defended, standing alone, with open ground all around, and it's stuffed full of weapons. It would be a perfect place to set up camp. But someone else got here first and we can't expect them to look after us."

"I don't want to stay here anyway," said Jack. "I want to get home."

"Then why the hell were you arguing so much with Jordan bloody Hordern?"

"He wound me up," said Jack. "I don't like anyone talking to me like that."

"I don't want to stay here either," said Matt. "I need to go on to St. Paul's. It's been ordained that—"

"Give it a rest, Matt," said Ed. "We're fed up with hearing about your bloody made-up religion."

"It's not made-up."

"Yes it is. Nothing has *been ordained*. It's all come out of your head."

"And what about this, then?" said Matt, angrily tapping his forehead.

"What about what?"

"The mark of the Lamb."

"It's a scab, Matt."

"It's the mark of the Lamb."

Ed laughed harshly, using his laughter like a weapon.

"It doesn't matter whether you believe us anyway," said Archie Bishop. "We want to carry on to St. Paul's. With or without you all—it doesn't make any difference."

"Doesn't make any difference?" Ed scoffed. "You'll be murdered out there by yourselves."

"The Lamb will protect us."

There were groans from the other tables, and people

started throwing things at Matt. Old discarded coffee cups, balled-up paper, empty cigarette packs.

Matt tried not to react, as if he were above it all, but they could tell he was getting riled.

"What does anyone else want to do?" Ed asked when things had calmed down a little.

"We want to stick with you," said Wiki. "We'll go wherever you say you want to go. If we stay together, it'll be safer. Like when fish form into schools. Even though they're a bigger target, individually they're safer, and harder for predators to focus on. The chances of being picked out from a big swirling mass are less than if they're swimming alone."

"Thank you, David Attenborough," said Jack, trying to cut him off.

"We could find another building to shelter in," said Jibber-jabber. "There's loads of places near the museum; I came here once with my dad, we had to park miles away and walk, there's all sorts of houses, I bet if we explored we could find something great; we don't need to stay here, I don't like Jordan Hordern or any of them, actually, although I liked the look of that game they were playing, I like toy soldiers, at home I've got hundreds; and now we've got our own gun and maybe they'll let us have some weapons from the museum, we could be like a commando squad, you're good fighters and—"

"Not all of us," said Bam darkly, looking at Kwanele.

"I never said I was a fighter," Kwanele protested.

"I thought we weren't going to go on about that." Ed sounded tired and fed up.

"Sorry." Bam bowed his head.

Frédérique suddenly let out a sob and collapsed facedown

on the tabletop, crying. Jack and Ed both put a hand on her, trying to comfort her. She was tugging at her hair, hysterical.

"What's the matter with *her*?" said Brooke snottily, and Aleisha jabbed her with an elbow. "What?" said Brooke. "I only asked what was the matter."

"What do you think?" said Ed. "If we weren't all trying so hard to act tough, we'd all be facedown on the table crying like babies. Because that's all we are. Just babies. This is all too much for any of us to handle."

"I ain't crying," said Brooke. "I ain't giving up."

Jack clapped sarcastically. "Well done, you."

"It's stupid," said Frédérique. "We are all going to die. What's the point of all this talking? Why must we argue?" She raised her head. Her face was blotchy and streaked with tears. "Why do we need to find somewhere safe? Why do we need to do anything? We are all going to die. I thought there was some hope. Greg was not ill. I thought if just one adult was not ill, there was hope for us. But he is ill, and there is no hope. . . ."

Frédérique was crying so much she started to choke, and she crumpled down again, weeping, coughing, and spluttering.

"Cheery soul, ain't she?" said Brooke, and Aleisha elbowed her again.

The big glass door opened and DogNut came in.

"Okay, listen up," he said, clapping his hands together. "Jordan Hordern's made a decision." He pointed at Ed. "You, whatsyourname . . ."

"Ed."

"Okay, Ed my man, you go and talk to the general. He's waiting for you. Chop-chop. The rest of you, chillax."

31

Ed and Jordan Hordern were sitting side by side in the front seats of a World War II Jeep, looking out across the atrium. It was cold, and the thin winter light that made its way through the massive arched glass ceiling did little to lift the gloom. Jordan had given Ed a furry blanket that he'd wrapped tightly about his body.

"You mustn't take any of this personally," Jordan was saying, staring straight ahead without looking at Ed.

"I don't," Ed replied. "I know where you're coming from."

"Good. I don't hate any of you. But I have to look after my people."

"It's cool. So you're booting us out?"

"Not necessarily. Like I said, we don't have enough food here to support any more people. But there's a simple answer. I'll let you take any weapons you want. There's way too many for us to use. And I'll let you stay here. . . ."

"Thanks."

"I ain't finished."

"Oh. Right."

"As I was saying. You can sleep here tonight. No conditions. I'll put you in the 1940's house."

"What's that?"

"Special exhibit, complete wartime house with all the stuff in it. Beds and everything. I figure the little kids you got with you will feel more at home in there. Less freaked out."

"Thanks."

"Then, after that, you can stay here as long as you want, so long as you can feed yourselves."

"What do you mean?"

"What I say. Don't worry about water, there's plenty in the tanks here, but if you want to eat, you gonna have to go out and find it."

"That sounds fair, I guess," said Ed. "I'll see what the others think about it. Can you let us have any food to keep us going?"

"Nope. I've given you my offer. I won't change it. They're pretty good guys, the guys here. You stick with us, we'll be strong. But you got to carry your weight."

Ed was thinking through how this arrangement might work. "Do you think there's food out there?" he asked.

"Don't see why not," said Jordan. "Take it from me, though, you won't find nothing fresh: no bread, no eggs, no milk, no fresh vegetables and fruit, nothing like that."

"Have you got any of that stuff?"

"Nope. We got cans and boxes of dry stuff. It ain't exactly healthy, but it keeps us alive."

"Where'd you get it all from?"

"We wasn't the only ones who had the idea to hole up in here. Some guys was here first. Men. Real nasty. They was well-armed with tools, and must have brought a load of supplies in with them, boxes and cans and whatever. I think maybe they'd robbed a supermarket or something. They killed off the security guards and settled in for a siege, but like everybody else they found out real quick that the enemy was inside, not outside. The sickness. Already eating away at them." Jordan paused, ran his fingers around the rim of the steering wheel.

"What happened to them?" Ed asked.

"Tore each other to pieces. The ones who was slower to get sick whacking the ones who got sick first. When we turned up, there was only five of them left. We got rid of them, but they took out a bunch of us. It was pretty heavy duty. Which is why we figure we earned the right to what's here."

"So there were more of you to start with?"

"Twenty-two. Five died in the attack. One died after of an infected wound. Two more got sick later on—turned out they was older than we knew—broke out in spots; we ejected them quick. Then four more left to try their luck elsewhere."

"What were you, all at the same school?"

"We're a mix. Family, friends, school, we all just sort of come together out on the streets, moving from place to place until we washed up here about five weeks ago."

"Okay." Ed sighed and got out of the Jeep. His muscles felt stiff and sore from being tensed for so long. "I can see why you want to protect what you've got," he said. "I'll go talk to the others. You sure you can't give us any food, though? They're all pretty hungry."

"You want to eat, you got to go shopping."

Ed was overcome with tiredness. Everything seemed such a struggle. He rubbed his face with his hands. "I just don't know where to start," he said.

"Can I make a suggestion?"

"Sure."

"What was you eating before you got here?"

"There was stuff on the bus."

"What I thought."

Ed looked at Jordan Hordern. His glasses were glinting in the half-light. "So what's your suggestion?" he asked.

"Go back to the bus," said Jordan. "See if there's any left."

Ed nodded. "Sounds like a good plan."

"But first," said Jordan, "you need to get yourselves some serious weapons."

32

The main exhibition gallery of the museum was on the next floor down, underground. Ed remembered coming here with the school. It was a big, dimly lit, windowless area filled with display cases and divided into various sections. There were exhibits covering the two world wars, and another covering conflicts since 1945. There were also a couple of special sections, like the Blitz Experience. The rows of glass cases were filled with dummies in uniform and hundreds of guns, grenades, knives, small artillery pieces, maps, banners, personal items, and equipment.

Six boys were coming down the stairs, their flashlight beams showing the way. Jack, Ed, Bam, and Jordan were at the front, followed by Matt and Archie Bishop. Ed's flashlight wasn't working properly; the beam kept going out. He rattled it, then banged it against his palm and swore.

"Not scared of the dark, are you?" Jordan asked.

"Not the dark," said Ed. "Only what hides in it."

As he said it, Ed's flashlight came back on. It landed on a face and he jumped. The others laughed.

"Only a dummy," said Bam.

Ed didn't like it down here. Everywhere he turned there was another dummy. He was surrounded by perfect, clean-faced young men, frozen at attention, or holding their guns ready for action. They looked very different from the men who now roamed London's streets with their bloated faces and ruined flesh, but they still gave him the creeps.

His heart was thumping. He felt like a silly little kid, frightened of ghosts. But he couldn't shrug off the feeling. He'd been strung out for so long, scared for so long, not sleeping, not eating properly, it was no wonder he was on edge.

And what if there were sickos down here? What if one had gotten in and was hiding in the dark? Waiting to jump him? What if . . . ?

He told himself not to be an idiot, but stayed close to the others all the same.

"Most of this stuff's no use to you," said Jordan. "Mostly guns without ammo, and you'd need a manual to figure out how to use them. There's some gear through this way you might like, though."

He led them into the World War I section and shone his flashlight into a trench warfare cabinet whose glass had been kicked in.

"I'd suggest you take a rifle or two," he said. "No bullets for these, but they've got straps to carry over your shoulder, and if you stick them bayonets on the end, you can use them like spears. I recommend the British Lee-Enfield. It's a good solid gun."

Ed reached in and took a rifle from the display, then found a bayonet that fit it.

"There's a load more weapons in the armory downstairs," Jordan explained. "And ammo too, but I'm keeping the best stuff for my boys, you understand."

"We understand," said Jack wearily. "You're keeping the best stuff."

Jack hadn't quite forgiven Jordan, but he had to admit that these weapons would be very handy.

"These are useful too," said Jordan, swinging his flashlight beam over to the case opposite, which held a selection of weapons for close-up, hand-to-hand fighting in the trenches. Clubs, knives, knuckle-dusters, knuckle-duster knives . . .

Ed and Bam tried some of them. Bam picked out a sturdy wooden club that was studded with bits of metal and nails. It looked completely evil, and Bam grinned, taking a few practice swings. Finally he turned to one of the dummies and caved its face in with one blow.

"This should do the trick," he said. "Very nice."

Matt and Archie were pressed up against one of the other cases, deep in conversation.

"What are you after?" Bam asked them. "A Holy Hand Grenade?"

"A what?" Archie and Matt looked confused.

"It's in *Monty Python and the Holy Grail*."

"Monty Python?"

"You must have heard of Monty Python," said Bam, as if he were talking to a couple of idiots. "They were like this old comedy team? They made films and everything."

"No."

"Well . . . I don't suppose you ever will see any of that now. But they were very funny."

"Right."

"So what *are* you looking for, then?"

"We need a banner," said Archie Bishop seriously. "There's a lot in the texts about banners."

"We will be the army of the Lamb," said Matt. "Modern crusaders marching under a banner. The pages have shown us that we are fighting a new war—we are soldiers of the Lamb."

"Yeah." Bam wasn't really listening. He was distracted by the scab on Matt's forehead. It was going a bit yellow and gungy around the edges and looked really horrible.

"Did you properly clean that?" he said, nodding toward it.

"No. It's the mark of the Lamb. The Lamb will heal me."

"It looks infected. You need to be careful."

Matt shook his head. "I don't need to worry about anything. I am being carried by the Lamb. His arms are around me."

Matt walked on in search of a suitable banner, and Bam held Archie back.

"Listen, mate," he said quietly. "If you're really serious about heading off to St. Paul's, just be a bit careful, yeah? You go wandering around out there singing hymns and waving flags, you'll attract every sicko in London."

"Banners, not flags."

"Same difference," said Bam.

"We'll be all right," said Archie.

"You reckon?" Bam asked, his face creased with a frown. "You really believe that the Lamb's going to protect you and all that?"

Archie shrugged. "I might as well believe in the Lamb as anything else, Bam. None of the old gods really helped anyone much, did they? My dad was a vicar; he got sick along with all the rest. Nothing we put our trust in before stood up to much. It's reassuring, you know, Matt being so, well, so *sure* of stuff. If I stick with him, I don't have to worry about anything else."

"Fair enough." Bam smiled.

"Think about it, Bam," Archie went on. "You're going to have to do something sooner or later. We're all going to have to try and work out how we're going to survive." Archie looked around the museum. "This is all right, I suppose, but it's not real life. You've got to have a plan, or you'll go crazy."

"Good point."

"I mean, how long are you planning to stay here?"

"I'm trying not to think more than about twenty seconds ahead, Archie. Never have. It's gotten me this far all right."

Jack had wandered away from the others, unsatisfied. He didn't know what he was looking for, but he hadn't seen it yet. The knife he'd picked out wasn't enough. He wanted something that when he held it in his hand he'd feel invincible. Feel its strength and power flowing into him.

He wished there were bullets for the various pistols on display; a handgun would have been perfect. He wondered whether he could persuade Jordan to let him see what was in the armory. Probably not. He'd gotten off to a bad start with Jordan. Misjudged him. The guy was hard and cold, but at least he was reasonable. Nothing he did was because of any twisted emotions. In a way, Jack respected him. But he didn't want to push his luck.

He wandered past the displays, impressed and appalled at man's ingenuity, the endless ways he'd found to kill other people. He stopped and reached into a broken cabinet to pick out a Russian World War II helmet. It fit perfectly and he kept it on.

"Come on, Jack. We're going." Ed's voice. "You got what you need?"

"Yeah, nearly," Jack replied. "I'm coming."

Jack headed back toward the entrance, flicking his beam from side to side, angry at himself for not choosing something, and then a flash of bright blue sky caught his eye. It was a uniform. He went over for a closer look. It was in a cabinet of outfits from another era, a time before camouflage and khaki and dull olive green. They looked so old-fashioned they might have been worn at the battle of Waterloo, but they were from just before the First World War, when soldiers still wore brightly colored uniforms to stand out on the battlefield and impress the enemy. They were officers' uniforms, covered in braid and gold buttons and fancy details.

And there, neatly displayed, was a sturdy-looking naval officer's sword. It looked to be a good length and was probably well made. Jack smashed the glass with the handle of his knife. The noise sounded like an explosion going off in the silent gloom of the gallery.

"What was that?" Ed's voice again. He was probably bricking it.

"It's all right. It's only me. I found something."

Jack lifted out the sword. It was clean and gleaming, the edge still sharp. The curators at the museum had obviously looked after everything very well. He smiled. The blade was perfectly balanced in his hand, a good weight. He sliced a long curve through the air.

That'd do it.

"Jack?"

He took the scabbard and belt from the dummy torso they were on and fastened them around his waist. It was a good fit. The scabbard hung well.

"You coming, Jack?"

"Yeah. I'm ready."

33

It was perhaps a five-year-old child's idea of a feast, but it was a feast all the same. Chips and cookies and Coke. Perhaps a five-year-old would have turned up his nose at the cans of cold sausages and beans, but to the hungry kids in the museum, it was the best food they'd ever tasted.

Jack, Ed, and Bam had done a mad dash to the bus and grabbed as much food as they could carry before Ed spotted a group of sickos approaching along the road. They'd made it back without having to use any of their new weapons, and were welcomed as returning heroes. The only bad moment had been when they'd spotted what they'd thought was a discarded pair of dirty trousers in the road. Ed had gone over to check them out and realized there were legs inside, with black shoes on the feet. And at the waist was a ragged tangle of guts and a stub of white spine.

It was all that was left of Piers.

They'd thought about rationing the food and trying to make it last a couple of days, but in the end they decided what the hell, they might as well scarf it all down and have a proper look for some decent food in the morning.

The Brain Trust and the girls had made an effort to tidy up the café and make it feel a little more welcoming. The tables had been wiped, the trash collected, and they'd put candles around the place, which helped give the impression that the room was warmer than it was. Even Frédérique had perked up and joined in. It had helped her to have something to do. Stopped her from sitting by herself and staring into space. She'd bustled about and chatted to the other girls, and now she was sitting at a table with Jack, Ed, Bam, and Brooke, and was even laughing as Brooke told a funny story about eating too much chocolate at Courtney's tenth birthday party.

"I puked my guts out!" she boasted. "It was like a fire extinguisher going off. Kersploosh! It went everywhere. All over the cake, all over Courtney, all over Courtney's mom, all over her presents . . . Sorry if I'm putting you off your dinner, Fred."

Frédérique couldn't stop laughing. It was a slightly hysterical, out-of-control laugh that was just a little unnerving. She'd taken a gulp of water and the puking part of the story had taken her by surprise. She was now mainly laughing at the fact that she was laughing and choking and dribbling and about to spit water everywhere. Somehow she managed to swallow it, but that caused her to start coughing and spluttering, which made the others laugh, which made her laugh. . . .

It hadn't been lost on Ed that Brooke wasn't sitting with her two girlfriends, who were at a table with the Brain Trust, enjoying playing mother for a bit with the younger kids.

Brooke had made a point of sitting right next to him, and she kept directing her conversation at him, and touching his arm and making eye contact. He found it quite flattering, but, to be honest, Brooke scared him. She was so loud and confident and unforgiving. She was one of those girls who used her friendship like a weapon, giving it and taking it away to reward or punish people.

He was just glad she was on his side for the time being. Maybe since Jordan Hordern had put him in charge she wanted to make sure she was at the top table.

Jack was making an effort with Frédérique. Trying to keep her spirits up and not let her slip back into her dark mood. But he reckoned he was fighting a losing battle. She seemed exhausted after her laughing fit, and the more Brooke talked about the past, the quieter Frédérique became. Slowly, the haunted look came back into her eyes and she retreated into herself.

"Hey," he said when he noticed that she was crying again. "It's going to be all right."

"No," she said. "Tomorrow there will be no more food, and you will go, and I don't know what I will do."

"I'm not going to abandon anyone," said Jack, and he caught Ed looking at him. "Okay? I'm not just going to leave you. Tomorrow morning, we'll go out and we'll find some food, and when I'm sure you're all going to be fine, I'll go home. But not before."

"Okay." Frédérique nodded.

"There's nothing to be frightened of anymore. Greg's gone. We've got good weapons. The sickos don't stand a chance, eh?"

Jack immediately wished he hadn't bothered. As soon as he said the word "sickos," Frédérique let out a huge sob, and the floodgates opened. The crying set her off coughing again. Jack whacked her on her back.

"Don't talk about them," she said.

"I'm sorry, Fred. I didn't mean to scare you."

"Greg is one of them now."

"Yeah, I guess, or else he's dead. Good riddance, I say. He was an asshole."

"But he said he would not get sick."

"Yeah, well, he could have said he could fly—we didn't have to believe him, did we? He thought he could cheat nature. He couldn't. Basically, if you're over sixteen, forget it."

Before Frédérique could say anything else, Justin the nerd came over to their table, looking embarrassed and secretive. He tucked in behind Jack's chair and leaned over to speak quietly into his ear. "Can I talk to you?" he said.

"Yeah, of course, Just. What's up?"

"Did you bring Greg's cooler back from the bus?"

"Yeah. Why? You want something from it?"

"No. Have you . . . have you eaten anything out of it?"

"Nope." Jack shook his head. "We thought we'd save it for breakfast. As a kind of treat. There's proper food in there."

"Only . . . don't eat the smoked meat."

"Why not?"

Justin shuffled about nervously. "We've been talking . . ." He glanced back at his table, where the Brain Trust was watching him. "About something Liam said before he, you know, died. . . . About the meat."

"Is there something wrong with it?"

Justin looked at the other kids sitting around the table, not sure how to say the next bit. Not sure if he should.

"Can we talk in, you know, private?"

"Yeah, sure."

Justin and Jack went over to the food counter, where nobody could hear them. The kids in the Brain Trust were still staring at them.

"Why all the mystery, Just?"

"I don't want to, you know, upset anyone," said Justin. "That French girl seems pretty freaked out by all this. I wasn't sure . . ."

Jack laughed. "You're not really a nerd, are you, Justin?"

Justin looked surprised. "What do you mean?"

"A real nerd wouldn't care about hurting anyone's feelings."

"Oh, well . . ." Justin blushed, and Jack laughed again.

"So, come on, then, Mr. Sensitive, tell me—what's wrong with the meat?"

"We think it's human meat."

"You what?"

"We think Greg butchered a boy down on that farm in Kent he was always going on about. We think that's what he was eating."

"Jesus Christ." Jack looked appalled. "So he was already sick?"

"In a way, maybe. Or maybe he was just trying to survive. He said the livestock on the farm got ill, so he . . . You know . . ."

Jack sighed and rubbed his eyes. Half of him wanted to laugh. The other half wanted to throw up.

"Thanks for letting us know," he said at last. "I'll chuck it out. Thank God we didn't eat any of it. And you were right, mate. Let's not tell anyone else about this. We'll stick to our sausages and beans."

"Mind you," said Justin, "the crap they put in those tinned sausages, you never know what you're eating. For all we know they've been putting human meat in them for years."

"You *are* still a *bit* of a nerd, aren't you, Justin?"

34

The 1940's house was a full-size replica of a mock-Tudor suburban house complete with green-painted front door, sloping tiled roof, Union Jack, and empty milk bottles on the doorstep. It was set up in a corner of the exhibition space to show children what life had been like during wartime when the German bombs had rained down on London. There was a little kitchen, a dining room, a living room, and a couple of bedrooms, all equipped and furnished as they would have been during the Second World War. There were already a few beds in here, but Jordan Horden's boys had dragged in some extra mattresses and sleeping bags and had lent the kids a small kerosene heater so that it was cozy and warm. They'd lit tea lights in glass jars, which gave a twinkling glow to the place, and for a while all the problems of the outside world were forgotten. The kids felt safe and excited at the same time, as if they were having a giant sleepover.

There was even a Morrison shelter in one room, like a big steel cage. During the Blitz, families would have slept in one of these; now it was the perfect place for Frédérique's cat, Dior, to come out of her box and spend the night.

Lying nearby on his mattress on the floor, Ed could hear her scrabbling about. He couldn't get to sleep. It wasn't just the noise of the cat and the grunts and snores and gurgling bellies of the other kids. He couldn't stop his mind from going over and over the events of the last two days.

He felt like he had failed. He could have done more. Sure, they were safe here for now, but how many friends had he lost along the way?

"You not asleep?"

It was Jack's voice. He was lying on a mattress on top of the Morrison shelter.

"No," Ed whispered. "You either?"

"No. Been looking at this poster on the wall. Wartime advice from the government. *Make Do and Mend. Save Fuel for Battle. Save Kitchen Scraps to Feed the Pigs. Don't Waste Water. Dig for Victory. Holiday at Home. Eat Greens for Health. Keep Calm and Carry On.*"

"Very good advice," said Ed. "Especially now."

"Is that where *Keep Calm and Carry On* comes from, then?" Jack asked quietly.

"I guess so. It was a wartime thing. The Blitz. Bombs falling all about."

"There was a real craze for that slogan recently, wasn't there?" said Jack. "People had it on posters and mugs and things."

"My mom gave me a T-shirt with it last Christmas." Ed smiled at the memory. "Wish I still had it. All I had to get stressed about before was exams."

"She didn't give you a T-shirt that said *Save Kitchen Scraps to Feed the Pigs*, then?"

"No." Ed smiled.

"Do you suppose in the war, in the Blitz, people thought it would go on forever?" Jack asked. "That it was the end of the world?"

"You mean like now?" Ed shrugged. "Probably a few did, but I bet most just wanted to try and carry on as if things were normal."

"Keep calm and carry on," said Jack.

"Exactly . . ."

"And holiday at home."

Ed laughed. "I prefer you when you're like this," he said.

"How do you mean?" Jack shifted and propped himself up on one elbow.

"Well, you know. This is like the old days, how things used to be. Us two just having a laugh. I've noticed with you, when things are safe, you know, quiet, like now, you're cool, we get on all right, but as soon as we're out there, in any danger, you get all aggressive and you start having a go at everyone, not just me. It's like you turn, like you're two different people."

"Oh right," said Jack, his voice harder, wary. "So I'm two-faced, am I?"

"Not exactly."

"You mean like with my birthmark? I'm like a villain out of Batman, or something. Two-Face?"

"I didn't say two-faced, Jack, did I? I just meant . . . Well, you're doing it now. One minute you're my best mate, and the next you're having a go at me. I'm not used to it."

Jack slumped back onto his mattress with a grunt and stared at the ceiling. "I can't help it, Ed," he said. "You're right—it's when I get stressed I lash out. It's like I know I'm doing it, I don't want to do it, but I can't stop myself. I'm so knackered all the time and strung out. I could sleep for a year . . . but I can't get to sleep."

"Let's try, though, eh?"

"Yeah. Good night, Ed."

"Good night, Jack."

35

It was morning. The rain had stopped, the clouds torn away by a strong cold wind from the south. The sun was shining, and the glistening, silvery streets were drying out.

There were two flower beds underneath the twin naval guns in front of the museum. Frédérique was kneeling down on the grass next to one of them with her cat box next to her.

There was a big wide-bladed army knife sticking up out of the flower bed like a tool. Frédérique looked like she might have been gardening, trying to sort out the tangle of over-grown plants. Except she was very still. Kneeling there with her hands by her chin, almost as if she were praying.

"Frédérique?"

Jack had emerged from the building and was coming down the steps. He was wearing his Russian helmet, and his sword was dangling at his side. He walked between two yellow artillery shells embedded in the sidewalk, scanning the area for any sign of sickos. Nothing moved anywhere. The park looked pretty in the sunlight. The drifts of trash piled up everywhere might have been early spring flowers.

When he got to Frédérique, she didn't look up.

"What are you doing?"

"I cannot keep Dior locked up. It is not fair. She will have a better life by herself. I must let her go. My father would have done the same."

"Are you sure?"

"She can find her own food, I think. Better than what I can give her. I have run out. The only problem is, she does not want to go."

Jack squatted down and peered into the cage. Dior was flattened against the box at the far end, looking out fearfully, her eyes wide.

"You should hurry," he said, straightening up. "The sickos can't easily get into the park, but if they spot us by ourselves, they might just try."

"You go in, Jack. I am all right."

"I'm not gonna leave you out here by yourself, Fred."

"Please . . ." Frédérique sniffed, coughed, and put a wad of tissues to her nose. She was crying again. Jack sighed. He didn't know what to do or say to make things better.

"Come back inside," he said. "We'll find food for the cat."

"Leave me." She said it so forcefully, even angrily, that Jack backed away across the grass, leaving her alone with the cat.

He watched as she made little encouraging noises, cooing to the cat in French until at last it crept cautiously out, tiptoeing and tense. It looked around, making quick nervous movements with its head. Frédérique closed the cage and sat back on her heels. The cat made its way into the flower bed. Frédérique coughed again and the cat darted away. In a moment it had disappeared. Frédérique stood up, head bowed, shoulders shaking. She dabbed her nose again with the tissues. Jack went to her and put his arm around her.

"Come on, it's cold out here. Admittedly, it's not much warmer inside, but you don't want to get ill."

Frédérique threw her arms around Jack and gave him a powerful hug. She was stronger than she looked. Jack hugged her back, but he still didn't know what to say.

Bam and Ed had now come out of the museum and saw Jack locked in his embrace with Frédérique.

"Ah, young love!" said Bam.

"Touching, isn't it?" said Ed, and they laughed.

Jack broke away from Frédérique and came over to join them.

"This is what we need to take on the sickos," he said as he passed the naval guns. "Bloody big cannon."

"We're not doing too badly with this stuff." Ed brandished his rifle, the bayonet stuck firmly on the end.

"We've got nothing to fear," said Bam, slipping two shells into his shotgun.

"Maybe," said Jack. "But, still, I'd be happier if there were a few more of us."

Even as he said it, there was a commotion at the doors, and Brooke came out, all in a fluster, carrying a long spiked club and whining back over her shoulder at someone behind her. "Get off my case, loserface, I never said I liked Justin Timberlake. . . ."

She stopped when she saw the others, and skinny DogNut followed her out of the museum, his head bobbing up and down as if he were listening to loud music.

Jack frowned at her. "What are you doing?"

"What's it look like? I'm helping. Didn't want you to have all the fun, did I?"

"This isn't a game, Brooke," said Jack angrily.

"What? And you think I don't know that? We survived a long time on the road, me and my girls. Don't think we can't look after ourselves."

"Yeah, but . . ."

"Yeah, but what? This is the twenty-first century, Jacko, or hadn't you noticed? Girls have a lot more to offer than just knitting and cooking and having babies."

"Making babies," said DogNut with a smirk. "Now you talking."

Brooke spun around and slapped DogNut hard in the face. His head seemed to wobble like it was on a spring, and he looked completely stunned.

Jack laughed.

"I've had just about enough of you, you loser," Brooke shouted. "Keep your big mouth shut or I will shove it so far down your throat you'll be smiling out of your ass."

"Yeah, okay . . ." DogNut mumbled, and Brooke turned her attention back to Jack.

"I'll admit I got freaked out on the bus, but I can handle it. You should have seen me whack Greg with that hammer thing. And now I've got something better than a hammer." She swung the club, and Jack had to jump back to avoid being spiked.

"I figured if I'm not going to be scared, I've got to stand up to them," Brooke went on. "This is how it is now, and the quicker I get used to it the better."

"What about him?" Jack nodded at DogNut, who still hadn't fully recovered from being hit.

"I can't shake him off. He's been tagging along behind me like a fart cloud all morning."

"You come to wave us off, have you, Donut?" Jack asked.

"Not Donut, *DogNut*."

"What kind of a name's DogNut?" Brooke asked with a withering look on her face.

"It's my gamer's tag. See, like the dog's nuts."

"So why ain't you called Dognuts?"

"Yeah, or Dogsnuts?" said Bam.

"DogNut sounds better," said DogNut.

"You reckon?" Brooke asked.

"You still haven't told me what you're doing out here," said Jack.

"I come to help, blood," said DogNut. "I'm pretty good in a mash-up, and I go mental being banged up in there. I need to get outside and feel the wind in my hair now and then, see? So let's bust some chops, eh? Hiyaa!" He did a bad kung fu kick, and Jack was forced to smile.

"Come on," he said. "Let's go."

"I am coming with you." Frédérique was standing by one of the yellow shells, the big knife in her hand.

"No," said Jack. "It's all right, Fred . . ."

"I want to."

"It's dangerous."

"I don't care. I will come with you. I am like Brooke. I do not want to be scared anymore. I want to help find food. I want to be useful."

"All right," said Jack. "I did say we needed more bodies,

though this wasn't quite what I had in mind."

"Oh good, you ain't left yet!"

More kids were coming out of the building. Big Courtney and little Aleisha, both carrying weapons that looked all wrong with their hair and their makeup and their bright clothing.

"We was worried you'd gone without us," said Aleisha. "Courtney took so long to get ready, you'd think she was going to a party or something, not on a sicko-whacking expedition."

"Hey, that ain't fair!" Courtney protested. "I couldn't get near the mirror in the bathroom this morning, not with Brooke putting on her makeup. 'Oh what d'you think? D'you think Ed would like this color of lipstick? Oh, do you think the spikes in this club go with these trousers?'"

"Shut it, Courtney!" Brooke shrieked. "That is *so* not what happened."

"It *is* so, darling."

"So, where we going, then, anyway?" Brooke asked Ed, trying to change the subject. "Back to the bus?"

"Maybe, if we don't find anything else," said Ed. "We didn't get it all last night, but we took the best of what there was. We need to find proper food, really."

"Chips *is* proper food where I come from!" said Courtney, and they all laughed.

"We should go down to Kennington," said DogNut. "There's a supermarket there, a big Tesco, near the gas tanks." He pointed to the road that ran down the west side of the museum. "Worth a look."

"You sure we shouldn't just search some of the houses around here?" Ed asked.

"I grew up in Kennington, blood," said DogNut. "I know it real good. There's lotsa shops there, eating places too, you know, like, restaurants and that, yeah? More than around here for sure."

"And what if we see any sickos?" asked Courtney, who had armed herself with a sword that was a bit too long and unwieldy for her to use easily.

"Depends," said Ed. "It's best to run rather than fight."

"We have to assume we *will* meet some of them," said Jack. "And we *will* have to fight. If anyone's got a problem with that, they should stay behind."

Nobody said anything.

"Let's go, then."

"I must be crazy coming along with you," Courtney said quietly to Brooke as they took the steps that led down into the park on the side of the museum.

"Sisters are doing it for themselves," said Brooke, and she gave Courtney a high five. Aleisha joined in, and then the three of them forced Frédérique to do one too. They giggled at her halfhearted effort.

"Get down, girl," said Brooke. "Don't be so snooty and, like, grown-up all the time. We're all kids in this together, yeah?"

"Yeah." Frédérique tried again, this time really slapping Brooke hard.

"That's more like it, sister!"

Halfway to the edge of the park they heard a shout from behind and turned around to see Justin the nerd running toward them, awkwardly carrying a rifle and bayonet.

"Now what?" said Jack. "Is he coming too?"

"Surely not," said Ed.

Justin was out of breath when he caught up with them, red-faced from running. "I'm going to help," he said.

"You sure about this?" Ed asked.

"Yes, I'm sure."

"We're not going on a picnic, Justin," said Jack, sounding a little harsher than he had meant.

Justin looked nervous and angry at the same time. He took a deep breath, and the words tumbled out of him. "You said something to me yesterday, Jack. You said I wasn't a proper nerd."

"I was mucking about, Just."

Justin was blushing now. "I know what everyone thinks," he said. "That just because I'm clever, because I study hard and don't do sports, just because I like computers and know how they work, because I like *Star Trek* and *Robot Wars* and have every *Doctor Who* DVD ever made, going right back to William Hartnell and including the rubbish one with Paul McGann, just because I've never had a girlfriend and don't know what type of jeans I'm supposed to wear, you all dismiss me. You all think I'm a useless nerd."

"We don't think that, Justin," said Ed.

"Yes you do. I know you do. You call me Justin the nerd. Nerdy Justin. El Nerdo. That's all I am. Nothing more than a nerd, hardly human. But I *am* human, and yes, I suppose I *am* a nerd, but I want to prove to you that I'm not a complete waste of space. I'll help you find some more food. I'll fight if I have to. I've been picked on and bullied all my life, so I've had to learn how to defend myself. I'm actually quite strong, if you want to know." Justin stopped and glared at

DogNut, who had snickered. DogNut looked embarrassed. He stopped snickering and walked on.

"Are there any more of you coming out?" Jack asked, amused, staring back at the museum.

"Don't think so."

"What about Chris Marker?"

"That geek! No way is he coming!"

36

At that moment, Chris Marker was exploring the museum, carrying an old oil lamp. He had discovered a series of interconnected rooms hidden away down one side of the building, which contained stack after stack of books, pamphlets, papers, letters, and documents of all kinds relating to the history of warfare in the last century. It would take several lifetimes to read all the words they contained.

He wasn't frightened being alone here in the dark. Instead he felt a deep peace. He was reminded of TV ads for plug-in air fresheners where some woman would stick the little plastic thing into a socket and animated fumes would waft out and everyone would lift their faces, close their eyes, breathe in deeply, and go "Aaaaaah." Like they were taking some kind of drug rather than inhaling chemicals. Well, the smell of all these old books and papers did that for Chris. He felt very calm.

This place was like a church for Chris, a cathedral. In the unlit gloom the great shelves of books could easily have been solid walls. Walls of information. A castle of words.

He was safe here. In the quiet, inside his wall of words, he could think clearly.

It was strange to be at peace in a library where most of the books had to do with war, but he would need to learn about war now. He picked a cardboard box at random from a shelf and opened it. Inside was a pile of old army manuals, with instructions about how to fire different rifles. Whole little booklets for each gun. He'd had no idea that guns were so complicated. He supposed that's why they trained soldiers. All those guns downstairs in the exhibits and the armory were useless without these manuals, little better than clubs or spears. It was only by using the power of these books that they could come alive.

He'd need time. Time to pick out what was useful. He'd start to make piles of books and pamphlets. Maybe he'd move a bed in here and live with the books. He'd only ever need to go out to eat and use the toilet.

He was smiling at the thought. It was the first time he'd been alone since this whole nightmare had started. Properly alone. It was a delicious feeling.

No, not really alone, when he came to think about it, because he had the books for company, and to him they were like living, breathing things. The writers were there among the book stacks with him, like friendly spirits. Whenever he opened a book and read the words hidden inside it, he was waking a ghost, and the ghost would talk directly to him. The long-dead writer would come alive.

One of Jordan's boys had told him that this part of the museum was supposed to be haunted by a real ghost, the Gray Lady. He wasn't scared by the idea. He could imagine her watching over him, watching over the precious books, the guardian of all the other ghosts they contained.

He was aware of a presence. Someone was there. He'd caught a flash of movement out of the corner of his eye. He looked along one of the book stacks. There was a woman there, dressed in gray. Crouched over, watching him. For some reason he still didn't feel scared.

"Hello," he said, but the woman didn't respond.

He walked toward her and, as the light from his lamp fell on her, she disappeared. One moment she was there, and then she seemed to dissolve into the books.

Chris had always seen ghosts. His mother had taken him to see a doctor who'd tried to explain that they weren't real.

What did doctors know?

Chris sat down on the floor.

He realized he was crying.

37

DogNut wouldn't shut up. Jack reckoned it was because he was nervous. Leaving the park had felt like stepping out of safety into danger. The road they were on, Kennington, was pretty wide, with a good view in both directions, and so far it had been weirdly quiet. They hadn't seen anyone else, but they all had a prickly feeling, as if they were being watched by unseen eyes. The others had tensed and gone silent, but not DogNut—he kept up a running commentary.

"Why's there never any zomboids around?" he was saying. "Where do they all go in the daylight? Where's all the dead bodies?"

"Maybe they've all been eaten," said Jack. His helmet already felt heavy on his head, and the sword banged against his leg as he walked. "They've got to eat something."

"True that," said DogNut. "Except they prefer fresh meat. The living. *Us.* But, I mean, think about it, there was so many people in London before. Where'd they all go? It's too spooky."

"You want to go back?" Jack asked.

"No way, soldier. I can't bust no moves stuck in that museum all day. Nice bundle will be a good way to get some exercise." He waved his arms about and took a few practice swipes with the samurai sword he carried.

"Watch what you're doing with that thing," said Jack.

"It's safe, man. Jordan makes us all do weapons practice. Drilling. But I'm telling you, blood, there's only so many war games you can play in a day. Don't try telling Jordan Hordern that, though. He's nuts about anything to do with war and the military. I reckon he thinks he's a real general."

"He seems pretty cold," said Jack.

"That's not the half of it, brother. He's bonkers, I reckon. He never talks about his old life. Never talks about nothing normal. Just stares at you and yaks on about war and fighting. I reckon he's some kind of an ick."

"A what?"

"You know, like he's autistic, or dyslexic, schizophrenic, alcoholic, something like that. Before all this he was just some sort of war-obsessed loony; now it's his cold freaky brain that's kept us all alive, which is why we do whatever he tells us to do. All hail the general!"

Bam was walking with Ed. He kept glancing up at the sky. Overhead it was still a clear pale blue, but ahead of them, to the south, it looked unnaturally dark.

He pointed it out to Ed. "Do you reckon it's storm clouds?"

"Dunno." Ed studied the blackening patch. "Can you see a kind of red glow along the bottom?" he asked after a while. "Or am I imagining it?"

Bam squinted. "My eyesight's not brilliant, to tell you the

truth, mate. I should have had an eye test ages ago, but I was too scared."

"Scared?" Ed shook his head, smiling. "You're Bam the man. You're not scared of anything."

"No word of a lie," said Bam. "I was a nervous wreck. I thought if I needed glasses I might not be able to play rugby anymore. Wouldn't be able to see the ball." He did a mime of someone fumbling to catch a ball, cross-eyed, hands going in all directions.

Ed laughed. "They make special sports contact lenses, don't they?" he said. Then he checked himself. "Or at least they used to."

"I know, I know, but it's not the same. Rugby's a pretty brutal sport. I'd have been worrying all the time."

"Well, it's too late to get your eyes tested now." Ed chuckled. "Let's hope you don't go blind."

"Can you imagine?" said Bam. "Being blind and trying to cope with all this."

"Dunno," said Ed. "Some ways it might make it easier. You know, you wouldn't have to look at their ugly pizza faces for a start."

"No," said Bam. "I don't even want to think about it. That would be just too frightening. Urgh!"

Ed laughed, but his eyes were firmly fixed on the black sky ahead. "I can definitely see what looks like a glow along the bottom," he said. "Can you not see it at all?"

Bam turned and bellowed at the girls. "Hey! What do you reckon that cloud is, ladies? Can you see a red glow in it at all?"

Aleisha nodded.

"Red or, like, orange," she said. "Flickering."

Bam sighed. "It's probably a fire, then."

"You think?"

"Yup."

"That's a shedload of smoke if it is," DogNut called from the front.

"Well, there's no one to put it out, is there?" said Bam. "Look at all these houses, packed right next to each other. There's so much stuff in them that'll burn really easily once a fire takes hold. This whole place could go up."

"Looks a long way off," said Ed. "I don't think we need to start panicking just yet."

"Well, you let us know, won't you, Ed," said Jack, with a slight mocking tone, "when we *do* need to start panicking."

"Guys?" Brooke sounded nervous. "I think that maybe *now's* the time to start panicking."

She was pointing down the road. There was a group of sickos ahead, crouching over something lying on the ground.

"What do you reckon?" said DogNut. "Fight them, or go around?"

"Come off it," said Ed. "We go around them, obviously. There's no point fighting if we don't have to. I mean, it's not like we can't go another way, is it?"

"I say we fight them," said DogNut. "They don't look like much."

"What's the point?"

"Show them who's boss. Show them we own these streets, blood."

"No," said Bam. "Ed's right. Let's go around. We should never fight if we don't have to."

"Yeah, let's take the chicken run," said Jack.

"What do you mean?" Ed asked, trying not to get angry.

"The Yellow Brick Road. The way the Cowardly Lion would go."

"I'm not saying we go around them because I'm scared," said Ed. "It's just stupid to get into a fight for no reason."

"I never said you were scared. I never said anything about you. Why do you assume I'm talking about you all the time? Don't be so touchy." Jack looked around at the others. "Did I say that Ed was scared?"

They shook their heads and shrugged.

"I'm not arguing with you, am I?" Jack said to Ed. "I'm agreeing with you. Let's go around them. Okay?"

38

Matt and Archie had found their banner. An old Austrian military standard with a two-headed black eagle on a gold background. They were sitting around a table in the café modifying it. One of Jordan's boys had directed them to a cupboard full of paint and brushes and various tools. They'd found some sheeting as well and cut out pieces that they'd glued on to cover the parts they didn't like. They would have preferred to sew the patches on, but didn't know how. The banner would look pretty scrappy, but it would do for now. When they had more time and resources they'd make a new one.

Matt had done some sketches for the design they were painting onto the scraps of sheet. It had taken him a while to get the picture right, but he'd finally drawn one he was happy with. The image was based on his vision. When you looked at it one way, it was a picture of two different boys, one behind the other. Looked at another way, it appeared to be a boy and his shadow. The main figure, the boy at the front, was fair-haired and dressed in white. The second boy, his shadow, was dark-haired and wore dark clothing. He was less detailed and looked sort of half-formed. Matt wasn't the greatest artist in the world, but there was something about his last drawing—a strange, haunting quality.

Transferring the image to the banner was like a school art project. Matt and Archie and their ten acolytes crowded around the banner, which was draped over the table, the edges dangling down. Matt had sketched in the outline with a big marker, and the others were filling in the shapes. They happily chatted away as they mixed the colors and daubed them on, utterly engrossed in their work.

"Red for the eyes!" said Phil, the youngest of the acolytes. "The Shadow Boy should have red eyes."

"It's not a poster for a horror film," said Matt.

"What color, then?"

"Just leave them dark. And he's not called the Shadow Boy. He's the Goat. The shining one is the Lamb; the dark one is the Goat."

"Should he have horns?"

"No. They're not a real lamb and a real goat. Just paint him as I've drawn him."

"If we put on yellow rays it'll look like the Lamb is glowing," said Harry Ryan, another of the acolytes.

"All right. But do it carefully."

"What's it going to say?" Phil asked.

"What do you mean, 'say'?"

"It has to have words on it."

"I don't know."

"Something in Latin," Harry suggested. "Like *Death to the enemy*. What would that be in Latin? Did anyone here take Latin?"

"I did," said Archie. "I think *Death to the enemy* would be something like *nex ut hostes hostium*, or *mors ut hostes hostium*, something like that. I'm not really sure."

"We can't put something on we're not sure of," said Harry.

"We should put the name of our Lord on it," said Matt. "The name of the Lamb."

"That's an easy one," said Archie. "That's *Agnus*, and *Agnus Dei* would be Lamb of God, or Lamb of the Lord."

"That sounds cool," said Phil. "*Agnus Dei*."

Harry had the best handwriting. He'd taken a calligraphy course at school, and Matt had been getting him to write down his teachings in a big notebook they'd scrounged from the museum gift shop. They were making their first testament. They'd argued for ages over what to call it. *The Book of the Lamb* sounded like a cookbook, and *The Book of Matt* didn't sound right either. *The Book of Matthew* sounded too much like the Gospel of Matthew in the Bible, and Matt had gone to great lengths to explain that their new religion had nothing to do with Christianity or any of the old religions, even though he'd nicked most of it from the Book of Revelation. In the end they'd decided to just call it *The Book*, and Harry had carefully drawn the words on the front cover in gothic script. After that he wrote down everything Matt came up with about his new religion. It turned out that Harry's spelling wasn't the best in the world, but his writing looked really cool, so Matt let him keep his job.

Harry had tried suggesting that maybe their new religion could have its own special new kind of spelling, but the others weren't convinced.

Once they'd filled in the two main figures, Harry started on the words. But after twenty minutes he was still working on the *A*, so they left him to it, sitting there, hunched over the banner at the table, his tongue between his teeth, a look of intense concentration on his face.

39

They had turned off the main road westward toward the river and had started to weave their way through the tangle of side streets, occasionally catching glimpses of the gas tanks they were using as a landmark. These giant steel drums, painted pale green, towered above the surrounding buildings, but when the kids got in among the tightly packed houses, their view of them was blocked.

There was no clear layout to the streets, and the kids had to make detours around housing estates, so their progress was slow. They felt really nervous now. There was much more evidence of the disaster on these side streets, reminders of all that had happened. Fires, wreckage, dead bodies. They also spotted two different roving gangs of sickos, and each time had to make another diversion to avoid them, ending up more lost and disoriented.

At last, though, by pure chance they came out onto a main road, and there ahead of them was the blue-and-white Tesco logo on the front of a long, low, ugly building next to the inevitable parking lot. The gas tanks were silhouetted against the sky behind them.

"What did I tell you!" DogNut cried triumphantly, and the kids cheered as they ran across the road.

Their excitement was short-lived, however.

The supermarket had been gutted.

The windows along the front were all smashed in, the shelves inside stripped clean. A few empty shopping carts stood forgotten and lonely among the debris of smashed registers and broken shelves.

The kids wandered around glumly, glass crunching underfoot, hoping they might find something that had been missed.

There was nothing.

"Well, that was a big waste of time," said Jack.

"It was worth trying, though," said Bam.

"Really? Was it?"

"Come on, Jack, maybe let's look on the bright side a little, yeah?"

"The bright side of what?"

"Well, at least there weren't any sickos waiting for us in here."

"I wouldn't be so sure about that," said Brooke, and they turned to see her staring into one of the aisles.

They hurried over to her.

A skinny mother, her naked arms sticking out like twigs from her down vest, was waddling toward Brooke. She was maybe twenty-five, with short spiky hair, and she walked stooped over on bent legs, unable to stand properly. She looked at the kids, her big blue eyes sad and confused, then opened her bloodstained mouth and tried to say something, but only a strangled gargle came out. She coughed and looked embarrassed as a wad of saliva dripped over her lower lip and hung from her chin.

She started to move toward them, half crawling, half crouching, feeling her way along with her spindly arms out to either side.

"Kill it, Bam," said Jack.

"Shoot it," DogNut added.

Bam shook his head. The mother looked so pathetic. "Don't know if I can."

Ed stepped forward, rifle raised, the tip of the bayonet pointing at the mother's face. She looked up at him, her eyes unnaturally large and shiny, as if she were about to cry. She reminded him of something. For a moment he couldn't place it, and then it came to him. One of those stupid big-eyed characters from a Japanese manga comic.

He gripped his rifle tighter. Told himself she wasn't human anymore. She was just a mindless thing now, eaten up by disease, probably dying.

"Do it, Ed." Jack's voice sounded hard. Ed knew he didn't believe he could.

Could he?

The thought of sticking the bayonet into her, feeling it sink into her flesh, pushing it hard enough to kill her, into her brain . . .

Could he do it?

Brooke pushed past him and grunted as she swung her

club at the back of the mother's head. The stricken mother collapsed facedown with a little whimper and lay still.

"See?" said Brooke. "Told you I wasn't totally useless. Not like you bunch of wimps. What's the matter with you all? She was just some stupid sicko. Why can't you just—"

Brooke stopped, clapped her hands to her face, and ran around the end of the aisle to be noisily sick.

"Let's get out of here," said Jack.

It was dark in the store. The strip lighting that ran in gray ranks along the low ceiling hung down dead and useless. When the kids trooped back outside, the suddenly bright sun caused them to blink and squint and shield their eyes, so it was a few seconds before they spotted a group of sickos tramping toward them across the parking lot.

There were about twenty of them, in various stages of decay. The worst were at the back—the slowest, most diseased. They were limping, hunched up, their skin almost totally covered in boils and sores, or else hanging off them in sheets. Their faces were unrecognizable as human—shapeless, raw, bloody, and swollen. Noses missing, ears missing, eyes missing, their cheeks either puffed out and swollen or rotted away, exposing their teeth. Those at the front were the healthier ones—younger, faster, and fitter, but still visibly sick, their flesh discolored and bloated, their bodies ravaged by the poison that was erupting from within.

At the front, as if he was leading them, was a tall black-haired father with crazed yellow eyes. He was wearing a long dark coat that flapped in the wind.

"Omigod, it's Pez!" Brooke gasped.

"What?" Jack had no idea what she was talking about.

"The one in charge, he looks like one of those Pez candy dispenser things. He was there before, at the bus. He must have followed us."

Despite everything, Jack laughed. She was right. The father's head was tilting back, leaving his unattached lower jaw dangling and his tongue lolling out over his lower lip. Jack had a strong urge to stand and fight, to stop running and hiding, to hack this human Pez down with his sword. He didn't want to put the others in any danger, though.

"Let's get away from here!" he shouted, and they ran.

They skirted around the supermarket and into an industrial area behind it. They could smell the gas from the towers here; its pungent odor was everywhere. After a couple of minutes of furious, breathless, lung-busting running, the kids darted into a sort of yard with garages and sheds around the edges and an alley at the back.

"Stop!" said Bam, looking around. "We should be safe here. I'll check to make sure they haven't followed us, but if we stay put for a while they'll surely give up searching and bug off."

DogNut and Bam went over to the entrance to the yard and peered out.

"No sign of them," said DogNut after a while. "I reckon we lost them."

"This is crazy," Courtney gasped. The big girl was fighting for breath, and she looked pale and scared. Her eyes kept flicking around, not settling on anything. "We don't know what we're doing. It's too dangerous out here. I think we should go back."

"I agree," said Aleisha. "We ain't gonna find nothing."

Then Jack's voice caused them all to turn around. "There's a truck in that alleyway."

"What?" Ed frowned at him.

"I said there's a truck in that alleyway."

"So what?"

"So I think it's a Tesco delivery truck. We should check it out."

"Wait a minute." Ed put his hands up, palms toward Jack. "Call me a coward if you want, but I don't think that's a great idea."

"Why?" said Jack. "What's going to happen?"

"It was like this when we were ambushed at The Fez."

"There's no one around, Ed."

"That's what it was like then. They came from nowhere. They were waiting for us. That truck could be a trap."

Jack laughed. "What bloody sickos are going to be able to drive a truck up an alley and hide it?"

"So why's it there, then?"

"I don't know, do I?" said Jack. "I'm just saying we should have a look."

"You weren't there in Rowhurst," Ed pleaded. "You don't know what it was like. . . ."

But Jack was already walking over to the alleyway.

Ed called after him, "Jack!"

The others could do nothing but follow. The alley was just wide enough to fit the width of the truck, which was about ten yards down. It sat there in the darkness, a solid menacing shape, blocking the way like some great beast in a lair ready to dash out and catch its prey. Before he was halfway there,

Jack wished he hadn't been so hasty. Ed was right—it would be too easy to get trapped in the narrow space. Then he heard his friends behind him, and it gave him the confidence to carry on.

The truck had a streamlined hood on top of the square blunt cab that clearly said Tesco, and there was a manufacturer's logo in the middle of the black grill: MAN. Jack smiled to himself. It was like a sign. It'd be funny if there actually *was* a man sitting there inside the cab like a neatly labeled exhibit, but it was too dark to see.

The truck was jammed in, making it impossible to open the doors. The grill, however, was made up of three bars, like the rungs of a ladder. Well, that was an invitation if ever Jack'd seen one. He reached for the wipers to get a grip and hoisted himself up.

There *was* a man sitting there, in the driver's seat, and Jack didn't know whether to laugh or scream.

He was dead, his skin bloated and puffy, covered with a layer of white mold that gave it a soft, fluffy look. His eyes were sunken into his swollen face like two little black holes. He reminded Jack of something.

A snowman.

It was quite uncanny. The resemblance was made even stronger by the fact that the driver had a vivid red nose, lumpy and crusted with blisters, like a carrot that had been left too long in the bottom of the fridge.

Hell, he was even wearing a little hat and a scarf.

Now Jack started laughing, and had to let go and jump back down.

"What is it?" said Bam, the first to join him by the truck.

"Look in there," said Jack, snorting with laughter. "There's a bloody snowman!"

Bam climbed up, and a moment later he was standing next to Jack, doubled over and barking.

"You are *sick*," he managed to gasp between laughs.

"Is that, like, a dead body in there?" said Courtney, too squeamish to look.

"Sure is," said Bam. "As dead as they come."

"Well, let's get out of here, then. That's creepy."

"We need the truck, Courtney," said Jack.

"What for?"

"What do you think? Can't you read?"

"Yeah, I can read."

"And what does that say?"

"Tesco."

"Exactly. It's a Tesco delivery truck. It could be full of food."

Courtney stared at the cab and wrinkled her nose. "Yeah, well," she said. "I can't see *him* driving it very far."

"I'm gonna check out the back," said Jack, and, using the bumper, the grill, and the side mirrors, he scrambled up onto the roof of the cab. Behind the cab was what looked like a long blue container. He climbed over the sloping hood and hopped up onto it. It was made of thin metal that banged and clanged beneath his feet as he made his way to the rear.

His heart was pounding, as much with hope as with fear. If the container was intact, it might be filled with food. A very valuable load. Why else would the snowman have driven in here if not to escape looters or hijackers? He'd probably been on his way to Tesco and had come down here to hide, and then tried to sit it out. He could have starved to death, or he could have been taken by the disease. It was impossible to tell.

Well. He might have escaped the marauding sickos, but in the end he hadn't been able to escape death.

Jack got to the end and dropped onto his belly. He peered over the edge, hardly daring to look. The back of the truck appeared to be untouched. Unopened.

He grinned from ear to ear.

He heard a clatter behind him and twisted around to see Ed and Bam climbing up onto the container.

"Well?" Bam called out to him. "Don't keep us in suspense."

Jack sat up, too excited to speak. He gave them a double thumbs-up.

"You think there might be food in here?" Bam asked, smiling too.

Jack nodded his head as Ed ran over to take a look.

"We need to check inside," he said. "It could be empty, or all rotted."

"Now who's the pessimist?" said Jack.

"I don't want to get everyone's hopes up and then find it's a truckload of shampoo or something."

"We have to get into the cab," said Bam.

"What for?" Ed frowned at him.

"Think about it. The snowman—he drove in here and you can't open the doors of the cab, right?"

"Right."

"That means he must still have the keys with him. We

can use them to open the back, and if it *is* food, we could just ditch the snowman and drive the whole bloody rig back to the museum and unload it back there."

"You know how to drive a truck?"

"Nope. But since things all went belly-up, I've learned a lot of new skills. I'd be happy to add truck driver to my list."

They returned to the front of the truck and climbed down. The other kids were waiting for them in the alley.

"Okay. We need to get the keys out of there," said Bam. "Any volunteers?"

Unsurprisingly there were none.

"Didn't think so."

"I'll help," said Ed.

"Help who?" said Bam.

"Help you," said Ed. "It was your idea."

"Oh, cheers."

"There's a little sort of skylight thing in the roof of the cab," said Jack. "You know, like a sunroof? If you could get it open, you could get in that way."

Ed and Bam climbed back up and, using Ed's bayonet and DogNut's club, they managed to batter and bend the sunroof up until it came away, leaving a rectangular hole in the top of the cab. Instantly, a foul stench of putrefaction wafted out, accompanied by a squadron of flies. The boys dropped back, groaning and gagging, their eyes watering.

"I will *never* get used to that smell," said Bam. "That is *rank*. I really don't think I can go in there, Ed."

Ed took a deep breath. "I'll do it."

He eased himself through the narrow hole, feeling for the passenger seat with his feet. Then he dropped down.

It was even worse inside the cramped cab. There were flies everywhere and the air was foul. Ed kept one hand clamped over his mouth and nose and tried not to look at the snowman, who was clutching the wheel with rotted hands. He got a brief glimpse of his face. There were maggots around his nostrils and lips. Ed leaned over him and fumbled around the steering column and dashboard, feeling for the keys. He had to press his body against the corpse. It felt soft and cold.

He tried to shut down his mind and just think about the keys, but it was hard. He could see the other kids outside staring up at him, and somehow that made it worse, seeing their looks of horror and disgust. He felt like a contestant on *I'm a Celebrity . . . Get Me Out Here!*

Your challenge, Ed, is to go in there with a dead man and several buckets of maggots and find the keys. Your reward will be meals for the whole camp for the next six months.

"I can't find anything," he called up to Bam.

"Try his pockets."

Oh, Jesus.

Ed steeled himself and patted the snowman's pockets, still trying not to look. First the jacket and then the trousers.

"There's something in there," he said.

"Keys?" Bam sounded excited.

"Could be."

"Get them out."

"I am *not* sticking my hand in there. It's all . . . wet."

"You're gonna have to, Ed."

Ed held his breath again and slowly, slowly slipped his fingers inside the pocket.

"God . . . it's disgusting. Oh, God."

"Are the keys there?"

"There's something . . . Yes! Got it!"

He jerked out his hand and proudly waved a chunky set of keys up at Bam. Then he looked at his fingers. They were covered in slimy green-and-yellow paste.

"Yaaaaah!" He dropped the keys as if they were red hot and frantically flicked his fingers, then he wiped them on the passenger seat.

Bam was laughing.

"Good work, Ed! You're a star!"

Ed found a rag among the trash inside the cab and cleaned the keys, then he tossed them up to Bam, stood on the seat-back, grabbed the rim of the sunroof, and hauled himself out.

The kids below cheered as Bam helped Ed to his feet, and then the two of them raced along the top of the truck and climbed down the far end.

There was a big steel shutter in the back that rolled up into the roof of the container. Ed tried the most likely-looking key and slotted it into the lock at the bottom. Right first time. There was a satisfying clunk as the shutter popped open.

"Yes!" Ed cried, and the two of them slid the door up.

The truck was filled almost to the door with rows of tall wire cages on wheels, held in place by red webbing straps. There must have been nearly fifty of them in all, and they were piled high with produce.

Canned fruit and vegetables, beans, cereal, toilet paper, fruit juice and soy milk, chocolate, peanut butter, jam, yogurt, chips, and nuts. It was like someone had taken a small supermarket and packed everything from it into the back of this one truck.

Ed and Bam grabbed each other by the forearms and yelled incoherently as they danced around in a circle.

"This'll last us weeks," said Bam when they'd calmed down a little. "And look! You're in luck. There *is* shampoo! We'll show that Jordan bloody Hordern. He'll be on his knees begging us for some of this stuff."

"We've still got to get it back to the museum, though," said Ed.

"We've got the keys. We've got the muscle. We're on a roll. Let's rock! The good times are here to stay. I feel good about today, Ed. No, I don't feel good. I feel bloody great!"

40

When Ed and Bam came back to tell the others the good news, they found DogNut and Jack lifting the driver out through the sunroof, pulling him up by his jacket. They both had scarves wrapped around their faces, but the smell alone was enough to make you retch.

"We figured from all that shouting there was food in the back," said Jack, his voice muffled.

"Tons of it," said Bam. "If we can get the truck back to the museum, we've got it made."

Jack looked around at Ed. "Still think we shouldn't have checked it out, you wimp?" he said.

"It was a good call, Jack."

"Yeah. Now give us a hand here."

Ed took a deep breath and grabbed hold of the body. Once it was clear of the opening, they tipped it over the front of the cab. It rolled down the windshield and flopped to the ground with a wet slap, spilling a small puddle of thin brown liquid.

The kids waiting below jumped back in alarm and swore

at the boys on the roof, who jeered at them.

"Make yourselves useful," Jack said. "Drag him away from here where we can't smell him. We've got to work out how to get this truck moving."

"I might be able to drive it," said Justin.

"You?" Jack scoffed. "What gives you that idea?"

"I used to play a computer game called Truck Simulator."

"I'll bet you did," Jack laughed. "I expect you played Starship Commander as well—doesn't mean you could fly a real rocket."

"A truck's a bit easier than a rocket," said Justin, trying not to get angry. "The principle's roughly the same as a car."

"Yeah? And can you drive a car, in principle?"

"Yes I can, actually. My dad gave me lessons on an old airfield near where we live. He was crazy about cars. Me too. But I'm more interested in trucks, really. Dad didn't have a truck to teach me in, though."

"You really think you can drive this?" Ed asked, slithering down.

"I watched Greg driving the bus," said Justin, with a shrug. "It's the same thing. I really think I could do it. I really do."

"I can drive and all," said DogNut. "Used to jack cars with me mates. I'll sit with him. Between us we can work it out, I reckon."

"All right, we're on!" Ed clapped his hands together.

"Hey, you lot!" Jack called down from the roof. "Who's moving that bloody body? It's stinking the place up."

He looked at Brooke and her friends. They made disgusted faces and backed away, shaking their heads.

"I'll do it," said Frédérique, stepping forward and picking

up one of the snowman's feet. She tried to pull him along, but couldn't shift him. She had a determined, slightly wild look on her face, but it was clear she wasn't going anywhere.

"Come on." Brooke nudged Courtney. "We ain't leaving her to do this. Makes us look bad. Grab a leg."

"Broo-ooke," Courtney protested.

"We didn't come along on this trip just to make sarcastic comments, did we?" Brooke said, grasping the other foot. "Or to hold the boys' coats for them while they had a fight. We got to pull our weight, or at least pull *his* weight." She snickered. "Come on, shake a leg."

Giving in to Brooke's bullying, Courtney and Aleisha joined Frédérique, and the four of them started to drag the body along the alley toward the yard, keeping their faces pointing resolutely forward, away from the snowman. Trying not to think about what they were doing.

They got him to the end of the alley and pulled him over to the row of garages. It had been dark in the alley, which lay in shadow, and the sun felt suddenly warm and cheerful as they stepped into its light.

Brooke let go of the snowman's foot and, closing her eyes, turned her face up to the sun, feeling its warmth on her skin.

"Oh, that feels so good," she said. "I have been *so* cold."

"Brooke," said Courtney. "Look at this . . ."

"What?" Brooke opened her eyes. Courtney was staring at the dead driver with a half-revolted, half-fascinated expression.

"I don't want to look," said Brooke. "It's going to be something horrible, isn't it?"

"Just look."

"I can't . . ."

"You've got to see this."

Brooke clenched her teeth and forced herself to look around at the dead driver, prepared for the worst.

For a moment Brooke thought the snowman was coming back to life. His skin seemed to be boiling, as if liquid were bubbling up from beneath it, pushing it out into rippling blisters. Before their eyes his body was swelling, blossoming, bloating. His tongue poked out from between his lips, the tip of it studded with more blisters that popped as they hit the air. His hands were moving, the fingers wriggling and writhing. His neck was getting fatter and fatter, until it was thicker than his head. Then there was a hiss and sigh as his throat burst open, squeezing out bright pink jelly.

The only way Brooke could deal with what she was seeing was to imagine that she was watching a film. Something with over-the-top special effects. The driver didn't look human anymore. She was absolutely mesmerized.

Someone tugged at her arm.

"What d'you want?" she said, turning around angrily, assuming it was one of the boys come to get her.

Instead she found herself looking into a black hole where a face should be. It was a young mother, with wavy hair that was once blond but was now showing dark roots. She had eyes and a lower jaw with a row of teeth with silver fillings, but nothing in between.

Brooke felt like she'd been kicked in the guts. Her windpipe clenched shut. Her lungs froze. She opened her mouth and tried to scream, but nothing came out.

While the girls had been watching the driver, a group of about fifteen sickos had entered the yard, attracted by the noise. They were all young adults, mothers and fathers, but they were in a terrible state, bloodied and battered, with parts missing, and skin ruined by craters and sores.

Aleisha, Brooke, and Courtney had left their weapons behind in the alley so their hands were free to drag the body, but Frédérique had her knife in a sheath on her belt. She pulled it out and started waving it at the sickos, yelling and screaming in French as the three other girls shouted for help.

Frédérique was like a wildcat, spitting with rage, a look of crazed fury on her thin face. Her blade slashed clumsily at the sickos, doing little real damage but confusing them enough to give the other three time to move away from where they'd been backed up against the garage doors. Frédérique at last managed to get close to a father. She gouged him in the neck, and he whined and went into a sort of stiff-legged dance. She stabbed again and again, the knife rising and falling like a piston.

"Leave him!" Brooke yelled. "Get away, Frédérique!"

Frédérique didn't hear. All her fear and anger and sadness was coming out. She turned from the father and lunged at a bald mother, who stepped to the side. She snarled, the knife scything through the air, and waded right into the knot of sickos. The knife flashed in the sunlight, then punched into a father, where it lodged in his armpit. Frédérique tried to tug it free, but two mothers barged into her arm, loosening her grip on the handle. A third got her from behind, knocking her to her knees. She put her arms around her head to protect herself, and curled forward, arching her back, defeated.

A father crouched over her, sniffing her hair. He was quickly joined by five others, who crowded around her, blocking her from view. Vultures on a carcass.

Unarmed, Brooke, Aleisha, and Courtney could do nothing to help. The rest of the sickos had gotten between them and Frédérique and were now advancing on the girls, dribbling and moaning softly, sniffing the air.

Ed came skidding around the corner, and when he saw what was happening he took hold of Aleisha and Courtney and dragged them back toward the alley, shouting at Brooke to follow.

Once in the alley, they retreated toward the truck, the sickos closing in after them.

"Where's Frédérique?" Ed asked.

"They got her," said Brooke. "They got her."

"We can't leave her."

"I ain't going back. Are you?"

Ed said nothing.

Bam and Jack were sitting on the roof of the cab. They could see the sickos advancing along the alley.

"Hurry up!" they shouted, waving their arms. "For God's sake, run!"

41

Justin and DogNut were inside the cab, struggling to get the engine started. They had the windows wide open, but it still stank something rotten in there. DogNut had found a whole pack of pine-tree-shaped air fresheners in the glove compartment and had ripped them out of their packaging and strewn them about the place. But he didn't think all the air fresheners in the world would be able to get rid of the smell of a fat dead truck driver left to rot in his seat.

Yelling encouragement, Bam and Jack reached out to the girls, ready to drag them up onto the roof. They got Aleisha first, as Courtney started to clamber up the grill by herself. Aleisha was so small she weighed almost nothing. Ed and Brooke waited their turn.

From inside the cab, all Justin could see was a tangle of arms and legs as the girls wriggled up the windshield. The engine didn't want to start. Probably because the diesel fuel had gotten too cold. He was running out of ideas. Every time he turned the key there was a cough and a rumble, then nothing.

"Swear at it," said DogNut.

"Do what?"

"Swear at it. It's what my dad used to do when his car wouldn't start. Sometimes worked."

"Okay," said Justin. "Bastard!"

"That word won't work," DogNut sneered. "Try something stronger."

"Knob-end!"

"No, like this . . ."

As Justin turned the key, DogNut let out a filthy obscenity and the next moment the engine jumped into life. They both roared. Then, as Brooke and Ed cleared the windshield, the two boys in the cab finally saw the sickos lumbering toward them, blocking the narrow alleyway, reaching toward them with scabby fingers.

"Bloody hell. We need to get motoring," said DogNut. "Put her in gear and let's get out of here."

Justin sucked a lungful of air in through his mouth, plunged the clutch pedal down with one foot, wrestled the gear stick into place, and pressed his other foot on the accelerator. It was much harder than the simulation on his computer, but it was basically the same idea.

He forced the accelerator down farther—and farther—and farther. It was nothing like a car. The engine was a monster and was pulling a monster load. There was no subtlety or delicacy involved. You had to work the pedals with heavy boots.

He could feel the whole rig shuddering, but it still didn't want to move. He was beginning to doubt whether he could do this after all. The size and power of the thing terrified him. He eased the clutch up and gave the engine yet more juice. There was a thump and he looked up.

The lead sickos had reached the cab and were battering on the windshield with dirty hands, leaving smears of pus and blood and filth.

"Get a move on, nerd-boy," said DogNut nervously, then saw to his horror that one of the sickos had gotten hold of a lump of concrete and was getting ready to lob it at them. He was a younger guy, a teenager, and showed little sign of the sickness. He looked pretty much like any of the older boys from DogNut's estate. Like a junkie after a heavy night.

There was a flash and a bang and the sicko was thrown back against the wall.

"That must be Bam," said Justin. "We'd be toast without him."

"Can we *please* get out of here," DogNut shouted.

Two mothers had climbed up onto the front of the cab. One of them was the blonde without a face.

"Jesus, that's rank," said DogNut. "I can see right down her throat."

Someone on top of the cab knocked the mother off and then took a swipe at the other sicko, catching her in the side of the head but failing to dislodge her.

The truck shuddered, jerked forward, and then stopped, throwing the mother clear.

The engine cut out.

"Do you want me to drive?" said DogNut.

"No," said Justin. "I'm getting the hang of it. Don't hassle me. I'm all right."

"Drive, dork, drive!"

Justin flushed red. He felt a cold rush of adrenaline wash

through him on a rising tide of anger. In his mind he swore at DogNut, using the same words DogNut had used to swear at the truck, and then told himself it was all okay.

Don't panic.

Engine on. Down with the clutch. Gear into position. Accelerator. Be brave. Do it.

The truck just needed to be treated more brutally than a car. It was hard to give it too many revs.

Clutch up. Right up.

Now it was straining to move off.

Stamp on those pedals with all your weight.

And now they were moving. Inching forward, nudging the rest of the sickos out of the way. They could hear shouts of triumph from the roof.

"You're doing it, man," said DogNut. "Oh my days, you're doing it, you knob-end, you're doing it!"

Slowly and steadily the truck plowed on. Justin didn't dare try shifting up a gear, so they stayed in first, crawling along, over-revving, fumes from the exhaust filling the alley.

The sickos limped and stumbled ahead of them, trying to get out of the way. A couple fell over, but the high clearance of the truck meant that it passed right over them.

As they broke out into the winter sunlight at the end of the alley, they saw someone standing directly in front of them. Justin was about to run it down when he realized it was Frédérique. He slowed, and she drifted out of their way in a daze.

Up on the roof, Jack spotted her. He called out her name and climbed down the side of the cab, using the open window as a footrest. He hung on the step for a moment, then jumped clear and ran over to Frédérique.

"What happened? Are you all right? I didn't even realize you hadn't come back with the others. You must be a better fighter than I thought."

"I'm all right," Frédérique mumbled, and indeed she looked untouched. Jack took her by the wrist.

"Keep moving!" he shouted to DogNut through the window. "Don't stop. I'll see you out on the road."

He ran ahead of the truck, pulling Frédérique along behind him.

Justin was sweating and trying not to panic. Going in a straight line was relatively easy, but turning was a different matter. The steering wheel was huge, and you had to force it around and around to make the wheels rotate even a little way. And then there was the immense length of the truck to deal with, plus the fact that it was jointed and turned in two parts.

Trying to ease past the garages, they smashed into the corner of a wall and demolished it. They scraped along, and Justin thought of the scene in *Titanic* when the ship hits the iceberg.

DogNut was laughing hysterically and swearing at him.

"If you would just shut up, I could handle this," Justin complained.

"No way you could, man," said DogNut. "You are *totally* out of control."

"I can't concentrate with you yelling at me."

"Nah, you need someone to light a fire under you, to get you rocking and rolling," DogNut laughed. "Now go for it, dweeb!"

"Shut up!"

They trundled out into the road and crushed a car before Justin managed to get the wheel turned far enough, and then he had to spin it all the way back in the other direction to straighten up. He didn't do it in time, and before he could stop, they'd crossed the road and trashed another car.

"This is insane!" DogNut shouted, but the engine stalled and the truck at last came to a halt.

Jack ran over and told Justin to wait until everyone was safely off the roof and then went around to open the back. Ed and Bam and the girls scrambled down and followed him, wide-eyed and excited, as if they'd all just been on the most thrilling theme park ride in the world. Finding Frédérique unhurt had been the topper. Ed reckoned the sickos must have left her alone to come after the richer pickings in the alley.

Jack whistled when he saw how much food was inside the truck, and there was an elated party mood as the others piled in to check it out. They were all talking at once, over each other, not listening, laughing, almost crying with joy.

There was just enough room for them to squeeze on, and once they were all safely on board, Jack shouted to Justin to get going. Then he climbed up the tailgate to join his friends inside. The whole truck shook as the engine started up again.

The truck slowly picked up speed until it was crawling along at a steady pace. Jack looked out at the road as it unspooled behind them. Then he made a quick decision and pulled Ed to one side.

"I'm going," he said.

Ed was still buzzing. He didn't really take in what Jack

had said. "Okay, cool," he said, and hugged his friend.

"Did you hear what I said?"

Ed shook his head. "Not really, no," he said, and laughed. "Was it important?"

"I'm going home."

"Back to the museum?"

"No, to Clapham, to my old house. Like I always said I would."

"What?" Ed stopped laughing instantly, as if someone had chucked a bucket of iced water over him. "What do you mean?"

"We're halfway there," said Jack. "I could be home in less than half an hour."

"Yeah, but I thought finding all this food . . . it's changed everything, hasn't it?"

"Why?"

"I mean, you can't leave all this."

"I'll come back. It's not far. I'll get my things and—"

"No, Jack. It's too dangerous."

"I don't care," said Jack bluntly. "I always meant to go home. And now I won't be leaving you guys in the crap anymore. Not now you've got all this."

"Jack—"

"You're all right, Ed," Jack interrupted, shaking Ed by the shoulders. "You've got food, you've got shelter, you've got friends, weapons, girls. You don't need me anymore."

"I do, Jack . . . You're my best friend."

"You said it yourself last night, though, Ed. I've been giving you a really hard time lately. I would've thought you'd be glad to get rid of me. I've been a huge pain in the ass, I know that. And that's why I need to get away. To clear my head. To go home. To get back in touch with how things used to be."

"And then you'll come back?"

"Of course I will. I'll probably be back tonight." Jack grinned at Ed.

"What if you don't come back, though? What if something happens?"

"I'll be all right." Jack slapped his sword. "I've got this."

"Jack . . ."

"You know me, Ed. Stubborn bastard."

Bam had been listening in. He leaned over and held the shotgun out to Jack.

"Take this, mate," he said. "With any luck I won't need it any longer."

"No, you keep it, Bam. You're the shotgun king. I'm fine with my sword."

"Well, then, let me come with you."

"No way, Bam," Jack protested. "I don't want to be responsible for anyone else. That's why I'm going. These kids, they need a dad to look after them, but I'm not ready to be a dad yet. It's hard work. Worrying about everything, looking after everyone. I used to laugh at my mom for getting anxious if I was out late. But I know what it feels like now, being responsible, being scared, and I don't like it. I'm going. Okay? This is my decision and it doesn't affect anyone else."

"And it's my decision to come with you, mate," said Bam. "My decision. My choice. My risk. I won't hold you responsible. You won't have to worry about me."

"I don't need anyone!" Jack turned away from his friends. The truck was snorting and hissing, shuddering as it started to accelerate. Justin was obviously getting the hang of the controls, risking a gear change. Jack jumped down off the back before it was too late.

Ed stared helplessly at him, thinking he might never see him again. And then Bam was on his way too. He vaulted over the back, stumbled in the road as he landed, then ran after Jack and slapped him on the back. Jack threw up his hands, then Bam said something to him and he laughed.

As Ed watched the two of them growing smaller, Frédérique came and joined him at the tailgate.

"What are they doing?" she asked nervously.

"Jack just wants to check out his old house," Ed explained, trying to play it down and not upset her. Not upset himself either, to be honest. "It's not far from here," he added, wanting to believe it. "He'll be back later."

His efforts were obviously failing. Frédérique looked terrified.

"He cannot go. He must not leave me."

"Hey, you're all right now, Fred. We're all gonna be all right. There's plenty of others at the museum who can look out for you until he's back."

"He must not go. . . ."

The truck was getting faster and faster. Jack and Bam were walking in the opposite direction, already two distant figures. Ed tugged at his hair. How could they be so reckless? So unafraid? Strolling off like that. Who knew what was out there? It was crazy.

He suddenly felt very alone. Something clicked inside him. He grabbed Frédérique and shoved her at Brooke.

"Make sure Fred's all right," he said to the startled blonde.

"Why, what's going on?"

Ed was light-headed, drunk almost. And yet everything suddenly seemed very clear and simple. It was as if he had just woken up and cast off a dark heavy suffocating blanket. He wouldn't be afraid anymore. He wouldn't be alone. He would be free and alive. Nothing really mattered, and as a result he could do anything he wanted.

He kissed Brooke and swung out over the tailgate, hanging there for a moment dramatically.

"We'll be home for supper!" he shouted. "And I expect a decent spread."

42

From the shadows of a burned-out house at the side of the road, a figure watched the three boys, with red sore eyes. He'd been following them all morning, waiting for his moment. He'd lost them a while back, but the noise of the truck had alerted him, and now here they were again.

Close enough to taste.

Not yet. Not yet. Wait some more. Watch some more. The time would come.

Shut up! Stop talking! Those voices in his head. Why wouldn't they just shut up? There was too many of them in there, all talking at once, too many to fit, crammed in, bursting his head. It was going to split open.

His head was going to split open. Split open. His head. Like a peach.

Not yet! Not yet!

Shut up!

He shook his head violently, a dog with a rat in its jaws. Spraying sweat everywhere.

He was shivering. Shivering and sweating at the same time. His nose was running, pouring snot down into his mouth. He hardly noticed. He noticed the itch, though, like stinging nettles under the skin. He would scratch his skin off if he could. Skin. Skin a rabbit. Dress it.

Why would you dress a rabbit? What is a rabbit? He couldn't remember. Why was it so hard to remember anything? An animal? Yes.

He rubbed his neck. It was ringed with boils, like a horrible shiny yellow scarf.

Never mind that.

The boys were there. The ones he wanted. The boys who had done . . .

What had they done? He didn't remember. He only knew he hated them. He wanted to smash them and crush them like insects. He wanted to tear the flesh from their bones. He would eat them. He would eat them, but first he would make . . .

Soap . . .

Soup?

He would make soup of them.

Soup? What was soup?

Something.

Rabbit soup.

His mind kept spinning away from him. But there was an important thing to pin down, fix there. Superglue. Yeah . . . the very important thing. The big thing. The thing that they had done wrong to him. To his boy.

His boy. That was it. His boy. His boy who was . . .

little . . . ? Little boy? He had a name, but the big boys had taken his name, they'd taken his son, they'd taken his son from him. His boy. Lee-am.

His Liam.

Yes. He grinned. And as his skin tightened, it pulled at the sores around his mouth, making them bleed. They'd tried to take Liam from him. But they couldn't—he was too clever for them. Clever clogs. That was him. Cleverer than them. Yes. He had kept Liam. They didn't know that, did they? Kept him with him. Kept him safe. Always.

But he would get the boys. He would fix them good. He would skin them. He would dress them. He would do it. He knew how to do it. He was a . . .

What was the word?

Pooch?

Butch?

Teacher?

Not a teacher—he hated teachers—a pusher.

No.

Come on, clever clogs, think!

A butcher.

That was it.

Mr. Clogs the Butcher. And he had the thing to prove it. The tool thing hanging at his belt. He'd had it with him all the time. Clever, see?

A clever. That was it. No, not a clever. A cleaner. A leaf cutter. A leaver. The thing the butcher used. A cleaver. A clever cleaver.

Boys . . . meet the cleaver.

A meat cleaver. He was a butcher. He had his cleaver and he would do butcher to them.

He smiled wider, the blood smeared around his mouth like a clown's painted smile. The boys were walking away. But he could follow because the meaty, juicy stink of them hung in the air like something he could see and touch.

He picked up his bundle, hugged it to his chest, and followed.

43

"rédérique's not too happy about you going, you know."

"That's exactly what I mean," said Jack. "I can't be responsible for everyone." His shoulders were hunched, his head drooping. "I can't look after her. I don't know how."

Ed wasn't going to give up. "She really likes you," he said, slinging his rifle on to his back. "Don't you like her?"

"Yeah, I think so. No, I *do*. I like her a lot," said Jack.

Ed leaned over and picked a long hair off Jack's coat.

"What's this I find?" he said, holding it between finger and thumb so that it twisted in the air. "Evidence!"

"You're going to start singing in a minute, aren't you?" said Jack.

"Singing what?"

"Jack and Fred sitting in a tree, k-i-s-s-i-n-g."

"Well?" Ed raised his eyebrows.

"It's not like that," said Jack, the white half of his face reddening. "She's just latched on to me."

"And you don't like her?"

"I'd like her more if she could stop crying for five minutes.

There's something making her miserable and I can't get through to her. I can't get her to tell me what it is."

"She's just freaked out by everything," said Bam. "We all are, and we all deal with it in different ways."

"How do *you* deal with it?" Ed asked.

"You know me," said Bam. "I do things. Get physical. Same way I've always done. Rugby's a good cure for real life." He paused and turned to Jack with a leer. "So, *do* you fancy her?"

"I haven't really thought about it."

"Yeah?" It was obvious Bam didn't believe him. "You reckon? Nice bit of French totty."

"All right," said Jack. "Maybe a bit."

"Ooh la la! Just a bit?"

"Look. She's all right. I like her. Okay? She's nice-looking. A bit thin perhaps . . ."

"Thin?" Bam snorted. "She's skinny as six o'clock."

"But she's okay," said Jack. "You know what I mean? Maybe if things had been different I might have done something about it, I don't know. I can never, like, *tell* with girls, whether they just like me as a, you know, just as a person, or whether they fancy me. I'm always scared of mucking up."

"Well, I reckon you're in there anyway, mate," said Bam.

"So what about you and Brooke, then?" Jack asked Ed, trying to move the spotlight onto someone else.

"What *about* me and Brooke?"

"When are you gonna make a move on her?"

Ed snickered, remembering. "You know what I just did back there?"

"What?"

"I kissed her."

"You never? What, in front of everyone?"

"It wasn't, like, a proper snog or anything," said Ed. "It was more like a sort of movie kiss. I was sort of acting. You know, like a soldier going on a dangerous mission kissing his girl good-bye. Maybe she'll wait for him, maybe she won't kind of thing."

"Oh, she'll wait for you. You're well in there, mate," said Bam.

"Yeah," said Jack. "She only goes for good-looking blokes, and I'm spoken for. There's no one else around she'd look twice at."

"Hey!" said Bam. "What about me?"

"What *about* you?" said Jack. "You're hideous, Bam. You're a kind of troll."

"I am *not*. I had a girlfriend back home, if you really want to know."

"A real one or an imaginary one?" said Jack.

"She was a picture in a magazine, I reckon," said Ed, joining in the game.

"She's a real girl, thank you," said Bam. "With arms and legs and everything."

"Everything?"

"Far as I know. We hadn't got much past the kissing stage. And now . . ." Bam sighed and gave a little grunt. "God knows if I'll ever see her again."

"What was her name?" Jack asked innocently. "John? Barry? Roger?"

"Cass, if you must know."

"I thought you only liked rugby, Bam."

"I'm a man of the world, Ed. There's more to me than you will ever know."

"There's certainly more to you than I will ever *want* to know," said Jack. "Already that's way too much information. The thought of you and poor Cass getting all loved up on a sofa somewhere . . ."

"Leave it, Jack," said Bam. "Why are you two picking on me, anyway?"

"We're only having a laugh, Bam," said Ed. He put an arm across Bam's shoulders and they walked a few steps linked together.

"So you're going to make a move on Brooke, then, are you, Bam?" said Jack.

"Brooke? No way! She's not my type at all. She's scary as all hell. You're welcome to her, Ed."

"She's all right once you get past her front," said Ed. "But in the past she wouldn't have looked twice at me. I'm not her type, really. I'd have thought she'd be more interested in someone like DogNut. And you can see he fancies her. He's always sniffing around."

"Oh, come off it, Ed!" Jack scoffed. "I thought you understood girls. You can tell she's not the slightest bit interested in him. He's like an over-affectionate dog, sticking his nose up your ass all the time."

The three of them laughed as they marched along. For one small moment they could forget about survival and pretend that nothing had changed.

They'd ended up back near the gas tanks, and they stopped so that Jack could work out which way they should be going.

"That gas sure does smell rotten," said Ed, wrinkling his

nose. "Stupid thing is, there's probably enough gas in those tanks to last us the rest of our lives, if we only had some way to get it out."

Bam wasn't listening. He was looking up at the sky and shading his eyes from the sun. The thick black cloud they'd seen earlier had grown larger.

"I don't think the smell's all from the gas tanks," he said. "That smoke's definitely getting worse. Either *we're* getting nearer to it, or *it's* getting nearer to us."

"Bit of both, I reckon," said Ed. "Must be some way off still, though."

He sniffed the air. "You reckon that's the smoke we can smell?"

"Yeah," said Jack. "Like a coal fire mixed with a sort of cooking smell."

"And something rotten, like food that's gone bad, unless that's the gas," Bam added. "Not nice at all. What if the fire spreads right up to the museum?"

"It won't," said Jack. "It's been too wet lately."

"If it's hot enough, it'll burn anything," Ed pointed out. "No matter how wet."

"Come on, guys," said Jack, moving off. "Let's get a move on. There's nothing we can do about it."

"Yeah," said Ed, and he coughed. He definitely tasted smoke in the air.

44

"Who's this Angus Day, then?"

The younger kids from the Brain Trust had come into the museum café to get away from Matt and the rest of his gang, who were out in the atrium having a religious discussion, and Harry was proudly showing off his fancy lettering.

"*Agnus* Day," he sneered, mocking their stupidity. "It says *Agnus* Day."

"Well, who's Agnes Day?" said Jibber-jabber. "And why have you made a flag for her? Is she your girlfriend?"

"It's Latin, dumbo," Harry explained, with as much scorn in his voice as he could. "It means Lamb of the Lord."

"That definitely says Angus Day, actually," said Wiki. "You've written *Angus*, not *Agnus*. And *Dei* is spelled D-E-I, not D-A-Y."

"You're joking," said Harry. "I've not got it wrong, have I? Matt'll kill me. We spent ages working on this."

"You're not even close," said Wiki.

"Shit, I knew I should have gotten Matt to write it down for me."

"Write what down?" said Matt, walking in with Archie Bishop and the other acolytes.

"The name of your new god," said Wiki.

"Why? What's he done?" Matt read the banner. "You idiot, Harry. What is that? You've ruined it. We'll have to start all over again now."

"Bit of a boring name for a new god, Matt," said Jibber-jabber. "Angus can't really compete with Thor or Zeus or Buddha."

"Yeah," said Wiki, joining in the fun. "Jehovah, Hades, Baal, Osiris, they sound really exciting, but Angus Day sounds more like a newscaster."

"Maybe it's on purpose," said Archie seriously, and everyone turned to look at him, including Matt, who was red-faced with anger and embarrassment.

"I didn't do it on purpose!" Harry protested. "I was doing my best. I really was. I thought I'd gotten it right."

"Exactly," said Archie. "So maybe the Lamb was working through you. It's like the pages and Matt's visions—we don't choose any of it. Everything has been shown to us by the Lamb. Isn't that right, Matt?"

"Er, yeah, that's right," said Matt, backing Archie up but not really sure where this was going.

"So the Lamb must have been working through Harry," Archie went on. "Showing him something that we wouldn't have seen otherwise. He *made* Harry put the wrong words on there. Except they're *not* wrong; they're right, you see? They're what he was supposed to paint on there all along."

"Angus Day?" said Jibber-jabber, not sounding convinced. "Why would he want you to write Angus Day?"

"We don't know why, not yet, but we'll find out," said Archie. "It'll be shown to us."

Matt stood there, struggling to find something good in this. He could see what Archie was doing. He was trying to make the best of it and stop the others from laughing at them. But Matt *really* wished that Harry hadn't gotten it so wrong. Not *both* bloody words.

Angus Day! If Matt wasn't so furious, he would have been laughing too.

One of Jordan's boys came in. He glanced expressionlessly at the banner, then looked around at the kids.

"Your friends are back," he said. "Nice flag. Who's Angus Day?"

45

The smell had gotten worse—deeper, thicker, more intense. It was a strange mixture of familiar, comforting smells, like bonfires and barbecues and wood-burning stoves, jumbled up with unpleasant smells that shouldn't go with them—rotting food, chemistry lessons, dust, and blocked toilets.

"How come we can smell rotting food and cooking food at the same time?" said Bam, wrinkling his nose as he walked.

"Maybe it's not rotting food," said Ed. "Maybe it's chemicals of some sort."

"Great," said Bam. "We're probably being poisoned as we speak."

"It's the gas from the tanks," said Jack. "Must be."

Ed stopped in the road. "Should we turn back?"

"You can cut out if you want," said Jack, who kept on walking. "But I'm not giving up now."

"Wait, guys, look at that."

Bam was staring at a big redbrick building that rose six stories high.

"That's the main stand of the Oval cricket ground," said Ed. "I was there last summer."

"I know what it is," said Bam. "I don't mean the Oval, I mean *that* . . ."

Ed and Jack peered at the building, trying to work out what Bam was going on about.

And then they saw it.

Clustered around the gates were police cars, military vehicles, crowd control barriers, and a broadcast van with a TV transmitter on the roof.

People moving about.

"Oh my God," said Ed, his insides lurching. "Is that for real?"

"Well, it's not a mirage, is it?" said Jack. "It's not like we're in the desert or anything. So I'd say, yes, it must be real."

Ed tried not to get his hopes up. Maybe, though, just maybe, they'd been wrong. Things hadn't fallen apart completely. His heart was racing, thoughts chasing each other around his tired mind.

"Civilization," said Bam. "If the police and the army are there, then, I mean, then we're saved. There are people still alive, proper people, adults not affected by the disease. You know what this means, don't you? There might be a cure after all."

"I don't know," said Jack. "I don't know what it means."

"Well, let's go and find out," said Bam.

"Be careful," said Jack. "I've seen movies where the survivors try to get help and the army thinks they're infected and they shoot them."

"Let's risk it," said Bam.

They moved out of the road onto the sidewalk, where they hurried along, staying close to the buildings even though Ed pointed out that there was a greater risk of being ambushed by any sickos who might be hiding in the area.

"Come off it," said Bam. "There won't be any sickos within a million miles of here, not with that crowd waiting for them over there."

"Guys?" said Jack, slowing down.

"What?"

"Why are we assuming that the police and the army and whoever are going to be alive?"

"Oh crap," said Ed, skidding to a halt and ducking behind a parked car. "Good point."

"But I can see people moving about," said Bam.

"What sort of people?" Ed asked.

"A couple of soldiers, a policeman."

"Are they diseased soldiers, or are they healthy soldiers?"

"It's too far away to tell with my lousy eyesight."

"Then we should be very, very bloody careful until we can be sure either way," said Jack.

Now they darted from car to car, trying to keep out of sight as they steadily worked their way closer.

"When I get back to the museum, I'm going to get a pair of binoculars," said Bam.

"I'm going to get a tank," said Ed. "Life would be a lot easier in a tank."

At last they were near enough to see clearly what was going on. They hid behind a big black 4x4 and peered ahead.

"Shit," Jack hissed.

There were two soldiers and a policeman walking around, but apart from that, nothing was moving. It looked like a scene from a DVD on pause. Some big disaster movie. The security forces lined up ready for action . . . but staying absolutely still.

There were more soldiers sitting in Jeeps, and policemen in vans, a small crowd pressed up against some barriers, and not one of them stirred.

"They're all dead," said Bam, deflated. "Apart from those three, they're all dead."

Now they became aware of more bodies, scattered everywhere. On the ground, in the vehicles, by the entrance gates to the Oval. It looked as if there had been a battle of some sort. Most of the dead bodies weren't in uniform. They were mothers and fathers, teenagers, many with bullet wounds.

"At least we know now what that smell was," said Bam, covering his face with his scarf. "It was two different things. The smell of the fire was masking the smell of dead bodies."

"What d'you think was going on here?" said Ed.

"No idea," said Jack.

"It looks like they were guarding something," Ed suggested.

"The Oval?" said Jack. "Why would the army want to guard a cricket ground? What were they—scared the public was going to break in and carry off the stumps?"

"You got a better suggestion?"

"Maybe there's something else inside," said Bam. "Maybe the government was stockpiling supplies, or weapons, or the crown jewels, or something?"

"We should take a look," said Jack.

"What?" Ed spluttered. "No way. We need to get far away from here. This has nothing to do with us."

"There's only three of them moving about," said Jack. "We could take them easy."

"But why bother?"

"Whatever's in there," said Jack, "it was obviously valuable enough for people to try and break in."

"Sick people probably," said Ed. "Sick idiots who don't know anything."

Jack sat in the road, his back against the car. "It's definitely worth taking a look," he said as the others squatted down next to him. "What if it's like Bam says? A huge emergency food supply? We'd be set for life. It'd make that truck look like chicken feed."

Ed had his hand clamped over his mouth and nose, trying to keep the stench out.

"Jack," he said. "I thought all you wanted was to get home."

"I know . . . I do . . . I really do. But we should still look. If we can get rid of those three mugs, we can find some more guns. There *have* to be guns there. Real modern working guns. And then we'll be invincible."

Ed ground his teeth in frustration. "Why don't we just go to your place?" he said. "Do whatever it is you need to do, then get back to the museum before dark? We could come back here in the morning with some of the guys, DogNut and the others, a proper fighting unit."

"You're such a coward, Ed," said Jack. "We'll be all right. Just think what might be inside there waiting for us. The place is huge. I mean it's the size of, well, the size of a cricket field, for God's sake. There might be food. There might be weapons. There might even be medicine. All three!"

"Come on, Ed," said Bam. "We're here now. Let's just find out what's in there, or we won't be able to think about anything else."

"All right, all right." Ed realized he was beaten. "We'll look inside. But let's see if there's any guns first, like Jack said."

They stood up and gave each other a high five, though Ed's slap was pretty halfhearted. Then they carried on toward the Oval, staying low and using cars for cover.

Finally they sneaked across the road to the line of security vehicles.

They checked whether there were any more sickos moving about. As far as they could see, though, there were just the two soldiers and the policeman.

One of the soldiers had a small machine gun hanging over his shoulder on a strap, but now that they were closer they realized he was pretty far gone, slow and clumsy, his face eaten away by disease. The other soldier was equally wrecked. In the boys' experience the sicker the adults were, the less likely they were to remember how to use any tools or weapons; they usually attacked with just their bare hands. The policeman was a complete mess, with one ear dangling down by his chin and his features replaced by a cluster of glistening blisters.

"I'll take the soldiers," Bam whispered, checking his shotgun. "You two go for the policeman."

"I can't do it," said Ed. "I can't just kill them."

"Come on," said Bam. "Look at them. We'll be doing

them a favor, putting them out of their misery."

"No." Ed squatted down behind a police van, covering his face with his hands. "You do it. I can't."

Jack tutted and drew his sword from its scabbard. "Wait here."

"All right."

Ed couldn't watch. He crouched there, hands over his face. He heard his friends' footsteps. There was a moment's silence, then there came two loud blasts, followed by the sounds of a scuffle and a body hitting the ground.

"You can come out now," Jack called to Ed in a slightly singsong way, as if talking to a toddler. "It's all safe."

Ed stood up, still not wanting to look. He walked around the van to where Bam and Jack were waiting for him. He was aware of the dark shapes of bodies on the ground.

He told himself that it didn't make any difference. These were just three more bodies to add to the piles of corpses that were already here. He forced his eyes around. He had to accept the way things were now. Somehow he had to become as hardened as Jack and Bam.

Jack was wiping his sword clean on the dead policeman's jacket. Bam was pulling the machine gun off the soldier. "You want this?" he said, offering it to Jack. "I'm sticking with my shottie."

"I sure do."

"Do you know how to use that?" Ed asked as Jack started turning the gun in his hands.

"No—but I can find out."

Parked on the other side of the outer wall that surrounded the grounds were four open-backed trucks. The kind builders used to remove rubble from building sites. They were piled high with corpses. Next to them was a fleet of ambulances, their back doors hanging open, paramedics lying by the wheels.

Whenever he'd watched the news he'd never imagined that one day he'd be part of a story. But now the news had come to town in a big way, and there was no one left to record it. The corpses by the TV cameras were blind and deaf. There were no zombified news reporters standing there giving the viewers the statistics.

"The whole population of London has been wiped out. . . ."

Ed went over to a military Jeep, where two grunts with blackened faces and hands sat in the front seats as if waiting to drive off. They were wearing white face masks, presumably to prevent them from breathing anything noxious. Above the masks their eyes were clouded. Flies crawled all over them.

They both had sidearms in holsters.

Ed carefully unbuckled the belt from the soldier in the passenger seat and strapped it around his waist. The pistol hung heavy and solid at his side. The driver had a pair of binoculars round his neck. Ed fished them off and chucked them over to Bam, who thanked him with a big cheesy grin.

Ed did a quick check of the bodies of the other soldiers and policemen. They were all wearing face masks.

He walked through the open gates and over to the line of ambulances, where he jumped up into the back of one. There was a green-clothed paramedic lying on the floor, his face lumpy with yellow spots. His face mask hadn't prevented him from getting sick, but Ed figured that if he could find one, it would at least keep some of the smell out.

With any luck there would be other useful stuff in here as well.

He took off his backpack and went through the ambulance, grabbing anything that looked like it might come in handy and stuffing it in the bag. Painkillers, antiseptic, bandages, antibiotics, scalpels, syringes, rubber gloves, it was all good stuff. And there, finally, in a taped-up cardboard box, a supply of spare masks. He dumped a handful into the top of the bag, but kept three out.

He hopped down off the ambulance. Jack and Bam were walking over, discussing how the machine gun worked. Neither of them really had a clue.

"You ready?" said Jack when he saw Ed.

"Here." Ed handed out the masks. "Put these on. They'll protect you from the smell, at least."

All the doors in the main stand were securely locked, so the boys circled the building, looking for another way in. Finally they came to a more modern part where the big glass doors stood open. There were more dead soldiers here, splayed out on the polished floor of a large entrance area. The boys peered cautiously into the gloom.

"You first," said Bam, with mock politeness.

"After you," said Jack. "I insist."

Ed pushed past them, shaking his head, determined to prove that he wasn't a coward. The other two followed, laughing and jostling each other. The air inside felt trapped and stale. The boys tried not to gag. Their masks helped a little, but there was still a stench of rotting meat mixed with a moldy, mildewy smell. There was also a humming noise, as if there might be some machinery working somewhere nearby.

They stepped over the bodies of two soldiers who looked like they were holding each other in their arms, and went up some stairs.

Ed was beginning to feel horribly faint and wobbly. He wanted to check out the stadium and then get the hell away from here as quickly as possible. He knew that dead bodies carried all sorts of diseases, like cholera and dysentery. Whenever there had been a natural disaster—and there seemed to have been loads before the big one, the sickness— the news bulletins always went on about the risk of disease from unburied bodies. Well, there must have been thirty or forty of them outside, not counting the ones in the trucks. The thought of all those germs . . .

This was a place of death.

They climbed the stairs, trying the doors on every level, until they reached the top and at last found a way out into the stands. Bam was first through. He took a couple of steps and stopped.

Ed heard him say two words.

"Holy cow . . ."

46

J ack and Ed followed Bam out into the sunlight. He was standing there, frozen to the spot, too stunned to say anything.

They were way up in the modern stands, a gleaming white construction of steel and concrete and glass. And below them was the vast expanse of the cricket pitch, every part of it filled with dead bodies. They were stacked in great mounds, like a giant garbage dump. The ones at the bottom were the most decomposed. If it weren't for their bright clothing and the bones sticking out here and there, they wouldn't have been recognizable as human at all. The ones at the top were the freshest, though even they had been eaten away by disease and decay.

There were several earthmoving vehicles standing idle. Diggers and bulldozers, even a couple of cranes with scoops dangling from their gantries. One scoop still held a few bodies.

And there were more bodies in the stands, dumped in the rows of green plastic seats, sitting there like dead spectators at the ultimate gladiator fight. How many dead? Five thousand, ten thousand, a hundred thousand? Looking out over the mounds of corpses, it was impossible to tell.

The noise Ed had heard was flies, millions of them, swarming over the dead. They were not alone. Crows hopped about, rats crawled, seagulls flapped and screeched and squabbled with each other. Two dogs were digging into one of the piles of flesh to get at the bones.

"Treasure beyond our wildest dreams," said Ed bitterly.

Jack and Bam said nothing.

Ed noticed several towers made out of logs and planks and scrap wood, like giant bonfires. They had large blue plastic canisters strapped to them. There were more canisters fixed around the stands.

"This place is one giant funeral pyre," he said. "Looks like they were planning to burn the whole bloody lot. Or blow it sky high."

"They had the right idea," said Jack.

Ed leaned over, pulled his mask down, and threw up onto a seat. His head was spinning and throbbed with an intense cold ache. "We've got to get out of here," he groaned. "This is hell."

But as they turned to leave, they heard the sound of heavy footsteps climbing the stairs.

Ed felt a wave of fear and panic. He didn't need to look to know what was happening.

The sickos were coming.

They were trapped now. They were going to die here. They were going to join this heap of human compost, forgotten, like bags of trash tossed out for the garbage collector.

Ed's mind was racing faster than his heart. He couldn't think straight. A tangle of images were tumbling in his mind, like the wheeling knot of seagulls over the corpse pile. Images of death and decay. But one thought kept poking through, beating all the others back, and he clung on to it.

He didn't want to die. It was as simple as that. He would do anything to stay alive.

The thought was terribly strong and clear.

He wanted to see the summer.

"We need to find another way out," he said. "There are sickos coming up the stairs."

"You don't know that."

"Then who is it, Jack? The undead police come to help us?"

Before Jack could say anything in reply, the first of the sickos appeared at the entrance to the stairs. Three fathers. Sniffing the air. Searching for their prey.

Jack raised his machine gun. Ed saw that it was trembling in his hands. "We could shoot them?"

"You don't know how to work that bloody thing," Ed snapped. "We can outrun them, though."

He looked around for an escape. There was an external staircase leading to the lower seating levels. They charged down it, crashing into the metal sides as they rounded the corners, until they reached the bottom. They quickly took in their situation. The nearest exit was blocked by one of the ominous stacks of blue canisters. The boys realized that the best means of escape would be to get down onto the pitch, where a narrow strip of open grass had been left around the side of the corpse piles. They started to climb over the seats, pushing past the bodies that had been dumped there.

As Ed was clambering over a middle-aged mother in a weird floral sun hat, however, she reached out a hand and tried to take hold of his jacket. He jumped back. The mother hauled herself up out of the seat and puckered her lips and dribbled at Ed, as if she were getting ready to kiss him. Ed shoved her away and she fell into the next seat, waking a hairless father, who flailed at Ed with long dirty fingernails.

"They're not dead," Ed yelled. "They're not all dead!"

All around them sickos were rising from the seats and shuffling toward them, and now Ed saw that there were more live ones down on the field, moving along the narrow pathways that divided the mounds.

The boys vaulted over seats, knocking sickos out of their way, stepping on dead bodies, slipping in filth, doing whatever it took to get down. As they reached the bottom, two young mothers on the edge of the field made a lunge for them, and Bam fired off both barrels of his shotgun, not taking any chances.

The mothers went down, and Bam fumbled to reload his gun.

One barrel at a time, he told himself, jiggling the shells into the holes. Just fire one barrel at a time. Keep something back.

"There's a way out over there," Ed shouted, pointing to an exit from the field over near the old stands. They sprinted toward it, past a wall of decomposing flesh on one side and the live sickos in the stands on the other. The sickos were all coming down toward the field, some walking, some crawling, the younger ones moving faster, others stumbling, barely able to move, and as they came they dislodged the ones who had given up, who fell out of their seats.

It was impossible to tell which were dead and which alive. They were all covered in sores and boils and soft rotten patches.

The boys thought they were home free—the exit was just a few feet away—but then something moved ahead of them, and a cascade of dead bodies tumbled down from one of the piles directly into their path.

They had no choice. They would have to climb over them.

They tried, but it was like wading through deep mud. The bodies were so soft they gave way beneath their feet, and the boys found themselves treading in shredded skin and innards.

"Look out!" Ed shouted.

A large group of sickos had gotten onto the field and was approaching from behind.

Jack raised his machine gun, fiddled with it, tried the trigger.

Nothing.

The sickos moved nearer.

He thumbed off the safety catch.

Tried the trigger again.

Nothing.

He swore and shook the gun, tried another catch.

He yelled as the gun suddenly jumped and jerked in his hands, seeming to fire itself, spraying bullets everywhere except at the advancing sickos. Jack let go of the trigger in fright, but one of the bullets must have struck a canister, for the next moment there was an almighty bang, and flames leapt into the air, along with an ugly mess of body parts and a horrible reddish-brown spray.

The boys, along with most of the sickos, were knocked off their feet. They went sprawling against the billboard around the edge of the stands and smashed painfully into the wood and plastic. They landed in a pile of sticky wetness, and Ed was insanely grateful for the mask that was still clamped to his face.

This really was hell.

It was raining rotten flesh. A fire had started. A clutch of sickos ran past them, clothed in flames. They crashed into another stack of canisters and there was a second explosion.

The whole stadium seemed to be alight now.

The boys seized their opportunity and stumbled, dazed and disoriented, toward the exit. The open gate was tantalizingly close. But they had to wade through body parts and unmentionable filth to get there.

"Come on!" Ed yelled, breaking away from the others. "We can do it—"

The next thing he knew, he was running in silence in midair. The ground beneath his feet seemed suddenly to rise up and then just disappear. At the same time, the air contracted around him, squeezing the breath out of him, crushing his chest, popping his eardrums. He didn't hear a bang so much as feel it. There was a blinding brightness and a bottomless darkness at the same time. Up became down and inside became out. Slowly, slowly, slowly an avalanche of dead bodies collapsed on top of him and smoke billowed toward him in a gray mushroom cloud that grew and grew until he was embraced by sweet, soft, silent oblivion.

47

Frédérique was alone in the women's toilet at the museum. Only her hands showed any signs of life as they fiddled in her lap, twining and intertwining, her fingernails picking at the skin. A drip of moisture fell from her nose and she shivered. Inside, though, she felt hot, like she was cooking. Her insides were writhing and churning. Her stomach cramping. Her heart beating too fast. Every few minutes she gave a little dry cough that sent a spasm of pain through her lungs.

She was in one of the stalls, sitting on a toilet with the lid down. The kids in the museum didn't use the restrooms anymore. They had buckets for that, which they emptied outside. The water they had was too precious to waste flushing down the toilet.

She had come here to be alone, away from the noise of the other kids. Their constant chatter was starting to hurt her ears. She knew she should be happy. The day had gone well. Justin had eventually managed to get the truck back to the museum, and they'd stopped around the back, near to some loading-bay doors. The boys at the museum had been ridiculously overexcited when they'd seen what Justin and DogNut and the girls had brought back for them. It had lifted the younger ones out of their state of hungry, depressed boredom, and they'd celebrated by having a proper lunch. Or as proper as you could get out of cold tins.

It was while they'd been eating lunch that Frédérique had started to feel unwell. The food tasted weird and smelled of rotting plants and cows and fields and compost and toilets. Even now, thinking about it, it was making her mouth fill with vinegary saliva, and bile was rising up her throat. She thought she might be sick. She could picture what she'd eaten, sitting in her belly, sending out roots and tendrils and spores, living inside her. . . .

Sitting there in the café, trying to eat, a headache had lodged behind her eyes that she couldn't shift, despite digging into the precious supply of painkillers she kept in her purse. The noise in the café, with all the kids talking at once, had slowly driven her mad.

She needed quiet. Only she couldn't find any quiet. Not even alone here in the restroom. There seemed to be a constant babble of voices inside her head, all shouting and arguing at the same time. Screaming sometimes. The pressure was awful. Just awful. Every now and then she put her head down between her knees and moaned softly, then the pressure would press down hard on her eyes and she got scared that they were going to fall out onto the floor or simply explode.

She rubbed the back of her head, at the base of her skull, trying to massage the tension away. It didn't make any difference, but she kept on anyway, rubbing and rubbing until her hand came away bloody.

If only Jack hadn't left. She could talk to him. Jack would know what to do. She'd been frightened of him at first, with that strange birthmark on his face. But not anymore. He was the nicest of them all, the kindest.

So why had he left? The bastard.

The sudden flare of rage burned itself out as quickly as it had come on.

Her stomach was gurgling. A boiling mess of acid bubbled up her throat, scalding it. She had eaten something bad. That was it. The food had been on the truck for a long time, after all. The stuff in cans had sell-by dates months away, but even so . . .

The voices in her head erupted, yelling at her.

It's not the food—not the food—you know what it is—why won't you admit it—you coward—it's not the food—the kids— they're all bastards—Jack left you—nobody gives a shit . . .

"Tais-toi!"

She clamped her hands to either side of her head and her fingers ran over a cluster of little bumps that were nestling behind her ears, like insect bites.

They hadn't been there before.

She stood up. All her muscles felt stiff and it hurt to move, but she forced herself to stand and walk out of the cubicle. The restroom was underground, and she had brought a little candle down with her that she had left by the sinks. It seemed suddenly very bright, and Frédérique gave a cry and shielded her eyes. She staggered over to the row of mirrors, eyes pressed nearly shut, and looked at her reflection.

She didn't like what she saw.

She was thinner than ever. Her lips were cracked and dry, peeling. Her eyes and nose rimmed with red. She lifted her long hair to look at the side of her neck.

"*Oh, mon Dieu, non. . . .*"

48

Bam didn't know if his eyes were open or not. He was in a world of blackness. As far as he could work out, the explosion had ripped through the ground and he'd ended up somewhere below the field. All he knew for sure was that he was sitting on a cold, hard floor with his back against a wall. The air was thick with dust and his mouth full of grit. He was bruised and aching all over, but the pain was bearable. His legs hurt the most. He could wiggle his toes, though, so he assumed that nothing was broken.

He could cope with a few bumps and bruises. What he couldn't cope with was the complete darkness. Either the light had been blocked by falling rubble, or the explosion had blinded him.

He had felt around with his hands when he had first regained consciousness. There was a dead body next to him. Long dead. It was cold and soft and putrid. He wanted to get away from it, but he was too scared, because there was something else moving about down here with him, snuffling and sniffing and searching in the dark. Every few seconds he could hear its feet scrape on the floor.

Bam was trying to keep utterly still and utterly quiet. It wasn't easy. He had to keep breathing. The dust in his mouth and nose made him want to sneeze. His left leg was at an awkward angle and he desperately wanted to move it. But he couldn't risk it. He was scared even to swallow in case it made a noise.

He still had the shotgun in his hand, which was something. As far as he could remember, he had reloaded it and cocked it before the cave-in, but he wasn't a hundred percent sure. There was a strong chance that he might pull the trigger and there would be a small, pathetic *click* and nothing more. He couldn't check it. It would give him away. He gripped the double triggers tightly. If the thing came too close, he would pull them and hope for the best.

He had no choice.

The thing, whatever it was, a mother or a father, there was no way of telling in the dark, moved again. He heard the dry rasp of its feet.

They could smell you, couldn't they? That's what they did. They sniffed the air. And there was probably more than one of them down here. They'd find him and he wouldn't be able to fight back because he couldn't see them. He couldn't see anything. He could imagine them, though, a group of them slowly creeping toward him in the darkness, worm-eaten, puffy, and insane. Closing in, step by step, leaving slippery trails of saliva on the floor.

There!

The scuff of a shoe.

It was definitely closer.

He could hear it breathing.

Bam was beginning to feel faint. He wasn't taking in enough oxygen. The darkness seemed to be closing in on him, shrinking around him, crushing him. He wanted to be out in the sunshine, in the fresh air, running up a sports field with a ball in his hands.

He wanted to see his enemy. In the daylight he was the bravest boy in the world. He would tackle players twice his size. He was Bam the tank.

Not down here, though, not in the dark, covered in filth, alone.

Another scuff. Closer still. Only feet away.

Where were his friends? What had happened to them? Had they died in the explosion? He wanted to cry out, to shout for help, but that would only bring the shambling thing in the dark nearer.

But where were they?

Where were his friends?

49

Jack, too, was in the dark, wandering lost and alone, moving as fast as he dared, desperately searching for Ed and Bam. His throat was hurting, raw, as if someone had scraped it with a wire brush. His vocal cords felt scalded and strangled. He'd tried to cry out, but the dust and the pain and the tightness had prevented him from making anything more than a gurgling, choking sound.

His head was ringing. He thought he might have been deafened by the explosion. All he could make out above the whistling, whiny noise that filled his ears were dull muffled sounds that could have been inside his head.

He'd been terrified that something like this would happen. He hadn't wanted to be responsible for the others, hadn't wanted Bam and Ed to come along with him. He'd tried to get away from them all, and now he *was* responsible. It was his fault they'd ended up down here. Wherever *here* was.

So now he had to find his friends, to rescue them.

It was up to him.

It wasn't easy. He was stumbling along, arms held out

in front, groping at the blackness, feeling for any walls or obstructions, head tucked down, cringing away from anything it might bash against. And all the while his sore, gritty eyes flicked around in their sockets, searching for any clues as to where he was and how he might ever get out of here.

Look!

Was he imagining it? No. It was real. A small chink of light. If he could just get to it, he'd be able to find his bearings. He had to admit he was no use to anyone like this, blind and dumb and confused. But if he could find a way out, he could go back to help the others. One of those dead soldiers or policemen outside must have a flashlight on them. Providing there still *was* an outside. Who knew how much damage that last explosion had done? Maybe he was buried down here under tons of rubble and dead bodies. . . .

Don't think about that.

The most important thing was to escape, and then sort himself out and go back to look for the others. Nothing could happen to Bam and Ed in the meantime, not down here in the dark.

He froze. Something had moved in front of him, shifted slightly. The tiny spot of light had flickered. There was something up ahead.

He stood as still as he could, straining to see anything in the pitch darkness, straining to hear anything. But there was only the throb and hiss of his own blood surging around his body.

He couldn't stay like this forever, though. He had to move.

Then a thought struck him. He couldn't see in the dark,

but neither could the sickos. They would be just as lost as him. He forced a smile. What was the worst they could do?

He got ready to run toward that welcoming chink of light.

50

Thirty-four, thirty-three, thirty-two . . .

Bam was counting down from fifty in his head. When he got to one, he would do something. Fight back. Get up. Take control. The sicko was still there, he could tell.

Eighteen, seventeen, sixteen, fifteen . . .

Come on, you diseased bag of pus. Let me know where you are. Move, damn you.

And then it did move. Suddenly it was coming straight for him. And coming fast.

Bam yelled in fright and pulled the trigger at the same time. Firing one barrel. There was a *whoomph!* and a bright flare as the charge in the cartridge exploded, sending shot spraying out toward his attacker. It was over almost before it had started. Like a camera flash going off. But it lasted long enough for Bam to see a body falling back, arms thrown wide, the white face splashed with red down one side, eyes wide in terror and surprise.

Jack's face.

51

The kids were playing in the atrium, the younger ones chasing each other around among the tanks and vehicles. Nobody could remember being this happy for weeks. Jordan Hordern had been to see them. He was impressed by the truck and had officially invited the newcomers to stay and share in everything they had. He'd organized some of his boys into a team to bring a few of the cages inside. Justin had even worked out how to operate the lift at the back of the truck that brought the cages down to the ground. There were too many to move in one trip, and they'd had to leave half of them on the truck, securely locked away from any marauding sickos.

Brooke, Aleisha, and Courtney sat on a bench watching the fun. Wiki, Jibber-jabber, Zohra, Froggie, and a couple of Matt's younger acolytes were dashing about yelling and shrieking. Frédérique had even joined in. She'd been moody since lunch, but now she seemed almost hysterically happy, like she'd become a little kid again.

Froggie ran over.

"Save me!" he shouted, and Aleisha jumped up. She was hardly taller than Froggie, but she wrapped her arms around him protectively.

"I'll save you!" she said. "Just pretend I'm your mom!"

Froggie pressed his face into her body. "Can I?" he asked quietly.

Aleisha smiled and kissed the top of his head. "'Course you can, little man."

Brooke jeered at her friend. "Look at you, being mom again. What's with you, girl?"

"She's nice," said Froggie.

"She's *too* nice," said Brooke. "It ain't right."

"What game you playing, anyway?" Aleisha asked.

"Zombies!" said Froggie.

"You are joking me! Zombies?" Aleisha shook her head, laughing in disbelief.

"They're doing the right thing," said Brooke. "You go for it, Froglet. Show them sickos we ain't scared of them."

"Ain't we?" said Aleisha.

"No we ain't," said Brooke. "We done it. We went out there and we got them good! We won. We wasn't just sitting around biting our nails and going, 'Deary me, whatever can we do, we're all going to die.' We fought back, yeah? That's what we gonna do from now on, fight back."

"You said it, girl." Courtney bumped Brooke's clenched fist, then turned to Aleisha. "They not so tough. By theyselves they rubbish, just weak and, like, stupid, yeah? But in big groups they way bad, they can, like, overdo you. No. What's the word? Not, like, overdo. Over something? Overword? Overwell?"

"I don't know what you mean," said Brooke. "What word?"

"When you get, like, overwhelmed by something."

"That's it! That's the word."

"What?"

"*Overwhelm*, you idiot."

"Oh yeah, I said it. *Overwhelm!*"

The three of them laughed. It felt so good. Whenever they laughed it felt as if heavy weights were being lifted from their backs.

Aleisha let Froggie go, and he ran off. Aleisha watched him for a while, then a cloud passed over her face and she grew serious.

"Are we alone?" she asked, sitting down.

Brooke looked at her.

"How d'you mean *alone*?"

"I mean—is this it? *Us* here. Are we, like, all that's left?"

"I don't know. Can't answer that."

"Is only because we haven't met no other kids since we got here. And we didn't see none out on the streets today, did we?"

"Don't mean there ain't none out there," said Brooke. "I reckon there must be loads more kids around. Somewhere. Hiding. All in they own little groups. I'll bet you there's an identical group of kids going through all the same things as we are, having their own adventures, living, dying, finding food . . . laughing."

"Farting," said Courtney.

"I'm serious, Courtney. We ain't alone."

"And I'm serious too." Courtney gave an evil grin and

then the others smelled it. They jumped up from the bench and backed away, holding their noses and cursing Courtney.

Frédérique ran past, her long hair flying. Eyes and mouth wide. She was chasing Zohra, who was screaming happily. Frédérique screamed too, copying the younger girl, forcing out a long, thin, impossibly high note that seemed to fill the whole atrium. It was the only way she could shut out the other sounds the kids were making. The loud breathing, hearts beating, blood flowing through veins, food being digested, the thoughts yammering inside their heads. So many voices. Drone, drone, drone, gibbering on about nothing.

It wasn't just her hearing that was better; all her senses had been boosted. She could smell so much more, feel so much more, see so much more. Things were so bright it hurt her eyes, blinding her. The light burrowed into her head. She could feel it as it came in through her eye then down the optic nerve straight into her brain. Like someone was shining a flashlight into her mind, lighting it up.

Everything was very clear now. Clear and sharp and glowing and bright. She understood so many things she hadn't known before. The light had unlocked all this hidden stuff, sent her brain spinning. The others couldn't know that, the children. The stupid little children.

Because that's all they were. *Children*.

Stupid–stupid–stupid . . .

What did they know? Her brain was supercharged, like a sports car; they wouldn't understand that. They were wandering in the dark, like cave people. Their brains were solid and heavy and slow; hers was spinning so fast in her head it was getting hot.

She bit her knuckle, tasted blood. Like touching battery terminals with your tongue. A flash of electricity, metal, food, red, water, life.

She was changing. That was it. Evolving into a higher being. Like a caterpillar becoming a chrysalis becoming a butterfly. Her brain was turning to liquid, and it would reform as something spectacular.

Yes.

She was becoming a super-being.

Not like these stupid-stupid-stupid . . . what was the word?

Enfants.

She laughed. Why had she been scared before? There was nothing to be afraid of. She was changing into something . . . magnificent.

Froggie and Wiki ran away from Frédérique and hid behind a tank.

Froggie was fighting to catch his breath.

"She's scary," he gasped. "I hope she doesn't catch me."

"You're fast," said Wiki. "You can outrun her."

"It feels really weird to be going crazy in a museum. You're never usually allowed to run around."

"It's actually quite funny you should say that, about going crazy here," said Wiki. "You know what this place used to be? This building?"

"No," said Froggie. "What?"

"Bedlam."

"What's that?"

"Its proper name was the Bethlem Royal Hospital. For insane people."

"A loony bin?" said Froggie, his big eyes wide.

"Yes. It was nicknamed Bedlam. It's where the word comes from."

"What word?" said Froggie.

"Never mind."

"Is there anything you don't know?" Froggie asked.

"There are lots of things I don't know," said Wiki seriously.

"What's the weirdest thing you know?"

"I know how to say 'the toenails of my grandfather's elder brother are stiff' in Indonesian."

"Yeah? Go on, then."

"Okay—*Kuku-kuku kaki kakak kakekku kaku kaku.*"

"You made that up."

"No I didn't. It's true. *Kuku-kuku kaki kakak kakekku kaku kaku* means 'the toenails of my grandfather's elder brother are stiff' in Indonesian. Now look out! She's coming!"

Frédérique could smell them. Hiding behind the tank. Oh, they were ripe. Fresh and ripe. Not like the muck she'd been forced to eat at lunch. That had been poisoned, she was sure of it now; the other children had tried to poison her— they'd never liked her. She was different in some way. And they knew it. She wasn't one of them.

She was French.

They'd been hiding the good food. Keeping it for themselves. But she knew how to get at it. It was inside them.

The smell of them was making her salivate. Her mouth was full of liquid. It spilled over her lips. God, but she was hungry.

There they were, the two boys, two little piggies. She

breathed in their stench, could already taste them. The smaller one, Froggie. He would be so tender. The soft flesh. The blood. Young and fresh and alive, electric, pulsing, pure, and full of red, red life . . .

She was gripped by a spasm that sent her whole body rigid. It felt like all her bones must break, snap under the strain. Electricity was running through her—power, fire, metal, red, food . . .

Zohra was watching Frédérique move in on Froggie and Wiki.

"Get away!" she shouted, glad it wasn't her over there. Frédérique was too good at this game. She was making it too real. Froggie and Wiki were bumping into each other and yelling as they tried to dodge the tall girl's grasping hands.

"Run, Froggie!" Zohra was laughing so much she thought she might be sick. The boys looked like something out of a speeded-up comedy film.

Then Frédérique howled and grabbed hold of Froggie's arm.

Froggie shrieked.

"She's caught me!"

Frédérique bared her teeth, brought Froggie's arm up to her mouth, and bit down hard.

52

"Jack, Jack . . . I'm sorry, Jack."

"You moron. You could have killed me."

"But you're not dead. Thank God. How bad is it?"

"What do you think? You shot me, you moron."

"I'm sorry. I didn't know it was you. I thought . . ."

"Well, it *was* me. . . ."

"Jack, what have I done?"

"You *know* what you've done. You've shot me."

"You're not dead, though. I didn't kill you."

"It only got me down the side. I'm bleeding a bit. It's not too bad, I think. Doesn't hurt too much. It's lucky you're such a rotten shot."

"I'm so sorry, Jack."

"It's all right, Bam. It's not your fault. I know you didn't mean it, but I wish to God you hadn't done it."

"I couldn't see. I thought you were a sicko."

"Yeah, I know. I thought you were one too. There was a light, I saw a light, I think it must have been something reflecting off your gun barrel."

"Jesus, Jack, I really thought I'd killed you."

"Yeah, well, you didn't. Better luck next time."

"Jack . . ."

"I'm still here, Bam. Just shut up about it. We've got to get out of here somehow."

"Help!" Bam's voice boomed out in the darkness. "Hello! Help . . . Ed! Are you there? Help us, Ed! Where are you? Ed . . ." Bam stopped shouting and the silence and the blackness felt deeper.

"Can you see anything?" Jack asked. "Any light anywhere?"

"No, Jack, but I can feel you. . . . You're soaked. It's bad, Jack, it's bad."

"I feel all right, Bam. It doesn't hurt too much. I can stand up, I think."

"Come on, then. I'll help you."

"Ow . . . don't hold me there, that hurts like hell. Ow. Okay. I'm okay. I'm okay. I'm up."

"Which way do we go? I can't see anything."

"Oh, Jesus, Bam, I don't think I can do this, put me down, put me down. . . ."

Bam realized that Jack had been faking it before. The injury was bad, and he was in a lot more pain than he'd been letting on. Tears came into Bam's eyes. He wiped them away and stared into black nothingness. And then a strange thing happened: a patch of the black started to break up and fall apart, to be replaced by a bright square that hung like a TV screen in the darkness.

He struggled to make sense of what he was seeing.

Light. A waft of smoke and dust. Then a silhouetted head and shoulders. A voice.

"Bam?"

"Ed? Is that you, Ed?"

A flashlight shone in, and Bam shielded his eyes.

"I heard you shouting." It was definitely Ed's voice. "I've been looking everywhere. Come this way. I'll pass you a flashlight. Is Jack hurt?"

"Just a bit," said Jack sarcastically.

"In the explosion?"

"No," said Bam, coming over to the small opening and taking the flashlight from Ed. "I shot him. I thought he was a sicko."

Ed swore. "We've got to get you out of there fast," he said. "See if you can pull down any more of this wall of rubble."

With Bam on one side and Ed on the other, they set to work, moving lumps of concrete until they'd made a big enough hole for Bam to get through. Then Ed shone his flashlight to guide Bam back to Jack. Bam saw that they'd fallen into some sort of underground sports hall. Part of the roof was caved in, and there was a mound of dead bodies at the far end.

He went back over to Jack and swore again when he saw the state of him. His whole left side was covered in bright red blood, crusted with dirt. His shirt and jacket were ragged. He groaned as Bam hauled him to his feet and manhandled him to the opening. Ed helped them both out into the corridor on the other side. There was smoke everywhere, and the sound of flames. The structure of the building had been badly damaged. Big cracks zigzagged up the walls, and chips of concrete and little rivulets of dust were falling everywhere.

Ed and Bam got under Jack's shoulders, and the three of

them blundered their way to a staircase that led up to ground level. Jack cursing. Bam fretting. Ed just glad they were all alive.

"I didn't fall through," he explained as they made it out of the stand through some shattered glass doors. It was a relief to get out of the building, although the air outside wasn't much cleaner. "The explosion threw me off the field into the stands," Ed went on. "I don't know how long I was unconscious, but when I came around I figured you two must have got buried underground somewhere. I managed to get outside and find this flashlight in an ambulance. It's crazy, the whole place is on fire, but at least it's gotten rid of the sickos."

"It's lucky you heard us shouting," said Bam.

"Yeah, well, when I got back here I thought it was hopeless," said Ed. "I went down to the lower level, and half the place was collapsed. Then I heard a shot. I couldn't believe it. When you started shouting, I finally worked out where you were."

They were skirting the stands, making their way to the main gates where they'd first come in. There was a creak and a rumble from the building.

"It's collapsing," said Ed. "We need to get far away from here, then we'll see how bad you are, Jack."

"I'm fine," Jack insisted. "It's not as bad as it looks."

"I hope so. Because it looks terrible."

Swirls of black smoke carrying ashes and cinders billowed around the security vehicles, and there was a sickening stink coming from the fire. Roasting flesh and blazing fat mixed with the bitter, choking stench of burning hair and bones, not to mention the smell of all the plastic and chemicals and building materials that were poisoning the atmosphere. Bam and Jack had lost their masks in the fall, and Ed stopped just long enough to hand them fresh ones from his pack. Then they struggled on, half carrying, half dragging Jack between them. Ed had had to get rid of his rifle. It had been damaged in the explosion—the bayonet had snapped in half—and it was too awkward trying to carry it and Jack at the same time. Bam was limping. His legs were more badly hurt than he'd realized, but at least he could walk. Jack grunted and complained as they jostled him along.

They headed to the main road and carried on southeast, toward Clapham. Behind them a vast column of smoke rose from the ruined Oval. Flames at the base of the column leapt and spurted skyward as if trying to escape. The roar was deafening, and the surrounding buildings were already getting covered in a layer of soot and ash. The boys hadn't gone far when they heard the first of the vehicles explode.

"Looks like we got out just in time," said Ed, glancing back at the devastation. "We need to keep moving."

They walked a long way before Ed reckoned it was safe to stop, and they broke into an office building. They thought it would be easier to fix up Jack in there than out on the street. There were no signs of any sickos. It was clean and dry and quiet. A black leather-and-chrome sofa stood in the reception area. They sat Jack down on it, and Ed took off his backpack.

Jack looked awful. His skin was almost bone white, making his birthmark stand out even more vividly. His torn clothes were soaked with blood.

"We need to take a proper look at you," said Ed.

"It's only on the surface, I think," said Jack. "It must be, otherwise why isn't it hurting more?"

"Whatever. You're still losing a lot of blood."

Ed opened Jack's coat and put his fingers to his shirt buttons, but Jack stopped him, pushing his hand away.

"Don't, Ed," he said. "Just leave it. I'd rather not know."

"If you don't want to look, fine. But we've got to at least bandage you, Jack."

Jack thought about it, biting his lip. "All right," he said, turning his head away.

Ed unbuttoned Jack's shirt and peeled it back.

"Oh crap, Jack. That does *not* look good."

Jack's left side was peppered with red marks that ran from his chest down to his trousers. Some were merely bloody dents, but some were actual holes.

"There's probably still shot in there," said Bam, looking at the nasty punctures that dribbled blood down Jack's pale skin. "If we don't get that out, you'll get infected, mate."

"*Can* we get it out?" Jack asked.

"I don't know." Bam shrugged. "I don't know, Jack. I don't know how deep it is. I'm not a doctor."

"Then I'm screwed, basically."

"We should get you back to the museum," said Bam. "Someone there might know what to do."

"No," said Jack angrily. "How many times do I have to tell you I'm going home? Look, what's this?"

Jack's hand clutched at something that was hanging around his neck on an old leather bootlace.

"It's a key," said Bam.

"Exactly," said Jack. "My front door key, to be precise.

I've kept it with me from the start. Because I always knew that one day I was going to go home and let myself into my own front door. I don't know why you two came along on this. All you've done is try and persuade me to go back. You'd do anything to stop me getting home, wouldn't you? Even shoot me!"

"It was an accident."

"I know it was a bloody accident, Bam. I was making a joke."

"Bam's right, though," said Ed. "I got some stuff from the ambulance, but you'd be better off back at the museum."

"My house is nearer," said Jack bluntly. "And I don't feel like I can go very far like this. Clean the wounds, bandage me up, and get me home. Anything you haven't got on you, I don't know, tweezers, scalpels, whatever you need, we can probably find there. And then we'll look at the damage properly. Deal?"

"All right, yes. We'll do that," said Ed, unpacking his medical supplies. "But you're a stubborn bastard, Jack."

"Exactly. Too stubborn to die, that's me! Iron Jack, the armor-plated man." He gave a little twisted smile, then closed his eyes before he started crying.

53

They'd been going for an hour. Along a very wide, very straight, and very dreary road. They'd passed an endless parade of small shops and businesses. It had taken them twice as long as it should have. Jack was walking more and more slowly. He was bandaged and smothered in antiseptic, but blood was already soaking through the dressings in dark patches, and now, as the adrenaline wore off, every step hurt him. He'd taken some painkillers. They'd done little more than take the edge off, and his mood was as black as the cloud of smoke that hung over south London. He knew that the chances of getting all the shot out cleanly were pretty slim. If it stayed inside him, the wounds wouldn't heal properly. It was hard enough trying to survive when you were fit and healthy, but like this . . .

He didn't want to think about it, but couldn't help himself. No matter where he steered it, his mind kept slipping back there. The bright flash, the stinging pain, the punch to his belly. The realization that everything had changed.

Ed and Bam tried hard to keep his spirits up, but it

irritated him as much as it helped. Bam irritated him most. Jack knew he shouldn't blame him for what had happened. It was an accident. But, even so . . . If it just hadn't happened. If he could turn back time. If he could have called out to Bam. If Bam could have called out to him. If Bam had aimed another foot to the right. If, if, if . . .

He played the scene over and over in his head with different outcomes, but it didn't make any difference. The reality was that he was full of lead shot and losing a lot of blood. His hands and feet were freezing. He had pins and needles in his face. He was feeling faint and feeble and dizzy and thirsty. They had water with them, and they stopped every few hundred feet so he could sip some more, but no matter how much he drank, he wasn't able to quench his burning thirst.

They were getting into Clapham. He was nearly home, but if they were attacked again, he wasn't sure he'd be able to do much.

Then he realized something else.

"My gun!" he said. "Where's my gun? My lovely machine gun?"

"You must have lost it in the explosion," said Ed.

"Why didn't you say something? Why didn't you get me another?"

"I did."

"What?"

"When I went for the flashlight I got another pistol."

"Not another machine gun?"

"Face it, Jack, you didn't really know how to use it, did you? You were more danger to us than anyone else."

"I could have learned, practiced."

"Yeah, and how many bullets would you have had left when you'd finished? Guns are all well and good, but without ammo, they're useless. Pistols are easier and safer, and they don't use up their ammo so quickly. I found a few extra clips as well. It's all in my pack. When you're stronger, I'll give it to you."

"Give it to me now. Give me the gun."

"It's too heavy, Jack. How would you carry it? You try and shove it in your waistband, you'll kill yourself."

"Yeah, all right . . ." Jack's voice softened. "Thanks, Ed. You did really well back there. But that machine gun was so cool. All those weapons outside the Oval. All burned up. It's tragic."

"You can have my shotgun if you want it, mate," said Bam.

"I never want to see that bloody shotgun again as long as I live."

"Sorry."

"Stop saying sorry. It only makes things worse."

"Sorry."

"Oh bloody hell, Bam."

They stopped for another sip of water and for Jack to catch his breath. Ed's back was stiff from propping him up under his shoulder.

"How much farther now?" he asked. Since leaving the Oval they hadn't seen anyone else, and he was hoping their luck was going to hold out.

Jack sat down on a car hood and looked around. They were by Clapham Common tube station; ahead of them lay the wide expanse of the common itself. A pack of dogs was running across it barking, but otherwise there were no signs of life.

"Only about five minutes," Jack said. "Maybe ten if we keep going at this speed. We're nearly there."

They looked back the way they'd come. The column of smoke from the Oval had gone miles up into the sky and had spread out to mix with the smoke from the other, larger, fire.

"London's burning, London's burning," Jack sang quietly, and the others forced a laugh. It wasn't the funniest thing anyone had ever said, but it encouraged Ed that Jack could still try to make a joke. It gave him some small glimmer of hope that perhaps things weren't as bad as they seemed.

He was searching for something funny to say himself when he saw a movement in the distance.

Luckily, Bam still had his binoculars firmly around his neck.

"Bam, take a look through your binocs." Ed pointed down the road. "I think I saw someone moving about, just past the traffic lights."

Bam put the binoculars to his eyes and scanned the area.

"No . . . can't see anything. Oh, wait a minute. Yes, I think it's a man, just one, carrying something. But he's ducked out of sight. He's a long way away, though. I don't think we need worry about him if we keep moving."

"You're sure there was just one of them?"

"Well, I only saw one, but that doesn't mean anything. They usually go around in groups, don't they? I mean, as I say, we need to get a budge on."

They hoisted Jack onto his feet and turned back in the direction they were heading.

Jack spat out a harsh swear word and sagged in their arms.

There were about fifteen sickos coming across the common toward them. They were mostly fathers, but there were three or four particularly raddled-looking mothers. They'd managed to get close while the boys were distracted.

Too close.

Bam and Ed quickly picked up Jack and staggered over to a side road to get away.

"We can't outrun them," Jack croaked. "You'll kill me. Give me my gun, Ed."

"We can't fight them all," said Ed. "Not with you like this."

He looked back. The sickos were steadily gaining on them.

"Come on, Bam!" They tried to speed up, but it was no use. Jack cried out in pain.

"Stop! Stop! Just give me the gun."

"It's in my pack."

"Then give me yours. I'm too weak to use my sword."

"Jack, you're too weak to do anything."

"Give me the gun!"

"All right."

They stopped and propped Jack against a car.

Ed ripped the pistol from the holster at his waist and gave it to Jack. Bam turned, raised his shotgun. He hadn't thought to reload it since shooting Jack at the Oval—he'd been too distracted—but he was fairly sure he still had one shell ready in the barrel. He took aim, squeezed the trigger, and felt the gun kick against his aching shoulder.

The lead father fell back.

Jack was ready now. He pointed the pistol and fired. The gun sent a shockwave of pain down his arm as it jumped in his hand. The bullet completely missed its target.

Bam fumbled in his jacket pocket for more cartridges and discovered to his horror that the pocket was ripped and hanging half off. There was only one lone shell left.

Jack slid down the side of the car and sat with his back against it. This time he held the gun firmly with both hands and fired two shots in quick succession. The next sicko went down.

Bam broke his shotgun, slotted in his last shell, and fired again. A third father fell.

Then he was out of shells, and the sickos were on them.

Ed had backed away as the sickos advanced, so that he was behind Bam and Jack. He watched as a mother made a grab for Jack, who feebly tried to bat her away with his pistol. Bam charged into the rest of them with a war cry, his shotgun reversed in his hands like a club. He whacked three sickos aside, barging into a fourth one and knocking her flat. He continued past the group until he was well clear, then turned and came flying back, barreling through the sickos like a mad bull.

Ed didn't know what to do. It had all happened so quickly. The sickos had come from nowhere. For a few seconds he stood there, unable to move. The mother who had gone for Jack had been joined by a father. They had hold of him and were dragging him away. He was too weak to resist.

Bam had gone down in a tangle of bodies and was trying to stand up with three sickos on his back.

Ed closed his eyes. And then it was as if something broke inside him, a wire that been twisted tighter and tighter and tighter had finally snapped. A weird calmness settled over him. An emptiness.

He opened his eyes.

"No." He spoke softly, quietly. Then louder. "No."

Finally he screamed, "No!" and ran at the two sickos who had Jack. He shoved the mother aside, kicked the father in the stomach, and then punched him in the nose, splattering it across his diseased and pockmarked face. He kept moving and snatched up the fallen pistol before pulling Jack clear and dumping him behind a van for safety. He leaned down, checked that Jack was conscious, then put the pistol back into his hands and took hold of the handle of his sword.

"I need this," he said, pulling it from its scabbard.

As he straightened up, he saw the father with the flattened nose coming right at him, arms raised. Ed slashed wildly at him, and he went down in a spray of blood. One of the mothers was right behind. Again Ed chopped the sword through the air. The mother hissed and collapsed to her knees, clutching her bloody face.

Ed could hear a horrible screeching, keening sound, high and angry, like some huge, hungry bird of prey attacking.

He realized he was making the sound. He had a bloodlust on him, a killing frenzy. He was no longer thinking about what he was doing. He wasn't thinking about anything. He had become a mindless animal. Outside he was this yelling, screaming monster, and inside there was that weird calm, as if he had become two people, one acting, one watching.

And he somehow knew that he would never be the same

again. The blade rose and fell, rose and fell, glinting as it cut through the air.

Almost in slow motion, a father came at him, and Ed plunged the sword into his belly. The flesh sucked at the blade, holding it hard, and as Ed tried to pull it free, the father fell sideways and twisted it out of his grip.

Ed didn't stop; he ran to Bam and got hold of an attacking mother by the hair. He wrenched her head back so hard he felt something snap, and carried on, kicking, gouging, snarling at the sickos, prying them loose one by one and tossing them aside. At last Bam was up, scratched and bloody, but all right. Encouraged by Ed's efforts, he was off again, charging the sickos and crunching into them.

Ed heard a gunshot. Jack was fending off another attack. The sickos had evidently singled Jack out as being the easiest target. Ed ran over just as a fat young mother got to him. He took her by the face, digging his fingers in. Her skin was thick with boils, and blood and pus ran down her neck as she twisted and writhed and thrashed about.

Jack shot at a father who was getting too close, and Ed threw the mother hard against the van, knocking the fight out of her. Then he went back for the sword and at last managed to wrench it out of the dead father.

He turned, sword raised . . .

But it was all over.

There were only three sickos left now. Two big fathers and a teenager. They looked at the carnage and had enough sense to get away. As they hobbled off, Jack rolled out from behind the van and fired off another three shots, taking down the teenager.

Bam stood there jeering at the fathers as they retreated. He was exhausted, his clothes torn and spotted with blood, but there was a look of crazy joy on his face. "Yeah, you useless buggers!" he yelled. "Get lost! You can't take us! We owned you. We're kings of the streets!"

Ed whooped and grinned at Bam, who went into a Maori war dance.

"That was easy," said Ed, drunk with happiness and relief.

Bam stopped dancing and rested his hands on his knees, laughing too much to carry on.

"Come and help me with Jack," said Ed.

"Okay." Bam straightened up, and as he did so, another father stepped out from behind the hedge of somebody's front yard. Ed saw a flash as he swung his arm at the back of Bam's head.

Bam grunted and fell facedown on the pavement with a horrible thud.

It was Greg.

He held a bloody meat cleaver in one hand and a large bundle under his arm. There were blisters on his face, and his mouth was ringed with scarlet. There was a look of unthinking madness in his eyes.

He took a step toward Ed.

"Get out of the way!" Jack yelled, and Ed instinctively ducked to one side.

Jack aimed the pistol and pulled back hard on the trigger four times.

There were four pitiful clicks, like a child's cap gun, but nothing else.

"Ed?" Jack yelled. "I need more bullets!"

"They're all in my bag," Ed replied, but even as he said it, he knew there wasn't time to get at them. Greg was walking fast toward him, legs wide, the meat cleaver swinging in long vicious arcs.

Ed realized he still had the sword. He lunged at Greg but misjudged the distance. The tip of the blade raked across his chest, slitting open his jacket and shirt but doing little harm.

Greg didn't even pause. Just kept on coming.

He swiped wildly downward, and as Ed jumped back, he felt the cleaver swish past his cheek.

He felt a sudden weird attack of dizziness. His cheek felt hot and there was a sharp pain, like a wasp sting. He put his hand to his face. It was drenched with blood, and more blood was already pouring off his chin and onto his jacket.

Ed felt anger rise inside him, filling the emptiness. He moved in and lunged again. It was either luck or some kind of dumb reaction, but Greg managed to bring his cleaver up just in time. The sword hit it with a clang that jarred Ed's arm. The blade shattered, but knocked the cleaver to one side.

Ed didn't wait. He dropped the useless sword and ran at Greg. It was like running into a solid wall. Ed was winded. Somehow, though, he got Greg's wrist and held the cleaver at bay. Greg didn't seem to want to drop whatever he was carrying under his other arm, so with his free hand, Ed was able to go for his throat.

Up close, Greg stank like a sewer. His body felt hot and damp. His breath came straight from a slaughterhouse. He was breathing through his mouth, and pink-flecked saliva foamed at his lips.

He may have been sick, but he was still stronger than Ed, who was losing his grip on Greg's wrist.

Then Jack was with him, making a grab for the cleaver.

"No, Jack!" Ed yelled. "You're hurt. I can do this."

"It's all right," said Jack.

Just then, Greg's arm slipped out of Ed's hand and the cleaver came around. Jack gasped and fell back, but Greg was thrown off balance. Ed let go of his neck and slammed the heel of his palm into Greg's windpipe. Greg coughed and went limp, dropping his weapon. As he staggered backward, taking tiny, dainty steps, Ed scrabbled to pick up the fallen cleaver.

His fingers closed around the slippery handle and he twisted around to face Greg.

He was standing there, fighting for breath, wide open, an easy target.

Ed didn't have to think twice. The killing rage was on him again. He moved in. . . .

And then he saw what Greg was carrying under his arm—what had looked at first like the sort of pitiful bundle of rags that a street person would carry around.

Only it wasn't rags. It was a small dead body.

"Liam?" said Ed.

It was like a switch had been thrown in Greg's head. The madness was gone, and for a moment he was human again. He looked down at the creased, purple face of his son and wailed in horror.

Then he looked at Ed, shook his head, and ran off down the road toward the common.

Ed ran a few paces after him, then stopped. He wanted

to follow him, to try to finish it, but he couldn't leave his friends. There might be other sickos around.

He went back. Jack was lying curled up into a ball, clutching his stomach. But, thank God, he was still alive. Ed knelt down and put a hand to him.

"Jack?"

"He cut me, Ed. He cut me open."

"I'll get you home."

"Don't worry," Jack grunted. "Too stubborn to die, remember? But how's that big idiot Bam? Is he okay? I want to tell him I don't blame him. It wasn't his fault."

Ed went over to Bam. It was no good. It was all crap. There were no happy endings. Nobody watching over them. Only misery and struggle. And what for? Good people died as well as bad.

Greg's cleaver had split open the back of Bam's skull.

He was gone.

Ed sat down in the middle of the road and wept.

54

Jack was unconscious. He felt as heavy as two people, and Ed could hardly put one foot in front of the other as he staggered down the road with his friend on his shoulder. He'd figured the best thing would be to deal with Jack's wounds when they reached the relative safety of his house. It was too dangerous to stay out on the streets. It would be growing dark soon, and then the sickos would emerge from their hiding places and go hunting for food.

It had been fine at first. He'd managed to coax Jack back onto his feet, promising all the while that he would get him safely home, reassuring him, encouraging him, until eventually Jack had started walking.

He'd been reasonably cheerful when they set off. He was able to talk, and, although clumsy and weak, he could at least hold himself upright, but he'd gradually become vague and confused, and finally he'd slumped against Ed, his feet dragging along the road. Now Ed was just pulling him along. He'd tried slapping him and yelling at him like they did in films, but it didn't seem to do anything. Luckily, Jack had given him pretty clear directions and an address before they'd set off again, but the journey seemed to be never ending.

Ed was really scared.

Jack's clothes were stained black from the bleeding, and his wounds were starting to smell. Ed's hand around his ribs was slick with blood. He worried that holding him like this was tearing him open, but he had no choice.

If they were attacked now, he doubted he could do much to defend his friend. He'd reloaded his pistol, and it dangled from his other hand, growing heavier with each step. He longed to shove it back in its holster, or even throw it aside, but he knew he had to keep hold of it. It might be the only thing between him and a horrible death.

He came to a junction and checked the street names.

Thank God.

They were there at last. A typically English street of semi-detached houses with pointy roofs, white painted porches with balconies over the top, and once-neat little front gardens behind low stone walls.

"Come on, Jack," he panted. "Help me. You're nearly home. Just take a step, yeah?"

Now that the end was in sight, Ed felt more exhausted than ever. This final leg was going to be the hardest. If only Jack would wake up and help him.

"Look, this is your street," he said. "That's your house up ahead. . . . Come on, I'm not sure I can do this. . . . Jack, walk, please walk, don't give up on me. They'll all be waiting for you. Your sisters, your mom and dad, they're all there. I can see them at the door, waving, calling to you; come on, Jack, do it for them."

Something inside Jack's brain must have been functioning, because he groaned, and Ed felt him stirring in his arms. Then his feet no longer dragged. They searched for a footing, took a step, then another. He was weak and uncoordinated, but he was walking again.

Ed laughed and cried at the same time.

"That's it. Come on, Jack, that's it." He looked at the house numbers as they passed. 67, 65, 63, 61 . . . Only another thirty to go. No, less, because this was the odd-numbered side of the street. Fifteen houses, fourteen . . .

He looked round at Jack. His eyes were open, rolling in his head, but he was struggling to focus. He recognized the street.

"You see," said Ed. "I told you I'd get you home. You can lie in your own bed again."

49, 47, 45, 43 . . .

They were going unbearably slowly, but they were still moving. Ed had all but forgotten his own wound, where Greg's cleaver had sliced his face open. There hadn't been time to do anything more than press a load of tissues against the cut. It was only when he put his hand up to wipe the sweat from his eyes that he felt the wad of paper still stuck there on the dried blood. As he tried to pull them away, it sent a flash of pain through his head.

It was nothing, he told himself, compared to Jack's wounds.

35, 33, 31 . . .

They were there at last. Ed looked up at the house. The same as all the others. The cars parked outside in the road told him that this was an expensive street, though the houses weren't that big.

He dragged Jack up the front steps and let him flop down

on the porch. He gently felt Jack's neck and took hold of the bootlace, then fished the key out. He lifted it over Jack's head and slipped the key into the lock. The door clicked open. It all felt so normal and familiar.

He put the key back over Jack's heart and then bent down to lift him up. It was the hardest thing he'd ever done. Jack wasn't helping, and Ed was very nearly done for. His back felt like it was going to snap. Somehow, though, he managed to haul his friend up and in through the door, which he kicked shut behind him. It was dark inside without electricity and with the windows covered in grime. There was just enough light to show that the house hadn't been looted or trashed by anyone. It smelled stale and slightly rotten, but otherwise Ed might have simply been entering a locked-up house after a long holiday. His mom and dad had taken him to Australia for a month one Christmas to visit a cousin, and when they'd gotten back, the house had felt all stuffy and kind of dead.

He pushed past a bike in the hallway, dumped Jack on the sofa in the sitting room, and took a quick look around. There were two photos on the mantelpiece of Jack and his family; one was just him and his sisters, the other was of the whole family, standing smartly dressed in a big garden, maybe at a wedding. There was Jack, looking shy and awkward. He'd never liked having his photo taken. And there were his mom and dad, just as Ed remembered them from the couple of times they'd met. His father wearing glasses, a bit bald, but with a nice open face and broad grin. His mom, small and thin, a little tired-looking, her smile slightly strained.

Both dead now, probably.

And as for Jack's sisters? What was the chance that either

of them would still be alive? Not his older sister. That was for sure. She would have been over sixteen when the disease broke out. Not necessarily dead, though, he supposed. Maybe just sick. Her pretty face covered in boils, her skin peeling . . .

Ed went into the kitchen. He opened the fridge; inside was a putrid mass of green mold and fungus. He went through all the kitchen cabinets. Apart from pots and pans and plates, they were empty. Anything edible was long gone.

In a cupboard under the stairs, though, full of mops and brushes and a Hoover, he found a cardboard box hidden at the back, stuffed with cans.

Jack's folks must have stashed it away there. Ed pulled it out with a wild excited cry of triumph. Peaches, tomatoes, spaghetti hoops, frankfurters, meatballs, chickpeas, fava beans. Ed realized he was actually drooling. He'd not had anything to eat since breakfast, and that hadn't been much to write home about. They'd left the truck in such a hurry, none of them had thought to stock up on food.

He opened a can of peaches and drained the liquid greedily before stuffing some of the fruit into his mouth.

What was he thinking? This wasn't his food.

He raced in to tell Jack the good news. He found him at the mantelpiece, holding the family photograph, tears streaming down his face. Ed put an arm around him and hugged him, and Jack hugged him back.

"Why is this happening, Ed?"

"Don't think about that," Ed whispered into his ear. "I've found some food, mate."

Jack feebly pushed him away, nodded, smiled. Ed slotted a peach slice between his lips, and Jack's whole face lit up like a little kid given ice cream. He worked his jaws, dripping juice and bits of peach down his front.

"I feel like someone in a cartoon," he said. "You know, when they've been shot and they drink a glass of water and it all spurts out of little holes all over them." He tried to laugh, but it hurt him too much, and Ed helped him back to the sofa.

"I need to look at you again," Ed said. "I need to sort out whatever Greg did to you and put some clean bandages on."

"Where's Bam?"

Ed didn't know what to say, whether he should protect his friend. He felt numb and blank.

In the end he simply said, "Bam's dead."

Jack just said, "Oh," and closed his eyes. The conversation had worn him out, and his brief rally was over.

Ed lifted his shirt, dreading what he would find. It was awful. Greg's cleaver had sliced through the original bandages just below Jack's ribs. It was impossible to tell how deep the wound was without prodding and probing and risking making it worse. Instead he set to with antiseptic and did what he could with the bandages, but he was no nurse.

When he was done, he gave Jack some water and some more peaches. It seemed to revive him a little, and he summoned the strength to speak. Although it was only one word.

"Bedroom."

"Come on, then."

Ed once again took Jack on his aching shoulder, and they stumbled awkwardly across the room, back out into the hallway, and over to the foot of the stairs.

"D'you think you can make it up?" Ed asked. Jack nodded and took hold of the banister.

Up they went, step by agonizing step, Jack growing weaker all the way. They made it eventually, though. How long had it taken? Half an hour? An hour? Ed had no real sense of time anymore. It was still light outside, though, so it couldn't be that late.

When they reached the landing, Jack was almost passed out again, and Ed had to look around for any clues as to which might be the door to his room. One of them had a KEEP OUT sign on it with a skull and crossbones dripping blood. How old had Jack been when he'd put it there, Ed wondered. For it must surely be Jack's room. It wasn't the sort of sign girls put up. He must have been maybe ten, younger even. Parents liked to hang on to ancient things.

They groped their way along to the door, and Ed pushed it open. A thin layer of dust covered everything, but otherwise the room looked untouched.

There was a narrow single bed along one wall, with a dark blue spread on it. Above the bed was an old poster for *Casino Royale*; one corner had come away and was hanging down, a flattened lump of putty stuck to it. Ed lowered Jack onto the bed and, without thinking, pushed the corner of the poster back up so that it stuck to the wall.

He sat next to Jack and took in the rest of the room. It was a typical boy's bedroom. There was a little desk and a bookshelf. Old books mostly. Jack had been at boarding school for the last couple of years. There was Harry Potter, Alex Rider, Melvin Burgess, Robert Muchamore. A stack of comics sat on the floor, a Marvel Zombies on the top. Ed recognized the Kev Walker cover. He'd read that one. Enjoyed it. On either side of the door were a poster of Lady Gaga and a framed print of a piece of Banksy graffiti—the two guys from *Pulp Fiction* with bananas instead of guns. There was a shelf of trophies near the window, for football and cricket and swimming, even one for trampolining. And there—Ed's heart snagged against his ribs—a photograph of the two of them, Jack and Ed, taken after the school team won a football tournament in Holland. Ed stood up and went over to take a closer look. He remembered clearly when it had been taken. It was two years ago; they would both have been twelve. They looked so young, another lifetime. Ed had long hair back then. Jack was happy and relaxed. The two of them stood with their arms around each other's shoulders, smiling straight at the camera, not a worry in the world.

As Ed was studying the photograph, he caught sight of a face reflected in the glass of the frame, and he spun around in fright, thinking he'd seen the face of a sicko.

Idiot. Jumpy idiot. Not a sicko.

There was a closet across the room with a mirror in the door. He went to it, hardly daring to look.

No wonder he'd mistaken himself for a sicko.

The boy who stood looking back at him was in a sorry state. Covered in blood, his face pale and plastered with soot and ash. Most of the tissue had fallen off his cheek, but a few crusty black scraps remained, stuck to a long gash that was mostly scabbed over, but still bled in a couple of spots. His left eye was bruised and swollen shut. His right eye was ringed with dark purple.

The young fresh-faced boy in the photo might have been a different person.

He went back over to Jack, who was lying on his back,

his eyes closed, his breathing shallow. Already the bedspread was darkening around him where his blood was soaking into it. He was shivering.

And then Ed remembered something.

There was a toy box in the corner. He lifted the lid and rifled through it. It was full of Legos, and old Action Men with no heads and arms. There were also bits of Bionicle and some half-painted Warhammer figures. Nearer the bottom were some plastic zoo animals. But no stuffed toys.

He closed the lid and looked around the room. A battered cardboard box sat on top of the wardrobe. He pulled it down, his shoulders screaming.

It was full of cuddly toys—a duck, a cow, three teddies, a snake—and there . . . a dog, with long floppy ears and a silly smile. One of the ears was worn away almost to nothing.

Floppy Dog.

He took it over to Jack and put it in his hands. Immediately, Jack's fingers found the frayed ear and started to rub at it.

Ed lay down next to his friend and put his arm around him. Jack felt very cold and still.

"Are you awake?"

"Yes," Jack whispered, barely making a sound.

"You're home, mate," said Ed. "In your own bed."

"I know. It's good. There's nothing like your own bed, is there? It doesn't hurt anymore, you know. I think I'm getting better."

"Yeah."

"When I was little . . . I wish I was little again . . ." Jack was finding it hard to speak. "At primary school. Nothing seemed to matter then. Everything was easy. There was nothing to worry about. Except when I had to cram to do the entrance exams for Rowhurst, but even that . . . It seems, as you get older, there's just more and more to worry about. I wish I was at home with Mom."

"You are home, Jack."

"Oh yes . . ." Jack opened his eyes and looked at his old toy. "Yay, Floppy Dog," he said, then closed his eyes again. "Is it all over now, Ed? Is it safe?"

"Yeah. It's safe, mate. We'll be safe now. In the morning we'll get up and have some breakfast, then go down to the shops—maybe they'll be open again. And then . . ."

"It's all right, Ed. You don't have to."

"Okay."

"You know, Ed, I'm sorry I ever called you a coward. You're not a coward. You're brave. You're really brave. You got me home. You didn't leave me. You're my best friend, Ed."

"And you're my best friend, Jack; you always will be."

"Thanks."

Neither of them said anything else. They didn't need to. There was nothing more to say. Ed watched the square of sky at the window as it faded to pink, then gray, then dark blue, then black. There was no moon tonight, but the sky was splashed with millions of bright stars, more than Ed had ever seen before. He pictured himself flying up out of the little room, up on into the night sky, and then out into the solar system, past the planets and out into the endless reaches of space. The two of them lying here, alone in the empty house, didn't really matter very much, did they?

55

Brooke, Courtney, and Aleisha lay squashed together on a couple of mattresses in the 1940's house. They could hear Froggie whimpering. Luckily, Frédérique's teeth hadn't broken through the sleeve of his sweater and drawn blood, but he had a nasty purple bruise in the perfect shape of her jaws, as if he'd been bitten by a miniature shark, and he was really upset by the incident. It was the shock more than the pain that was making him cry now. For a little while they'd all felt safe. Happy. Not anymore. They knew that an attack could come from anywhere at any time.

The girls couldn't get the image out of their minds—Frédérique, with her teeth clamped on the little boy's arm, not letting go, her long hair falling about her face. The other kids milling about shrieking and yelling, nobody knowing what to do. In the end, Jordan Hordern had rescued Froggie. He'd come down from the upper floor, calmly walked over to Frédérique, and chopped her in the side of the neck with his hand.

DogNut and Jordan had then taken her limp body away.

"Is that gonna happen to the rest of us?" Aleisha asked, staring at the flickering night-light, glad of the warmth of her two friends on either side of her.

"Don't think about it," said Brooke. "Get some sleep."

"I can't. Whenever I close my eyes, all I can, like, see is *her*, coming at me, like a witch, saying all this, like, French stuff, like *bonjour*, *mercy*, *Moulin Rouge*...."

"French is a stupid language," said Courtney, "and France is a dump."

"Don't be scared of her," said Brooke. "She's locked up. She can't hurt you now."

"What if she gets out, comes creeping through the museum? I don't like it here."

"I always found her creepy," said Courtney. "I never trusted her. I had, like, a what you call it, sick sense."

"You was just *jealous*," said Brooke.

"Wha-aat?"

"Yeah, because she's, like, thin, and you're, like, fat."

"Bro-ooke!" said Alesiha, appalled. "What you saying? You didn't ought to say things like that."

"Yeah," said Courtney. "I ain't fat. I'm big."

"Yeah, big and fat." Brooke gave a snort of laughter. "I don't know how you do it, girl, with what we get to eat. You're like that fat guy in *Lost*, Hurley. Crashes a plane on a, like, desert island, where there's no McDonald's or nothing, and doesn't get any thinner after, like, *weeks*."

"I ain't fat, Brooke!"

Brooke laughed and leaned over Aleisha to give Courtney a little squeeze.

"I don't love you any less because you're XL, girl. You

are who you are. My mate. I don't care what you look like. I'm just saying you didn't like Lady Ooh-La-La because she's skinny. Ain't that right?"

"No," said Courtney. "I don't like Frédérique because she's a sicko who tried to eat Froggie."

"Can we talk about something else?" said Aleisha. "It's freaking me out. I don't feel safe no more. The sooner the boys get back, the better."

56

When Ed woke, there was light in the sky. For a long while he didn't move. His whole body was stiff and chilly, gripped by a knotted web of aches and pains. At last he gently untangled his arm out from under Jack's head and then very carefully closed Jack's eyelids. Jack's skin was completely cold now, except for the strip along his side where Ed's body had been pressed against him.

"Good-bye, mate," said Ed, but he had no more tears inside him.

At least Jack had died happy, at home, in his own bed, among his old familiar things. He looked very peaceful, lying there with his old dog for company.

Ed hoisted himself up off the mattress and stood on the carpet, trying to stretch some of the stiffness away. When he felt strong enough, he went down into the kitchen and looked out at the garden. The plants were shaking and bending in a strong wind. Shrubs and nettles and brambles and weeds were being tossed about as if some giant hand were stirring them.

It was morning, but still gloomy. The dark smoke cloud now filled most of the sky, and there was the red glow of fire nearby. He could smell the smoke. It reminded him of when they'd broken into the church and found Mad Matt and the others passed out.

How long ago was that? It felt like weeks. But it wasn't, was it? It had only been three days.

He coughed. He would have to hurry. The fire was obviously blowing closer. There was a row of books on a dresser. He scanned the titles. They were cookbooks mostly, but he was searching for something that you could be pretty sure of finding in every house in London. An *A to Z*.

There!

He pulled it out. It was filled with maps of all the streets in London. He looked up Jack's address and followed the route back to the Imperial War Museum with his finger. He checked it and rechecked it, memorizing street names. Once he was sure of what he was doing, he slipped the *A to Z* into his back pocket and then went over to one of the drawers he'd looked through last night and fished out a box of matches. Finally he grabbed a cookbook at random, then went back upstairs.

He opened Jack's bedroom window and looked out onto the road. The wind was blowing trash along, but there was no sign of any people out and about. Before he'd finally fallen asleep last night, he'd heard them, the sickos who came out after dark, wandering the streets, fighting, looking for food, but none had come near the house.

He tore a handful of pages from the cookbook, balled them up, and put them under Jack's bed. Then he packed in anything else he could find that would burn—more books, comics, teddies, clothes—and set it all alight with a couple of matches. In a few moments there was a blaze going and the room was filling with smoke.

"See you, Jack," he said. He tucked Floppy Dog into his friend's arms, kissed him on the forehead, and went out.

He ran down the stairs, stuffed as much food as he could carry into his pack, shoved his pistol into its holster, grabbed the bike from the hallway, then opened the front door and went out into the street. He looked up at the house. Already Jack's bedroom was filled with flames, and smoke was pouring out of the open window.

At least Jack wouldn't be found by any scavengers.

Ed turned away, got on the bike, and started pedaling.

57

Frédérique was humming softly to herself. A familiar tune, but she couldn't remember the name of it, or the words. Papa used to sing it to her when she was a little girl. She felt calmer now, out of the light. She was wrapped in darkness, and it meant she could think clearly. The light punched your brain. It hurt. The darkness was kind and gentle, like . . .

She moaned and pushed her fingers through her hair. All across her scalp there were lumps and bumps. It was as if her brain were expanding, forcing these new growths out of her head. If she concentrated really hard as she ran her fingertips over them, she could read them like Braille, all the thoughts coming out of her head. . . .

She would think of a way to escape from where they had trapped her. She would get away and punish them for what they had done to her.

The first thing she had to do was work out how to get

her hands free of these things they'd clamped around them, these bracelets, these *menottes*.

She'd figure it out.

She was clever now.

Cleverer than them . . .

58

E d couldn't get the reek of smoke out of his nostrils. It was everywhere, blown on a hot wind. It stung his eyes so that he wept as he cycled. He felt itchy under his skin. On edge. There was a weird, tense atmosphere to the day, as if the world had been screwed up tight. Everything felt wrong. It was dark when it should have been light, so that it was somehow day and night at the same time. The wind tugged at him like an annoying child, making him jumpy. He had every reason to be nervous. The events of yesterday had really shaken him up, and he'd lost two good friends.

His last friends.

It looked like today wasn't going to be any easier. The empty street he'd seen from Jack's window had given false hope. There were more sickos out on the streets than he'd ever seen. They were everywhere, spooked as badly by the approaching fire as he was. He expected to be attacked again any minute.

He had a dreadful feeling of hopeless doom he'd never known before. The dark sky seemed to press down on him with an awful heaviness. The sky was a lid, slowly closing, suffocating the world, trapping the smoke and the fire and wind. He was reminded of all those myths and legends where the sky was a solid thing that had to be held up. There was a giant, wasn't there, who lifted it on his shoulders?

Atlas. That was it. Atlas holding the sky up.

Well, it felt like Atlas had fallen.

He cycled as fast as he could, but it wasn't easy. The roads were blocked everywhere by abandoned vehicles and he had to keep swerving around them. It hadn't been so noticeable yesterday when they were walking, but riding a bike was different. You were aware of every bump and hole and obstruction. Driving a car would have been nearly impossible.

In fact, every now and then he would come to a car that had been set on fire and was now reduced to a pile of twisted metal and plastic. There was other debris as well, strewn everywhere, trash and cans and dead bodies, occasionally a row of burned-out buildings that had collapsed. He longed for an open stretch, but he had resigned himself to the fact that it wasn't going to happen.

He had already had to change the route he'd planned. The area around the Oval was an inferno. The flames had rapidly spread to the surrounding buildings, so that there were now two big fires that threatened to link up and engulf the whole of South London. He had to stop every couple of minutes to check the *A to Z* and adjust his plans based on which roads he felt were safe to ride down.

The sickos didn't help either. There seemed to be gangs of them whichever way he went, standing in the road looking up at the sky, or just wandering aimlessly. Once he had to make a detour around a small group of them who were fighting like drunks, the sort of addled street people you used to see in the cities, arguing with each other and throwing clumsy punches.

He kept moving, though, and in his roundabout way he was getting gradually closer to the museum and safety. He just wished his heart wasn't beating so hard against his ribs and his breathing wasn't so quick and painful.

As he rode, images flashed through his mind, switching back and forth. Jack and Bam, alive and laughing. Bam doing his Maori war dance. And then Bam lying in the gutter, cold and still, and Jack in his bed holding Floppy Dog. The living and the dead.

The dead.

All those bodies at the Oval. The red fountain of flesh rising over them when the first canister went off. He wondered how many other sites there were around London like that, stacked with corpses. He knew a lot of people had left the city when the disease had started killing people. He'd seen it on the news—traffic jams miles and miles long. Those were some of the last images they'd shown on television before it went off the air. It had all happened so fast.

Ed tried to picture the rest of the world like this, falling into chaos and ruin. The numberless dead bodies everywhere. And, worse, the living. Zombies. Stranded between life and death. He remembered the sensation of being pressed up against Greg. The stink of him, the heat and the damp. The craziness in his eyes. Struggling over the meat cleaver . . .

And Greg was still out there somewhere.

With poor little Liam.

He told himself to just concentrate on the road and not dwell on anything else. But try as he might, he couldn't get those images out of his head.

What was it about Greg?

There was something more. Something worse.

When Ed had looked into his eyes, seen the madness there, he'd recognized something, and now he understood what it was. They were the same, the two of them; they'd both been helpless in the grip of a killing frenzy. When Ed had found his courage yesterday, he'd lost something precious in the bargain. He'd lost part of what made him human.

He was a different person now, and not a better one. Oh, he could fight, he could swat sickos like flies; he was a bloody hero, wasn't he? He was Death himself. Riding a bike. But in the end, all he was doing was adding to the score of the dead.

Was that all a hero was, then? A killing machine without a heart?

Stop it, Ed. Stop thinking. Keep pedaling, keep those wheels turning. Get back to the museum. See the others. Your new friends.

That would help fight the sadness and blow away the darkness inside him that was spreading, suffocating him like the black clouds in the sky.

Jack lying there on the bed, cold and still with Floppy Dog in his arms.

Pedal. Just pedal. These tears are because of the smoke. . . .

Concentrate on the living. Justin the truck-driving nerd and the little kids in his Brain Trust, mouthy Brooke and the girls, big Courtney and little Aleisha, strange Chris Marker with his face in a book, even Mad Matt and his acolytes. He missed them all.

And don't forget Jordan Hordern and DogNut and Frédérique. . . .

God. Frédérique. What was he going to tell her? She really liked Jack. She'd come to rely on him. How could he break the news to her? She was most likely going to be tipped deeper into her own sadness.

Ed wasn't used to giving people bad news. Up until a few weeks ago there hadn't really *been* anything bad in his life. Bad news was something that adults had to deal with. Not kids. Oh, yeah, he'd had a mate whose mom had died in a road accident. The boy had left school. But it hadn't really touched Ed. He'd soon forgotten about it. Now the sickness had forced them all to behave like adults. To take on adults' worries and responsibilities.

He stopped.

The way ahead was completely blocked.

He'd come to a railway bridge where there had been a train crash. Something had derailed an engine and it had tumbled off the bridge, dragging the lead cars behind it and half demolishing the structure. There was a pile of mangled metal and bricks in the road. Two cranes stood nearby, next to several emergency vehicles, and there were bodies under tarps, a few more still on the train. They'd all just been left there. Abandoned.

No, not completely abandoned. Now that Ed looked closer, he saw a bunch of sickos squatting down, eating a corpse.

They hadn't spotted him yet, but he'd obviously have to go a different way. He checked his options and saw that more sickos were approaching from the direction he'd come. The only other route was along a side road that branched off at a right angle, but that, too, was busy with people.

He had to get off the street. He made a quick decision and darted into the front yard of one of the houses that lined the road. He dumped his bike behind the hedge. Even if any of the sickos did find it, they wouldn't know what to do with it. Keeping low, he checked out the building. Steps led up to the front door. If he went up them, though, he'd risk being seen. There was a wide bay window on the raised ground floor, and beneath that a narrow basement window that overlooked a sort of shallow well below the level of the yard.

That would have to do.

He crawled over to it. It looked just big enough for him to fit through if he could get it open. He turned around, dropped onto his belly, and kicked out a pane of glass, hoping the sickos wouldn't be attracted by the noise. Then he slithered down into the well, reached through the broken section, and lifted the latch. In a few seconds he had swung the window up and was crawling through the opening feetfirst.

He lowered himself down until he was on solid ground, then quickly took up a position from where he could see out the corner of the window.

Sickos were passing on the street. Luckily, none of them made a detour into the front yard. He'd gotten away with it. All he had to do now was sit it out until the coast was clear.

He pulled his pistol out of its holster and rested against the wall, nose close to the glass. For the moment he was safe. He could rest, recharge his batteries, which were being drained by the constant stress. He was so tired all the time.

He closed his eyes and let out his breath in a long sigh. Then froze. There was an answering sigh. Then the sound of movement behind him. He hadn't checked out the room when he'd climbed in backward. It had been dark, and he'd been concentrating on what was going on outside.

Slowly he turned around, hardly daring to look. There was just enough light from the broken window to show him that he was in a large basement kitchen.

And it was filled with people.

They were lying on the floor, packed together, too many to count. Sickos. Hiding from the daylight. And they were starting to wake up, blinking in the gloom. The smell of smoke in the air had masked their stink, but now Ed became aware of it. A horrible toilet smell. And he could feel the heat coming off them. The one nearest to him belched and sat up, sniffing. He reached out toward Ed's leg, and Ed kicked him away. That caused a commotion, and soon a gaggle of them were struggling to their feet.

Ed thought about trying to climb back out of the window, but all the sickos around him were awake and clawing at his clothes now. They'd pull him down before he could get halfway.

To the right, about fifteen feet away, there was a staircase leading up to the next floor. Ed shoved a tall pockmarked father aside and set off toward it. A mother stood up, barring his way, and without thinking, Ed put the pistol to her chest and pulled the trigger. The bang startled all the other sickos in the room, and for a moment they stopped. Ed seized his chance and ran for it, barging through the few remaining adults who blocked his path.

He raced up the stairs and crashed through the door at the top into the hallway. He kept on moving until he reached the front door, then started fumbling with the various locks and chains that secured it. The sickos were evidently using some other way to get in and out of the house, but he didn't have time to look for it. He could hear them coming up the stairs, their feet thudding on the wooden steps, their arms brushing against the walls. The last lock didn't want to open, though; he obviously needed a key. He pulled at it and swore at it and battered the door violently.

"Come on!"

It made no difference. He was stuck here.

He turned around and fired off a shot at the lead sicko, who tumbled backward. And then he had an idea.

In how many movies had he seen it done?

Did it really work?

He aimed his gun at the lock and pulled the trigger three times.

The hallway was instantly full of flying bits of metal and splintered wood. A piece took a chunk out of his neck, but he hardy felt it.

He tugged the handle, the remains of the lock fell away with a clatter, and the door swung open.

To hell with what was out there—anything was better than being trapped inside with a bunch of them. He leapt down the front steps, holstered his pistol, grabbed the bike, and charged out into the street.

There must have been twenty or thirty sickos, stretched right down the length of the road. They were a bad bunch, far gone, walking corpses, rotten and confused. But they were still a threat.

The side road was about a hundred yards away. If Ed was

quick, he might just make it. The sickos weren't in a pack. They were mostly in ones and twos. There was a chance he could get around them.

He got back into the saddle and stood on the pedals, swerving around a couple of warty-looking mothers, then careered through the middle of another group. He ignored two ancient fathers with no hair or teeth who flailed at him with stick-thin arms as he passed. The side road was approaching fast. He leaned into the curve and pedaled hard.

But as he turned the corner, he saw nothing but more sickos, packed into this much narrower space. He skidded to a halt and thought about turning around. But the sickos from the main road were filtering down this way now. He was trapped.

59

If Ed had just kept on pedaling when he'd first rounded the corner, he might have been able to smash his way through the lurking sickos, but he'd waited too long now. They were bunching into a mob. There was nowhere to go in either direction.

He dismounted and drew his pistol. Maybe he could just blast his way through? He was using up a lot of his ammunition. He'd wanted to save his bullets for an emergency.

Hell, whichever way you looked at it, this *was* an emergency.

He fired, keeping his arm as straight and steady as he could. Then fired again. And again. All the while wheeling his bike forward. His aim wasn't brilliant. He clipped two of them, though, and the others stood there, not sure what to do. Not sure what was happening.

Ed kept on walking and firing, his bike acting as a shield to his left. How many bullets in a clip? Ten? Twenty? What would he do when he ran out?

He swore at the sickos.

Although he was moving, he was really only getting deeper and deeper into the heart of the mob. They were closing in behind him as he passed, waiting for their moment. For when the shooting stopped.

At last the gun clicked empty, and Ed reckoned it was all over.

He swore again. Wished he had another weapon. Hated it to end like this.

And then he saw an extraordinary sight. A column of schoolboys wearing red blazers and carrying clubs, marching in step down the road, with packs on their backs. Like a unit off to fight in the Napoleonic Wars.

The column was two wide and maybe ten deep. The boy at their head, with jet-black hair and chalk white skin sprayed with freckles, was shouting orders. The boys stayed in formation, and as they reached the rear of the bunched-up sickos, they started to lash out and hack their way through to Ed.

Using his bike as a battering ram, Ed forced his way toward them.

"This way!" called the boy at their head, pointing to a walkway between two rows of houses. Ed hurried, shoving sickos away to either side. When he got to them, the boys closed ranks around him, forming a protective wall. Then, still keeping their discipline, they backed down the walkway, leaving the confused sickos behind.

The boys followed the walkway through a small housing estate, clubbing a few stray sickos as they went, and soon found their way onto a relatively clear street, where they stopped to get their bearings.

Ed was so relieved and amazed and confused he didn't know what to say. In the end all he managed was a pathetic "Thanks."

"We heard gunshots," said the boys' leader. "And we know that strangers can't use them."

"Strangers?"

"That's what we call the people with the disease. I suppose everyone calls them something different."

"Why strangers?"

"We were always taught to be careful of strangers."

"Stranger danger?" said Ed.

"Exactly."

Ed looked at the boys, who were staring at him in silence. "Where the hell did you all come from, anyway?" he asked.

"We're from St. Hilda's in Surrey," said the leader.

"St. Hilda's school?" Ed grinned, which sent a spasm of pain up his wounded cheek. "I know St. H. We used to play you lot at rugby. *And* football. I'm from Rowhurst."

"Rowhurst? God, I know you buggers!" Another boy stepped forward, a big keen-looking guy with fluffy hair, his shirt collar turned up and sticking out of the top of his sweater.

"You're a Rowie, are you?" he went on. "We came over in the autumn term. Good game too. You had a killer prop forward. Guy called Bam. Do you know him?"

"Of course!" Ed cried excitedly, and then a twinge of sadness got him and he bit his lip.

"What about Johnno?" said the St. Hilda's boy. "Piers?"

"I know them all," said Ed quietly.

"Are they with you?"

"No," said Ed. "They *were*. They . . ."

A lump formed in his throat, stopping him from saying anything else. The boy obviously got it, though, and didn't press Ed any further.

"Bad luck." He stuck out his hand. "I'm Pod, by the way. What's your name?"

"Ed Carter."

"Pleased to meet you, Ed."

"Ed Carter?" A boy with a big nose jostled to the front of the crowd. "I know you. Andy Thomas," he said, patting his chest. "I remember you from the football team."

"Yeah, hi," said Ed, smiling at Andy, although in truth he couldn't remember him at all.

"You all right? That looks bad," said Andy, pointing to Ed's cheek.

Ed shrugged. "I think it *is* bad," he said.

"So, are you just wandering the streets, or do you have a safe place to go?" said the boys' leader.

"Safe place," said Ed. "I was trying to get there. The Imperial War Museum, actually."

The leader looked interested. "Could you take us there?"

"I could," said Ed, "but I'm not in charge. The guy who runs the place is . . . well, he's not very welcoming. He's got a good setup and he doesn't want to spoil it. He doesn't really want any newbies."

"I'll deal with that when we get there," the boy said confidently. "I'm David, by the way, David King. I was head of the junior school at St. Hilda's. Now, shall we get going?"

"Sure." Ed dug out his *A to Z* and checked it quickly. The museum was much nearer than he'd realized.

They set off, Ed wheeling his bike at the head of the column with David. There were black ashes blowing in the wind, which had grown even fiercer and hotter. Ed had to raise his voice to be heard over the noise of it. "Have you walked all the way from your school?" he asked.

"Yes. There were quite a lot more of us when we started."

Ed looked around at the matching red blazers. "You haven't picked up anyone else on the way?"

David smiled. "Your chap who runs the museum," he said, "he's got the right idea. Look after your own. May I see your gun?"

"Sure." Ed passed it to him.

"A gun is a very valuable thing," said David, weighing it in his hand.

"You're telling me."

Ed looked at David. He had a very serious, slightly snooty expression. It was quite funny in a way, on a boy his age, but Ed knew better than to laugh at him. "I get it," he said, a note of amusement in his voice. "You weren't trying to rescue me, you were trying to rescue the gun!"

"Something like that," said David. "But now you can help us at the War Museum, so it's worked out quite well all around, really, hasn't it? We can get you there safely, and you can get us in."

"I'll try," said Ed. "But there may be certain conditions."

"I'm good at negotiating." David sounded very sure of himself.

"Yeah?"

"Yes. I suppose, really, I should keep this as a reward for saving your life."

David aimed the pistol at him. Ed smiled, not sure if David was being playful, but giving him the benefit of the doubt.

"I went through a lot to get that gun." Ed kept his voice flat and calm. "So I'm afraid I'm not going to give it up." He gently took the gun from David and put it in his holster. "You can have this bike instead, though, if you want."

"No thanks," said David. "I could have shot you then, you know?" he added.

"No you couldn't," said Ed, forcing another smile, though it badly hurt his face. "It's not loaded."

60

"You've got to come and see this." DogNut was standing at the main doors, looking out at the open ground in front of the museum. "It's the bloody red army."

The boy who was on guard duty came over to join him, and he laughed at what was going on outside.

David was marching up the pathway at the head of his column with Ed at his side. The St. Hilda's boys were keeping in perfect step and singing as they went.

The column marched right up to the doors, Ed's bike bumping up the steps.

"Hey!" Ed called out. "Open up! It's me."

DogNut came out to meet him. "Where'd you pick this lot up, brother?" he asked. "You got yourself an escort?"

"I needed one."

DogNut looked at Ed's ruined face with a pained expression. "Yow," he said. "You want to get that seen to."

"Yeah, I will," said Ed, moving toward the doors. "Let's go inside. I need to sit down."

DogNut put up a hand. "You know Jordan's rules," he

said, and nodded toward David and the others. "They can't come in."

"Oh, don't be so silly," said David, and before DogNut could do anything, he pushed past him and took his boys inside.

DogNut turned to Ed, looking panicked. "Ed!"

"I'm not responsible for them, DogNut."

"You brought them here."

"Had no choice, really."

"Hold up." DogNut looked puzzled. "Where's Jack and Bam? Ain't they with you?"

Ed followed David inside. "No," he said bluntly over his shoulder as DogNut hurried after him.

"What do you mean?" said DogNut. "Where they at? They coming back?"

"No," said Ed. "They're not coming back."

"You mean they—"

"DogNut!" Ed snapped. "They're dead, all right?"

"Shit . . ."

Inside the museum it was chaos. David's boys were milling around, and Jordan's guards were shouting at them.

"Ed, you got to sort this out, man," said DogNut.

"Not my problem."

Kids were filtering out of the café to see what was going on. Brooke was among them. When she saw Ed, she broke out into a broad eager smile and trotted over to him. Halfway there, though, she caught sight of his wounds and stopped dead, one hand up to her mouth, her eyes wide.

"Oh, Ed," she said into her fingers. "What have they done to you?"

Ed felt suddenly deflated. Everything that had happened in the last few days came tumbling down on top of him. What *had* they done to him? Tears came into his eyes. Someone pushed past. He ignored it. The angry shouting of the boys in the atrium sounded a million miles away. Through a film of tears he saw Brooke shaking her head, backing away, horrified. Before he could say anything, Jordan appeared at the head of the stairs.

"Be quiet!" he shouted, and miraculously, everyone fell silent. All eyes turned as he came down, his long military coat rustling on the stone steps.

"What's going on?" he asked, and David stepped out of the crowd.

"I'm David King," he said. "We brought Ed Carter back for you."

"He doesn't belong to me."

"He lives here, doesn't he?"

"Yes."

"And you're in charge, aren't you?"

"I am."

"Then he belongs to you." David was holding his hand out. "You must be Jordan Hordern," he said.

Jordan looked at David's hand through his thick glasses, but didn't make any attempt to shake it.

"Thanks for helping Ed," said Jordan. "But I'm afraid you're gonna have to leave now. We haven't got enough food for you all."

"I understand that," said David. "I would do the same in your position. But might I talk to you for a minute?"

"You might," said Jordan, intrigued by David's strange,

stiff, grown-up manner. "Your boys can wait outside, though."

"They'll wait inside, actually," said David. "I don't want them exposed to any danger. I've gotten them all the way here from Surrey. I'm *responsible* for them. They stay with me." He was so firm, so sure of himself, that Jordan was taken aback. He looked around at the scattering of red blazers.

"Fair enough," he said. "But they stay here in the atrium. And no trouble. Whatever you and I agree on, they don't argue about, okay?"

"They won't be any trouble. They'll do whatever I tell them."

David shouted some orders, and the boys began to take off their packs and find places to sit.

"You got 'em well drilled," said Jordan as he led David back upstairs.

"Without discipline we would all be dead," said David. "Wasn't it the explorer Roald Amundsen who said 'Adventure is just bad planning'?"

"Was it?"

"I think it was."

"You remind me a lot of me," said Jordan. "And that is not necessarily a good thing. There's not room here for two generals."

"I appreciate that," said David. "But I'm sure we can come to some arrangement."

Jordan laughed briefly. "We'll see about that," he said.

DogNut put a hand on Ed's shoulder.

"I'm sorry about Jack and Bam," he said. "They was good people."

"Yeah," said Ed. "The best. We should never have gone. Just three of us." He looked toward the café. Brooke had disappeared. "Is everyone all right here?"

"Need to talk to you about that, blood."

"What?" Ed looked at DogNut. He'd been assuming that the rest of the bus party were safe.

"It's the French girl," said DogNut.

"Frédérique? What's happened to her?"

"You better come see for yourself. Don't sweat, everyone else is fine. It's just her."

"Where is she? Is she hurt?"

"We had to lock her up in the Blitz Experience," said DogNut, leading Ed to the back of the atrium. "To keep it safe."

The Blitz Experience was a mock-up of a wartime air-raid shelter and part of a bombed-out London street. Ed had visited it once a couple of years ago. He remembered sound effects of planes going over, and air-raid sirens and falling bombs and explosions, with radio announcements and cheesy recorded cockney voices taking you through it all. None of that was working now. It was dark and silent in there without power for light and sound.

DogNut fetched a candle and a rifle with a fixed bayonet and gave them to Ed. As they went down to the next level, he briefly explained what had happened.

"D'you want me to come in with you?" he asked as he unlocked the doors. "Just in case?"

"I don't know." Ed waited by the entrance. "Is she dangerous?"

"She's locked up. Handcuffed to a chain. But don't get too close."

"I'll see her alone." Ed stepped through into the darkness. "She knows me. She might be better with just one other person."

"All right. Good luck, brother," DogNut said as he closed the door behind him.

61

The way in was through the fake air-raid shelter, little more than a concrete box with benches down the sides and reproductions of old wartime propaganda posters. Ed walked to the far end and went through to the main exhibit. There was a ruined street here with a view of a miniature London skyline. He saw Frédérique at the far end, by a bomb-damaged shop, sitting on an old wooden chair. She was hunched over, hugging herself, her arms tight over her stomach. She was bundled up in a big puffy jacket and a long skirt. A loop of chain snaked out from under her chair to an iron railing that was part of the set. There was a plate of untouched food next to her, a plastic bottle of water, and a bucket that she hadn't used. Lying on the floor next to the plate was what looked like a small half-eaten chicken leg.

"Frédérique . . . ?"

As Ed approached her, she raised one hand to cover her eyes and gave a little gasp. Ed shielded the flame.

"I'm sorry," he said. "Is that better?"

"It's too bright," said Frédérique.

Ed wondered whether to blow the candle out—it was clearly distressing her. Instead he took it to the far end of the exhibit and put it behind the flat front of the London skyline. The flickering light gave a feeble impression of the old flame effect they'd used to bring the blitzed cityscape alive. He left the rifle down here as well so as not to frighten Frédérique.

As he made his way back to her, she watched him intently with staring eyes, her pupils so wide they looked like great black holes in her head.

Ed sat down on a piece of scenery. "Is that better?"

Frédérique sniffed the air. *"Oui."*

Ed's eyes were slowly growing used to the dark. He could see that there was moisture glistening around Frédérique's nose and mouth and a run of spots in the shadow beneath her chin.

"How are you doing?" he asked gently.

"It is better in here." Frédérique's voice sounded low and dull. "Outside it was too bright. The sun was too hot. I couldn't think right. You know? In here it is more quiet. The voices in my head are asleep. Where is Jack?"

"He's . . . he's okay. He wanted to stay longer at his house." Ed couldn't bear to tell her the truth. "There were things he wanted to do," he added lamely.

"I would like to see him. To talk to him."

"You can talk to me."

"All right."

But Ed didn't know what to say to her. How to approach

what had happened. He sat there for a long while just looking at her while she stared into the distance, hardly moving, leaning forward, folded in her arms.

In the end, Ed realized there was no easy way to ask what he wanted to, so he just came straight out with it. "Frédérique?"

"*Oui?*"

"How old are you?"

Frédérique sighed. She closed her eyes. Her head dropped so that she was curled into a ball on her seat. "Sixteen," she said quietly.

"Right . . ." Everything became very clear to Ed. It had been staring them in the face all along, but they'd misread all the signs. "That's what you were scared of, wasn't it?" he said. "Not the adults. The disease."

"Yes. I thought that maybe when Greg was not sick, there was some hope for me. But then . . . even he . . . I am very hungry, Ed."

"There's food here. They've given you food."

"I can't eat this. I need . . . Oh . . . I did not used to eat meat. Now . . . all I want . . . I don't know what I want . . . what I don't want."

"I'm so sorry, Fred."

"I'm going to die, aren't I?"

"Not necessarily, I mean, not everyone . . ."

Frédérique gave a short bitter laugh. "No," she said. "You are right. Not everyone dies. You think that will be good, yes? To be like them. I have seen them. I don't want to be like them. They are . . . red." Again Frédérique sniffed.

"Red?"

"The word, I don't know, the English word . . . red . . . *rouge* . . . *sang* . . . Oh . . ."

Frédérique mumbled something in French that Ed didn't understand.

"How bad is it?" he asked.

Snot ran out of Frédérique's nose, and she snorted it back in. "I have a, what you call, *un mal de tête*?" she said.

"A headache?"

"Yes. And my stomach is bad. It is alive. My skin itch. I want to scratch all the time. Scratch-scratch. In the light I can't think. In here I am safe. But I don't know how long . . ."

She raised her head and looked at Ed with her wide black eyes, the whites tinged with pink. Her nostrils widened and she sucked in air through her nose. It bubbled and rattled in her throat.

She sighed, licked her dry lips, then pulled her long hair back from one ear.

"Look."

Ed leaned closer. There was a growth of ugly fat boils, full of pus. They clustered around her ear and inside it, blocking the hole. From there they ranged down her neck and under her chin, getting smaller as they went.

"That is not the worst," she said. "My body is the worst. Oh, Ed, I do not want to be sick. I do not want the red to have a baby."

"Sorry? What? I don't get it."

"I didn't mean to say that. I . . . I want to say . . . I don't know. I need to eat. But I am so dry. Do you have some water, please?"

"There's a bottle there," said Ed. "Do you want me to open it for you?"

"Thank you, you are very kind, a kind of *méchant*."

"What's that?" Ed asked, picking up the bottle. "Is that a French word?"

"I don't know. Why is it so dark?"

"You said the light hurts your eyes," said Ed, unscrewing the lid.

"What?"

"You asked me why—"

"I didn't say anything."

"Here. Drink some of this." Ed kept his distance and stretched the bottle out toward her. Even from where he was he could smell a wet-dog stench coming off her.

She made no move to take the bottle, and he shuffled closer. She was a pathetic figure. He felt sorry for her, not scared. Then he heard a drip and looked down to see that there was a puddle of blood beneath her chair.

There was something wrong about this.

He looked at the bottle, the plate of food, the scrap of raw chicken on the floor. The skin white. Raw.

No. That didn't make sense.

Why would they give her raw chicken?

She wasn't an animal.

And *that* wasn't chicken.

He looked again.

It was a human thumb. With a bloody flap of skin around the base and the white stub of a broken bone sticking out.

Ed swallowed. His mouth was dry as dust.

Whose thumb was it?

It must be hers.

But why would she tear off her own thumb?

And then he got it. Too late. Frédérique was up out of her chair and coming at him, arms outstretched. The handcuffs dangling from one wrist, the other hand, the free hand, missing its thumb. There was blood all over her arms and down her front.

She came fast, and before Ed could react, she got hold of his shirtfront and shoved him hard up against the wall with more force than he'd imagined she was capable of, winding him. He tried to pull away from her, but she held him tight. His head was spinning. He was worn out from carrying Jack yesterday, and all his muscles ached. He didn't think he had the strength to fight her off. She bared her teeth. There was saliva bubbling between them. She put her face closer. The whites of her eyes were almost solid red. Thin trickles of blood came out of her tear ducts and ran down either side of her nose. Her jaws opened wide and she forced her mouth toward Ed. Her strength was appalling. Her breath stank like an animal house at the zoo. Ed was on the verge of fainting.

She stuck out her tongue and licked the length of Ed's scabby wound.

"No!" he yelled. "Get off me!"

Somehow he managed to twist away and jab an elbow into her side, knocking her over. She howled and came straight back at him on all fours. This time Ed knew she was going to bite him. He kicked her in the jaw and she fell back.

Ed just had time to get to the rifle and hold it out in front of him before Frédérique recovered. She squatted there, writhing and spitting.

"Frédérique, stop it!"

Then the poor girl doubled over in pain and started to retch, bringing up a sticky, silvery stream of liquid that spattered onto the fake cobblestones.

With that, the fight went out of her. She slumped down, pressed her face against the floor, and started to weep.

"Kill me, Ed," she pleaded. "Please kill me. I cannot go on like this."

"No, Fred, no. . . . It's all right. You'll be all right. . . ."

How many lies was he going to tell her today?

Just one more.

"Wait here," he said. "I'm going to get something that will help."

"Okay . . ."

Ed backed away from her and knocked on the door for DogNut to let him out.

62

Ed walked quickly into the center of the atrium, where the two rival gangs of boys were eyeing each other suspiciously.

"Right!" he shouted. "Listen to me. I need you all to get your weapons and make two rows, leading from the stairs at the back to the front doors. Make a sort of passage, like, you know, running-the-gauntlet type of thing. I'm bringing someone through. She's sick, okay? But she's one of us, so I don't want anyone to hurt her. I just want to get her out of the building and away from here."

"You sure you know what you doing, man?" DogNut had followed Ed up from the lower level, his small head bobbing on his skinny neck, agitated.

Ed took him into the front entrance area. "We can't keep her locked up in there like an animal," he said quietly and urgently. "She'll only get worse. If I let her out, she can at least try and look after herself."

"So you don't have to deal with her?"

"No. Maybe. Yeah."

"But if you let her out, Ed . . ."

"She's a friend."

"She's a sicko now," said DogNut. "That's the word you lot like to use, innit? *Sicko*. And sickos ain't our friends."

"But *she* was. . . ." said Ed. "She *was* my friend. She'll just die in there."

"True that." DogNut pointed through the doors at the gardens. "And out there she's free to attack any kid she wants."

"So?" Ed shouted angrily. "What do you want me to do? Shoot her? Stick my bayonet into her guts?"

"I dunno. . . ."

"Well, neither do I. So I'm going to let her out. Open the doors. And be careful—she got out of the handcuffs."

"How the hell she do that?"

"She bit her thumb off."

"Holy Jesus . . ."

DogNut didn't argue anymore. He opened the front doors and then formed the kids into a gauntlet as Ed went back for Frédérique.

The boys stood there in two long lines, each bristling with sticks and bayonets, swords and clubs. They waited, some laughing and making sharp remarks, others quiet and thoughtful, like kids organized into a game whose rules they didn't really know.

After a while Frédérique emerged, blinking and confused, covering her eyes with her good hand, the cuffs rattling.

She flinched from the weapons as she shuffled between the lines. A group of Jordan's boys snickered at her, and a couple made crude comments. Then she brought up her injured hand and they shut up.

Ed followed, his rifle ready in case Frédérique tried to turn and run back.

She didn't. She just kept slowly walking toward the main entrance. When she got there, she halted. Cringing away from the sunlight, hunched over.

Ed came up behind her. "You have to go," he said.

She turned and gulped at him. She looked so sad suddenly, so normal, just a frightened little girl. She shook her head.

Ed turned his rifle around and prodded her with the butt. "Please, Frédérique. Just go."

There were bloodstained tears running down her cheeks. Her lower lip was trembling.

"Ed," she said.

"Just go!" Ed snapped, and shoved her so that she went sprawling onto the front steps.

DogNut swung the doors shut.

Frédérique got up, came over to the glass, and pawed at it. DogNut winced when he saw the ragged tear where her thumb had been. She was pleading in French and sobbing.

"I'm sorry," said Ed, and Frédérique threw herself at the window, slobbering against it, smearing it with filth. An animal again.

Ed didn't want to see. He turned away and left her there, thumping and mewling and clawing at the glass. He couldn't believe how quickly she'd gotten sick, how fast she'd changed, fallen apart.

Would it be worse now that she was outside in the light? Quicker? He didn't know how the disease worked, but he'd seen enough to know that sunlight accelerated it.

He tried to shut her out of his mind. Walked away between the lines of silent boys.

DogNut stayed where he was. Not looking at the girl, but up at the sky.

He felt a cold hard lump in his guts.

63

Jordan Hordern was sitting at his desk. He had taken over the director general's office in the corner of the museum on the first floor. He had a bed against one wall and spent a lot of time reading and planning. The rest of his boys slept in the boardroom next door, which they'd turned into a dormitory. Both rooms looked out over the park and had good lines of sight.

David King was sitting opposite Jordan at the desk, his legs neatly crossed, listening as Jordan explained the rules. They were no different for David than they were for the bus party. If he and his boys could feed themselves, they were welcome to stay.

"We might not want to stay."

"That's your decision."

"You said yourself we can't have two people in charge," David went on. "I think I know best, and I don't want to be told what to do by anyone else."

"Fair enough, soldier. Where were you heading anyway, before you found Ed?"

"Somewhere central. Somewhere with a good supply of food and water. Somewhere safe. Somewhere like this, really."

"Yeah, well, I'm afraid we got here first."

"Yes."

"Why London, though?" Jordan asked. "Wouldn't you have been better off in the countryside?"

"For the next few years we are going to be a scavenger society," said David. "Living off what the adults have left behind. This place, for instance, is full of weapons that we couldn't hope to make ourselves. Not until we learn the skills."

"True."

"So London is the obvious place to come. The country-side will be fine when it's safer, when the Strangers have all died off, when we can learn how to grow our own food. But at the moment it's pretty terrible out there. Funnily enough, it's quieter here in town."

"You'll find somewhere else to hole up," said Jordan.

"I doubt we'll find somewhere else with as good a supply of weapons, though."

"Okay," said Jordan. "That's what this is all about, then? Weapons?"

"You've surely got more than you can use."

"Not necessarily. Who knows how things are going to go? Who knows what we might need in the future?"

"Twenty rifles," said David. "That's all I'm asking for. Give me twenty rifles. You must have hundreds here."

"What about bullets?" said Jordan.

"I hadn't thought of that."

"Most of these guns are useless. There's no ammo for them. We did find some others in the armory, and some bullets, but I ain't Father Christmas."

"Well then, if some of the guns aren't of any use to you," said David, "why not give them to us and let *us* worry about ammunition?"

"If I give you guns, will you move on?" Jordan asked, but David wasn't listening. He had his head cocked to one side.

"Can you hear that?" he said.

"What?"

"Sounds like shouting."

64

A huge argument was raging in the atrium. David's boys against Jordan's. It seemed that with their leaders not around, both crews had lost all their discipline. There was a lot of childish name-calling going on. David's boys were from a privileged public school; Jordan's boys were mostly from the local estates. No one was quite sure what had started it, but there was now a fierce slanging match going on, with each side insulting the other in the crudest possible way.

David and Jordan came down the stairs shouting and trying to restore some sense of order. But the argument had been allowed to get out of hand, and there was no easy way of stopping it. The two sides were acting like rival football teams who had gotten into a fight on the field and were using Jordan and David as referees. And the bus party kids were acting as spectators, nudging each other and pointing, enjoying the spectacle.

It looked like there were going to be a few flags on the field today. The big rugby player, Pod, was particularly angry.

"You have to get them to apologize, David," he kept saying, and David tried to ignore him.

In the end, David lost his cool and snapped at him. "Just shut up, Pod!" he shouted. "All of you shut up."

The noise died down a little.

"What have you two decided, anyway?" Pod asked. "Although, to tell you the truth, I don't really want to stay here with this bunch of morons."

"Loser," someone shouted.

"We hadn't finished talking, if you must know," said David, sounding calmer.

"Can't they give us some guns and we'll get going?" said Pod.

"Yeah, get lost!" came a voice from the crowd.

"There's a lot to sort out," said David. "And you all aren't making it very easy for me. You're behaving like a bunch of kids."

"David," said Andy, the guy with the big nose, "we *are* kids."

"I won't have you fighting like this. I can sort things out, but I have to be able to leave you alone for five minutes without you fighting."

"They started it," said Pod.

"We did not!"

"It might not matter anyways," said DogNut, coming in from the front entranceway. "You'd better come take a look at this."

65

Ed, Jordan, David, and DogNut were on the roof of the museum. The sky was almost completely covered by roiling black smoke, which was visibly spreading from the south-east, like ink staining a bowl of water. There was a roaring, crackling sound like a distant waterfall, and they could see great flames leaping into the sky in the distance. The hot wind carried ash and cinders. Birds were flying past, and skinny moth-eaten dogs were appearing, trotting along the road with their tails between their legs.

"The fire's driving them this way," said David.

"It's getting serious," said DogNut.

"We're in open ground here, aren't we?" Ed asked. "I mean, the park goes all the way around, doesn't it?"

"Not at the back," said Jordan. "We're close to some other buildings there. If the fire gets really out of control, it could spread to the museum. I guess we could maybe try and fight it off somehow."

"The thing is, though," said David, "if everything around

you burned down, you wouldn't want to stay here, would you? It would be a wasteland."

"At least there'd be no sickos left," said Ed.

"There'd be nothing," said David. "You'd be stranded here."

"We're not leaving," said Jordan. "We fought hard for this place."

"But you said yourself it could catch fire," said Ed.

"We'll take that risk."

"For real?" DogNut was alarmed. "I do not like fire, captain. I'm telling you, if them flames get too close, I am *out* of here."

"DogNut's right," said Ed. "I saw what happened at the Oval. When a fire gets hot enough, it just burns everything."

"Maybe the wind will drop?" said Jordan. "Change direction."

This was the first time Ed had seen Jordan show any doubt, any hesitation.

"I saw a program about bushfires once," said David, staring at the sky. "In California and Australia. Whole towns just turned to ash and rubble. Cities rely on firefighters. Without them, fires can spread unchecked, and there's nothing you can do to stop them. I'm taking my boys and I'm going. But first you're going to give us some guns, Jordan. There's no point in leaving them here to get burned."

"I'm with David," said Ed. "I'm going to at least get ready to pull out. You should too, Jordan. Pack everything up, put it on the truck if you want."

"I can't leave the museum."

"Bloody hell, Jordan. Look at that! The whole horizon's covered with fire. You can always come back afterward. See if the museum's still standing. I'm not risking it, though. I'm going to start loading our food back onto the truck. If it looks too hairy, we'll head north, across the river. At least the Thames will stop the fire from spreading any farther. Honestly, Jordan, just let it burn itself out and come back when it's all over."

"I'm not leaving."

66

After the dogs came the children. A steady trickle of them heading for the bridges. Boys and girls, bedraggled, exhausted, terrified. In small groups mostly, some riding bikes, some pushing shopping carts full of belongings, quite a few with suitcases on wheels, a handful packed into cars, driving slowly down the choked streets.

Jordan posted guards at all the entrances to the museum to stop anyone from trying to break in, but nobody wanted to stop. They'd seen the fire, they knew what it was capable of, and they just wanted to get far away.

Ed organized the bus party into a team; they grabbed all the food they'd carefully unloaded the day before and packed it back onto the truck, along with their sleeping bags and blankets. DogNut helped, and stayed outside with Ed to make sure no passing kids stole anything. Twice a small group of tough nuts made a detour and came over for a look, but when they saw the boys' weapons, they kept going by, jeering and throwing things.

One group, though, three boys and a girl, stopped and

asked for water. Ed gave them a bottle and asked them for details about the fire.

"We was hiding out in a tower block down Brixton," said one of the boys. "There was loads of us there. Last night the fire lit up the whole sky. This morning you could see it. We was up high and you could watch it jumping from building to building. There ain't nothing gonna stop it. You getting out?"

"Probably," said Ed.

"Don't wait too long, man. It moves fast. It's a firestorm. If it gets close, you can't outrun it. We're getting over the river, take our chances on the north side, though I've always hated north London. It's just that *now*, well there ain't hardly no south London left."

"Honestly," said the girl. "Don't leave it too late. There's crazies back there. Thousands of them, being driven up this way by the fire. Every last one in south London most likely."

Wiki and Jibber-jabber were arranging the food in the back of the truck with Zohra and Froggie.

"Could we be burned?" said Froggie, his big bulging eyes wider than ever.

"Yes," said Wiki.

"Will the whole of London be burned?"

"Probably not. The wind will drop, or it might rain, then there's the river that acts as a natural firebreak. But in the Great Fire of London in 1666, thirteen thousand houses went up in smoke. There were eighty thousand people living here then. About seventy thousand of them lost their homes. In 1906 in San Francisco, twenty-five thousand buildings were destroyed by fire—admittedly there had been an earthquake as well, but even so . . ."

Ed came around to see how they were getting on. He had the rest of the bus party with him. There was Kwanele, wheeling his suitcase, immaculate in an admiral's uniform he'd found. Chris Marker followed, for once not reading a book. Justin the nerd was carrying a Sten gun for protection. It had no bullets in it but looked menacing enough and gave him a feeling of security. Then came Mad Matt and Archie and the acolytes, carrying their ridiculous banner. The scab on Matt's forehead was really gungy now, but he displayed it proudly as a badge of honor. Bringing up the rear were Brooke, Courtney, and Aleisha, quieter than normal, subdued and fearful.

Brooke nodded toward the kids that were streaming along the roads. "See, Aleisha," she said. "We ain't alone. I told you."

They all crowded nervously around, watching the skies. Ed shouted to get their attention. "There's only twenty-three of us left." Word had gotten around about Jack and Bam, although it was clear Ed didn't want to talk about it. "And we're not going to lose any more. Okay? So this is how it is. The fire's spreading this way and spreading fast."

"We're moving north," said Matt, sounding very sure of himself. "We were never meant to stay here. The Lamb has sent the fire."

"Please, Matt . . ."

"We have to cross the river and go to the temple in the city, to St. Paul's. Isn't it obvious?"

"No, it's not bloody obvious." Ed was trying not to lose

his temper. "Why would we want to go to St. Paul's? We'll decide where we're going when we get across the river."

"We should hurry," said Froggie. "I don't want to get burned up."

"There's a few things I need to do before we leave," said Ed.

"We're going to St. Paul's," Matt insisted.

"Shut up. Let me finish!" Ed glared at Matt until he was sure he wouldn't interrupt again, then went on. "Kwanele, I want you to go and find Jordan, tell him if he wants to load anything onto here he'd better hurry, okay? Justin, I need to talk to you and Wiki about something inside. The rest of you stay with the truck."

"We need to rescue the books," said Chris.

"What books?"

"There's a whole library of books up there. I'll need everyone to help me save the most useful ones."

"We don't need books now, Chris."

"Yes, we do," said Chris bluntly. "If we want to survive, we need knowledge. And books contain knowledge. Trust me. Books will save our lives just as much as weapons."

"All right, all right. Brooke, you're in charge of helping Chris. You go with him, bring down what he wants, and load them into one of these empty cages. Just one, okay? Then get it onto the truck. Don't argue with him. Don't be pissy about it. Just do it."

"Sure thing, boss."

"And be quick, it's getting late."

"Right."

"Who does that leave to guard the truck?"

"We'll do it," said Matt.

"You?"

"We're well armed."

Indeed, Ed saw that Matt and his followers had gotten themselves some guns and were loaded down with knives and swords.

"All right," said Ed, "but don't get any stupid ideas about leaving without me." He turned to Justin and Wiki. "Come with me. We need to talk."

67

"Frédérique's gone. I guess you all know what happened to her?"

"Yes," said Jibber-jabber.

Ed was in the museum shop with Justin and Wiki. Jibber-jabber had insisted on coming along as well. He and Wiki couldn't be separated, and now he was off on one of his breathless monologues.

"She got the sickness, she went nuts and tried to eat Froggie. You see, like a wildcat? That's what she looked like, it was really scary, not as scary as when Greg went psycho on the bus, but it wasn't nice at all; she must have lied to us about her age."

"We never asked her," said Ed. "We just assumed."

"It explains a lot," said Justin.

"Exactly. She's sixteen."

"What's going to happen to her?" asked Wiki.

"God knows," said Ed. "She's on her own now. She went for me while I was trying to talk to her. She seemed almost normal at first. Why is it that when they get sick, all they want to do is attack us?"

"Is that what you wanted to talk to us about?" said Justin.

"Well, the main thing is . . ." Ed paused, not sure if he should carry on.

"What?"

"Okay. But you've got to promise not to tell anyone else."

"Fine."

"I'm fifteen now," said Ed. "What I'm asking is—am I going to get sick like Frédérique?"

The other three just sat there staring at him.

Ed pressed on. "I mean—what happens to us as we get older? Are we all going to become sickos?"

Still the others just sat there in silence.

"Come on," said Ed. "Say something."

"We don't know, Ed," said Justin. "How can we know?"

"You must have some ideas."

"Well . . ." Justin bit his lip. "Okay. If I had to say either way, I'd say it doesn't look too bad for you."

"Why?"

"You have to consider the evidence," said Wiki.

"Yeah, yeah, what evidence?"

"We've been talking about this in the Brain Trust," said Justin. "Sometimes when you talk about something, it makes it less frightening. So we've been talking about why the sickos want to eat children."

"Yeah, I can see how that might make Froggie a little less frightened," said Ed sarcastically.

"It does, actually," said Justin. "If you can understand

something, you can control it. Now, there's obviously something different between us and the sickos."

"Yeah, just a bit," said Jibber-jabber. "They're nuts!"

"And we've thought about it in a Darwinian way," Justin went on, ignoring Jibber-jabber.

"Get to the point," said Ed. "We haven't got long. What's a Darwinian way?"

"Survival of the fittest. Genetics, mating rituals, alpha males, queen bees, ant colonies, all the sort of stuff you get in a David Attenborough series."

"What's that got to do with me?"

"We're animals just the same as any other," said Justin. "And everything we do is to survive. Sickos as well."

"Put it like this," said Wiki. "Whatever the sickos do—it's not random. So we have to assume that the sickos eat us in order to survive."

"Oh, bloody hell, we know that!" Ed tried not to laugh at the ridiculousness of the conversation. Wiki and Justin being so serious and wannabe scientific. "They need to eat something, so they try to eat us."

"But why us?" said Justin. "Why, out of all the available food sources, do the sickos choose us first? I mean, from what we can gather, if there's no children around, they'll eat other things to survive—rats and cats and dead pigeons—any food they can find. Chips even, I suppose, if they could get the bags open. But given the choice, they'd *rather* eat children. Even though we fight back. Even though we kill them. Offer them a nice steak and they're not interested; they'll try to bite your hand off and eat that instead."

"Yeah, okay. I get that."

"Well," said Justin, twining his fingers together like some crusty old school teacher. He was really enjoying this. "In the wild, animals know what to eat and what not to eat. There's no food labeling, no sell-by dates, no nutritional advice or cooking programs for them. They even eat some things as a sort of medicine."

"You see my dog?" said Jibber-jabber. "He used to eat grass to make himself sick, he'd chew away at it then cough it up; he used to look quite funny, but it was still disgusting."

"Exactly," said Justin. "A lot of animals do things like that. They don't know why they do it, but they do. They have an impulse. Their bodies seem to know what they need even if their brains don't."

"Are you saying that the sickos *need* to eat us, somehow?" Ed asked, getting interested now. "To survive?"

"That would seem to be the most obvious answer," said Justin. "Let's look at the facts." He counted on his fingers. "One—as soon as anyone gets the disease, what's the first thing they do?"

"They attack."

"Right. Two—why didn't Greg get ill as quickly as most other adults?"

"I don't know. Why? I've no idea."

"Come on—what was he eating? That smoked meat."

"Oh, yeah. And you reckon that was human meat?"

"Not just any human meat. Child meat."

"Okay. I get you, I think." Ed smiled. "Yeah. You're saying that if they eat us, it helps to keep the sickness away? Is that it?"

"Maybe." Justin stood up and started to walk up and

down. "Look at the most successful sickos. They're not so diseased, are they? So they can catch us kids easier. But maybe it's a chicken-and-egg thing? Maybe the two things are connected? The more kids they eat, the less sick they get, and the less sick they get, the more kids they eat."

"You're saying we're like a sort of medicine for them?"

"In a way, yes."

"Bloody hell." Ed rubbed his temples and slowly shook his head, trying to take this in.

"We think there's something in us that adults need to eat in order to stay alive," said Wiki. "That means that the reason we didn't get the sickness is that we're different from them. Biologically different somehow. Everybody born less than sixteen years ago has something inside them that prevents them from getting the disease."

"What is it?"

"We've got no idea," said Justin. "But the sickos can sense it. Not consciously. I don't know, they can smell it, maybe. Remember what happened to Frédérique when she was attacked at the truck? The sickos weren't interested in her. They left her alone and went after the other kids. And that explains why they don't eat each other, well, not unless they're absolutely desperate. Their primary impulse is to attack and kill and eat children because we are the *only* thing keeping them alive. Why do some die of the disease and some live? They live because they eat children. And the more they eat, the longer they live."

"That's not a very nice thought."

"Yes, but like I said, all knowledge is power," said Justin.

"The more we can understand them, the more we can defend against them."

"And what about sunlight, then?"

"What do you mean?"

"Why does sunlight make them worse?"

"Does it?" Justin was frowning. This was new information for him.

"Oh, come on, Justin," said Ed, pathetically pleased that he knew something that Justin didn't. "You must have seen it. When you put a dead sicko into the sun—"

"They turn into popcorn," Jibber-jabber interrupted. "Like exploding caterpillars."

"Yes," said Justin. "Go on."

"They prefer to stay in the dark," said Ed. "Not come out in the daylight. Frédérique kept saying the sunlight hurt her."

"Maybe there's something in the electromagnetic radiation from the sun," said Wiki. "Maybe the ultraviolet, or something. The sun's rays could accelerate the disease. There are people who are allergic to sunlight. They have to stay in the dark or their skin blisters. It's called polymorphus light eruption."

"There's obviously a lot we still have to learn about the disease," said Justin, sitting back down.

"Maybe you should catch some sickos and do experiments on them," said Ed.

"Yes," said Justin. "It'd be dangerous, but if we really want to understand what's going on, then we should."

"Justin, I was joking!" said Ed. "You can't start doing human experiments."

"They're no longer human, Ed. We're the only humans left."

"If you say so." Ed sighed and started drumming his fingers on the table. "But you haven't really answered my original question. Am I still going to be human after my next birthday?"

"You say Frédérique tried to attack you."

"She looked at me like I was lunch," said Ed. "Came at me with her mouth wide open."

"Then you must have inside you whatever prevents the disease."

"Yeah, but will it still be there when I get older?"

"Logically, I would say yes." Justin smiled at Ed. "You're probably all right."

"Probably?"

"It's very hard to say anything definite in science," said Justin. "*Probably*'s the best we can offer."

"It's better than nothing." Ed smiled back at Justin. "Thank God for the nerds of this world."

"But at the first sign of a cough or a cold," Justin added, "or a fever, or a rash, or spots of any kind, you get far away from me, okay? And stay away!"

Before Ed could reply, there was a flash and a thud. The whole building shook and several windows cracked.

"What the hell was that?" said Jibber-jabber, jumping up.

"An explosion of some sort, I reckon," said Justin. He pointed toward the broken windows. "Coming from that direction."

"The gas tanks," said Ed. "I'll bet it was the gas tanks. That decides it. We're getting out of here now."

68

Looks like we ain't going nowhere. I guess we gonna stay loyal to the general." DogNut made a gun of his fingers and fired two imaginary shots into the air. "Brap-brap!"

"You're staying?"

"Yup."

Ed shook his head. "You're crazy."

"You know it, bruv!"

There was still a steady flow of bedraggled-looking kids tramping past the park, staring sullenly over at the museum. Ed and DogNut were standing at the back of the truck. Justin had parked it on the grass to the side of the museum, ready to get away. The fire was obviously getting nearer. The sky was now filled with sparks and billowing smoke that burned their throats. The wind was so hot it was like opening an oven door.

Ed threw up his hands in despair. "This whole place is gonna go up," he said, raising his voice to be heard over the noise of the fire.

DogNut shrugged. "I dunno, bruv. It's all we got. We

leave here, where we gonna go? What we gonna do? Maybe we need to make a stand. Get me?"

"You can't make a stand against fire."

"Jordan Hordern can. He's one tough brother. Big boy on the road."

"All right. Suit yourself. But we're pulling out." Ed slapped him on the shoulder and walked toward the driver's cab. "Good luck!"

"Wait a minute!" DogNut called him back. "The general gave me some gear for you. Thought you might find it useful." He waved to a boy inside the museum, who came out the side entrance wheeling a cart piled high with weapons. Ed saw rifles, swords, axes, clubs, bayonets . . . a proper arsenal.

He felt like weeping.

"Jordan Hordern's gone soft," he said, picking out a rifle with a fixed bayonet. "He's not as tough as he makes out, is he?"

"Don't worry," said DogNut, with a twisted grin. "He ain't jazz. He kept all the best stuff for hisself."

"What about David?"

DogNut sucked his teeth. "He got his guns."

Even as DogNut said it, David and his boys emerged from the building and marched outside, proudly carrying their rifles on their shoulders. David shouted an order, and they stopped to line up next to the truck, trying to look all serious and military but breaking into childish grins as they checked out one another's new toys.

David came over to Ed. "We're willing to act as an escort," he said. "I think if we stay together we stand a better chance of making it across the river."

"That's very good of you, David," said Ed. "What do you want in return?"

"Some of your food, obviously."

Ed exchanged a look with DogNut. "Fair enough," he said. "But will you be able to keep up with us?"

"Look at it," said David. "The roads are jammed. It was hard enough traveling on them before, but now it'll be nearly impossible. We can clear a way for you. You *really* don't want to get stuck, after all."

"Okay." Ed looked along the line of red-blazered boys. "You got bullets for those things, by the way?"

"A few."

Ed walked back to the building with DogNut. "Last chance, DogNut." Ed put an arm over the skinny kid's shoulders. "You sure you're not coming? We could use someone like you."

"The DogNut is staying, blood. It's not like Jordan's forcing us or nothing. It's our choice. We a team. We stay here. And we fight for what we got. Took a whole lot to win this place."

"Say good-bye to him for me," said Ed. "And thanks."

"Good luck, bro," said DogNut. "Come back and see us when the fire's gone out."

Ed laughed, exchanged an awkward high five with DogNut, and went back over to the truck, where the bus party kids were waiting for him.

"Right," he shouted. "Justin up front. I'll ride with you. And Brooke?"

"Yeah? What?"

"You as well, in with me and Justin. The rest of you in the back."

As Justin climbed up into the cab, Brooke took Ed aside. "What you want me in the front with you for, then?"

Ed sighed. "I know you all want me to be the leader and make all the difficult decisions," he said, "but I'm not sure I always know the best thing to do."

"Yeah? So?"

"So you're the only other one around here who gets any respect from the others. From now on, you and me, Brooke, we're going to work together, okay?"

Brooke shrugged, flattered, but a little scared at the same time. "Okay."

Ed had been facing south, trying to figure out how far away the fire was. Now he turned back to look at Brooke. "You ready, then?"

Brooke winced and shrank away from him. She didn't want to look at the gash down the side of his face, but she was ghoulishly fascinated at the same time. "I'm sorry," she said. "I keep forgetting. I still ain't used to your, like, *cut*. It looks awful, Ed. You ain't even cleaned it properly or nothing. Couldn't you have got one of Jordan's crew to help you?"

Ed sighed and fingered the scab. His face hurt like hell, and his eye was still swollen shut. He hoped it wasn't damaged. "I haven't had time," he said.

"Ed, you got to—you don't want it to go bad. You'll look like crap."

Ed had been too busy before to think about his wound, and that was how he wanted it to stay; there was enough other stuff to worry about. "What do you reckon they could do about it anyway?" he snapped. "Stick a Band-Aid on it and kiss it better?"

"You don't get that seen to, there ain't no one ever gonna want to kiss you again, man," Brooke muttered grumpily, annoyed by Ed's manner.

"I'll sort it out later," said Ed. "We've got to get going. It'll be dark soon, or at least it would be if it wasn't for the fire."

"At least let me clean it," said Brooke. "You got, like, toilet paper and stuff stuck to it. It looks really nasty."

Brooke reached out a hand toward Ed's face, then snatched it away with a grimace. "You look like one of them," she said. "You ain't turning into Frédérique, are you?"

"Just get in the truck, Brooke, and let's get out of here."

69

The truck plowed through the railings at the side of the park, flattening them, and the kids in the back cheered. As soon as they hit the road, however, they had to slow down. It was choked with fleeing children. The truck rumbled forward at a snail's pace, David and his boys clearing a path, shoving aside kids to stop them from being run down, shifting piles of debris that were blocking the street, shunting away broken-down cars. It seemed that every few feet there was another obstacle in the road. Once they even had to move a collapsed billboard.

As they cleared a railway bridge, they finally came to a complete stop. There was yet another abandoned car in their way. David's boys fussed about as the truck sat there shaking and hissing, and Ed grew more and more frustrated. He hated being stuck in the claustrophobic cab, not able to do anything except watch. Justin was sweating and swearing, teetering on the verge of panic. Brooke was moody and twitchy, being separated from her friends. She kept sneaking disgusted glances at Ed's face. In the end, Ed could stand it no longer. He kicked the door open and jumped down to help David's group with the car.

Once the road was clear, he decided to stay and walk with them for a while.

From down here the truck looked huge as it moved slowly through the crowds. He was reminded of those old dinosaur movies, where the dying dinosaurs have to escape some terrible natural disaster. There would be lots of small fast-moving dinosaurs, maybe even the odd early mammal or two, and there, in the middle of it all, a lumbering, hulking apatosaurus or the like.

It was taking too long. Behind them the fire was growing ever closer, traveling faster than they were, steadily eating away at London. Ed could hear the roar and crackle of it and see unbelievably big flames clawing at the sky over the rooftops of the houses. There were distant screams, but it was impossible to tell, in all the confusion, from which direction they were coming.

At last they reached the river, where the road opened out. Ahead of them was a large traffic circle, and on the far side of it was Lambeth Bridge, flanked by two tall stone obelisks that were topped with what looked like pineapples. To the left was a modern glass-and-steel apartment block with curved walls; to the right, in sharp contrast, was what looked like a medieval church; and beyond that the square redbrick Tudor buildings of Lambeth Palace. The church sat in its own gardens, which were filled with children waiting to cross the bridge.

A major road ran along the river, and it, too, was packed. The sheer number of kids was causing a dangerous bottleneck, and nobody seemed to be moving. Traffic was stuck on the bridge, and children had to climb over cars or squeeze past them to get anywhere. It was chaos. There were dogs barking, horns blaring, boys and girls of all ages sitting in the road clutching their pathetic bundles of belongings. As more and more kids arrived, they milled around, pushing and shoving each other.

"We'll never get over," said one of David's boys, staring at the solid mass of people on the bridge.

"We have to," said Ed. "None of the other bridges will be any better. And we'd never get to them in time anyway."

Somewhere off to the left there was an explosion. A fountain of vividly colored sparks shot up into the air, and a second later, everyone felt the force of it as a shockwave passed through the crowd, starting a panic. There was a stampede, but with nowhere to go, the mass of kids surged in all directions, knocking each other over and trampling smaller kids underfoot.

Ed tugged at his hair and bit the skin around his fingernails. Was this really happening? The black mood of despair settled over him again. He didn't have the energy to cope. He'd used up everything he had. He slipped his rifle off his shoulder, closed his eyes, slid slowly down one of the huge rear tires of the truck, and sat on the pavement. He put his hands over his ears to block out the sound of screaming.

They were all going to die here, on this stupid bloody road. And it was his fault. He should never have led the kids away from the safety of the museum.

70

The fire had reached the museum. Fanned by the strong winds, it had torn through the houses at the rear and leapt up into a line of big trees at the edge of the park. Now, finally, one of the trees toppled over and crashed into the corner of the museum, ripping it open.

Smoke started to spread through the galleries.

Jordan was up in his office making plans with a small group of boys. DogNut was outside by the naval guns, watching the chaos and confusion. Smoke wafted in clumps across the park, which was garishly lit up by the nearby fires.

DogNut was beginning to wish he'd gone with Ed and the others. The sheer power of the fire was terrifying. He'd never known anything like it. It was an unstoppable elemental force. Could they really hold out here?

He went back inside. Boys were sitting with their heads bowed, exhausted by the fear and stress. DogNut blinked. His friends looked vague and hazy, as if there were a veil hanging in the air between them. He looked up at the Spitfire dangling from the ceiling. It was lost in a gray fog.

DogNut swallowed. His throat hurt.

"Look at that." One of the boys was pointing to the back of the atrium.

A long tendril of smoke was crawling across the floor. It looped around one of the tanks.

Then DogNut became aware of a hissing, shuffling sound. Like waves raking over small pebbles on a beach.

Was it fire making the sound, or something else?

Footsteps. Heavy breathing.

A father came shambling up the stairs, drool hanging from his lower lip. Behind him, other dark shapes were emerging from the smoke.

DogNut drew his katana from its sheath.

"They're in!"

71

"Get up!"

Ed tilted his head back and squinted at David. He was standing over him, clutching his rifle, a black shape against a fiery sky.

"Why?"

"Get up, Ed."

"What's the point?"

David took hold of Ed's jacket and hauled him to his feet.

"You might want to sit here and get barbecued," he said, "but I don't. Everyone needs to do his part. I've sent Pod and three others forward to try and find out what's happening on the bridge. The rest of my squad is guarding the truck. We can't let anything happen to the cargo."

Ed took a deep breath. "Maybe we should just abandon it," he said. "If everyone got out and walked, it'd be a lot easier to get across."

"Is that really what you want to do?"

Ed sighed. "No." In truth he couldn't bear the thought of

abandoning the truck. It had their whole lives on it, as well as being a safe place for the kids. There was no getting away from the fact, though, that the conditions on the bridge were only going to get worse. More and more kids were arriving from every direction and filling the space around the traffic circle, and the longer they sat here waiting for it to clear, the closer the fire was going to get. The wind was still blowing strongly in this direction. The smoke in the air was so thick it scoured Ed's eyes and throat so that he couldn't stop coughing.

David shoved him back against the side of the truck and fixed him with a cold hard stare. "Are you just going to give up?" he asked.

Ed shrugged. He wanted to curl up under the truck and go to sleep.

"Is that what your friends would have wanted?" David went on.

"No."

"Then do it for them."

David was right. What had it all been for? To have come through everything, to have fought so hard, for Jack and Bam and the others to die . . .

Ed wearily picked up his rifle. "I'll fight," he said.

"Good." David looked at his watch. "It's after six o'clock. We have to push on. What we haven't considered is exactly what's on the other side. The Strangers will all be coming out of their hiding places. The quicker we get to a place of safety, the better."

There was a shout, and David turned to see Pod returning with his scouting party.

"Some morons in cars have crashed," Pod explained when he arrived. "They're arguing and fighting with each other. More cars have come up behind and tried to get past, and they're just making it worse. They're blocking the whole bridge."

"We'll have to clear it," said David.

"How?" Ed asked, amazed at David's confidence.

David raised his rifle. "We've got these, haven't we?"

"You can't shoot everyone on the bridge."

"I'm not going to," said David, as if he were talking to a complete fool. "But it'll give us some authority. Come on, Pod, bring everyone; we're going to make a path for the truck."

David's troops marched toward the bridge, David yelling at the milling kids to get out of the way. Miraculously, they did. Ed went along to the cab and shouted at Justin to follow, but now they were vulnerable to the hordes of angry kids who couldn't go anywhere. They were tired and hungry and desperate. If they knew what was in the back of the truck, they could easily be tempted to attack.

As the truck rolled slowly forward, Ed jumped onto the running board and leaned in the driver's window. "Don't let the gap close," he told Justin. "David's going to try and cut a way through. Keep your doors locked and your windows up. Brooke, you stay here with Justin. You're in charge of the truck now."

"What are you going to do?"

"Stay out here and make sure nobody gets any bright ideas about hijacking us."

"Okay."

Ed dropped down and pushed his way to the back of the truck. The shutter was rolled halfway up, the kids staring out at the crowds from among the cages.

"I need help," he said, climbing up onto the tailgate. "David's group is going on ahead, and I need more bodies down here protecting the truck."

At first nobody moved, then Matt and Archie Bishop and their acolytes clambered down, awkwardly carrying their banner. Courtney and Aleisha, looking scared but determined, came after them. Kwanele, Chris Marker, and the younger kids made no move to follow.

Ed couldn't blame them. It was getting pretty intense out here.

"You two stay at the back," Ed said to Chris and Kwanele as he swung down into the road. "Keep off anyone who tries to get in. We won't be far away."

Chris nodded, his face white. Kwanele picked up a rifle with a fixed bayonet and came over to the opening. The weapon was shaking in his hands. He looked out. There was a field of faces peering up at him from the road, and behind them there was a flickering red-and-orange glow above the buildings. Every few seconds a great shower of sparks would blossom up and spiral into the sky.

For a while it went okay. The truck crept forward, and Ed's small band patrolled the back and sides. So far nobody was bothering them; they were all too intent on trying to get over the bridge themselves. The people being barged out of the way at the front weren't too happy about it, but when they saw the rifles in David's boys' hands, and the massive truck rumbling and fuming up behind them, they didn't argue.

Justin managed to get the truck across the traffic circle, but as they approached the start of the bridge, there was shouting from behind, and the crowd surged forward. People were being knocked over in the panic, and others were rushing to fill the gap David had cleared in front of the truck. The crush of kids was soon going to be too great to let them move any farther.

Ed thought at first that the fire must have gotten close, but when he looked up he could see no change. The flames still seemed to be a few streets away.

So what was spooking everyone?

He rounded up his little band.

"We need to see what's going on," he said. The others nodded, though he could tell they weren't happy about going too far from the truck.

"Stick together," he said, and they fought their way back through the crowd toward the rear. It was impossible to see anything in the chaos, and Ed was just about to give up when there was another stampede, and a whole section of kids fell over almost as one, offering a clear view all the way back to the line of buildings.

Aleisha was the only one to speak, but she summed up what everyone was thinking.

She simply said three words.

"Oh—my—God . . ."

Packed together in a featureless mass of ruined flesh were hundreds of sickos. Limping and shuffling up the road, angry, confused, and as desperate to get away from the approaching fire as the kids. This first wave was going to be the fittest, the least diseased, the most dangerous.

Behind them would come the ones who were nearly dead.

And behind them the flames.

Already, the younger boys and girls in the road around them were screaming and climbing over each other as they tried to get away. Ed pulled a little girl to her feet and passed her to her friends.

"We've got to stop them from panicking," he called out to his gang. "We've got to hold the sickos back."

He pushed through the crowd, grabbing anyone who carried a weapon of some kind, or who looked bigger or tougher or less afraid.

"Come with me!" he yelled at them. "We have to hold them off. We can do it, come on!"

Most of the kids pulled away and swore at him or barged past toward the bridge, but a few understood what he was trying to do and joined him.

When they got to the edge of the crowd, they could see the sickos more clearly. They were pouring in from every direction, some of them covered in blood, some of them blackened by soot. Their fear had turned them completely crazy. They snarled and bared their teeth and shook their arms.

Ed saw a girl who looked about ten running toward him. She tripped and was immediately swamped by sickos. An older boy went back to rescue her, and he too disappeared into the mass of bodies. Another group of kids turned to make a stand by the church gardens. They had no choice. There was nowhere for them to run. But they were too few and only armed with sticks and broom handles, which they thrashed vainly at the advancing tide. They didn't have a hope in hell of holding them back. In a minute they were going to be massacred.

Ed drew his pistol, fumbled with the safety catch, and fired into the wall of rotting bodies. He had no idea if he hit anything, but the noise was enough to draw everyone's attention to him, kids and adults alike.

For a second it was as if time froze. Ed stepped forward out of the ranks of children. "We have to fight them off!" he bellowed, his voice hoarse. "All of us. Together. Turn around and stand your ground!"

He reholstered his gun. It would be a pointless waste of bullets to shoot anything else into that near-solid mass.

"Anyone with a weapon come to me," he said, holding his rifle above his head with one hand.

"The Lamb will protect you!" Matt shouted, lifting his banner, and he, too, stepped clear of the crowd. Nobody had any idea what he was talking about or what the banner meant, but it seemed to offer some sort of hope, and kids began to rally around him.

Now they charged forward to reinforce the smaller group by the church garden. They managed to beat the first wave of sickos back, and form a line. Ed found himself with Courtney and Aleisha on his left and a big square-headed boy armed with a garden hoe on his right. The boy was swearing under his breath and grinding his teeth. "Come on, come on, you sick bastards, come and get it. . . ."

After briefly dropping back, the sickos came forward again. And soon they were close enough for Ed to pick out individuals. A mother with no lips; a teenager with a broken arm, the bones sticking through the skin; a fat father with bulging eyes, whipping his head from side to side. And there . . .

Pez.

His lower jaw flapping at his chest.

Ed sensed the blood fever coming on again. He could feel that weird out-of-body calmness settling over him and, behind it, something wild and furious and out of control like a crazed beast rushing out of the darkness.

It was as if he were splitting into two people.

"Take it to them!"

72

David was on the bridge with his boys, pushing steadily forward, the truck inching along behind them. The crush of kids around them was getting worse, and they were in danger of being totally overwhelmed. He was aware that something was going on to the rear—there had been shouts and screams, and then a gunshot. This had thrown the kids on the bridge into even more confusion, and David was nearly knocked off his feet. The gunshot had given him an idea, though.

He fiddled with his rifle, pulled back the bolt, and managed to shunt a bullet up out of the magazine into the chamber. They had all done CCF at school—the Combined Cadet Force—where they'd learned the basics of being a soldier, including how to fire rifles. The old Lee-Enfield .303s they were carrying were similar to the .22s they'd trained with, but the reality of using rifles in some sort of combat situation was very different to the calm and ordered atmosphere of a rifle range.

The first thing was to get everyone's attention.

He aimed at the sky and pulled the trigger. The gun kicked, there was a loud bang, and the bullet ripped up into the black smoke cloud that hung over the bridge.

"Get out of the way!" he shouted, aiming his rifle at the kids in front of him who had turned around to see what was going on. His boys also leveled their guns, some of which had fixed bayonets, and instantly a pathway cleared.

"Forward!" David commanded, and his boys marched in formation, the truck following.

They soon got as far as the stalled cars. There were two gangs of boys fighting around them, other kids shouting from the edges of the scuffle, yet more crammed into the various stalled vehicles. By the side of the road, a double-decker bus was on fire, adding to the chaos.

"Stop what you are doing and move these cars!" David barked. The boys barely looked at him. Some didn't even hear him, so once again he fired into the air.

Now they listened.

"Get these cars out of the way," he said firmly, reloading the rifle. "You're blocking the whole bridge."

"Shove it up your ass," said a stocky kid with a flat, blunt face. His friends laughed. David lowered his gun, aimed it at the boy's chest, and fired.

The boy grunted and fell over backward. Pod swore, not quite believing what had happened. Everyone else fell into a stunned silence.

David glared at the circle of kids that had formed around him.

"I said, get these cars out of the way."

Instantly, everyone jumped to life, starting engines,

releasing brakes, pushing stalled cars, shoving back the crowd. In a minute there was a clear path down the center of the bridge, and David marched on.

Sitting in the driver's cab, Brooke was appalled. She looked down to where the stocky kid was being cradled by two crying girls. He wasn't moving, but whether he was dead or not was impossible to tell.

"You can't do that," she said. "You can't go around shooting people."

"He's cleared the bridge," said Justin.

"Justin, he *shot* that boy. Just like that."

"If we don't get everyone over the bridge," said Justin, "a lot more people are going to die."

"Yeah, but . . . I mean, you can't just shoot people; it ain't right."

"It's not right, no," said Justin. "But it's done."

"You listen to me, Justin. Soon as we get across, soon as the road is clear, we got to get away from this nutter. You put your foot down, okay?"

"What about Ed?"

"We got to hope he's with us. I ain't getting out to look. I doubt we're the most popular people on this bridge right now."

Ed stabbed his bayonet into the fat father and twisted. There was a splash of blood and a howl. He jerked the blade free, reversed the rifle, and slammed the butt into a mother's face. He didn't stop now, but stabbed again, hacking into the sickos, splitting skulls, opening guts, hardly aware of what was going on. The square-headed boy was at his side, swearing with each jab of his hoe, thrusting and grunting and kicking. Courtney and Aleisha were also still with him, but he was somehow alone, lost in a world of redness, channeling all his frustration and terror through the rifle into his bayonet.

Pez stared through red sore eyes. Seeing little more than shapes. But he could smell them.

And he could taste them.

His belly hurt, burning with a cold fire. The only thing that would make the fire go away was the blood of one of the small ones. He was so hungry. He couldn't eat anymore, though. He tried, but he couldn't chew. His jaws wouldn't work.

He tilted back his head. Such a pain around his mouth. His tongue felt over his teeth like a feeding parasite looking for scraps of food. There was no food.

He howled in frustration. Why wouldn't his jaws work? He didn't know that they were unconnected, that his lower jaw hung uselessly down, the cheeks and tendons gone. All he knew was that he was hungry and he needed to kill.

Aleisha was terrified. This was way worse than yesterday. What was she doing here? She'd gone along with Courtney without really thinking. She'd wanted to be helpful, and now here she was in the middle of a full-on freaking battle, surrounded by kids, yelling and screaming as they hit with fists and feet, bits of wood and garden tools, sports equipment, and the odd proper weapon. But the sickos just kept on coming. A mindless wall of them pushing forward, smelling like raw sewage.

She hung back behind Courtney and another big girl, poking her club at any sicko that got close. She might as well not have bothered. She was too small for this, not nearly strong enough, and totally unused to fighting. Any minute now she was going to lose it big-time.

She looked along the line. Ed was there, his rifle swinging through the air. He had cut himself a wide circle and resembled something out of one of her little brother's computer games, with the scar down his cheek, the gun in his hands, and the blood all over him. He was wild-eyed and unhinged, grunting viciously as he hacked and stabbed at the sickos. The kids around him were keeping well away, obviously as scared of him as they were of the sickos. If she hadn't known him, she'd have been scared too.

The gap closed up and she lost sight of him. The sickos were advancing. She spotted Pez wading through the ranks of the adults, spit running down his lower jaw and onto his chest.

And then the line of kids broke, and the sickos surged forward.

73

As soon as Ed cut one sicko down, another took its place. It was like trying to empty an ocean with a bucket. He was plastered with blood and pus that stiffened as it dried. His arms ached from the wrists to the shoulders; the rifle felt as heavy as a telephone pole. All around him the road was littered with bits of bodies, and his feet kept slipping in puddles of blood. Wounded sickos crawled away or sat there stunned among the shapeless lumps of their dead companions.

The kids were completely boxed in now, crushed up against the front line of the sickos. They'd been reduced to just pushing and shoving in a great heaving mass of bodies. Ed stopped a beat too long, and even he was swamped. One moment there was still room to swing his rifle, the next he was wrestling with a sweaty policeman who seemed to be trying to speak.

"Hold them," Ed croaked. "We've got to try and hold them!"

But then something gave way behind them. The crowd of waiting kids moved, and Ed found himself staggering backward. He stumbled over a corpse, got his footing back, and then tripped again as three mothers charged at him.

He went down heavily, jarring his spine. A knee got him in the face, and for a moment he was dazed. He was in a tangle of legs, like when he fell over in a rugby scrummage.

Another boy had fallen near him and was being dragged away by a group of fathers as he twisted and squirmed in their hands and tried to pull free.

There was another scuffle going on to his left. Sickos had gotten to a girl. He could only see her lower half. A young mother had hold of her club, another was tugging at her sleeves, and the girl had nothing to fight back with.

She was pulled to the ground, and Ed realized to his horror that it was Aleisha. Even if he could get back on his feet, there were too many people between the two of them to get to her in time.

He watched helplessly as a teenage girl with long hair flapping in her face lunged down at Aleisha. Aleisha struggled, but the other girl took hold of her and sank her teeth into her forearm. Aleisha screamed and hit out at her attacker with her free hand. The long-haired teenager ignored the feeble blows and dragged Aleisha deeper into the ranks of the sickos.

Ed remembered his pistol. He forced himself into a kneeling position, wrenched the gun from its holster, and aimed.

For a second the crush of bodies parted and he had a clear shot.

The girl with the long hair turned. Her hair whipped back, and Ed could clearly see her face. She stared at Ed, and suddenly the wildness drained out of her features.

It was Frédérique.

She frowned and smiled sadly at Ed. Then she held out her hands toward him like someone begging for money.

Ed pulled the trigger.

One moment Fred was there, the next she was gone.

And then Ed was knocked over again. His face hit the pavement and he saw stars. Somehow he managed to wriggle onto his back, spitting and half blinded, only to find himself looking up into the gaping, dripping, wet face of Pez, his lower jaw swinging like a pendulum.

Ed tried to bring the gun around, but he could barely move. His body seemed to be working in slow motion. Pez dropped on top of him, trapping his arm against his chest. The stink coming out of the red hole of his throat made Ed retch. He thought he would throw up. Pez pressed his mouth against Ed's face, but he couldn't bite. Ed felt his tongue slithering over his skin, saw his mad, pink eyes. Felt his fingers clawing at him.

He groaned.

And then there was a movement. Ed was dimly aware of someone plunging a weapon into the sicko. Pez flopped to the side, wriggled horribly, his feet drumming on the ground, and then fell still. Whoever had attacked him put a foot on the dead body.

It was the square-headed boy.

"Filthy bloody animal," he said, pulling his hoe out of Pez's chest. And then he reached down and hauled Ed to his feet.

Ed filled his burning lungs with oxygen, and his head

began to clear. He glanced around. Matt and his bunch were in the middle of the church gardens, waving their banner. They appeared to be singing and chanting. Other kids were regrouping around them. Ed and the boy with the hoe cut their way over to them, picking up Courtney as they went. She had Aleisha with her, thank God. She looked terrible, though, bleeding badly and trembling, her face tight with shock.

When they got to the gardens, there was some degree of protection from the railings that surrounded them, and Ed quickly took stock of their situation. There was progress on the bridge finally. Kids were pouring across it. The truck was more than halfway over. But Ed's war party had become separated from the main group, and the way back to them was cut off by sickos.

To make matters worse, the fire had finally reached them and was rampaging through Lambeth Palace and the apartment block on either side of the road. It wouldn't be long before it reached the small church.

Ed had a strong urge to give up again, but then he realized the boy with the hoe was grinning at him.

"This is fun, isn't it?" he said.

"Dunno about that." Ed shook his head. "But thanks for saving my ass. What's your name, by the way? I'm Ed."

"Kyle," said the boy.

"Well, Kyle"—Ed pointed toward the bridge—"we're gonna have to get over there somehow, or we're gonna be stuck here."

"Okay." Kyle's grin widened. "I'm with you, mate."

Ed smiled. Somehow the boy's insane enthusiasm had

gotten to him. Maybe it wasn't impossible. The two of them formed the remaining kids into a tight unit, with the best fighters along the outer edge, ready to battle their way through the sickos.

"Make some noise!" Ed yelled when they were ready, and then they charged out of the gardens, roaring a battle cry.

It was hopeless, though; a case of two steps forward, three steps back. There were just too damned many sickos blocking their way. Instead of moving toward the bridge, the kids were being forced off to the right, onto the road that ran eastward alongside the river. The bridge was getting farther away. Ed looked for the truck but couldn't see it anymore. He hoped that the other kids at least were going to get to safety.

74

Zohra was sitting at the back of the truck, pointing out at the London skyline.

"You see that, Froggie?" she said. "What's that?"

Froggie leaned over his sister and peered along the river. His bulgy eyes opened wide.

There it was, silhouetted against the flame-bright sky, sparks exploding in the air behind it.

"The London Eye."

"See?" said Zohra. "Looks just like it does on the telly at New Year, doesn't it? With the fireworks and everything."

"Yeah," said Froggie, lost in the magic of it. "It's amazing."

"And there's the Houses of Parliament, with Big Ben and that."

"Yeah." Froggie smiled at his sister, his wide frog mouth stretching from ear to ear. She put her arm around him.

"We're gonna be all right, little frog," she said.

Chris Marker sat with the cage of books he'd rescued from the museum, but for once he wasn't reading anything. He didn't know if it was caused by the fear and stress, the tiredness and hunger, but he was seeing things. Out of the corner of his eye: a gray shape that would dissolve if he tried to look at it straight on. He was sure it was the ghost from the museum, the Gray Lady. When he closed his eyes he could picture her clearly. Her skin was as gray as her old-fashioned clothes, but she didn't look diseased; instead she looked beautiful, as if lit by an inner light. There was a half smile on her lips.

She'd come with him, to look after her books. He felt comforted by her presence. He imagined that she was wrapping her arms around him, holding him and whispering in his ear.

Like a proper mother.

Not like that mob out there, the sicko mothers. And not like his own mother. She'd never been any use to him.

The Gray Lady was a ghost mother. The mother of all the writers of the books he'd saved. She would protect him.

As long as he protected the books.

75

Ed's group was surrounded on three sides now, with the Thames at their backs and the bridge to their right. They'd been forced off the road and onto the walkway that bordered the river. Ed was slashing and hacking at the enemy, but there was nowhere for either side to go. They would have to fight till the last man standing. And it looked like the sickos were going to win. They were starting to get in among the kids, biting and scratching, and the kids were exhausted. He doubted they could hold out much longer. It was only a matter of time before they were overrun by the army of disease-ridden adults.

What was the point? What was the point of killing any more of them? Why keep fighting? He'd done his duty. He'd saved the others and honored the memory of his fallen friends. He'd shown David he wasn't a quitter. He'd stood his ground like a hero. And now he was going to die a hero's death, massacred by a much bigger force.

What was the point?

But somehow his rifle kept on moving, stabbing, battering,

rising and falling, rising and falling, and somehow his legs didn't buckle. He had no idea what reserves of energy he was running on; he'd gone beyond tiredness. He was little better than a machine.

The sickos seemed far, far away, and nothing mattered to him anymore. He was shutting down his conscious mind and letting his body fight on without him.

And then he heard gunshots. Shouting. And a shudder passed through the ranks of the diseased.

"Someone's attacking them from the rear," Kyle shouted. "Come on! Let's show them who's boss!"

Ed came alive again, turned to his exhausted friends. "Don't give up!" he bellowed, tears in his eyes. "There's help coming!"

He sensed a fresh fight along the line. In front of them the sickos were falling away, turning to the side, trying to get clear, trapped between Ed's group and whoever was pressing them from behind.

A mob of sickos broke and stumbled away, and now Ed could see. . . .

It was Jordan Hordern and his crew from the museum. Well armed, well drilled, and fresh. They moved mercilessly through the fleeing sickos. Chopping down anyone that got in their path.

At their head was Jordan himself, shouting orders, his sword flashing in his hand.

And there was DogNut, fighting just as hard with his katana.

Ed's group gave a cheer and with savage fury laid into the sickos that remained. The two groups fought their way toward each other until at last they linked up.

Jordan saluted Ed.

"What happened?" Ed panted, ready to drop.

"Couldn't stay," was all Jordan replied. "What about you?"

"We got separated from the others," Ed explained, looking toward the bridge. "We have to get over there."

"No chance," said Jordan flatly. "You all are finished and there's hundreds of the bastards between here and the bridge. Plus, the fire's just about on us. We managed to stay a few yards ahead is all."

"Then what?" said Ed, feeling his new hope slipping away.

"There," said Jordan, nodding.

A small pier jutted out into the river. A metal gangplank ran down to four sightseeing boats.

"We could get across on one of those," said Jordan.

"You reckon?"

"Do we have any choice?"

"Fall back!" Ed bawled. "Get onto that pier!"

They fought their way to the café at the end of the pier and then swarmed past it and out along the gangplank.

The surface of the Thames was alive with reflected light. Vivid reds and oranges, golds and yellows made ever-changing patterns on the normally black water. Pieces of garbage and wreckage and the bodies of people and animals flowed past serenely on the current.

The kids kept moving down the gangplank and scrambled onto the nearest boat, a blue-and-white cruiser with an enclosed lower deck and an open-sided upper deck.

Jordan made his way to the wheelhouse at the front. DogNut and one of his friends went around throwing off the mooring ropes. Ed helped the other kids climb aboard and checked that everyone was all right. Along with Jordan's crew, there were about twenty others who'd fought alongside them. The casualties from his own gang weren't as bad as Ed had feared. Three of Matt's acolytes hadn't made it; the others were bruised, but they had no serious cuts. Ed himself was painted with gore from head to foot—as far as he could tell, though, none of it was his.

Last to board were Courtney and Aleisha. Aleisha's arm was soaked with blood, and she was in a lot of pain. Her dark skin was gray, and she looked smaller than ever, as if she had shrunk in on herself.

"Take her below," said Ed. "Sit her down and stay with her. When we get to the other side we'll catch up with the truck and get some antiseptic and bandages and stuff."

"The truck," said Aleisha, perking up for a moment. "Did they make it?"

Ed smiled. "They made it."

"Woo-hoo." Aleisha tried to shout, but didn't have the strength.

"And we're going to make it too," Ed said defiantly. "We'll get your arm fixed up. . . . Actually . . ."

Ed grabbed Kyle, who was going past with his garden hoe. "Kyle," he said, "there must be a first-aid kit somewhere on board. See if you can find it and sort these two out."

"Aye, aye, skipper!" Kyle saluted and blundered off along the rocking deck.

The sickos didn't try to get onto the boat, and the kids on

the boat laughed and jeered at them as DogNut came running over to Ed.

"There's only one rope left," he said. "Shall I let her go?"

Ed took a last look back. Lambeth Palace was now completely engulfed in flames, which were spreading to some of the trees along the riverside. The noise was deafening and the whole sky to the south looked like something out of a war film.

The sickos were starting to cross Lambeth Bridge. The truck was somewhere on the north side, with all their food, water, bedding, extra weapons, everything they needed to survive. If Ed and the others couldn't get to it, if they couldn't get over in time, and Justin couldn't hang on for them . . .

Then they'd have to start over again, with nothing.

"What are you waiting for?" he said. "Let's go!"

DogNut cast off and they drifted out onto the Thames. The boat started to turn slowly in the water. The Thames was tidal, which meant that the water could be pushed back up from the sea when the tide was high. Ed reckoned it must be high now, because the flow wasn't too fast. They would still be pulled downstream on the current, though, and would have to try to somehow steer across.

Ed hadn't thought about that. He hoped Jordan knew what he was doing. All he wanted was to collapse onto one of the benches and sleep.

Not yet.

He had to check that somebody was in control of the boat.

He went to the front and climbed the steps to the wheelhouse.

There was broken glass on the floor where the window had been smashed. Jordan was at the wheel; with him were Matt and Archie Bishop. As Ed came in, the three of them were arguing about something.

"Nothing will work without any power," Archie Bishop was saying.

"It's doing something," said Jordan. "The wheel's turning."

"Let me do that," said Matt, stepping forward, his face beaming with eager excitement.

"Why you?" Ed asked. "Do you know about boats or something?"

"This was all meant to be," said Matt.

Ed sighed. "What are you on about now?" he asked. "This isn't the time for your religious crap."

Matt turned his beam on Ed.

"No, Ed, don't you see?" he said. "We're being sent downriver to the temple."

"Please don't start up about St. Paul's again, Matt."

"Listen to me!" Matt shouted, jabbing a grubby finger at the scab on his forehead and making it bleed. "I have the mark of the Lamb on me. I know the truth!"

"We're not going downriver, Matt," said Ed. "We just need to get across to the other side to meet up with the others."

"No. It was not meant to be like that. We're supposed to go to the temple of the Lamb. This boat was given to us."

"He's right," said Archie Bishop. "It's all written in the papers. The fire, the flood, the battle, the river of blood."

"What river of blood?"

"Look at it!"

Ed gazed out at the Thames, washed with scarlet.

"*The third angel poured out his bowl on the rivers and springs of water, and they became blood,*" said Matt, his voice low and urgent. "*Then I heard the angel in charge of the waters say: 'You are just in these judgments, you who are and who were, and you have given them blood to drink as they deserve'* . . ."

"You're not helping, Matt," said Ed, weariness eating away at his last few scraps of patience.

"We're crossing to the promised place," said Matt.

"Bullshit," Ed snapped. "We just need to get to the other side. Once we're there, if you want to bugger off down to St. Paul's with your silly flag and your silly bits of burned paper, feel free, but we're not coming with you. Okay?"

"We'd have to cross the whole of London, though," Matt protested. "This boat can take us straight there."

"We might not have much choice," said Jordan. "The river's taking us that way."

"Just go across diagonally," said Ed. "We need to be near the truck."

"I'm trying. Believe me, I'm trying."

"The river is taking us where we are supposed to go," said Matt.

"No way," said Ed.

"My way!" Matt yelled, and he threw himself at Jordan.

76

Matt tried to wrestle the wheel out of Jordan's grasp, puffing and panting with the effort.

"What are you doing?" Jordan snapped, and batted Matt away. The backhander didn't look like much—Jordan hardly seemed to move—but Matt flew across the wheelhouse and crashed into the door with a grunt. It didn't stop him, though. Instantly, he and Archie came back at Jordan and grabbed hold of an arm each.

"Help me, Ed," Matt gasped.

"Are you nuts?" said Ed, not sure whether to laugh or get angry. He got past the three struggling boys and took the wheel. It was hard to tell which way he should turn it; the boat was drifting out of control in the current, spinning slowly.

Jordan threw Matt and Archie off, sending them sprawling onto the floor. Now Matt coiled his arms around Jordan's legs, and Archie got up and tried to push him over. Jordan kept his balance and knocked Archie down before kicking Matt away.

Whichever direction Ed spun the wheel, it didn't seem to be having any effect on the boat. He soon had no idea which way they were facing, and felt a rising sense of panic.

Then he heard Jordan say, "Is that loaded?" And he turned to see Matt waving an old British Army Browning revolver.

Matt nodded, his face twisted by a wild excitement. It was clear that Jordan didn't know whether to believe him. Did Matt even know how to fire it?

But it would be stupid to risk testing him.

Jordan looked at Ed.

"Do something."

"I'm not responsible for him," said Ed.

"He's one of yours."

Ed gave a nervous laugh. "He doesn't follow me. He follows the Lamb."

"Will he shoot?"

"He's crazy enough."

Now Matt spoke. "Get the wheel, Archie," he said. "Steer us downriver to St. Paul's."

Archie was shaking. His nose was bleeding and one eye was bruised. He pushed Ed out of the way, took hold of the wheel, and tried to take control of the boat.

"I can't do it, Matt. I don't know how."

"Let the Lamb guide you!"

"Use the Force, Luke," Ed scoffed, and Matt glowered at him.

"I can't do it," Archie shouted, his voice high and wobbly.

"Yes you can!"

77

O n the lower deck, Aleisha was shaking and holding her arm tight to her belly. She was sitting on one of the benches with her back against the windows. Kyle had found a first-aid kit, and he and Courtney had disinfected the wound and bandaged it. It had looked bad—ragged and torn by Frédérique's teeth. Aleisha was trying to stay cheerful, but was slipping into shock, shivering, her teeth clattering, her eyes rolling up in her head.

Courtney put her arm around her. "We're all right now, babe," she said, and Aleisha forced her gray lips into a smile.

"Yeah."

Kyle looked out the windows into the night. "I'm going to see what's up," he said. "We're all over the place. Doesn't feel like anyone's driving this thing."

He walked off, but as he got to the exit, there was a horrible crunch, and the boat lurched to the side. Everyone was thrown to the floor, and Courtney was aware of a massive stone bulk passing the windows.

"We've hit something!" she shrieked.

The windows all down the side where Aleisha had been sitting were cracked. Two of them had smashed completely, letting in smoke and the rushing, roaring, gurgling din of the river. There was also a screeching, scraping noise and the sound of splintering wood and breaking glass.

Courtney looked for her friend. Aleisha had fallen to the floor and hit her head on the table on the way down. She was still conscious, but dazed. Courtney took a step toward her as the boat gave another sudden lurch and tilted over at a crazy angle. Kyle grabbed Courtney to stop her falling. Aleisha rolled against the side.

"Hold on, Aleisha!" Courtney tried to break free from where Kyle was holding her steady, and the next moment, with a deafening crack, the boat split completely open. A gush of water burst through, reaching in like a giant black hand, and closed around Aleisha. And then it withdrew, sucked out as the boat tilted back the other way.

"Aleisha!" Courtney screamed, but her friend was gone.

"You idiot, Matt!" Ed shouted, picking himself up from where he'd been thrown to the floor by the force of the collision. "That was Westminster Bridge."

"We're sinking," said Archie, clinging to the wheel to keep from falling over.

"It's worse than that," said Jordan, looking out the windows. "We're breaking up. We need to find the lifeboats."

"Out there, look!" Archie nodded through the window of the wheelhouse. There was a short deck in front of them with two dinghies tethered to it.

"We'll never all fit on them," said Ed. "There must be at least thirty of us."

"Look for more," said Jordan, struggling over to the door. "I'll take care of these two."

Matt was staring out at the flames that raged over the south side of the river, his face lit with writhing yellows and scarlets.

"The third angel sounded his trumpet," he said quietly. *"And a great star, blazing like a torch, fell from the sky on a third of the rivers and on the springs of water—the name of the star is Wormwood. A third of the waters turned bitter, and many people died from the waters that had become bitter."*

78

Kyle had gotten rid of his garden hoe and swapped it for a fire ax. He was up on the roof of the top deck with three of Jordan's boys, hacking through the ropes that held four more lifeboats in place. It was tricky and dangerous work with the cruiser lying at such a steep angle; every few seconds the boat gave a sharp jolt as the water tugged at it, slowly tearing it in half.

Ed appeared and helped them, clinging on to some rope to keep from falling off. Amazingly, Kyle still seemed to be enjoying himself, as if this were all some crazy game.

Kids were swarming over the boat in a panic. There was nowhere to go except up to the roof or onto the short deck at the front. Ed heard DogNut down below yelling at them not to jump in. He leaned over and shouted down to him. "There's lifeboats up here. We'll get them into the water, but be careful getting in. Jordan's got two more boats at the front."

The next few minutes were a nightmare. Ed was only dimly aware of all that was going on around him. Kids trying not to fall off the cruiser as she broke up. Other kids trying to get the boats into the water without losing them. Dead bodies and bits of floating wreckage knocking into them. Screams. Shouts. Arguments. Hands burned on ropes. Clothes drenched with water. Courtney yelling in one ear about Aleisha. DogNut yelling, "Hurry up! Hurry up!" in the other.

Then the kids were spilling off the cruiser as she sank lower in the water, packing the lifeboats and threatening to capsize them. Jordan was in control at the front, snarling at the kids to slow down. Ed was trying to keep some sense of order on the roof.

"Don't aim directly for the lifeboats," Ed barked as kids lowered themselves over the side, or jumped, or slipped. "You'll sink them. You've got to land in the water next to them. The guys in the boats can pull you in."

The water between the cruiser and the lifeboats was soon thick with splashing kids. It was too dark and too chaotic to tell if anyone was sinking or being swept away. Ed just prayed that most of them would make it.

Now it was his turn. If he left it any longer, the cruiser was going to sink and drag him under.

He launched himself into the air. Hit the water with a punch to his guts. The cold snatched his breath away. He reached out for the nearest lifeboat, and then it was gone and he was under the water. Someone had landed on top of him, forcing him down. He felt hard shoes kicking at him. It was freezing, and he could sense his body shutting down. A pale face looked at him through the murk, the features frozen into a scream, eyes wide, mouth gaping, then it floated away and he was alone again. The current pulled at him. He wanted to shout but had his mouth clamped shut against the poisonous waters of the Thames.

Then suddenly he was in the fresh stinging air. The light of the fire was blinding him. Strong hands had hold of his jacket, and he was being pulled into one of the boats.

It was Kyle, still grinning like a madman. "Nearly lost you there, chief," he said, dumping Ed into the bottom of the boat. Ed lay there, useless as a landed fish.

"How many of us made it?" he croaked once he'd got his voice back. Nobody heard him, so he struggled to sit up. He saw Courtney packed in among the other kids next to DogNut. She was crying.

Ed looked back at the cruiser. It had finally split in two. The back half had sunk, but the top half was still afloat and drifting down the river, half submerged.

Then he saw an amazing sight. Matt and Archie and the four remaining acolytes were standing on top of the wheel-house roof, like the crew of a submarine coming into harbor. They were holding their banner upright, their faces reflecting the fire that raged over south London. They didn't look scared or worried at all. Rather, they appeared to be quite calm and at peace.

Ed looked at the banner. It was brightly lit by the flames, and the image of the golden boy on it seemed to be glowing. Behind him, the other boy, the shadowy one, looked as if he were made of smoke. The way the banner fluttered, the Lamb and the Goat appeared to be alive, moving. And then the lifeboat passed under Waterloo Bridge, and that was the last Ed saw of Matt.

79

The last stragglers were crossing the bridge; the feeblest, the weakest, the sickest, shambling along as behind them the flames tore at the sky, raining down ash and soot.

He'd stayed behind to eat a part of one of the small bodies lying in the road. The others, the stupid ones, just wanted to get away from the fire. Not him. He knew he had to eat. Meat Is Life. He'd stayed there squatting in the road as the fire ripped into the buildings. It was pretty. He liked fire. Always had.

The fire couldn't get him, though. It couldn't leap across the road or the round thing, the thing the cars went around, around, the roundabout, the magic roundabout. But there was nothing left for him here. He belched. He was full. He picked up his bundle and walked toward the bridge. They were over there, the ones he needed. He could smell them. The living food.

There was water below him now. He stopped to look. And over there . . . he knew those houses, the big boys lived there, the bastards, he knew the name. . . .

HP sauce, or something, the jolly green giant.

Big Ben.

Aaaah, it was all too much for him.

All he knew was that the bastards lived in there, in the spiky buildings. The ones who made the laws . . .

Politicians.

You see. He still had the words in him.

Politicians.

He looked down into the river. It was full of fire and death and pigs.

No, not pigs . . .

He looked at the boiling colors. He wanted to drop something in, see it splash. That's what you did, wasn't it? There was a game.

Pig sticks.

No.

Not pigs.

Pooh.

Pooh sticks.

Race them under the bridge. Two sticks. See which one came out first on the other side. He'd played it with him, the little one, the boy, what was his name . . . ?

Gone now.

They'd played it, racing sticks under a bridge in the park. Played the game. He wanted to drop something in now. He had something. This thing in his hands. Didn't know what it was. Why was he carrying it?

It weighed nothing, just a bundle of scraps and twigs.

A stick, yeah. It was a sort of stick.

He propped it on the wall of the bridge, then pushed it

over, watched as it turned and fluttered in the air, as if it were trying to fly away. And somehow it turned into a boy. A little angel, flying down . . .

Down and down it fell.

And then the tiny splash.

Watched it float away under the bridge.

Now what? There was something he was going to do, something about a race and sticks and pigs and a jolly green giant.

It had gone.

No mind. No mind. Get over the water to the other side. Get home. Go see his boy.

His Liam.

That was it. Get home to see Liam.

He turned and walked on.

80

The first lifeboat bumped into the pier, and the kids cheered. They'd been beginning to wonder if they'd ever be able to make it to the north bank, or whether they were going to be swept all the way down to the estuary and out to sea. They'd managed to lash the boats together, which gave them greater stability and protection, but steering the giant raft had proved difficult. There were powerful eddies and currents in the Thames, and the raft had a tendency to spin. The force of the water seemed to grow stronger and stronger, and no matter how hard they tried to aim toward the edge, they kept being pulled back into the center, where the flow was strongest. After bumping against Hungerford Bridge, they passed under seven more bridges, and each time it caused a mad panic among the kids. The water bunched up and foamed between the pilings, and they nearly lost two of the boats in a collision. But as they cleared London Bridge, they hit a clear straight stretch of river and finally managed to get some sort of control over the raft. Inch by inch, yard by yard, they made their way closer to the side. Then they'd seen a modern steel pier sticking out into the river, and it had given them something to aim for.

They clawed at the water, sticking their bodies half over the sides and kicking, scrabbling with the few oars they had. At last they'd stopped.

They were on a wide, open reach of the Thames. On the far side was the great hulk of the battleship HMS *Belfast*, which had been run as a tourist attraction. Ahead were the twin gothic towers of Tower Bridge. On this side of the river were the high walls and turrets of the Tower of London.

Ed planted his feet firmly on the steel deck of the pier and hugged Courtney. The two of them were cold and wet and exhausted. They clung to each other, laughing and crying at the same time.

The fire hadn't spread this far downriver, so it was quite dark, though the sky to the west was lit by an angry red glow. Ed broke away from Courtney, wiped his face, and looked up at the ramparts of the Tower, silhouetted against the sky.

"It was Wiki, wasn't it?" he said. "Or was it Jibber-jabber? One of them, anyway, said we should come here."

"I don't know," said Courtney. "Where are we?"

"Don't you recognize it? It's the Tower of London."

"It looks like a castle."

"That's because it *is* a castle." Ed laughed. "The oldest bit was built by William the Conqueror, I think."

"Who's he?"

"It doesn't matter." Ed shook his head. "All that matters is that we've washed up in just about the safest spot we could. This is the perfect place to hide out. No sickos could get to us in there."

Jordan Hordern was already organizing the kids, shouting at them to form into groups. "We need to know who's made it and who we've lost," he barked.

Ed checked his crew. It didn't take long. He and Courtney were the only two left. Jordan had lost five of his boys, either in the fight or when the boat had sunk. Of the third group, the kids who'd joined the fight at the roundabout, nobody really knew how many there had been to start with. Some kids talked of losing friends, but again it had all been so confusing—for all they knew their friends could have crossed Lambeth Bridge safely. Though one or two were certain their friends had disappeared in the water. Ed remembered that pale face sinking past him when he'd gone under.

He tried to shut the image out of his mind.

"We need to get inside the Tower," said Jordan, who had evidently come to the same conclusion as Ed. "In the morning we can find food and water, but for now we need somewhere to get warm and dry and safe. We have to assume, though, that there's already people inside. So be ready for a fight." He took off his glasses and wiped them clean. "If you all work together and do what I say, you'll be all right. But just remember—I'm in charge. Okay? DogNut here is my second in command, directly responsible for my boys. That's Ed over there. The one with the scar. He's in charge of everyone else. You do what he says, he does what I say."

"Who says he's in charge of us?" said a short kid with thick arms and a fat neck.

"I do."

"And who says you're in charge?"

Jordan walked over to the short kid. He didn't stare at

him directly, but stood right next to him and looked out across the river at HMS *Belfast*. Somehow it was more intimidating than if he'd gone eyeball to eyeball with him.

"Don't argue with me," he said quietly.

"Listen—" said the kid, but Jordan cut him off.

"So you want to be in charge, do you?"

"Maybe?"

The short kid looked around for support. Nobody seemed keen to back him up.

"Do you not think I'd better be in charge?" asked Jordan. His voice low and steady.

"Yeah, all right," said the short kid, and Jordan walked away.

"I like him. I like his style," said Kyle quietly as he came over to stand next to Ed, still holding his fire ax. Then he raised his voice and addressed everyone else. "I ain't got no problems with Ed," he said, and gave a big smile. "He knows what he's doing. I saw him fight. This man is a *maniac*! Now, let's get shifted. I'm freezing my ass off here."

The castle was ringed by two walls: a plain outer wall, and a higher inner wall studded with round towers. The main entrance was via a large turreted gatehouse connected to the castle by a narrow walkway over the wide, dry moat.

The gates in the gatehouse were too big and solid to force, but there were drainpipes up the outer wall of the castle, and DogNut and Kyle volunteered to see if they could climb them. Jordan gave them the go-ahead, and they vaulted the railings by the edge of the moat and then sprinted across the grass to the other side.

They stopped at the bottom of the wall and looked up.

"What d'you reckon?" DogNut asked.

"No problem," said Kyle. "Used to break into houses all the time when I was younger. Race you!"

It proved to be quite easy. The two of them scrambled up the drainpipes and were over the top of the wall in less than a minute. It was another easy climb down the other side, where they found the main castle gates unguarded and secured only with a metal bar.

They lifted the bar, and five minutes later the kids were tramping into the Tower. Some of them had visited recently with their schools, and they showed the party to a gateway through to the inner courtyard. There was a big open space. Around the edges were various ancient castle towers and a mismatched jumble of redbrick, Tudor, and Victorian houses. The oldest part, the White Tower, a tall square building with a turret at each corner, stood in the center of the grounds on a low mound.

The kids assembled in an area to one side that felt like a village green, with a chapel at one end and timber-framed houses at the other.

"Looks like there's no one about," said DogNut.

"Let's find out," said Kyle, and before anyone could stop him, he started shouting, "Hey! Wakey, wakey! Anyone at home?"

Jordan hurried over to shut him up. "What are you doing?" he said. "If there is anyone here, we don't want to wake them up. We'll lose the element of surprise."

"Why, what was you gonna do?" asked Kyle, with a mad grin. "Slaughter them in their beds? Cut their throats while they sleep?"

"Makes no difference now," said Jordan. "Here they come."

Figures were emerging from one of the houses. Ed had lost his rifle, but he still had his pistol in its holster. He was just about to slip it loose when he saw that they were only other kids, three unarmed boys and a girl, wrapped in coats, looking cold, sleepy, and confused.

"Who are you?" said one of the boys, with a yawn. He looked like he hadn't eaten in days. He was tall and thin with sunken cheeks and a bad cough. "How'd you get in?"

"Who's in charge here?" asked Jordan.

"No one really." The boy shrugged.

"What about Tomoki?" said the girl.

"Yeah, Tomoki, I suppose."

"Go and get him."

"What?"

"Go and get this Tomoki," said Jordan. "I want to talk to him."

"He'll be asleep."

"Then wake him up."

"I'll go," said a younger boy, and he trotted off toward the timber-framed building.

The two groups stood there staring at each other. Ed was shivering and just wanted to go inside and get warm. But Jordan wasn't moving.

"How many of you are there living here?" he asked the boy with the cough.

"Dunno," he replied. "Maybe thirty?"

"Okay," was all that Jordan said.

In a minute the small boy returned with an older boy

who had long, straight black hair and oriental features.

"What's going on?" he said sleepily as he approached. "Who are you?"

"I am Jordan Hordern. Are you Tomoki?"

"Yeah." Tomoki stopped and squared up to Jordan.

"And you're in charge in here?"

"I suppose so."

"No sa seems very sure of it."

"All right, yes," said Tomoki. "I *am* in charge here."

"Not anymore, you're not," said Jordan.

"What?"

"From now on, I'm in charge."

Tomoki laughed. "You can't just walk in here and—"

"That's just the point, though, isn't it?" said Jordan.

"What do you mean?"

"We did just walk in here." Jordan stepped toward Tomoki with such an air of quiet menace that Tomoki fell silent and backed away. He was shorter than Jordan and much less confident.

More kids were emerging from the buildings, curious and sleep-addled. Some were armed, but they held back. They didn't look like they had the stomach for a fight.

"You've got the best site in London," said Jordan, looking at the White Tower rather than at Tomoki. "The perfect place to live. A castle. Easy to defend. Full of weapons. And what are you doing? There's no guards posted. The gates weren't even locked. All we had to do was climb a couple of drainpipes and we were in."

"Yeah, well, mothers and fathers can't climb drainpipes, can they?" Tomoki protested.

Jordan pressed on. "You don't deserve to be in charge here," he said. "And if you don't care about running this place properly, then you shouldn't be worried that I'm taking over."

Tomoki gave a dismissive shrug and a grunt. He'd been half asleep when he came out, with no idea what was going on. Now he was pulling himself together.

"We outnumber you," he said evenly. "So let's not get into an argument, okay? Now, I don't mind you staying here—we need all the help we can get, quite frankly. It hasn't been easy for us. But you can't expect to walk in here and take over just like that."

"I agree," said Jordan. "Let's not get into an argument. I don't like arguments."

"Good."

"So I'll fight you for it."

"You want to fight me?" Tomoki sounded incredulous.

"Yes."

"That's not the way things are decided."

"It is now," said Jordan. "The world's changed. So, come on."

"No," said Tomoki, and he backed away as Jordan advanced on him.

"Fight me," said Jordan.

He kept on coming, and Tomoki was stumbling backward. In the end he put up a hand to Jordan's chest to try to stop him.

Jordan clipped him. The movement was fast and casual at the same time. Tomoki's head jerked to the side and he crumpled to his knees.

Jordan stood over him for a moment, then helped him

to his feet. Tomoki wobbled on shaking legs, stunned and groggy.

"Nothing personal," Jordan said quietly, and then he turned to face the ring of kids who had come out to see what was going on.

"If the rest of you want to fight us, that's fine. But you will lose. We've battled our way across town to get here—you will not be able to beat us. Tomoki can keep his position here, as your representative, but from now on we all work together, and you all do what I say. If anyone doesn't agree with me, come over here and I will talk to you."

Nobody moved.

Ed felt an uncomfortable mixture of embarrassment and pride. He didn't like Jordan's cold bullying tactics, but he couldn't deny that he was probably the best man for the job; and when it came down to it, Ed, like everyone else, just wanted to get this over with quickly so that he could go and lie down somewhere and fall asleep.

"Good," said Jordan. "Then it's decided."

Ed sighed and closed his eyes.

Safe at last.

81

The morning sun was bright. Blinding him. He covered his face with his hands. He knew this place. A big open square, a pill, a pillar, big stone pillar in the middle. The statue of a man on the top. The man had a name. He was a hero. Yeah, what was his name? He had one eye and a hat.

Nelson.

Yes. He grinned. He still knew things. He was going to beat the disease. Hadn't he told them? He was going to live. He was going to go home and live a happy life.

Home.

He knew the way to go now. He knew this bit of . . . Where was he? What was the name of this place?

Nelson.

Lord Nelson. Not Nelson. Lord Lumsden. London. Lord London. London Town.

As he limped across the square, a mess of birds took flight all around him, swirling up into the sky and confusing him. He flailed at them, cursing and swearing.

They were pigs.

Pigs might fly.

Pigeons too.

The next thing he knew he had one in his hand. He'd caught it in midair. Like a golfer. A goalie. His grin grew wide. He was king of this place. He should be up on top of that pillar. Lord London! That was him. He squeezed the bird until he could feel its bones crack. Then he stuffed the corpse into the pocket of his jogging pants. He was cold. He'd lost his shirt in a fight over a dead boy. It had been ripped anyway.

The boy done that. Before.

He'd make that boy behave himself.

He'd won the fight but lost his . . . what was the word? He'd had it just now. Save it for later.

Shirt. Yes. His shirt.

Something glittering caught his eye. An overturned stall. It had scarves and hats and . . .

Souvenirs.

That was a good word. A hard word to remember. How many people knew that word?

He shouted it.

"Souvenir! Souvenir! Souvenir!"

He came to the stall and rifled through the stuff, throwing aside rubbish and junk and souvenirs.

Junk. Junky souvenirs.

Then he found a sleeveless vest. He held it up. It looked good. The colors pleased him. There was a pattern on it, a picture, red stripes, one way and the other way.

A crisscross.

Cross.

He saluted.

"Lord Nelson, sir," he said, the words clear in his head but coming out as a slurred grunt.

It was a flag.

The cross of his country.

He pulled it over his head. Yes. He was the king now. The king of London, the king of the world. And he was going to get strong and take his revenge on those boys. Those clever-clever schoolkids who thought they could beat him.

Him! Lord Nelson. Lord London. King of souvenirs.

And worse. They done bad. They took his Liam from him. Yes. They killed him. He'd been looking after Liam and they killed him.

They couldn't do that to him. He was a hero. He was Charlie George. Saint Charlie. Saint George, the pigeon slayer. Not a pigeon, a dragon. Yes. Saint George. And he was going to kill every dragon in the world.

But first he was going to go home and see his boy. And he was going to take his boy to the football. To the big church, what were they called? Catherine wheel? No. Catholic. Cathedral. Yes. His own cathedral. The stadium. The theater of dreams.

Home.

The Arsenal.

ONE YEAR LATER

Ed was standing on the battlements with Kyle, looking at the Thames as it flowed sluggishly past. It had rained the night before, and everything glistened wet. Now, though, a patch of blue appeared in the sky, the sun broke through the clouds, and everywhere was lit up gold and silver.

He turned his scarred face toward Kyle and smiled. "The sun actually feels warm," he said.

Kyle grinned back at him. "You're right, skipper," he said. "Soon be summer."

"Slow down a bit," said Ed. "We haven't had spring yet."

"I never did work out which way around the seasons went." Kyle laughed. "Account of me dyslexia. If you asked me, I couldn't even tell you how long we been here."

"Feels like forever."

Ed thought back to when they'd first arrived. The first few weeks at the Tower had been very busy. Jordan had kicked everyone into shape, insisting that the key to survival was organization. Left to themselves, the kids would have behaved like kids. They would have drifted into anarchy and squabbling. But Jordan wasn't going to let that happen. He had a vision, and he had drive. He was going to make sure they survived.

He'd started by organizing a military system. Guards and soldiers and scavenging parties. The White Tower was full of weapons and armor, and the buildings were well protected. Ed was made captain of the Tower Guard, in charge of defending the castle. He was a strong, solid figure whom everyone trusted. Knowing that he was watching out for them made the younger kids feel safe and secure. Kyle acted as a sort of personal bodyguard. Ed could do nothing to shake off the big square-headed boy; wherever he went, Kyle was at his side.

When spring arrived, the dry moat had been dug over and planted with seeds. The kids had been inspired by old photographs they'd found showing the moat during wartime, when it had been turned into a giant vegetable garden.

Spring had turned into summer, and the kids' spirits had been lifted by the light and warmth and sense of new life. But summer had drifted into autumn and autumn into winter. Food was always short. The scavenging parties had to search buildings farther and farther away to find stuff to eat. Twice they'd struck lucky and found warehouses stacked with provisions, but despite rationing, even those had soon started to run low.

The worst part was the lack of fresh food. The vegetable gardens hadn't been very productive. The kids had a lot to learn, and in the autumn the Thames had risen and flooded the moat, so they'd lost all their crops. They raided health food shops and chemists for supplements, vitamins, and minerals, but they were no substitute for real fruit and vegetables. Lots of the kids had gotten sick; with their poor diet and no proper doctors there was nothing they could do about it. Too many had died.

With the winter had come the cold and the dark, and attacks on the scavenging parties from sickos had become more frequent. They'd been just as desperate and hungry as the kids. It had snowed in January, and while some of the kids enjoyed playing in it, the relentless freezing dampness made everyone miserable. At night they'd huddled together in big piles like hibernating insects. The death rate rose. The kids were kept busy carting bodies away to be dropped into the icy Thames.

To Ed it had seemed like the winter was never going to end, so now feeling the sun on his back filled him with fresh hope. A year. They'd survived for a whole year. Hard to believe. And now it was possible, just possible, that they were going to make it. The world wasn't going to end.

Ed had been so busy, so tired at night, so distracted by everything that needed to be done, that his birthday had come and gone without him even noticing. He'd realized with a shock one day that he must be sixteen. He'd kept to himself for a few days, but he had shown no symptoms apart from a mild cough, and as all the kids had constant sore throats, coughs, and colds, he didn't worry too much about that.

He smiled. He was sixteen now. It looked like Justin had been right. Whatever the sickos had caught, the kids weren't going to get it.

"We're alive," he said, and Kyle looked confused.

"What d'you mean?"

"I mean we're *alive*, Kylo. Against all the odds we're standing here, breathing." He slapped the top of the wall and gave a great whoop of joy. Kyle shook his head and looked at him like he was nuts. Kyle didn't ever think too deeply about anything.

There was a shout, and DogNut appeared. He'd shown his strength and reliability in the last year and was well respected by the other kids. Jordan had made him captain of the Pathfinders, the name he'd given to the scavengers.

"See that!" he said cheerily, turning his face to the sky. "Sun's out at last!"

Ed smiled at him. "Better get some of your guys to find us some sunblock," he said.

DogNut laughed and settled next to him, arms over the wall. "Feels good."

"I was just thinking back to when we first arrived," said Ed.

"I think about them crazy days in south London sometimes," said DogNut, "and it all seems like a dream, or a movie I watched once a long time ago."

"I know what you mean," said Ed.

"Do you ever wonder what happened to the others?"

"Used to," said Ed. "Not so much anymore. Hardly remember them, to tell you the truth."

"You must remember them," said DogNut. "They was your mates."

"All my close friends died," said Ed quietly. "Malik, Bam, Jack . . ."

"What was the nerd called, who drove the truck?"

"Justin," said Ed. "Couldn't forget him. And there was little Wiki and his pal, Jibber-jabber. Then there was, God, what was he called?"

"Who?"

"Guy who was always reading? Chris Marker! That's it, and Kwanele."

"Which one was Kwanele?" DogNut asked.

"Guy who was always really well dressed."

"Oh, yeah. The Zulu dude. See, you *do* remember!"

"Yeah. Just needed to jog my brain."

"What was he called, the religious nut?" DogNut asked.

"Mad Matt," said Ed quietly. "Good riddance to him, I say. It was his fault the boat sank and Aleisha drowned. He could have killed us all. But the others. I hope they made it all right. They had all that food on the truck, and that weird kid, David, watching out for them, so I guess they're probably holed up somewhere like us."

"Don't you never think about Brooke?" DogNut asked.

"Oh, yeah, Brooke." Ed blew out his breath noisily through his nose. "Think about her now and then, I guess."

"I think about her all the time, man," said DogNut. "I mean, back in the day, I knew I was waiting my turn. She was hot for you—"

"Until I got this," Ed interrupted, putting a hand to the jagged scar that pulled his face out of shape.

"Is that why you ain't interested in her?" DogNut asked.

"What d'you mean?"

"You think she won't like you no more?"

"I don't really care," said Ed.

"Don't you want to find out what happened to her?"

"I've not really thought about it, to tell you the truth, DogNut. There's been too much going on, just trying to stay alive. Yeah, I mean, obviously now and then I do wonder."

"I do more than wonder," said DogNut. "She had her

problems, but she was *tough*, man, and I like that in a girl. She's the sort of chick you *need* in times like this. Plus, she was fine, bruv, *really* fine."

"What're you saying, DogNut?" Ed asked. "You want to go and look for her?"

"We should be finding out what other kids are up to out there, man," said DogNut. "We can't just sit behind these walls and pray that the world's gonna go away."

"But you're captain of the Pathfinders."

"Yeah, so I should be exploring! I'll clear it with the general. He won't have no beef with me. Things is quiet here. I've talked to some of the other kids, and a few of them want to come along. They got split up from brothers and sisters and best friends. Courtney, too, she misses Brooke."

"Well, good luck to you, mate," said Ed.

"Reason I'm telling you, Ed," said DogNut, "I thought you might want to come with us."

Ed turned away and looked back at the castle grounds. Kids busy everywhere. Safe. It was like a little town.

"This is my home, DogNut," he said. "*These* are my people now."

In the days after DogNut left, Ed thought about their conversation. He hadn't told the whole truth to DogNut. His friends were still with him more than he'd let on. He had bad dreams most nights, dreams in which Jack was still alive. He'd come at him out of the darkness, his wine-colored birthmark splashed down one side of his face. He always looked sad and angry, and always asked Ed why he'd abandoned him and left him for dead, and then Ed would see boils on Jack's skin and realize he had the disease, and he'd wake up gasping for breath.

All the kids were plagued by nightmares. It was understandable really, but there also seemed to be something strange about this part of town. This was the edge of the old City of London, the historic heart of the capital since Roman times. It was easy to believe that there was some ancient magic living deep in the stones here. The kids never went into the City itself, what had been the financial district before the collapse, an area of offices and skyscrapers and old, old churches. They'd made it a no-go zone. Not only was there little food to be found in those concrete-and-glass canyons, there was also a creepy, unsettling atmosphere, and the sickos who lived there were dangerous and unpredictable.

One rainy evening, Ed and Kyle were out guarding a works party that was securing the gates at the Tower Hill underground station. The kids had been meaning to seal the place up for some time. The dark tunnels below were a potential hiding place for sickos. The boys were alert and well armed. No kid would have dreamed of leaving the castle grounds without some kind of weapon. Ed carried a knife, a heavy sword in a scabbard, and a crossbow. His pistol had long since run out of ammunition, but he kept it by his bed as a reminder of the old days. Kyle carried a halberd. It was the perfect defensive weapon, a cross between a spear and an ax.

It had been an unsettling day. There had been some sort of disturbance in the no-go zone. Sickos were on the move. They usually kept well away from the Tower—they knew it was dangerous for them there—but today the normal rhythm had been upset, and scouting Pathfinders reported seeing gangs of them as near as Aldgate and Fenchurch Street.

"I'm gonna take another look 'round," said Kyle. "I'm getting itchy standing here doing nothing."

"All right," said Ed, "but be careful."

Kyle grinned and slapped him on the back. "When am I ever careful?" he said, and walked off with his halberd over his shoulder, chuckling and muttering to himself.

Ed felt his face, running his fingertips along the bumpy scar that ran from his forehead down almost to his chin. The wound was aching tonight—aching and prickly. He wasn't a superstitious boy, but when his scar hurt like this, he sometimes had the feeling it was trying to warn him of something. He never talked about this with any of his friends, for fear that they would accuse him of turning into Harry Potter.

He heard footsteps and the jangle of metal, and saw a group of kids coming through the underpass that ran beneath the main road next to the Tower. Jordan Hordern was at their head. He was wearing a breastplate and helmet that looked slightly incongruous with his battered old spectacles. The four boys with him all carried halberds.

"Weird night," he said when he saw Ed.

"You can feel it too?" Ed asked.

"Yeah," said Jordan. "Everyone's on edge. Maybe there's a thunderstorm coming. What're you doing out here, anyway?"

"Finally getting around to sealing off the station. The way things are, we wanted to try and get it all done today. The guys are just finishing."

"You should bring them in," said Jordan. "Whether they're finished or not. It's not gonna be safe out here tonight."

"They should be packing up now."

They walked over to the station gates, where, sure enough, the works party were putting their tools away. Jordan and his team helped them by priming the windup flashlights that they carried, and aiming the beams at the tool bags.

Just as they were all ready to go, Kyle came back, looking concerned. "You need to come and look at this," he said quietly.

"What is it?" Jordan asked.

"See for yourself."

Jordan told the others to stay out of sight, and he and Ed and one of his guards followed Kyle back the way he had come. Sticking close together, they walked past an old bit of Roman wall and along the side of an ugly modern gray brick building that offered them some cover, moving quickly and silently. When they got to the end of the office block, Kyle stopped and nodded toward the road. Ed crept forward to the corner and cautiously peered around.

He looked up the road toward the railway bridge and gasped, sucking in air and holding it in his lungs. He couldn't quite believe what he was seeing.

He pulled back and turned to Jordan. "Take a look," he said.

Now it was Jordan's turn. Ed waited for his response, wondering if it would be the same as his. Had he really seen what he thought he'd seen? He frowned and rubbed his scar. It was aching again. He told himself he was being stupid, he was imagining things, haunted by the weird atmosphere of the day.

At last Jordan ducked back from the corner and looked at Ed. "It can't be," he whispered.

Ed made a move to take another look, when Kyle grabbed

him and pulled him back. The four of them crouched there in the darkness as two people walked past the end of the building along the road toward the Tower.

They were two small boys. They couldn't have been more than nine or ten years old, dirty and exhausted, wide-eyed, delirious even. They looked like they could hardly stand up, let alone walk. They were soaked by the thin rain that drizzled relentlessly.

But what caused Ed to hold his breath was that the two of them exactly resembled the boys on Matt's religious banner. The one that everyone had laughed at when Harry Ryan had written "Angus Day" on it.

The Lamb and the Goat.

One boy was slightly in front of the other, just as the Lamb had been depicted on the banner. He was wearing a filthy white sweatshirt and had fair hair and pale skin; the second boy had wild dark hair, and his skin was so grubby he looked almost black. He was hanging back behind the first kid like his shadow.

"It's a coincidence," Ed whispered. "It has to be."

"We should be careful," said Jordan. "They've come from the no-go zone. There's something not right about them."

Ed was getting freaked out. "Bloody hell, Jordan," he whispered. "Don't tell me you're starting to believe in Matt's crap?"

"You thought exactly the same thing as I did when you saw them, Ed."

"Come off it, Jordan, they're just little boys."

But even as he said it, Ed doubted his own words.

Strange things had happened in the world. If Matt had been right, those boys just might be God and the Devil over there, walking right past them, not five yards away.

Don't be an idiot.

Ed straightened up. "Stand still. Don't move."

The boys froze.

"We're kids," the fair-haired one shouted, without turning around. "Only kids."

"Let's hope so," said Ed under his breath, then he shouted back at the boy. "I can see that. Where have you come from?"

"Waitrose," said the kid.

Ed wanted to laugh, but stopped himself. It was too ridiculous. They hadn't come from heaven. They'd come from a supermarket.

"Waitrose?"

The little boy turned around. "In Holloway."

"Where's that?"

"North London. Past Camden Town."

Ed tried to figure out how far that was. His geography of London wasn't great, but he was pretty sure that Camden was a fair distance away.

"You've come all the way from there?"

"Yes—I'm trying to get to Buckingham Palace."

This was getting more and more surreal.

"Well, you're more than a little lost," he pointed out.

"I know," said the boy. "Please, we're very tired and hungry. We've been running from grown-ups all day." He sounded scared and shaky, not like a god at all.

"Is it just the two of you?"

"Yes."

Ed and the others walked into the road and approached the boys.

"Will you help us?" the dark-haired boy called to them. "We can't go on. These are our last legs."

Ed whispered to Jordan. "You satisfied? They're just kids."

"I know," said Jordan. "But you can't be too careful. It's been an unusual day. And you must admit . . ."

"Yeah, I know, but I mean . . ." Ed paused. He was trying to convince himself more than Jordan that there was nothing supernatural about these two boys. "You don't . . . *feel* anything?"

"You said it, Ed, they're just kids."

"Yeah."

Ed went over to the boys, taking off his helmet. The boys looked at his scar with wide eyes. He knew the effect it had on people, so he smiled so as not to scare them, and knelt down in front of them.

"How old are you two?" he asked.

"Nine," they both said together.

"And you've made it all the way here from north London?"

"The shrimp did," said the dark-haired kid. "I been living around about Spitalfields, but I got into the tunnels and I was sore lost and—"

"Whoa, hold on, not so fast." Ed put up his hand to stop him. "So, you've been in Spitalfields? Who's been looking after you?"

The dark-haired kid shrugged. "No one. There was some other kids with me one time, but they're all dead now, you can count on it. It was only me. But then I found the hobbit. We been helping each other. We're pals."

Ed shook his head and snorted with laughter. "And here we were thinking we were pretty clever living in the Tower— pretty tough. You two kids have shown us up as a bunch of wimps."

"Is it safe there?" said the fair-haired boy.

"In the Tower?" Ed thought about it. "Safe enough."

"You sure?"

"You've been through a lot, haven't you?"

The fair-haired boy nodded.

"Well, it's as safe as anywhere, I guess. Safer than out here on the streets. Safer than down in the tube tunnels, that's for sure."

"Will you take us there?"

"Sure. Why not?"

"And we'll really be safe? It's just you? Just kids?"

"There's sixty-seven of us living there," Ed explained. "All kids. All ages. It's not the greatest life in the world. But it's a life. You're safe now, mate."

The two boys burst into tears.

Ed nearly joined them. He held them to his chest until they stopped crying, and then picked them up so that they sat against his hips, and carried them toward the Tower.

As they walked along, an image of the banner came into his head once again.

Maybe, just maybe, Matt had been right all along.

DON'T MISS THE NEXT FRIGHTFULLY THRILLING INSTALLMENT IN THE ENEMY SERIES:

THE FEAR

PROLOGUE

THE COLLECTOR

*S*tuff . . . *more stuff . . . Get more stuff . . . good stuff . . .*

It was dark outside, safe to leave now. He squeezed his great bulk down the hallway and out the front door, sniffing the air. A curtain of greasy hair flopped in front of his eyes and he pushed it back with an enormous fat hand, smearing a shiny yellow streak across his face from a burst pustule on his cheek.

He smiled. He was going out to find stuff.

More stuff.

All he had ever really been interested in was stuff. Things. Gadgets. Toys. Gizmos. His tiny basement apartment had always been full of it. Days and nights he had spent down there on his computer—TV on, music blaring, playing games: playing and playing and playing until he lost all track of time. He had been so happy down there, surrounded by his stuff, his shelves of DVDs, CDs, old vinyl, comics, *Star Wars* figures, manga figures, *Star Trek* collectibles, books and magazines, take-out food cartons, toy robots, keyboards and amps and screens. . . . Nothing ever chucked away. Old computers piled in corners, mobile phones, cameras, tangled piles of cords and plugs . . .

Stuff. *A life of stuff.*

Eventually he had made holes in the walls, burrowed out of his flat, taken over the basements on either side, and when they were full, he had moved upward, floor by floor, filling the building ever fuller with stuff.

And now he was off out to find more stuff. It was so easy.

Everything was just lying around waiting for him to come and pick it up. He held a sturdy shopping bag in each meaty hand, though he didn't think he'd need them tonight. Tonight he was looking for toys. His last toys were broken beyond repair. They'd stopped moving, stopped entertaining him with their jerky actions. Stopped making their funny noises. What use were toys if you couldn't play games with them anymore?

When they no longer worked, he simply ate them.

Collecting stuff and eating, that was all he did now. When his toys broke, he would sit on his sofa and stare at the blank screens of his TVs, waiting for night to fall. Sometimes he would sit at the computer, tapping away at the keyboard, some deep memory stirring inside him. For hours on end. Tap, tap, tapping. Making a strange kind of music.

But now he had a purpose.

He waddled slowly down the road, taking great care with each step. There was enough light from the thin moon and distant stars to pick his way along. He didn't mind the dark. In truth he had always been nocturnal, sitting with the curtains drawn, no interest in sunlight or fresh air or other people.

He was careful, though. If he fell down, it would be hard for him to get up again. His bare feet landed solidly and squarely on the filthy surface of the road he knew so well. Night after night he would come out here and move from shop to shop, house to house, looting them for more stuff. Like some huge clumsy bear ransacking people's trash cans, his strong arms ripping and tearing to get at what he needed.

He was tempted by the massive building down the road. The department store. So many nights he'd spent in there removing stuff. But it was getting too dangerous now. Others had gotten in and made nests, and they sometimes tried to attack him as he trundled about, searching for anything he'd missed. They couldn't do him any real harm—he was too big, too heavy, too solid—but he liked to hunt for his stuff in peace. So he had taken to breaking into houses instead. There was always stuff in them. This had been a rich neighborhood. He would tear out stereo systems, pull flat screen TVs from walls, dig through drawers for cameras and navigation systems and iPods and cell phones, cramming them into his bags to carry home and add to his collection.

Not tonight, though. He had to concentrate, not forget what he was looking for.

Toys.

He'd heard them the night before. Smelled them. On his way back home with bulging shopping bags. He'd tried to get to them where they were hidden in a building, but the sky had started to brighten over the tops of the roofs and he had slunk back to his cellar to hide until the darkness returned.

He hated the sun. It burned his skin, blinded him, sent his thoughts spinning so that he couldn't think straight. The darkness was warm and comforting, like an old blanket. He would sit slumped on his sofa through all the long day: waiting, dozing, dreaming. And now . . . now he had the whole night to break in and get at the toys.

He smiled as he pictured all the fun he was going to have when he got the toys back to his collection. Prodding them, and making them skitter about on the floor. Letting them get away, then pulling them back. He chuckled, the sound a wet gurgle in his throat.

Stuff . . .

He only wished they would last longer and not break so quickly, because it was hard work catching them. They ran about and made too much noise. Most broke before he could even get them home.

He followed the scent down the street, wiping away the snot that bubbled permanently from his nose. He was dribbling, too. Sticky saliva falling onto his stained T-shirt.

Stuff . . .

It took him ages to make his way down the street, around the corner, and onto the next road. Each footfall landing softly on the asphalt. He hoped no one had gotten there before him. The smell of the toys was very strong.

Here was the place. A shop he used to come to a lot. A gadget shop. Long since cleaned out, but the toys had slipped inside. He'd passed it last night and the good sweet smell had hit him like a hammer blow. He'd tried to get in, but there were wooden boards nailed across the front.

He had plenty of time tonight, though.

He smiled again.

Stuff . . .

Good stuff. Cool stuff. More stuff. Nice stuff. More stuff. Stuff stuff stuff.

There was nobody else around. The streets were quiet tonight. He walked over the road, his legs making a swishing sound as they rubbed together. He put his face to the gap between two of the wooden boards and breathed in.

He had to be sure. Sometimes their smell could linger for days, even if they'd moved away. *No.* They were still in there. His toys. He leaned his weight against the boards, heard them creak and groan, felt them bend. He moaned with delight. That was the way to do it. Last night he'd made the mistake of trying to pull the boards down with his hands. Better to push. He walked backward. Put down his bags. Then moved forward, not exactly running, but gaining speed. Until . . .

THUD.

He hit the boards, heard a crack and then sounds on the other side. Scurrying. Whispered voices. The toys were awake.

He backed off, farther this time, then went forward again, the breath hissing through his nose.

THUD.

And again. Again and again and again—slow, unthinking, patient—until at last the wood splintered and fell away from him and he was inside. In the dark.

Stuff . . . Come on . . . Where's the cool stuff?

The smell of the toys was more intense now. Filling his head and making him feel drunk. He closed his eyes and smacked his lips together, then stuck out his tongue, tasting the air. They were nearby. If he could just catch two, maybe three, of the toys, he would have the whole night ahead of him to play with them before he went to sleep. After that? How long? A few days, maybe, before they broke.

But where were they? He stopped moving and stood very still so that he could listen. There was a scraping sound, a rattling and banging. More whispers. *Ssss-sss-sss-sss-sssssssss . . .* He moved toward the sound, groping his way through the darkened shop, past the empty shelves and on into the back.

There they were. Four of them. Trying to open a back door. They'd barricaded themselves in with no way out. He spread his arms wide and belched. The toys all turned around together, their faces white blurs. One of them ran at him, but he barely felt it. Like a moth bumping at a window. They were shouting. Why did they always shout? Why not just come quietly?

Come on . . . stuff . . . make it easy for me. . . .

They were on the small side, easy to carry but easy to break, too. He picked one out, trying not to be distracted by the others. The smallest one. He backed it into a corner while the rest of them battered at his back. Just moths.

There. He had it. He picked it up and tucked it into his armpit, the weight of his arm holding it still. The rest of them kept on hitting him, shouting, their thin voices irritating him. Maybe if they'd run they might have gotten away from him, because they were faster. He would have tracked them all night, slowly and steadily, following their scent, and he knew that the smaller ones couldn't keep going for long—they always got tired before he did. But these ones had stayed to fight, so this way it would be easier.

Two of them had sticks. The biggest two. Their blows fell harmlessly on his flesh, no more than a tickle. He sighed and swept his free arm wide, flinging one against the wall. He knew that would break it, but he couldn't take all of them home anyway. The smashed toy fell to the floor, and he managed to scoop up the other small one. Two was enough. He tucked it away neatly in the great folds of his flesh.

Maybe he should try for a third, hold it by the neck. Sometimes they broke, though, when he did that.

No. He'd leave the other one. Maybe it would stay close and he could come back for it tomorrow.

He sighed again and headed back toward the front.

The fourth toy followed him through the shop. It had found a bigger stick. It was sharp. The toy was screaming very loudly as it jabbed at him with the stick. It might follow him out onto the street, all the way home, and its noise would attract the others. Then they would fight him for his treasures.

He stopped, turned, and pushed his huge belly against the toy, forcing it against the wall. He pressed harder and harder, watching the soft blubber fold itself around the toy until it was invisible. He could feel it wriggling feebly.

It wriggled and wriggled and then, at last, was still.

The Collector moved away and the small body was pressed into his gut. He took it by the hair and trudged out into the street. It would be no good for playing with, but he could dump it on his food pile.

And so, with a toy under each arm, he dragged the third broken toy down the street toward home.

He would leave the shopping bags where they were. He had plenty more. He had stacks and stacks of them among his stuff. He felt a little pang, though. He hated to leave anything behind.

The toys under his arms kicked and struggled, but by the time he reached his front door they had stopped, exhausted. He was pleased with himself. This had been a good night's work. He had more cool stuff. New toys. They would keep him happy for a few days. He dreamed of all the things he would do with them, all the games he would play. First, though, as soon as he got them inside, he would have to snap their little legs. He had learned the hard way that they could escape if you didn't do it. Why did they always try to run away? Why wouldn't they just stay and play nicely? Why did they always have to make things so difficult?

And why, in the end, did they always have to break?

The Supreme Court and

the Commander in Chief

EXPANDED EDITION

The Supreme Court and the Commander in Chief

By CLINTON ROSSITER

EXPANDED EDITION

WITH AN INTRODUCTORY NOTE AND ADDITIONAL TEXT

By RICHARD P. LONGAKER

Cornell University Press ITHACA AND LONDON

International Standard Book Number (cloth) 0-8014-1052-5
International Standard Book Number (paper) 0-8014-9161-4
Library of Congress Catalog Card Number 76-12815
Printed in the United States of America by Vail-Ballou Press, Inc.
Librarians: Library of Congress cataloging information appears on the last page of the book.

Preface 1951

LIKE most students of the government of the United States, I have observed with interest the varied and delicate relationships among its three great independent branches. I have often thought that the true study of our system of government begins with these points of contact —between President and Congress, Congress and Supreme Court, and Supreme Court and President—rather than with the powers and functions of any one of the three branches.

This study is directed to the third of these relationships. It attempts to show how the Supreme Court, in deciding several hundred cases involving the scope of the national war powers, has interpreted the President's status and authority as commander in chief. Perhaps it should bear the title "The Supreme Court and the War Powers of the United States," but the figure of the President looms so large—in the use of these powers and in their interpretation at the hands of the Court—that I feel safe in treating this problem as one important strand in the nexus of relationships between the executive and judicial organs of our uniquely three-part government. In any case, this is a limited study of a limited aspect of one of our three fundamental intragovernmental relationships. I trust my readers will bear this fact in mind.

PREFACE 1951

I am indebted for aid and comfort to my two distinguished friends and teachers, Edward S. Corwin of Princeton and Robert E. Cushman of Cornell, and to my excellent contemporaries, John P. Roche of Haverford and T. L. Tolan, Jr., of the Milwaukee Bar. Miss Shirley Ford of Van Etten, New York, has been the best of all possible typists. And after the silence of two former prefaces in which I was forbidden to mention her name, I am now permitted to acknowledge that my wife, Mary Crane Rossiter, has taught me all I know about grammar, style, and taste.

CLINTON ROSSITER

Ithaca, New York
October 1950

Preface 1976

IN preparing this new edition of Clinton Rossiter's classic study I have not found it necessary to rewrite the original text or to change the substance of his argument. Both form and argument are beyond improvement. *The Supreme Court and the Commander in Chief* is durable: it is durable in the elegance of the author's style, his careful historical analysis, and his insightful interpretation of constitutional development. It is sound history which embraces an essentially sound thesis. Thus, the corpus of the original work remains intact with the exception of a few bracketed insertions to orient the reader to the year of writing; and where, in a few instances, such phrases as "the recent war" or "the recent conflict" have been changed to "World War II."

In accord with Rossiter's plan to "examine the decisions of the Court as they have followed one another in history" (page 13) I have added an Introductory Note and, in Part III, "The Constitution and the Commander in Chief after 1950," an analysis of some events which even Clinton Rossiter, with all of his prescience, could not have fully foreseen. The new material, while not intended to comprehend all constitutional developments regarding the commander in chief since 1950, is designed to point up some significant changes which I believe a quarter of a century has brought light. It describes some events which have had an effect on our constitutional evolution, but particularly the impact of the broadening sweep of presidential prerogative.

Where there is error of interpretation or fact I am, of course, solely responsible. But where there is merit and insight I owe a profound debt to my mentor, the original author. More immediately, I am indebted to my colleagues Douglas S. Hobbs and Robert S. Gerstein, who had the uncommon experience of reviewing earlier drafts when facts and ideas were in disarray and tried their best to set me right. And I will always be deeply grateful to my wife, Mollie, who is so important in confirming that beyond the capriciousness of words there is something of value.

RICHARD P. LONGAKER

Los Angeles, California
May 1976

Contents

ix

CONTENTS

Introductory Note

CLINTON ROSSITER had just completed *The Supreme Court and the Commander in Chief* when President Truman dispatched troops to Korea. In so doing, the President confirmed a major theme of Rossiter's study: in times of stress a President can comfortably assume that he can act without systematic institutional restraints from other sectors of American government. More specifically, Rossiter argues that a President need concern himself little about restraints imposed by the judiciary. The principal thread of his rich analysis is the existence in the American experience of judicially accepted, if not judicially noticed, power in the presidency to preserve the peace and security of the nation, especially in times of emergency. The peacetime words of such cases as *Ex parte Milligan* and *Duncan v. Kahanomoku*,[1] cases in which Presidents were chastised for the excessive use of military power are, to Rossiter, mere rhetorical jousting at accomplished wartime deeds. Although he concludes that control must be found in the "political" branches, not the judiciary, he also presents abundant evidence that the acquiescence of Congress in the deeds of the commander in chief has been the rule and not the

[1] 4 Wallace 2 (1866); 327 U.S. 304 (1946). See Rossiter's discussion of these cases, pp. 26–39, 57–59, 127–130, below.

exception. Thus for the most part restraint has been imposed in practice only by the President, his conscience, and his sense of history.

The perceived necessity for action during domestic or foreign crisis breeds an inexorable demand for executive initiative, and any would-be intervention by courts or Congress is subject to this pressure. In time of crisis constitutional limitations bend to other needs, or, if invoked, a presumption runs strongly against them. The principal challenge, a quarter of a century after Rossiter's study was first published, is to determine what gloss the intervening years have put on the underlying soundness of the author's findings and the historical experience which he so lucidly relates. For any such assessment several developments with constitutional implications are of critical importance.

One was the acceptance by all post–World War II Presidents of a common core of attitudes related to the primacy and singularity of presidential power in foreign and military affairs. The executive self-denial associated with William Howard Taft's classic response to Theodore Roosevelt's heroic "stewardship" theory—in which Taft asserted that executive opportunities for leadership were strictly limited by the Constitution—became a doctrinal antiquity.[2] Presidents unabashedly spoke of power, not limitations. And they were encouraged by events. The broadening concern for national security added a new dimension to the application of executive power. The military engagements in the Korean and Vietnam wars blurred, if they did not destroy, the time-of-peace, time-

[2] Edward S. Corwin, *The President: Office & Powers* (New York, 1957), 152–153.

of-war distinction which had guided past interpretations of the Constitution. And, internal suspicion as well as the civil disturbances of the 1960's and 1970's stirred new questions about the scope of the President's power, as chief executive and commander in chief, to preserve the domestic peace by electronic surveillance and the use of troops. But especially, there was the celebration of the presidential mystique, publicized by academicians and journalists, nourished by recollections of power effectively used during World War II, dramatized by Korea, and captured in an idealized form during the Cuban missile crisis.

Whether before Congress or the courts, when the executive had occasion to specify the sources and scope of presidential power, the clause giving power to the President as "Commander in Chief of the Army and Navy" was an essential companion to other constitutional clauses in justifying presidential primacy. When a President's responsibility to see to the faithful execution of the laws and the commander-in-chief clause were joined with the thematic description, in *United States v. Curtiss Wright*, of "the very delicate, plenary and exclusive power of the President as the sole organ of the Federal government" [3] in foreign affairs, the presidency took on an exalted status in constitutional theory. This interpretation claimed for the President a special discretion and independence in moments of perceived crisis as well as in the day-to-day administration of foreign affairs.

[3] Justice Sutherland was referring in part to remarks made by John Marshall before he became Chief Justice of the Supreme Court in a debate in the House of Representatives in 1800. 10 *Annals of Congress* 613; *United States v. Curtiss Wright Export Corp.*, 299 U.S. 304, 319–320 (1936).

Such assertions were not without judicial precedent. The case law relied upon a handful of regulars: *United States v. Curtiss Wright, United States v. Belmont,* the *Prize Cases, Chicago and Southern Air Lines v. Waterman, In re Neagle,* and *In re Debs.*[4] These decisions,

[4] "It is important to bear in mind that we are here dealing not alone with an authority vested in the President by an exertion of legislative power, but with such an authority plus the very delicate, plenary and exclusive power of the President as the sole organ of the federal government in the field of international relations." See *United States v. Curtiss Wright Export Corp.,* 299 U.S. 304, 320 (1936) (Congressional delegation to the President of discretion to impose an embargo on the shipment of arms); *United States v. Belmont,* 301 U.S. 324 (1937) (the President may negotiate executive agreements on his own authority to implement his decision to recognize a foreign nation); the *Prize Cases,* 2 Black 635 (1863) (a President may use force to counter force on his own independent initiative); *C. & S. Air Lines v. Waterman,* 333 U.S. 103 (1948) (the judiciary will not intervene in presidential decisions which are essentially political and where a judicial decision cannot be the final, definitive one), Mr. Justice Jackson emphasizing (111): ". . . the very nature of executive decisions as to foreign policy is political, not judicial. Such decisions are wholly confided by our Constitution to the political departments of the government, Executive and Legislative. They are delicate, complex, and involve large elements of prophecy. They are and should be undertaken only by those directly responsible to the people whose welfare they advance or imperil. They are decisions of a kind for which the Judiciary has neither aptitude, facilities nor responsibility and which has long been held to belong in the domain of political power not subject to judicial intrusion or inquiry" (This is the essence of the "political" question doctrine as it relates to the presidency; see footnote 14, p. 145); *In re Neagle,* 135 U.S. 1 (1890) (a President, in order to execute the law may use means which have no specific statutory origins); and *In re Debs,* 158 U.S. 564 (1895) (a President may use troops domestically to remove obstructions to federal activities), which states (578–579, 582): "The entire strength of the nation may be used to enforce in any part of the land the full and free exercise of all

while somewhat ambiguous on close inspection,[5] have language which reinforced generous interpretations of presidential power. At the same time, they can be interpreted to limit judicial intervention, except, arguably, intervention to legitimate that power. These sparse but powerful precedents are supported by historical references to executive independence as well as to the common sense of the matter, particularly in foreign affairs, that only the presidency has the necessary institutional attributes for the making of foreign policy—access to information and singleness of purpose—and, in its execution, for "decision, activity, secrecy, and dispatch."[6] These themes were supported by an overarching formulation of presidential prerogative, in which executive power was conceived as superior and independent, emphasizing

national powers and the security of all rights entrusted by the Constitution to its care. The strong arm of the national government may be put forth to brush away all obstructions to the freedom of interstate commerce or the transportation of the mails. If the emergency arises, the army of the Nation, and all its militia, are at the service of the nation to compel obedience to its laws." See Rossiter, p. 40, below.

[5] See especially Charles A. Lofgren, "*United States v. Curtiss-Wright Export Corporation:* An Historical Reassessment," *Yale Law Journal,* LXXXIII (1973), 1–32; Francis D. Wormuth, "The Nixon Theory of the War Power: A Critique," *California Law Review,* LX (1972), 648–649, 666–669, 693–695; Raoul Berger, "War-Making by the President," *University of Pennsylvania Law Review,* CXXI (1972), 69–75. Compare Louis Henkin, *Foreign Affairs and the Constitution* (New York, 1972), 19–35, *passim.*

[6] "That unity is conducive to energy will not be disputed. Decision, activity, secrecy, and dispatch will generally characterize the proceedings of one man in a much more eminent degree than the proceedings of any greater number; and in proportion as the number is increased, these qualities will be diminished." *The Federalist,* number 70 (Mentor edition, 1961), 424.

the view that special discretion was constitutionally allowable and justified by the nature of the office. The theory, in its many permutations, relied upon specific Article II powers of the President and the traditional designations of presidential power as residual, resulting, inherent, implied, exclusive, autonomous, and discretionary. Assertions of prerogative power, under whatever name, were present during the post-World War II period when Presidents sought to justify initiatives in foreign affairs or independence in the execution of military policy.

The formulation was put to another use, however. When turned inward to embrace "national security," presidential power affected an even larger domain. Thus one finds variations on the prerogative theme utilized to justify ever broader presidential claims to independent power over matters as various as covert surveillance, the impounding of funds, the proliferation of executive agreements, internal loyalty-security programs, and restrictions on access to vast amounts of information held by the executive branch. Congress might contribute to policy by action or inaction; but where Congress did act, such action was viewed by the more generous interpreters of presidential power as a welcome convenience, a gesture of support, rather than a constitutional necessity.[7] And it was presumed that the judiciary in such large matters of state not only should be, but would be, deferential.

The theory was disturbed on occasion during the

[7] *National Commitments, Senate Committee on Foreign Relations, Report No. 797,* 90th Cong., 1st Sess. (1967), 7 (hereinafter, *National Commitments Report*).

1950's but was not really shaken until well into the next decade. During the so-called "Great Debate" about the presidential dispatch of additional troops to Europe in 1951, elements in Congress led by Senator Robert Taft attempted to place restrictions on President Truman's determination to give further support to the North American Treaty Organization (NATO). The President based his claim on the commander-in-chief clause and his prerogative power; his opponents contended that any movement of troops into an area where hostilities might start at any moment had to be shared with Congress under its war powers. The debate ended in a draw. In a resolution on the question, Congress seemed to accept the President's power to dispatch troops independently but added, ambiguously, "Congressional approval should be obtained on any *policy* requiring the assignment of troops abroad." [8]

Several months later Senator John W. Bricker of Ohio began his crusade for the adoption of a constitutional amendment to restrict the President's power to negotiate treaties and make executive agreements, in the latter case by requiring congressional review and consent. The immediate concern was that treaties and agreements might be used under the supremacy clause of the Constitution to give internal effect within the United States to decisions by international agencies such as the United Nations without specific congressional participation. The Eisenhower administration's opposition was decisive in undermining support for the proposed restrictions on presidential power; but even Eisenhower's prestige did

[8] *Senate Report No. 175*, 82d Cong., 1st Sess. (1951), 2–3. Emphasis added.

not fully deflate concern in Congress and, as it turned out, in the courts. In 1957 the Supreme Court stirred itself in a significant holding to decide that executive agreements made in implementation of a treaty were suspect if they clashed with the Bill of Rights.[9] Further congressional anxiety about the legislative role in such agreements did not focus itself clearly until well over a decade later when Senate committees began to examine the escalating use of independently negotiated executive agreements, many of them secret, in lieu of more open treaty procedures.

The most portentous constitutional event affecting the presidency in the 1950's was the Supreme Court decision in the *Steel Seizure Case*. When the decision was handed down it received popular and congressional acclaim. But among many learned commentators it was viewed as a dangerous attack on the powers of the presidency, a judicial invasion into matters traditionally beyond the Court's power. For some it was a decision without foundation in principle, a "judicial brick without straw." [10] It proved to be more.

[9] *Reid v. Covert*, 351 U.S. 1. This development is discussed on pp. 155–158 below.

[10] *Youngstown Sheet and Tube v. Sawyer*, 343 U.S. 579 (1952). The disparaging description is from Edward S. Corwin, "The Steel Seizure Case," *Columbia Law Review*, LIII (1953), 53–66; see also Paul A. Freund, "The Year of the Steel Seizure Case," *Harvard Law Review*, LXVI (1952), 89–95; Glendon A. Schubert, "The Steel Seizure Case: Presidential Responsibility and Judicial Irresponsibility," *Western Political Quarterly*, VI (1953), 61–77. But see Paul G. Kauper, "The Steel Seizure Case: Congress, the President, and the Supreme Court," *Michigan Law Review*, LI (1952), 141–182.

President Truman seized the steel mills after negotiations failed to settle a strike which was interrupting the flow of matériel to the armed forces in Korea. The President seized the industry pending settlement of the strike or action by Congress. He did so solely on his authority as commander in chief and by virtue of his power to "see to the faithful execution of the laws." In the ensuing action by the steel companies in the courts to recover their property, government counsel set forth executive prerogative power as a defense. It appears with greatest clarity in an exchange between government counsel, Holmes Baldridge, and Judge David A. Pine in the United States District Court for the District of Columbia:

MR. BALDRIDGE: . . . We base the President's power on Sections 1, 2 and 3 of Article II of the Constitution, and whatever inherent, implied or residual powers may flow therefrom. . . . We say that Article II . . . which provides that the Executive power of the Government shall reside in the President, that he shall faithfully execute the laws of the office and he shall be Commander-in-Chief of the Army and Navy and that he shall take care that the laws be faithfully executed, are sufficient to permit him to meet any national emergency that might arise, be it peace time, technical war time, or actual war time. . . .

THE COURT: Then, as I understand it, you claim that in time of emergency the Executive has this great power.

MR. BALDRIDGE: That is correct.

THE COURT: And that the Executive determines the emergencies and the Courts cannot even review whether it is an emergency.

MR. BALDRIDGE: That is correct.[11]

In a rich and cacophonous decision, the Supreme Court majority found against the President, their agreement hanging on the slender but constitutionally significant thread that Congress had explicitly denied the power of seizure to the President when it had considered amendments to the Taft-Hartley Act. Whether those in the majority would have found otherwise had Congress been silent on the question, or if the emergency had been more severe, is an open question. Chief Justice Fred M. Vinson, joined by two others in dissent, did consider the emergency sufficiently severe. Relying upon an inherency approach and the supposition that Congress had implicitly accepted seizure in other statutes, the dissenters said the exercise of power was justified as a wartime act.

Beyond the central finding that Congress had denied the seizure power to the President, there was little unity in the six separate opinions for the majority. But there were some gifts of doctrine. Justice Black, in the opinion

[11] *Oral Argument, Youngstown Sheet and Tube Co. v. Sawyer, Transcript,* 371–372; House of Representatives, 82d Cong., 2d Sess. (1950), H. Doc. #534, Part I. Although the government softened its arguments somewhat, the parameters were the same. See the government's brief, spelling out the same theory with greater care, appearing in *ibid.,* Part II, 799 ff. President Truman was unchastened and affirmed the theory in his *Memoirs: Years of Trial and Hope* (New York, 1956), II, 478: "The President, who is Commander in Chief and who represents the interests of all the people, must be able to act at all times to meet any sudden threat to the nation's security. A wise President will always work with Congress but when Congress fails to act or is unable to act in a crisis, the President, under the Constitution, must use his powers to safeguard the nation."

for the Court, seemed to conclude that no eventuality would justify presidential action in an emergency without express congressional authorization; Justice Tom C. Clark thought that seizure would be constitutional if the nation were in grave and immediate danger. And Justice Robert H. Jackson in a brilliant concurrence described for the first time in the Court's history a hierarchy of alternatives keyed to the separation of powers: where the President acts pursuant to the explicit or implicit authorization of Congress his powers are at their fullest; when Congress is silent a President, in practice, may have independent power although subject to the concurrent powers of Congress once they are activated; but where presidential action is contrary to the express or implied will of Congress, as the seizure was, the President's power is "at its lowest ebb," and courts must look askance at any exercise of power by the President that would disturb "the equilibrium established by our constitutional system." There is little breathing space for presidential prerogative in Jackson's formulation.[12]

Although the case was dismissed by many as a constitutional deviation, the Court had in fact intervened in the President's war power, even if some of the Justices who concurred seemed to do so under the fiction that it was a domestic issue. Moreover, the Court had invoked the separation of powers and, by indirection through the medium of property rights, the Bill of Rights. It revived, for the moment, the notion that Presidents were subject to congressional limitations in foreign affairs. And it put in question the free-floating view of presidential power long associated with Justice Sutherland's language

[12] 343 U.S. 579, 634–640.

in *United States v. Curtiss Wright* by insisting that presidential power was based only on the language of the Constitution. The *Steel Seizure Case*, in short, provided a benchmark for a positive judicial role in determining constitutional limitations on the presidency. The *Steel Seizure Case* was there, in the words of Justice Jackson in an earlier and more regrettable decision interpreting presidential power, "like a loaded weapon" ready for those who might be inclined to use it.[13]

The trend toward intervention quickened in the years following this decision because of the activism of the Warren Court and the increasingly popular expectation that the Supreme Court would and should interject itself into matters once thought more fitting for treatment by other branches of government. The divisions in the Court about the appropriateness of judicial activism are not of first significance. Nor is the fact that in the 1950's and well into the 1960's the Court's interventions in the national security field were generally supportive of presidential and congressional initiatives. Where the decisions were not supportive, they were often wary or wavering.[14] What is of significance is that the symbol of an "active" Court and the development of doctrine about the First Amendment, and criminal procedure, once joined with intensely complex constitutional issues regarding the

[13] See Kauper, "The Steel Seizure Case," *Michigan Law Review,* LI (1952), 175. The quotation is from *Korematsu v. United States,* 323 U.S. 214, 246 (1944).

[14] For some examples see *Kent v. Dulles,* 357 U.S. 116 (1958), and *Zemel v. Rusk,* 381 U.S. 1 (1965); *Watkins v. United States,* 354 U.S. 178 (1957), and *Barenblatt v. United States,* 360 U.S. 109 (1959); *Dennis v. United States,* 341 U.S. 494 (1951), and *Scales v. United States,* 367 U.S. 203 (1961).

exercise of presidential power and heightening awareness of the separation of powers, invited the possibility
that the Court would not remain aloof.

In some of the issues chosen for analysis in Part III the
Court elected to intervene; in some it did not—or its
consideration did not reach the underlying constitutional
questions. But common to all of the issues was a freshen-
ing attitude that somehow the scope of presidential
power might properly be resolved in the judicial forum.
And whether or not the judiciary chose to intervene,
there were gradually accelerating expectations that Congress should reassert its constitutional responsibility. To
do so would be in harmony with the holding in the *Steel
Seizure Case*. More broadly, however, it would be in
harmony with the structural design envisioned in 1787.

Introduction

WARS and rumors of war have set us to thinking about the shape of the national government in an atomic catastrophe. There is much talk of *power,* and thus of the final power of national self-preservation in the American constitutional system: the immense authority of the President as commander in chief. There is little talk of *limitations,* of the techniques through which the uses of this authority can be confined to paths of constitutional righteousness. We seem grimly prepared to submit to strong and arbitrary government in the event of atomic attack, but we avoid consideration of the methods through which we can render such government trustworthy and temporary.[1]

On the assumption that it is never too late, even in an age of vast sociopolitical flux, to speak of constitutional limitations, this book examines the operation of one order of restraint upon presidential power in which millions of Americans continue to put their special trust. More specifically, it relates the "natural history" of the Supreme Court's role as overseer and interpreter of the war powers, especially the power of the President as commander in

[1] See generally Clinton Rossiter, "Constitutional Dictatorship in the Atomic Age," *Review of Politics,* XI (1949), 395–418, and references there cited.

chief. These are the questions for which it seeks answers: What use has the Court, whether under Taney or Chase or White or Stone, made of its opportunities to speak with authority on this most awful of presidential powers? When has it been bold, when silent amid the clash of arms? Under what circumstances have Court and President met in head-on disagreement, and what effect upon the latter's course of action did the censures of the judiciary actually have? What permanent influence on the extent and content of the war powers has been worked by the Court's decisions? What future trust can we place in the Court as defender of constitutionalism in time of great national crisis? In fine, the purpose of this book is to evaluate the effectiveness of the momentous American doctrine of judicial review in an area of presidential-military power that may well hold our future in its flexible grasp. It is a study in the realities of constitutional law.

In exercising his lofty prerogatives as "Commander in Chief of the Army and Navy of the United States" the President would seem to enjoy a peculiar degree of freedom from the review and restraints of the judicial process. His powers in the broad field of national defense are largely discretionary, and the exercise of military discretion is one species of official action that American courts have always held themselves particularly unqualified to control. The recruiting and training of personnel, the stationing of troops in peace and their deployment in war, the appointment and removal of "high brass," the selection of corporations with which to let contracts for matériel, the determination to buy more B-36's and halt work on ultramodern carriers, the decisions on when and how fast to produce atomic bombs and where and when

2

to use them—these are matters over which no court would or could exercise the slightest measure of judgment or restraint. For his conduct of such affairs the President is responsible, so far as he can be held responsible, only to Congress, the electorate, and the pages of history. It would seem at first sight that the Supreme Court could do nothing to control or even interpret the President's authority to command the forces and wage war, and that the war powers would therefore have no judicial history.

Yet the 340-odd volumes of the *United States Reports* are crammed with cases familiar to all students of American government—*Martin v. Mott*, the *Prize Cases*, *Ex parte Milligan*, *Arver v. United States*, *Korematsu v. United States*, to mention a few of the more notable—in which some element of the President's military competence was directly before a Court that was constitutionally and often practically in a position to restrain the free play of his martial will. The war powers of the United States, especially as brought to bear by the commander in chief, can play hob with personal and property rights, and a number of injured individuals have had enough determination and resources to push their cases through to the highest level, and thus to force the Supreme Court to examine critically some of the most high-toned of the military powers of President and Congress. A passing glance at such volumes as 7 *Wallace* or 321 *U.S.* will demonstrate the amazing number of cases in which the legality of the government's interference with private or property rights was sufficiently dubious to permit close judicial scrutiny. Lincoln could not be challenged in court for placing Ambrose E. Burnside in command of the Army of the Potomac, but his blockade of the South, suspension of

3

the writ of habeas corpus, and trial of civilians by military commission were all put to judicial test. Roosevelt gave no thought to the Supreme Court in deciding when and where to invade Europe, but he, i.e., his Attorney General, thought long and hard (and not too well) about the constitutionality of the evacuation of the west coast Japanese-Americans and the seizure of Montgomery Ward. And he, too, was challenged seriously on four or five major exertions of his martial powers.

The first part of this study examines the Court's construction of the President's power of martial rule, of all his powers the most basic, spectacular, and injurious to private rights. The second deals with five other problems arising under the war powers on which the Court has discoursed with varied results for presidential authority. By way of introduction to the whole subject, we shall reverse the usual procedure in such matters and establish at the outset a number of general propositions concerning the Court's historic attitude toward the President's war powers. In mounting the attack upon the specific from a solid base of generality, we should be better prepared to follow the twists and turns of the Court's opinions. A long and painstaking consideration of the hundreds of important cases in which the Court has declaimed on the Constitution-at-war would appear to lead to these conclusions:

First, the Court has refused to speak about the powers of the President as commander in chief in any but the most guarded terms. It has been respectful, complimentary, on occasion properly awed, but it has never embarked on one of those expansive flights of dicta into which it has been so often tempted by other great constitutional questions.

4

It has moved well beyond the limited concepts of Hamilton in *The Federalist,* number 69 ("It would amount to nothing more than the supreme command and direction of the military and naval forces, as first General and admiral of the Confederacy"), and of Taney in *Fleming v. Page* ("His duty and his power are purely military"),[2] but not nearly so far as have the Presidents themselves. The breath-taking estimates of their war powers announced and acted upon by Lincoln and Roosevelt have earned no blessing under the hands of the judiciary.

Second, the pronouncements of the Court have been as general as they have been guarded. It has fixed neither the outer boundaries nor the inner divisions of the President's martial authority, and has failed completely to draw the line between his powers and those of Congress,[3] except to proclaim such self-evident dogmas as that Congress cannot direct campaigns nor the President declare war. The thinking of the Court on this point was best expressed by Justice Swayne in *Stewart v. Kahn:* "The measures to be taken in carrying on war and to suppress insurrection are not defined. The decision of all questions rests wholly in the discretion of those to whom the substantial powers involved are confided by the Constitution." [4] It is apparently for the President, not the Court, to be specific about his powers.

Third, the Court's estimate of its ability to intervene in an improper exercise of the war powers has been one thing at one time, another at another. Often in one period,

[2] 9 Howard 603, 615 (1850). See also *U.S. v. Sweeny,* 157 U.S. 281, 284 (1895).

[3] See Chief Justice Chase's inadequate attempt in his concurring opinion in *Ex parte Milligan,* 4 Wallace 2, 139–140 (1866).

[4] 11 Wallace 493, 506 (1870).

or even in one case, its attitude has been quite ambivalent. Counsel for injured interests can always quote an over-powering and apparently conclusive array of decisions and dicta proving that the Court will actively defend the Constitution against the havoc of war; but the government's lawyers can come right back with an equally impressive array, plucked in many instances from the very same cases, proving the incapacity of the Court to put a bridle on the war powers. Of course, by now almost all great constitutional problems have respectable lines of precedents on both sides, as the present Court reminds us repeatedly with its split decisions. Yet in this area of the war powers it is particularly striking how unsure the Court has been about its real or nominal authority to substitute its judgment for that of Congress, the President, or his military subordinates. This unsettling fact will become especially evident in the analysis of the opinions in *Duncan v. Kahanamoku* and *Korematsu v. United States.*[5]

Fourth, the Court has made it a practice never to approve a challenged presidential or military order solely on the authority of the commander-in-chief clause if it can find a more specific and less controversial basis. The judges, that is to say, will do everything in their power to avoid considering an unusual action in terms of the President's power alone, and will seize with manifest relief on any evidence of congressional approval. In the outstanding cases to arise from World War II there are dozens of remarks such as, "We have no occasion to consider whether the President, acting alone, could lawfully have made the curfew order in question," or, "It is unnecessary for present purposes to determine to what ex-

[5] Below, pp. 48–59.

cuting agencies of our Government are as vital to the success of our great experiment in securing "the Blessings of Liberty to ourselves and our Posterity" as are the checks and balances which have been imposed upon our representatives.[14]

[14] 327 U.S. 304, 338. Two other "realistic" cases, *U.S. v. Curtiss-Wright Export Corp.*, 299 U.S. 304 (1936), and *Lichter v. U.S.*, 334 U.S. 742 (1948), should be carefully noted as first cousins to the Burton-Frankfurter thesis.

tent the President as Commander in Chief has constitutional power to create military commissions without the support of Congressional legislation" [6]—each followed by reference to some act of Congress that could be cited in support of the President's extraordinary action. This preference for statutory over constitutional authority actually works to the President's advantage, for the merger of his military powers and those of Congress produces something known simply but grandly as "the war powers of the United States," under which just about any presidential wartime action can be brought within the limits of the Constitution. Both President and Congress have constitutional powers of their own in military and foreign affairs; when these powers are merged they are virtually irresistible, at least in the courts. This is one instance in which two plus two equals five. And the powers, of course, are his to wield.

Finally, the Court has usually been quite realistic about the constitutional ability of this nation, led by its President, to wage war. There have been several occasions, as in the post-Civil War case *Ex parte Milligan*, on which it has been lured into saying things about limits on the war powers that were simply not true. For the most part, however, it has agreed with Chief Justice Hughes's famous observations that "the war power of the Federal Government . . . is a power to wage war successfully" and that "so, also, we have a *fighting* constitution." [7] This does not

[6] *Hirabayashi v. U.S.*, 320 U.S. 81, 92 (1943); *Ex parte Quirin*, 317 U.S. 1, 29 (1942).

[7] *Home Building and Loan Association v. Blaisdell*, 290 U.S. 398, 426 (1934); "War Powers under the Constitution," *American Bar Association Reports*, XLII (1917), 238.

mean that the Constitution goes to pieces in the event of war, for, as Hughes also remarked, "While we are at war, we are not in revolution." [8] It does mean that the Court has recognized, always *bello flagrante* and almost always *post bellum*, the cogency of Hamilton's contention in *The Federalist*, number 23, that the war powers "ought to exist without limitation, *because it is impossible to foresee or define the extent and variety of national exigencies, or the correspondent extent and variety of the means which may be necessary to satisfy them.*"

In another post-Civil War case, *Miller v. United States*,[9] Justice Strong observed, "Of course the power to declare war involves the power to prosecute it by all means and in any manner in which war may be legitimately prosecuted." Just what he meant by "legitimately" he did not go on to say, but other opinions have made clear that the war powers must be wielded in accordance with the great qualifications found "in the Constitution or in applicable principles of international law." [10] Yet the latter is today simply a moral limitation [1950]; the new view of the former, like so many new views simply an echo of Hamilton's illustrious voice, is that the Constitution encourages rather than discourages the use of the war powers. It has been fashionable among the justices in recent years to be a little more tough-minded, or simply resigned, on the nature and scope of these powers. The Constitution, said Justice Burton in an austere dissent,

[8] "War Powers under the Constitution," 232.

[9] 11 Wallace 268, 305 (1870).

[10] *U.S. v. Macintosh*, 283 U.S. 605, 622 (1931). See also *U.S. v. Russell*, 13 Wallace 623, 627 (1871); *Hamilton v. Kentucky Distilleries*, 251 U.S. 146, 155–156 (1919); *U.S. v. Cohen Grocery Co.*, 255 U.S. 81, 88–89 (1921).

was written by a generation fresh from war. The people established a more perfect union, in part, so that they might the better defend themselves from military attack. In doing so they centralized far more military power and responsibility in the Chief Executive than previously had been done. The Constitution was built for rough as well as smooth roads. In time of war the nation simply changes gears and takes the harder going under the same power.[11]

And his brother Frankfurter, some two years before:

The provisions of the Constitution which confer on the Congress and the President powers to enable this country to wage war are as much part of the Constitution as provisions looking to a nation at peace. . . . Therefore, the validity of action under the war power must be judged wholly in the context of war.[12]

At another point in the same opinion he protests against the timid, unrealistic concept of the war powers that would

suffuse a part of the Constitution with an atmosphere of unconstitutionality. . . . To recognize that military orders are "reasonably expedient military precautions" in time of war and yet to deny them constitutional legitimacy makes of the Constitution an instrument for dialectic subtleties not reasonably to be attributed to the hard-headed Framers, of whom a majority had had actual participation in war.[13]

And as a final touch, again Justice Burton:

Within their proper spheres, the robust strength and freedom of action allowed to the policy making and policy exe-

[11] *Duncan v. Kahanamoku*, 327 U.S. 304, 342 (1946).

[12] *Korematsu v. U.S.*, 323 U.S. 214, 224 (1944).

[13] 323 U.S. 214, 225.

PART I

The Supreme Court and the President's Power of Martial Rule

AS commander in chief and chief executive the President is empowered, indeed obliged, to preserve the peace of the United States against domestic violence and alien attack. The mandates of the Constitution, a procession of statutes dating back to 1792,[1] and the logic of history and political science have combined to place in his keeping a virtually uncontrollable discretion in employing the armed forces to defend the nation, execute the laws, and maintain national authority on every foot of American soil. Although this is a presidential power equally serviceable in peace and war, it is generally treated in the context of the war powers because it derives the substance of its authority from his status as commander in chief and because its most precedential uses have taken place in periods of armed conflict, especially those of the Civil War and World War II.

It is impossible to define with precision the scope of what we have conveniently labeled "the President's power

[1] *United States Code,* Title 50, secs. 201–204. See also Hamilton's provident words in defense of "energy in the executive" in the first paragraphs of *The Federalist,* number 70.

of martial rule," for it runs the gamut of military action from the mere threat of force to outright martial law. For the sake of convenience, his power may be broken down into three general, closely related categories: (1) *the power of martial law,* under which he may, with some show of formality, extend military government to domestic areas in case of invasion or rebellion; [2] (2) *the power simply to "call out the troops,"* which might involve anything from placing a platoon on a mail train moving through a strike-bound area to summoning the entire militia to preserve the Union; and, (3) *the power to suspend the writ of habeas corpus,* which may or may not accompany martial law, and which, as we shall shortly see, may or may not belong to the President!

Just where one of these powers leaves off and the other begins is something Presidents themselves would have trouble explaining. The uses of emergency powers have not been carefully institutionalized in this country, and Presidents like Washington, Lincoln, Cleveland, Wilson, and Franklin D. Roosevelt have wielded military force in time of crisis without much thought about the forms that their display of authority might assume. A major strike touched with violence, a wartime strike blocking the flow

[2] For a discussion of martial law, which is to be carefully distinguished from military law as well as military government of conquered areas, see Clinton Rossiter, *Constitutional Dictatorship* (Princeton, N.J., 1948), 9, 139–150, 215–217, and the many references there cited, especially Charles Fairman, *The Law of Martial Rule* (2d ed.; Chicago, 1943). In *U.S. v. Diekelman,* 92 U.S. 520, 526 (1875), Chief Justice Waite remarked, "Martial law is the law of military necessity in the actual presence of war. It is administered by the general of the army, and is in fact his will. Of necessity it is arbitrary; but it must be obeyed." For "general of the army" we may read "President."

12

of munitions, a great fire or flood accompanied by riots and looting, a localized rebellion with which the state authorities cannot cope, a major insurrection, the threat or actuality of alien invasion—all these are situations into which our armed forces have moved decisively under the direction and in the name of the President. In each instance it has been for the President himself to decide what type and degree of force was necessary to remedy the abnormal situation. As the exigencies of the emergency, the character of the incumbent, and the state of public opinion have varied, so, too, has the shape of the President's action.

Now it goes without saying that any such use of presidential power must inevitably interfere drastically with the normal exercise of private rights and civil liberties, whether those of a single person or a class or a particular area or the entire nation, and the courts have always been open—if not during the emergency, then at some later date—to hear the complaints of citizens unnecessarily restricted or too roughly handled by the forces acting under the President's direction. The Supreme Court has had occasion in about ten major cases to pass judgment on the President's military authority to circumscribe the normal liberties of the people in defense of the nation. Since judges have experienced just about as much difficulty as Presidents in defining with precision the boundaries and components of the power under scrutiny, we would be hard put to it to treat this subject any other way but chronologically. The plan, therefore, is to examine the decisions of the Court as they have followed one another in history.

The Element of Discretion:
Martin v. Mott and *Luther v. Borden*

Although the first seventy years under the Constitution were replete with emergencies calling for strong presidential action to preserve the peace—the Whiskey Rebellion, the Embargo troubles, the War of 1812, Nullification in South Carolina, the Mexican War, to name the most important—on only two occasions did the Supreme Court have a chance to say anything of note about martial rule, in the justly famed cases *Martin v. Mott* and *Luther v. Borden.*[3] Neither went to the root of the matter under present consideration, yet together they illustrate, and are still cited in support of, a fundamental principle of judicial review of the President's power of martial rule. Perhaps the best way to define this principle is to quote, with the aid of italics, the significant words of the two great judges who delivered these opinions.

Story for the Court in *Martin v. Mott* (1827):

The power thus confided by Congress to the President is doubtless of a very high and delicate nature. A free people are naturally very jealous of the exercise of military power; and the power to call the militia into actual service is certainly felt to be one of no ordinary magnitude. . . . It is, in its terms, a limited power, confined to cases of actual invasion, or of imminent danger of invasion. If it be a limited power, the question arises, by whom is the exigency to be judged of and decided? . . . *We are all of opinion that the authority to decide whether the exigency has arisen belongs exclusively to the President, and that his decision is conclusive upon all other persons.*

[3] 12 Wheaton 19, 29–33 (1827); 7 Howard 1, 42–45 (1849).

14

The law does not provide for any appeal from the judgment of the President, or for any right in subordinate officers to review his decision, and in effect defeat it. Whenever a statute gives a discretionary power to any person, to be exercised by him upon his own opinion of certain facts, it is a sound rule of construction that the statute constitutes him the sole and exclusive judge of the existence of these facts. . . . Such is the true construction of the act of 1795. It is no answer that such a power may be abused, for there is no power which is not susceptible of abuse. The remedy for this, as well as for all other misconduct, if it should occur, is to be found in the constitution itself. In a free government the danger must be remote, since in addition to the high qualities which the Executive must be presumed to possess, of public virtue and honest devotion to the public interests, *the frequency of elections, and the watchfulness of the representatives of the nation, carry with them all the checks which can be useful to guard against usurpation and wanton tyranny.*[4]

Taney for the Court in *Luther v. Borden* (1849):

After the President has acted and called out the militia, is a Circuit Court of the United States authorized to inquire

[4] This was an extremely important decision from the point of view of the federal system, for three New England governors in the War of 1812 had asserted that it was for them, not the President, to decide whether and when the militia was to be called out. For other cases constructive of the militia clause and laws, and of the President's powers thereunder, see *Houston v. Moore*, 5 Wheaton 1 (1820); *Presser v. Illinois*, 116 U.S. 252 (1886); *Johnson v. Sayre*, 158 U.S. 109, 115 (1895); *McLaughry v. Deming*, 186 U.S. 49 (1902); *Arver v. U.S.*, 245 U.S. 366, 381–387 (1918); *Cox v. Wood*, 247 U.S. 3, 5–6 (1918). The Court has been quick, as in the last of these cases, to repel the attempts of various citizens to shackle the war power with sophistries about the nature and purpose of the militia. Whether there are limits to the use of the militia is for the President to decide. See 29 *Opinions of the Attorney General* 322.

whether his decision was right? . . . If it could, then it would become the duty of the court (provided that it came to the conclusion that the President had decided incorrectly) to discharge those who were arrested or detained by the troops in the service of the United States. . . . *If the judicial power extends so far, the guarantee [of a republican form of government] contained in the Constitution of the United States is a guarantee of anarchy, and not of order.* Yet if this right does not reside in the courts when the conflict is raging, if the judicial power is at that time bound to follow the decision of the political, it must be equally bound when the contest is over.

It is said that this power in the President is dangerous to liberty, and may be abused. *All power may be abused if placed in unworthy hands. But it would be difficult, we think, to point out any other hands in which this power would be more safe, and at the same time equally effectual.* When citizens of the same State are in arms against each other, and the constituted authorities unable to execute the laws, the interposition of the United States must be prompt, or it is of little value. The ordinary course of proceedings in courts of justice would be utterly unfit for the crisis. *And the elevated office of the President, chosen as he is by the people of the United States, and the high responsibility he could not fail to feel when acting in a case of so much moment, appear to furnish as strong safeguards against a wilful abuse of power as human prudence and foresight could well provide. At all events, it is conferred upon him by the Constitution and laws of the United States, and must therefore be respected and enforced in its judicial tribunals.*

The common element in these opinions would seem to be a genuine judicial reluctance to speak in a situation where the voice of the Court, even if heard, could not have

16

any effect. More than this, both Story and Taney seem to share the suspicion, unusual in them, that under a popular form of government there are certain questions that the political branches must be trusted to answer with finality.

It would be dangerous and misleading to push the principles of these cases too far, especially the doctrine of "political questions" as implied in *Luther v. Borden*. Given the opportunity to afford a grievously injured citizen relief from a palpably unwarranted use of presidential or military power, especially when the question at issue falls in the penumbra between the "political" and the "justiciable," the Court will act as if it had never heard of this doctrine and its underlying assumption that there are some powers against which the judiciary simply cannot be expected to act as the last line of defense. In the main, however—indeed, in 99 cases out of 100—the principle of *Martin v. Mott* and *Luther v. Borden*, expanded into a general rule for judicial review of presidential military action, will be faithfully applied. And that principle is this: When the President decides to use military force to preserve the peace, neither the decision itself nor the methods employed are open to question in the courts of the United States. In such instances, his discretion must control, and the courts cannot intervene and grant relief. Powerless in fact, they have chosen likewise to be powerless in law.[5]

[5] Two instructive cases of judicial scrutiny of a state governor's decisions in regard to martial law are *Moyer v. Peabody*, 212 U.S. 78 (1909), and *Sterling v. Constantin*, 287 U.S. 378 (1932).

17

Who Can Suspend the Writ of Habeas Corpus?

Ex parte Merryman

This is another of those constitutional posers that the framers, probably because they entertained no doubts and anticipated no troubles on the subject, left as an unanswered legacy to generations of lawyers, professors, and commentators. The Constitution grants this great emergency power to no one; it assumes its existence as a matter of fact and common law, and merely qualifies its employment in these terms: "The privilege of the writ of habeas corpus shall not be suspended, unless when in cases of rebellion and invasion the public safety may require it." No court has ever doubted that Congress could suspend the writ of habeas corpus in a condition of necessity. The point of controversy has been: Does the President, too, possess this power?

Constitutional theory answers *no*. The great commentators from Story to Willoughby,[6] relying on the location of the habeas corpus clause in the legislative article and supported by a dictum of Marshall in the early case *Ex*

[6] Joseph Story, *Commentaries on the Constitution* (Boston, 1833), secs. 1338–1342; W. W. Willoughby, *Constitutional Law of the United States* (New York, 1929), III, 1611–1615. See also J. N. Pomeroy, *An Introduction to the Constitutional Law of the United States* (7th ed.; Boston, 1883), 473–474; William Winthrop, *Military Law* (Washington, 1893), II, 54–56; J. R. Tucker, *The Constitution of the United States* (Chicago, 1899), II, 642–652; H. von Holst, *Constitutional Law of the United States* (Chicago, 1887), 196–197; C. K. Burdick, *The Law of the American Constitution* (New York, 1922), 84–85. This list is representative, not exclusive; there could be many additions.

parte Bollman,[7] have assumed with virtual unanimity that Congress alone possesses this authority. Historical fact, on the other hand, answers *yes.* In the one period in our history when the suspension of the writ became an overriding necessity, a President, Abraham Lincoln, suspended it on his own authority, not once but several times, without substantial interference from Court or Congress.[8]

Unfortunately for the purposes of this study, fact and theory have never clashed at the highest level. The Supreme Court has yet to speak directly on the constitutionality of presidential suspension. There is no doubt that the Court had several chances in the course of the rebellion to come to grips with this unsolved problem; but enough members of the Court were wary (and Attorney General Bates downright fearful) of a final trial of strength between executive and judiciary to prevent a conclusive decision.[9]

In the lower courts, however, this problem was directly at issue, and although some courts agreed with the opinion of Bates, several intrepid judges spoke out fearlessly in defiance of Lincoln's assumption of this spacious power.[10]

[7] 4 Cranch 75, 101 (1807).

[8] On Lincoln's suspension of the writ, see the admirable study of J. G. Randall, *Constitutional Problems under Lincoln* (New York, 1926), chaps. 6–8.

[9] Randall, *op. cit.*, 132.

[10] See the interesting opinions in *In re McDonald*, 16 Fed. Cas. 17 (1861), No. 8751; *Ex parte Benedict*, 3 Fed. Cas. 159 (1862), No. 1292; *Ex parte Field*, 9 Fed. Cas. 1 (1862), No. 4761; *McCall v. McDowell*, 16 Fed. Cas. 1235 (1867), No. 8673. As splendid examples of the critical attitude of some of the state courts, see *Jones v. Seward*, 40 Barb. (N.Y.) 563 (1863), and *In re Kemp*, 16 Wisc. 359 (1863). It was the adverse decision in the latter case that Bates advised Stanton to let go unappealed.

To the strictures of these lower-court judges Lincoln paid no heed, but on one opinion, we may feel sure, he dwelt with careful attention. Whatever his ideas in 1863 and 1864, he was not at all certain of his authority in the early months of the war, and an opinion of the Chief Justice denying that the President could ever suspend the writ of habeas corpus was certain to win a careful reading.

The case, of course, was *Ex parte Merryman*,[11] decided by Taney May 28, 1861, in the circuit court in Baltimore, not, as is commonly asserted, in the capacity of circuit justice, but as Chief Justice of the United States pure and simple, acting under section 14 of the Judiciary Act of 1789,[12] which provided that "either of the justices of the supreme court, as well as judges of the district courts, shall have power to grant writs of *habeas corpus* for the purpose of an inquiry into the cause of commitment." The circumstances of this case attracted a great deal of popular attention, and the elements of melodrama are in it even today. At no other time in all the long history of the Court have a President and a Chief Justice, or any justice for that matter, come into such direct conflict over an exercise of presidential power.

John Merryman, a leading citizen of the state of Maryland, had succeeded in making himself, through a variety of secessionist activities, a thorough nuisance to the military authorities trying to maintain order along the Philadelphia-Washington line of communications. Having

[11] 17 Fed. Cas. 144 (1861), No. 9487. For graphic accounts of this incident, see C. B. Swisher, *Roger B. Taney* (New York, 1935), 547–560; B. C. Steiner, *Roger Brooke Taney* (Baltimore, 1922), 490–504.

[12] 1 *Stat.* 72, 81.

been arrested and confined in Fort McHenry, one of the few places in seething Baltimore where the star-spangled banner yet waved, he petitioned for a writ of habeas corpus. Under ordinary circumstances he would have turned to the district court with his prayer, but a judge of that court had already been successfully defied by a major at Fort McHenry. It was plain that it would take a good deal more prestige than that of a district judge to tip the scales for justice in this unequal balance of the judicial and military powers. With the Supreme Court out of session, its members who remained in Washington were available to issue the writ, and who could have been more eager to do just that than the justice in whose circuit the court in Baltimore happened to fall? It is now an accepted fact that Taney, old and worn as he was, or perhaps because he was old and worn and had little to fear ("I was ever a fighter, so—one fight more, the best and the last!"), went from Washington to Baltimore for the specific purpose of entertaining Merryman's application. He did this, of course, in full knowledge of the President's order of April 27 authorizing the Commanding General of the United States Army or the proper officer to suspend the writ of habeas corpus "at any point or in the vicinity of any military line which is now or which shall be used between the city of Philadelphia and the city of Washington." [13]

The scenes of this drama unrolled at a pace that left the actors little time for reflection on the implications of their words and deeds. Merryman was carried off from his country estate at 2:00 A.M. on May 25, and petitioned for a writ of habeas corpus the very same day. On May 26

[13] J. D. Richardson, *Messages and Papers of the Presidents* (Washington, 1896–1899), VI, 18.

Taney issued the requested writ, directing General George Cadwalader to bring Merryman before him. At the appointed hour on May 27 the general's aide-de-camp, armed with his sword and girded in a bright red sash, appeared before the Chief Justice and politely but flatly refused to produce the prisoner, citing as authority the President's order of April 27. At the same time, he made clear the general's desire to postpone the action "until he can receive instructions from the President of the United States, when you shall hear further from him." Taney, who by now considered himself the last barricade between the Constitution and despotism, would have none of it, and ordered that an attachment for contempt be issued immediately against Cadwalader, returnable the following day.

The final scene was played on May 28. The Chief Justice, informed by the United States marshal that the guard at Fort McHenry had not permitted him to serve the attachment, excused him from any further action on the ground that "the power refusing obedience was so notoriously superior to any the marshal could command." To the several thousand people who had flocked to the courtroom half expecting to see Lincoln and Taney have it out face to face, he announced four points: that the President had no power under the Constitution to suspend the privilege of the writ of habeas corpus; that the military had no power, either of its own or by order of the President, to detain a civilian "except in aid of the judicial authority," which was clearly not the case in this affair; that Merryman was entitled to immediate discharge; and that he would file an opinion in writing within the week.

There is little that need be said about the content of this

22

opinion. A brief, straightforward exposition of the exclusive power of Congress to suspend the great writ, it relied heavily on Blackstone, Marshall, Jefferson, Story, and the location of the habeas corpus clause in the legislative article. The central proposition in Taney's argument, as in that of all those who deny this power to the executive, was as simple as this: "And if the high power over the liberty of the citizen now claimed, was intended to be conferred upon the president, it would undoubtedly be found in plain words in this article."

At the end of his opinion Taney pointed directly to the person who bore the responsibility for this action and who alone could correct it:

In such a case, my duty was too plain to be mistaken. I have exercised all the power which the constitution and laws confer upon me, but that power has been resisted by a force too strong for me to overcome. It is possible that the officer who has incurred this grave responsibility may have misunderstood his instructions, and exceeded the authority intended to be given him; I shall, therefore, order all the proceedings in this case, with my opinion, to be filed and recorded in the circuit court of the United States for the district of Maryland, and direct the clerk to transmit a copy, under seal, to the President of the United States. It will then remain for that high officer, in fulfillment of his constitutional obligation to take care that the laws be faithfully executed, to determine what measures he will take to cause the civil processes of the United States to be respected and enforced.

What Lincoln did with the copy sent to him, or what he thought of the entire incident, has never been disclosed. Taney returned to Washington unmolested; Lincoln went right on exercising the power that the Chief Justice had branded palpably unconstitutional; [14] and Merryman, after languishing a short time in Fort McHenry, was turned over to the civil authorities, indicted for treason, and eventually released. In his famous July 4 message to the special session of Congress Lincoln acknowledged that "the attention of the country has been called to the proposition that one who is sworn 'to take care that the laws be faithfully executed' should not himself violate them." He insisted that the question had been left open by the framers and that, in effect, the emergency of April, 1861, had answered it. In any case, he promised an "opinion at some length" from the Attorney General and left further action "entirely to the better judgment of Congress." On the following day Bates announced his opinion that the President shared with Congress the power to suspend the writ.[15]

Professor Swisher has written, "It is futile to argue whether the President or the Chief Justice was *right* in the matter, for back of their legal differences were fundamental differences of opinion on matters of public policy," and with this severely neutral judgment we can generally

[14] See particularly his sweeping suspension of the writ by proclamation of September 24, 1862, in Richardson, *op. cit.*, VI, 98–99. Lincoln plainly regarded the Act of 1863 (12 *Stat.* 755), authorizing him to suspend the writ, merely as declaratory.

[15] Richardson, *op. cit.*, VI, 20–31, especially 24–25. The opinion of Bates is in 10 *O.A.G.* 74–85, especially 81–85. Lincoln's chief unofficial support came from the distinguished lawyer Horace Binney. See his *The Privilege of the Writ of Habeas Corpus* (Philadelphia, 1862), and other works. In criticism of this stand, see S. G. Fisher, "The Suspension of Habeas Corpus during the War of the Rebellion," *Political Science Quarterly*, III (1888), 454–488; there is an invaluable bibliography at 485–488. The mixed attitude of Congress is depicted in G. C. Sellery, *Lincoln's Suspension of Habeas Corpus as Viewed by Congress* (Madison, Wisc., 1907).

agree.[16] Taney was a judge, Lincoln an executive. Taney was from Maryland and had delivered the opinion in *Scott v. Sanford;* Lincoln was from Illinois and had ridiculed that holding. It certainly cannot be said that Taney had one shred more respect than Lincoln for the rights of his fellow citizens, especially the rights of those who disagreed with him. Indeed, we know that the contrary was true. In the end, it was simply a question of this: Taney as Chief Justice was anxious to preserve respect for the law; Lincoln as President was determined to preserve the Union.

It would seem equally futile to argue over the present location of this power, for it is a question on which fact and theory cannot be expected to concur. Today, as ninety years ago, the answer to it is not to be found in law but in circumstance. The one great precedent is what Lincoln did, not what Taney said. Future Presidents will know where to look for historical support. So long as public opinion sustains the President, as a sufficient amount of it sustained Lincoln in his shadowy tilt with Taney and throughout the rest of the war, he has nothing to fear from the displeasure of the courts. If he should misread the necessity and find public opinion overwhelmingly against him, he can always, like Jackson at New Orleans, submit to the court with a speech to the gallery and turn the incident into a personal triumph! The law of the Constitution, as it actually exists, must be considered to read that in a condition of martial necessity the President has the power to suspend the privilege of the writ of habeas corpus. The most a court or judge can do is read the President a lecture based on *Ex parte Merryman*. And the chief

[16] Swisher, *Taney,* 555.

end that such a lecture will doubtless serve—it was certainly true of Taney's opinion—will be that of a handy weapon for agitators, obstructionists, and haters of "that man in the White House."

The Great Exception:
Ex parte Milligan

Of all the arbitrary executive practices in which Lincoln found it imperative to engage, certainly the most dubious and judicially assailable was the trial of civilians by military commission. It was one thing for him to proclaim a blockade of the South, suspend the writ of habeas corpus along the nation's most important line of communications, raise the limits of the regular forces in the absence of Congress, or even issue the Emancipation Proclamation while denying that Congress had any such power. It was quite another, certainly in a country that could trace its legal history back through the Petition of Right, to authorize military trial of disaffected civilians in areas where the civil courts were open and functioning. Yet this is precisely what Lincoln did in his proclamation of September 24, 1862. The importance of this document demands that it be quoted in full:

Whereas it has become necessary to call into service not only volunteers, but also portions of the militia of the States by draft in order to suppress the insurrection existing in the United States, and disloyal persons are not adequately restrained by the ordinary processes of law from hindering this measure and from giving aid and comfort in various ways to the insurrection:

Now, therefore, be it ordered, first, that during the existing insurrection, and as a necessary measure for suppressing the same, all rebels and insurgents, their aiders and abettors, within the United States, and all persons discouraging volunteer enlistments, resisting militia drafts, or guilty of any disloyal practice affording aid and comfort to rebels against the authority of the United States, shall be subject to martial law and liable to trial and punishment by courts-martial or military commissions; second, that the writ of *habeas corpus* is suspended in respect to all persons arrested, or who are now or hereafter during the rebellion shall be imprisoned in any fort, camp, arsenal, military prison, or other place of confinement by any military authority or by the sentence of any court-martial or military commission.[17]

One year later, September 15, 1863, he issued a second proclamation suspending the privilege of such persons to the great writ, and this time cited as authority the Habeas Corpus Act of 1863.[18] He did not mention the subject of military commissions, and it is extremely important to note that Congress did not authorize them in this act. Whatever military trials of civilians took place during the war found their authority in the President's position as commander in chief.

Here, it will be said, was the point at which the courts of the United States, led by an indignant Supreme Court, called a halt to the President's cavalier treatment of the Constitution. Certainly the constitutional guarantee of jury trial and the procedural rights outlined in Amendments IV, V, and VI prevented trial by military commission in areas where the regular courts were open, whatever might have become of these rights in Kentucky or

[17] Richardson, *op. cit.*, VI, 98–99; 13 *Stat.* 730.
[18] *Ibid.*, 170–171; 13 *Stat.* 734.

Tennessee or reconquered Louisiana. Certainly they did, and yet there is no case on the records of the Supreme Court or other federal courts in which this practice was impugned in the course of the war; first, because trials of this nature in areas where the regular courts were functioning were extremely rare, since the normal method of dealing with persons suspected of treasonable activity was arrest without warrant, detention without trial, and release without punishment; second, because most federal courts went out of their way to avoid a brush with the military authorities; and, third, because the Supreme Court itself put a damper on attempts to challenge the constitutionality of these controversial trials by military commission through an interesting decision announced in February, 1864.

The case in question, *Ex parte Vallandigham*,[19] involved the petition of the notorious Peace Democrat Clement L. Vallandigham "for a *certiorari*, to be directed to the Judge Advocate General of the Army of the United States, to send up [to the Supreme Court] for its review, the proceedings of a military commission" by which he had been tried in Cincinnati in May, 1863 (on a charge of publicly expressing sympathy for the enemy), and had been sentenced to prison for the duration. A few days after the trial the President commuted this sentence to banishment to rebel territory. Vallandigham, who apparently didn't think much of the celebrated query, "If he doesn't like it here, why doesn't he go back where he came from?" made a grand circuit through Bermuda and Halifax, and within six weeks was settled down across the river from Detroit. From this vantage point he ran for Governor of Ohio on

[19] 1 Wallace 243 (1864).

28

the Democratic ticket and watched his case pushed through to the Supreme Court.[20]

The Court refused to touch it. Seizing with evident relief upon the circumstance that the district court in Cincinnati had refused to issue a writ of habeas corpus to General Burnside and had thus forced Vallandigham to take his case directly from military commission to Supreme Court, the judges beat a unanimous retreat to the fortress of technicality. They declined to accept the case, on the ground that the military commission was not a "court" within the meaning of the Constitution or the section of the Judiciary Act of 1789 that granted the Court its appellate jurisdiction.[21] Moreover, the doctrine of *Marbury v. Madison* concerning the sharply defined limits of the Court's original jurisdiction forebade it to issue a writ of habeas corpus to the military authorities. Thus was staved off a potentially explosive judgment on the validity of the arrests and military trials ordered by Lincoln and Stanton.

The only indication of the Court's attitude on this great question was a cryptic remark at the close of Wayne's opinion: "And as to the President's action in such matters, and those acting in them under his authority, we refer to the opinions expressed by this court, in the cases of *Martin v. Mott,* and *Dynes v. Hoover.*" In each of these opinions, the latter of which Wayne had delivered,[22] the Court sup-

[20] In June, 1864, he slipped back into Ohio and spent the rest of the war agitating, while Lincoln looked the other way. Carl Sandburg, *Abraham Lincoln: The War Years* (New York, 1939), III, 109.

[21] 1 *Stat.* 73, 81.

[22] 20 Howard 65 (1857). The case involved a challenge on technical grounds to the jurisdiction and sentence of a Navy court-martial.

ported strongly the jurisdiction and sentence of a court-martial. In the first was expressed, in the second implied, an equally strong opinion that the President in acting under his military powers should be accorded great if not conclusive discretion. Since the three justices (Nelson, Grier, and Field) who concurred in the decision of *Ex parte Vallandigham* but not in the opinion were with the extreme limitationists in the next case of this type to come before the Court, it seems safe to assume that with this remark Wayne went out of his way to make clear that no censure of the President was to be implied from this decision. This, however, is circumstantial conjecture. As a final observation on this case, Wayne's opinion was based squarely on the reasoning of Judge Advocate General Holt, just as squarely as an opinion could be on argument of counsel at the bar.

Nothing more concerning the legality of military commissions was heard in the courts of the United States until the end of the war. Then, on April 3, 1866, some 353 days after Lincoln's assassination, a Supreme Court that included five of his appointments announced its unanimous conviction that the President had acted unconstitutionally in instituting trial by military commission during the war in areas where the civil courts were open and functioning. Five of the judges (Davis, Nelson, Grier, Clifford, and Field) went further and denied this power to Congress as well; the other four (Chase, Wayne, Swayne, and Miller) refused to join in this far-reaching dictum. At first, the decision went virtually unnoticed, for the opinions were not delivered until December 17, 1866, nor made public until two weeks later. Then, however, the country erupted into the most violent and partisan agitation over a

30

Supreme Court decision since the days of Dred Scott. The views of the majority on the lack of power in Congress to institute military tribunals, which were not necessary to the decision and could only be regarded as a gratuitous salvo against the plans of the Radicals for congressional reconstruction, split the nation, or at least its press, into two hotheaded camps.[23] Mr. Lincoln and his commissions were all but forgotten in the exultation of the Democrats and recriminations of the Radicals.

Today, of course, we remember this case for its construction of the President's war powers as well as for its celebrated defense of the inviolability of the Constitution in time of crisis. It is from this point of view that we should set out the facts and evaluate the opinions in *Ex parte Milligan.*

Lambdin P. Milligan, a "Son of Liberty" who had done a great deal more than merely give speeches in defiance of Lincoln and the Union, was arrested October 5, 1864, at his home in Indiana, tried by a military commission established under presidential authority, and sentenced to be hanged May 9, 1865, for disloyal activities. This sentence was approved by President Johnson. At the time of his arrest and trial the circuit court in Indianapolis was open for business and fully prepared to take cognizance of his case under the procedures outlined in the Habeas Corpus Act of 1863. Sections 2 and 3 of this law provided in sub-

[23] See the magnificent account of this affair in Charles Warren, *The Supreme Court in United States History* (New York, 1926), II, 423–449. To me this is easily the most fascinating part of a great, if unbalanced and uncritical, book, even though I cannot agree that *Ex parte Milligan* "has since been recognized by all men as the palladium of the rights of the individual." See also Samuel Klaus, *The Milligan Case* (New York, 1929).

stance that lists of prisoners arrested under authority of the President were to be furnished by the Secretaries of State and War to the circuit- and district-court judges. If grand juries returned no indictments against them, they were to be discharged by judicial order upon taking an oath of allegiance and entering into recognizance for good behavior. Where such lists were not furnished, a judge could discharge a prisoner on a writ of habeas corpus if satisfied of his loyalty. This process had been completely ignored in Milligan's case.

On May 10, 1865, with the noose practically around his neck, Milligan sued out a writ of habeas corpus to the circuit court in Indianapolis, and on a division of opinion the case was brought before the Supreme Court. The linchpin that had been missing in *Ex parte Vallandigham* was supplied by a circuit court able and willing to be heard in military circles. The arguments in this case, which took place in March, 1866, pitted the illustrious team of Attorney General Speed, Attorney General-to-be Stanbery, and General Benjamin F. Butler against the still more illustrious team of David Dudley Field, James A. Garfield, and Jeremiah S. Black. Lest it be thought that these gentlemen were arguing over the disposition of a corpse, it should be remarked that Milligan was very much alive. His sentence of hanging had been stayed on May 10 and had later been commuted to life imprisonment by President Johnson. Apparently no one had bothered to inform the Court, for at one point Davis paused to remark, "Although we have no judicial information on the subject, yet the inference is that he is still alive; for otherwise learned counsel would not appear for him and urge this court to decide his case."

It is impossible to express in capsule form the right-eousness, one might say self-righteousness, of Davis' opinion for the Court. He, like Taney, elected to turn a fairly simple case into a defense of "the very framework of the government and the fundamental principles of American liberty," with the obvious difference that Taney had been in the trenches, while Davis was well to the rear. In any case, he made the specific points that this presidentially authorized military commission had no jurisdiction to try and sentence Milligan, that the writ of habeas corpus ought immediately to issue, and that the prisoner should thereupon be discharged from custody. His general holding has already been mentioned: The President has no power under the Constitution to institute a military commission for trial of civilians in areas where the regular courts are open for business. It was his further observation that an invasion of American soil had actually to be under way, not merely threatened, to permit a state of martial law, and that Congress itself could not have authorized these commissions, which drew the fire of four of the justices. "We think," said Chase, thinking of his friends in Congress and the election of 1868, "that Congress had power, though not exercised, to authorize the military commission which was held in Indiana." All nine agreed, however, that Lincoln, whose name was never mentioned in argument or opinion but with reverence and awe, had gone well beyond the limits of his authority as commander in chief to maintain order among the civilian population. Finally, although both Davis and the Chief Justice had a great deal to say about the writ of habeas corpus, neither attempted to decide the question upon which Lincoln and Taney had clashed.

33

There remain to be quoted the most famous lines of Davis' opinion:

The Constitution of the United States is a law for rulers and people, equally in war and in peace, and covers with the shield of its protection all classes of men, at all times, and under all circumstances. No doctrine involving more pernicious consequences was ever invented by the wit of man than that any of its provisions can be suspended during any of the great exigencies of government. Such a doctrine leads directly to anarchy or despotism, but the theory of necessity on which it is based is false; for the government, within the Constitution, has all the powers granted to it which are necessary to preserve its existence; as has been happily proved by the result of the great effort to throw off its just authority.[24]

A great deal of praise and condemnation has been heaped indiscriminately upon *Ex parte Milligan*. For that reason, it is necessary to stand back a little from this case, look once again at its history and opinions in the light of facts and not legends, and attempt to appraise its true value as a restraint upon and interpretation of the exercise of the President's power as commander in chief.

As a restraint upon a President beset by martial crisis it was then, and in 1950, of practically no value whatsoever. It cannot be emphasized too strongly that the decision in this case followed the close of the rebellion by a full year, altered not in the slightest degree the extraordinary methods through which that rebellion had been suppressed, and did nothing more than deliver from jail a handful of rascals who in any event would have probably gained their freedom in short order. For Johnson it was, if anything, an extra round of ammunition to be fired at

[24] 4 Wallace 2, 120–121.

Thad Stevens. And upon all Presidents who have come after, it has had precious little demonstrable effect. True, it has been urged upon the Court many times in the hope of restraining some unusual presidential or congressional action, but never yet has it gained an important victory. No justice has ever altered his opinion in a case of liberty against authority because counsel for liberty recited *Ex parte Milligan.* Judges, too, are practical men, and when they decide for liberty, as happily they often do, they do it for better reasons than the fact that once upon a time a Supreme Court scolded a President who had saved the Union and had been shot for his pains, especially since that same Court with but one change in personnel had failed to scold him earlier when it might have done some good.

It is often argued that, quite apart from the practical influence this case has had or could have as a weapon for Court, Congress, and people to use in keeping a crisis-minded President in line, the moral value of Davis' opinion as a lecture to all future Presidents must assign it a place high on the list of the great cases. But this is to ignore the fact that no President, certainly not Cleveland or Wilson or the two Roosevelts, seems to have given it the slightest thought in determining the scope and form of his martial powers, and that in any case Davis so overstated his point as to render his observations wholly meaningless for a constitutional government determined to stay alive in a strife-torn world. The Constitution of the United States does *not* cover "with the shield of its protection all classes of men, at all times and under all circumstances," and there is nothing to be gained by insisting that it does. Would that it did—or, better, would that it could.

As an interpretation of presidential power the Milligan case has considerably more standing. It was important, even at that late date, to announce that there were, after all, some limits to the President's power over the civilian population well behind the lines. The use of military commissions in Indiana in 1864 was, it must be agreed, plainly unconstitutional, and even Lincoln's defenders could wish that he had shunned this extraordinary practice. It is no answer to point out that the regular courts, principally by reason of the jury system, were more hindrance than help to the cause of the Union; for if the military authorities did not trust the civil courts, they had only to keep their suspects locked up until the danger had passed. This, indeed, was the usual method of handling these cases. In other words, it was arguable that, under the conditions then obtaining, Milligan should be denied the privilege of the writ, but it was not necessary to go further and place him on trial before a military court. To this extent, Davis' opinion rested on solid ground.

But on several other points it flew far too high and wide. It is simply not true that "martial law cannot arise from a *threatened* invasion," or that "martial rule can never exist where the courts are open." These statements do not present an accurate definition of the allowable limits of the martial powers of President and Congress in the face of alien threats or internal disorder. Nor was Davis' dictum on the specific power of Congress in this matter any more accurate. And, however eloquent and quotable his words on the untouchability of the Constitution in time of actual crisis, they do not now, and did not then, express the realities of American constitutional law.

Finally, viewed simply as a conspicuous link in the long

chain of decisions on liberty and authority that stretch from 1 *Dallas* to the present, *Ex parte Milligan* was an exhibition of judicial self-hypnosis of which no clearheaded friend of the Court could possibly be proud. It is not easy for the layman to see the alleged decisive difference between *Ex parte Vallandigham* and *Ex parte Milligan*. The decision in the former has a hollow ring, which makes the echo of the latter even more hollow. If the Court had been at all anxious to test the President's reading of his powers —if, for example, Davis had really believed that the Constitution meant what it said about trial by jury—it would have been no trouble at all to alter Vallandigham's petition from one for certiorari to one for a writ of habeas corpus, returnable before one of the justices, if not the Court itself.[25] The Court could certainly have done what another Court was later to do in *Ex parte Grossman:* [26] entertain as an original suit the petition for a writ of habeas corpus of an individual unable to get justice from a recalcitrant (or spineless) lower federal court.

The answer, of course, is that Vallandigham got the ear of the Court in February, 1864, Milligan in March, 1866. Davis himself, at the outset of his opinion, betrayed this crucial point in these remarkable words:

During the late wicked Rebellion, the temper of the times did not allow that calmness in deliberation and discussion so necessary to a correct conclusion of a purely judicial [sic!] question. *Then,* considerations of safety were mingled with the exercise of power; and feelings and interests prevailed which are happily terminated. *Now* that the public safety is

[25] See 2 Wallace 243, 252 for the Court's shaky explanation of its inability to do this.
[26] 267 U.S. 87 (1925).

assured, this question, as well as all others, can be discussed and decided without passion or the admixture of any element not required to form a legal judgment. We approach the investigation of this case, fully sensible of the magnitude of the inquiry and the necessity of full and cautious deliberation.[27]

And, he might have added, entirely free to decide against the executive power without inviting the accusation that the Court was obstructing the President's efforts to lay the rebellion. It is one thing for a Court to lecture a President when the emergency has passed, quite another to stand up in the middle of the battle and inform him that he is behaving unconstitutionally. There is no intention here to deride the Court for executing its retreat of 1864. At that time discretion was indeed the better part of valor, and the Court practically confessed the futility of judicial restraint on a President actively exercising his war powers in defense of an embattled nation. There is, however, a clear intention, openly avowed and resolutely pursued, to blast that "evident piece of arrant hypocrisy," [28] *Ex parte Milligan*. Perhaps this assessment has been too hard on Davis and his brethren. He was a good and patriotic man, and so were most of his associates. He was a confused man, too, for on one hand he had been a great friend of Lincoln, and on the other he was deeply concerned over the spirit of disrespect for the Constitution that the war had touched off and that reconstruction was fanning ever higher. His anxieties, and his muddleheadedness, too, are plain in this passage:

This nation, as experience has proved, cannot always remain at peace, and has no right to expect that it will always

[27] 2 Wallace 109. The italics are his, not mine.
[28] E. S. Corwin, *The President* (2d ed.; New York, 1941), 165.

have wise and humane rulers, sincerely attached to the principles of the Constitution. Wicked men, ambitious of power, with hatred of liberty and contempt of law, may fill the place once occupied by Washington and Lincoln; and if this right is conceded, and the calamities of war again befall us, the dangers to human liberty are frightful to contemplate.[29]

He was doing his sincere best to preserve our constitutional future, but even here he tripped over his own ambivalence, for the one thing upon which all nine justices were agreed was that Lincoln had *not* been "sincerely attached to the principles of the Constitution." If this Court had not been willing or able to restrain that "wise and humane ruler," how could any future Court, even if armed with *Ex parte Milligan,* be expected to check a "wicked man, ambitious of power, with hatred of liberty and contempt of law"? In effect, he was rejecting the sound advice of Story in *Martin v. Mott* and Taney in *Luther v. Borden* that the character and devotion to duty of the President himself must ever be the principal checks on the abuse of executive power.

In sum, *Ex parte Milligan* is sound doctrine in forbidding the presidential establishment of military commissions for the trial of civilians in areas where the civil courts are open—but it is little else. Its general observations on the limits of the war powers are no more valid today than they were in 1866. Here again the law of the Constitution is what Lincoln did in the crisis, not what the Court said later.[30]

[29] 2 Wallace 125.

[30] One other Civil War case, which will be treated at length below (pp. 68–77), should be mentioned here. In the *Prize Cases,* 2 Black 635, 671–674 (1863), the majority held, in effect, that the President could brand and treat as enemies of the United States

Martial Rule in World War II:
The Case of the Japanese-Americans

From *Ex parte Milligan* to the second year of World War II only one major case concerning the President's power of martial rule came to the Court for decision. In *In re Debs* a unanimous Court gave its unqualified blessing to the President's authority, even in defiance of the wishes of a state governor, to call out the troops in defense of the nation's interests, property, and powers.

"We hold it to be an incontrovertible principle, that the government of the United States may, by means of physical force, exercised through its official agents, execute on every foot of American soil the powers and functions that belong to it. This necessarily involves the power to command obedience to its laws, and hence the power to keep the peace to that extent."

The entire strength of the nation may be used to enforce in any part of the land the full and free exercise of all national powers and the security of all rights entrusted by the Constitution to its care. The strong arm of the national government may be put forth to brush away all obstructions to the freedom of interstate commerce or the transportation of the mails. If the emergency arises, the army of the Nation, and all its militia, are at the service of the nation to compel obedience to its laws.[31]

---

all inhabitants of an area in general insurrection against the federal government. This pushes his power of martial rule to fantastic extremes. See also *Ford v. Surget,* 97 U.S. 594, 604 (1878).

[31] 158 U.S. 564, 578–579, 582 (1895). The first paragraph was a quote from Bradley's opinion in *Ex parte Siebold,* 100 U.S. 371, 395 (1879), in which he was discussing the power of United States marshals to perform certain duties in connection with elections.

40

The strong bias of the justices in favor of corporate property and against Governor Altgeld led them farther down the road to the Jackson-Lincoln-Roosevelt theory of the Presidency than the Court is usually inclined to go. Yet Brewer painted a remarkably accurate likeness of the President's actual powers to protect the peace. The Court had already made clear, in the memorable case *In re Neagle*,[32] that the "peace of the United States" would require a good deal of protection. In the light of the Debs and Neagle cases, it might easily be argued that there are no judicial limits to the President's real or alleged "inherent" power to protect the peace of the United States.

Otherwise these seventy-five years were barren of judicial discussion of this momentous problem. The Spanish-American War certainly raised no controversies of any basic importance over presidential or congressional war powers, and even World War I came and went without presenting the Court a single opportunity to lecture the President on such matters as habeas corpus, military commissions, martial law, and the use of troops. Wilson, recognizing the profound differences in character between his war and Lincoln's, made it clear from the outset that he was opposed to military trial of sedition and espionage cases as unconstitutional and as bad policy. Although numbers of Americans of questionable loyalty were roughly handled in the course of the war, in each instance it was at the hands of a civil court and a jury of fellow citizens acting under the broadly permissive terms of the Espionage Act of 1917, the "Sedition Law" amendment of 1918, and provisions in several other acts. In *Schenck v. United States* and *Abrams v. United States* the power of

[32] 135 U.S. 1, 58–68 (1890).

41

Congress to pass these laws, and of the Department of Justice to enforce them, was strongly, perhaps a little too strongly, upheld.[33]

World War II, however, was a different matter, for it brought in its wake three unusual exercises of military power over civilians, all grounded on the President's authority as commander in chief: the evacuation of the west coast Japanese-Americans, the declaration and maintenance of martial law in Hawaii, and the sixty-odd seizures of plants and industries in which labor disputes were injuring the war effort. Each of these programs was attacked in the courts by persons who had received arbitrary treatment at the hands of the military.

The evacuation of the Japanese-Americans is by now so familiar a tale that it will be retold here only so far as necessary to establish its significance for the President's power of martial rule, the ability of the Court to restrain that power, and the present standing of *Ex parte Milligan*.[34] The facts in brief are these: On February 19, 1942, in response to an overwhelming combination of military, journalistic, and congressional pressures, President Roosevelt issued Executive Order 9066,[35] which endowed the Secretary of War "and the Military Commanders whom he may from time to time designate" with broad discretionary authority to establish "military areas" from which

[33] 40 *Stat.* 76, 217, 411, 553; 249 U.S. 47 (1919); 249 U.S. 211 (1919); 250 U.S. 616 (1919).

[34] See generally the books and articles cited in Rossiter, *Constitutional Dictatorship*, 280–282; the first-rate study of Morton Grodzins, *Americans Betrayed* (Chicago, 1949); the legal literature cited by Grodzins at 351, especially the articles of Dembitz, Fairman, Rostow, and Freeman; and Leonard Bloom and Ruth Riemer, *Removal and Return* (Berkeley, Cal., 1949).

[35] 7 *Federal Register* 1407.

"any or all persons" might be excluded in order to prevent espionage and sabotage. The Secretary was directed to provide food, shelter, and transportation for such persons as were to be evacuated from a military area, and "the use of Federal Troops" to assist in enforcing compliance with his orders was authorized. All this was done "by virtue of the authority vested in me as President of the United States, and Commander in Chief of the Army and Navy." Although the order spoke in general terms that permitted the Secretary of War the fullest discretion to use this grant of power anywhere in the United States, it was a notorious fact that the Japanese-American population of the Pacific states was the target in mind. In all this Mr. Roosevelt acted in good faith, relying, as perforce he had to rely, on the opinions and advice of his civil and military subordinates.

The following day Secretary of War Henry L. Stimson delegated this authority to Lieutenant General J. L. De-Witt, commanding the so-called Western Defense Command. General DeWitt in his turn established by proclamation "Military Areas Nos. 1 and 2," consisting of the three westernmost states and part of Arizona. By a series of 108 separate orders he then, with the aid of the troops under his command and the War Relocation Authority (established by another executive order on March 18, 1942),[36] proceeded to remove all persons of Japanese ancestry from these two areas. This process was not finally completed, be it noted, until October, 1942. Both the coastal and eastern portions of the designated states were in this manner cleared of some 112,000 persons who answered the racial criterion established by DeWitt's orders.

[36] 7 *Fed. Reg.* 2165.

Fully 70,000 of this number were full-fledged citizens of the United States, by every legal, constitutional, and moral standard enjoying all the rights and privileges of all other citizens of the United States. Yet New Year's Day, 1943, found them locked up in a chain of camps in the interior hundreds and even thousands of miles from their homes. Many of the homes had already been occupied by fellow citizens fortunate enough to lack Japanese blood. The official explanation for this enforced mass evacuation was that it was a "military necessity." In the event of a Japanese assault on the Pacific coast, said the Army, the presence of thousands of disloyal or unpredictable people of Japanese descent might easily prove an element of confusion that the enemy could exploit to excessive advantage. Nor was there time for individual examination to separate the loyal from the disloyal.

Lest it be assumed that Congress looked askance at this extraordinary move by the President, it should be recorded that on March 21, 1942, by a voice vote, the two houses passed a law that substantially ratified and confirmed Executive Order 9066 by making a federal misdemeanor (punishable by a $5000 fine, a year in jail, or both) of any action in violation of the restrictions and orders laid down by the President, Secretary of War, and military commanders.[37] This eleven-line statute became law on March 21.

The judicial history of the Japanese-American evacuation consists primarily of three leading cases: *Hirabayashi v. United States,* decided June 21, 1943; [38] *Korematsu v.*

[37] 56 *Stat.* 173; 88 *Congressional Record* 2722–2726, 2729–2730.

[38] 320 U.S. 81 (1943). See 46 Fed. Supp. 657 (1942). See also *Yasui v. U.S.,* 320 U.S. 115 (1943).

United States, decided December 18, 1944; [39] and *Ex parte Endo,* decided the same day.[40] Even the dates of these cases give pause for sober reflection.

Hirabayashi v. United States. Gordon Hirabayashi, an American citizen and a senior at the University of Washington, was tried and convicted in the district court for violating two orders issued by General DeWitt: one directing him to report at a certain time to a "civil control station" (a preliminary to evacuation), the second a curfew regulation. He was sentenced under the Act of March 21, 1942, to imprisonment for three months on each count, the sentences to run concurrently. The circuit court heard his appeal and certified questions of law to the Supreme Court, whereupon the latter ordered the entire record brought before it.

The Court was in a position to follow either of two paths, one short and smooth, the other rocky and full of traps. It could review Hirabayashi's conviction on both counts, in which case it would have to examine the legality of the order commanding him to report to the control station, and thus might be forced into considering the constitutionality of the entire program of evacuation. Or it could confine itself to one count, and, if it found him guilty, could then ignore the other count, since the two sentences ran concurrently.[41] The Court selected the second path, fixing its attention rigidly on the much narrower issue of the curfew violation.

A unanimous Court found the general's order valid and sustained the conviction. Chief Justice Stone had little

[39] 323 U.S. 214 (1944); 140 Fed. 2d 289 (1943). Rehearing denied February 12, 1945; 324 U.S. 885.

[40] 323 U.S. 283 (1944).

[41] On this point, see *Brooks v. U.S.,* 267 U.S. 432, 441 (1925).

trouble repelling the two principal attacks on the curfew order. To the contention that the Act of March 21 was an unconstitutional delegation of legislative power, he retorted with the well-worn formulas and citations of the *Brig Aurora* and *Opp Cotton Mills v. Administrator*.[42] To the more serious contention that a curfew regulation discriminating between "citizens of Japanese ancestry and those of other ancestries" violated the Fifth Amendment, he replied that "the actions taken must be appraised in the light of the conditions with which the President and Congress were confronted in the early months of 1942." A nine-page review of these conditions—the Japanese victories, the exposed condition of the west coast, the unusual number of defense plants in that area, the peculiar problem of the Japanese-American population—led the Chief Justice to this conclusion:

We cannot close our eyes to the fact, demonstrated by experience, that in time of war residents having ethnic affiliations with an invading enemy may be a greater source of danger than those of different ancestry. Nor can we deny that Congress, and the military authorities acting with its authorization, have constitutional power to appraise the danger in the light of facts of public notoriety. We need not now attempt to define the ultimate boundaries of the war power. We decide only the issue as we have defined it—we decide only that the curfew order as applied, and at the time it was applied, was within the boundaries of the war power. In this case it is enough that circumstances within the knowledge of those charged with the responsibility for maintaining the national defense afforded a rational basis for the decision which they made. Whether we would have made it is irrelevant.

[42] 7 Cranch 382 (1812); 312 U.S. 126 (1941).

Hirabayashi v. United States is perhaps the most clear-cut case on record of the Court's tendency to insist that unusual military actions be grounded, whenever possible, on the combined powers of President and Congress, which when merged are called simply "the war powers of the United States." In this instance, thanks to the Act of March 21, the Court could state, "We have no occasion to consider whether the President, acting alone, could lawfully have made the curfew order in question or have authorized others to make it." With the aid of this formula, and confining itself strictly to the simple problem of a fairly reasonable curfew regulation, the Court had no trouble sustaining the government. Justices Douglas, Murphy, and Rutledge, in concurring with the result, warned that there were limits to this sort of thing. "In my opinion," said Murphy, "this goes to the very brink of constitutional power."

Ex parte Endo. Not until eighteen months later did the Court again find it necessary to think publicly about the Japanese-Americans, when two cases came before it for decision. The plea of Mitsuye Endo, an American citizen of demonstrated loyalty (she was a permanent employee in the California Civil Service), was simple and easily satisfied. She was evacuated in 1942 from Sacramento to a relocation center near Tule Lake, California, from which place she petitioned the district court unsuccessfully for discharge on a writ of habeas corpus. (Her petition was filed in July, 1942, and denied in July, 1943.) On appeal to the circuit court and certificate of questions of law to the Supreme Court (April 22, 1944), the entire record was passed up for final scrutiny. In the meantime Miss Endo had been removed to a camp in Utah, from which

47

she could gain release only under a series of conditions designed to prevent "a dangerously disorderly migration of unwanted people to unprepared communities." By the date of the decision the military areas had been disestablished and the relocation centers were being broken up. Under the circumstances the Court had no trouble in sidestepping the great constitutional issues—for which it was castigated by Justice Roberts in a separate opinion—and in holding that Miss Endo had been entitled all along to an unconditional release by the War Relocation Authority. In other words, even if evacuation of a loyal person from California had been warranted, detention in Utah had not been—definitely not by statute or order, probably not by the Constitution. The fact that she had been detained for several years and was already free to go her way in peace was not mentioned.

Korematsu v. United States. It was in the case of this citizen, convicted in the district court for remaining in his home in San Leandro, California, contrary to an exclusion order of General DeWitt,[43] that the Court was finally brought to an unavoidable consideration of the great constitutional questions raised by the evacuation. In a 6–3 decision, with Justice Black speaking for the majority and Justices Murphy, Roberts, and Jackson filing separate dissents, the Court upheld the program, and thus the exclusion order, as a valid exercise of presidential-military-congressional power, "as of the time it was made and when the petitioner violated it," and rejected the

[43] The general had the Japanese-Americans "coming and going." One order forbade them to leave the area, another to remain in it! The result, fully intended, was to force them to report to the evacuation stations. This is what Korematsu would not do. In effect, he was punished for sitting in his own home.

charges of counsel for Korematsu that it violated Amendments IV, V, VI, VII, and VIII.

Black's brief opinion was based on these very simple propositions: "There was evidence of disloyalty on the part of some, the military authorities considered that the need for action was great, and time was short. We cannot —by availing ourselves of the calm perspective of hindsight—now say that at that time these actions were unjustified." He denied that the evacuation was founded in racial prejudice, pointing out that the authorities had made their decision on the purely military basis of security against invasion, espionage, and sabotage. And to the Japanese-Americans he said:

We are not unmindful of the hardships imposed . . . upon a large group of American citizens. But hardships are part of war, and war is an aggregation of hardships. All citizens alike, both in and out of uniform, feel the impact of war in greater or lesser measure. Citizenship has its responsibilities as well as its privileges, and in time of war the burden is always heavier. Compulsory exclusion of large groups of citizens from their homes, except under circumstances of direct emergency and peril, is inconsistent with our basic governmental institutions. But when under conditions of modern warfare our shores are threatened by hostile forces, the power to protect must be commensurate with the threatened danger.

Since the Court had decided that it was constrained to accept the military's judgment of the extent of this danger, it was likewise constrained to accept its judgment of the extent of "the power to protect."

Justice Roberts dissented in a biting opinion. "This is not a case of keeping people off the streets at night as was *Hirabayashi v. U.S.* . . . On the contrary, it is the case of

49

convicting a citizen as a punishment for not submitting to imprisonment in a concentration camp based on his ancestry, and solely because of his ancestry, without evidence or inquiry concerning his loyalty or good disposition towards the United States." He would not go so far as to hold that an evacuation of this sort would never be justified, but declared that "no pronouncement of the commanding officer can . . . preclude judicial inquiry and determine" whether a sufficient emergency had in fact existed. In this instance, he was certain, it had not.

Justice Murphy's words bit even deeper. "This exclusion . . . goes over 'the very brink of constitutional power' and falls into the ugly abyss of racism." He had apparently bothered to read the military and congressional reports on the evacuation, and had been shocked by the evidences of naked prejudice that ran like angry veins of poison through its entire history. Admitting frankly that the judgments of the military "ought not to be overruled lightly by those whose training and duties ill-equip them to deal intelligently with matters so vital to the physical security of the nation," he nevertheless felt that such a judgment "based upon such racial and sociological considerations is not entitled to the great weight ordinarily given the judgments based upon strictly military considerations." Against the arguments of urgent necessity advanced by the government's attorneys he set the fairly leisurely pace with which the evacuation had proceeded and the fact that "conditions were not such as to warrant a declaration of martial law." Nor could he forbear contrasting the manner in which the English in 1940 had examined 74,000 enemy aliens individually and that in which Americans in 1942 had declined to make any attempt to separate the loyal from the disloyal in the Japanese-American population. To him the whole scheme was rankly unconstitutional and deserved to be labeled as such in the bluntest terms. "I dissent, therefore, from this legalization of racism."

Finally, Justice Jackson:

It would be impracticable and dangerous idealism to expect or insist that each specific military command in an area of probable operations will conform to conventional tests of constitutionality. When an area is so beset that it must be put under military control at all, the paramount consideration is that its measures be successful, rather than legal. . . . No court can require such a commander in such circumstances to act as a reasonable man; he may be unreasonably cautious and exacting. Perhaps he should be.

In short, the Court had no power to obstruct this unconstitutional program. At the same time, Jackson palliated this abdication of judicial oversight of military power by remarking that "if we cannot confine military expedients by the Constitution, neither would I distort the Constitution to approve all that the military may prove expedient." The fact that the courts could not prevent the execution of this program did not mean that they were therefore bound to lend a hand in enforcing it. Murphy and Roberts, in disapproving the evacuation, were wasting their time; the majority justices, in approving it, were creating a "loaded weapon ready for the hand of any authority that can bring forward a plausible claim of an urgent need." The correct thing to do, Jackson seemed to say, was to ignore the whole affair. "I should hold that a

51

civil court cannot be made to enforce an order which violates constitutional limitations even if it is a reasonable exercise of military authority." [44]

It would be easy to write ten or twenty or a hundred pages on the many astounding aspects of the great evacuation—the long history of prejudice against the Japanese-Americans, the economic and social pressures behind the demands for their removal, the mind of General DeWitt as laid bare in his own reports and those of investigating committees, the all but unanimous support tendered the Army by local and state officials, the time schedule, the actual record (which is no record at all) of espionage and sabotage on the Pacific coast, the further efforts to do justice to these people, and a dozen other points of interest or incredulity. It would be easier still to analyze the various opinions in these three cases sentence by sentence, an exercise in judicial semantics, constitutional interpretation, and moral confusion that no student of the Court should fail to tackle. But that is not the purpose of these recollections of the evacuation. Their purpose is simply to evaluate the role of the judiciary, and especially that of the highest court, in this amazing assertion of presidential power. What are the lessons of these three cases?

In the first place, the very fact of this evacuation should be convincing proof that the courts of the United States, from highest to lowest, can do nothing to restrain and next to nothing to mitigate an arbitrary presidential-military program suspending the liberties of some part of

[44] 323 U.S. 243–248. Compare the dissent of Justice Rutledge in *Yakus v. U.S.*, 321 U.S. 414, 460–489 (1944), especially his thoughts at 467–468.

the civilian population, even when it takes months to carry through. There was no court, no writ, no show of judicial power that could be expected to check the President, Secretary Stimson, General DeWitt, or any of his officers in the immediate execution of this dictatorial decision to clear a racial minority out of an area announced to be "threatened with enemy invasion." This, then, is a first lesson of the evacuation: The courts are powerless to prevent a President from going into action with his powers of martial rule. And a second lesson, the inevitable result of the slowness of the judicial process, the difficulties in the path of an aggrieved individual bent on speedy relief, and the impossibility that one writ of injunction or even ten could halt an operation on this scale: The courts are likewise powerless to prevent him or his subordinates from carrying their plans through to conclusion. And a third lesson, which does little more than repeat what we have learned before: The courts will not, even when the necessity has clearly passed, presume to substitute their judgment for that of the military acting under presidential orders. Whatever relief is afforded, and however ringing the defense of liberty that goes with it, will be precious little and far too late.

The fact is that *Korematsu v. United States* makes perfect hash of the general principles of *Ex parte Milligan*. There was no suspension of the writ of habeas corpus, no declaration of martial law, no trial by military commission. But there was something that cut even deeper into the liberties of the American people: the wholesale invasion, based on a racial criterion, of the freedom of person of 70,000 citizens, an invasion of American liberty made all the more reprehensible, as Justice Murphy pointed out, by the fact that there was indeed no occasion for martial law. Nor can much stock be placed in the Court's numerous efforts to tie the whole program up with the string of the Act of March 21 into a conclusive bundle labeled "the war powers of the United States." From start to finish this was a naked display of the President's power of martial rule. The law in question simply made it easier to deal with the tiny handful of Japanese-Americans who were not overpowered by DeWitt's show of force. The Army could just as easily have "gone and got" Korematsu and hauled him off to Utah. And certainly Justice Jackson had no illusions that a refusal by the Court to help enforce the exclusion orders would in any way have cramped the general's style.

Again, perhaps, we have been too harsh with the Court. The majority justices would not use hindsight on the President and the Army; we should not use it on them. It should suffice to state the facts as they indubitably exist: The government of the United States, in a case of military necessity proclaimed by the President, and a fortiori when Congress has registered agreement, can be just as much a dictatorship, after its own fashion, as any other government on earth. The Supreme Court of the United States will not, and cannot be expected to, get in the way of this power.

Martial Law in Honolulu and Military Seizure in Chicago

The story of martial law in Hawaii is considerably less disturbing and has a slightly happier ending than the tribulations of the Japanese-Americans.[45] On December 7, 1941, for reasons that need no explanation, Governor J. B. Poindexter, acting upon a clear grant of authority in section 67 of the Organic Act of the Territory of Hawaii,[46] suspended the writ of habeas corpus, declared martial law throughout the islands, and turned over to the Commanding General, Hawaiian Department, the exercise of all his normal powers "during the present emergency and until the danger of invasion is removed." In conformance with the requirements of the statutory grant, a message was rushed off to President Roosevelt asking for approval of this action, and confirmation was immediately forthcoming. Through this action the President took full legal and constitutional responsibility for the initiation of military government.

The regime of martial law thus instituted was no mere paper transfer of power. The military assumed the entire governance of the islands. The civil authorities who continued to function did so at the pleasure and for the convenience of a military command that was legally and actually superior to them. The manner in which criminal justice was administered will be illustration enough. The Army took over courtrooms and offices; dispensed with such trappings as grand jury indictments, trial by jury, and rules of evidence; and handled criminal cases by summary procedure. There was no slackening in this regime until March, 1943, when the strong protests of Governor

[45] The literature on this subject is voluminous. See Rossiter, *Constitutional Dictatorship*, 284, and references there cited. Charles Fairman, "The Supreme Court on Military Jurisdiction," *Harvard Law Review*, LIX (1946), 833–882, especially 834–866, leaves virtually nothing to be said.

[46] 31 *Stat.* 141, 153.

Ingram M. Stainback, who had in the meantime replaced Poindexter, finally persuaded the military to restore eighteen functions of civil government to the regular authorities, although with the reserved right to resume them at any time. The important features of military law continued, however, with most crimes being tried by military courts. Despite a rising wave of criticism, especially after the Battle of Midway and the commencement of the great offensives eighteen months later, the state of martial law was not finally terminated until October 24, 1944, when a presidential proclamation cut short a regime that the military would just as soon have prolonged until the end of the war.[47]

With the writ of habeas corpus suspended, the civil courts of the territory, although fully prepared to perform their normal tasks, were powerless to give relief to the hundreds of civilians who were punished for the usual run of crimes and misdemeanors by military courts and summary procedures—powerless, that is, until a doughty district judge named Delbert E. Metzger got tired of waiting and in August, 1943, issued a writ of habeas corpus in the case of two naturalized Germans interned by the Army.[48] Lieutenant General Robert C. Richardson, then in command of the area, countered with an order, with penalties attached, forbidding any judge in the islands to

[47] 9 *Fed. Reg.* 12831.

[48] For the facts of this seriocomic episode, see Garner Anthony, "Martial Law, Military Government and the Writ of Habeas Corpus in Hawaii," *California Law Review*, XXXI (1943), 486 ff. Anthony, Attorney General of the Territory, was counsel for Duncan in the Supreme Court. See also Claude McColloch, "Now It Can Be Told," *American Bar Association Journal*, XXXV (1949), 365–368, 444–448.

entertain a petition for a writ of habeas corpus and incidentally naming Metzger specifically. The judge, who had apparently been reading up on the Hall-Jackson vendetta at New Orleans in 1815, followed through with his grand riposte: a $5000 fine ($4000 more than Hall fined Jackson) for contempt of court! This head-on collision of determined exponents of two widely differing views of the Constitution was finally resolved by a compromise worked out by special emissaries of Attorney General Biddle and Secretary Stimson, through which the President remitted the fine (reduced to $100) and the general withdrew his order. The territorial courts were empowered to issue writs of habeas corpus, but prisoners were to gain release only on successful appeal to higher courts.

It was thus in early 1944 that two civilians—White, who had been convicted by a military tribunal in August, 1942, on a charge of embezzling stock, and Duncan, who had been similarly convicted in March, 1944, on a charge of assaulting two Marine sentries in the Pearl Harbor Navy Yard—were able to petition the territorial district court for writs of habeas corpus.[49] In each instance the district

[49] There had been one earlier attempt to challenge the military regime. Hans Zimmerman, a citizen arbitrarily detained by the Army, had sued unsuccessfully in February, 1942, for a writ of habeas corpus in the territorial court. Although he was locked up, his wife was free, and managed to get a review of his case in the circuit court (9th circuit) on the mainland. Failing to get a reversal, 132 Fed. 2d 442 (1942), she pushed on to the Supreme Court. On March 3, 1943, the Army removed Zimmerman to San Francisco and there, March 12, the day before she applied for a writ of certiorari, released him unconditionally. The Solicitor General brought this to the Court's attention, and the Court held the case moot, *Zimmerman v. Walker*, 319 U.S. 744 (1943). The possibilities of this road to freedom from military imprisonment were not further explored, but one man at least had gone up it to victory.

court held that the trials had been without authority and that the prisoners were entitled to their freedom. These holdings were appealed in tandem to the circuit court and there reversed. The Supreme Court granted certiorari in early 1945, heard arguments in December, and finally handed down its decision February 25, 1946.[50]

The Court held 6–2 that the prisoners had been unlawfully tried by the military tribunals, but as ever the decision was confined to the narrowest possible scope. The gist of Justice Black's opinion for the majority was that the "martial law" authorized by section 67 of the Organic Act did not extend so far as to justify the trial of civilians by military commission when the civil courts were in fact fully prepared to function normally. In other words, the opinion of the majority was based on the construction of a statute and not, as Justice Murphy insisted in a concurring opinion that it should have been, on constitutional grounds. Chief Justice Stone concurred in the result, but went on record as granting a wider scope to section 67. Justice Burton, joined by Justice Frankfurter, announced his conviction that the military governor had not exceeded the permissible range of discretion under the circumstances shown to have existed. Burton even went so far as to state, "I am obliged to dissent from the majority of this Court and to sound a note of warning against the dangers of over-expansion of judicial control into the fields allotted by the Constitution to agencies of legislative and executive action."

The majority justices, in deciding that these military trials could not be brought within the meaning of section

[50] *Duncan v. Kahanamoku, White v. Steer,* 327 U.S. 304 (1946); 146 Fed. 2d 576 (1944).

67, had to go behind the testimony of the military authorities concerning the necessities of the moment, read the facts of life in Hawaii in 1942 and 1944 for themselves, and substitute their own judgment for that of the authorities—something they had refused to do in *Korematsu v. United States.* In that case they had accepted at face value what Justice Murphy termed "an accumulation of much of the misinformation, half-truths, and insinuations that for years have been directed against Japanese-Americans by people with racial and economic prejudices." In this case, as if stung by Murphy's bitter words, they accepted nothing. The question inevitably arises: What would they have decided in *Duncan v. Kahanamoku* a year or two years or three years earlier? The most that can be said for this case is that two men got some extremely belated relief and that the Court indirectly upheld the Constitution. But the people of Hawaii lived under martial law from December, 1941, to October, 1944.

The third spectacular display in World War II of the President's power of martial rule—the seizure before, during, and after hostilities of some sixty plants or industries in which labor disputes had impeded (or threatened to impede) the war effort—had nothing to do with habeas corpus, martial law, or military commissions. Nevertheless, the wartime commandeering of private industry may be properly treated as an instance, however extraordinary, of this presidential power, for it was as commander in chief, with the use of federal troops, that Presidents Roosevelt and Truman engaged in this severe practice.[51] Not

[51] For a more complete treatment of this power, see Clinton Rossiter, "The President and Labor Disputes," *Journal of Politics,* XI (1949), 100–105.

even the extreme exponents of the strong presidency have argued that the President holds this authority in time of peace.

Wartime seizure is a relatively new departure. In the first World War President Wilson seized factories or industries on two occasions, in each instance under a grant of statutory authority. It remained for Franklin D. Roosevelt to base this practice on the exalted plane of the President's constitutional authority. The pattern of presidential power was set in the very first seizure of the "unlimited national emergency," that of the North American Aviation plant in Inglewood, California, in June, 1941. The President announced that he was acting pursuant to the powers vested in him "by the Constitution and laws of the United States, as President of the United States and Commander in Chief of the Army and Navy of the United States." [52] Just what these laws were, and there were several, Mr. Roosevelt did not trouble to say. Both he and Mr. Truman generally cited all their authorities for seizure in one jumbled sentence, leaving it to the commentators to determine which was the most reliable in any particular case. In 1943 the President was specifically granted the power of seizure in section 3 of the controversial Smith-Connally (War Labor Disputes) Act,[53] but in view of his status as commander in chief and the numerous actions of this nature he had already taken on that basis, this grant was at best declaratory, even supererogatory. It should be pointed out that all but a few seizures were occasioned by employer or union defiance of the directives of the

[52] 6 *Fed. Reg.* 2777.

[53] 57 *Stat.* 163, passed over Mr. Roosevelt's veto. This act came to an automatic end June 30, 1947.

National War Labor Board and its predecessor, the National Defense Mediation Board.

Only once in the course of the war was this power challenged in the courts, with results that must be set down as extremely disappointing for the purposes of this study. On December 28, 1944, by order of the President,[54] the Secretary of War took possession of nine of the plants and facilities of Montgomery Ward and Company. This bold move, the climax of an ill-tempered struggle between the War Labor Board and Mr. Sewell Avery that had kept the nation entertained for almost three years, was accompanied by an action in the district court in Chicago for a declaratory judgment to establish the legality of the seizure and for an injunction forbidding Avery and his officers to interfere with the government's possession. Normally the government would not have bothered with this quest for judicial approval, but the well-known nature of Ward's business was so different from that of the other plants that had been seized that it was considered good policy to have a ruling.

Solicitor General McGrath's argument made two points: (1) that the seizure was justified under section 3 of the Smith-Connally Act, which had authorized the President in the event of a dispute to seize "any plant, mine, or facility equipped for the manufacture, production, or mining of any articles or materials which may be required for the war effort or which may be useful in connection therewith"; (2) that, even if Ward's could not be brought within this formula, the President could seize these prop-

[54] 9 *Fed. Reg.* 15079. See 40 *O.A.G.* 312, in support of the first seizure, for the Attorney General's views of the President's authority to do this.

erties "under his general war powers." Both of these contentions were rejected by Judge Philip L. Sullivan on the general distinction, for which he consulted several dictionaries, that Ward's was engaged in "distribution" and not "production." His interpretation of the President's war powers was something less than Rooseveltian.[55]

The circuit court reversed this decision by a 2–1 vote. Again the question was: Does "production" include "distribution" within the meaning of the Smith-Connally Act? This time, after a slightly more careful examination of the statutory and judicial precedents, the answer was yes.[56] The court did not find it necessary to decide whether the President could have seized Montgomery Ward simply in his capacity as commander in chief, although it made no bones about its interest in this momentous question. "Active participation in its decision is intriguing," said Judge Evans, while refusing to be tempted from his secure position.

Certiorari was granted by the Supreme Court November 5, 1945, but hopes for a full rehearsal of the great arguments for and against Mr. Roosevelt's reading of his war powers, and for a major judicial pronouncement on this still unsettled question, were dashed by the Court's agreement with the Solicitor General that the case was moot.[57] The properties had been turned back to Mr.

[55] 58 Fed. Supp. 408 (1945).

[56] 150 Fed. 2d 369 (1945).

[57] *Montgomery Ward and Co. v. U.S.*, 326 U.S. 690 (1945). Certiorari had been denied at the previous term of court, 324 U.S. 858 (1945), on the ground that "application has been made prior to judgment of the Circuit Court of Appeals." It is also interesting to note that on the occasion of the government's first seizure of Montgomery Ward, in 1944, the properties were returned the day

Avery October 18, 1945. The Supreme Court's decision was vigorously protested by counsel for the company, who were anxious for a trial of strength in their own interest and in that of "a dispassionate review of one of the most ominous invasions of civil liberties which the late conflict encouraged," [58] but to no avail.

It is not likely that the Court would have held against the government in this important case. Undoubtedly it would have confined its attention to section 3 of the Smith-Connally Act and, having agreed with the circuit court that Montgomery Ward's business could be brought within its terms, avoided any statement concerning the President's constitutional war powers. Nor can there be any doubt that under the conditions of modern war the President has a broad constitutional power to seize and operate industrial facilities in which production has been halted, a power which, like his other powers of martial rule, is virtually impossible to define or control. Certainly it extends far into civilian territory, in view of the government's contention in the course of this litigation that the company deserved seizure because its defiance of the War Labor Board's orders threatened "the disintegration of the wartime structure of labor relations which . . . cannot survive successful repudiation by a company of the size and economic importance of Montgomery Ward." The activities of Mr. Roosevelt and inadequacies of the

---

before the district court was to announce a decision on the government's prayer for an injunction—thus rendering the case moot. For a somewhat similar case in World War I, see *Commercial Cable Co. v. Burleson,* 250 U.S. 360 (1919).

[58] *Memorandum on Behalf of Montgomery Ward and Company,* In the Supreme Court of the United States, October Term, 1945, No. 408, 7.

courts have forged yet another weapon of presidential martial power.

There is little to say in conclusion to this extended account of the judicial history of the President's power of martial rule, especially in the light of the estimates already voiced in connection with *Ex parte Merryman, Ex parte Milligan,* and *Korematsu v. United States.* There are many questions that go still unanswered—Can the President suspend the writ of habeas corpus? Can he declare martial law as a precautionary measure? Can he seize *any* plant that defies the decisions of his presidential wartime boards? Can he intern or evacuate citizens at his discretion?—but they are questions concerning the details of presidential power rather than its sweep, which the Court itself has acknowledged to be tremendous.

And if Lincoln and Roosevelt used this power without regard to the Court, what of the first President to face an atomic war? The only restrictions upon him as he invokes the fateful authority of martial rule will be his own political and moral sense, "the forbearance of a distracted people," [59] and the judgments of history. And *Ex parte Milligan* is proof enough that the judgments of the Court do not necessarily serve as the judgments of history.

[59] W. A. Dunning, *Essays on the Civil War and Reconstruction* (New York, 1898), 15.

PART II

The Supreme Court and Other Aspects of the War Powers

Ex parte Milligan and *Korematsu v. United States,* dramatic and controversial as they may be, by no means tell the whole story of judicial review of the war powers. There have been at least five other perplexing constitutional questions—Who can start a war? When is a war "over," and who is to end it? What are the war powers of Congress, and to what extent may they be delegated to the President? How independent of the Supreme Court are courts-martial and presidential military commissions? What are the President's powers in conquered areas?—that the Court has been begged to answer with some show of finality. Let us see if the Court has acted any more boldly and clearheadedly in dealing with these problems than it has in pronouncing the law of martial rule.

The President's Power to Wage Defensive War

One of the truly unique provisions of the American Constitution is the clause that confides to an independent legislature the power "to declare war." The Senate's searching debate in 1949 over the implications of article 5 of the North Atlantic Pact served as a dramatic reminder of this canon of our constitutional system: that the nation cannot be finally and constitutionally committed to a state of war without the positive approval of both houses of Congress.[1]

At the same time, it is a matter of history that most of our wars were in full course before Congress could get around to declaring the fact, and it has therefore always been assumed that the President, as commander in chief, could order the armed services to "meet force with force." [2] The extent of his powers of defensive war remains a much-argued problem, however, and Congresses, Courts, commentators, and even Presidents [3] have experienced con-

[1] But of course the President could veto a declaration of war, something that Cleveland for one was probably quite ready to do—in the case of war with Spain. See generally S. E. Baldwin, "The Share of the President of the United States in a Declaration of War," *American Journal of International Law*, XII (1918), 1–14.

[2] See the exhaustive discussion of this problem in C. A. Berdahl, *War Powers of the Executive* (Urbana, Ill., 1922), chap. 4, and the various works cited in his notes. See also T. S. Woolsey, "The Beginnings of War," *Proceedings of the American Political Science Association*, I (1904), 54–68; A. H. Putney, "Executive Assumption of the War Making Power," *National University Law Review*, VII, No. 2 (1927), 1–41; C. C. Tansill, "War Powers of the President of the United States with Special Reference to the Beginning of Hostilities," *Political Science Quarterly*, XLV (1930), 1–55; J. B. Moore, *Digest of International Law* (Washington, 1906), VII, 162–172.

[3] Particularly Jefferson, as might be expected. See his faint-hearted message to Congress, December 8, 1801, Richardson, *op. cit.*, I, 327, as well as a second message, December 6, 1805, *ibid.*, 388–390. Hamilton's scornful and realistic comment on Jefferson's doubts is in his *Works*, H. C. Lodge, ed. (New York, 1886), VII, 200–206.

siderable difficulty in fixing the boundaries of his power to fight without a declaration and in answering the important legal question, "When is the United States in a state of war as regards neutral rights, other third-party interests, the operation of wartime statutes, and other such matters?"

The framers of the Constitution, who had some first-hand knowledge of this sort of thing, recognized frankly that this nation could be embroiled in major hostilities without an express declaration. On August 17, 1787, in the course of a debate whether Congress should be given the power "to make war," Madison and Gerry "moved to insert 'declare,' striking out 'make' war; leaving to the Executive the power to repel sudden attacks," and the motion was carried.[4] The need for executive defensive action was also acknowledged in the militia clause (Art. I, sec. 18, cl. 15), as well as in statutes of 1792 and 1795 empowering the President to call forth the militia in actual or threatened invasion.[5]

The subsequent history of the Republic has justified the prescience of the framers and early legislators, for we have several times been factually and even legally at war without an express declaration by Congress. In at least four instances—1798–1800, 1801–1805, 1815, and 1914–1917—we have fought a public war without any declaration at all.[6] Generally, however, Congress has been only too will-

[4] Max Farrand, ed., *Records of the Federal Convention* (New Haven, Conn., 1911), II, 318–319.

[5] 1 *Stat.* 264, 424.

[6] See generally J. G. Rogers, *World Policing and the Constitution* (Boston, 1945), 45–55. In *Hamilton v. McLaughry*, 136 Fed. 445, 449–450 (1905), the period of the Boxer Rebellion was held to be a "time of war" within the meaning of the 58th Article of War.

ing to acknowledge by declarative resolution that war has been thrust upon us, and has expressly or by implication approved the acts of war for which the President's power as commander in chief was up to that moment the sole constitutional justification.

Fortunately for commentators and constitutional historians, as well as for Presidents anxious for impeccable judicial support for their more questionable acts of defensive war, there is a major Supreme Court decision favoring the President on this very point. Even more fortunately, the decision was not unanimous, and limitationists have hardly less impeccable precedents of their own to cite in defense of strict construction of the war-declaring power.[7] The decision, easily one of the most momentous in the history of the Court's interpretation of presidential power, was the celebrated *Prize Cases*, argued before the Court February 10–25 and announced March 10, 1863.[8] In this instance the Court was brought face to face with one of the most controversial actions of Lincoln's great eleven-week "dictatorship," the blockade of

---

See also *Thomas v. U.S.*, 39 Ct. Cls. 1, 6–9 (1903), and *Warner, Barnes and Co. v. U.S.*, 40 Ct. Cls. 1, 28–30 (1904), in which the Philippine Insurrection was likewise held to be a public war.

[7] Note the weight that Willoughby accords the dissent in his *Constitutional Law*, III, 1559–1560. A more recent authoritative statement of the limited view of the President's warmaking powers is that of Senator Taft, delivered June 28, 1950, at the beginning of the Korean crisis. See *Daily Congressional Record*, 9460–9461. The advocates of untrammeled presidential power rely heavily on Nelson's opinion in *Durand v. Hollins*, 4 Blatch. 451 (1860), which sustained Pierce's authorization to a naval commander to bombard Greytown, Nicaragua, in retaliation for a mob assault on the American consul. Had this litigation been decided in the Supreme Court, it would have been one of the four or five leading cases in this book.

[8] 2 Black 635 (1863).

the Confederacy effected by his proclamations of April 19 and 27, 1861.[9] Four ships—two American, one Mexican, one British—had been captured by Union naval vessels enforcing the blockade and had been brought into various ports to be libeled as prizes. "The libels were filed by the proper District Attorneys, on behalf of the United States and on behalf of the officers and crews of the ships, by which the captures were respectively made. In each case the District Court pronounced a decree of condemnation, from which the claimants took an appeal." Once again the capricious mechanics of "government by lawsuit" had forced the Supreme Court to decide the constitutional validity of an important exercise of presidential power. Indeed, the problem of public policy before the Court was even more sweeping than that, for as counsel for one of the shipowners boldly reminded the justices, "The question here is, how can the United States, under the Constitution, be involved in war?"

The complexities of this great case attracted much popular attention. More important, they attracted a display of legal and forensic talent rarely equaled in the history of the Court, nine ornaments of the bar—including Attorney General Bates, William M. Evarts, James M. Carlisle, and Richard Henry Dana (who had learned the law of the sea the hard way)—all fully prepared to range far and wide upon the law of nations, the war powers of the President, and the legal subtleties of "intestine conflict." The arguments, which consumed twelve full days of the Court's unforced attention, make exciting reading even today. For eloquence, passion, and depth of learning they have never been surpassed in our judicial history.

The Court was faced with a personal problem of no

[9] 12 *Stat.* 1258, 1259.

little magnitude. For one thing, its stock of popular support had never been lower; the ghost of Dred Scott would not be laid. For another, the peculiar nature of this case and the war that had produced it made certain that, no matter what the decision, the Court would not please everybody and might not please anybody. The possibilities of this situation have been graphically stated by Taney's biographer:

The Supreme Court was in a position greatly to embarrass the government in either of two ways. It might hold that the conflict was not a war and not covered by the laws of war, and that the prizes had been illegally taken and foreign trade with southern ports illegally broken up. Such a position would make the government liable for huge sums in damages, and its psychological effect would be such as seriously to cripple the conduct of the war. On the other hand the court might hold that the Confederacy was an independent sovereign power, and, although holding the blockade to be legal, it might do it in such a way as to encourage the recognition of the Confederacy by foreign governments. Such a decision would be only less serious than the other.[10]

The Court escaped neatly but narrowly from this beckoning trap. To the precise question for which the justices agreed to find an answer—"Had the President a right to institute a blockade of ports in possession of persons in armed rebellion against the Government, on the principles of international law, as known and acknowledged among civilized States?"—five judges (Grier, Wayne, and the three Lincoln appointees then on the Court, Swayne, Miller, and Davis) answered *yes;* four (Nelson, Clifford,

[10] Swisher, *Taney,* 563–564. Quoted by permission of the Macmillan Company.

70

Catron, and Taney) answered *no*. The heart of Grier's decision was his belief that the insurrection of the southern states was a "state of war" in contemplation of domestic and international law, and that the President's proclamation of blockade and the capture of these prizes were therefore entirely legitimate. At the same time that he accorded the Union full belligerent rights from the beginning of the insurrection, he did not accord any rights of sovereignty to the South, even by implication. This, of course, was the extraordinary conception of the nature of this conflict to which Lincoln had come at an early date. He could not have asked for a more favorable opinion.

The essential passages of Grier's opinion, quoted hundreds of times since by champions of the strong presidency, are these:

If a war be made by invasion of a foreign nation, the President is not only authorized but bound to resist force by force. He does not initiate the war, but is bound to accept the challenge without waiting for any special legislative authority. And whether the hostile party be a foreign invader, or States organized in rebellion, it is nonetheless a war, although the declaration of it be *"unilateral."* . . .

This greatest of civil wars was not gradually developed by popular commotion, tumultuous assembles, or local unorganized insurrections. However long may have been its previous conception, it nevertheless sprung forth suddenly from the parent brain, a Minerva in the full panoply of *war*. The President was bound to meet it in the shape it presented itself, without waiting for Congress to baptize it with a name; and no name given to it by him or them could change the fact. . . .

Whether the President in fulfilling his duties, as Com-

71

mander-in-chief, in suppressing an insurrection, has met with such armed hostile resistance, and a civil war of such alarming proportions as will compel him to accord to them the character of belligerents, is a question to be decided *by him,* and this Court must be governed by the decisions and acts of the political department of the Government to which this power was entrusted. "He must determine what degree of force the crisis demands." The proclamation of blockade is itself official and conclusive evidence to the Court that a state of war existed which demanded and authorized a recourse to such a measure, under the circumstances peculiar to the case.[11]

At one point in his opinion Grier turned aside to observe, with some show of irritation, that these third parties could hardly ask the Court "to affect a technical ignorance of the existence of a war, which all the world acknowledges to be the greatest civil war known in the history of the human race, and thus cripple the arm of the Government and paralyze its power by subtle definition and ingenious sophisms." [12] The expression "subtle definition and ingenious sophisms" is worth quoting and remembering. It sums up neatly not only the character of Nelson's dissenting opinion but also the whole history of this extraordinary process, repeated in every one of our wars, through which injured private interests have set out to embarrass the war power of the United States in the hope of personal redress. The great legal arguments over the extent of this power have been carried on not between opposing branches of the government with national ends in view, but between a government anxious to enforce its laws and private persons anxious to evade their admittedly

[11] 2 Black 668–670. See also *Matthews v. McStea,* 91 U.S. 7, 12–13 (1875).
[12] 2 Black 669–670.

harsh application. Subtle definition and ingenious sophisms have been the chief weapons of these interests since time out of mind.

In this particular instance the dissenting justices agreed with Carlisle's brilliant, if entirely too legalistic, argument that "war did not exist; blockade did not exist; and there could be no capture for breach of blockade, or intent to break it." Not everything the President had done to meet the insurrection had been illegal. He was certainly empowered to wage war upon the rebels "under the municipal laws of the country," but he could not take any action "under the law of nations." He could march his legions up and down the South, but he could not, no matter how many supply ships were sailing in and out of Confederate ports, proclaim a blockade that neutral third parties were bound to respect—not until Congress had recognized the situation through a declaration of war. This step had not been taken, Nelson asserted, until the Act of July 13, 1861.[13] Prizes taken between April 19 and that date could not be libeled in the courts of the United States. In short, the President could "meet the adversary upon land and water with all the forces of the Government," but not with all the forces of the law!

The telling passages of Nelson's opinion are these:

Now, in one sense, no doubt this is war, and may be a war of the most extensive and threatening dimensions and effects, but it is a statement simply of its existence in a material sense, and has no relevancy or weight when the question is what constitutes a war in a legal sense, in the sense of the law of nations, and of the Constitution of the United States? For it must be a war in this sense to attach to it all the consequences

[13] 12 *Stat.* 255.

that belong to belligerent rights. Instead, therefore, of inquiring after armies and navies, and victories lost and won, or organized rebellion against the general Government, the inquiry should be into the law of nations and into the municipal fundamental laws of the Government. For we find there that to constitute a civil war in the sense in which we are speaking, before it can exist, in contemplation of law, it must be recognized or declared by the sovereign power of the States, and which sovereign power by our Constitution is lodged in the Congress of the United States. . . .

So the war carried on by the President against the insurrectionary districts in the Southern States, as in the case of the King of Great Britain in the American Revolution, was a personal war against those in rebellion, . . . with this difference, as the war-making power belonged to the king, he might have recognized or declared the war at the beginning to be a civil war . . . , but in the case of the President no such power existed: the war therefore from necessity was a personal war, until Congress assembled and acted upon this state of things. . . .

I am compelled to the conclusion . . . that the President does not possess the power under the Constitution to declare war or recognize its existence within the meaning of the law of nations, which carries with it belligerent rights, and thus change the country and all its citizens from a state of peace to a state of war.[14]

What then can we say of the decision in the *Prize Cases* and its significance for the President's military powers? For Lincoln, the result and the majority opinion were entirely satisfactory. Nelson's opinion, too, was no balm to the South and, as an isolated instance of minority judicial disapproval of certain phases of the war, of little more

[14] 2 Black 690, 694–695, 698.

satisfaction to Lincoln's detractors. In particular Lincoln was encouraged to believe that his ever-broadening interpretation of the commander-in-chief clause would encounter no substantial restrictions in the future decisions of the Court. It was a fact of considerable importance for the conduct of the war that the Court, although clearly in a position to do all sorts of legal and moral damage to the cause, did not go out of its way to castigate Lincoln's theory of his powers (as expounded by Dana) or invite other challenges to the effective prosecution of the war. Although direct evidence on the subject is impossible to find, it seems reasonable to believe that the *Prize Cases* went far to discourage determined assaults on the validity of the Conscription Act of 1863, the Legal Tender Act of 1862, the Emancipation Proclamation, and the various arbitrary suspensions of free speech and press, all of which were considered palpably unconstitutional by Chief Justice Taney.[15] The decision in the *Prize Cases* was a welcome addition to the arguments of the Union men, and Lincoln fought his war with no more thought about the Supreme Court than was necessary in making his five appointments.

For future occasions when Presidents would be forced to fight without prior congressional authorization, the case was as important as a case can be in shaping the contours of presidential power, especially since there have been no further decisions on this tremendous constitutional and practical problem.[16] After the two points of

[15] Swisher, *Taney*, 566–572.

[16] For the Court's opinion on the date of commencement of the Spanish-American War, see *The Pedro*, 175 U.S. 354, 363 (1899); for World War II, see E. M. Borchard, "When Did the War Begin," *Columbia Law Review*, XLVII (1947), 742–748. In *New*

view of the *Prize Cases,* which can certainly be expanded into general theories of the President's authority in foreign as well as domestic war, there is really little more to be said. The split in the Court was a pretty accurate reflection then, and remains so [1950], of the division of informed opinion on an unsettled question. In this case, as in so many others, the two views of the Constitution—as grant of power and as catalogue of limitations—clashed head on. Five of the judges were, for various reasons, thinking in terms of power, four in terms of limitations, and probably all nine would just as soon have found some middle ground.

Yet war, even as fought by the constitutional Americans, always has been a question of power, and it seems more than providential that the decision, however closely fought, should have been in favor of the Union rather than the Constitution. In the final analysis, the facts of history and the doctrine of the *Prize Cases* dovetail rather neatly, and both bear impressive witness to the cogency of Richard Henry Dana's sweeping view of presidential warmaking powers in his argument for the United States:

It is not necessary to the exercise of war powers by the President, in a case of foreign war, that there should be a preceding act of Congress declaring war.

The Constitution gives to Congress the power to declare war.

But there are two parties to a war. War is *a state of things,* and not an act of legislative will. If a foreign power springs

---

York Life Insurance Co. v. Bennion, 158 Fed. 2d 260 (1946), it was held, for purposes of construction of a life insurance policy, that the war began legally with the Japanese attack on Pearl Harbor. Certiorari in this case was denied by the Supreme Court, 331 U.S. 811 (1947).

a war upon us by sea and land, during a recess of Congress, exercising all belligerent rights of capture, the question is, whether the President can repel war with war . . . or whether that would be illegal? . . .

It is enough to state the proposition. If it be not so, there is no protection to the State.[17]

Yet Carlisle, the opposing counsel, in summing up Dana's argument, and therefore overstating it for effect, was an even better if unwitting prophet for war in the atomic age:

The matter then comes . . . to the pure question of the power of the President under the Constitution. And this is, perhaps, the most extraordinary part of the argument for the United States. It is founded upon a figure of speech, which is repugnant to the genius of republican institutions, and, above all, to our written Constitution. It makes the President, in some sort, the impersonation of the country, and invokes for him the power and right to use all the forces he can command to *"save the life of the nation."* The principle of self-defense is asserted, and all power is claimed for the President. This is to assert that the Constitution contemplated and tacitly provided that the President should be dictator, and all constitutional government be at an end whenever he should think that "the life of the nation" is in danger.[18]

The Supreme Court's Lack of Power
to Declare Peace

In sharp contrast to the clear-cut words of the Constitution on the power to declare war is its casual silence on the power to make peace. The failure of the framers to

[17] 2 Black 659–660.
[18] 2 Black 648.

include a positive statement of the location of this power was not entirely accidental, for Madison's *Journal* records that on August 17, 1787, Pierce Butler's motion to add the words "and peace" after the words "to declare war" was voted down unanimously [19]—principally, as Story was later to write, "upon the plain ground that it [the power to make peace] more properly belonged to the treaty-making power." [20] It seems clear that an overwhelming majority of the framers considered that the power to make peace was first of all lodged with President and Senate in their treaty-making capacity.

As a matter of historical practice the government of the United States has "declared peace" by several methods other than that of the solemn constitutional treaty, although the latter has always remained the most important technique. A 1948 opinion of the Supreme Court acknowledges that a state of war "may be terminated by treaty or legislation or Presidential proclamation," [21] and adds significantly, "Whatever the mode, its termination is a political act." Thus the Court at one time or another has given full support to the action of the political branches in terminating war by treaty (the Spanish-American War),[22] by proclamation of the President (the

[19] Farrand, *op. cit.*, II, 319, also 540–541.

[20] *Commentaries*, sec. 1173.

[21] *Ludecke v. Watkins*, 335 U.S. 160, 168–169 (1948).

[22] *Hijo v. U.S.*, 194 U.S. 315, 323 (1904). In *MacLeod v. U.S.*, 229 U.S. 416, 432 (1913), the Court stated that "a state of war as to third persons continued until the exchange of treaty ratifications." On treaties of peace, see also *Haver v. Yaker*, 9 Wallace 32 (1869); *U.S. v. Anderson*, 9 Wallace 56, 70 (1869); *Dooley v. U.S.*, 182 U.S. 222, 230 (1901).

Civil War),[23] and by joint resolution (World War I).[24] Nor does this exhaust the techniques of peacemaking that could be constitutionally employed—employed, that is to say, by the President and tolerated as a "political act" by the Court. An executive agreement with or without specific congressional authorization would seem one way to end a war, should the political-international situation demand such action; Congress could also authorize the President to proclaim the official termination of a state of

[23] It was held several times by the Court that the Civil War ended on two different dates in two different parts of the South— by presidential proclamation of April 2, 1866 (14 *Stat.* 811), in all states except Texas, and by proclamation of August 20, 1866 (14 *Stat.* 814), in the latter state. See especially *The Protector*, 12 Wallace 700, 702 (1871), as to the legal dates for the beginning and ending of the war. See also *Masterson v. Howard*, 18 Wallace 99, 105–106 (1873), and *Burke v. Miltenberger*, 19 Wallace 519, 525 (1873). The power of the President to terminate a foreign war by proclamation is a question to which the future alone can offer a satisfactory answer. It is important to note that President Wilson denied categorically that he possessed any such power. See his letter to Senator Fall, printed in the *New York Times*, August 22, 1919, 2. For sound comment on this problem, see J. M. Mathews, "The Termination of War," *Michigan Law Review*, XIX (1921), 833–834.

[24] The famed joint resolution of July 2, 1921 (42 *Stat.* 105; see also 41 *Stat.* 1359), was accorded full respect by the Court in *Commercial Trust Co. v. Miller*, 262 U.S. 51, 57 (1923); *Swiss Insurance Co. v. Miller*, 267 U.S. 42 (1925); and many similar cases. For a fuller ventilation of the constitutional problems involved in making peace, see Berdahl, *War Powers*, chap. 14; Willoughby, *Constitutional Law*, I, 534–536; E. S. Corwin, "The Power of Congress to Declare Peace," *Michigan Law Review*, XVIII (1920), 669–675; Quincy Wright, *The Control of American Foreign Relations* (New York, 1922), 290–293; Coleman Phillipson, *Termination of War and Treaties of Peace* (New York, 1916).

war after ascertaining certain facts, in other words, largely at his own discretion. Something of this sort is to be found in several sections of certain important statutes enacted during the first World War.[25] And it is altogether possible, especially in this atomic age, that an enemy would be so completely reduced to a state of impotent anarchy as to leave no authority with which we could negotiate a peace. In such an eventuality the President or Congress, or preferably both, would probably make an official statement to this effect, which the courts would doubtless accord judicial recognition.[26] Finally, it need only be mentioned in passing that the power to terminate actual hostilities by an armistice or other agreement is a strictly military power, belonging to the President as commander in chief, that no litigant has ever been so brazen as to question.

This reference to the President's power to negotiate an armistice should remind us that there is something more to war than war itself. Not only do we have the "war before the war"; more important, we have the war after it, a war that can "rage" for some years after the shooting has died down. This is a fact of huge consequence for the scope and effect of presidential power. No one who lived through the years after World War II could fail to feel the effects of the vast power that had been left by the American people in the possession of their government, especially in the hands of the President, simply because they are [1950] not at peace with Germany or Japan, or finished with the unlimited national emergency declared

[25] 40 *Stat.* 276, 283–284, 411, 412.

[26] The reverse of this situation, the *United States* in "impotent anarchy," is something about which we might also give a thought.

by President Roosevelt May 27, 1941. Reconversion and rent control were only two of the many areas into which the war power of Congress continued to reach, while Mr. Truman dealt with a variety of problems from Russian intransigeance to railroad strikes as a commander in chief with abnormal constitutional and statutory competence. To accept, as accept we must, the theory that every state of war extends for an indefinite number of years beyond the end of hostilities is to acquiesce in an immense expansion of national, congressional, and especially presidential power.

It is therefore highly important to record that the Supreme Court, although repeatedly requested to declare that occasion for the exercise of this or that war power had in fact ceased, has uniformly, if not altogether unanimously, favored the government's contention that war does not end with the last shot, nor for some years thereafter. A case or two from each of our last four major wars may be briefly examined to illustrate the Court's historic attitude on this much debated question.

In *Stewart v. Kahn* [27] (1870) the Court, which in a variety of opinions had already announced or assumed that the Civil War continued until President Johnson's two proclamations of 1866, took special pains to remind the litigants that the war power of the United States "is not limited to victories in the field and the dispersion of the insurgent forces. It carries with it inherently the power to guard against the immediate renewal of the conflict, and to remedy the evils which have arisen from its rise and progress." The implications for presidential authority of

[27] 11 Wallace 493, 507 (1870). See also *The Protector*, 12 Wallace 700, 702 (1871).

this eminently practical doctrine are better imagined than specifically catalogued. It opens the door to an undefined and therefore virtually unlimited exercise of the war power after the war, with impact on enemy and citizen alike.

Hijo v. United States [28] affords ample evidence that Chief Justice Fuller and his election-following Court subscribed without reservation to the doctrine that war with Spain did not terminate until the exchange of ratifications of the Treaty of Paris in April, 1899. A Spanish corporation's contention that the war had ended with the protocol and presidential proclamation of August 12, 1898, suspending hostilities, was met by Justice Harlan with passages from Kent's *Commentaries* brought to the Court's attention by Assistant Attorney General James Clark McReynolds.[29]

Hamilton v. Kentucky Distilleries and *Ruppert v. Caffey* [30] were the leading cases in which the Court was asked to re-examine this problem during the postwar years of World War I. It is the first of these that is generally cited as the basic case in this particular field; but the latter, too, invites our attention, chiefly because of the appearance for Ruppert's Beer of Mr. Elihu Root and his eloquent, and nearly successful, appeal to the shade of Lambdin P. Milligan. In addition, both these cases present a splendid example of the manner in which injured private

[28] 194 U.S. 315, 323 (1904). See also 22 *O.A.G.* 190.

[29] The passages in the *Commentaries* may be found in the second edition (New York, 1832), I, 159–161.

[30] 251 U.S. 146, 158–163, 165–168 (1919); 251 U.S. 264 (1920). See also *Commercial Cable Co. v. Burleson,* 255 Fed. 99, 104–106 (1919), which exhibits Judge Learned Hand at his learned best.

interests can force the Court to stand up and be counted on a major issue of national policy, even if most of the justices will say nothing more than "count us out."

The interests in these cases *had* been injured heavily, even disastrously. There could be no doubt of their right to a day in the highest court of the land, for the enforcement of one controversial law, enacted by Congress under the approving eye of President Wilson, meant, and was supposed to mean, nothing less than the indefinite and uncompensated suspension of their business. This, of course, was the famed War-Time Prohibition Act of November 22, 1918,[31] an exercise of the war power (ten days after the cessation of hostilities) that made it "unlawful to sell for beverage purposes any distilled spirits, . . . for the purpose of conserving the man power of the Nation, and to increase efficiency in the production of arms, munitions, ships, food, and clothing for the Army and Navy." Among the arguments put forward by the Kentucky Distilleries, which obviously represented every distillery in America, was the assertion that the act "became void before these suits were brought [October 10, 1919] by reason of the passing of the war emergency." A unanimous Court, speaking through Justice Brandeis, rejected this contention with force and finality. With approving references to *Hijo v. United States* and *Stewart v. Kahn,* as well as to the numerous postwar actions of President Wilson explainable only in terms of a continuing emergency, the Court refused to "enquire into the motives of Congress" or the "wisdom of the legislation."

In view of facts of public knowledge, . . . that the treaty of peace has not yet been concluded, that the railways are

[31] 40 *Stat.* 1045.

still under national control by virtue of the war powers, that other war activities have not been brought to a close, and that it cannot even be said that the man power of the nation has been restored to a peace footing, we are unable to conclude that the act has ceased to be valid.[32]

At the same time, Brandeis remarked "that it would require a clear case to justify a court in declaring that such an act, passed for such a purpose, had ceased to have force because the power of Congress no longer continued," a statement that seemed to leave other laws and presidential actions open to challenge. And in *Ruppert v. Caffey*, argued at the same time and decided only three weeks after *Hamilton v. Kentucky Distilleries*, four justices decided that the war power stopped short of Colonel Ruppert's beer. Justice McReynolds, a border-state gentleman who could tell bourbon from beer, summed up his opinion in this characteristic passage:

The argument runs—This court has held in *Hamilton v. Kentucky Distilleries* that under a power implied because necessary and proper to carry into execution the above named powers relating to war, in October, 1919, Congress could prohibit the sale of intoxicating liquors. In order to make such a prohibition effective the sale of non-intoxicating beer must be forbidden. Wherefore, from the implied power to prohibit intoxicants the further power to prohibit this non-intoxicant must be implied.

The query at once arises: If all this be true, why may not the second implied power engender a third under which Congress may forbid the planting of barley or hops, the manufacture of bottles or kegs, etc.? [33]

[32] 251 U.S. 163.
[33] 251 U.S. 305–306.

And with the aid of two full pages of *Ex parte Milligan* Justice McReynolds had no difficulty substituting his judgment for that of President and Congress in determining whether prohibition of nonintoxicating beer was a valid use of the war power one year after the cessation of hostilities. This, of course, was a very special case of that power interfering with a legitimate private interest, and these justices, troubled at the sight of a major industry singled out for annihilation under a strained reading of the war powers, simply decided that here was a proper place to call a halt. The only basis for distinguishing their stands in the Hamilton and Ruppert cases is that whiskey is one thing and beer another. On a variety of such distinctions is our jurisprudence grounded.

The pattern of World War I was repeated in the years after V-E and V-J Days. In two major cases, *Fleming v. Mohawk Wrecking and Lumber Co.* (April 28, 1947) and *Woods v. Miller Co.* (February 16, 1948),[34] the Court evidenced few qualms in rejecting the contentions of private interests that the war emergency had come to an end; in a third, *Ludecke v. Watkins* (June 21, 1948),[35] involving the arbitrary handling of an enemy alien under a sweeping and ancient statutory grant of presidential power, the Court decided only 5–4 in favor of the govern-

---

[34] 331 U.S. 111, 116 (1947); 333 U.S. 138, 141–147 (1948). See also *U.S. v. Shaugnessy*, 70 S. Ct. 309, 314, decided January 16, 1950. For informative further comment on this problem, see Theodore French, "The End of the War," *George Washington Law Review*, XV (1947), 191–201, and the learned note—an outstanding example of what a good law-review note should be—"Judicial Determination of the End of War," *Columbia Law Review*, XLVII (1947), 255–268.

[35] 335 U.S. 160 (1948).

ment and questioned bluntly the unqualified existence of a state of war.

The exercise of war power under attack in the Fleming case was an executive order of December 12, 1946,[36] consolidating the OPA and three other agencies into the Office of Temporary Controls. The order was issued under authority of the First War Powers Act of 1941,[37] which granted the President a broad power of administrative reorganization "only in matters relating to the conduct of the present war" and "during the continuance of the present war and for six months after the termination of the war." The Court denied without dissent the argument of counsel for the Mohawk Company that President Truman's proclamation of a "cessation of hostilities" on December 31, 1946,[38] had ended the state of war. Full reliance was placed on *Hamilton v. Kentucky Distilleries* and *Stewart v. Kahn.* "The cessation of hostilities," said Justice Douglas, "does not necessarily end the war power. . . . Whatever may be the reach of that power, it is plainly adequate to deal with problems of law enforcement which arise during the period of hostilities but do not cease with them."

In *Woods v. Miller Co.* the exercise of war power was a far-reaching statute, the Housing and Rent Act of June 30, 1947,[39] passed by Congress more than twenty-two months after the last shot was fired. Again the Court found the war power sufficient. Said Justice Douglas:

[36] 11 *Fed. Reg.* 14281.
[37] 55 *Stat.* 838.
[38] 12 *Fed. Reg.* 1.
[39] 61 *Stat.* 193.

The legislative history of the present Act makes abundantly clear that there has not yet been eliminated the deficit in housing which in considerable measure was caused by the heavy demobilization of veterans and by the cessation or reduction in residential construction during the period of hostilities. . . . Since the war effort contributed heavily to that deficit, Congress has the power even after the cessation of hostilities to act to control the forces that a short supply of the needed article created. . . .

We recognize the force of the argument that the effects of war under modern conditions may be felt in the economy for years and years, and that if the war power can be used in days of peace to treat all the wounds which war inflicts on our society, it may not only swallow up all other powers of Congress but largely obliterate the Ninth and Tenth Amendments as well. There are no such implications in today's decision.[40]

Justice Jackson, in concurring, made even more articulate the Court's feeling that there must be some limit somewhere beyond which it would refuse to go in support of the war powers. "I cannot accept the argument that war powers last as long as the effects and consequences of war, for if so they are permanent—as permanent as the war debts." For Jackson the fact that "we have armies abroad exercising our war power and have made no peace terms with our allies, not to mention our principal enemies" was sufficient to justify this act and its enforcement.[41]

Finally, in *Ludecke v. Watkins*, some three years after the fighting had ended, the Court was forced to consider

[40] 333 U.S. 142–144.
[41] 333 U.S. 147.

the applicability of the Alien Enemy Act of 1798,[42] which gave the President broad authority to restrain and remove alien enemies "whenever there is a declared war between the United States and any foreign nation or government." The decision was 5–4 in favor of the government. The question of "war or no war?" was not presented or answered in a clear-cut manner, principally because the hard problems of civil liberty for alien enemies and of judicial review of administrative action were uppermost in the minds of the dissenting justices, but it did evoke significant comment. Said Justice Frankfurter in his majority opinion: "Whether and when it would be open to this Court to find that a war though merely kept formally alive had in fact ended, is a question too fraught with gravity even to be adequately formulated when not compelled." And the Liberal Four (Black, Douglas, Rutledge, and Murphy) rushed through this opened door to announce that the doctrine of *Stewart v. Kahn* and *Hamilton v. Kentucky Distilleries* could not be stretched to cover this set of facts. Said the first of these, "I think the idea that we are still at war with Germany in the sense contemplated by the statute controlling here is a pure fiction," and, "Whatever else that fiction might support, I refuse to agree that it affords a basis for today's holding that our laws authorize the peacetime banishment of any person on the judicially unreviewable conclusion of a single individual. The 1798 Act did not grant its extraordinary and dangerous powers to be used during the period of fictional wars."

Will the logic of this dissent appeal to a majority of the Court and thus serve as a check to the hitherto unbounded post-bellum sweep of the war powers? The an-

[42] 1 *Stat.* 577, as amended by 40 *Stat.* 531.

swer to this question would seem to be *yes*. In a case such as this, one in which the check upon the political branches would be confined to a particular exercise of the war power and would affect only the parties to the suit, it is altogether possible that the Court would refuse to accept the fiction of a state of war. But in a case in which an adverse decision would interfere on an important scale with the domestic and diplomatic policies of President and Congress or alter the rights of millions of individuals, it would be idle to expect the Court to go to the mat with the government. In other words, *Hamilton v. Kentucky Distilleries*, with all its implications for national and presidential power, remains good law and sound politics, while the dissents in *Ruppert v. Caffey* and *Ludecke v. Watkins* constitute a footnote to that case which may yet become a definite qualification. However that may be, the Court has yet to disagree officially with the President's lawyers on this momentous issue, and if it ever does, we can be sure that the case will be one with a narrow range. We cannot expect the Court to end our wars.[43]

Judicial Review of the War Powers of Congress

The President cannot conduct our wars simply on the basis of his constitutional authority as commander in chief. His powers of command are spacious, but first he must have something to command. Congress alone can supply the men, money, and munitions with which he pursues the success of our arms. He must also rely on the legislative will for all those supplementary statutory

---

[43] On the problem of emergency, see the interesting decision in *East New York Savings Bank v. Hahn*, 326 U.S. 230 (1945).

powers that are especially necessary in modern war. However narrow the intentions of the framers in granting the President the command of the armed forces, an intention that carried over into the limited views of such authorities as Hamilton and Taney, the nature of modern war has added an entirely new element to this authority: the power to wage the "war at home"—to regulate labor-management relations, commandeer plants and whole industries, control the production of munitions and distribution of necessities, sequester enemy property, reorganize the administration, even initiate prohibition. And though he can do wonders with that simple phrase "He shall be Commander in Chief," [44] he needs the support of Congress to bring the home front to the proper pitch of production and co-operation.

Congress has rarely been known to refuse this support. No less concerned with getting on with the war than the President, it has been no less eager to wield its own huge accumulation of constitutional war powers in the grand manner. The fact that the President, both as chief execu-

[44] On the special problem of the President's right as commander in chief to issue "rules and regulations" for the government of the armed forces—a power that, to judge from the famed "Lieber's Code" (General Orders, No. 100, *Official Records, War of Rebellion*, ser. III, vol. III; April 24, 1863), is hardly less sweeping than that of Congress "to make rules for the government and regulation of the land and naval forces"—see *U.S. v. Eliason*, 16 Peters 291, 301–302 (1842); *Kurtz v. Moffitt*, 115 U.S. 485,503 (1885); *Smith v. Whitney*, 116 U.S. 167 (1886). Congress has granted the President wide power to issue regulations, and these, the Court has held, have the "force of law." See *Gratiot v. U.S.*, 4 Howard 80, 117 (1846). On the distinction between regulations issued under constitutional and under legislative authority, see *Matter of Smith*, 28 Ct. Cls. 452, 459 (1888), and cases there cited. See also 6 *O.A.G.* 10.

tive and as commander in chief, controls the execution of the far-reaching laws that accompany each war, and therefore gains new strength almost every time Congress exercises its powers, gives the legislators only temporary pause. While the pages of the *Congressional Record* fill up with cries of "dictator!" "despot!" and "one-man government!" the pages of the *United States Statutes* fill up even faster with grants of authority—to seize factories, draft men, fix prices, raise money—that make him, at least in theory, all those things and a great deal more. The scope of this transfer of power can be perceived in volume 12 or 40 or 55 of the *United States Statutes*.

Inevitably, Americans being Americans even (or especially) in time of war, the authority of Congress to grant these powers, and of the President to make use of them, has been heavily challenged in a multitude of lawsuits during and after each of our three great wars. Once again the Court has been offered several excellent opportunities to call President and Congress to task and put an effective check upon the former in his often arbitrary activities as commander in chief. And once again it must be recorded that the Court has seized few, if any. For one thing, the Court, too, likes to win wars, and especially in the twentieth century has been quick to recognize the cogency of Hughes's remark that "we have a *fighting* constitution." For another, the difficulties of the judicial process and the calculated reluctance of the executive to push doubtful suits to a final decision keep many questionable laws out of the courts while the war rages, and after it as well. Thus, for example, there were no major tests of the controversial Conscription, Habeas Corpus, and Legal Tender Acts during the Civil War. The Overman Act of 1918 and the Lend-Lease Act of 1941 were likewise never challenged in the courts, principally because it was virtually impossible to raise a justiciable issue over them. And, third, whenever presented directly with the question of the validity of a wartime statute, the Court has somehow found a technical reason to avoid a straight-out ruling or, forced willy-nilly to rule, has stretched the Constitution to cover the law. All this has meant simply another vast increase in presidential power over which the Court has been unable or unwilling to exercise any real control. A brief review of the important cases is in order.

The Civil War. The two most controversial grants of power to come in due course to the Supreme Court for judgment were the Confiscation Acts of 1861 and 1862 [45] and the Legal Tender Acts of 1862.[46] The former were given approval and wide application in about thirty cases spread over ten or twelve years, the most important of which were *Miller v. United States* and *Stewart v. Kahn* [47] The latter were brought squarely before the Court in the midst of the war in the interesting case *Roosevelt v. Meyer;* [48] but the canny justices, a majority of whom unquestionably regarded this law as beyond the financial or war powers of Congress, announced that they lacked jurisdiction, relying upon a very narrow construction of section 25 of the Judiciary Act of 1789.[49] Only Justice

[45] 12 *Stat.* 319, 589. See also 12 *Stat.* 820.

[46] 12 *Stat.* 345, 370. See also 12 *Stat.* 259, 338, 352, 532, 709.

[47] 11 Wallace 268, 304–307 (1870); 11 Wallace 493, 506–507 (1870).

[48] 1 Wallace 512 (1863).

[49] Eight years later the Court acknowledged this construction to have been in error, in *Trebilcock v. Wilson,* 12 Wallace 687, 692–694 (1871).

Nelson was prepared to meet the greenback question squarely. With the war safely past, the Court, much to its sorrow, again listened to arguments on the Legal Tender Acts, and on February 7, 1870, in *Hepburn v. Griswold* [50] held 4–3 that the recent attempt to make legal tender of paper currency had, among other faults, not been "an appropriate and plainly adapted means for carrying on war." Fifteen months and two new justices later this decision was reversed in *Knox v. Lee* [51] by a 5–4 vote, the majority opinion of Justice Strong (one of the new men) according a remarkable scope to the war powers of Congress. The less said of this unhappy incident the better for the memory of Ulysses S. Grant and a number of others, but it should be noted that the man who delivered the majority opinion in *Hepburn v. Griswold* and stuck to his guns in *Knox v. Lee*, Chief Justice Chase, had in 1862 as Secretary of the Treasury reluctantly agreed that Congress must pass this act as a much-needed spur to the war effort! His peroration on the act of 1862 is worth hearing:

It is not surprising that amid the tumult of the late civil war, and under the influence of apprehensions for the safety of the Republic almost universal, different views, never before entertained by American statesmen or jurists, were adopted by many. The time was not favorable to considerate reflection upon the constitutional limits of legislative or executive authority. If power was assumed from patriotic motives, the assumption found ready justification in patriotic hearts. . . . Not a few who then insisted upon its necessity, or acquiesced in that view, have, since the return of peace, and under the influence of the calmer time, reconsidered their conclusions,

[50] 8 Wallace 603, 617–622 (1870).
[51] 12 Wallace 457, 540–541 (1872).

and now concur in those which we have just announced. These conclusions seem to us to be fully sanctioned by the letter and spirit of the Constitution.[52]

Is it possible that we have one Constitution in peace and another in war?

World War I. The major grants of power in the first of the total wars were the Selective Service Act of 1917, Emergency Shipping Fund Act of 1917, Food and Fuel Control (Lever) Act of 1917, Trading with the Enemy Act of 1917, Railway Control Act of 1918, Executive Co-ordination (Overman) Act of 1918, Control of Communications Act of 1918, and War-Time Prohibition Act of 1918.[53] All these save the Overman Act had one or more days in the Supreme Court. The challenges to the validity of the Trading with the Enemy Act and the Railway and Communications Acts were hardly brisk, and the constitutionality of these acts was assumed virtually without argument in the important cases in which the Court construed their application.[54] The War-Time Prohibition Act was upheld strongly in *Hamilton v. Kentucky Distilleries*, less forcefully in *Ruppert v. Caffey*, two cases discussed earlier in this book.[55]

A huge but altogether justifiable grant of power was

[52] 8 Wallace 625.

[53] Respectively, 40 *Stat.* 76, 182, 276, 411, 451, 556, 904, 1046.

[54] Respectively, *Central Union Trust Co. v. Garvan*, 254 U.S. 554 (1921); *Northern Pacific Railway Co. v. North Dakota*, 250 U.S. 135, 148–150 (1919), a powerful statement of the "complete and undivided character" of the "war power of the United States" and its dominance over the rights of the states; *Dakota Central Tel. Co. v. South Dakota*, 250 U.S. 163, 183 (1919).

[55] 251 U.S. 146 (1919); 251 U.S. 264 (1920). See above, pp. 82–86.

94

approved with dispatch in *Arver v. United States*, the case in which Chief Justice White, announcing the judgment of a unanimous court that the Selective Draft Law of 1917 was a valid exercise of the war power, dispelled once and for all time the notion that there is something inherently unconstitutional, or perhaps extraconstitutional, about drafting men to fight our wars.[56] The law was attacked on about a dozen counts, stretching all the way from the First to the Thirteenth Amendment, but was deftly defended by the old soldier of the Confederacy. This was an outstanding instance of a case that the Court could not possibly have decided any other way, but in which it was important and altogether proper for the Court to speak in stentorian tones and give unanimous expression to the national will. In so doing it approved a war statute delegating unparalleled discretionary authority to the President, who in both our twentieth-century wars has raised armies pretty largely on his own terms.

The Emergency Shipping Fund Act of 1917 was an astounding wartime intrusion upon private interests, remarkable alike in the power asserted by Congress and in that granted the President. It authorized him virtually to

[56] 40 *Stat.* 76; 245 U.S. 366 (1918). See also *Cox v. Wood*, 247 U.S. 3 (1918), on the power of Congress to draft men to fight overseas; *McKinley v. U.S.*, 249 U.S. 397 (1919), on its power to protect the health and morals of the armies it raises, especially against "houses of ill fame, brothels, or bawdy houses." The Conscription Act of 1863 (12 *Stat.* 731) was never brought before the Supreme Court directly, but was apparently assumed to have been entirely constitutional in *U.S. v. Scott*, 3 Wallace 642 (1865); *Tarble's Case*, 13 Wallace 397, 408 (1872); *In re Grimley*, 137 U.S. 147, 153 (1890); and *Jacobson v. Massachusetts*, 197 U.S. 11, 29 (1905). An important state case upholding conscription in the Civil War was *Kneedler v. Lane*, 45 Penn. St. 238 (1863).

take over the shipbuilding industry in America. He could commandeer any yards or facilities, purchase ships at what he considered a reasonable price (with provision for subsequent revision by the courts in the event the seller deemed it unfair), or simply contract for the building of ships by negotiation. The Court, oddly enough, although construing the act on about a dozen occasions, never had occasion to discourse on its constitutionality until two months after the start of the second World War. Then, in *United States v. Bethlehem Steel Corporation,*[57] while upholding the latter's claims in a dispute over a contract, Justice Black thought it opportune to recall some truths about the war power:

We cannot regard the Government of the United States at war as so powerless that it must seek the organization of a private corporation as a helpless suppliant. The Constitution grants to Congress power "to raise and support Armies," "to provide and maintain a Navy," and to make all laws necessary and proper to carry these powers into execution. Under this authority Congress can draft men for battle service. Its power to draft business organizations to support the fighting men who risk their lives can be no less.

Finally, the single important case in which any part of the vast body of regulatory legislation enacted in World War I was held unconstitutional should be briefly mentioned. In *United States v. Cohen Grocery Co.*[58] the Court, dividing 6–2 on the constitutional question, invalidated

---

[57] 315 U.S. 289, 303–305 (1942).

[58] 255 U.S. 81 (1921). See also *Weeds, Inc. v. U.S.*, 255 U.S. 109 (1921); but see, too, *Highland v. Russell Car Co.*, 279 U.S. 253 (1929).

several lines of section 4 of the Lever Act,[59] which had made it "unlawful for any person wilfully . . . to make any unjust or unreasonable rate or charge in handling or dealing in or with any necessaries," as contrary to certain safeguards of the Fifth and Sixth Amendments, especially in that they failed to set up "an ascertainable standard of guilt." This was hardly a blow to presidential power. For one thing, there had never been any concerted attempt to enforce these provisions of the Lever Act, the words in question being little more than hortatory. For another, the date of this decision was February 28, 1921, and three days later Congress terminated the act and many others by joint resolution.[60] There were many brave words about the tenacity of the Fifth and Sixth Amendments in time of war, but the effects of the decision were negligible.

In a word, the Constitution was altogether equal to our first great foreign war.

World War II. In the matter of presidential use of delegated power World War II followed rather closely the pattern of the first World War. At some points—price control, rationing, rent control, plant seizures, priorities — the powers cut a little deeper into the lives and economy of the people; at other points—communications, railroads, prosecutions for treasonous or obstructive speech—the government's touch was lighter. At no point did the Court find fault with the laws themselves and only rarely with their use.

Judicial battle lines were drawn between the adminis-

[59] 40 *Stat.* 276, 277, as amended by 41 *Stat.* 297, 298, attaching penalties.

[60] 41 *Stat.* 1359.

tration and private interests over only one prominent statute. In three major and several additional minor engagements the Supreme Court doggedly defended the Emergency Price Control Act of January 30, 1942,[61] against a host of outraged businessmen and landlords. The attack upon the constitutionality of the act was launched with the aid of those time-honored weapons with which war statutes are always belabored: the principle forbidding delegation of legislative power, and the Fifth Amendment. In *Yakus v. United States* the price-fixing authority of OPA was held to be a valid exercise of the war powers; [62] in *Bowles v. Willingham* rent control was likewise found constitutional.[63] And in *Steuart and Brothers v. Bowles* [64] the highhanded practice of "indirect sanctions," through which the President aided OPA, WPB, NWLB, and the rest to enforce their orders by resorting to his powers under other statutes,[65] was looked upon, if not with equanimity, at least with tolerance. In this in-

[61] 56 *Stat.* 23.

[62] 321 U.S. 414 (1944).

[63] 321 U.S. 503 (1944). See also *Lockerty v. Phillips*, 319 U.S. 182 (1943), on the power of Congress to withdraw equity jurisdiction to restrain the enforcement of OPA regulations and orders from all other courts, state or federal, except the Emergency Court of Appeals set up in the Price Control Act. Rent control was confined to much narrower limits in World War I, yet barely escaped being declared unconstitutional in *Block v. Hirsh*, 256 U.S. 135 (1921), and *Marcus Brown Co. v. Feldman*, 256 U.S. 170 (1921). In *Chastleton Corp. v. Sinclair*, 264 U.S. 543 (1924), the Court decided that the emergency had passed, and refused to enforce a 1922 extension of the 1919 District of Columbia Rent Act.

[64] 322 U.S. 398 (1944).

[65] And to his constitutional powers and prestige as well. See J. L. O'Brian and M. Fleischmann, "The War Production Board," *George Washington Law Review*, XIII (1944), 1–60.

stance the President had delegated to OPA the power given him in the Second War Powers Act of 1942 to "allocate" materials to "promote the national defense." [66] The latter had used this power to withhold scarce fuel oil from a retail dealer found guilty of loose practice in the matter of ration coupons, thereby using the authority of one act to punish him for violating regulations issued under another. This was obviously a far easier and cleaner way to deal with people who disregarded OPA regulations than the attempt to get a conviction for misdemeanor, as authorized in the Price Control Act itself. In refusing to interfere with this summary method of penalizing the Steuart Company, the Court acquiesced in an exercise of presidential war power that would seem to have infinite and explosive possibilities. And in approving, in the Yakus case, a novel and summary technique for enforcing administrative orders, it virtually abdicated its responsibility for defending the whole pattern of due process against wartime encroachment by such agencies as OPA.

Concerning the other major statutes of World War II there is little to record. In the joint resolutions declaring war against Japan, Germany, and Italy, Congress "authorized and directed" the President "to employ the entire naval and military forces of the United States and the resources of the Government to carry on" the war,[67] and this sweeping mandate was supported with some remarkable delegations of power. Few were attacked; all were held constitutional, often without so much as a word of opinion. Typical was the Court's handling of the Selective

[66] 56 *Stat.* 176, 178, 180; 7 *Fed. Reg.* 2719.
[67] 55 *Stat.* 795–797. This formula was borrowed from the declaration of war of April 6, 1917. 40 *Stat.* 1.

Service Act of 1940.[68] Although the draft was attacked and defended on constitutional grounds in many lower-court cases, the Supreme Court refused to add a single word to White's great opinion in *Arver v. United States*. A petition for certiorari to review an important lower-court case was denied without opinion.[69]

These few examples should be proof enough that in time of war Congress can pass just about any law it wants as a "necessary and proper" accessory to the delegated war powers; that the President can make just about any use of such law he sees fit; and that the people with their overt or silent resistance, not the Court with its power of judicial review, will set the only practical limits to arrogance and abuse. And as if these examples were not enough, two other handy congressional weapons have yet to be mentioned. Neither has been employed for some years now, but certainly could be dusted off quickly in case of need; each has obvious uses in these troubled times. One, congressional authorization to the President to fight a "limited war," was upheld as long ago as 1800, in a notable case arising from the French Spoliations, *Bas v. Tingy*.[70] The

[68] 54 *Stat.* 885.

[69] *Brooks v. U.S.*, 324 U.S. 878 (1945); 147 Fed. 2d 134 (1945). See also *Weightman v. U.S.*, 142 Fed. 2d 188 (1944); *Heflin v. Sanford*, 142 Fed. 2d 798 (1944). The Act of 1940 was assumed by the Supreme Court to be constitutional in dozens of cases, for example *Bowles v. U.S.*, 319 U.S. 33 (1943); *Bartchy v. U.S.*, 319 U.S. 484 (1943); *Falbo v. U.S.*, 320 U.S. 549 (1944); *Billings v. Truesdell*, 321 U.S. 542 (1944).

[70] 4 Dallas 37 (1800), seriatim opinions by Justices Moore, Washington, Chase, and Paterson approving the acts of May 28, June 13, 25, 28, and July 9, 1798, and February 9 and March 3, 1799 (1 *Stat.* 561, 565, 572, 574, 578, 613, and 743), under all of which the naval war with France was fought. See also *Talbot v. Seeman*, 1 Cranch 1, 28 (1801). The joint resolution of April 22,

other, the so-called indemnity act, through which Congress protects executive and military officials from suits for illegal actions taken in an emergency, came into prominence during and after the Civil War. The normal method was to make any order of the President or of someone acting under his authority "a defense in all courts." The omnibus provision in section four of the Habeas Corpus Act of March 3, 1863, found judicial approval in terms that made plain the Court's conviction that Congress could ratify any action that it could have authorized in the first place.[71]

Whether Congress could protect someone who acted illegally under a presidential order when it could *not* have authorized the action itself seems doubtful, but it is a matter of record that the indemnity acts of May 11, 1866, and March 2, 1867, designed to protect officers who had executed the Lincoln-Stanton program against disloyalty (in other words, designed to discourage suits based on *Ex parte Milligan*), were assumed to be constitutional by the Court in several cases.[72] And since we are entitled to assume from past performances that the Court regards the war powers of Congress as limited only by the necessities

---

1914 (38 *Stat.* 770), declaring Wilson's use of troops at Vera Cruz justified but disclaiming any purpose to make war, was one example of this power. E. S. Corwin, *Total War and the Constitution* (New York, 1947), 29, describes the Lend-Lease Act of 1941 as "to all intents and purposes . . . a qualified declaration of war."

[71] 12 *Stat.* 755, 756. *Mitchell v. Clark,* 110 U.S. 633, 640 (1884).

[72] 14 *Stat.* 46, 432. *Bean v. Beckwith,* 18 Wallace 510 (1873); *Beard v. Burts,* 95 U.S. 434 (1877); *Beckwith v. Bean,* 98 U.S. 266 (1879). For a third example of Congress' power to intervene decisively in support of executive emergency power, see *Wilson v. New,* 243 U.S. 332 (1917).

of the case, which are for Congress to ascertain, there is apparently nothing the President cannot do *constitutionally* if war should strike the country. This puts him in a position hardly less favorable than that of the Prime Minister of Great Britain, who in time of emergency can do anything that Parliament will subsequently approve. The indemnity act may be due for a revival.

The President's Authority over Courts-Martial and Military Commissions

The President is the fountainhead of military justice. As commander in chief he could not be otherwise, and Congress, in enacting and re-enacting the complexity of regulations that govern the conduct of all persons in the armed forces, has always recognized that he was, in effect, the supreme court of military law. With the normal enforcement of the federal Uniform Code of Military Justice,[73] which consolidates and revises the Articles of War and the Articles for the Government of the Navy, he has little concern. Naturally he is required to take action only in important matters. For example, Article 71 of this Code provides that a sentence of death or one "involving a general or flag officer" must be approved by him before it can be carried into execution. Article 22 authorizes him to appoint general courts-martial, a provision that, in the light of his status as commander in chief, would appear to be merely declaratory of an existing power. In these various ways Congress has recognized and

[73] *P.L.* 506, 81st Congress, 2nd session; to take effect May 31, 1951. For a blistering attack on the underlying assumptions of this code, see A. J. Keeffe and M. Moskin, "Codified Military Injustice," *Cornell Law Quarterly*, XXXV (1949), 151–170.

confirmed the primary position of the President in the system of military justice. And it should always be remembered that his pardoning power extends to every cranny of this intricate system.

The relationship between the courts-martial and the regular federal courts is extremely tenuous. The latter have always acknowledged that the courts-martial were part of an entirely different system of law. The Court has stated that a member of the armed forces belongs to a "separate community recognized by the Constitution." [74] If there is any one rule to which the civil courts have held, it is that they have no general power to review the proceedings and sentences of courts-martial.

With the sentences of courts martial which have been convened regularly, and have proceeded legally, and by which punishments are directed, not forbidden by law, . . . civil courts have nothing to do, nor are they in any way alterable by them. If it were otherwise, the civil courts would virtually administer the rules and articles of war, irrespective of those to whom that duty and obligation has been confided by the laws of the United States, from whose decisions no appeal or jurisdiction of any kind has been given to the civil magistrates or civil courts. [75]

[74] *Carter v. McLaughry*, 183 U.S. 365, 390 (1902).

[75] *Dynes v. Hoover*, 20 Howard 65, 82 (1857). For similar statements, see *Wales v. Whitney*, 114 U.S. 564, 570 (1885); *Kurtz v. Moffitt*, 115 U.S. 487, 500 (1885); *Carter v. Roberts*, 177 U.S. 496, 498 (1900). For some indications of the continued viability of this doctrine, see *Wade v. Hunter*, 337 U.S. 684 (1949); *Humphrey v. Smith*, 337 U.S. 695 (1949); *Hiatt v. Brown*, 70 S. Ct. 495, decided March 13, 1950. For other instructive cases on the relationship of military and civil law, see *Coleman v. Tennessee*, 97 U.S. 509, 512–514 (1878); *Ex parte Mason*, 105 U.S. 696, 699–700 (1881); *Smith v. Whitney*, 116 U.S. 167, 175–186 (1886);

At the same time, even in this broad statement of nonintervention there appear certain qualifications, one might say descriptions, of those circumstances under which the civil courts would take jurisdiction of a soldier's plea for justice. The occasions for intervention have been best expressed in a noted opinion in the Court of Claims by that remarkable judge, Charles C. Nott:

The proceedings of these military tribunals cannot be reviewed in the civil courts. No writ of error will lie to bring up the rulings of a court-martial. . . . When the record of a court-martial comes into a civil court in a collateral way, the only questions which can be considered may be reduced to these three: First, was the court-martial legally constituted; second, did it have jurisdiction of the case; third, was the sentence duly approved and authorized by law.[76]

And through these narrow openings the Supreme Court has peered occasionally at the legality or jurisdiction of a court-martial. In a number of these cases some aspect of the President's position as chief dispenser of military justice has been under scrutiny, but rarely if ever has that position been challenged or impaired. Indeed, the Court, feeling somewhat shamefaced for allowing itself to be dragged by the heels into heathen territory, has excused

---

Johnson v. Sayre, 158 U.S. 109, 118 (1895); *Grafton v. U.S.,* 206 U.S. 333, 351–352 (1907); *Franklin v. U.S.,* 216 U.S. 559, 567–568 (1910); *Caldwell v. Parker,* 252 U.S. 376, 385–388 (1920); *Collins v. McDonald,* 258 U.S. 416, 418 (1922); and the important World War II case (important for draftees, at any rate) *Billings v. Truesdell,* 321 U.S. 542 (1944).

[76] *Swaim v. U.S.,* 28 Ct. Cls. 173, 217 (1893). See also *Wise v. Withers,* 3 Cranch 331, 337 (1806); *Ex parte Watkins,* 3 Peters 193, 208 (1830); *Keyes v. U.S.,* 109 U.S. 336, 340 (1883); *In re Grimley,* 137 U.S. 147, 150 (1890); *Givens v. Zerbst,* 255 U.S. 11, 19 (1921).

its presence by unnecessarily low bows in the direction of the commander in chief. The usual outcome of one of these cases has been to strengthen the President's hand. Thus, for example, in *Martin v. Mott* [77] the Court granted conclusive discretion to the President and his officers in such matters as fixing the number of officers, between the statutory limits of five and thirteen, for any particular court-martial; in *Swaim v. United States* [78] it spoke in approving terms of the inherent constitutional authority of the President to convene a general court-martial "in the absence of legislation expressly prohibitive"; and in a series of cases it cut the heart out of the only decision in which it had ever attempted to restrict the President, *Runkle v. United States.* [79] In that case the Court had interpreted the old sixty-fifth Article of War, which required presidential confirmation of a sentence cashiering an officer, to mean his personal approval, to be shown affirmatively on the record. In *United States v. Page, United States v. Fletcher,* and *Bishop v. United States* [80] it was announced, in effect, that he could turn over this duty to the Secretaries of War or Navy. In such case, their actions were presumed to be his in contemplation of law.

The refusal of the Court to interfere with the President's

[77] 12 Wheaton 19, 34–35 (1827). See also *Mullan v. U.S.*, 140 U.S. 240, 245 (1891).

[78] 165 U.S. 553, 558 (1897). See also 15 *O.A.G.* 290, 297–303.

[79] 122 U.S. 543, 556–560 (1887). In *McLaughry v. Deming,* 186 U.S. 49 (1902), the Court held illegal the trial of an "officer of volunteers" by a court-martial composed entirely of regular officers.

[80] 137 U.S. 673, 679–680 (1891); 148 U.S. 84, 88–89 (1893); 197 U.S. 334, 341–342 (1905). For another case in which the President and his subordinates were accorded considerable latitude by the Court, see *Ex parte Reed,* 100 U.S. 13, 22–23 (1879).

activities in the area of military justice was most vividly illustrated in *Swaim v. United States*,[81] something of a *cause célèbre* of the Arthur administration. This litigation was especially interesting in that the President was involved in it just about as deeply as a President could be. The facts are these: David G. Swaim was appointed Judge Advocate General of the Army on February 22, 1881, with the rank of brigadier general. Accused of fraud and improper dealings with a banking firm in Washington, he was tried by a general court-martial convened by the President in November, 1884. Found guilty of "conduct unbecoming an officer and a gentleman," he was sentenced to be suspended from "rank, duty, and pay for three years." Dissatisfied with this sentence, which he believed not "commensurate with the offenses as found by the court," President Arthur returned the record to the general court-martial. A new sentence, suspension for one year and reduction to the rank of major, was fixed, and was likewise found unsatisfactory by the President, principally because it would require a new appointment to office. This time the court-martial did its best to please the President by sentencing Swaim to twelve years' suspension on half pay. Arthur found this, too, a stupid performance, and said as much publicly, but finally approved it "for the public interest that the proceedings in this case be not without result." After brooding over his fate for several years, and having seen Chester Alan Arthur go to his grave, Swaim at length brought suit in the Court of Claims for back pay, on the grounds that the general court-martial had been unlawfully constituted and that he had been unlawfully

[81] 165 U.S. 553 (1897), on appeal from 28 Ct. Cls. 173 (1893).

tried and sentenced. Rebuffed by that court, he took an appeal to the Supreme Court.

The Court, speaking through Justice Shiras, took up his contentions one by one, punctured them neatly, and decided unanimously for the United States. It may be instructive to set out his contentions and the Court's rejoinders:

SWAIM: The President had no power to appoint a general court-martial when my commander was not the accuser. SHIRAS: His power to appoint general courts-martial cannot be hedged in by technicalities, especially when he probably has an inherent power to convene such courts.

SWAIM: The President, by his order appointing the court-martial, became himself the accuser. SHIRAS: "Wholly unfounded."

SWAIM: The court-martial was constituted in violation of the seventy-ninth Article of War, which provides that "officers shall be tried only of general courts-martial; and no officer shall, when it can be avoided, be tried by officers inferior to him in rank." A majority of the court-martial was composed of officers inferior to me in rank. SHIRAS: "The presumption must be that the President, in detailing the officers named to compose the court-martial, acted in pursuance of law." The President had his reasons, and this Court cannot search for them.

SWAIM: One of the officers on the court-martial was of known hostility to me. SHIRAS: The decision of the court-martial to seat this officer despite challenge cannot be reviewed by a civil court in a collateral action.

SWAIM: The judge advocate was not appointed by the convening officer, nor was he sworn in; evidence for the

United States was improperly received; evidence in my behalf was improperly barred. SHIRAS: Such matters are questions of procedure and cannot be attacked in a civil court.

SWAIM: The facts did not support the conviction. SHIRAS: We cannot review.

SWAIM: The action of the President in twice returning the proceedings and urging a more severe sentence was "without authority of law." SHIRAS (in effect): Since it is not specified how many times he may do this, he may apparently do it as many times as he sees fit. And finally:

As we have reached the conclusion that the court-martial in question was duly convened and organized, and that the questions decided were within its lawful scope of action, it would be out of place for us to express any opinion on the propriety of the action of that court in its proceedings and sentence. If, indeed, as has been strenuously urged, the appellant was harshly dealt with, and a sentence of undue severity was finally imposed, the remedy must be found elsewhere than in the courts of law.[82]

This summary makes clear the two important principles adhered to consistently by the Supreme Court in cases of this type: (1) if a court-martial is legally constituted, has jurisdiction of the accused [83] and the offense, and awards a sentence authorized by law, which is then duly approved, it exists in another world from the regular courts;

[82] 165 U.S. 566. In 1894 Cleveland finally gave in to Swaim's importunities, appointed him Judge Advocate General, and retired him immediately with the rank of brigadier general.

[83] For another newsworthy case in which the Supreme Court held that a court-martial lacked jurisdiction over the accused, or at least over the offense with which he had been charged, see *Hirshberg v. Cooke*, 336 U.S. 210 (1949).

(2) the exercise of discretion by the President as the fountainhead of military justice is not to be questioned in the courts of the United States.

So much for courts-martial. But there is another type of military tribunal that the President may institute, the so-called military commission, which has been characterized by a leading authority as "merely an instrumentality for the more efficient execution of the laws of war." [84] As such, the military commission is wholly the creature of the commander in chief or of one of his ranking officers in the field. Congress, too, may occasionally authorize the establishment of military commissions, as the southern states learned in the period of Reconstruction. In general, however, they are executive creations. Their jurisdiction, composition, procedure, and powers are for the President alone to determine and supervise. One use of this extraordinary type of military court was held unconstitutional in *Ex parte Milligan*. Another use is for the summary trial of civilians indicted for crimes in conquered areas. Still another is for the trial, when trial is thought at all necessary, of captured spies and enemy combatants accused of violating the laws of war.

The employment of a military commission is thus an exercise of command, hardly open to collateral attack in the civil courts of the United States, and for that matter rarely attacked. Nevertheless, there have been three outstanding uses of this type of tribunal, two of them under direct order of the President, upon which the courts have been asked to look with disfavor. The facts of these trials

[84] William Winthrop, *Abridgement of Military Law* (Washington, 1887), 330. See generally the same author's *Military Law*, II, 57–82.

and the general lesson to be drawn from them should be briefly stated.

Easily the most spectacular of all military commissions was the tribunal of nine officers authorized by President Johnson May 1, 1865, to try the assassins of Abraham Lincoln.[85] Concerning this trial and the intervention of the regular courts in its notoriously irregular proceedings there is practically nothing to say, which for our purposes is the most important fact about it. Brought to life by the President in an exercise of pure constitutional authority, the commission was based on the overwhelming conviction of an outraged people that, in the words of one of the commission's chief defenders, "The assassination of ABRAHAM LINCOLN was a military crime. While actually in command of the national forces, he was killed in a city which was his headquarters, strongly fortified and garrisoned, with a military governor. . . . Not only was the murdered commander-in-chief, to use the words of the Constitution, '*in actual service in time of war,*' but it was a time of '*public danger.*' " [86] The specification drawn up by Judge Advocate General Holt never mentioned "Abraham Lincoln, President of the United States" without adding "and Commander-in-Chief of the Army and Navy thereof."

[85] Richardson, *Messages and Papers of the Presidents*, VI, 334–335. Attorney General Speed's approval is recorded in 11 *O.A.G.* 297. For the facts and fancies of this melodrama, see Benn Pittman, compiler (and expurgator!), *The Assassination of President Lincoln* (Cincinnati, 1865); D. M. DeWitt, *The Assassination of Abraham Lincoln* (New York, 1909), and *The Judicial Murder of Mary E. Surratt* (New York, 1895); Ben: Perley Poore, *The Conspiracy Trial*, 2 vols. (Boston, 1865–1866); T. M. Harris, *The Assassination of Lincoln* (Boston, 1892).

[86] Poore, *op. cit.*, I, 3.

From start to finish this was a military trial. It was never seriously considered that it could be anything else. No civil court ever looked into the commission's authority, composition, jurisdiction, proceedings, or sentences. Under the circumstances no court could have been expected to raise its voice.

One bold attempt to gain civil justice was made in behalf of Mrs. Mary E. Surratt. At 3:00 A.M. of the day set for execution, July 7, 1865, Judge Andrew Wylie of the Supreme Court of the District of Columbia was persuaded by her counsel to issue a writ of habeas corpus to Major General W. S. Hancock, who as Commanding Officer of the Middle Military Division had custody of the doomed prisoners. At 11:30 A.M. General Hancock, accompanied by the Attorney General, surprised the skeptics by appearing before Judge Wylie. Acknowledging with respect the serving of the writ, he nonetheless declined to produce Mrs. Surratt. His authority for refusal was unimpeachable, for endorsed upon the writ were these words:

To Major General W. S. Hancock, Commander, etc.

I, ANDREW JOHNSON, President of the United States, do hereby declare that the writ of habeas corpus has been heretofore suspended in such cases as this, and I do hereby especially suspend this writ, and direct that you proceed to execute the order heretofore given upon the judgement of the Military Commission, and you will give this order in return to this writ.

Signed, ANDREW JOHNSON, President

With regret but discretion Judge Wylie gave way: "The jurisdiction of this court yields to the suspension of the writ of habeas corpus from the President of the

111

United States." Two hours later Mrs. Surratt was dead.[87]

After the decision in *Ex parte Milligan* the unfortunate Dr. Samuel Mudd, from his cell at the Dry Tortugas, applied for a writ of habeas corpus to Wayne and Chase. Mudd and the three other surviving culprits had been purposely sent to that faraway prison because Stanton, so Gideon Welles reported in his priceless diary, thought it "best to get them into a part of the country where old Nelson or any other judge would not try to make difficulty by *habeas corpus*." [88] The Chief Justice denied the writ on the ground that he had no power to issue it outside his own circuit.[89] The pardoning of the three surviving accomplices in 1869 put an end to any possibility that the legality of this military commission would ever be tested in the courts. Whether it was legal or not is now of little significance. What is significant is that in April, 1865, the military commission seemed to almost all men the natural way to deal with Booth's gang, and that when a lone judge dared to intervene, public opinion approved overwhelmingly the personal suspension of the writ of habeas corpus by the President of the United States. The Supreme Court, incidentally, was not in session, but several justices were present in Washington. Also incidentally, the two other presidential assassins, Czogolz and Guiteau, got their due from civil courts.

Three wars and seventy-seven years later, July 2, 1942, Franklin D. Roosevelt issued a proclamation appointing a military commission of seven members to try the well-

[87] See the lurid account of this last day in the *New York Times*, July 8, 1865, 1.

[88] *Diary of Gideon Welles* (Boston, 1911), II, 334.

[89] Warren, *The Supreme Court*, II, 443–444.

remembered "Nazi Saboteurs" for offenses against "the law of war and the Articles of War," and fixing various procedures to be followed by the commission. In a simultaneous proclamation he declared that enemy adherents apprehended in the act of entering the United States "to commit sabotage, espionage, hostile or warlike acts" were to be tried by military courts and denied access to the civil courts.[90] In all this he acted "by virtue of the authority vested in me as President and as Commander in Chief of the Army and Navy, under the Constitution and statutes of the United States, and more particularly the Thirty-Eighth Article of War." This article gave the President a general power to prescribe procedures for military courts.[91]

The saboteurs had landed from a submarine in two groups, one on Long Island June 13, the other in Florida June 17, but had apparently got nowhere with their plans to blow up assorted factories and bridges when picked up in Chicago and New York within two weeks by the FBI. Their trial began in Washington July 8. On July 28, with the case closed except for arguments of counsel, the saboteurs petitioned the District Court for the District of Columbia for a writ of habeas corpus, asserting their right to be tried in a civil court. The writ was refused, but the electrifying announcement had already been made that the Supreme Court would meet in special session July 29 to hear their petitions for writs of habeas corpus. Whether the Court was willing to hear their petition as an exercise

[90] 7 *Fed. Reg.* 5103, 5101. See generally Cyrus Bernstein, "The Saboteur Trial," *George Washington Law Review*, XI (1943); 131–190; Corwin, *Total War and the Constitution*, 117–121.

[91] *United States Code*, Title 10, sec. 1059.

113

of original jurisdiction is a matter of speculation, for by the time (July 31) the Court handed down its judgment, an appeal had been perfected through the Circuit Court of Appeals for the District, and the case had gone thence to the Supreme Court on certiorari.

The Court's unanimous decision in *Ex parte Quirin*, delivered *per curiam*, was that the military commission had been lawfully constituted and that the saboteurs were clearly subject to its jurisdiction. The motions for leave to file petitions for writs of habeas corpus were therefore denied, the orders of the district court affirmed. The military trial resumed, the prisoners were found guilty, and on August 8 the President announced that six of the saboteurs had been electrocuted and two sentenced to long prison terms.

Not until three months later, when the Court met for its regular October term, was its reasoning made public. In an elaborate twenty-two-page opinion Chief Justice Stone took up one by one the principal contentions of counsel for the saboteurs and disposed of them with the aid of history and military law. The complexities of this opinion need not detain us.[92] It will be sufficient to our purposes to mention these few of the many points made by the Chief Justice: (1) the President's proclamation did not "preclude access to the courts for determining its applicability" to this particular case; (2) it was not necessary for the Court to discuss the President's power as commander in chief to create this commission, for Congress, in the fifteenth Article of War, had in effect "au-

[92] 317 U.S. 1 (1942). The Chief Justice's arguments are neatly summarized in R. E. Cushman, "The Case of the Nazi Saboteurs," *American Political Science Review*, XXXVI (1942), 1082–1091.

thorized trial of offenses against the law of war before such commissions"; (3) the offenses charged against the saboteurs were offenses against the law of war, which has always recognized that unlawful combatants are subject "to trial and punishment by military tribunals for acts which render their belligerency unlawful"; (4) the procedural guarantees of Amendments V and VI were never intended to apply to military trials (again the emphasis is on two separate and distinct systems of law); (5) *Ex parte Milligan* did not apply to this situation, and indeed must be confined closely to the facts under which it arose; and (6) the President could validly fix the procedures to be followed by the commission.

There have been two general estimates of the value of *Ex parte Quirin*. One opinion holds that the willingness of the Court to assemble and inspect the legality of a presidentially sponsored military trial was in itself a fact of no little moment for constitutional law and civil liberty. The prisoners did, after all, get through to the highest court in the land to have their questions answered, and the Court "stopped the military authorities and required them, as it were, to show their credentials. When this had been done to the Court's satisfaction, they were allowed to proceed." [93] The other opinion regards the Court's participation "as little more than a ceremonious detour to a predetermined goal intended chiefly for edification." [94]

The truth lies somewhere between these two extremes. Even as a solemn pageant masking the naked power of the President to have these surreptitious invaders shot on the

[93] Cushman, *loc. cit.*, 1091.
[94] Corwin, *op. cit.*, 118.

115

spot, the convocation of the Court had its good points, especially as a warning to future Presidents and military commissions to proceed in such matters in a careful way. And yet the whole affair was a shadow play without blood or substance. There was something a little pathetic about the Court's eagerness to hear the pleas of the saboteurs, and something a little odious about the comparison of the ready hearing accorded these scoundrels with the glue-footed course of justice for the Japanese-Americans and citizens of Hawaii. The brave arguments of Colonels Cassius M. Dowell and Kenneth Royall, who wrung the last drop of support out of the suffering corpse of Lambdin P. Milligan, were likewise hollow with unreality. When the Attorney General remarked, "The President's power over enemies who enter this country in time of war, as armed invaders intending to commit hostile acts, must be absolute," he had said all that was really necessary to say. And yet when asked by the Chief Justice, "Does the Attorney General challenge the jurisdiction of the Court?" Mr. Biddle replied, "I do not." In that simple exchange was summed up the total value of *Ex parte Quirin*.

From this trial to that of General Tomoyuki Yamashita was but a step, although from the point of view of judicial oversight of executive-military authority it was a step to the rear. In this instance the Court examined the authority of a military commission established in 1945 by order of General W. D. Styer, Commanding General, United States Army Forces in the Western Pacific, to try General Yamashita for offenses against the law of war, especially his failure to restrain his troops from committing atrocities against Americans and Filipinos.[95] Once again the Court asserted its right to scrutinize the authority and proceedings of a military commission, and once again found them either satisfactory or unreviewable. It was upon this latter element of the majority opinion—the unreviewability of the manifestly irregular methods employed in Yamashita's trial—that Justice Rutledge seized in an elaborate dissent, and in these terms pointed directly to the logical conclusion of the majority holding:

> The difference between the Court's view of this proceeding and my own comes down in the end to the view, on the one hand, that there is no law restrictive upon these proceedings other than whatever rules and regulations may be prescribed for their government by the executive authority or the military and, on the other hand, that the provisions of the Articles of War, of the Geneva Convention and the Fifth Amendment apply.[96]

It was his belief, and Justice Murphy's as well, that the military commission had disregarded flagrantly the accepted standards of procedural due process—for example, in accepting depositions and hearsay evidence—and should have been called to task by the Supreme Court. The majority regarded the procedure and rules of evidence of a military commission as reviewable only by higher military authorities.

There would be little profit and much confusion in

[95] *In re Yamashita,* 327 U.S. 1 (1946). See generally Charles Fairman, "The Supreme Court on Military Jurisdiction," *Harvard Law Review,* LIX (1946), 866–881, and the bristling attack by A. F. Reel, *The Case of General Yamashita* (Chicago, 1949).
[96] 327 U.S. 81.

examining the many constitutional, moral, and international-legal questions raised for consideration in the Yamashita case, and in the dozens of other petitions for writs of habeas corpus on behalf of captured generals, politicians, and even privates that flooded the Court between 1946 and 1950.[97] Their lesson for this study may be very simply phrased: The Supreme Court of the United States cannot be expected, indeed has no right, to set itself up as a sort of supermilitary commission to oversee the worldwide activities of the punitive tribunals that the President has authorized, often in conjunction with our allies, to

[97] See the excellent article of Charles Fairman, "Some New Problems of the Constitution Following the Flag," *Stanford Law Review*, I (1949), 587–645. The most important of these quests for relief were: (1) *Homma v. Patterson*, 327 U.S. 759 (1946); motion for leave to file petition for writ of habeas corpus denied *per curiam* on authority of *In re Yamashita*, with vigorous dissents by Justices Murphy and Rutledge. (2) *Milch v. U.S.*, 332 U.S. 789 (1947); similarly disposed of, although four of the justices wanted an argument on the jurisdiction of the Court. (3) *Hirota v. MacArthur*, 335 U.S. 876 (1948), 338 U.S. 197 (1948); with the addition of Justice Jackson, back from Nuremberg, to the four inquisitive judges of *Milch v. U.S.*, the Court heard arguments as to its jurisdiction, but declared itself as "satisfied" (with Murphy dissenting, Rutledge reserving decision, and Douglas concurring separately) that the international tribunal set up by General MacArthur to try the Japanese war criminals was "not a tribunal of the United States." For other citations, see Fairman, *loc. cit.*, 589n., 591n., 594n., 600–603nn.; for an important (and consistent) further case, see *Johnson v. Eisentrager*, 70 S. Ct. 936, decided June 5, 1950. Though I cannot agree with, I can admire deeply, the dissenting stand of Justices Black, Douglas, and Burton. Even more admirable was the opinion of Circuit Judge E. Barrett Prettyman, 174 Fed. 2nd 961. That this whole issue has not been decided with finality is made plain in P. B. Perlman, "*Habeas Corpus* and Extraterritoriality," *American Bar Association Journal*, XXXVI (1950), 187–190, 249–252.

pursue the laws of war to their harsh but imperative conclusions. If we did commit a moral and practical blunder
at Nuremberg and Tokyo and Manila, the man to correct
it, if correction were even possible, is the man whom
history will hold accountable, the President of the United
States. What he and his commanders have done in the
occupied countries they have done *politically*, in the
purest sense of the word, and the trials of these alleged
war criminals were part of that pattern. The brave and
angry and altogether understandable protests of Justices
Murphy and Rutledge notwithstanding, the Court was
right in recognizing its constitutional and practical incapacity to bring justice to Yamashita, Milch, Homma,
Hirota, and the rest. We can sympathize strongly with
Rutledge's anxiety that trials of this sort meet the high
standards of the Anglo-American legal tradition, but that,
too, is for the President or Congress to decide; even an
expression of national shame by the Court lies beyond the
end zone of the judicial function. The trials of the war
criminals are one type of "judicial" proceeding in which
the standards are set and maintained by the President,
not the Court. His sins the justices may lament, but not in
public. This would seem to be the general rule for the
Supreme Court's review and control of these extraordinary military commissions.

One final fact, just a little too curious to be relegated
to a footnote: In one of these cases Colonel Willis M.
Everett, Jr., chief defense counsel in the military trial
at Dachau of the Germans charged with perpetrating the
massacre at Malmedy, sought to file a petition in the
Supreme Court for a writ of habeas corpus for Bersin, one
of his clients. There was nothing unusual about this move,

but in making it he named the President (as Commander-in-Chief of the Armed Forces of the United States), the Secretaries of Defense and Army, the Chief of Staff, and the Attorney General as respondents! The case, as it will be cited in the years to come, bears a President's name for the first and only time since *Mississippi v. Johnson*. It might have been *In re Bersin;* it turned out to be *Everett v. Truman!* [98]

The President's Authority over Conquered Territory

The task of governing our defeated enemies was front-page news for more than five years. The toils and trials of Clay and McCloy in Germany, MacArthur in Japan, and Clark in Austria captured the continuous attention of the American people. Did they capture the Court's as well? Not as a court, certainly, for our military and civil governors, acting directly as agents of the commander in chief, were spared the necessity of justifying their activities to the Supreme Court of the United States.[99]

It was not always thus. There were times—after the Mexican War, Civil War, and Spanish-American War—

[98] 334 U.S. 824 (1948).

[99] For an informative survey of some of the problems of military government in World War II, see Charles Fairman, "Some Observations on Military Occupation," *Minnesota Law Review,* XXXII (1948), 319–348. See also C. J. Friedrich *et al., American Experiences in Military Government in World War II* (New York, 1948); Harold Zink, *American Military Government in Germany* (New York, 1947); Friedrich and Connor, eds., *Military Government* (Philadelphia, 1950).

when the Supreme Court was fairly flooded with litigation that demanded close examination of the President's powers of military government over conquered enemy territory.[100] Those were the days when American traders, and other nationals as well, could get loose in Vera Cruz or New Orleans or San Juan about one day after (if not before) the fighting had ceased, and could get involved in the most complicated squabbles with the military authorities. A disproportionate number of these came in time to the Supreme Court, which in settling them said just about everything that can be said about this interesting aspect of presidential power. No branch of his martial authority has been quite so fully explored and precisely defined. Although the chief reason for the absence of judicial oversight of our occupying activities is the absence of private interests in a position to push their suits, the fullness with which the Court has already expounded the President's powers of military government, and has given them the widest possible scope, would be enough to discourage the most gravely injured litigant. Another reason, of course, is the Court's constitutional and practical inability to oversee the joint activities of allied military government, a fact made clear in *Hirota v. MacArthur*. The condominium has no place in our constitutional law.

An unlimited number of pages might easily be devoted to the dozens of cases on this subject, especially since many of them provided the judicial climax to some rather colorful clashes between civilians at their most clever and soldiers at their most stupid. Yet all point in the same di-

[100] After the War of 1812 there were a few cases dealing with this problem in reverse. See for example *U.S. v. Rice*, 4 Wheaton 246 (1819).

rection, toward presidential autonomy, and thus may be disposed of in short order.

The central doctrine of military government, adhered to by the Court rigidly and almost with a sigh of relief, is that the President governs all conquered territory in his capacity as commander in chief, and that his determinations when an area is ready for military government,[101] what shape such government is to assume,[102] how far it is to dispossess or make use of existing law and institutions,[103] and when it is to cease [104] are conclusive and not to be questioned in any court of the United States. His powers are absolute, limited neither by the Constitution and laws of the United States nor by those of the conquered area, but only by the "laws of war." [105] Although in one of the *Insular Cases* the Court remarked of the President's military commander that "while his power is necessarily despotic, this must be understood rather in an administrative than a legislative sense," and that "his power to legislate would not be without certain restrictions—in other words, they would not extend beyond the necessities of the case" [106]—it is clear that the President

[101] *U.S. v. Pico*, 23 Howard 321 (1859); *U.S. v. Yorba*, 1 Wallace 412, 423 (1863); *Hornsby v. U.S.*, 10 Wallace 224, 239 (1869).

[102] *New Orleans v. Steamship Co.*, 20 Wallace 387, 393–394 (1874); *Dow v. Johnson*, 100 U.S. 158, 170 (1879). See also *Cross v. Harrison*, 16 Howard 164, 190 (1853); *Texas v. White*, 7 Wallace 700, 729–730 (1869).

[103] *Leitensdorfer v. Webb*, 20 Howard 176, 177–178 (1857); *Coleman v. Tennessee*, 97 U.S. 509, 517 (1878).

[104] *Neely v. Henkel*, 180 U.S. 109, 124 (1901).

[105] *Dooley v. U.S.*, 182 U.S. 22, 230–231 (1901).

[106] 182 U.S. 234. See also *Raymond v. Thomas*, 91 U.S. 712, 716 (1875), and *Lincoln v. U.S.*, 197 U.S. 419, 428 (1905), for examples of purely technical limits that the Court has occasionally

alone may judge of these necessities. It is also for him to decide how justice is to be administered—by what manner of court and under what law.[107] And certainly his orders have the force of law, superior law.[108]

Military government may be as arbitrary and absolute as the President and his commanders care to make it. He may authorize the requisitioning of private property and "exaction" of contributions from the local population, or order it, as Polk did in the Mexican War.[109] Or, if he should want to support the occupation in a more normal fashion, he may impose the necessary taxes and customs duties.[110] In any case, he governs the area in every aspect without interference from any source. His will is law, and the Court has no power to hold it in check. Several hundred cases all say the same thing, that to all intents and purposes military government under the commander in chief is "an absolutism of the most complete sort." [111]

---

set upon the actions of occupying military commanders, although hardly upon those of the President.

[107] *The Grapeshot*, 9 Wallace 129, 132–133 (1869); *Burke v. Miltenberger*, 19 Wallace 519 (1873). A technical limit is set in *Jecker v. Montgomery*, 13 Howard 498, 515 (1851).

[108] *Cross v. Harrison*, 16 Howard 164, 190 (1853).

[109] *Diary of James K. Polk* (Chicago, 1910), III, 156–157; Winthrop, *Abridgement of Military Law*, 324–325. See *Herrera v. U.S.*, 222 U.S. 558, 571–572 (1912).

[110] *Mechanics Bank v. Union Bank*, 22 Wallace 276, 295–297 (1874); *Dooley v. U.S.*, 182 U.S. 222, 231–232 (1901); *MacLeod v. U.S.*, 229 U.S. 416, 425 (1913).

[111] A. H. Carpenter, "Military Government of Southern Territory," *American Historical Association Reports*, I (1900), 496. Other important sources on military government are D. Y. Thomas, *A History of Military Government* (New York, 1904); W. E. Birkhimer, *Military Government and Martial Law* (3d ed.; Kansas City, 1914); Elihu Root, *The Military and Colonial Policy of the United States* (Cambridge, 1916).

This type of government normally extends until the withdrawal of our troops under the terms of a peace treaty or other agreement with the occupied power. If the United States is to acquire the territory permanently, the President's exclusive power of military government is considered to cease at the time of *de jure* transfer of sovereignty. The Court has several times had occasion to agree that "it is a well-recognized principle in the United States that, when a territory is annexed by the United States or comes in any manner under its jurisdiction, Congress has an absolute right, from the moment of any acquisition, to determine the political rights and governmental organization of that territory." [112] Generally, of course, Congress is not prepared to extend civil government immediately to such an area. The Court has indicated clearly the proper substitute:

The civil government of the United States cannot extend immediately and of its own force over conquered and ceded territory. Theoretically, Congress might prepare and enact a scheme of civil government to take effect immediately upon the cession, but, practically, there always have been delays and always will be. Time is required for a study of the situation and for the maturing and enacting of an adequate scheme of civil government. In the meantime, pending the action of Congress, there is no civil power under our system of government, not even that of the President as civil executive, which can take the place of the government which has ceased to exist. . . . Is it possible that, under such circumstances, there must be an interregnum? We think clearly not. The au-

[112] Berdahl, *War Powers of the Executive*, 252; *Cross v. Harrison*, 16 Howard 164, 193–195 (1853); *Downes v. Bidwell*, 182 U.S. 244, 345 (1901). See Lawson Reno, "The Power of the President to Acquire and Govern Territory," *George Washington Law Review*, IX (1941), 251–285.

thority to govern such . . . territory is found in the laws applicable to conquest and session. That authority is the military power, under the control of the President as Commander-in-Chief.[113]

Although this interesting fission of the President into two halves, one civil and the other military, is not exactly sound constitutional theory, the Court's words do give an accurate picture of his power in this field. Whether as commander in chief or as beneficiary of specific congressional authorization, he governs our permanently conquered territories for an indefinite number of years. In any event, these are matters for political, not judicial, determination. The President's powers of military government comprise a field in which the Court has done a great deal of interpreting and exercised no control, indeed has been a sort of judicial handmaiden to perfect absolutism.[114]

[113] *Santiago v. Nogueras*, 214 U.S. 260, 265 (1909).

[114] Another problem that used to agitate the Court occasionally and is now, with the arrival of total war, of purely antiquarian interest is the power of the President in the field against the enemy, especially in connection with the confiscation of enemy and requisition of friendly property. Among the cases of this type, almost all of them litigations in which the Court held for the government and against the assaults of injured private interests, are *Brown v. U.S.*, 8 Cranch 110, 122–129 (1814); *Mitchell v. Harmony*, 13 Howard 115, 132–135 (1855); *Mrs. Alexander's Cotton*, 2 Wallace 404, 418–421 (1864); *U.S. v. Padelford*, 9 Wallace 531, 540–541 (1869); *Miller v. U.S.*, 11 Wallace 268, 304–307 (1870); *U.S. v. Russell*, 13 Wallace 623 (1871); *Young v. U.S.*, 97 U.S. 39, 58–61 (1877); *U.S. v. Pacific Railroad*, 120 U.S. 227, 239 (1887); *Hijo v. U.S.*, 194 U.S. 315, 322 (1904); *Juragua Iron Co. v. U.S.*, 212 U.S. 297, 305–310 (1909), and the many cases there cited. In *Totten v. U.S.*, 92 U.S. 105 (1876), the Court upheld the power of the President to employ secret agents behind enemy lines and to make his secret promise of payment a contract binding on the government.

Conclusion

THIS discussion of the war powers of the President has already spawned so many generalizations and conclusions that there is not much left to pronounce by way of summation. Nevertheless, it might be helpful to pull together the main strands of fact and law that have appeared repeatedly in the decisions in this field. The total performance of the Court in and after our three great wars leads to these observations concerning judicial review and control of the President's actions as commander in chief:

First, the wealth of cases is somewhat misleading. Actually, the Court has been asked to examine only a tiny fraction of his significant deeds and decisions as commander in chief, for most of these were by nature challengeable in no court but that of impeachment—which was entirely as it should have been. The contours of the presidential war powers have therefore been presidentially, not judicially, shaped; their exercise is for Congress and the people, not the Court, to oversee.

Second, even when presidential or military actions work questionable inroads upon private rights and raise clearly justiciable controversies, it is extremely difficult for injured persons to obtain definitive judicial scrutiny of them, at least in time to do anyone much good. It is interesting to speculate as to which agency—the United States Army, the Department of Justice, or the Supreme Court—is most reluctant to see a highly charged presidential-military action forced through to a final decision at the law. The Army and the government lawyers apparently have no scruples about staving off an unpredictable judicial pronouncement, for we know that they will release interned prisoners and hand back seized factories the day before attorneys for these injured interests are to begin arguments in Washington. The Court in its turn will gladly agree that the case is moot, or it will seize with relief upon a technicality preventing it from taking jurisdiction, or, if forced to speak, it will decide the issue on the narrowest possible grounds. The picture is not pretty, especially when the subjects are decent and patriotic judges, soldiers, and lawyers. The explanation, of course, is that a challenge to an evacuation order or a plant seizure or a suspension of habeas corpus or an emancipation proclamation raises a question so politically explosive that the very notion of "government by lawsuit" becomes unthinkable. Whatever we allow this process to settle in peace, we cannot submit to its vagaries in time of war. The judges appear to realize this truth; perhaps in time more of them will come right out and state it.

Third, whatever limits the Court has set upon the employment of the war powers have been largely theoretical, rarely practical. Even admitting that *Ex parte Milligan, United States v. Cohen Grocery Co.,* and *Duncan v. Kahanamoku* have their uses as warnings to the political branches to fight our wars constitutionally, the warning is merely moral.[1] Future Presidents are likely to pay about

[1] The attempt to read morality into this part of the Constitution reached its zenith in Taney's opinion in *Fleming v. Page,* 9 Howard

127

as much attention to these decisions as did Lincoln, Wilson, and Roosevelt; the first and third were long dead, Wilson but three days from the end of his term, when the great limiting decision of each one's particular war was announced by a stern-visaged Court. Justice Burton, dissenting in the Duncan case, clearly overrated the significance of these decisions when he warned,

It is important . . . that in reviewing the constitutionality of the conduct of our agencies of government in time of war, invasion or threatened invasion, we do not now make precedents which in other emergencies may handicap the executive branch of the Government in the performance of duties allotted to it by the Constitution and by the exercise of which it successfully defended the nation against the greatest attack ever made upon it.[2]

Fourth, enough evidence is in from our three great conflicts with which to construct a definite, henceforth predictable pattern of wartime judicial review. *Bello flagrante* we may expect such performances—both good and bad, but all pointing to *power*—as the *Prize Cases, Roosevelt v. Meyer, Ex parte Vallandigham, Arver v. United States, Yakus v. United States,* and *Korematsu v. United States. Post bellum* we will hear about *limitations—Ex parte*

603, 614 (1850), in which he wrote that "the genius and character of our institutions are peaceful, and the power to declare war was not conferred upon Congress for the purposes of aggression and aggrandizement, but to enable the general government to vindicate by arms, if it should become necessary, its own rights and the rights of its citizens.

"A war, therefore, declared by Congress, can never be presumed to be waged for the purpose of conquest or the acquisition of territory." The context of these comments was the Mexican War.

[2] 327 U.S. 357.

Milligan, Hepburn v. Griswold, United States v. Cohen Grocery Co., and *Duncan v. Kahanamoku.* We may even expect occasionally to hear the existence of this pattern frankly confessed, as it was by Davis in the Milligan case and by Chase in *Hepburn v. Griswold.*[3] There do indeed seem to be two Constitutions—one for peace, the other for war.

Fifth, the Court has had little success in preventing the precedents of war from becoming precedents of peace. We might even go so far as to say that the Court has made a positive contribution to the permanent peacetime weakening of the separation of powers, the principle of non-delegation, the Fifth Amendment, and the necessary and proper clause as applicable limits to governmental power. Certainly its decisions in *Hamilton v. Kentucky Distilleries* and *Woods v. Miller Co.,* in which it confessed its incapacity to call a halt to the postwar exercise of the war powers, have helped project the loose principles of the Constitution-at-war into present interpretations of the Constitution-at-peace. Even more certainly, the doctrine of *Ex parte Milligan* and *United States v. Cohen Grocery Co.* has actually backfired on the Court. By insisting that the two Constitutions were really only one, the Court has contributed heavily to that emphasis on the Constitution

---

[3] See above, pp. 37–38, 93–94. Instructive, too, are Jackson's concurring thoughts in *Woods v. Miller Co.,* 333 U.S. 138, 146 (1948): "No one will question that [the war] power is the most dangerous one to free government in the whole catalogue of powers. It usually is invoked in haste and excitement when calm legislative consideration of constitutional limitation is difficult. It is executed in a time of patriotic fervor that makes moderation unpopular. And, worst of all, it is interpreted by judges under the influence of the same passions and pressures."

129

as grant of power that dominates present [1950] constitutional law. No man ever expressed this truth more clearly than that great limitationist, Justice Field, in his mordant dissent from *Juilliard v. Greenman*,[4] in which the peacetime issuance of notes as legal tender was held constitutional: "What was in 1862 called the 'medicine of the Constitution' has now become its daily bread. So it always happens that whenever a wrong principle of conduct, political or personal, is adopted on a plea of necessity, it will be afterwards followed on a plea of convenience." It is the Court itself that has had the most trouble distinguishing medicine from bread.

Sixth, the Court appears at last to have realized this situation, and is now launched upon a long-range trend away from the fatuous indignation of *Ex parte Milligan* and toward the tough-mindedness displayed by Justices Jackson, Burton, and Frankfurter in their several opinions in *Korematsu v. United States* and *Duncan v. Kahanamoku*. Increasingly the justices are speaking and interpreting in terms of "the *fighting* Constitution," and this trend, if not carried too far, could be a welcome departure. If the Court would be a little more clear-voiced about the general power of this nation to make war, it could then turn around and deliver a great deal more relief in specific instances of individual injustice, which was all it was supposed to do in the first place. In short, the less it pretends, the more it can defend.

Seventh, the criterion of this fighting Constitution is and will be the "reasonable decision," as arrived at by that irrepressible fellow, the "reasonable man." The "allowable limits of military discretion" that the Court will tolerate

4 110 U.S. 421, 458 (1884).

are those that a reasonable man would have determined in the circumstances with which the defendant official was actually faced. This, of course, is a formula of practically no value for judicial review of executive-military action. It is the soldier charged with military success, on the spot and at the time, not the judge charged with dispensing justice, in the court two years later, who must determine "reasonably" the extent of the war power in any particular situation. And the ultimate identity of the "reasonable man" is, as everyone knows, the President of the United States, whom no court of law is likely to brand unreasonable.

Finally, the implications of this study for constitutional law in the atomic age should be crystal clear. As in the past, so in the future, President and Congress will fight our wars with little or no thought about a reckoning with the Supreme Court. Such major constitutional issues as the hotly contested question of the President's authority to station troops in Europe will be resolved politically, not judicially. Most important, the defense of the Constitution rests at bottom exactly where the defense of the nation rests: in the good sense and good will of the political branches of the national government, which for most martial purposes must mean the President and his military commanders. This is a sad moral to proclaim after so long a journey, but it is one that we should have firmly fixed in our constitutional understanding. In the clear, cold words of Justice Jackson:

Of course the existence of a military power resting on force, so vagrant, so centralized, so necessarily heedless of the individual, is an inherent threat to liberty. But I would not lead people to rely on this Court for a review that seems to me

131

wholly delusive. . . . If the people ever let command of the war power fall into irresponsible and unscrupulous hands, the courts wield no power equal to its restraint. The chief restraint upon those who command the physical forces of the country, in the future as in the past, must be their responsibility to the political judgments of their contemporaries and to the moral judgments of history.[5]

[5] *Korematsu v. U.S.*, 323 U.S. 214, 248 (1944).

132

The Constitution and the

Commander in Chief after 1950

THE transitional period between World War II and the Cold War lasted only a fleeting moment. Similarly, the tradition of presidential supremacy in times of crisis, so effectively described here by Clinton Rossiter, was held in abeyance only briefly before the reality of new international tension made itself felt. Postwar America was to witness increasingly confident executive demands for discretion and independence, secrecy and privilege, as foreign commitments mounted and as national security turned inward. Well into the 1960's there was a heavy burden on those who would question the accumulating authority of the presidency, although, as noted earlier, momentary restiveness in Congress about the treaty power and executive agreements in the mid-1950's and the Supreme Court's invoking of the separation of powers and the Bill of Rights in the *Steel Seizure Case* and *Reid v. Covert* were, with the benefit of hindsight, harbingers of things that might come. It was inevitable, as long as the constitutional structure retained any vitality, that as executive power burgeoned and as Vietnam shaded into Watergate, pressure would increase within Congress for a re-examination of its role and whether it would claim its share of power or abdicate its responsibility. And in a society in which judicial activism was becoming a widely accepted norm it was inevitable that there would be strong expectations that presidential power would be weighed in the judicial forum. When challenges to executive authority did arise, however, they were confronted by a formidable theory of presidential prerogative, particularly but not alone in the proclaimed right of the president to independently commit troops abroad.

Presidential Power and Commitments Abroad

The Dispatch of Troops. When President Truman ordered American troops into Korea in June, 1950, a new era in the use of presidential power began. The constitutional rationale for the President's action was spelled out by the Department of State soon after issuance of the order to intervene. While secondary reliance was placed on the United Nation's Charter and the Security Council's resolution requesting support for those resisting North Korean aggression, primary reliance was on plenary presidential power and its exercise independent of other agencies, including Congress. Observing that there was "a traditional power of the President to use the armed forces of the United States without consulting Congress," the State Department emphasized:

The President, as Commander in Chief of the Armed Forces of the United States, has full control over the use thereof. He also has authority to conduct the foreign relations of the United States. Since the beginning of United States history, he has, on numerous occasions, ultilized these powers in sending armed forces abroad.[1]

The entry into Korea was an unalloyed act of independent power. A few months later Secretary of State Dean Acheson brought it full circle. In testimony before the Senate Committees on Foreign Relations and Armed Services, which were then meeting jointly to explore President Truman's determination to send four additional divisions to Europe in support of the NATO alliance, Acheson commented:

Not only has the President the authority to use the Armed Forces in carrying out the broad foreign policy of the United States and implementing treaties, but it is equally clear that this authority may not be interfered with by the Congress in the exercise of powers which it has under the Constitution.[2]

The President's prerogative was complete.

It is generally agreed [3] that there were two constitutional legacies of the Korean war. On the one hand there was the exercise of greater caution in the use of troops by the Eisenhower administration; on the other there was the legacy which said that President Truman had established a clear precedent for later presidential initiatives.

[1] Members of Congress were consulted informally and after the fact. The Department of State's rationale appears in "Authority of the President to Repel the Attack in Korea," *Department of State Bulletin*, XXIII (1950), 173–174.

[2] *National Commitments Report*, 17.

[3] "Congress, the President and the Power to Commit Forces to Combat," *Harvard Law Review*, LXXXI (1968), 1771–1805, 1792–1793; and Charles A. Lofgren, "Mr. Truman's War: A Debate and Its Aftermath," *Review of Politics*, XXXI (1969), 231 ff.

For example, some thirty years later Assistant Attorney General William H. Rehnquist referred to Korea as justification for the incursion by American troops into Cambodia under the Nixon administration, remarking upon "the value of the incident as a precedent for Executive action in committing United States armed forces to extensive hostilities without a formal declaration of war by Congress." [4] But immediately after the Korean war there was considerably more uncertainty. The uncertainty is evidenced most clearly in the Formosa and Middle East resolutions. In the first instance President Eisenhower sought and received from Congress "authority" to use American forces to protect Formosa and the Pescadores against the Communist Chinese; but at the same time he stated that "authority for some of the actions which might be required would be inherent in the authority of the Commander in Chief." [5] The 1957 Middle East resolution omitted any reference to "authority" originating in Congress, thus implicitly assuring the President that authority rested in his hands. Similarly, the Cuban resolution, which Congress passed one month before the Cuban missile crisis, avoided any suggestion that congressional authorization was required for subsequent presidential action. President Kennedy reminded

[4] "The President's Constitutional Authority to Order the Attack on the Cambodian Sanctuaries," in *Hearings Before the Subcommittee on National Security Policy and Scientific Developments of the Committee on Foreign Affairs, House of Representatives*, 91st Cong., 2nd Sess. (1970), 542 (hereinafter cited as *Hearings, House Subcommittee on National Security Policy*).

[5] *National Commitments Report*, 17; and 104 *Cong. Rec.* 13903–13904 (July 15, 1958). See the valuable discussion in Arthur M. Schlesinger, Jr., *The Imperial Presidency* (Boston, 1973), 159–163.

his advisors that the source of his authority did not originate with Congress. In the words of Theodore Sorensen,

He was acting by Executive Order, Presidential proclamation and inherent powers, not under any resolution or act of the Congress. He had earlier rejected all suggestions of reconvening Congress or requesting a formal declaration of war, and he had summoned the congressional leaders only when hard evidence and a fixed policy were ready.[6]

Consequently, when the United States became deeply involved in Vietnam in the mid-1960's there was no firm grounding, in either post-World War II precedent or practice, for the proposition that Congress needed to "authorize" the use of troops abroad if their use was to be constitutional. On the contrary, the presidential position was that while any formal support that Congress might wish to extend in a given instance would be welcomed, the independent power of the executive was sufficient. Variations on this theme appeared until the end of the Vietnam war.

The Gulf of Tonkin resolution, which preceded by several months the massive buildup of troops in Vietnam by President Johnson in 1965, in specific terms "authorized" nothing, but supported a great deal. So did subsequent appropriations for the war. In the resolution, Congress approved "the determination of the President

[6] Theodore C. Sorensen, *Kennedy* (New York, 1965), 702. Nor did President Kennedy seek congressional approval when he introduced the first substantial numbers of American troops into Southeast Asia in 1962. See "War Powers Legislation," *Hearings Before the Senate Committee on Foreign Relations*, 92nd Cong., 1st Sess. (1971), 91.

as Commander in Chief, to take all necessary measures to repel any armed attack against the forces of the United States and to prevent further aggression." The clause added little to constitutional theory, for it was generally recognized that a President could repel an armed attack against the nation or its forces on his own authority. The second clause was even more expansive. Congress, adopting language prepared by the executive proclaimed:

the United States is . . . prepared, as the President determines, to take all necessary steps, including the use of armed force, to assist any member or protocol state of the Southeast Asia Collective Defense Treaty requesting assistance in defense of its freedom.[7]

The operative phrases were "as the President determines" and "all necessary steps." The usage banished any presumed limitations on the power of the President to use military force and accomplished an apparent delegation of the putative war powers of Congress without a clear understanding of the scope of their exercise. Not surprisingly, the administration took the resolution to be "the functional equivalent" of a declaration of war.[8]

[7] House of Representatives, Joint Resolution 1145, 80th Cong., 2d Sess., 78 *Stat.* 384 (1964). For the background of the resolution see David Halberstam, *The Best and the Brightest* (New York, 1972), 411–422, and Schlesinger, *The Imperial Presidency*, 177–182.

[8] Schlesinger, *op. cit.*, 182 ff; *National Commitments Report*, 22. The position was accepted by many learned authorities including most judges in the lower federal courts. See "The Power to Commit Forces to Combat," *Harvard Law Review*, LXXXI (1968), 1804–1805, for a discussion of the issue. Many took exception to the functional equivalent theory. Alexander Bickel, citing *United States v. Curtiss Wright*, argued that Congress possesses no authority to delegate away its powers without determining standards

The central paradox of the Johnson administration's response to the Tonkin Gulf resolution was that, while the administration requested the resolution and employed it openly as the justification for the use of armed forces in Asia, the administration also declared that the resolution was not necessary. President Johnson said as much in a press conference in 1967,[9] and the position was increasingly formalized in testimony before congressional committees and in other official pronouncements. The most definitive statement appeared in 1966. Writing in the Department of State *Bulletin*, the legal advisor to the Department asserted that the President under his Article II powers as commander in chief and chief of foreign relations has "very broad powers, including the power to deploy American forces abroad and commit them to military operations when the President deems such action necessary to maintain the security and defense of the United States." He reasoned, moreover, that the generally accepted power of the President to repel attack on the United States or its forces had expanded with a shrinking world, for, as the world has grown smaller "an attack on a country far from our shores can

for the delegation. He said that clear standards are not found in the resolution and that the proceedings in Congress when the resolution was being considered were not only confused as to the implications of the resolution but, perhaps more significantly, seemed to be guided by the assumption that if the President wanted to act after the attack in the Gulf of Tonkin, he could do so independently in a way and to an extent that he alone would determine. See Bickel, "Congress, the President and the Power to Declare War," *Chicago-Kent Law Review*, XLVIII (1971), 137–139; and his excellent "The Constitution and the War," *Commentary* (July, 1972), 52.

[9] *The New York Times*, August 19, 1967.

impinge directly on the nation's security." A President is empowered, therefore, to meet force with force anywhere or even anticipate it. His decision need be based only on his own judgment and authority. Having taken this position, the spokesman found, however, that the use of force in Indochina was not based alone on inherent power. The nation's history, he argued, provided abundant precedent for presidential use of troops either with congressional acquiescence or acts of support short of a declaration of war. In so saying, the Johnson administration melded history, the Southeast Asia Treaty Organization (SEATO) treaty, the Tonkin Gulf Resolution, and continuing military appropriations with the theory of inherent presidential powers to make the constitutional case.[10] The key question was how this rationale might weather the growing disenchantment with the war and the Nixon administration's adjustment to a changing situation, including disengagement from the war itself.

As congressional disillusionment intensified, the opposition went through several mutations—sense resolutions, threats to cut off funds, and, especially, repeal of the Tonkin Resolution. Similarly, the purported reasons for the use of force shifted as the war wound down and led to variations in the constitutional rationale. First, the Nixon administration abandoned reliance on the SEATO

[10] See generally Francis D. Wormuth's stimulating and comprehensive study, "The Nixon Theory of the War Power: A Critique," *California Law Review*, LX (1972), 623–673; Leonard C. Meeker, "The Legality of the United States Participation in the Defense of Vietnam," *Department of State Bulletin*, LIV (March 3, 1966), 474–489.

Treaty which, at best, had always been a dubious basis for American involvement. Then, when the Tonkin Gulf Resolution was repealed, the administration relied upon argumentation based on historical precedent—some 150 instances in which troops had been used abroad by Presidents—and the alleged ratification of the war by continuing appropriations and other legislation, including the renewal of the Selective Service Act. And, even without these verifications of its support there was the President's independent power as commander in chief over forces committed in the field.[11]

This independent power was, at it has always been, substantive authority to dispatch and command the armed forces; but now it was viewed by the administration more broadly as the power of the President to use force as a negotiating instrument to assure the independence of Vietnam and to protect American troops during the process of withdrawal from the war. Approval was said to be implicit in military appropriations by Congress. And, by a turn of inverse interpretation, any sense resolutions by the House or Senate, or both, which attempted to place limits on the executive were said to be not binding. Thus, when Congress "advised" the President in the Mansfield Amendment to the Military Procurement Act to limit his actions solely to bring about the negotiation of a cease-fire and the withdrawal of all American forces, President Nixon stated that the limiting amendment was "without binding force or effect.

[11] Wormuth, "The Nixon Theory," *passim;* "War Powers Legislation," *Hearings Before the Senate Committee on Foreign Relations,* 539–544.

. . . My signing of the bill that contains this section, therefore, will not change the policies I have pursued and that I shall continue to pursue toward the ending of the war." [12]

It took another year and a half to extricate American troops from Vietnam. Another half year was needed to bring the war to a "conclusion." When the troop withdrawal was completed in March, 1973, reliance on the commander-in-chief clause for further military action in the Asian theater seemed to be undermined if not demolished. Moreover, opposition in Congress to the war had reached an intensity which severely strained the argument that there was continuing implicit authorization in congressional acquiescence. And when, with the departure of all American forces from Vietnam, the President ordered bombing of Cambodia and Laos, his constitutional resources became exceedingly thin. He could not rely on his power as commander in chief to repel attacks on American forces. There were none left to be attacked.

In May, 1973, Congress passed the Eagleton Amendment ordering an absolute cutoff of funds for combat activities in Cambodia and Laos. The bill was vetoed. In the same month the Department of Defense published a memorandum, "Presidential Authority to Continue

[12] *Congressional Quarterly*, XXIX (1971), 2371; Wormuth, "The Nixon Theory," 641. For Alexander Bickel's agreement with the President on this point, see "The Constitution and the War," *Commentary* (July, 1972), 49. The President's use of budgetary authority to transfer funds as one way of paying for the war is set out in compelling fashion by Louis Fisher, *Presidential Spending Power* (Princeton, 1975), 107–118.

Combat Operations in Cambodia." The memorandum reasoned:

Unilateral cessation of our United States air combat activity in Cambodia without the removal of North Vietnamese forces . . . would undermine the central achievement of the January [Paris] Agreement as surely as would have a failure by the United States to insist on the inclusion in the Agreement of Article 20 requiring North Vietnamese withdrawal from Laos and Cambodia. *The President's powers under Article II of the Constitution are adequate to prevent such a self defeating result.*[13]

In other words, the Paris Agreement was interpreted to require the withdrawal of all foreign armed forces from Cambodia and Laos to prevent their use as staging areas for continuing attacks on Vietnam. If these conditions were violated it was understood that the United States Air Force would respond. Actual termination of the war, then, was contingent in this view on the implementation of the agreement. The constitutional basis for the bombing (although the logic could embrace other military activities) was the Article II conjunction of the President's power as commander in chief and his responsibility as chief executive to see that an executive agree-

[13] Emphasis supplied. The memorandum appears in 119 *Cong. Rec.* 14993–14994 (May 9, 1973). The memorandum was a response to a House Armed Services Committee message "directing" the Department to answer a specified list of questions related to the bombing in Cambodia and Laos, including queries on tonnage, losses, sorties, and the authority for the attacks. See Thomas F. Eagleton, "The August 15 Compromise and the War Powers of Congress," *St. Louis University Law Review*, XVIII (Fall, 1973), 1–11.

ment (the Paris Agreement) was enforced—in other words, to enforce presidentially negotiated conditions of peace.

In June 1973, Congress and the President moved toward a direct confrontation when the Senate attached an absolute cutoff of funds to the Debt Ceiling Act and the House did likewise with a Continuing Resolution. A presidential veto, if upheld, would have left the government without funds to operate in the new fiscal year. The confrontation was avoided when Congress received assurance from the President that he would not veto the legislation; in turn, Congress tacitly agreed that the bombing could continue until August 15, but not beyond that time. Congress had, at long last, spoken unambiguously, and the President acceded. The immediate resolution of the issue in August, 1973, was that Congress refused to share further in the responsibility for military action in Cambodia. The presidential theory of unlimited authority over the disposition of American troops, the constitutional talisman of the post-World War II era, ran head on into the brute fact of the appropriations power. But these polar positions represented the extremes of constitutional confrontation, not constitutional principle.

The compromise was a tenuous political resolution of a profound constitutional question about the degree to which the war powers are to be shared by President and Congress. Whether, from the turmoil of the Vietnam experience, there was any accretion to constitutional doctrine other than an abundant and unrestricted theory of presidential power was the unanswered question.

At least two developments merit attention. One was

a sustained pattern of avoidance by the Supreme Court of any determination on the constitutionality of the war in Vietnam, which stance obscured growing restlessness in the courts below. Another was the passage of the War Powers Resolution (discussed below) by Congress in 1973. In the first instance, the Supreme Court did not reach the merits of the war's constitutionality, nor did the Court specify reasons for rejecting appeals from the decisions of the lower federal courts. Because there are no determinative opinions, it can only be deduced that a majority of the Court viewed the issue of constitutionality as a "political" one for other branches of the government to decide.[14] At the same time there was some

[14] The only decision which the Supreme Court affirmed (without opinion) was *Atlee v. Laird*, 347 F. Supp. 689 (E.D. Pa., 1972), *aff*. 411 U.S. 911 (1973), which rested fully on political question grounds. The doctrine has been described as more "amenable to description by infinite itemization than by generalization." John P. Frank, "Political Questions," in *Supreme Court and Supreme Law*, Edmund Cahn, ed. (New York, 1971), 36. See also Michael E. Tigar, "Judicial Power, the 'Political Question Doctrine,' and Foreign Relations," *UCLA Law Review*, XVII (1970), 1135–1179; and Fritz W. Scharpf, "Judicial Review and the Political Question: A Functional Analysis," *Yale Law Journal*, LXXV (1966), 517–597. The underlying principle is that the Court will not decide issues which by their nature, or by a determination that they are delegated to the other branches under the separation of powers, are not fitting for judicial resolution. In regard to presidential war powers it is said that traditional judicial standards and reasoning which may have bite in other areas of constitutional interpretation cannot be utilized where delicate questions of military judgment and foreign policy are involved. Moreover, traditional remedies (such as injunctions which might trigger volatile or unpredictable consequences in a war situation) are instruments a prudent judiciary should never use. Such issues, it is said, are political, with distinctly political consequences, and are beyond judicial competence.

movement in the lower federal courts. The persistent efforts by opponents of the war to litigate the constitutional issues and the increasing unpopularity of the war led to a greater inclination, as time passed, to hear argument about the war's constitutionality. Although many of the federal courts finally wrapped themselves in the protective mantle of the political question doctrine, especially during the depths of American involvement, several were willing to treat the war as a justiciable issue. The sum total of all of the Vietnam cases, seventy in number, left no coherent legacy. But in significant instances the political question doctrine crumbled noticeably, and standards began to emerge. It was a significant indication that the judicial deference which was assumed as a judicial fact of life in the immediate post-World War II years could no longer be taken for granted in the 1970's.

The cases most worthy of notice include the *Berk-Orlando* and *Holtzman* series.[15] The former were liti-

For a list of the Vietnam war cases in the courts see Robert P. Sugarman, "Judicial Decisions Concerning the Constitutionality of the United States Military in Indo-China: A Bibliography of Court Decisions," *Columbia Journal of Transnational Law*, XIII (1974), 470–481. See also Leon Friedman and Burt Neuborne, *Unquestioning Obedience to the President* (New York, 1972). On varying occasions three members of the Supreme Court seemed to show an interest in hearing argument. See, for example, *Mora v. McNamara*, 389 U.S. 934 (1967); *Massachusetts v. Laird*, 400 U.S. 886 (1970); *DaCosta v. Laird*, 405 U.S. 979 (1972).

[15] *Berk v. Laird*, 429 F. 2d 302 (2d Cir., 1970); *Orlando v. Laird*, 317 F. Supp. 1013 (E.D. N.Y., 1970); *Berk v. Laird*, 317 F. Supp. 715 (E.D. N.Y., 1970); *Orlando v. Laird*, 443 F. 2d 1039 (2d Cir., 1971); *Holtzman v. Schlesinger*, 361 F. Supp. 553 (E.D. N.Y., 1973); rev'd. 484 F. 2d 1307 (2d Cir., 1973); stay upheld, 414 U.S. 1304 (1973).

gated while the war was in full sway, the latter after American forces had been withdrawn, at a time when the August 15 bombing cutoff date was fast approaching. Those initiating the litigation in *Berk-Orlando* had at first asserted that the Constitution required a declaration of war by Congress for the Vietnam hostilities to be lawful. The rigidity of this formulation gave way quickly to the more persuasive proposition that short of a formal declaration of war by Congress, congressional responsibilities under the war powers could be fulfilled constitutionally by an explicit authorization for the use of force as a substitute for a declaration of war. It was argued that because the Constitution conferred the war power on Congress there was a manageable judicial standard available to the judiciary to make an explicit authorization mandatory. The lower federal courts did not accept this reasoning in full, nor did they accept the conclusion. Nevertheless, they shifted significantly from the absolute bar of the political question doctrine by asserting that there was the functional equivalent of an authorization in other congressional action, including continuing appropriations for the war.[16] Relying in part on the *Steel Seizure Case*, the court agreed that there must be some evidence of "mutual participation" by Congress in prolonged hostilities. In short, the political question doctrine did not foreclose judicial inquiry into whether there had been mutual participation. But the form and the "propriety" of the participation, that is, whether or not an

[16] Beyond appropriations, those legislative acts said to be the equivalent of an authorization were, *inter alia*, the renewal of the Selective Service Act and, before its repeal, the Gulf of Tonkin Resolution.

147

explicit authorization was required, was a political question for Congress, not the judiciary, to decide.

The *Holtzman* cases were litigated in a more fluid setting. American troops had been withdrawn; there was a peace agreement and, although the bombing continued, Congress had restricted its use by means of the August 15 compromise, a compromise which could be interpreted either as a declaration of congressional nonparticipation, a tactic to avoid a presidential veto, or as an agreement with executive strategy which had a firm ending date. In the only case of its kind known to American constitutional law, a federal district court enjoined the further use of air power. The court reasoned that earlier cases had presumed *continuing* mutual participation by the President and Congress in the use of force. Noting the withdrawal of American troops and the resolution of Congress which specified the date on which appropriations could no longer be used to sustain hostilities in Southeast Asia, the court found that the August 15 compromise could not be viewed as an affirmative authorization by Congress. Judge Orrin G. Judd concluded that the August 15 compromise was constitutionally flawed because it was a tactic forced on Congress in an effort to avoid a presidential veto. Judd reasoned, "It cannot be the rule that the President needs a vote of only one-third plus one of either House in order to conduct a war, but this would be the consequence of holding that Congress must override a Presidential veto in order to terminate hostilities which it has not authorized." The court said, in effect, that a constitutional one-third plus one could not determine the will of all, especially in the light of evidence of considerable congressional disapproval for continued bombing. Moreover, the court said that the situation had changed with the withdrawal of troops and that past authorizations in no way could be interpreted to cover a changed situation. Thus, mutual participation was lacking. Citing the *Steel Seizure Case* the court concluded that in whatever way the executive might interpret an emergency, emergency does not create power unless Congress shares in giving authority for its use. Affirmative authorization was found neither in past acquiescence in a war, the character of which had changed, nor in a compromise which had been forced on Congress by the threat of a veto. The court issued an injunction against the further use of armed force but stayed its order until it could be reviewed by the court of appeals.

In a decision which exposed judicial ambivalence, the court of appeals concluded that the nature of military tactics used by a President to wind down a war was a political question beyond the capacity of courts to judge; moreover, it was beyond the judicial function to determine whether a military situation had changed to such an extent that a renewed authorization was required from Congress. But, in an afterthought which gave an indication that the mutual-participation theory had retained some of its force, the court concluded that the August 15 compromise could be interpreted, in its terms, as an act of mutual participation. It was recognized, at least, that the theory could not be dismissed out of hand.[17]

[17] The court, in so saying, suggested what some other lower courts had affirmed, namely that there were judicially discoverable and manageable standards—in this instance the August 15 cutoff—which the courts could examine as to the sufficiency of mutual participation. *Holtzman v. Schlesinger*, 361 F. Supp. 553

This thin edge of doctrine found its legislative expression in the War Powers Resolution of 1973, an enactment which found its origin, in part, in the very failure of the courts to take a more active role in determining the scope of presidential power to commit troops abroad. With increasing antagonism toward the use of presidential power in Vietnam, Congress attempted to sys-

---

(E.D. N.Y., 1973); 484 F. 2d 1307 (2d Cir., 1973). In a companion case, which also indicated that the doctrine of mutual participation was taking hold, and that the courts might have to become involved, a federal district court found that the August 15 compromise was a clear demonstration that President and Congress were not in conflict. But if Congress had not compromised, "we would have a clear issue of conflict before us that would have required judicial determination." See *Drinan v. Nixon,* 364 F. Supp. 854, 858 (D.C. Mass., 1973). *Holtzman* was appealed to the Supreme Court. The issue of independent presidential power might have been presented squarely if it had reached the Court after the August 15 date, then a week away, and if the President had continued the bombing past that date. It is likely that given the force of the *Steel Seizure Case* the conflict would have created votes sufficient at least for arguments to be heard. Instead, with presidential compliance virtually assured, the Court, not then in session, with Justice Marshall speaking from his circuit, refused to issue a stay. The refusal led to an exchange with Justice Douglas which exposed the volatility of the issue and arguably the Court's wisdom in avoiding it. See *Holtzman v. Schlesinger,* 414 U.S. 1304 (1973); *Holtzman v. Schlesinger,* 414 U.S. 1316 (1973); *Schlesinger v. Holtzman,* 414 U.S. 1321. It is of considerable significance that Marshall referred positively to "a respectable and growing body of lower court opinion holding that Art. I, Sec. 8, cl. 11, imposes some judicially manageable standards as to congressional authorization for warmaking . . . [and] as a matter of substantive law, it seems likely that the President may not wage war without some form of congressional approval—except, perhaps in the case of a pressing emergency or when the president is in the process of extricating himself from a war Congress once authorized" (414 U.S. 1311–1313).

tematize the flow of presidential power in situations where hostilities were actual or imminent. The Resolution was legislative recognition, in a procedural mode, of the theory of mutual participation. Briefly described, the Resolution requires a President to report to Congress within forty-eight hours the circumstances, the scope of military action, and the basis of his authority if he commits troops to armed action or substantially increases the number of troops prepared for combat in a foreign country. Such operations must cease unless Congress gives affirmative approval within sixty days, with the exception that a commitment can continue for thirty additional days if such action is necessary to protect American forces. At any time from the date of initial commitment of troops, Congress may order, by a concurrent resolution not subject to the President's veto, the commitment of troops to end.[18]

Whether the Resolution imposes rigidities incompatible with a salutary presidential discretion in foreign affairs, or whether it may in fact enhance rather than restrict presidential power are questions still unanswered.[19] So, too, is the question whether Presidents will

[18] *Public Law 93–148, 93rd Cong., House of Representatives, Joint Resolution 542,* November 7, 1973. The Resolution was passed over President Nixon's veto, a veto which raised important constitutional questions. *Congressional Quarterly,* XXXI (1973), 2855–2856. See generally, Jacob K. Javits, *Who Makes War* (New York, 1973) and Thomas F. Eagleton, *War and Presidential Power* (New York, 1974).

[19] It can be argued that the most damaging aspect of the War Powers Resolution is its very existence, not the specificity of its provisions. It tends to remove the threatening imminence of the use of force by the President in dealing with other nations as an omnipresent calculation for others to take into account without

feel bound by an arguably unconstitutional statute. But it is of significance, whatever may happen in practice, that the cautious suppositions of some lower federal court judges paralleled the underlying constitutional concern that Congress expressed in the passage of the legislation.[20] The dispatch of troops, in theory, if not in practice, was no longer unencumbered. Among many remaining

---

being time-bound by the resolution's procedures. For other evaluations see especially Schlesinger, *The Imperial Presidency*, 301–307; Thomas Ehrlich, "The Legal Process in Foreign Affairs: Military Intervention—A Testing Case," *Stanford Law Review*, XXVII (1975), 637–652; Eugene V. Rostow, "Great Cases Make Bad Law: The War Powers Act," *Texas Law Review*, L (1972), 833–900; and Charles L. Black, "The Working Balance of the American Political Departments," *Hastings Constitutional Law Quarterly*, I (1974), 18–21.

[20] There is no doubt that Congress wanted to leave undisturbed the President's power to respond to sudden attack. The exception was specified in the Resolution. And there seemed to be general acceptance during the final evacuation of Vietnam that the inherent right to protect American lives—not mentioned in the Resolution—lay within presidential power. As for the removal of South Vietnamese citizens during the evacuation President Ford said that he acted on moral grounds. The Mayaguez incident, involving the seizure of an American freighter by Cambodia, was not decisively instructive about the reach of the Resolution. The President informed congressional leaders of his decision to use force and after the incident reported to Congress referring to the Resolution; but it cannot be said that there was "consultation" about whether to make the decision he made. Moreover, in his report he referred to the operation as being conducted "pursuant to the President's constitutional executive power and his authority as commander in chief." *Congressional Quarterly*, XXXIII (1975), 1340–1341. See also, John C. Crudin, "The War Making Process," *Military Law Review*, XLIX (1975), 35–139, 124–130; and J. Terry Emerson, "The War Powers Resolution Tested: The President's Independent Defense Power," *Notre Dame Lawyer*, LI (1975), 187–216.

questions was whether Presidents could continue to enjoy, in constitutional terms, uncontrolled discretion in other relations with nations abroad.

Presidential Authority and Executive Agreements. Executive agreements with other nations have traditionally had one or more constitutional sources: agreements made by a President in pursuance of a treaty; agreements implementing a congressional resolution or other legislative authorization; and agreements made under a President's power as chief of foreign relations and commander in chief. With justifications similar to those offered for the comitment of troops abroad, Presidents over the last quarter of a century have amply interpreted their authority to make agreements without any binding obligation to inform Congress.

Numbers tell part of the story. In 1930 the United States concluded twenty-five treaties and only nine executive agreements. By 1950 the proportion had risen to eleven treaties and 157 executive agreements. The trend continued upward. In 1971 seventeen treaties and 214 executive agreements were negotiated. More significant, however, was the accumulation. As of 1972 the United States was party to 4,000 formal international agreements other than treaties, with an estimated 200 agreements being added each year. Additionally, some 1,000 treaties were then in force. But these figures do not tell the full story; in fact, they may distort it. In 1972 the Department of State estimated that only 3 percent of the then extant executive agreements were based alone on presidential authority.[21] But the problem,

---

[21] The figures vary and, of course, the numbers are not as important as the nature of a given agreement may be. *Congres-*

as it pertains to presidential discretion, centers on the difficulty of describing an executive agreement with sufficient precision. Agreements can range from explicit documents to shadowy statements of presidential intent to other heads of state or their agents. Moreover, while during the post-World War II years the constitutional grounding for the exercise of authority remained the same as it had for such singularly important agreements as those made at Yalta and Potsdam, the character and the tempo of the process changed. The effect of increased numbers was intensified by their importance. For example, a myriad of executive agreements drew the country step by step into deep involvement in Southeast Asia and eventually into full-scale war; and it was a unilateral executive assurance by President Nixon to President Thieu, during the peace negotiations in January, 1973, promising that the United States would "respond with full force" to any violations of the peace settlement, that could have brought about a renewal of the war. The agreement was never reported to Congress, in all of its implications, confidentially or otherwise.[22]

There was also an increasingly casual preference for the use of executive agreements in place of the more complicated treaty mechanism, even for agreements of great moment. At the same time, an expanded treaty network invited a vast expansion of executive agreements

sional Quarterly, XXXII (1974), 3283–3284; "Transmittal of Executive Agreements to Congress," Hearings Before the Committee on Foreign Relations, 92d Cong., 1st Sess., 58–59 (1971); Schlesinger, The Imperial Presidency, 310–319; Raoul Berger, "The Presidential Monopoly of Foreign Relations," Michigan Law Review, LXXI (1972), 33–48.

[22] See Congressional Quarterly, XXXIII (1975), 845.

for their implementation. Above all, there was a growing proclivity for secret agreements involving critical policy matters in which the veil of secrecy served military security, as well as a continuing presidential wish to be free from the inconveniences which informing Congress might bring.

For many years this was accepted by Congress as standard operating procedure. After the mid-1950's, and the abortive Bricker movement, few questioned the policy of presidential independence. It was said to be affirmed by such Supreme Court decisions as *United States v. Belmont* and *United States v. Pink,* by dicta in *United States v. Curtiss Wright,* and by an ample reading by Presidents of their inherent powers as chief executive and commander in chief.[23] By the early 1970's, however, doubts began to emerge. While there was full acceptance of the utility of executive agreements as necessary instruments in the administration of foreign affairs, there was increasing concern about their scope. For example, although in many instances the agreements were only contingency arrangements, it was argued that if a given contingency arose the agreements might stimulate serious military or foreign-policy commitments without congressional foreknowledge or participation. In the background was the ghost of concern raised in the early 1950's that somehow executive agreements might be used to capture the war power from Congress or otherwise forefeit constitutional limitations.

In the late 1950's, in *Reid v. Covert,* the Supreme

[23] For a judicial reference to inherency, see *United States v. Guy W. Capps Inc.,* 204 F. 2d 655, 659 (4th Cir., 1953). The limitations of the case are discussed in Louis Henkin, *Foreign*

Court looked askance at the proposition that treaties and executive agreements might be used to limit the application of the Bill of Rights. The decision had implications for the employment of discretion in international agreements as well as for civilian control over the military. It also foretold an emerging role for the judiciary in the years ahead. *Reid v. Covert* and its companion cases came about when the magnitude of American troop commitments abroad brought to light the potential impact of military law on the rights of civilians accompanying the troops.[24] In each of the cases, Status of Forces

---

Affairs and the Constitution (New York, 1972), 180–181. And see *Consumers Union v. Rogers,* 352 F. Supp. 1319 (D. D.C., 1973).

[24] For earlier cases involving civil-military relations, see Rossiter's discussion above, pp. 40–64, 102–120; *Reid v. Covert,* 354 U.S. 1 (1957) (military trial of service dependents for noncapital offenses is unconstitutional); *McElroy v. United States ex. rel. Guagliardo,* 361 U.S. 281 (1960), and *Grisham v. Hagan,* 361 U.S. 278 (1960) (American civilian employees of the armed forces overseas cannot be tried by military courts for capital or noncapital offenses). Efforts to apply a "time of war" exception in the legislation for the trial of civilians during the Vietnam war were frustrated in *Latney v. Ignatius,* 416 F. 2d 821 (D.C. Cir., 1969), and *United States v. Averette,* 19 U.S.C.M.A. 363 (1970). *Reid v. Covert,* 354 U.S. 1 (1957), reversed a decision which the Court had handed down a year earlier in *Reid v. Covert,* 351 U.S. 470 (1956). The reversal was in part the result of the retirement of two justices (Reed and Minton), two Justices who changed their minds (Harlan and Frankfurter), and the appointment of Justice Brennan. *Reid v. Covert* stands out among a line of important cases imposing judicial control over military trials and, more broadly, civilian control over the military. See Rossiter's discussion of *Duncan v. Kahanomoku* above, pp. 54–59; see also *Toth v. Quarles,* 350 U.S. 11 (1955) (discharged service-

Agreements, made incident to such treaties as NATO, had been negotiated as executive agreements to implement provisions of the Uniform Code of Military Justice. The agreements gave military courts jurisdiction to try American civilians who accompany American troops abroad. The underlying question in each of the cases was whether Congress, under its power to "make rules for the government and regulation of the land and naval forces" and to make treaties, or whether the President acting under his power to make executive agreements pursuant to treaties, could displace the right of civilians to the protections of the Fifth and Sixth Amendments. In *Reid*, the principal issue was the right of a serviceman's wife, charged with the murder of her husband, to a grand jury indictment and trial by jury. The Court concluded that the words of the Constitution "to make rules for . . . the land and naval forces" meant just that and no more. To bring civilians within the jurisdiction of the Uniform Code, as Congress and the President had done, was to violate specific constitutional limitations. Significantly, the Court refused to accept the government's bold argument that congressional action in establishing the jurisdiction was a "necessary and proper"

---

man cannot be subjected to court martial for offenses committed in the service); *O'Callaghan v. Parker*, 395 U.S. 258 (1969) (for a crime to be within military jurisdiction it must be service connected); and Edward F. Sherman, "Legal Inadequacies and Doctrinal Restraints in Controlling the Military," *Indiana Law Journal*, XLIX (1974), 561–565; Thomas M. Strassburg, "Civilian Judicial Review of Military Criminal Justice," *Military Law Review*, LXVI (1974), 1–66. But see *Parker v. Levy*, 417 U.S. 733 (1974).

action and, therefore, a constitutional means for implementing international agreements. As Justice Black wrote, referring to "the steadfast bulwark of the Bill of Rights,"

It would be manifestly contrary to the objectives of those who created the Constitution, as well as those who were responsible for the Bill of Rights [to permit] the United States to exercise power under an international agreement without observing constitutional prohibitions. . . . The prohibitions of the Constitution were designed to apply to all branches of the National Government and they cannot be nullified by the Executive or by the Executive and the Senate combined.[25]

Although the Supreme Court did not undermine the rationale of *United States v. Belmont,* which concluded that a President has independent power to make executive agreements, in its burst of activism it established that there were limitations emanating from the Bill of Rights and staked a claim for the judiciary in determining those limitations.

As for Congress, many years passed after the *Reid* decision before concern about executive discretion produced a constructive reaction. Finally, after a series of investigations exposed secret military agreements with such countries as Ethiopia, Laos, Thailand, Spain, and Portugal, in 1972, Congress passed a mild measure requiring that all executive agreements be reported to Congress within sixty days. The reporting procedures included the proviso that those agreements which involved sensitive national security material were to be

[25] *Reid v. Covert,* 354 U.S. 1, 17.

submitted as classified documents to the House and Senate foreign-affairs committees. The measure did not invade the shadow area of presidential communications of the kind which might be interpreted by other nations as national commitments with a force equivalent to formal executive agreements; nor did it require an affirmative response by Congress to put the agreements into effect. Throughout the first half of the 1970's, Congress continued to explore alternative procedures to cover such contingencies.[26] Nevertheless, the reporting procedures, in much the same way as the decision in *Reid v. Covert*, put in question the executive assertion that international agreements, not pursuant to a treaty or legislative authorization, were the exclusive province of the presidency. Taken together these steps can be viewed as flickering concern by Congress and the judiciary about structural imbalances which could affect the Bill of Rights and the separation of powers in this one phase of national security policy. It remained to be seen whether the same concern might make itself felt elsewhere.

Presidential Power and the Domestication of National Security

Before World War II the penetration of the war power into the domestic realm was serious but transient. So, too, were exceptions to constitutional limitations in the

[26] *Public Law*, 92–403 (1972), *United States Code*, Title 1, *sec. 112* (Supp. 1974). For discussion of more elaborate congressional control see "Congressional Oversight of Executive Agreements," *Hearings, Subcommittee on Separation of Powers of the Committee on the Judiciary, United States Senate*, 92nd

name of national security. Lincoln's constitutional "dictatorship" gave way to *Ex parte Milligan* and the politics of Reconstruction. The severe violations of constitutional rights that took place during World War I and the subsequent Red Scare surrendered to the politics of normalcy. No such surcease followed World War II. There was a brief though uncertain period of quiet, but it was soon troubled by the real and imagined necessities of strategic security in an unstable world, changing military technology, ideological confrontation, and sensitivity about internal security.

The Berlin blockade and the Korean war formed the watershed internationally, President Truman's loyalty-security program domestically. By the end of the 1940's external security and internal security were fast becoming fused into the notion of national security. This inchoate yet potent formulation helped to dignify the release of executive power into the domestic sphere and under a broadened presidential prerogative. But quite apart from assertions of prerogative power by the executive, there were abundant statutory resources as well as established legislative-executive patterns which could be relied upon, appealed to, or interpreted as support for a President's use of power. Before the Watergate era it would have been unneccessary to add that executive practices were not necessarily uncongenial to comity with Congress, unremittently insensitive to constitutional rights, or lacking—either on constitutional or policy grounds—an arguable basis for their exercise.

The two limitations which experienced the greatest

Cong., 2d Sess. (1971), 7–9, and *Congressional Quarterly,* XXXIII (1975), 1712–1717.

stress and, perhaps paradoxically, the greatest theoretical enrichment in this period, were the Bill of Rights and the separation of powers. From a constitutional perspective, the formulation which contributed most to the stress was the notion of inherent executive power and a broad reading of presidential discretion. In this formulation a positive value was assigned to secrecy and confidentiality, administrative discretion, and executive expertise. And, the President's electoral accountability was said by some to replace or pre-empt a strict reading of more direct constitutional limitations.[27]

Judicial passivity, reinforced by the political question doctrine, was presumed by some of the advocates of a strong presidency to be the rule in the national security area. On the other hand, where a judicial function was accepted, it was viewed as a validating one, "balancing" in favor of the security interest when weighing that interest against constitutional limitations. The range of presidential activism—which intensified during the Nixon administration but neither originated nor, one can suppose, ended there—was vast. It extended through the impounding of appropriated funds, electronic surveillance in the name of national security, executive privilege, and executive secrecy. Each assertion of authority was linked, tenuously, to the President's responsibilities as chief executive, commander in chief, and chief of foreign relations. Each had serious domestic implications.

The Impoundment of Funds. The impoundment con-

[27] See Schlesinger, *The Imperial Presidency*, 377, for a trenchant description of this view, tying it to the philosophy of the Nixon administration.

troversy, which generated special heat during the Nixon administration, turned squarely on the separation of powers. In monetary terms, impoundment reached a high point in 1973 with the refusal of the President to spend some 12 billion dollars appropriated by Congress.[28] The practice of impounding was of course not without precedent. It goes back at least to the Jefferson years. Beginning with Franklin D. Roosevelt's administration and World War II it became a recurring issue, first in regard to defense expenditures and the setting of fiscal priorities in wartime, later over expenditures which were not directly related to defense policy. And during the Johnson and Nixon administrations, but particularly the latter, impoundment was used outright to reorder expenditures over a wide range of defense and nondefense matters to shape executive policy preferences contrary to officially stated congressional intent.

The constitutional contours seemed at first to be simple: Congress under its Article I powers has the sole authority to legislate and appropriate funds; the executive under its Article II powers has the responsibility, without discretion, to execute such laws. The situation, however, was more complex. Presidents could claim that several statutes afforded them discretion, and, where these statutes or the conditions under which the funds were to be expended were ambiguous, Presidents were entitled, under Article II, to act on their own power. Moreover, it was asserted that acquiescence by the courts and Congress in the practice of impounding since the earliest days of the Republic had, by implication, em-

[28] The precise figure differs, depending on the basis for calculation. See *Congressional Quarterly*, XXXI (1973), 270–274.

bedded it in the Constitution.[29] There was also the direct constitutional assertion that the President, as commander in chief and chief executive, had independent authority to refuse to expend funds for weapons systems which in his judgment were unsound or where appropriations designated for domestic purposes would be inimical to the execution of foreign policy. Thus, President Truman refused to spend $735 million appropriated to increase the Air Force from 48 to 58 groups largely on his authority as commander in chief. Similarly, President Eisenhower set aside $137 million appropriated for the initial procurement of Nike-Zeus missiles, and President Kennedy refused to release $180 million for the development of the B-70 bomber. During the Vietnam war, Presidents Johnson and Nixon impounded nondefense funds purportedly to reduce the inflationary impact of the war, a practice which the Nixon administration continued after the war had come to a close.

Prior to the 1970's there was a fragile but real distinction between impoundment of appropriations for weapons systems and the impoundment of other funds. There was some force in the argument that the President's power as commander in chief gave him a special responsibility to utilize or not utilize funds based on his

[29] Among the statutes are the Antideficiency Acts of 1905, as amended (33 *Stat.* 1257; 34 *Stat.* 49), and The Employment Act of 1947 (60 *Stat.* 23). See especially Louis Fisher, "The Politics of Impounded Funds," *Administrative Science Quarterly,* XV (1973), 361–377; and Fisher, *Presidential Spending Power;* Ralph S. Abascal and John R. Kramer, "Presidential Impoundment (Part I); Historic Genesis and Constitutional Framework," *Georgetown Law Journal,* LXII (1974), 1549–1618; and Nile Stanton, "History and Practice of Executive Impoundment of Appropriated Funds," *Nebraska Law Review,* LIII (1974), 1–30.

strategic estimates and to control the special pleading of the services and the cluster of interest groups around them. But with the massive impounding by the Nixon administration the distinction between defense and non-defense expenditures became blurred to the point of vanishing. It was argued that, quite apart from any statutory authority a President might or might not have to impound funds, there was independent power to impound rooted in the executive's singular role in foreign affairs. Thus, presidential power to impound was not restricted to defense expenditures but extended to matters within the domestic sphere which might have an effect, however indirect, on national security. No line was drawn; the theory had come full circle.[30] Presidential

[30] The definitive statement of the theory appeared in a response by the Deputy Attorney General to a congressional query: "It is generally conceded that the President has substantial authority to impound funds in the areas of defense and foreign relations. . . . [I]t must be recognized, moreover, that galloping domestic inflation may impinge significantly upon the President's responsibilities as Commander-in-Chief, and as the Nation's representative in foreign relations. Domestic inflation dilutes the effectiveness of the defense dollar, and aggravates a host of difficult and inter-related foreign problems, such as our balance of payments. This is not to argue that the President's authority to impound domestic program money flows directly from his constitutional powers in the military and foreign affairs areas. It is to suggest, however, that these powers may not properly be viewed in isolation. Their exercise is profoundly affected by domestic inflation, and they therefore lend support to his constitutional authority to alleviate inflation through impounding money for domestic programs." *Joint Hearings Before the Ad Hoc Subcommittee on Impoundment of Funds of the Committee on Government Operations and the Subcommittee on Separation of Powers of the Committee on the Judiciary,* United States Senate, 93rd Cong., 1st Sess., 838 (1973). President Nixon, after referring to President Truman's impound-

control over matters normally thought to be in the domestic sphere—sewage treatment facilities or urban mass transit, for example—were said to fall within the "area of defense," that is, national security, and thus were subject to the President's authority.

In the flood of litigation during the early 1970's around the President's authority to impound funds, the constitutional contention that it was a power based on national security was never squarely reached. Lower federal court decisions and the one impounding decision handed down by the Supreme Court turned on statutory interpretation about the degree of discretion which Congress intended to give the executive. In the few cases where the constitutional powers of the President as chief executive were invoked directly—revised in meaning to read "the most fiscally responsible" execution of the laws—the execu-

---

ment as a precedent, stated that "the constitutional right for the President of the United States to impound funds . . . is absolutely clear." *Congressional Quarterly,* XXXI (1973), 185. The administration's formulation of the power of the commander in chief as a source of authority into which Congress cannot "intrude" was spelled out by Deputy Attorney General Joseph Sneed. Citing *United States v. Curtiss Wright,* he said: "It is clear that any [congressional mandate that funds be spent] is subject to at least two important qualifications. The President has substantial authority to control spending in the areas of national defense and foreign relations. Such authority flows from the President's constitutional role as Commander-in-Chief of the Armed Forces and from his relatively broad constitutional authority in foreign affairs. In those areas, congressional directives may intrude impermissibly into matters reserved by the Constitution to the President." *Joint Hearings,* 368. The much cited Rehnquist memorandum, that a President had to comply with congressional directives to spend funds, specifically excepted refusals based on his power as commander in chief. *Ibid.,* 394.

tive was informed by the judiciary that there were no inherent powers in this area. There was uniform reliance on the *Steel Seizure Case* and its admonition that the President was to execute the law; he was not "the lawmaker." [31]

A more definitive restriction on the power to impound, however, was the passage of the Congressional Budget and Impoundment Control Act of 1974 [32] which allows a President to defer an expenditure of funds unless his reported deferral is overturned by a resolution of either

[31] The Supreme Court's first impoundment decision was *Train v. City of New York*, 420 U.S. 135 (1975), and its companion case *Train v. Campaign Clean Water, Inc.* 420 U.S. 136 (1975). Besides the *Steel Seizure Case*, the most active precedent was *Kendall v. United States*, 12 Pet. 524 (1838) (the obligation imposed on an executive officer to perform ministerial duties does not imply a power to forbid their execution). See *Pennsylvania v. Lynn*, 362 F. Supp. 1363, 1372 (D. D.C., 1973); *Campaign Clean Water, Inc. v. Ruckelshaus*, 361 F. Supp. 689, 696 (E.D. Va., 1973); *National Council of Community Health Centers v. Weinberger*, 361 F. Supp. 897, 901 (D. D.C., 1973); *Local 2677 v. Phillips*, 358 F. Supp. 60, 77 (D. D.C., 1973); but in another vein, *Harrington v. Schlesinger*, 373 F. Supp. 1138, 1141 (E.D. N.C., 1974) where it was said that in the instant case the administration of appropriations for military expenditures in Southeast Asia was a matter of executive discretion. J. Timothy Gratz, "Impoundment—Separation of Powers," *Wisconsin Law Review*, Vol. 1975 (1975), 211–212, 230; Abner J. Mikva and Michael F. Hertz, "Impoundment of Funds—The Courts, the Congress and the President: a Constitutional Triangle," *Northwestern Law Review*, LXIX (1973), 335–389, 380–381.

[32] Public Law, 93–344, 88 *Stat.* 336 (1974). With good reason a highly regarded constitutional scholar compares the Act to the War Powers Resolution of 1973, remarking that they both represent "congressional action of an unusual and especially important nature. Instead of congressional directives regarding substantive governmental policies, [they delineate] structures and processes.

the House or Senate; or, to rescind an appropriation only if the House and Senate approve the action within 45 days. The legislation reflects the *Steel Seizure* principle that if Congress prohibits the executive from acting, or provides alternative means for acting, he is constitutionally bound by the limitations. There is also a touch of the mutual-participation theory which had surfaced in the Vietnam war cases. Because the legislation is soundly rooted in the primacy of the congressional appropriations power under the Constitution, it would be difficult for a President now to assert that a discretion to spend or not to spend in the national security field arises independently from his own powers. Whatever conclusions might be drawn about the wisdom of the legislation and its impact on constructive executive discretion,[33] the action of the federal courts and Congress seemed, by the mid 1970's, to have foreclosed further constitutional debate over the question. Such a lack of ambiguity was not to be the case in other instances where the President invoked national security as a source of power.

National Security Surveillance. In the last twenty years national security has been used to justify surreptitious activity that has been patently criminal (Watergate), criminal or excessive (some of the domestic

---

It is legislation that can be viewed as quasi-constitutional in nature, for it seeks to clarify and define basic relationships among the branches of government." Gerald Gunther, *Constitutional Law* (9th ed.; New York, 1975), 416.

[33] For early difficulties with the Act see *Congressional Quarterly*, XXXIII (1975), 860–867; and Ralph S. Abascal and John R. Kramer, "Presidential Impoundment: Judicial and Legislative Responses (Part II), *Georgetown Law Review*, LXIII (1974), 149–185, 177, 184.

activities of the CIA and the FBI), and, from a more dignified perspective, assertedly lawful (the gathering of information about foreign agents, foreign agencies, and their alleged domestic sympathizers). John Ehrlichman typified the first when in his testimony before the Senate Watergate Committee he referred to the burglarizing of Daniel Ellsberg's psychiatrist's office as "within the President's inherent constitutional powers." [34] The dignified argument was put forward by several Presidents before the 1970's in internal memoranda and public statements. But the most bountiful theory was that proclaimed by the Nixon administration regarding the authority to use electronic surveillance and other clandestine means to monitor the activities of domestic dissidents.

From its inception in the 1940's the justification for electronic surveillance was based on the exceptional theory that the President's powers as commander in chief and chief of foreign relations allowed executive agencies to monitor conversations and activities of suspected subversives. While so doing they were not bound by the Fourth Amendment requirement that there be judicially approved warrants, based on probable cause, as a prerequisite for such surveillance. After 1968, when Con-

---

[34] Cited in Harold W. Chase and Craig R. Ducat, *Constitutional Interpretation* (St. Paul, 1974), 315; *New York Times*, July 25, 1973; see also Schlesinger, *The Imperial Presidency*, 255–266, for some of the activities of the Nixon administration including the proposed Huston Plan. Ehrlichman's defense that surreptitious entry was lawful because the President had authorized such activities for national security purposes was rejected by Judge Gerhard A. Gesell in *United States v. Ehrlichman*, 370 F. Supp. 29, 33–34 (D. D.C., 1974).

gress passed the Omnibus Crime Control and Safe Streets Act, the President's power was said to be supported further by legislation. While the Act required warrant procedures for wiretapping in domestic criminal cases, it was argued that the legislation made an exception to the warrant requirement for national security surveillance, including internal security. The Act was said to affirm by implication that inherent presidential power had been a pattern of executive practice extending back at least to 1940.[35]

The first Presidents to invoke inherent power were committed but cautious. Franklin D. Roosevelt, in a confidential memorandum directed to Attorney General Robert Jackson in 1940, authorized the Attorney General to use agents to wiretap telephones to protect "the defense of the nation" against the "fifth column" danger from "persons suspected of subversive activities . . . including suspected spies." The reference to the fifth column presupposed that Nazis and Nazi sympathizers

[35] *United States Code*, Title 18, secs. 2510–2520. Prior to the passage of the Act, the Communications Act of 1934 was said to govern. Although the Act seemed to prohibit all wiretapping, its language in terms prohibited "intercepting and divulging" information from wiretaps. This was interpreted by the FBI and other agencies as permitting interception as long as the information was not "divulged," that is, the information could not be used as evidence in court. See also *Katz v. United States*, 389 U.S. 347, 358 (1967), which established that electronic surveillance was a Fourth Amendment search and seizure and that evidence attained thereby would be excluded if warrant and probable cause requirements were not met. The decision reserved the question whether the principle extended to national security surveillance. For an excellent treatment of this history, see "The National Security Interest & Civil Liberties," *Harvard Law Review*, LXXXV (1972), 1248–1270.

would receive the most attention. The President asked the Attorney General to oversee the taps personally, to limit them in number, and to restrict them, in so far as possible, to aliens. The directive was clearly a wartime measure.

The substance of the same memorandum was brought to the attention of President Truman by Attorney General Tom Clark in 1946. Clark recommended that the President's wiretap authority be used in peacetime because of the troubled international situation and an "increase in subversive activity here at home." Clark took the liberty of extending the scope to ordinary criminal cases "where human life is in jeopardy." [36] Twenty years later, President Johnson, ostensibly because of his concern about the misuse of wiretapping and its potential for violations of privacy, set standards for its use which, while cautionary in requiring the Attorney General's approval for the use of telephonic taps, affirmed wiretapping and other means of electronic surveillance for national security purposes. There were

[36] Some of this material is to be found in the Appendix to the federal court's opinion, *United States v. United States District Court*, 444 F. 2d 651, 669–671 (6th Cir., 1971). A suggestion that Attorney General Tom Clark omitted some of President Roosevelt's self-imposed restrictions without informing President Truman of the implications is found by comparing Roosevelt's "Memorandum for the Attorney General," May 21, 1940, with "Attorney General Clark to the President," July 17, 1946 (*Harry S. Truman Library Files*). See also "National Security," *Harvard Law Review*, LXXXV (1972), 1250–1252. Wiretaps were viewed by the executive as intelligence-gathering devices, not as the principal means for gathering evidence, since the statutes still precluded "divulgence," including divulgence of the information as evidence in the courts.

no clear specifications about the meaning of "national security," however.[37]

The first opportunity grasped fully by an administration to spell out a theory of presidential power and electronic surveillance for domestic "subversion" was occasioned by national unrest over the Vietnam war in the early 1970's. The theory appeared in capsule form in arguments before the federal courts in *United States v. United States District Court.*[38] The Nixon administration was resisting a court-ordered disclosure of wiretap information demanded by the defense in a case alleging a domestic conspiracy to bomb, and the actual bombing of, a CIA office in Ann Arbor, Michigan. The conversations in question had been monitored by the government without meeting the Fourth Amendment charge that a warrant be obtained and that probable cause be judicially established.

The government's position was that there are constitutionally allowable exceptions to the warrant requirements specified in the Fourth Amendment. In this

[37] Johnson's directive is cited in 444 F. 2d 670–671; for the Kennedy experience see Victor S. Navasky, *Kennedy Justice* (New York, 1971), 72–95, 135–155. For the widespread misuse of this power by every President since Franklin D. Roosevelt, see the details of the report by the Senate Select Committee on Intelligence Activities in *Congressional Quarterly*, XXXIV (1976), 1019–1025, 1111–1114.

[38] *Brief for the Petitioner, United States v. District Court*. See "*United States v. United States District Court:* Warrantless Wiretapping Surveillances and the 'National Security,'" *University of Pittsburgh Law Review*, XXXIII (1972), 573–588; and Charles R. Nesson, "Aspects of the Executive's Power Over National Security Matters: Secrecy Classification and Foreign Intelligence," *Indiana Law Journal*, XLIX (1974), 399–421.

instance the exception was governed by the President's power as commander in chief and chief executive to safeguard national security by gathering so-called preventive intelligence about dissident groups. The government argued that because the Fourth Amendment prohibits only "unreasonable" searches and seizures, the peculiar circumstances of national security made some procedures reasonable which under other circumstances would be constitutionally unacceptable. Quite apart from reserving to the President a "unique" responsibility in the national security field, there were immediate practical considerations, according to the government, which made surveillance reasonable under the Fourth Amendment. For example, it was asserted that the probable-cause requirement did not have to be met, because the government's activities were essentially investigatory probes into future, and not always predictable, disorders. In such instances probable cause would be difficult if not impossible to prove; conversely, by the time probable cause might be established a violent step may have been taken and the damage done. As for the warrant procedures themselves, they would require judges to make delicate estimates regarding national security, a subject which was inappropriate to the judicial function and well beyond judicial expertise. If there had ever been any doubt about presidential authority, the government reasoned that Congress had settled the question in the Omnibus Crime Control and Safe Streets Act by refusing to include national security matters among the normal criminal categories requiring warrants and the establishment of probable cause.

It followed that the balancing of the competing values

of the Fourth Amendment and the preservation of "the fabric of American society" from both foreign and domestic subversion was singularly executive in nature. Where, in the government's words, forces might be gathering to undermine the very "functioning of society," the executive must tip the balance toward the preservation of the system as a sovereign entity unrestrained by customary constitutional limitations:

> The President, in his dual role as Commander in Chief of the armed forces and Chief Executive, possesses . . . serious power and responsibility [to safeguard] the nation against those who would subvert the Government by unlawful means. This power is the historical power of the sovereign to preserve itself.[39]

To meet this responsibility, and because there was no viable distinction between domestic and foreign threats, the government concluded that the President has the authority "to maintain our on-going intelligence apparatus necessary to deal with those forces, whether foreign or domestic, which threaten the national security."[40] National security was thus domesticated.

From the maelstrom created by such arguments, including Watergate itself, Congress launched in the mid-

[39] *Brief for the Petitioner, United States v. District Court*, 5–15; and the court quoting the government's *Memorandum of Law*, "The power at issue in this case is the inherent power of the President to safeguard the security of the nation" (444 F. 2d 651, 658). In the words of the Sixth Circuit Court of Appeals: "The sweep of the assertion of the Presidential power is both eloquent and breathtaking" (*ibid.*, 658).

[40] *Reply Brief for the United States, United States v. District Court*. See generally, "National Security," *Harvard Law Review*, LXXXV (1972), 1189–1245.

1970's a series of investigations into the misuse of investigative techniques, including electronic surveillance, against reputed domestic subversives by such agencies as the FBI, the CIA, the National Security Agency, the Department of Defense, and the White House.[41] Congress also considered extending the warrant requirement to all national security surveillance cases, while the Ford administration tried to initiate some policies of self-limitation within the executive branch.

Well before Congress began to investigate these matters actively, however, the Supreme Court stepped forward in 1972 with a decision which some authorities rank in importance with *Ex parte Milligan* and *Youngstown Sheet and Tube v. Sawyer*. Whether time will continue to place *United States v. District Court* [42] among that company is not certain, but because the Court invoked elements of both the separation of powers and the Bill of Rights as limitations on presidential authority in the national security field, it was a decision of considerable significance. Until the Supreme Court acted in *District Court*, both the courts and Congress had avoided interference with presidential use of electronic surveillance in

[41] Article II of the House impeachment charges against President Nixon concerned the misuse of surveillance, *Congressional Quarterly*, XXXII (1974), 2021. In the only case that reached the Supreme Court relating to the development of dossiers for domestic dissidents by the Department of Defense, the Court avoided the merits on technical grounds with the admonition that nothing in the holding could be "seen as giving any indication that actual or threatened injury by unlawful activities of the military would go unnoticed or unremedied" in a case properly before the Court. See *Laird v. Tatum*, 408 U.S. 1, 17 (1972).

[42] *United States v. United States District Court*, 407 U.S. 297 (1972).

the national security field. And, although the finding was a narrow one, i.e., that warrant procedures were required by the Constitution where purely domestic organizations are the target of investigation, the tone of the opinion put past assumptions about presidential discretion in serious question.

Justice Powell, speaking for a unanimous court, reasoned that neither the statutory language nor the legislative history of the Omnibus Crime Control Act would support the executive's claim that Congress had intended to recognize independent power in the executive to engage in electronic surveillance whenever and whereever a President said it was necessary. On that question, Powell said Congress had remained "neutral," intending only to leave presidential power where it had found it, that is, undefined. The Court thus was charged with examining *de novo* presidential power as it affected domestic organizations.

Powell affirmed the President's power under his Article II duty "to preserve, protect and defend" the government against those who would overthrow it by unlawful means. He conceded that in so doing a President may find it necessary to use electronic surveillance. But once the subjects are domestic entities the Fourth Amendment erects a barrier to protect the citizen's right to privacy. Moreover, because the very notion of national security can raise important issues of political free speech, quite apart from the Fourth Amendment, the First Amendment also casts a shadow over unrestricted discretion. When the Court balanced "the duty of Government to protect the domestic security, and the potential danger posed by unreasonable surveillance to individual privacy and free expression," it found that these rights could not be properly protected if surveillance were to be "conducted solely within the discretion of the executive branch." The judiciary must be an intervenor. The Court was not impressed by the government's reassurance that the executive, acting alone, would be responsible.

> The Fourth Amendment contemplates a prior judicial judgment [by a neutral and detached magistrate], not the risk that executive discretion may be reasonably exercised. This judicial role accords with our basic constitutional doctrine that individual freedoms will best be preserved through a separation of powers and division of functions among the different branches and levels of government.[43]

And in response to the government's contention that security matters are beyond judicial competence Powell remarked tartly, "If the threat is too subtle or complex for our senior law enforcement officers to convey its significance to a court, one may question whether there is probable cause for surveillance." [44]

The Court had made serious inroads into an all-encompassing national security formulation. In doing so it relied on judicial responsibility for the Bill of Rights. While inherent presidential power to use surveillance in situations more directly related to foreign relations was for the moment left untouched, its exercise against domestic entities was subject to prior judicial examination. The limitation, furthermore, was put on a constitutional footing, not the arguable exception the government seemed to find in the Omnibus Crime Control Act. In

[43] *Ibid.*, 317.   [44] *Ibid.*, 320.

sum, the President was not above the conventional procedures found in the fundamental law.[45]

Many questions remained about the scope of presidential power after *District Court*. Not the least among them was the continuing use by governmental agencies of unlawful surveillance of a kind which was beyond the case-by-case reach of judicial decisions.[46] A solution to this widespread problem lay with Congress and the executive, not with the judiciary. But even the judicial limitations, beyond the basic principles enunciated in *District Court*, required a further interpretation. For example, the Court had defined a domestic organization to signify a group "composed of citizens of the United States . . . which has no significant connection with a foreign power, its agents, or its agencies." The Court

[45] Justice Powell suggested that Congress might want to adjust the standards specified in the Omnibus Crime Control and Safe Streets Act for domestic security purposes. "It may be that Congress, for example, would judge that the application and affidavit showing probable cause need not follow the exact requirements [of the Act] but should allege other circumstances more appropriate to domestic security cases; that the request for prior court authorization could, in sensitive cases, be made to any member of a specifically designated court (e.g., the District Court for the District of Columbia or the Court of Appeals for the District of Columbia Circuit); and that the time and reporting requirements need not be so strict as those [in the Act]." *Ibid.*, 323.

[46] "Foreign Security Surveillance and the Fourth Amendment," *Harvard Law Review*, LXXXVII (1974), 995–997; Alan Meisel, "Political Surveillance and the Fourth Amendment, *University of Pittsburgh Law Review*, XXXV (1973), 53–71; John A. Merrigan, "Wiretapping in Domestic Security Cases," *Loyola Law Review*, XX (1974), 199–213; J. H. F. Shattuck, "National Security Wiretaps," *Criminal Law Bulletin*, XI (1975), 7–28. For guidelines and proposals by the Ford administration to govern surveillance, see *Congressional Quarterly*, XXXIV (1976), 417–420, 596.

admitted that there were difficulties in distinguishing between "domestic" and "foreign" organizations. It left it to the lower courts and another day to develop the distinction more clearly and to give a more functional meaning to a "significant connection." It also left unanswered whether a warrant would be required where foreign powers were actively or solely engaging in an activity of such a nature as to justify surveillance. However, an important constitutional protection had been imposed by the Supreme Court with an invitation for others in the judiciary and Congress to explore the question further.[47] At least, insofar as the judiciary could have an impact on the temptations of electronic convenience, unlimited presidential power in the search for "national security" information had been inhibited.

Governmental Secrecy and the Withholding of Information. Recent history has made it demonstrably clear

[47] In an important federal court of appeals decision regarding surveillance associated with threats and demonstrations by the Jewish Defense League against Soviet agencies in the United States, including the Soviet delegation to the United Nations, the court put a significant gloss on *District Court.* Judge Skelly Wright in *Zweibon v. Mitchell,* 516 F. 2d 594, 614 (D.C. Cir., 1975), concluded that merely because an activity "affected" foreign relations it could not escape the strictures of the Fourth Amendment. Basing his reasoning on *District Court,* he fashioned the rule that "a warrant must be obtained before a wiretap is installed on a domestic organization that is *neither the agent of nor acting in collaboration with a foreign power,* even if the surveillance is installed under presidential directive in the name of foreign intelligence gathering for protection of the national security." (Emphasis supplied.) But see, *United States v. Brown,* 484 F. 2d 418 (5th Cir., 1973); *United States v. Butenko,* 494 F. 2d 593 (3rd Cir., 1974). For an excellent discussion of the situation in the courts see Morton H. Halperin, "National Security and Civil Liberties," *Foreign Policy* (Winter, 1975–1976), 125–127.

that the withholding of information by the executive branch has both noble and ignoble purposes. The "secret" bombing of Cambodia (unknown to the American public and Congress but not to other agencies and foreign powers) and the selective secrecy in which the Watergate tapes were wrapped, by normal constitutional standards, are in the ignoble category. The protection of codes, details of pending negotiations with foreign powers, and internal advisory memoranda, together with a myriad of other presidential confidences, fall distinctly within the former. In justifying executive withholding of information, Presidents have referred to their constitutional powers, tradition and usage, as well as statutory recognition of their authority to keep state secrets inviolate.

In recent years, constitutional controversy has swirled around two interrelated assertions of such power: presidential authority to withhold information from the public at large, and the right to deny access to information to Congress and the judiciary. More specifically, the controversy has involved two analytically separable but practically related policies: secrecy classification, and executive privilege. And together with the issue of whether there should be access to information is the critical question of which institution is to be the ultimate arbiter of conflicting claims. The presidential position until the very end of the Nixon administration was that decisions as to the substance of what is withheld are presidential. Deference should always be given to national security needs as specified by the executive. Contending arguments reached a high point in intensity, if not lucidity, in briefs in two of the most famous Supreme

Court cases of the 1970's, the *Pentagon Papers Case* and *United States v. Nixon.* The arguments appeared in other forums as well: in executive representations before congressional committees, in other cases in the federal courts, and in public debate as policy developed and was applied.[48]

One source of presidential power to control the dissemination of information is found in the secrecy classification system. The key document is President Eisenhower's Executive Order 10501, which codified and broadened classification systems used by earlier Presidents. The executive order and its progeny are based on the Article II powers of the President, including his power as commander in chief and his responsibility to see to the faithful execution of the laws. The authority is supported by statutes which make it a crime for a federal employee to give certain types of information regarding national defense to unauthorized persons. The statutes purportedly affirm the President's independent power by implication. More pointedly, the Freedom of Information Act of 1966, which established procedures for broadening access to information held by the government, specifically excludes from disclosure information which is "required by Executive Order to be kept secret in the interest of the national defense or foreign policy." [49]

[48] See, for example, the invocation of executive privilege against Congress to protect intelligence documents, *Congressional Quarterly,* XXXIII (1975), 2589–2590; and the Ford administration's revised secrecy provisions, *ibid.,* XXXIV (1976), 417–420.

[49] "National Security," *Harvard Law Review,* LXXXV (1972), 1198–1199; and the Freedom of Information Act, *United States Code,* Title 5, sec. 552 (1970). For commentary on the 1974 amendments to the Act, see footnote 59, below.

Using these various sources of authority the executive branch has classified masses of material in the name of national security, even though the material may have no direct security implications. One result has been to deprive other institutions, public and private, of the best opportunity to engage effectively in public policy determination and evaluation.[50]

Whatever other motives history will assign to the self-help release of the Pentagon Papers by Daniel Ellsberg, certainly among them must have been the impulse to overcome the excessive use of secrecy regarding the Vietnam war and to counteract the manipulation by officials of information solely available to the executive. Whatever the merits of the release of the Papers, it is only necessary for present purposes to describe the theory of presidential power which was used to justify the government's request for a court injunction to prohibit their further publication.[51] The motion for the injunction brought the First Amendment presumption against prior restraint of publication by the press into

[50] Several attempts were made by formal executive action to revise the classification system and to make information in certain categories more available to the public. See "National Security," *Harvard Law Review*, LXXXV (1972), 1203–1205.

[51] The decision by the Supreme Court, which was to become known as the *Pentagon Papers Case*, is *New York Times v. United States*, 403 U.S. 713 (1971). The Pentagon Papers was popular nomenclature for the multivolume top-secret government study of the Vietnam war relating primarily to the Kennedy-Johnson period. For a thorough treatment of the issues, see Martin Shapiro, *The Pentagon Papers and The Courts* (San Francisco, 1972); and Sanford J. Unger, *The Papers and the Papers* (New York, 1972). The text is found in Neil Sheehen et al., *The Pentagon Papers* (New York, 1971).

conflict with the asserted needs of government secrecy. Thus, national security interests insinuated themselves into the legal right of the press to publish.

The day after the.publication of the first segment of the Pentagon Papers by the *New York Times,* and after seeking a voluntary agreement to cease further publication, the government sought its injunction. The government's case in the lower federal courts was based on prohibitions which it said were found in the Espionage Act and in the authorization to withhold information embodied in Executive Order 10501. The government also referred to its inherent power "to protect itself in its vital functions." [52]

The government had mixed success in the lower courts. In the United States District Court for the Southern District of New York, Judge Murray I. Gurfein reasoned that the sections of the Espionage Act which most clearly seemed to cover the Pentagon Papers situation did not reach actual "publication." Further, after *in camera* examination of the portions of the Papers not yet published, he found that while the documents might be embarrassing if published, they could not be said to "vitally affect the security of the nation" or present the possibility of irreparable injury which alone might justify prior restraint against publication.[53] When two separate

[52] Citing, among other authorities, *In re Debs,* 158 U.S. 564 (1895), and *United States Code,* Title 18, sec. 793. See James C. Goodale, *New York Times Company v. United States: A Documentary History* (New York, 1971), 658–659.

[53] For relevant portions of Judge Murray I. Gurfein's opinion see Goodale, 665–666. In another jurisdiction Judge Gerhard A. Gesell commented that there was a failure to show "an immediate, grave threat to the national security, which in close and narrowly

Courts of Appeals differed about the right of the government to prohibit publication, the Supreme Court accepted the case. At this stage the government abandoned the argument that there was a statutory basis for its action and rested the case squarely on the President's right to utilize his inherent powers, particularly those powers exemplified in Executive Order 10501, that the judiciary should exercise its independent powers to stop publications. The courts were to act as enforcers of the President's responsibility "to protect the nation against publication of information whose disclosures would endanger national security," and, by recognizing the President's obligation, determine that it outweighed First Amendment guarantees.[54] Moreover, the government's theory supposed that the judiciary would accept the executive assessment of the "immediacy and irreparable quality" of the national security threat in determining whether to enjoin publication. In such determination the burden of proof would lie against those who claimed the right to publish material classified secret by the executive branch under the President's inherent powers. In sum, the courts were to become the executors of the President's discretion.[55]

---

defined circumstances would justify prior restraint on publication." See *United States v. Washington Post*, 446 F. 2d. 1328, 1327 (D.C. Cir., 1971).

[54] Goodale, "Brief for the United States," 1172.

[55] The government brief, conveniently, and perhaps understandably, cut two ways: it was said that judges were not equipped to evaluate "national security" matters, but, equally, they could still use *in camera* proceedings to reassure themselves of the seriousness of the government's plea about national security. See generally, *ibid.*, 1161–1182.

The decision hurriedly handed down by the Supreme Court in response to this theory was truly a confusion of tongues.[56] The holding of the case was in a short *per curiam* opinion which spoke in the narrowest terms for the six-man majority; in addition each of the nine justices filed an opinion expressing his own views. The majority could agree on only one manifest proposition, that is, that any prior restraint on publication bears a heavy presumption against its validity and that the government bears a similarly heavy "burden for showing justification for the imposition of such restraint." Employing a preferred-position approach, four of those in the majority attempted to balance the government's interest in national security against the use of injunctive processes to limit freedom of the press. They concluded that the government had not met the heavy burden of proving necessity; however, they appeared to acknowledge that there might be occasions where prior restraint could be applied if Congress explicitly authorized it. Two members of the majority, Justices Black and Douglas, declined to engage in balancing and asserted that any prior restraint on publication was prohibited by the First Amendment.

The three members of the Court in dissent expressed strong reservations about deciding a case of such magnitude in a situation pressured by time and emotion. They

[56] *New York Times v. United States,* 403 U.S. 713 (1971). The first segments of the Pentagon Papers were published by the *New York Times* on June 13, 1971. The *Washington Post* published portions five days later. On June 15, the Justice Department sought an injunction to prevent publication. After consideration by the lower federal courts, argument was heard by the Supreme Court which handed down its decision on June 30, 17 days after the initial publication.

seemed to conclude that prior restraint was acceptable under some circumstances, while the constitutional issues should be allowed to season in the course of measured thought and argument in the lower courts. The rhetoric of their opinions, however, gives ample indication that, if they had reached the merits, secrecy would have outweighed a right to publication. As it was, Justice Harlan was the only dissenter to attempt to fashion a standard to justify prior restraint. He did so by referring to the sensitive nature of foreign affairs and the singular presidential responsibility for national security. The responsibility presumably gave the President the right to expect that the courts would use their injunctive power to stop publication of official secrets. The only inquiry that the judiciary could make, according to Justice Harlan, was whether the matter subject to prior restraint fell within "the compass of the President's foreign relations power." If so, the courts should not inquire further.

The "precipitate timetable," in the words of Justice Harlan, certainly contributed to the proliferation of opinions.[57] But there were other factors, not the least of which was the complexity of the issue itself and its newness to constitutional law. Divisions were exacerbated by constitutional sensitivity in weighing the protection of secret data against the First Amendment right to publish. Additionally, there were delicate questions of interpretation of statutes governing the release of secret informa-

---

[57] Only two or three were carefully reasoned. Justice Black reaffirmed the absolutist position which he had developed over the years. Justice Harlan, a very ill man writing his last opinion, did his best. But see, especially, Justice Marshall's thoughtful treatment (403 U.S. 713, 740–748).

tion as well as the legal issues associated with the strong medicine of the injunctive processes. Emotions about the Vietnam war seeped into many of the opinions, most particularly those written by Justice Black and Justice Blackmun, as did concern expressed by others about the mounting overclassification of documents. Although neither the justness of the war nor the wisdom of the security classification system were relevant to a decision on the merits, such considerations did arise peripherally and intensified divisions on the court.

Consequently, it is not surprising that the unsigned *per curiam* decision's "heavy burden" test is all that emerges as a commonly accepted standard. However, other possibilities surface in the majority opinions. The doctrinal glue which held the majority together was a mixture of First Amendment and separation of powers values. Viewing the case in this way, three members of the Court, while playing down First Amendment considerations, secured their finding in the separation of powers. They concluded that Congress had on at least two occasions considered making criminal sanctions available to punish the transmission or publication of state secrets; on each occasion, however, Congress had had specifically rejected the use of injunctions to prohibit publication. They suggested that if Congress had passed criminal statutes allowing prior restraint the court would have been confronted with an out-and-out First Amendment question. But, for the Court to interject its injunctive power and join with the President in upholding prior restraint on publication would, in the absence of such legislation, make the courts and the President, not Congress, the lawmakers. Thus the *Steel*

Seizure Case emerged as the controlling precedent, for there, too, Congress had specifically refused to give a President power which he later sought to use on his own authority.

The other three justices in the majority, while not ignoring the separation of powers argument, emphasized First Amendment considerations. Each suggested that even if Congress had passed legislation authorizing the use of injunctions against publication and had, consequently, accepted prior restraint, the legislation would have been unconstitutional. Seemingly, in a case where both the separation of powers and the First Amendment were at play, the majority was held together by the dual proposition that the Court would prohibit that which Congress could not authorize or, alternatively, that which Congress did not authorize. More definitively, the majority was bound together by a mutually accepted doctrine that prior restraint was suspect. It was suspect to the three in the majority because Congress had not authorized it; it was suspect to the remaining members of the majority because of the dangerous counterprecedent which it would establish against prevailing First Amendment values.

One authority has commented that quite apart from the decision on the merits, *New York Times v. United States* has an "aura of importance which goes beyond the profile of technical doctrine" in contributing to the First Amendment tradition.[58] A part of that aura, also, was

[58] Harry Kalven, Jr., "Even When a Nation Is At War," *Harvard Law Review*, LXXXV (1971), 26. See especially, Peter D. Junger, "Down Memory Lane: The Case of the Pentagon Papers," *Case Western Reserve Law Review*, XXIII (1971), 3–75; Louis

the Court's refusal to render judicial assistance to a President attempting to exercise inherent powers. But of equal importance was the acceptance of a judicial role in measuring the scope of the President's power over national security, a role encouraged by the Court's First Amendment activism as well as precedential force and reasoning characterized by the *Steel Seizure Case*. The Court assumed, if only for the moment, that even in sensitive national security matters it was the final monitor of constitutional limitations.[59]

Henkin, "The Right to Know and the Duty to Withhold: The Case of the Pentagon Papers, *University of Pennsylvania Law Review*, CXX (1971), 271–280; Alexander M. Bickel, *The Morality of Consent* (New York, 1975), 78–82.

[59] The federal criminal laws for espionage, theft, and conspiracy, of course, remained intact, and Daniel Ellsberg was indicted under these statutes. He was granted a mistrial because of unlawful governmental activities in gathering evidence. For legislation which attempted to incorporate and broaden these restrictions, in what some have called the American equivalent of the British Official Secrets Act, see *Congressional Quarterly*, XXXIII (1975), 2388. The judicial treatment of other secrecy issues, not involving prior restraint, is found in supportive statutory interpretations of the national security exception for the release of information under the Freedom of Information Act (*United States Code*, Title 5, sec. 552 [1970]) in *Environmental Protection Agency v. Mink*, 410 U.S. 73 (1973); and *Epstein v. Resor*, 421 F. 2d 930 (9th Cir., 1970) and, generally, "The Freedom of Information Act: A Seven-Year Assessment," *Columbia Law Review*, LXXIV (1974), 895–959. The Act was amended in 1974 to allow *in camera* judicial participation to determine whether a claim of national security is justified and to review information in order to determine whether it is properly classified. See "Freedom of Information Act—Procedural Requirements Amended," *Tulane Law Review*, XLIX (1975), 678–685 (1975); and John F. Murphy, 'Knowledge Is Power: Foreign Policy and Information Interchange Among Congress, the Executive Branch,

The withholding of information took on a different character three years later when it became associated with the abuses of presidential power in the Watergate cover-up by the President and his associates and in the Supreme Court's decision in *United States v. Nixon*.[60] The case involved an appeal to vacate an order by Judge John Sirica of the federal District Court for the District of Columbia requiring the President to release tapes and transcripts of sixty-four White House conversations among persons specified as co-conspirators, including the President, for use in the Watergate cover-up trial. The

and the Public," *Tulane Law Review*, XLIX (1975), 505–554. A close parallel to the *Pentagon Papers Case* emerged when a past employee of the CIA was enjoined by the courts from publishing an exposé of the agency before submitting the manuscript for agency review and making certain deletions. In proceedings before the Court of Appeals for the Fourth Circuit in *United States v. Marchetti, New York Times v. United States* was referred to only briefly in a footnote. The case is arguably distinguishable since the author, when employed by the CIA, had signed an agreement pledging himself to secrecy. The court found the agreement constitutional. See *United States v. Marchetti*, 466 F. 2d 1309 (4th Cir., 1972), cert. denied, 409 U.S. 1063 (1972); and *Alfred A. Knopf Inc. v. Colby*, 509 F. 2d 1362 (4th Cir., 1975), cert. denied, 422 U.S. 1049 (1975).

   [60] *United States v. Nixon*, 418 U.S. 683 (1974). The decision reached only executive privilege as it related to the judiciary and not presidential power to withhold from Congress. Court decisions in that controversial area are virtually nonexistent; but see *Senate Select Committee v. Nixon*, 370 F. Supp. 521 (1974). See *Congressional Quarterly*, XXXIII (1975), 2097–2099, for congressional proposals for dealing with executive privilege in this realm, and the *New York Times*, December 15, 1975, for President Ford's invocation of executive privilege against the efforts by Congress to extract information from Secretary of State Kissinger regarding covert activities abroad. A possible court test was narrowly avoided by compromise.

defendants included a past Attorney General, John Mitchell, and members of the White House staff, John Ehrlichman, H. R. Haldeman, and Charles Colson. All were charged with obstruction of justice and conspiracy to defraud the United States. The President resisted on grounds of executive privilege.

Unlike the *Pentagon Papers Case* evidence in a criminal proceeding was at issue, not the First Amendment. But still brooding in the background was the constitutional principle on which the President placed his primary reliance, the separation of powers. In contrast to the theory of presidential power put forward in the *Pentagon Papers Case*, the courts were not to be participating agents in support of the independent powers of the President to withhold information; they were said to have no role at all. Not only was the President, in this formulation, immune from court processes, but it was asserted that he alone could determine what information was privileged and what could thus properly be withheld. The position was spelled out most elaborately by the President in stratagems and arguments marking resistance to the release of the White House tapes. At various stages there was a national security component. That a theory of privilege, which included a national security privilege, might have untoward domestic effects is evidenced by its use. As many surmised at the time, and, as subsequent release of other tapes revealed, the claim was tainted. The following exchange regarding strategy for dealing with the Watergate break-in, is indicative:

PRESIDENT: How you keep it out, I don't know. You can't keep it out if Hunt talks . . .

190

JOHN DEAN: You might put it on a national security grounds basis.

PRESIDENT: National security. We had to get information for national security grounds. . . . With the bombing coming out and everything coming out, the whole thing was national security.

JOHN DEAN: I think we could get by on that.[61]

Before the courts the President's counsel stood on higher and more meritorious grounds, as had government counsel in earlier cases involving executive privilege.[62] The central issue was, Who was to decide what could be held privileged, whether or not on grounds of national security? It was stated in argument that executive privilege had been used since the early days of the Republic, but that it had taken on special institutional force during the Eisenhower administration when it was invoked against the McCarthy investigations and other congressional inquiries. Since the privilege was based on the separation of powers and the President's inherent powers, it guaranteed a similar immunity from judicial inquiries. Behind the constitutional principle was the practical claim that there was a profound administrative need to maintain confidence and encourage candor within the executive branch if the President was to exercise his powers effectively in domestic and foreign affairs.

[61] Cited in Berger, "The Incarnation of Executive Privilege," *UCLA Law Review,* XXII (1974), 27. And see *The White House Transcripts* (Bantam edition, 1974), 163.

[62] See especially *United States v. Reynolds,* 345 U.S. 1 (1952). For a complete description of the government's secrecy arguments and the judiciary's partial rejection of them, see the lower court decision in *Reynolds v. United States,* 192 F. 2d 987 (3rd Cir., 1951).

As for national security, that component of the executive privilege argument loomed larger in the earlier phases of the movement of *United States v. Nixon* through the courts than it did during the final presentation of the President's case before the Supreme Court. Doubtless the argument was ultimately discarded because of its implausibility in the Watergate context, particularly as the selective release of some of the tapes by the President indicated that something else was afoot. Moreover, the national security contention may have been played down in the final briefs before the Supreme Court because of calculations of what the Court would not accept and its failure to impress in the lower courts. The President elected to take his final stand on a claim of "generalized" or absolute privilege—which was beyond judicial scrutiny. However, a trace of national security was still in evidence. The President's counsel, referring to the President's "sole discretion to decide what Presidential communications he will disclose" elaborated further:

Of course, international relations and national defense have very special claims to secrecy, but the importance of the President being able to speak with advisers "freely, frankly, and in confidence" is not confined to those matters. It is just as essential that the President be able to talk openly with his advisers about domestic issues. . . . The wisdom that free discussion provides is as vital in fighting inflation, choosing Supreme Court Justices, deciding whether to veto a large spending bill, and dealing with the myriad other important questions that the President must confront in his roles as Chief of State and Chief Executive, as it is when he is acting as Chief Diplomat or as Commander-in-Chief. . . . It is true that the President has more substantive freedom to act in foreign and military affairs than he does in domestic affairs, but his need for candid advice is no different in the one situation than in the other.[63]

The argument, presumably, was designed to convince the Justices that where executive privilege was in question presidential roles could not be differentiated. But the mention of national security concerns suggested that the ultimate privilege over state secrets cast a protective shadow over executive privilege exercised elsewhere. The main body of the opinion, in *United States v. Nixon*, disposed of the President's claim of a generalized, absolute privilege for all presidential communications against judicial inquiry. In his opinion for a unanimous Court, Chief Justice Warren E. Burger denied that there was an unquestionable privilege protecting all presidential communications from the reach of courts of law. Citing *Marbury v. Madison*, among other cases,[64] Burger said it was well established that it was the duty of the judiciary to interpret the law and to pass on the legitimacy of the use of power by other branches. Such a duty included defining the scope of executive privilege. In the first judicial statement of its kind, the court stated unambiguously that there was an executive privilege.

[63] "Brief for the Respondent, Richard M. Nixon, President of the United States," in Leon Friedman, ed., *United States v. Nixon: The President Before the Supreme Court* (New York, 1974), 361–362 *et. seq.*

[64] 1 Cranch 137 (1803). The other precedents which played leading roles were *Youngstown Sheet and Tube v. Sawyer*, 343 U.S. 579 (1952); *Powell v. McCormack*, 395 U.S. 486 (1969); *Branzburg v. Hayes*, 408 U.S. 665 (1972); and *United States v. Burr*, 25 Fed. Cas. 187 (1807).

Moreover, it was especially weighted. There was a presumptive privilege for the confidentiality of all presidential communications, a privilege "fundamental to the operation of the government and inextricably rooted in the separation of powers." But it was not unqualified. The privilege must give way to the rule of law. More specifically, it must be weighed against the Fifth and Sixth Amendment protections of the Bill of Rights, balancing "the importance of the general privilege of confidentiality of presidential communications in performance of his responsibilities against the inroads of such a privilege on the fair administration of criminal justice." In striking the balance, the Court not only concluded that the tapes and documents should be released to the lower courts, but that executive privilege could not immunize a President from judicial proceedings, including judicial orders.

Neither the doctrine of separation of powers, nor the need for confidentiality of high level communications, without more, can sustain an absolute, unqualified presidential privilege of immunity from judicial process under all circumstances.[65]

Even though the Court ruled against the President, in dicta which future Presidents will no doubt rely upon, the Court touched upon a possible exception for military, diplomatic, or sensitive national security documents. The Court suggested that such matters may not be subject to *in camera* inspection by federal judges, for they are in a realm where courts "have traditionally shown the utmost deference to presidential responsibilities."[66] But there

[65] *United States v. Nixon*, 418 U.S. 683, 706.
[66] *United States v. Nixon*, 418 U.S. 683, 710–711, citing *C. & S. Air Lines v. Waterman*, 333 U.S. 103 (1948), and *United*

was enough in the basic holding of the Court—that the President is subject to law—together with uncertainties about the force of the precedents mentioned and inconsistencies in the decision itself to question that there was any measured intention to place an absolute bar on such matters.[67] At most, the Court seemed to be saying that national security would weigh heavily in balancing executive privilege against a competing constitutional claim.

The legacy of the opinion is that the President is under law. The Supreme Court had established a judicial role in determining the validity of a claim of executive privilege and, when it was properly invoked, even as to

---

States v. Reynolds, 345 U.S. 1 (1952). These precedents, cited in dicta in *Nixon,* do not seem apposite or unambiguous. Both were civil cases. And, further, the language of *Reynolds* includes the statement, "The rationale of the criminal case is that, since the government which prosecutes an accused also has the duty to see that justice is done, it is unconscionable to allow it to undertake prosecution and then invoke its governmental privileges to deprive the accused of anything which might be material to his defense," adding, "judicial control over the evidence in a case cannot be abdicated to the caprice of executive officers." 345 U.S. 1, 9–10, 12. Moreover, a footnote in *United States v. Nixon,* 418 U.S. 683, 715, fn. 21, seems to contradict dicta elsewhere in the case regarding *in camera* inspection of documents with national security implications, for the lower court was ordered to look at such documents.

[67] See Paul A. Freund, "On Presidential Privilege," *Harvard Law Review,* LXXXVIII (1974), 32–34; Kenneth L. Karst and Harold W. Horowitz, "Presidential Prerogative and Judicial Review," *UCLA Law Review,* XXII (1974), 64. Compare Raoul Berger, "The Incarnation of Executive Privilege," *UCLA Law Review,* XXII (1974), 26–29. See also William Van Alstyne, "A Political and Constitutional Review of *United States v. Nixon,*" *UCLA Law Review,* XXII (1974), 117–118.

the presidency. At the same time the Court secured in constitutional law the notion of a presumptive privilege for presidential communications as a fundamental need for the efficient administration of the presidency.

In some respects *United States v. Nixon* was a narrow decision for it dealt only with the withholding of information in the setting of a criminal trial. But, more broadly, it extended further the range of judicial authority. As others have described its significance:

> The lasting importance of the decision—apart from its "affirmative pregnants" about executive privilege—would seem to lie at the level of abstraction represented by the . . . use of the *Youngstown* precedent. Justice Jackson, in his eloquent *Youngstown* concurrence, said: "With all its defect, delays and inconveniences, men have discovered no technique for long preserving free government except that the Executive be under the law. . . ." In *United States v. Nixon,* the most important thing the Court did was to reaffirm that truth by subjecting the President's claim of discretionary power to the limits of law.[68]

Just as profoundly, the decision, which itself helped to trigger the President's resignation, contributed notably to redress the constitutional balance which had experienced such severe strain in the preceding years.

The Use of Troops during
Domestic Disturbances

The assertions of presidential authority discussed above came to be viewed by the executive as part of the

[68] Karst and Horowitz, "Presidential Prerogative," *UCLA Law Review*, XXII (1974), 67.

day-to-day management of the office. Given the unremitting demands of national security, such assertions were not considered extraordinary in the scheme of things, at least not until the courts or Congress spoke. In some executive circles the use of electronic surveillance, the exercise of government secrecy policy, and the assertion of executive privilege were, before the 1970's, considered to be unexceptional behavior.

What distinguishes such interpretations of executive power from the claimed emergency power to use troops in domestic situations is that the latter was considered an exception to the norm, an exertion of executive power in the face of extraordinary events, temporary in nature, oriented toward the solution of immediate, if not transient, problems, and momentary in its impact. In theory, troops were to be used only in the event of severe disruption, in order to return the system to a state of orderly functioning. But domestic pressures in the last quarter of a century helped to bring about subtle changes in the use of troops in the domestic sphere and, as a result, an interpretive broadening of presidential power.

Apart from any autonomous presidential power to use troops to protect "the peace of the United States," which reputedly is found in a broad interpretation of the Constitution in such cases as *In re Debs, In re Neagle,* and *Ex parte Siebold,*[69] a firm statutory basis for presidential use of force domestically has existed since the early years of the Republic. Whether the statutes prohibit any independent exercise of power by the President is an unsettled question. There is no doubt, however, that the

[69] 158 U.S. 564 (1895); 135 U.S. 1 (1890); 100 U.S. 371 (1879). The cases are discussed by Rossiter at pp. 40–41 above.

statutes authorize the use of presidential power, if they do not strictly confine it.

There are several statutes which deal directly with presidential power to use troops to implement a President's role as commander in chief and chief executive. The principal statutes appear as Sections 331, 332, 333, and 334 of the United States Code.[70] Section 331 authorizes the President to respond to a state's request for armed forces to put down an "insurrection" against the state government. Section 332 authorizes the President to use troops when he finds that there are unlawful obstructions, combinations, assemblages, or rebellion against the authority of the United States which make it "impracticable" to enforce federal law by the ordinary course of judicial proceedings. Section 333 allows the President to take measures, including the use of armed force, to suppress any "insurrection, domestic violence, unlawful combination, or conspiracy" if the execution of either state or federal law is hindered in a manner that deprives a person or a class of persons of a constitutional right, or if the activity obstructs the execution of the

[70] *United States Code*, Title 10, secs. 331–334 (1970); *United States Code*, Title 18, sec. 1385 (1970) prohibits the use of the Army or the Air Force as a *posse comitatus*. The emphasis on federal statutes here does not overlook the fact that the states have the power to use the National Guard and other force to deal with civil disturbances. Governors have used such force on many occasions in recent years. On this general topic see the excellent treatment by Joseph W. Bishop Jr., *Justice Under Fire: A Study of Military Law* (New York, 1974), chap. 6; and "A Comprehensive Study of the Use of Military Troops in Civil Disorder," *University of Colorado Law Review*, XLIII (1972), 399–446; Dominic Campesi, "Honored in the Breach: Presidential Authority to Execute the Laws with Military Force, *Yale Law Journal*, LXXXIII

laws "or impedes the course of justice" of federal law. This section does not require that a state request assistance or agree that force be used. In fact, originally, one of the purposes of the section was to allow the use of force when a state was either unable or unwilling to enforce federal law within its borders. Section 334 requires the President to issue a proclamation ordering the dispersal of "insurgents" before he uses troops under Title 10 authority. Presidents have also relied in recent years upon House Joint Resolution 1292, passed in 1968, which allows the Secret Service to request assistance from the armed forces in the performance of its duties, as well as the Economy Act of 1932.[71]

These statutes have been used on several occasions

(1973), 130–152 (hereinafter cited as Campesi, "Honored in The Breach"). See also *Report of the Advisory Commission on Civil Disorders* (Bantam, ed.; New York, 1968), 497, 532–533.

[71] 82 *Stat.* 170 (1968); *United States Code,* Title 31, sec. 686 (1970). These statutes have been viewed by some as exceptions to the Posse Comitatus Act (*United States Code,* Title 18, sec. 1385 [1970]) which by inference prohibits the use of troops to aid in the enforcement of local or federal law without a proclamation invoking authority under *United States Code,* Title 10, secs. 331–334 (1970); that is, it is designed to prevent the casual use of troops by local or federal law-enforcement officers either as a posse comitatus or unless specifically authorized by statute. The original purpose of the Act was to restrict the use of federal troops by United States marshals, *inter alia,* to enforce the Reconstruction Acts. The Act reads, "Whoever, except in cases and under circumstances expressly authorized by the Constitution or Act of Congress, willfully uses any part of the Army or Air Force as a posse comitatus or otherwise to execute the laws shall be fined not more than $10,000 or imprisoned not more than two years, or both." See Campesi, 'Honored in the Breach," 141–149; David E. Engdahl, "The New Civil Disturbance Regulations: The Threat of Military Intervention," *Indiana Law Journal,* XLIX

since 1950 by Presidents to enforce the law, put down civil disturbances, or to assure the "normal" functioning of the government. President Johnson, for example, relied upon Section 331 for the use of troops in the 1967 riots in Detroit and during the riots following the assassination of Martin Luther King in 1968. Section 333 was used during the Washington riots of the same year. Sections 332 and 334 provided the principal statutory base for the use of troops by President Eisenhower to enforce a federal court order regarding school desegregation over a governor's opposition in Little Rock in 1957. President Kennedy utilized the same sections to federalize the National Guard and to send troops to enforce federal court desegregation orders affecting the University of Mississippi and the University of Alabama. Kennedy also positioned troops at military bases near Birmingham during the civil rights demonstrations there in 1963, but the troops were never used.[72] In the late 1960's some 6,000 troops were used to assist the Secret Service in law enforcement and covert intelligence mis-

(1974), 581–617, 601; and Clarence I. Meeks, "Illegal Law Enforcement: Aiding Civil Authorities in Violation of the Posse Comitatus Act," *Military Law Journal*, LXX (1975), 83–136.

[72] The state of Alabama contested his authority to do so, but the Supreme Court avoided the issue in *Alabama v. United States*, 373 U.S. 545 (1963), saying that the action of the President was "merely preparatory" in making ready to use troops under Section 333, and therefore there was no basis for relief. The Kennedy administration's reluctance to use troops for this purpose was expressed by Deputy Attorney General Nicholas Katzenbach. He saw sections 332–334 as limited to situations where there had been a "complete breakdown" of law and order that could not be handled by local authorities. See "Riot Control and the Use of Federal Troops," *Harvard Law Review*, LXXXI (1968), 649, 650.

sions during the Democratic National Convention and during both of President Nixon's inaugurals. Troops were also dispatched to guard the White House during antiwar demonstrations in 1969, 1970, and 1971, and to the Democratic and Republican National Conventions in 1972.[73]

What characterized the actual or contemplated use of troops during the Nixon years—and to some extent in the last years of the Johnson administration—was an ample, even strained, reading of the statutes. When this penchant for loose statutory construction was combined with a reaffirmation of inherent presidential power it provided the opportunity for the possible use of federal troops in situations where past practice and interpretation had presupposed that other law-enforcement measures were to be used. For example, it seemed to be the legislative understanding that House Joint Resolution 1292, which authorized armed-forces support for the Secret Service in fulfilling its duties, was meant to signify logistical support—communications and the like—not the actual use of troops. And it required considerable interpretive flexibility to find authorization for the use of troops in the following words in the Economy Act:

Any executive department . . . of the Government . . . may place orders with any other such department . . . for materials, supplies, equipment, work, or services, of any kind that such requisitioned Federal agency may be in a position to supply or equipped to render.[74]

[73] Campesi. "Honored in the Breach," 130, 146.

[74] Ibid., 144–145; United States Code, Title 31, sec. 686 (1970). See also Engdahl, "The New Civil Disturbance Regulations," 605.

201

Yet President Nixon relied on the Economy Act to place troops on domestic air carriers to prevent high-jacking and under the same expansive authority used troops to process the mail during the postal strike in New York City.

But above all, the Nixon administration's recodified Civil Disturbance Regulations, designed to implement the civil disturbance sections of the United States Code and the President's Article II powers, put a new gloss on presidential discretion. The regulations do not always seem to sit squarely on the statutes. By way of illustration, the regulations seem to presume that Sections 331–334 of Title 10 of the United States Code authorize "Federal action, including the use of military forces, to protect Federal property and Federal governmental functions," while the same regulation, designated as "the Emergency Authority" states even more broadly:

Prompt and vigorous Federal action, including use of military forces, to prevent loss of life and wanton destruction of property and to restore governmental functioning and public order, when sudden and unexpected civil disturbances, disasters, or calamities seriously endanger life and property and disrupt normal governmental functions to such an extent that duly constituted local authorities are unable to control the situations.[75]

[75] In one instance the new regulations seem to interpret legislation which reads "laws of that State, and of the United States within that State" to mean "execution of State or Federal law," thus suggesting that intervention is possible when only state laws are being violated, an interpretation which flies in the face of the express intent of Congress. Engdahl, "The New Civil Disturbance Regulations," 609–610; and Campesi, "Honored in the Breach," 130.

This is lush growth indeed from the infertile ground of the statutes. So is the wording which says that the authority for use of troops is based on the "inherent legal right of the U.S. Government—a sovereign national entity under the Federal Constitution—to insure the preservation of public order and the carrying out of governmental operations within its territorial limits, by force if necessary.[76] So also are the suppositions implicit in the revised regulations that no local request for assistance is required, that federal property and federal law do not have to be involved, and that prepositioning of troops as well as the preventive gathering of intelligence by the armed forces are acceptable modes of procedure.[77] The language of the revised regulations, in literal meaning as well as in tone, clearly presumes that the President has an independent source of authority and that the statutes are to be viewed as alternative paths for the exercise of power, not as restrictions on its use. If there could be any doubt that the Nixon administration meant what it said, the administration's response to the 1971 May Day disturbances in Washington surely dispelled them. When queried about the authority for the use of troops on that occasion the administration replied:

The President has the inherent power and the duty under the Constitution as Chief Executive to insure the continued functioning of the government and to protect government property. The troops were used to insure that federal employees had access to their places of employment so that

[76] Engdahl, "The New Civil Disturbance Regulations," 607–608.
[77] Ibid. pp. 607–609, 614–615. See Laird v. Tatum, 408 U.S. 1 (1972); but compare, Gilligan v. Morgan, 413 U.S. 1 (1973).

203

they could carry on the government's work and to protect the government's property.[78]

There is no doubt that the revised regulations were inspired in part by the unparalleled stress put on government operations by such incidents as the May Day antiwar demonstrations. It is equally true, whatever the necessity, that the revisions were designed to systematize broadened presidential discretion by codified executive definition of the occasions when military force might be used, a codification which went beyond past statutory, if not constitutional, understanding.

The revised regulations have not been put to direct judicial test, nor has Congress seen fit to clarify the law by legislation.[79] The Supreme Court has given some at-

[78] Harold W. Chase and Craig R. Ducat, *Corwin's, The Constitution and What It Means Today* (Princeton, 1973 ed.), 150. For one account of the event, see Michael S. Wald, "Mayday Revisited," Parts I and II, *Criminal Law Bulletin*, X (1974), 377–436, 516–543. See also *Sullivan v. Murphy*, 478 F. 2d 938 (D.C. Cir., 1973), for judicial rejection of the disturbance procedures.

[79] Congress has studied intensively, and legislated to a lesser extent, to place some control over the broader emergency powers which have accumulated at least since the Depression years. The accumulation is represented by some 470 statutes and hundreds of executive orders and includes executive power to seize commodities, to organize and control industrial production, and to commandeer communications facilities in time of proclaimed emergency. *Hearings Before the Special Committee on the Termination of the National Emergency*, Senate, 93rd Cong., 1st Sess. (1973), Parts I, II, III; and the *Report* of the same committee, *Senate Report* No. 93–549 (1973). For congressional action see *Congressional Quarterly*, XXXVII (1975), 1958; and Richard P. Longaker, "Emergency Detention: The Generation Gap, 1950–1971," *Western Political Quarterly*, XXVII (1974), 395–408.

tention to the use of troops in domestic disturbances over the years, but it has done so with a caution appropriate to the dangers inherent in judicial entanglement in judgments about the propriety of the use of force or in speculation about the degree of force needed to prevent anticipated disturbances. And with possibly two or three exceptions the cases, as noted below, have dealt with the use of troops by state executives, thus leaving some uncertainty as to analogous exercises of power by the commander in chief. However, there is nothing in the decisions to prevent a willing Court from applying the precedents at the federal level.[80]

For many years one standard of review was represented by *Moyer v. Peabody*, in a decision rendered by the Supreme Court in 1909. During a labor dispute in Colorado the governor had proclaimed martial law and authorized the use of troops to put down violence. The Court concluded that the governor's determination of necessity as well as the means used to restore order were conclusive on the courts. The judiciary would not intervene as long as the action was taken in "good faith."[81]

[80] Note that in *Sterling v. Constantine*, 287 U.S. 378, 399 (1932), the Court in restricting the powers of a state executive makes parallel reference to the presidential power. *Ex parte Milligan*, 4 Wall. 2 (1866), and *Duncan v. Kahanomoku*, 327 U.S. 304 (1946), imply limits and, in other settings *Martin v. Mott*, 12 Wheat. 19 (1927), *Luther v. Borden*, 7 How. 1 (1849), and *Korematsu v. United States*, 323 U.S. 214 (1944) do not. See Rossiter, pp. 14–17, above. And, generally, "A Comprehensive Study of the Use of Military Troops in Civil Disorders," *University of Colorado Law Review*, XLIII (1972), 422–430. For comment, see "Martial Law," *Southern California Law Review*, XLII (1969), 546–577; and "Riot Control and the Use of Federal Troop," *Harvard Law Review*, LXXXI (1968), 638–652.

[81] *Moyer v. Peabody*, 212 U.S. 78, 85 (1909).

The doctrine prevailed until the mid-1930's, when the Court, in *Sterling v. Constantin,* responding to the use of troops by the governor of Texas to control the production of oil and the purported violence arising from the production controls, concluded that the governor had absolute discretion to declare an emergency and to determine the exigency for the use of troops. But the Court declared that the measures taken were themselves reviewable. In the words of Chief Justice Charles Evans Hughes, "What are the limits of military discretion, and whether they have been overstepped in a particular case, are judicial questions." [82] The Court determined that the measures taken were not directly related to quelling disorder.

Sterling was an important step forward, for it did away with the apparent absolutism of the *Moyer* principle, while declaring more broadly that the use of military force could not escape constitutional limitations and judicial review. Implicit in the Court's holding was the assertion of civilian control, including control by an independent judiciary, over the use of military force domestically. There was, however, a distinct tension between the acceptance of an executive's declaration of "necessity" and judicial evaluation of the "means" used, particularly when the presumption in lower-court opinions was more often than not weighted toward acceptance of executive assessments of both the need and the means.

In any event, the issue, except in such wartime cases as *Korematsu v. United States* and *Duncan v. Kahanamoku,* did not find its way to the Supreme Court again until the

[82] *Sterling v. Constantin,* 287 U.S. 378, 399–401 (1932).

1970's in *Scheur v. Rhodes.*[83] *Scheur* was one of several cases emerging from the Kent State tragedy in 1971 when several students were killed by National Guard troops dispatched by the governor of Ohio. In considering the technical legal issues which had been presented to it, the Court put an important gloss on *Sterling* when it stated that, while a declaration of emergency by an executive is entitled to great weight, it is not conclusive and, citing *Sterling*, neither can the measures used be free from judicial review. Thus, executive discretion in the declaration, the finding of necessity, and the measures used, were, according to Chief Justice Burger subject to judicial review.

The Court had squared its own precedents and, in its rhetoric, had attested significantly to both civilian control over the military and access to judicial review. *Scheur* did not seem to leave room for injunctive prohibitions on executive initiatives nor, in the nature of urgent and confused emergency situations and customary pru-

[83] 416 U.S. 232 (1974) in which the principal question was the extent of executive immunity from action under the Civil Rights Act of 1871, an issue not of immediate relevance here. In another case growing out of the Kent State tragedy the Supreme Court a year before found that the requested use of an injunction to prohibit future premature use of allegedly poorly trained National Guardsmen was a nonjusticiable political question vested in the other branches and was beyond judicial competence. *Gilligan v. Morgan*, 413 U.S. 1 (1973). It is not without significance that the Court emphasized (as it did also in *Scheur v. Rhodes*, 416 U.S. 232) that "It should be clear that we neither hold nor imply that the conduct of the National Guard is always beyond judicial review or that there may not be accountability in a judicial forum for violations of law or for specific unlawful conduct by military personnel whether by way of damages or injunctive relief." 413 U.S. 1, 10–11.

dential deference to the executive, could the judiciary be expected to intervene readily. Nonetheless, there was a fresh assumption that executive discretion in domestic emergencies was not untrammeled and was clearly reviewable.[84] The further task of clarifying federal statutes and administrative regulations having to do with the dispatch of troops would, within the limitations on the judicial function, seem to be a legislative one.

Conclusion

Few would disagree that the growth of presidential power after 1950 was the result of the pressures of the contemporary world, not personal ambition or self-aggrandizement alone. Moreover, most observers would concede, in spite of the executive excesses that mar this period of our history, that vigorous executive leadership is not only necessary but can be used for beneficial purposes and with a fundamental respect for the Constitution; any effort to impose restraints on executive power by means of pervasive judicial intervention against a proper presidential discretion or overweening legislative restrictions on presidential initiative can be damaging to the nation's larger security interests as well as to the constitutional scheme itself. There can be no doubt, however, that as constitutionalists retrace the years since 1950 they can take comfort in the fact that excessive exercises of presidential power did not go unquestioned

[84] For activity in the lower courts see Clarence I. Meeks, "Illegal Law Enforcement: Aiding Civil Authorities in Violation of the Posse Comitatus Act," *Military Law Journal*, LXX (1975), 132–134.

and that judicial and legislative sensitivity to limitations on the presidency seemed to have matured into a special concern for the Bill of Rights and the separation of powers.

Increasingly, in the years after 1950, the more profuse exertions of executive power became entangled in the perpetual contest which the framers had built into the Constitution. And the contest took place on a broader and more undulating field than could have been imagined in the years immediately after World War II. The situation was affected by many unforeseen conditions, including the virtual disappearance of "war" in its traditional terms, unremitting emphasis on national security, social disruption and suspicion domestically, and increasingly unembarrassed assertions by Presidents of their broad prerogative power. For many years such assertions were widely accepted. Congress, although frequently dubious and unsettled, by and large acquiesced in an expansive theory of presidential power, at least until the Vietnam war brought its institutional anxieties to the surface. Much the same can be said for the public at large. As for the judiciary, the *Steel Seizure Case* and the cautionary warning about executive agreements in *Reid v. Covert* at first seemed scarcely noticeable things of the moment. By the end of the 1960's a series of events began to dramatize the constitutional limitations on presidential power. The events ranged from President Johnson's deception about the escalation of the war in Vietnam to President Nixon's private war in Cambodia; they included overt resistance to the right of Congress to inform itself about the exercise of presidential power, the excrescences of security surveillance, and finally, the national disgrace of Watergate. All were bottomed on executive prerogative. As these and similar developments became attached to generous interpretations of presidential power, their very accumulation pointed up the increasingly severe structural imbalance in the constitutional scheme. The critical question is, What weight can now be given to the varied institutional responses, but particularly the judicial response, to this imbalance? The evidence is scattered and fragile but permits of some generalization.

First, the judiciary did interject itself into matters affecting the presidency, matters which had been assumed traditionally as beyond judicial competence or concern. The *Steel Seizure Case* and *Reid v. Covert* were bellwethers, for they signaled the basic rationales for later intervention by the courts, that is, the separation of powers doctrine and the Bill of Rights. These limitations were to appear in later cases involving the presidency, perhaps in their purest form when the Court considered the constitutionality of presidential use of electronic surveillance in *United States v. District Court* and executive privilege in *United States v. Nixon,* but invariably in other cases as well. Moreover, nonjusticiability—a theory of judicial avoidance which an earlier generation might have thought applicable to such issues as executive privilege, presidential impoundment of appropriated funds, or the war power—began to lose its vitality. The judiciary, certainly with mixed results in the Vietnam war cases, but more surely elsewhere, was more inclined than in the past to probe for manageable standards by which the use of power might be measured. Judicial exploration ranged widely in inquiries which were encouraged by heightened expectations about intervention. These expectations, however excessive they may have been in constitutional matters other than those dealing with presidential power,[85] were largely met. Viewed collectively, the cases were not devoid of significant doctrine, particularly as they affected presidential prerogative.

Second, a more rigorous form of constitutional inquiry began to emerge. It can be contrasted, for example, with the relaxed view of presidential power in the landmark case, *United States v. Curtiss Wright,* whose easy reference to the President as "the sole organ" of the nation in foreign affairs had guided so many Presidents over the years. Adjudication and judicial inquiry became more focused, partly because of a maturing of theory about the Bill of Rights. But judicial inquiry also involved a growing awareness of the problem of structure within the national government. Specifically, one finds in several of the decisions discussed above an awareness of the separation of powers, not as power alone, but as structure, in which each branch possesses independent constitutional footing with independence tempered by the requirement that powers must be shared unless the basic nature of a given constitutional role dictates otherwise.[86] For instance, in the *Steel Seizure Case,* the *Pentagon Papers Case,* and in some of the Vietnam war cases, the sharing of power seemed to be elevated to a constitutional requisite. With a somewhat different emphasis, *United States*

[85] For one account of the excesses see Philip B. Kurland, *Politics, the Constitution and the Warren Court* (Chicago, 1970).

[86] See especially Charles L. Black, Jr., *Structure and Relationship in Constitutional Law* (Baton Rouge, 1969).

v. Nixon assigned independent roles within the structure to both the judiciary and the President in regard to executive privilege; similarly, in the impounding cases, dealing with presidential refusal to spend appropriated funds and in the warrant procedures for surveillance in *United States v. District Court,* independence was respectively recognized for Congress and for the judiciary. These determinations were not made, as presidential theory would have it, on the basis of exegesis from a given clause in Article II or from a broad reading of the President's power "under the Constitution," but rather on the basis of a more explicit inquiry into what was properly independent and what was properly shared within the constitutional scheme. While the courts were moving toward analysis based on structural considerations, Congress was making similar calculations. In the 1970's, Congress finally declared its own view of independence by using its appropriations power to close out the hostilities in Southeast Asia, and expressed its conviction about the sharing of power by President and Congress in the Budget and Impoundment Control Act and the War Powers Resolution. As others have noted, these measures were not momentary expressions of public policy but addressed themselves fundamentally to matters of constitutional design.[87]

Third, this increased inclination toward judicial intervention and the critical attention which was paid to problems of structure combined to establish with unprecedented clarity that the President is accountable to the law. The easy generality that a President was ultimately responsible only to the people, the President's reliance on

[87] See footnote 32, above.

his own reading of the Constitution, and on his own conscience, no longer seemed sufficient. A more studied examination of the roots of presidential power in the Constitution or in legislative enactments took place, and inquiry about where power stopped and started narrowed considerably. The beginning of the end came with the *Steel Seizure Case,* when a President's confident claim of uninhibited power received critical judicial examination. The later cases received similar scrutiny, with the possible exception of the cases involving the constitutionality of the Vietnam war. But even in the war cases—and the refusal of the Supreme Court to hear argument—there was unprecedented judicial unrest about the issue, unrest which was arguably restrained only because the war came to an end.[88] In another vein, after careful examination of the source of presidential authority to engage in electronic surveillance, the Court in *United States v. District Court* could not find authority either in the statutes or the Constitution, while in the impounding cases the notion was rejected that the authority to execute the laws included the right to refuse to execute those with which the President disagreed. And, whatever other legacy it may represent in *United States v. Nixon* —where the Court was drawn together in unanimity not only by the momentous issue before it but by the President's unwillingness to commit himself to obey a judicial decree—the Court ruled unambiguously that the Presi-

[88] By 1973, if one includes Justice Thurgood Marshall's expressed sentiments appearing in the final hours in *Holtzman v. Schlesinger* (414 U.S. 1311–1313, 1316 [1973]), four members of the Court seemed to be increasingly sympathetic toward hearing argument. Whether the Court should have heard argument, however, is another question. See footnote 17 above.

dent was under the law and resolved a long-standing uncertainty when it declared that the President himself was amenable to the judicial process.

Finally, a word should be said about the impact of these considerations on the theory of prerogative which was immanent in many of the exercises of power by post-World War II Presidents. Any reconstruction of the theory depends upon an awareness of the use of power during this period and of the presidential pronouncements alluded to above which were used in way of justification. It also requires a careful culling of such inchoate phrases as resulting powers, residual and autonomous powers, implied powers, and inherent and exclusive powers, which were said to justify presidential authority. When all are considered, the latter two seem to contribute the greatest substantive clarity to the theory of prerogative power, because they embrace all of the others and were constant, intertwined themes throughout the period.

The doctrine of inherency describes the origin of power; the doctrine of exclusivity, the independent exercise of power. Inherent power, under the theory of presidential prerogative, finds its source in the specified powers under Article II—for example, in the commander-in-chief clause and the President's responsibility to see to the faithful execution of the laws—but more notably its source is in the nature of the office itself, the unique position of responsibility of a popularly elected executive to act as "sole organ" of the nation in foreign affairs, in keeping the peace, and in protecting national security. Secret surveillance, executive privilege, the use of troops abroad and at home were all at one time or another justified as prerogative acts based on the inherent powers of the President. The doctrine of exclusivity is inextricably bound up with inherency. It exclaims that there is no constitutional requirement which invariably necessitates that the exercise of power be shared in a system of separated powers. It also speaks to the reach of presidential discretion. Thus, Presidents Johnson and Nixon denied that their constitutional powers needed to be shared, as a matter of right, during the hostilities in Southeast Asia. The doctrine also assumes that the President is the final interpreter of the scope of his discretion. Thus, for example, President Nixon maintained that executive privilege was discretionary and absolute, that there was no recourse from his discretionary power to refuse to spend appropriated funds, and that the scope of national security surveillance was for the executive alone to determine.

Both doctrines were seriously eroded by the mid-1970's in constitutional theory, if not in political fact. As for inherency in the early cases after 1950 (namely, the *Steel Seizure Case* and *Reid v. Covert*), in the first, inherency as a source of power seemed to be denied, by implication, for domestic seizures of property, even when related to a foreign emergency. In *Reid* there was neither affirmation nor denial of inherent power for the President to negotiate executive agreements on his own authority. Whatever these cases do tell about inherency, however, they definitely confirm that it can be confined by the judiciary and Congress acting in tandem or by the judiciary alone. As for cases in the 1970's, the impounding cases and congressional legislation restricting presidential determinations not to expend funds provide no residue of inherency, with the possible exception of decisions regarding the specific use of funds for troops in the field. In the Vietnam war cases, those which said that the political question doctrine was a bar against judicial determination of the war's constitutionality contributed nothing, since none turned directly on the doctrine of inherency; but when some of the lower courts saw fit to make a substantive determination, inherency was overwhelmed by the doctrinal requirement of mutual participation by Congress and the President in the use of war power. Inherency retained its strength only as an exception for dire emergencies, such as an attack on the United States or its armed forces, an exception which also is found in the War Powers Resolution. Similarly, in *New York Times v. United States,* while the Court seemingly denied judicially enforced inherent power to impose prior restraint on publication, at least six of the nine opinions can be read to admit of prior restraint where the results will be dire and immediate, but only then. On the other hand, the decision in *United States v. District Court* is an outright denial of inherency as applied to electronic surveillance against domestic entities without foreign ties, although the question of inherent power to use surveillance over foreign groups or those associated with foreign groups was left unresolved. As for the domestic use of troops, the Court, in *Scheur v. Rhodes,* particularly when considering other cases in its lineage, admits the possibility of inherent powers in emergencies. And *United States v. Nixon,* by its positive determination that executive privilege is rooted in the Constitution and the nature of the office, positively affirms the existence of an inherent power. In short, while

the doctrine of inherency was not subject to blanket rejection in every instance, inherency as a source of presidential power was subjected to narrow application.

The doctrine of exclusivity was subject to similar inquiry, touching on both its principal elements: the sharing of power and the reach of presidential discretion. In
the *Steel Seizure Case,* the *Pentagon Papers Case,* and in
some of the lower-court opinions on the Vietnam war—
buttressed as they were by the War Powers Resolution—
it was mandated that executive power be shared with
Congress. The impounding decisions, together with the
Budget and Impoundment Control Act of 1974, did more
than mandate sharing; they re-established congressional
dominance. In *United States v. District Court* and *Scheur
v. Rhodes* judicial participation was reinforced: in the
former because of the judicially imposed warrant requirement for electronic surveillance, and in the latter because
of the affirmation of a judicial role in estimating the
appropriateness of the use of troops domestically. In the
nature of things *Scheur* allows considerable discretion
in the initial determination of the need for troops in
emergencies; but beyond this, the only cases which
show strong deference toward the exercise of presidential
discretion are *United States v. Nixon,* because of the
presumptive right which the Court arguably gave the
President to protect state secrets, and, possibly, *United
States v. District Court,* if only because the Court failed
to reach the question of allowable discretion over surveillance involving those associated with foreign powers.
And, of course, in all the cases, the judiciary by their
very involvement, affirmed the right, or did not definitively surrender the right, to determine the standards by

which exercises of discretion might be measured. Exclusivity, both in its denial that power had to be shared and in its claim that the executive was the ultimate interpreter of its own discretion, was seriously undermined.

In sum, the doctrinal support for the theory of presidential prerogative lost much of its sweep. It may be that inherency was put where it belongs, supporting powers which are uniquely related to the nature of the office and Article II, such as the right to use force to preserve the functioning of government in urgent and exceptional domestic and external emergencies, to gather information secretly in the most sensitive dealings with foreign powers, and, as in *United States v. Nixon,* to protect the integrity of the office itself. When this more restricted meaning of inherency is considered in conjunction with the serious inroads made into the doctrine of exclusivity, unimpeded prerogative power ceases to exist in judicially ratified interpretations of constitutional theory.

It may be that this analysis puts too great a burden on a handful of cases which could be interpreted as good for one day, and one day only. On the other hand, the future may find the accumulation of insights about the constitutional structure in these cases a more coherent collection of precedents than the truly disparate decisions which Presidents have depended upon in the past to justify their exercise of power. It is likely that this process of discovery will continue. At least the burden on those who would test presidential power in the courts diminished; nor can Presidents any longer assume that executive actions will be judicially validated. There is too much in these cases of the separation of powers and the

Bill of Rights and too much in the future which will entwine them with the broadly conceived notion of national security.

But one should not ask too much of the courts. The judiciary cannot for long go it alone in setting doctrine uncongenial to the other branches, and it cannot be assumed that judicial doctrine will become public policy without acquiescence or positive action elsewhere in the political system. There is a congressional responsibility to continue efforts to devise means which will sustain a constitutional balance without suppressing a salutary executive discretion. And, equally, there must be executive sensitivity to principle and an inclination to work with the grain of constitutionalism. Without these fundamental undertakings, nourished or not by the judiciary, there can only be continuous constitutional imbalance, structural confusion, and, in operative reality, a presidency limited only by responses to the misuse of power too long delayed.

Table of Cases

220

TABLE OF CASES

Index

Library of Congress Cataloging in Publication Data

Rossiter, Clinton Lawrence, 1917–1970.
  The Supreme Court and the Commander in Chief.

  Includes bibliographical references and index.
  1. War and emergency powers—United States.
I. Longaker, Richard P. II. Title.
KF7220.Z9R6   1976   342′.73′062   76-12815
ISBN 0-8014-1052-5
ISBN 0-8014-9161-4 pbk.